MW01641457

THE CAGELING

THE CAGELING

Napoleon's Forgotten Son:
A Biographical Novel

ANN VAN DAN

VANTAGE PRESS
New York

Cover picture
The Duke of Reichstadt
from the illustrated work
of Octave Aubry/©Flammarion

This is a work of fiction.
However, due to the historical nature of this work, where appropriate, the author endeavors to use the names of actual historical characters, places, and events in the context of the subject matter.

FIRST EDITION

Published by Vantage Press, Inc.
419 Park Ave. South, New York, NY 10016

Manufactured in the United States of America
ISBN: 0-533-15396-4

Library of Congress Catalog Card No.: 2005909990

0 9 8 7 6 5 4 3 2 1

To my mother,
and
To my sister-in-law, Annette

THE CAGELING

1

February 2, 1810

Long before the night sky began to blush at the first hint of daybreak, a bright and steady orange glow illuminated a row of windows at the Tuileries palace. The candles had been burning non-stop, far into the night and up to the new day.

In a few hours, a less ardent winter sun might manage to shine—if only halfheartedly—over Paris, the capital of a fabulous empire that geographically corresponded approximately to the ancient West Roman Empire and to the later dominion fought for and assembled by the King of the Franks, Charlemagne. But France now was a republic, having beheaded her most recent king to replace him with a hereditary, Corsican-born emperor.

The French emperor had been hard at work to further secure the foundations of his self-made empire, a splendid monument to his military genius and untiring industry. And at this early hour, he was quite satisfied to have accomplished what he had set out to do.

His over-worked secretary could only suppress a yawn. Claude François Baron de Menéval did not look up when his sovereign stopped pacing to lean over his shoulder. Instead, his sleepy eyes focused on the plump and almost alabaster-white hand whose tapering index finger drew an imaginary line to underscore the words he had just written.

As usual, the dictation had been incredibly brisk, perhaps the most taxing aspect of Menéval's extensive secretarial duties. He was also required to work long hours and could count on being summoned out of bed in the middle of the night—as he presently had been—if his indefatigable master so demanded.

Menéval's wrist positively ached, and he more than welcomed the pause. Then the sonorous voice—so awe-inspiring to those not so well-acquainted with the thickset man hovering over him—trumpeted in triumph in his ear with a friendly, familiar ring.

"Excellent! No equivocation is possible now! The Tzar will have to recognize that the initiative is all mine! You will dispatch this at once!"

Even though it was presently four in the morning, it made no difference. Like Menéval, couriers were also on-call at any time of night or day.

"Right away, Sire. But what about the closing?"

"I leave this to you," Napoleon Bonaparte said briskly. "It must be amicable, of course!"

The secretary nodded in appreciation. He knew a letter to the Russian emperor Alexander I, regardless of the palatability of its contents, ought at all times express protestations of friendship and pious sentiments. Therefore he would close it with the usual phrase beginning with, "And hereupon, I pray God etc, etc, . . ." and think of some special expressions of regards which Alexander would most likely ignore.

"That will take a few more minutes, Sire," he pointed out, and immediately set himself to the task.

Napoleon grunted in acknowledgment and resumed pacing the floor with that jogging gait that had become as famous as his gray surtout and wide cocked hat. Alexander's anticipated displeasure at the refusal, or rather the rejection, could not be avoided.

Two years ago at Erfurt, the possible marriage between Napoleon and one of Alexander's sisters had marked the beginning of the French emperor's all-consuming preoccupation with producing an heir. At the time, the proposition seemed to have charmed the Russian emperor; but now, it was becoming evident that Alexander was either growing leery of Napoleon's invincible might, or simply felt adverse to what he might be considering a misalliance. And he had been consistently avoiding a firm commitment to the match.

All for the better! Napoleon thought, locking his hands behind his back. His decision to forgo a Russian alliance through a marriage had come as an after-thought while Alexander kept him waiting. A union with Grand Duchess Anna was fraught with too many complications: the Russian Orthodox religion she professed, and her age—she was only fifteen—was a matter of no less concern. I am nearly forty-one, Napoleon mused. I am not lusting after a barely nubile girl. I need a womb ready to give me a lusty son by next spring! Accordingly, the dispatch would apprise Alexander of the decision, the abysmal difference between their ages given as an excuse.

Napoleon needed a son and quickly! The survival of the formidable empire he had built hinged on having an heir. As it stood, the French Empire, for all of its glory and power, was no more than a redoubtable but vulnerable military machine. Of course, he knew the mere extension of his flesh would not suffice to stabilize and firm the remarkable yet perilous situation in which France found herself. Surrounded by despotically ruled countries and reviled by them for having committed regicide, France could only endure if Napoleon's heir could claim the *distinction of royal ancestry.*

Legitimacy!

The revival of this principle so vital to the existence of European monarchies and which Napoleon repudiated as false, was now indispensable. But his royal bride wasn't going to be a pubescent Russian princess.

He had come up with a far better alternative.

He had cast his eyes elsewhere. On the much more mature relation of another former foe he had subjugated like the Tzar: nineteen-year-old Marie Louise, daughter of Francis I of Austria, buxom, broad-hipped and, if anything like her mother, undoubtedly fertile enough to give him the heir he wanted.

Now he tingled with anticipation. "Menéval, have you finished?" he asked impatiently.

"Yes, Sire," Menéval replied, carefully blotting the wet ink on the page and handing it over.

Napoleon snatched the letter and began to read it with care.

Obliquely, Menéval observed him with undiminished interest. Only five feet, three inches tall—with his boots on—the French emperor was, by the power he wielded, a gigantic man.

Practically a whole continent was under his rule.

But if some strain was beginning to show on the face whose glowing pallor and fine features wore the distinction of classical antiquity, Menéval rather suspected that the recent annulment of the Emperor's first marriage pronounced by the Officiality of Paris may have largely contributed to it. The trauma of the separation had left its marks.

Menéval had served Napoleon long enough—eight years to this day—to perceive that the Emperor still felt bound to his ex-wife by a feeling of romantic indebtedness. It was common knowledge that Josephine, six years his senior, had been the first woman to kindle in Napoleon the fire of passion. As Napoleon soared to the pinnacle of power, Josephine also shared his prestigious ascent. He had married her, crowned and anointed her his Empress, and would have kept her, had their union been blessed with children.

There was no question in Menéval's mind that Napoleon had been patient and would have continued hoping for a son had Josephine given him a baby girl even. But after fourteen years of marriage, nothing. Not even a miscarriage. After some time, Napoleon had confided in Menéval that he was having doubt about his reproductive ability because Josephine had borne her late husband a boy, Eugene, and a girl, Hortense, both of whom Napoleon formally adopted.

Yet, on this early morning of February, quietly observing Napoleon go over the letter that would clear the last hurdle standing before his impending marriage to Marie Louise, the secretary could appreciate the Emperor's newfound confidence in his virile power: Napoleon had learned that his Polish paramour, twenty-one-year-old Marie Walewska, was soon to give birth, secluded in a castle in Poland.

Presently Napoleon lifted his eyes from the page he'd finished reading and said thoughtfully, as if sharing Menéval's reflection, "You know, I owe *all this* to Marie Walewska. . . ."

He kept an abiding remembrance of a passionate, gentle young girl, long after they had gone their separate ways. Etched in his memory was the day he had first seen her in the glittering ballroom of the ancient palace of Poland's kings. While musing over the fate of that long-suffering nation, his eyes had plucked her out of the crowd. Marie, honey-haired, shy and sweet, was in her teens and married to a senile but wealthy nobleman. The marriage had obviously been arranged by her kin as the sole means to save her from destitution.

Marie's relatives had urged her to yield to his burning advances, hoping she might be instrumental in the unification of Poland. He was aware of that, and also sensed that Marie had set her scruples aside only to help her country, and he admired her for it and found her even more desirable. Then she had fallen deeply in love with him and responded to his passion with unwavering constancy. Of this, he was certain. No gossips ever touched her. The few women with whom he had been intimate could never give him the same guarantee, for they had also been generous in the dispensation of their favors to others. But with Marie, there could not be any doubts. The child was his!

He *owed* her this assurance! Without it, he might not have attempted to embark upon a new matrimonial venture. He would have had to settle for the naming of a successor—an utterly useless, pointless, even ludicrous alternative. Besides, none of his brothers and sisters were of a caliber to encourage reliance. Joseph, the eldest, to whom he had given the Spanish crown, was headstrong and light-minded. Louis, the recipient of the throne of Holland, continued to be an inveterate dreamer. Lucien, impetuous, intensely ambitious and amoral, preferred adventure to discipline. Jerome, crowned King of Westphalia, was impossibly frivolous. Elisa had no modesty, no sense of decorum, and would prance in pink tights on the stage of amateur theatricals. Caroline, designing, petty, and envious, never ceased to whine, even after he had offered her husband, Murat, the kingdom of Naples. Of them all, Pauline proved the least troublesome and remained the only sincere, good-hearted and peaceable relative. Indeed, without an heir born of his seed, and descended from a princely ruling house on the mother's side, he could never guarantee France a long and lasting hegemony. . . .

Nearly tearing the paper, Napoleon scratched his name at the bottom of the letter. Carefully, Menéval dried the ink, folded the page, and affixed the imperial cachet. Within minutes the document was dispatched by special courier.

Menéval half-hoped he would be given at long last permission to retire, but no such invitation came. Napoleon seated himself on a settee, and by the preoccupied air on his face, indicated that he was mulling over the next order of business.

Dutifully, Menéval remained at his desk, awaiting further orders.

"Now listen carefully," Napoleon said. And he began pouring out directions and queries with the briskness of a commander taking dispositions for a battle. The Emperor's fondness for his step-children had in no way altered since his divorce from their mother; he had entrusted his step-son, Eugene, with a special task in preparations for his forthcoming marriage.

"Prince Eugene," he reiterated, "is to carry the formal announcement to Prince Schwarzenberg tomorrow. Has the interview been confirmed?"

"Yes, Sire. The Austrian ambassador is expecting him."

"The marriage contract," Napoleon continued in a rapid, precise recapitulation, "is to be signed on the very same evening. By the time Berthier arrives in Vienna, all arrangements must be completed so that he can wed the bride in my name on precisely March the second. The Archduchess may stay in the capital until the end of the Carnival, but she is to set off for France on Ash Wednesday. No later! Again, Berthier is to be reminded not to use the title of Prince of Wagram." Saying this, Napoleon shook a warning finger, adding, *"Ah! Surtout pas!"*

"The Prince of Neuchâtel is bearing this in mind, Sire," Menéval assured, according Berthier—Napoleon's most constant companion-in-arms—the only title permitted in the circumstances since at Wagram, only a year previous, in one of his most brilliant victories, Napoleon had defeated his father-in-law-to-be, forcing Austria to conclude an armistice six days later.

Leaning back, Napoleon cogitated, reviewing more details. The draft of the marriage contract had been sent to the French ambassador in Vienna; the appointments of the gentlemen and ladies who were to wait on the new Empress had been confirmed by a decree; the dazzling trousseau and carefully selected gifts packed in crates. . . .

Now came the terrible business of writing to his future father-in-law. It would be a chore, but Napoleon could no longer put it off. He heaved a deep sigh and finally sent Menéval away, fondly suggesting that he take a bath for relaxation, but not before complaining, "I am afraid I am going to have to write to the Emperor of Austria in my own hand. Courtesy, you know. But before you send the letter, be sure to rectify badly written words."

Menéval smiled. "Dot your i's and cross your t's, Sire. If that is not too much trouble."

Napoleon grimaced and made an amiable gesture of dismissal.

Left alone, he took a heavy sheet of paper emblazoned with France's Coat of Arms and began writing in an illegible scrawl: *To His Majesty, Sire, my Brother, the Emperor of Austria. . . .*

Friendly opening. Protocol. Pure formality. Nothing Napoleon would write could give the man once called Francis II any margin for action. More humbled than ever by Napoleon, Francis had been forced to renounce the crown of the Holy Roman Empire. At this juncture, he should be content to be recognized as Francis I, Emperor of Austria, and appreciate the honor of being called upon to give away his daughter in marriage to the man who had defeated him. Taking as a wife the daughter of a vanquished Habsburg caused Napoleon no embarrassment. He was marrying into a family of international prestige, and no degree of humiliation was ever known to have tarnished that prominence. Besides, Habsburg women were reputed to be prolific.

Napoleon suddenly frowned, wondering to what extent Francis I, who was soon to be counted among his relations, would oppose him should a serious crisis between them arise. . . .

With a slight jab of anxiety, he focused meditatively on the salutation. The word "brother," a purely ceremonious form of address used between sovereigns, now stressed a consanguinity of sorts. For after all, Francis would be the grandfather of the child to be born. And Francis could not conceivably behave ruthlessly toward his own flesh and blood. Instead, he should have his grandchild's interest at heart and by extension France's as well. . . .

Somewhat reassured by that thought, Napoleon resumed writing.

"I feel," Schwarzenberg reported to Vienna, "that the Emperor Napoleon did not propose. He just disposed!"

The very to-the-point remark only brought a smile on the cherry-red lips of Austria's newly appointed Minister of State, Clement Wenceslas Nepomuck Lothar, Count Metternich. There was no denying that the Archduchess's hand had not been sought but rather appropriated forthwith. And this time, Napoleon's cavalier proceedings did not ruffle a placidity born of calculating patience.

Metternich had set to work quietly and relentlessly toward the culmination of a masterful revenge. The Minister's loyalty to Austria was rooted in a profound aversion to anything that might cause the disruption of the *status quo,* which the European monarchies were struggling to conserve. He could not claim Austria as his homeland, but her possible subjugation touched upon the survival of a cause he sought to protect.

Born in Koblenz of a noble Rhenish family, thirty-seven-year-old Metternich had acquired from his father, Count Franz George von Metternich-Winneburg, a taste for privilege, money, and social standing. This taste became the foundation of Metternich's life. The French Revolution in 1789 was considered by him the work of modern barbarians set on wrecking social conventions he considered of quintessential value. In Metternich's eyes, Napoleon was the very incarnation of that malicious, destructive force, and he had declared himself a life-long enemy of revolution, of changes, of Napoleon.

For his part, Francis I of Austria found nothing to smile about. Furrow-browed and in the glummest mood, he seethed with anger and disgust at the proposed marriage between His Majesty the Emperor Napoleon, King of Italy, Protector of the Confederation of the Rhine, Mediator of the Swiss Confederation, and his daughter, Her Imperial and Royal Highness Marie Louise.

On this day of February 16, 1810, he felt helplessly trapped. The sun rays that filtered through the window panes of his study fell on his ash-blond hair with the cruelest of irony. Crowned with the light of heaven, Francis's inclined head had suffered the affront of being denied ever wearing again on this earth, the gem-studded diadem of the Holy Roman Emperors. Never had Austria been so hopelessly low!

Embittered, feeling utterly defeated, he sat at his desk sifting the innumerable grievances he had suffered at the hands of his future son-in-law. Because of Napoleon, after nearly one thousand years, the most prestigious political entity of all time, the Holy Roman Empire, had ceased to exist. To Francis, this inconceivable reality hurt him more deeply than the loss of Italy, the Belgian provinces, and the left bank of the Rhine. And apart from that irreparable shame that fueled his rancor, he positively ached at the mention of Austerlitz and Wagram. Then the fact that his summer palace of Schönbrunn had been twice occupied by Napoleon, who, not content at having brought Austria to her knees, was about to sully his race by this marriage, mortified him further.

Standing in the shadow of the draperies, Metternich, dapper and self-assured, luxuriated in astute satisfaction. Events were going his way, ripe for him to intervene and lead Austria out of her present ruin. He had watched and waited for this opportunity, and it had to be acted upon with utmost diligence. There was no time to lose!

Francis's sullen inaction was beginning to grate on his nerves. He entertained serious doubts concerning the Emperor's aptitude to govern aggressively. The crisis that now confronted them was of ominous proportion. Stripped of a fifth of its domains, Austria had tacitly become a French province. Metternich knew that total subjection was next, and he had worked assiduously to avert this catastrophic eventuality.

So far, he'd been respectful of Francis's somber reverie; kept silent while itching to see the Emperor put his signature to the marriage contract spread out before him. A marriage that was not entirely Napoleon's doing. With enterprising insight, Metternich had had an important part in engineering the match which, in his calculations, could assist Austria in coming to terms with a threatening neighbor. Francis had only rallied to the Minister's scheme when placed before the alternative of seeing Austria fall under French dominion.

No longer able to contain his impatience, Metternich stepped up to Francis's side. The Emperor had had plenty of time to study the document before him.

"Sire . . ." he said tentatively.

Francis still balked, ruminating the caustic cud of an unappeasable acrimony.

Notwithstanding Metternich's forceful exposition of all the good that would come of the marriage, his long, angular face was set in a tenacious sulk. The whole business trampled on his dignity. Touched to the quick of his pride, he could do no more than stare with obvious revulsion at the marriage contract awaiting his signature.

Francis needed a final urging. Disregarding the Emperor's wish to be left to this unproductive moping, Metternich resolutely egged on, "Sire, seeing that Your Majesty fully realizes the necessity to go with the marriage, I beg Your Majesty to sign without delay. If this contract is not ratified within the time prescribed by the Emperor Napoleon, the whole matter will be dropped."

Francis glared at the document. Then, with intense bitterness, he spat out, "Even in these circumstances we are faced with an ultimatum!"

"Things are not what they seem," Metternich soothed. "Your Majesty's consent to this union may prove to be Your Majesty's most successful move!"

"And my poor daughter is cast as a sacrificial victim to this . . . this French Minotaur!" Francis replied angrily, slapping the flat of his hand on the desk.

"The Archduchess will be the avenger, Sire."

Francis only shuddered. He would have preferred a political alliance, more concessions if needed; but Metternich had been adamant on the profitability of sealing the compact with a commingling of the races. "Kinship," he had told Francis, not without cynical insight, "is the milieu where guile flourishes best." Still, Francis felt deeply and irreparably dishonored. The House of Romanoff had not put up with the disgrace of an alliance by blood, so why should the House of Habsburg consent to it? Why can't defeat retain an element of pride, a sense of commitment to violated ideals?

"But our principles, Clement," he protested mulishly, "what of them?"

"They are in no way altered, Sire," Metternich responded, his patience wearing down to plain irritation. "Your signature . . ." and he delicately flipped the pages of the marriage contract to the place where the Emperor would be putting his autograph, ". . . attests to their immutability. In the present situation, however, we must adapt, Sire. In order to triumph, we must comply and flatter, until the day of reckoning."

Francis heaved a deep sigh, turned up his lace cuffs and eyed the quill and inkwell. His hand began to move, then stayed suspended in mid-air. One last detail still bothered him—the validity of Napoleon's divorce from Josephine. It troubled him now, when no one else gave the matter any more thought. Certainly, there had been some difficulties, but they no longer existed, having been smoothed away by the diligent proceedings of the French civil and religious authorities. The nullification of Napoleon's marriage, according to the findings of the Officiality of Paris, was based on the non-observance of formalities that were essential in the Roman Church to validate a religious union. As these formalities were declared to be lacking, there had not been any true marriage between Napoleon and Josephine. To everyone's satisfaction, the Archbishop of Vienna himself no longer raised any questions. . . .

In a quandary, Francis wrangled with the thought: Should he, Francis, set himself above the archbishop? The concept was absurd! It would be best to defer to the supreme authority from which he derived his own mandate.

"Clement, do you see in all this the hand of God guiding us?" he asked dourly, at long last reaching for the quill.

Francis's neurotic piety was another subject upon which the Minister could ponder for hours, and he answered obligingly only to speed up the conclusion of this whole vexing business. "Most definitely, Sire. I see it as the renewed assurance that Your Majesty will continue to rule successfully with divine help!"

Francis looked gravely at Metternich. "I pray never to ask God's forgiveness for deviating from the mandate I have received from Him to rule wisely our beloved homeland," he announced with solemnity. Then, he carefully signed his name on the marriage contract, not realizing the full portent of the declaration he had just made.

2

A tear fell.

The dew-like drop left a deeper-hued dot on the pale blue satin gown draped over Marie Louise's lap. In its voluptuous hollow, her hands nestled, idle, the fingers plaintively curled over a crumpled lace handkerchief.

March, though nearly gone, retained the harshness of winter. A chilling damp wind drove blinding sheets of pounding rain against the glass-plated windows of the carriage in which she sat—the saddest of brides for anyone to behold. And the deluge, she was sure, betokened Providence's compassion for the miserable lot that was hers.

Marie Louise could swear that no misery compared to that of marrying an old and evil man. Yet her father had said that she could not aspire to anything more noble than consenting to be the wife of their arch-enemy. He had explained that she would be saving her people from the wrath of Napoleon.

Of course she had submitted. And presently, riding to her doom, she *was* Empress of the formidable French Empire and the consort of that "horned devil"!

Now, fearful of the new life awaiting her, she sought comfort in thinking of Countess Lazansky, her devoted *aja,* a word of Portuguese origin that simply meant "auntie" but which, by some quirks of tradition, had come to designate the First Governess of the imperial brood.

Another tear fell.

She had just been separated from the Countess who was the only "mother" she had ever had. Her real mother, Maria Theresa of Bourbon-Sicily, Francis's second wife, devoted all of her energy and time to child-bearing. Tragically, the Empress had died in childbirth after her seventeenth pregnancy. Marie Louise had no idea how rattled Francis had felt, finding that his successive wives were succumbing one after the other under the demands of his unrelenting sexual ardor. His first empress, a princess of Wurtemberg, lasted only one year because, it was murmured, of the relentless usage he made of her.

And wasting no time after the death of his second wife, Francis had remarried and presented his family with a third wife, his cousin, Maria Ludovica of Este. And there again, Marie Louise hadn't realized, even to this day, that her father's piety forbade him to seek immediate carnal satisfactions outside the conjugal bed. Francis's latest wife was only four years older than Marie Louise, whose affection for her step-mother took on the form of a sisterly attachment. They found in one another the kindred climate of being both young and also shared a profound aversion to Napoleon.

The vivid impression of Maria Ludovica's grief, as she shed bitter tears upon seeing her bewildered step-daughter off on her journey to her new homeland on the gloomy and raining morning of March 13, 1810, started Marie Louise on the dour exercise of reckoning.

Fifteen days ago! She thought bitterly to herself. *Still raining and still on the road!*

Pressing and terrifying questions crowded her mind. Under her plumed toque, her forehead hurt. How was this all going to end? Would Napoleon treat her contemptuously? And how could the Devil incarnate that he was act otherwise? Oh, he had written letters that were sweet, and sent her gifts of incredible splendor, the likes of which her own experience of luxury had never seen nor could imagine. But again, was not Satan known for dazzling his victims with tricks? She had heard such bloodcurdling tales about him. Did he not burn priests alive and had he not strangled two of his generals with his bare hands because they had behaved like cowards during the battle of Aspern? Jesus! Mary! Now this abominable man was her husband! She couldn't expect to be anything more to him than his hapless booty!

But sadly, she had been dispatched to this unhappy fate with great pomp accompanied with joyous dins! Bells pealed, cannons thundered, and the Viennese crowded the Kärtnerstrasse and all other available passages surrounding the Hofburg palace to see her off.

When she had crossed the suburb of Mariahilf, the sight of the tricolor flags displayed in her honor accentuated the irrevocability of her departure. Driving past Schönbrunn she had begun to cry hopelessly. Countess Lazansky, who at the time still rode with her, squeezed her hands hard. "Child, child," she consoled, "do not lose heart. . . . It is not all so terrible. . . . Your dear father would never allow any harm to come to you, would he?" Marie Louise heaved a sigh. Well perhaps her *aja* was right. No harm would be coming to her. . . .

Then a thought that had remained buried under the accumulation of less intimate concerns, a thought that held something a little frightening but in a titillating sort of way, pushed past all her other dreads and rekindled a germinating curiosity—the idea of being a wife!

The seed had been planted at St. Polten where her father had been waiting to bid her a final farewell. Just before kissing her goodbye, Francis had drawn her aside and said, "As soon as you are alone with Napoleon. . . ." He hesitated. His daughter's ignorance of the facts of life had been carried to such unbelievable extremes! It was not enough that the physical aspect of love had never been mentioned to her—she had also been kept in utter darkness as to the physiological differences between the sexes. No male animals had ever been included in her numerous pets.

"Ah . . . err, I mean," he'd floundered, at a loss for the proper words, "really alone with him when everybody else will have gone to bed . . . then just do whatever he will tell you." Then a glance, sly and oddly enticing, cast sideways on his virginal daughter, accompanied the assurance: "I promise you that you will not mind being alone with your husband at all . . . and afterward, you will like nothing more than being alone with him."

This said, Francis again had praised Marie Louise's courage, reiterated the lofty character of her mission, but at the same time left her not unpleasantly puzzled.

Now she wondered, What had he meant? And whom could she ask? Suddenly, a gut-wrenching feeling of utter abandonment overshadowed her meager satisfaction at having achieved a semblance of self-control. Ever since Braunau, a little Austrian town on the frontiers of the Confederation of the Rhine, another creation of that redoubtable Napoleon, she had regained some composure, crying only intermittently and putting her trust in God's goodness and wisdom and in her own sense of worth. Desperately, she had clung to the King of Saxony's encouraging estimation of her sacrifice. She was an Angel of Peace, he had said. And she would help her papa win over evil.

Braunau was one of the many stops she remembered with acute desolation because there she had experienced true separation from her father's protection when she had been handed over to her French escort. At that point, she also underwent a cultural shock. The staid, frugal, and lusterless ambiance of her father's court had not prepared her for the taste-conscious and ebullient brilliance of French ways. Braunau boasted no palace, and the few houses requisitioned for her use were far from lending an appropriate setting for her glittering train, but the food, however, had been fit for the Empress that she was—tons of meat and fish kept on beds of ice. And to the mouth-watering aroma of seemingly endless banquets, a whiff of France's feminine frivolity had been added. Caroline, the plump and piquant Queen of Naples whom Napoleon had selected to meet and welcome his bride, had stripped her and seen that she would be bathed, perfumed, and dressed according to the latest Parisian fashion.

Then the harrowing journey had resumed, taking her reeking of a sweet, heady scent to Gunzbürg where the lunch had indisposed her; on to Munich where the festivities had given her a headache; then Strasbourg. . . .

As the cavalcade now headed toward Soissons through the pouring rain, Marie Louise's head still hurt and drooped from fatigue. She felt completely alone and homeless.

A third tear fell.

But the conviction of the angelic part she had agreed to assume to save Austria came to her rescue. She decided she must stop crying altogether. Such display of emotion could be misconstrued for ill will, an attitude her father exhorted her to repress.

Fortunately for Marie Louise, Queen Caroline, who had been riding with her since Braunau, had been steadfastly looking at her side of the road, at the rain that seemed to fall more heavily than ever, and didn't see the tears.

The mood of Napoleon's sister matched the weather. Caroline seethed with frustration and jealousy, vexingly conscious of her social inferiority and loose living. She hated her new sister-in-law's class and irreproachable innocence. Obviously, the girl was not only a virgin in body, but also in mind. Caroline's expertise in sexual indulgences could detect the purity of a girl's mentality in minutes, and she had concluded that her brother's bride was totally benighted on the subject of reproduction. Only one detail in Caroline's personal life mildly consoled her—she could boast to have had for a lover none other than Count

Metternich whom she had met four years ago during his ambassadorship in Paris. So much for class!

Since the abrupt dismissal of Countess Lazansky at Munich on Caroline's order, the two women had scarcely said anything to each other. Out of spite, the Queen of Naples took immense pleasure in tormenting the shy and frightened teen-aged archduchess by every available means, however petty, and discouraging any attempt at conversation during the last leg of the trip was one of them. To succeed in distressing a true princess gave her a feeling of importance.

Presently the monotonous jolting of the moving carriage slackened and Marie Louise realized the cavalcade was slowly coming to a halt. Peering through the window, she could see the facade of a church and a group of men with their hats pulled low over their faces huddling under its wind-swept, and rain-drenched porch. Timidly Marie Louise broke a long and strained silence. "Are we already in Soissons?"

Following her gaze, Caroline pouted. The town was not unfamiliar to her and the stop defied explanations.

"No, Madame," she answered, nonplused, "this, I am sure, is Courcelles."

"Then why are we stopping here?"

"Shhh . . ." Caroline silenced. In spite of the noisy spattering of the rain, she listened carefully, thinking she had heard some rather loud shouts.

Suddenly, the door of their carriage was yanked open followed immediately by a rush of cold damp air which set the two women shivering. An equerry hurriedly lowered the folding steps, and the duty chamberlain bellowed, "The Emperor!"

Caroline involuntarily shrieked in surprise as a hunched figure, sodden, dripping, and clad in the famous gray field coat, leaped into the coach and loomed over Marie Louise.

Her china-blue eyes grew wide with astonishment, then shut in a rush of panic mingled with vague expectation as she gave herself up to sensations never before experienced—strong arms clasping her with possessiveness and wet, hard lips pressing searchingly against her mouth. She gasped and struggled feebly, like a fledgling trapped in a net, then yielded to an ardor that sent not unpleasant chills up her spine.

As she grew limp and willing, Napoleon released the prize he should have been waiting to collect at Compiègne, as originally planned. But laying down the rules, he could undo them. . . .

Waiting at Compiègne had unnerved Napoleon, and he had gone from impatience to near frenzy by the total inability to draw from those who had actually seen Marie Louise, such as dispatch-riders, an accurate description of his bride. The vague accounts he received left him fearing she was hideous, especially when one courier he interrogated, depicted succinctly the Archduchess as "engaging."

"In which way?" Napoleon demanded, not without lust. Procreating should not, after all, be an irksome business.

"Her Majesty the Empress is very stately, Sire."

That told him nothing. "How are her features?" Portraits, Napoleon knew were not always reliable, especially when they were commissioned on the occasion of a betrothal. The artist was bound to flatter the model.

"They are . . . in proper order, Sire," the courier stammered, eyes downcast.

"I have heard enough!" Napoleon sighed, convinced that his bride must be unattractive beyond description.

Waiting at Compiègne had been frustrating in other ways. . . .

Resigned to the fact that he was marrying only a womb, yet wanting to make a good impression himself, Napoleon had been taking dancing lessons. His step-daughter, Hortense, Queen of Holland since her marriage to his brother, Louis, tried to teach him the waltz with pitiable results.

"Sire," she had chided fondly, "this is a dance. We are not on maneuvers! We must go: one, two, and three! Oh, and remember to turn at the same time!"

But again, he had stepped on her toes. Utterly discouraged by the inability to learn what any young fop could master without being taught, the master of Europe muttered, "Dancing is frightful business. . . . And I am too old!"

Marie Louise felt quite differently. As she opened her eyes and looked up at Napoleon, she found him incredibly young-looking for his age. In that respect, he could have been her father, for Francis of Austria was only one year the French emperor's junior. With pleasure she discovered that her husband's face was smooth and had the healthy, virile swarthiness of the warrior she knew him to be.

Examining him more closely, she observed that Napoleon's eyes, nose, and mouth were beautifully formed, his lineament impressed with the mold of a Roman imperator. The warm and lustrous chestnut-brown hair felt like it would be soft to the touch once it dried, and she was particularly attracted by a forelock that swept across his broad forehead.

Smiling at her with irresistible charm, his white teeth gleamed. Then she felt him nibble amorously at her shoulder after he'd quickly leaned over to kiss it, totally oblivious of Caroline. Drawing away, he said, "Madame, I had to see you! And I am absolutely delighted!"

For Napoleon, Marie Louise's foremost attraction would always reside in the fact that she was a Habsburg, and through her impressive lineage, his long-awaited heir, on the French side of the Bourbons's line, would be the great-nephew of Louis the XVI and Marie Antoinette.

Yet, to his surprise and relief, he also found her physically attractive—plump, rosy, and fair. As it was the fashion, her décolleté dress and the high-empire waistline raised to the underside of the breasts combined to emphasize a bust of generous proportions.

Essentially she was no true beauty, and her features reflected the dull family strain evident in countless portraits of her relatives and ancestors that hung in the palaces of Spain and Austria. She had a narrow, elongated face with flat, high cheekbones, and her protruding eyes were singularly slanted, hooded under heavy lids that gave her an air of bovine placidity.

But most of all, her lower lip gave her away. Fleshy and pendulous—the famous Habsburg lip! All of which Napoleon found enchanting.

As he stared at her, Marie Louise could sense that Napoleon was in some awe of her, but there existed such an abysmal difference between their backgrounds that she would never grasp the true nature and depth of his wonderment—a wonderment Napoleon savored second by second as he gazed at his Austrian bride. He had not quite contemplated earning the vertiginous honor of possessing someday the daughter of the Caesars! Never had he envisioned a career that would take him from the craggy wilderness of his native Corsica to *this!* The Bonapartes were poor and Napoleon remembered as a child how his mother Letizia struggled to feed her brood.

Shyly and blushing, Marie Louise ventured a compliment. "The portrait you sent me does not do you justice."

Utterly charmed, Napoleon laughed explosively, pulled her to him and covering her lips with his, slipped his tongue inside her mouth.

This time Marie Louise did not resist. Instead, she wrapped her arms around him, and abandoned herself to the thrill of experiencing the novel and strange invading prod, knowing no sweeter comfort than pressing herself closer to him when his hands began to explore a little.

As those eager hands gently fondled her, Marie Louise began to feel the suggestion of a yet unexplained pleasantness which coursed through her body and dispelled the somber and terrifying picture she had formed of their marriage. Catching her breath, she suddenly kissed him back with progress he found amazingly rapid, and she caught herself thinking something she would have sworn unthinkable a few minutes earlier—Thank God they were married! And thanks for Papa's wisdom in granting this holy happiness!

The Queen of Naples thought it best to look the other way. The fact that her Germanic sister-in-law was clinging to her brother within minutes of meeting him hinted that she might very well be oversexed for all her innocence, and Caroline now disdainfully thought her behavior unseemly and common.

For his part, Napoleon felt pleasantly surprised and flattered. The girl had succumbed to his charm! He had expected a certain reserve, a haughty distancing from his passionate advances, but that had not happened. Maladroitly—and this was all the more exciting—she was returning his attentions with equal ardor.

Giggling, Marie Louise snuggled up against his broad chest after he had taken off his coat and given order for the cavalcade to resume its progress toward Soissons. Soon, they were chatting as if they had known each other for a long time, and she listened rapturously to some nonsensical ghost stories he was fond of telling in feminine and familiar company. The subject was perfect. As she would pretend fright, exclaiming, "Oh cousin! This is giving me chills!", he would use this as a pretext to fondle her a little more intimately under the guise of reassurance, while emphatically reminding her not to call him cousin.

"I am your husband now," he told her, his thumb gently rubbing the underside of her breast.

Though "cousin" was strictly a term of courtesy used in official intercourse between princes of royal houses, Marie Louise thought, Thank heaven, we are not even that closely related!

"Shall I call you Nana?" she asked lightly, feeling impish and gay.

"Louise," Napoleon mouthed her name as though tasting it, enjoying the familiarity, "that would be different."

Impetuously, she kissed the lobe of his ear, and Napoleon suddenly decided on another change of plan. He could not wait to be alone with his bride. . . .

They reached Soissons shortly after dark, but passed it without stopping. The procession thundered through the town leaving waiting officials with mouth agape and a lavish banquet unsavored. Only a little curious, Marie Louise lifted her head from her husband's shoulder and gave him a questioning look. Napoleon explained briefly they were going directly to Compiègne. But she did not care anymore how long and how far she would be riding, provided it would be in the company of her wonderful Nana.

"Ah," she said nuzzling his chest, "I do feel tired and should like to go straight to bed when we arrive."

Napoleon smiled in the ara feathers of her toque, trying not to sneeze as they tickled his nostrils. "You will . . . I will see to it!" he promised.

A little after ten the same evening, the chateau of Compiègne came into sight with its facade ablaze in light. The rain had finally stopped.

As soon as the coach came to a halt, Marie Louise was helped out and alighted in a courtyard lit with an abundance of torches while an outdoor orchestra played a tune she thought rather melancholy. Through a colorful throng of mud-stained marshals, generals, chamberlains, equerries and pages, she made her way to the perron leaning languidly on Napoleon's arm. She could never imagine ever being apart from him. He was not a devil, but a lamb, a husband she would trade for no other. At that moment, she promised herself to promptly inform Francis of the wonderful discovery and change of heart. . . .

In the state room, the Court awaited with tingling curiosity, but no one was given the opportunity to become familiar with the new Empress. Instead, Napoleon hurried through the introductions and enjoined the Duchess of Montebello, one of Marie Louise's newly appointed ladies-in-waiting, to take the Empress to her apartments.

Then at long last, Napoleon took note of his sister. "Oh, Caroline," he said brightly.

The Queen of Naples appeared to be sulking. "Sire," she answered with surliness, intent on provoking him.

He noted her tone of voice, but without annoyance. Caroline's lapses into that sort of disposition was in no way unusual; and besides, he was in a splendid mood. Never had he felt so well disposed and more observant of ladies' fineries. He found that his sister looked absolutely ravishing in her sea green gown. A tight fitting gold filigree tiara encrusted with pearls and emeralds encircled her low, obstinate forehead.

The gems seemed to sparkle with a more brilliant fire against the ebony sheen of her impeccably arranged curls. Women, he thought, were decidedly enchanting creatures!

"Caroline," he continued amiably, "you will be supping with the Empress and me upstairs in the royal apartments. Afterward . . ." He smiled at another breach of protocol, "as I shan't be sleeping at the hotel de la Chancellerie tonight, you will prepare the Empress for bed."

Ten minutes later, while washing up and sousing himself with his favorite scent, eau de Cologne, Napoleon undertook to prepare the court Grand Almoner, his uncle Cardinal Fesch, for a much more delicate task.

"Am I," he asked him brusquely, "really married?"

"Yes," replied the Cardinal. "According to civil law, Your Majesty is married."

"And what of canon law?" he pressed.

There was a silence, and Napoleon darted an impatient look at Letizia's brother, a humble relation like the others whom he had raised to the dais of some significance.

Fesch stood, tight-lipped, in his gorgeous crimson robe, the very symbol of a spiritual power whose constant interference with temporal affairs had always disturbed his willful nephew. The Bonapartes were Catholic, but Napoleon's ideas of religion had always disquieted his pious mother. The Church, he held, was just as conniving as any secular institution. It lorded over Christendom not as a good shepherd, but as a body jealous of keeping its sways and privileges. In his opinion, the Church had not endured by the power of the Holy Spirit, but through cunning exploitation of mankind's fear of death and longing for perfection and eternal happiness.

Yet Napoleon would credit the institution with the convenient ability to explain away sufferings and inequalities in fortune as the will of God, thus rendering miseries and poverty more tolerable. Above all, he valued the influence of the Catholic Church, which for hundreds of years had provided a quantum of social order. But beyond this last consideration, Fesch had better not stand in his way. . . .

Actually, the Cardinal was not absolutely certain of the soundness of the base upon which the marriage stood. From the Vatican there had been a vexing silence concerning the proceedings regarding Napoleon's divorce, and if one were to delve seriously into the question, the present union might very well turn out to be null and void. But Fesch owed his appointment to the cardinalate to Napoleon's influence and thought it best to conform to the general attitude of approval.

Finally he spoke. "In a short while, Your Majesty will be married according to canon law."

But Napoleon felt a powerful attraction for a nineteen-year-old virgin.

"Can't the religious ceremony be performed by proxy now?"

"No, Sire. It is a sacrament," answered Fesch, clasping his hands nervously.

The peevish declaration that followed confirmed the Cardinal's suspicion.

"Then the civil marriage is worth noting where it concerns us tonight!"

Fesch cleared his throat. "Not for what Your Majesty intends to do," he said, lowering his gaze. And because it was his duty as a priest, he exhorted with meekness, "The religious marriage, as Your Majesty well knows, will take place in less than a week. It is a very short time to wait . . . then all will be in order."

Napoleon frowned. He thought of the fine supper by a log fire. He had ordered two roasted pheasants and three bottles of champagne to be served in the privacy of the royal apartments so as to create the proper atmosphere for the consummation of his desires, which presently had narrowed down exclusively to pure sensual appetite. . . .

Suddenly he decided not to let anything spoil the vivid and erotic picture of Marie Louise lying naked between scented sheets. But what if she entertained scruples and clung to them? The girl, according to reports, was said to have been raised in the strict observance of rules. That too, must not stand in the way.

With finality, Napoleon declared, "After supper tonight I shall take the Empress to bed forthwith. The Empress should be . . . spiritually prepared for this."

Fesch flinched a little. Napoleon's imperious ways did not encourage self-assertion. Nevertheless, in a last attempt to preserve the sanctity of the proceedings, he said, "The Empress will only listen to a priest."

"Who is also a cardinal!"

Fesch gave a start, not caring to be drawn into an unholy collusion. "Me, Sire?"

"Precisely," Napoleon laughed, yet his tone was commanding. "Princes of the Church are most fit to counsel princes of the world. She will listen to you!"

3

Sitting in a hot bath, Napoleon was whistling softly to himself when it suddenly occurred to him that he might be behaving with inexcusable callousness. Then he reconsidered. No! He *must* unwind, calm down, because there was nothing else *he* could do. Just for once, he had to relinquish all control and simply submit.

Submit to the mysteries of Nature.

Childbirth!

A drama of sorts, in which his wife assumed the lead while his role consisted of merely watching and worrying, though his First Physician, Baron Corvisart had assured him that giving birth was really a "trifling matter," especially in one young and strong like the Empress. Yet, from what Napoleon had seen, she wasn't very brave. The previous evening, the Empress had experienced the first labor pains and gone through severe fits of depression and several frightful panic attacks.

It was now past five in the morning, and still nothing. Napoleon had decided to take a bath to relax if at all possible. He'd just left Marie Louise sleeping peacefully—at long last, her form bloated under the sheet, the child within her setting its own pace and time.

"By God!" he thought, luxuriating in the sudsy warmth enveloping him like a blanket, this sanguinary life-giving process that awed and disgusted him was about to take place! Today, March 20, 1811! The date was to mark another victory for him, one of a very personal nature: the joy and pride of having his very own legitimate child. And if a boy, this birth was going to be a resounding triumph with far-reaching political echoes.

The glowing prospect was beginning to work its calming effect upon him. Or perhaps at this point, the nerve-wracking vigil had somehow finally worn his sensitivity down. He could feel now a soothing rush of confident exhilaration.

Besides, he told himself, the Empress was in excellent hands. She was attended by five doctors, including his personal physician, Dr. Corvisart; and the odds in her favor were very good. Marie Louise came from a child-bearing race of sturdy women, and most likely would not die in harness at the first attempt. Very little could go wrong.

Since Compiègne, nothing had. . . .

The Empress had *more than fully* cooperated. Cardinal Fesch must have been extremely persuasive. In fact, during their first time at love-making, she had giggled all along. Then on the first of April, before a glittering assembly of princes, ambassadors and high ranking clergymen, and with Cardinal Fesch officiating the religious ceremony of their marriage, she had noticeably blushed knowing that her white satin gown scintillating with diamonds bore witness to a spurious virginity. He'd only wished at the time she was already with child.

Thereafter, he'd watched for signs, like vomiting, and this she did. But those frequent attacks of indigestion had been caused by an over-indulgence in cream tarts, which she devoured in great quantity. As she grew plumper all in the right places, just the way he wanted his women to put on weight, her belly had not swelled significantly. And not from lack of his amorous incursions, which she welcomed. Actually, the innocent girl he had married seemed insatiable in bed as well as at table.

Finally, in July, not to be outdone by the unpublicized birth of a baby boy to Marie Walewska, Marie Louise was certain of being pregnant. He had needled Corvisart for precision. "Since when?"

The doctor answered vaguely, "It's all very difficult, Sire. The Empress's periods have been extremely irregular. . . ."

Sickening! That aspect of femininity upset him and he wanted to hear no more. After that, he was content with an approximation. Then by August, there was no longer any doubt that his "Good Louise" was in the second month of her pregnancy!

He remembered getting dizzy from joy. The Empire was safe! Fortune was eating out of his hand. All seemed to defer to his desires. "The child is going to be a boy!" he told Dr. Corvisart. It had to be! To have come such a long way, and climbed so high, surely deserved a final boon.

He also remembered getting on his wife's nerves by watching her girth expand like she was going to explode. When they were alone, he would lift her petticoats and lower her drawers to admire and caress her belly. She'd slapped his hands and cried, for she hated the way she looked.

He did not mind in the least. Her condition held him in thrall and he dreamed happily of the vast and splendid Empire he would be passing on to his boy. It stretched from Lubeck on the Elbe to the Pyrenees, and from Holland to Rome! He had made a tiny concession, though. Just in case the baby should be a girl, he was prepared to title her Princess of Venice.

But he clung to his belief that it was going to be a boy, and tailored all his preparations for the arrival of a prince. By a Senatus Consultum, his son was to receive the title of King of Rome. He had seen to every detail concerning the establishment of his son's household. Twenty nine people in all, from governess, nurses, and cradle-rockers to equerries, ushers, pages, grooms of the chambers, house stewards, and carvers. The infant would have a choice of three cradles in which to sleep—one made of yew, one of elm root, and the last, silver-gilt with a sculpted eaglet about to take flight perched at its foot, and standing at its head, on the world, a Winged Glory holding up a laurel wreath.

On the heights of Chaillot, facing the bridge that commemorated his victory at Jena, he'd planned for his son's use the construction of a stately palace that would equal in splendor the wondrous citadels of ancient Babylon.

The grounds had already been broken. . . .

Napoleon squeezed his eyes shut, and vigorously splashing his face with the bath water, muttered to the child to be born, "I am ready! And sooner than *you* are."

"Ah, Sire! . . ."

He opened his eyes.

Dubois, the accoucheur, livid, quite incapable of saying anything more, stood before him, mouth gaping.

The full impact of momentous events usually affected Napoleon afterward, leaving his mind at the moment of disclosure, alert and collected for practical directives. And from the expression on Dubois's face, he expected the worst possible news.

"Dubois," he said quietly, as if another self were speaking, "if you've come to tell me that the Empress is dead, you can be sure that we'll give her a proper burial."

The accoucheur regained the use of his tongue and blurted, "Sire, it's the water! It has broken too soon and the baby is not presenting itself properly!"

"The water. . . ." Napoleon repeated in a daze.

"The fluid surrounding the fetus, Sire!"

"Damn it! I know what *that* water is!" Napoleon roared, finally reacting to the actual peril of the situation. "Then do something!"

"The forceps . . . I'll have to . . . to use them," Dubois stammered.

Napoleon's voice went hoarse with anxiety. "Any danger?"

"Sire, it may come down to choosing between the mother or the child!"

"The mother, of course!" Napoleon cried, slamming his fist in the bath water and causing a considerable splash. "Save her! She can give me other children!"

Dubois retreated drenched from head to toes.

"Dubois!" the Emperor's voice thundered after him.

"Yes, Sire?"

"Treat her like an ordinary housewife! A cobbler's wife! And so help me, I'll have you quartered if you lose her!"

After Dubois had gone, Napoleon leaped out of the tub and dressed as quickly as possible, not even taking time to dry off. Still dripping under his clothes, he hurried to the Empress's chamber and found Marie Louise screaming and struggling to be left alone.

The sight of Dubois manipulating his instruments had terrified her.

Feeling gauche and totally inadequate, Napoleon tried to calm her. "Take heart, dear," he heard himself say rather primly, "all is going to be well!"

Haggard, she bawled. "Don't 'dear' me! I'm going to die, Nana! Do you want me to die?"

"No, silly!" He didn't know if it was water or sweat dripping from his forehead. "How can you say that?"

"Then, tell them not to touch me . . . Ahhh! . . ." The pain sucked the color out of Marie Louise's face.

Napoleon winced. As a hardened warrior, the gores and sufferings displayed on the battlefields touched in him a rational chord that sounded off an intellectual grief, and he had never flinched at the sight of blood. But this! A woman in the throes of labor pain . . . stained sheets on a bed in which they'd made love. That was more than he could endure.

It made him faint-hearted.

"Sire, please allow me. . . ." Napoleon felt a hand on his arm.

Madame de Montesquiou, wife of the Grand Chamberlain, Baron de Montesquiou and Count of the Empire, had approached the bed. She was the governess who would be responsible for the yet unborn child. In a cold sweat, and feeling nauseated, Napoleon gratefully moved to the side and took flight to hide in the adjoining lavatory.

The governess leaned over the Empress and said in a soothing voice, "Two of my children have been delivered this way with perfect safety. Your Majesty has nothing to fear."

In spite of the reassurance, Marie Louise persisted in refusing to let herself be touched. Finally, a pitiable struggle followed during which the doctors succeeded in holding her still while Dubois tried to free the baby, which appeared in the worst possible position—presenting its hip.

The Duchess of Montebello, Marie Louise's favorite lady-in-waiting, also in attendance, loitered without displaying much concern. As her mistress paid no heed to the governess's reassuring words, she felt wickedly happy because the idea that *anyone* but herself could have any soothing influence over Marie Louise galled her. Moreover, the Duchess had aspired to the post that had gone to the Countess—but only for the prestige and honor attached to it. Now she could savor Madame de Montesquiou's complete failure at calming Marie Louise with a glare full of vitriolic envy.

Her back turned on the Duchess, the governess's attention was totally directed at the progress of the Empress's delivery, and in her heart she said a prayer to the Mother of all mothers: "Holy Mary, pray Jesus to let the child come! Let the baby go free!"

Almost instantly her plea was answered. Dubois's skillful manipulation of the forceps turned the baby in a more deliverable posture, and after twenty-six agonizing minutes it came into the world feet first. A boy! The Prince hung limply head down as Corvisart held him up to his mother.

The infant appeared dead.

Immersed in the terror of giving birth, Marie Louise averted her face, and without ceremony the infant was placed on the carpet. The doctors thought it more urgent to fuss over the mother, especially as Napoleon came in to clasp the Empress in his arms.

From his wife's side, he cast an indifferent glance at the viscous little form which lay unattended on the floor and thought with dreamlike calm and cruel detachment: *It's dead. . . .*

But someone remained unconvinced. The very woman whom Napoleon had appointed to the enviable position of looking after the Imperial Prince because he saw in her a person of rare merit, rose to the occasion and may well have, by her intervention, prevented her charge's death.

Quickly, Madame de Montesquiou knelt beside the abandoned baby which was by no means puny in size. She estimated it must measure twenty inches in length. Carefully, she lifted it in her arms. The child was also heavy—at least nine pounds or thereabouts.

At that moment, the Duchess of Montebello's lips crinkled in a reproving pout and crossing over to the governess, she scolded, "Madame, you may not touch this child!"

"And why not?" asked the Countess, dumbfounded by the nonsensical interdiction.

"Have you forgotten?" the Duchess returned in a cutting tone of voice, "Etiquette requires that the Prince is not to be handled *by you* before the arrival of the Arch-Chancellor!"

May God take pity on such heartlessness! Madame de Montesquiou thought. She was pious, a sincere and good Catholic, but her charitable dispositions, given this emergency, would stretch no further. She could be sharp-tongued when provoked with reason.

"I don't see how the saving of a life can wait for anybody!" she retorted abruptly. Then with authority: "Doctor! Quick!"

Immediately, Corvisart came to the rescue. He dipped the baby in warm water; slapped it on the back, wrapped it in a blanket and forced a few drops of brandy into its mouth. At that moment, Arch-Chancellor Cambacérès made his grand entrance but was ignored.

Corvisart kept looking at his watch counting the seconds. Finally, on the seventh leap of the little hand, the child cried.

The pitiful, ear-piercing mew jerked Napoleon back to his senses. He had been in a daze, but as he realized his son was alive, he recognized that it was grief that had numbed his reaction when he thought the boy dead.

Leaving Marie Louise's side, he briskly strode over to the boy and snatched him from the governess's arms. As he cradled the baby, he was overwhelmed with indescribable happiness. All that he ever wanted seemed to be in that little wrinkled face peeping rosily from the sweet-smelling folds of wool. His son! To be known in the history of his dynasty as Napoleon, François, Charles, Joseph, Bonaparte! The future Napoleon II!

But when the double doors of the Empress's apartments opened, the Court and the world greeted the child by the name solemnly shouted by an usher, "The King of Rome!"

A salute of one hundred and one guns roared and echoed throughout the country.

The celebration of the Prince's birth was conducted on a scale reminiscent of a fairy tale. Pages galloped to the four corners of the Empire. Work stopped. Open-air banquets for the people were laid out. Wine flowed freely from barrels and fountains. The thunder of cannons and the peal of bells filled the air with a counterpoint of songs and cheers. From the Baltic to the Adriatic illuminated cities formed an immense garland of light.

Later, the pageantry that attended the Prince's christening was similar in splendor to that of a coronation. On that day, huge crowds lined the streets to watch an endless procession of gilded coaches flanked by squadrons of Mamelukes—retained after Napoleon's Egyptian venture—in addition to Dutch and Polish cavalry units which pranced in a dazzling flurry of multicolored plumes and shimmering uniforms.

The little King rode to his baptism in his own private carriage with handsome young pages dressed in white and gold clinging to the front and back. In his governess's lap, the newborn heir to the French Empire lay in a billow of white English point of lace, sashed with the vermilion grand cordon of the Legion of Honor—an order created by his father to credit bravery.

It took the sumptuous cortege two hours to reach the imposing Gothic cathedral of Notre-Dame built on the Ile de la Cité, an islet in the middle of the Seine which the French sentimentally regarded as the very cradle of Paris.

Napoleon was positively brimming over with joy. The occasion, the pomp, and the splendor attested to the durability and solidity of his empire.

When the ritual sets of questions were put to the godparents by Cardinal Fesch, Napoleon focused his attention on the one which meant the most to him.

"What name do you give this child?"

"Napoleon."

The crown to all his desires . . .

In spite of a glowing happiness, one thing disappointed Napoleon. The baby did not capture Marie Louise's interest beyond the time of her daily visits to the nursery. And although she was reasonably fond of the child, she did not care to fondle it. At his request she would kiss the baby, but was reluctant to hold it, invoking her own clumsiness and her fear of dropping their son.

This son was Napoleon's passion, the focus of his wakeful hours, the charmer of his dreams and the constant object of his worship. He was not afraid to handle the infant and did so adroitly and with gentleness, covering the little face and hands with kisses. Often he would go to the Prince's room late at night just to watch him sleep in the silver gilt cradle that so perfectly symbolized the glory he had worked so hard to pass on to the child.

In those moments, Napoleon envied his son's luck. Unaware of his good fortune and unsuspecting of the lofty destiny that awaited him, the little King of Rome slept with peaceful indifference, his tiny fists balled in rosy nuggets of tender flesh. His father's gaze lingered on the baby's hands and he thought how very simple it would be for him! All the child would have to do was to open them and reach for the world, whereas Napoleon had had to work indefatigably to master it.

But babies know of bounties only in terms of physical well-being.

The Prince was thriving as though Providence's generosity knew no bounds, and Napoleon took a particular pleasure in watching his son being bathed because the sight of the boy's nakedness kept him well appraised of his prodigious growth.

The baby King was strong. At five weeks he could lift his head off the pillow, and with immense pride, Napoleon admired the sturdy limbs, the rounded chest, the uncoordinated but energetic movements of the well-made body nourished from the excellent milk of Madame Auchard, the carefully chosen wet nurse.

As the months passed, the most pleasant moments for Napoleon moved from the nursery to the outdoors. At the palace of Saint Cloud, under the cool shade of chestnut trees, he would lunch holding his thirteen-month-old son on his knees and playfully entice the Prince to taste some Chambertain from his glass. The boy disliked the wine but seemed extremely intrigued by his father's medals and sword, which he tried to unsheathe.

Startled, but immensely pleased, Napoleon marveled, "So soon?" And he smothered his son with kisses, saying with a laugh, "Oh, my precious baby, you must grow a little more!"

A grown boy!

The prospect made him seethe with impatience. At his age, time was precious. Moving too fast and yet passing too slowly. He longed to share with his son the ideas that went through his mind. Communication between the two of them would be stimulating. He also felt great love, a love he yearned to see recognized and understood. But that, too, would have to wait till the day the child would finally emerge from the mental limbo of babyhood.

Meanwhile Napoleon became insufferably doting, but that was forgiven him. For the boy, born of a mother whose attraction could only be credited to her youth and of a father not so uncommonly fine-featured, was already arrestingly beautiful to behold. Moreover, the Prince was further distinguished by an air that hinted at remarkable intellectual endowment. Young as he was, his eyes had none of the absent stare quite normal in infants. On the contrary, they focused on people with sparkling concentration.

With increasing delight, Napoleon thought of him as a star child!

4

"Sweet child, perhaps one day, you will come to know the sacrifice I've made for you!" Saying this, ex-Empress Josephine went down on her knees before the little King of Rome and burst into tears, sobbing uncontrollably.

The visit, all pre-arranged and held in utmost secrecy so as to not arouse Marie Louise's displeasure, had been approved by Napoleon. He still kept feelings of tender affection for his first wife, and she knew in her heart that had she been able to give him this boy, he would not have repudiated her. She found the toddler entrancingly beautiful, and could only envisage for him a promising future and a happy existence.

But the specter of war was again looming over France.

Alexander had grown overtly hostile, and Napoleon's boundless confidence in the invincibility of his Grand Army was the decisive factor that led him to consider, then accept, the idea of meeting the Tzar on his own territory.

The arguments in favor of a bellicose Russian stance were cogent. Napoleon's decision to discontinue paying court to Grand Duchess Anna had not only been interpreted as an insult but was also regarded as signaling the start of an unshakable alliance with Austria since his marriage to Marie Louise. This would deprive Russia of a valuable former ally.

In addition, Alexander feared a restoration of Poland when Napoleon had added a buffer state with the creation of the Grand Duchy of Warsaw by the treaty signed at Tilsit in 1807. Lastly, Napoleon's obsession in annihilating England by undermining her credit through the strangulation of her trade, was on the verge of ruining the Russian economy.

The idea of moving the theater of war to Russian soil was a matter of grave concern to Napoleon's marshals. To wage a war in that God-forsaken land would be to court disaster.

The Emperor allowed them to speak their minds, conceding a few points with no intention of backing down. It was true that there were very few mills in Kovno where he proposed to send all the grains collected from German ports. And it was also out of the question to carry fodder for one hundred and fifty thousand horses. But this was not going to stop the preparation under way and cancel the conscription of half a million men. If he had to, he would build those mills! As for the horses. . . .

"In June, gentlemen, the grass will be green. We shall wait until then!" Napoleon decided.

Early in June, Napoleon crossed the Memel with his gigantic array of troops, with no trace of the enemy in sight. This deeply troubled the Prince of Neuchâtel, whom the Emperor called his "wife," so inseparable were they.

"Where are we going, Sire?" he dared ask.

"Smolensk," answered Napoleon. "Not even that far," he corrected after a pause. "Minsk!"

Berthier thought disconsolately of his sumptuous mansion in Paris, of his magnificent estate in the suburb, and all the gifts from a munificent master who required his presence wherever he went. What manner of favors were these when he could scarcely enjoy them? He compared his fate to that of poor Tantalus, the fabled Greek King who was condemned in Hades to reach for tasty fruits that forever eluded his grasp.

With a sigh he said, "That is far enough, Sire."

Napoleon looked straight ahead into the verdant and warm Lithuanian summer. By the time they would see the first snow, they would be well prepared for it.

"We will winter in Vilna," Napoleon declared confidently, "and live off the land. I have intelligence the Tzar is in Vilna, and we may just secure peace there."

"What if the Tzar refuses to make peace?"

"We go to the heart. Moscow, St. Petersburg!"

That same month, Napoleon's army reached Vilna without obstruction, but the Tzar was gone, and so was the Russian army. From the outset, Alexander's generals adopted a tactic of evasion, but not for strategic reason. They had no desire to pit themselves against the greatest army ever assembled up to that time.

As the Russians retreated, Napoleon marched on. In the stifling heat of July, the Grand Army advanced through a wasteland. The air, acrid from the smoke of burning villages and towns set afire by the fleeing population, stung the lungs, and the stench of dead horses, which had fed on rank grass suffocated the troops.

In this strange war, men, too, were falling victim to disease and exhaustion. Deaths rose to nine hundred a day in the Bavarian Corps alone—and without a shot having been fired. Constantly throbbing in everyone's mind was the same haunting, maddening question? *Where is the enemy?*

The Tzar had made an astounding discovery. The initial timidity of his generals was producing very good results. The French army had been seriously weakened without any engagements and casualties on the Russian's side. A strategy of sorts germinated in Alexander's mind. With God's help, there must not be any battle ground!

Napoleon marched on. Smolensk, a charred carcass of a town, then Borodino, had been left far behind. On to Moscow!

As there is no absolute infinity under the heavens, the nightmarish succession of plains ended on the evening of September fourteenth. Twelve hundred spires topped with turquoise cupolas and studded with golden stars rose majestically in the setting sun.

Moscow!

The front guard of the French army stood in awe at the sight, which seemed to have been conjured up from the fabulous tales of ancient Arabia. All mouths hung open.

Napoleon trained his binoculars on the city. Alexander had been just a little too confident. The fall of Moscow into Napoleon's hands could only prelude peace.

"Sire?" A voice interrupted his quiet jubilation.

Napoleon turned to the estafet sent to him by Murat, who'd gone ahead on a reconnaissance foray and asked, "Well, what does the King of Naples have to say?"

Obviously, Murat was sending words that he was about to lead out the civil, military, and religious authorities. They were about to present Napoleon with the keys of the city in conformity with the old Roman custom attending a surrender. Quite ready to receive them, he thought of the food heaped in cellars, of the comfort of houses to shelter an army worn out by hunger and disease. There, the wounded could receive better care and the dying could pass on in relative peace . . . Moscow intact! Little Mother Russia wasn't going to weep over Moscow!

"The town," said the messenger, "appears to have been stricken by a plague."

Without as much as a blink, Napoleon shot back, "Then we will have to burn the corpses!"

The short silence that followed denoted embarrassment at being misunderstood. Then the estafet said apologetically, "I pray Your Majesty to forgive the liberty I have taken . . . It is only a figure of speech."

As usual, Napoleon had reacted in a reflex, proposing an immediate course of action before becoming emotional.

"A plague is a plague!" he exclaimed.

"It's nothing of the kind, Sire."

"Speak then! What did the King of Naples find in the city?"

Another silence. Then, quite shaken, the estafet replied in a low voice, "No one, Sire."

"What?"

"All the houses are empty, Sire. There isn't a soul about."

But there was. A handful of galley slaves under the orders of Count Rostopchin, Governor of Moscow, had yet to attend to some unfinished business. The splendid city of Moscow was to be sacrificed and turned into a funeral pyre. The existing fire engines, it would be discovered later, had been mysteriously made away with so the destruction would be complete.

The next day, to the horror of the French, the city, mostly built of wood, became a sea of flame. In an urgent dispatch, Napoleon appealed to Alexander's reason: "Sire, my Brother . . ." The Tzar's systematic devastation of lands and properties smacked of madness. The destruction of Moscow, Napoleon assured him, proved totally needless as the city's provisions had not been touched by the conflagration owing to the fact that they were stored in cellars. "And I entertain no animosity toward Your Majesty." He concluded, "In the name of our past friendship, there is still time for peace between us."

Closeted behind the walls of his palace in St. Petersburg, Alexander did not reply.

The Emperor's staff began to voice their concern about the weather. It was still warm, but the winter was less than two months away, with the supply of provisions dwindling fast.

Bent over a map of Poland, Napoleon cogitated. With the Tzar shunning conciliation, the French could take up winter quarters on Polish soil.

At this proposal, Daru, chief commissary of the army, shook his head. "The army is in no condition to get there, Sire. Our meager resources to feed it would be promptly exhausted in view of the extra physical demands imposed on troops on the move. Rationing would weaken them further and preclude any successful outcome if we were to fight off an attack by the enemy. But rationing now, while we are fairly safely encamped here, would give us time to recoup. We should winter here, Sire, and wait for reinforcement from Lithuania. Then in the spring we can march on St. Petersburg."

Napoleon made no immediate reply. While Daru spoke, a matter of grave import had just occurred to him.

Slowly, he folded his compass and straightened up, staring absently at the thick walls around the room, walls so thick that the fire that had reduced Moscow to ashes had caused very little damage to this ancient fortress the Russians called the Kremlin and in which he had established his headquarters. Daru's proposal showed spirit, the kind of spirit he did not lack and fully appreciated. Unfortunately it had to be discarded because of another pressing consideration.

It was no longer a question of *even wintering in Moscow now.*

In the grip of a sudden premonition, Napoleon finally said, "Politicians and soldiers do not mix well, Daru. You speak like a fine soldier. But I have to contend with politics. It may be disastrous for the politician to be a soldier at this juncture. If I stay away six more months, France may very well think she can do well without me. . . ."

Immediately, his audience grew tense, and all eyes converged upon him. A faint, agitated murmur rippled and swelled into a hubbub, which silenced Napoleon in the middle of his sentence. Then everybody grew quiet again, and there was a terrible pause. It weighed on the assembly even more heavily than the giant cross of solid gold which had been taken down from the cupola of St. John's church. At this instant, no one had any thought of showing off the splendid trophy destined to surmount the dome of the Invalides in Paris. Instead, they all thought of Paris, yes! Of France! But only in a context no one dared verbalize. All silently lamented: So it must come to this! *Retreat!*

". . . Therefore," continued Napoleon, himself undismayed, "I have come to a decision. I give the order that the whole army is to turn back!"

General Rapp, overwhelmed by the horrible futility of the efforts and sufferings so far endured, played dumb. "How far back, Sire?" he asked innocently.

The rebuke came swift and so familiar that it did not offend. "Home, you, ninny! Home, of course!"

The retreat of Napoleon's Grand Army began with one great disappointment: The Kremlin, marked for destruction, did not crumble as expected, for the calculations of the Corps of Engineers had gone awry. Then General Sebastiani lost six guns to a horde of marauding Cossacks while napping at his bivouac in the early hours of dawn.

As for Napoleon, a brush with an attempt at abduction by these fierce horsemen prompted him to procure for himself poison from his physician. "Alexander will not have the satisfaction of having me as his prisoner. At least not alive," he said, fingering the small pouch he now wore as a pendant around his neck. He abhorred suicide, but in this particular case, he deemed it a necessity.

Necessity! Out of necessity he must retreat and suffer the incalculable humiliation of a monumental miscalculation. It dogged his steps as he walked in temperatures ranging between twelve and eighteen below zero in an infernal nightmare of snow and ice, lashed by a vengeful buran.

There were scarcely any horses left and nearly everyone, including the Emperor, trudged on foot. Not a mighty army anymore, but a stream of ghosts in rags, leaning on sticks staggered across Russia, ignominiously retracing their steps. Then the heroic crossing of the Berezina under a heavy Russian attack turned into a tragedy brought up from the bowels of hell. Twenty thousand men drowned, but it saved Napoleon and the tattered remnant of his Grand Army from capture.

Several days from Smolensk, nine-tenths of the men had perished . . .

Then, three days from Smolensk, news of a near-disaster at home struck. The empire Napoleon had so painstakingly established and consolidated with the birth of an heir had almost collapsed. Baron de Menéval, whose secretarial duties by no means exempted him from the hardship of accompanying Napoleon to Russia, tried to calm the Emperor by stressing that at least the plot had been frustrated.

Livid nevertheless, Napoleon stared at the jibbing canvas of his tent and tried to interpret the incredible events. The rumor of his death cleverly spread all over Paris by a rebellious general named Mallet had induced his ministers to accept as a matter of course the creation of a provisional government!

"This teaches me something!" he growled, thinking the incident to be a providential test as well as a warning against complacency. "These dunces are showing me what a failure they are! Had I really died, *they should have immediately thought of my son!*"

"Thank God, Sire, the offender has been shot," soothed Menéval.

Napoleon gesticulated violently. "And I would like to shoot a dozen more! Do you know what I mean?" he fumed.

Silence answered him, and Menéval thought sadly that loyalty, alas, could not be legislated.

But it could be hammered into those numbskulls by sheer authority . . . so long as this authority held.

"I," Napoleon raged on, stressing the personal pronoun, "must get to Paris ahead of the army in order to put some sense into my ministers' heads!"

5

The phrase borrowed from a system Napoleon judged expedient to make his own, commanded the Emperor's thoughts: *The King is dead. Long live the King!*

Those idiots! Couldn't they have thought of that? Had they taken the oath of allegiance to the Constitution of the Empire like brainless parrots? Was he, in fact, ruling over a flock of fickle, feather-brained birds?

As the sledge glided westward across the snow-covered plains of Poland and Germany, leaving behind a disintegrating Grand Army under the provisional command of Murat, Napoleon remained deeply disturbed and shaken by the unreliability of his ministers and the failure of a system he had thought foolproof. This all pointed to the appalling fragility of the Empire he had thought well established by the birth of the King of Rome. Alas! it appeared that it only rested on the foundations of his own ephemeral existence and undiminished might.

He bit hard on his lips, nearly drawing blood. The debacle of the Russian campaign *had* to be glossed over! There was no doubt in his mind that this appalling setback could be repaired. But at this moment, the attempt at a takeover—though unsuccessful—ignited in Napoleon such a furor that the matter of a catastrophic retreat was relegated to the background.

The aborted coup had rattled Marie Louise only briefly and the constitutional provision that her son should succeed his father never entered her mind.

At half-past eleven on this evening of December 18, 1812, the Empress sat up in her bed alerted by murmuring voices outside her bedroom door. She recognized her lady-in-waiting Mademoiselle Katzener's high-pitched voice, which though muffled, seemed to echo a deep-toned hum that presently rose to an impatient inflection. Then there was a faint cry, a silence and a thud, as though a body had fallen to the floor. A few more silent seconds elapsed, at which point Marie Louise decided to get out of bed.

As she stood in her nightdress, the door was suddenly thrown open and a short figure, hooded and heavily swathed in furs, strode in. When the garment came off to reveal the familiar uniform of the Imperial Old Guard, she ran to her husband and clung to him with shrieks of surprise and joy.

Napoleon devoured his wife with hungry kisses, not having seen her in over seven months. She kissed him back no less ardently, mumbling German words of endearment, after which she panted happily in French, "Did you have to knock my lady over?"

"I almost had to," Napoleon replied, mildly amused. "She deserves a citation for bravery. At the peril of her life, she wouldn't let me in. Didn't recognize me under this hood and coat. Then when she finally did, she fainted in good hands. Caulaincourt is with her."

Marie Louise said ecstatically, "And you are here! With me!"

Then noticing the somber expression that had settled over his face, she pouted. "You are not happy to see me?"

"Do you know why I am here?" His tone sounded a little short, and she took umbrage.

"Nana, why are you angry with me?" she asked plaintively.

He'd expected to hear something like, "Thank God you are home! I've been so upset over the attempted takeover!" And he was about to remark on her failure to communicate her anxiety, but stopped, studying her worriedly, curiously, too.

How was she bearing the stress of having had to face the coup alone, he wondered. Poor Louise! She must be taking the whole frightful incident with more sang-froid that he gave her credit for, something which he valued over hysterical behavior.

"I am not angry," he said gently. "Just tired."

"I know, I know," she promptly soothed. "Come sit on the bed. Hold me. I've missed you!"

Complying, he decided not to bring up the subject of the conspiracy that night.

But she did.

As she sat herself on his lap and began to unbutton his uniform, she said in a casual sort of way, "You shouldn't leave me alone, Nana. . . ." She peered at him and continued as if his sudden return had been prompted by a mere whim. "You must have heard about the conspiracy. This nasty *complot* has soured my complexion. See?" She brushed a finger to her cheek.

"You look fine to me," he muttered absently, shocked by her frivolous perception of an unquestionably alarming event. Then he realized how little he knew about her. Yet he thought it best to take her attitude with indulgence. She might just be pretending levity not to burden him with her own misgivings. One thing was certain: she was hot and good in bed. . . .

When she pulled him down to her and arched herself up a little, he said dismissively, "Fear nothing. Malet is no longer a menace."

He knew the man to be a monomaniac at conspiracy—had been as far back as 1806. Since that time, he'd been adjudged mentally disturbed and confined to a nursing home from which he had escaped to play his pranks. This one, in view of the devastating consequences which would have accompanied a successful outcome, cost him his life. Malet, captured, had been sent to conspire his fill in the nether world.

Beneath her husband, her hands diligently working on the side opening of his breeches, Marie Louise gave him a smug look and said lightly, "I really don't have any reason to fear anything, Nana."

"No, dear. Because it's my job to protect my wife and my child," he replied distractedly, aroused by the fumbling touch of her fingers.

Marie Louise emitted a low throaty laugh.

"Besides," she purred into his ear, "no one would ever think of harming the Emperor of Austria's daughter!"

Immediately Napoleon froze.

He had fallen out of desire and scrambled to his feet as if a courier had just brought news that a strategic position had been overrun. At once, he thought of his son, imperiled by such an immature, irresponsible stance.

Profoundly disturbed, he demanded, his voice shaking, "Louise! Is that all you have to say?"

She looked at him with an air of perfect innocence. "I'll always be his daughter," she said, obviously bewildered by his reaction.

He glared at her. "You are my wife! You are Empress of the French!" he scolded. He was going to add: "You are not an object on loan or a guest here! Where is your loyalty? And what of our son's rights? Don't you care to safeguard them?"

But he didn't.

The sudden discovery that she was beyond the reach of such considerations swept over him with chilling clarity. All the more so, when she complained in a child-like tantrum.

"Why are you so *méchant* with me?"

"It's hopeless," he moaned inwardly. They'd been married nearly three years and he'd never raised his voice to her. He apologized with all the contrition he could pretend having.

"I'm sorry. I am not being mean to you, Louise. Must be my nerves. . . . It's been a long day!" And quickly leaned over to graze her mouth with a hurried kiss.

Marie Louise's cat-eyes gleamed in pure anticipation. She expected her husband to make up to her by throwing himself upon her like he had done on their first night at Compiègne. . . .

But Napoleon had already pulled away, driven by an urgent need to see the little King, whom General Malet was reported as having planned to place in a foundling home had the coup been successful.

Hastily, he made for the door, fastening the buttons she had undone.

Her whine stopped him. "Oh, Nana! Where are you going at this hour?"

"Our son," he said huskily, half-turning. "I want to kiss him."

"But it's late!" she said in a plaintive voice. "You can kiss him to-morrow."

He forced himself to smile. "I won't wake him," he promised.

The next morning, another promise made a few days from Smolensk was duly carried out in a tempest of reproaches, and Napoleon's ministers visibly flinched under the cold, steely look he darted at them.

"So! At the mere rumor of my death, you were about to hand over the reins of the government to a lunatic who belongs in a sanitarium!" he roared. "Gentlemen, you too, are in need of a cure! What of my heir? What of the hereditary system I've put in place to save France from anarchy and prevent her from falling prey to foreign manipulation? Your inconceivable conduct during this stupid episode makes me dread the future! *Bon Dieu!* Isn't there anyone in whom I can trust? Is there?"

Silence.

The ministers' heads hung in self-examination. Now viewed in retrospect, the whole incident was stupid indeed. A flimsy deception. And they had fallen for it. Imagine! General Malet, impersonating a higher-ranking officer, had managed to secure within three hours, three-quarter of Paris with spurious orders and proclamations.

Fortunately, Count Hullin dared demand proof of the Emperor's demise, a sensible initiative which he paid for with his life. And with equal presence of mind, his chief of staff, recognizing Malet for who he really was, took it upon himself to arrest the impostor. But the fact that a minor officer had earned the distinction of saving the Empire, left those in the official capacity of protecting it, utterly confounded.

This infuriated Napoleon. "I find no comfort knowing that you, whom I have empowered to act in time of crisis, could have failed so miserably! You have forfeited your mandate by letting a subordinate frustrate the conspiracy! If the security of the Empire is to rest on such haphazard procedures, then what need have I of you?" he bellowed.

Hurt to the quick, they protested their willingness to make amends. They realized they had sinned against the Constitution and repented.

Napoleon immediately used the overture to the utmost. France, appalled at her losses, might clamor for peace even if that meant some concessions of her vast territories, but Napoleon knew that to give up that which he had so arduously conquered, also entailed the abdication of his claim to reign over her. France was similar to a mistress he must blandish with glory or he would be forced to give her up in defeat.

Those imbeciles were really willing to make it all up to him. And he knew exactly how!

He spoke his mind.

The Russian campaign had by no means ended. He intended to raise a fresh army. Not soon, but at once, before his alliance with Prussia—which he had reduced to quasi-vassalage—could deteriorate, and before the authority he held over the Princes of the Confederation of the Rhine had a chance to wane. He spoke of the retreat in terms of a calamity, not a rout. The excessive cold had been the bane of the Grand Army. Its valor and heroism had in no way been tarnished. Its capacity to recoup was no myth, and the ministers must convince the Senate of that fact.

The ministers nodded in agreement, pleased at being needed after all.

Confidently Napoleon declared, "By spring, gentlemen, I expect to raise a new army of six hundred thousand men!"

The Senate was amenable and voted the necessary appropriations, and preparations were soon underway. Still, a fresh political victory did not lessen Napoleon's anxiety concerning the stability of his dynasty.

The system had broken down once, and more than likely, if left unremedied, it could break down again *while he might be faraway from home.*

Indeed, he could trust no one save perhaps—and this was his last resort—a device so ingrained in old traditional statesmanship that it would force France to remember his son next time, should something happen to him: The child and his mother must be consecrated by a solemn coronation. If this could better bind people to their oaths, then he would turn for aid to a sacrosanct ritual he always held as having no rational value.

Succession would be insured by Divine Right!

On the evening of January 19, 1813, Napoleon rode to the palace of Fontainebleau located some fifty kilometers from Paris. Once the favorite residence of the kings of France, the chateau presently housed a recalcitrant old man who stubbornly refused to close his harbors to English ships. Pius VII, caught in defiance of Napoleon's orders, had suffered the humiliation of seeing the Papal States annexed to the Empire and was kept a virtual prisoner at the castle.

Purposefully Napoleon came unannounced. And unless he could succeed in mollifying the Pope in some way, the Pontiff might not be willing to perform the ceremony.

At the sudden appearance of the Emperor, an assembly of bishops scattered in surprise. Their retreat disclosed a frail figure clad in traditional, immaculate white, seated on a sturdy high back chair facing a crackling fire. A folded blanket covered the Pope's knees, and it almost slipped to the floor as he, too, was startled at the sight of his imperial jailer.

The Pope was seventy-three years old. Graced with a fundamentally gentle disposition, he could be swayed. He had excommunicated Napoleon and refused to allow thirteen cardinals to attend Napoleon's wedding, thus casting doubts on the validity of the ceremony.

In a glance, both men took measure of the other—the younger reassessing the advantages of a sequestration, while the older pondered over the effect of the excommunication he had pronounced against a man whom, he thought, some driving inner demon must have placed on the pinnacle of the world.

Solicitously, Napoleon waited on the Pope. He readjusted the blanket and kissed the Pontiff's ring, a gesture of fealty he had not used to greet Pius VII when he had come to Paris for his coronation.

"It gives me pleasure to see Your Holiness. . . ."

The Pope remained silent. Napoleon had to be after something, for he wouldn't have come all this way to enjoy the pleasure of his company.

Napoleon glanced quickly at the prelates who had regrouped in a protective semi-circle behind the Pope's chair. "I wish to speak to Your Holiness in private," he said.

Pius hesitated. Alone, he might weaken and concede too much out of sheer weariness.

"It is not regarding a contentious matter, Your Holiness," Napoleon insisted calmly, stifling his impatience.

Contentious? Pius VII wondered, and what else was there? Unless the Papal States were going to be restored to him, no contention would be left indeed. . . .

Piqued with a hopeful curiosity, the Pope waved a hand of dismissal to the silent group waiting bating their breath.

Nevertheless, upon finding himself alone, and left to his own devices to face the Emperor, the old man shivered perceptibly. Promptly, Napoleon added some logs to the fire, then pulled up a small taboret in preference to a chair so that when seated, his head would be lower than that of the Pontiff. The latter took note of this: The jailer was intent on playing the role of the supplicant.

Napoleon declared after a brief hesitation, "The situation in which I am forced to place Your Holiness does not please me. With God's help, our disagreement must be resolved."

"How?" asked the Pope, gazing at the fire. He felt helpless, tired. He'd cast away the burdensome expectations weighing down on his frail, drooping shoulders. He saw himself now as an ordinary old man and longed for a much needed rest and simple quietude.

Napoleon came straight to the point. "I propose a solution to Your Holiness's situation."

"And what else must I surrender in exchange?" the Pope asked suspiciously.

"Nothing that Your Holiness could not *freely grant!*"

"Ah . . ." Pius murmured, lost in the reminiscence of the despoliation he had suffered, "I have nothing more to give." Then wistfully he said, "Christendom is homeless!"

"Holy Father," Napoleon replied, expressing only a half-truth, "this is the subject that brings me here tonight. . . ."

And for over an hour he spoke of the ills plaguing them, of the senseless misunderstanding. Must the temporal and the spiritual be at all at variance? By no means! In fact, spirit and matter were so meant to coexist in harmony that the Lord in His infinite wisdom had promised the ultimate reunion of the soul to the flesh beyond mortal life. Shouldn't they set to mend a quarrel that was tearing Christ's flock asunder?

And since Christendom was in need of a rallying point in a geographical location, this, being strictly symbolic of Christ's otherworldly kingdom, must the location be Rome? The Holy See could very well be established at Avignon permanently. The fine French city possessed a splendid basilica and a huge palace where Popes had lived at one time. That certainly would obviate any qualms the Pontiff may have about being unfriendly to the British by being forced to close his ports to them.

From Avignon, with no such political cares and considerations, Pius VII could continue tending souls as a cherished and revered guest. Why endure the heartache of feeling unjustly treated when it was merely an impression created by an attachment to a few particular square miles whose location was totally irrelevant to the salvation of mankind?

The Pope's head bobbed from exhaustion, and he felt quite incapable of arguing.

He would accept Avignon.

Napoleon moved on swiftly. "In return, Holy Father, I desire that you crown my son! Crown him on his birthday!"

"That is a most splendid gift," the Pope murmured.

"Will Your Holiness do it?"

Pius joined his hands and propped his chin on the steeple they formed. Deep in his heart, he still wished Napoleon well, and most certainly had no quarrel to pick with an innocent little child.

"I shall crown him," he finally said.

"And my wife," Napoleon added distinctly.

"The Empress, too, of course," Pius answered after a brief hesitation.

The subtle choice of the word "empress" was duly noted, and Napoleon's jaws grew taut. He bit his tongue. This was hardly the time to let his temper show. He simply mentioned that Marie Louise longed to have an audience with His Holiness. The imperial couple would have six days to visit the Pope and seal the reconciliation with a new Concordat. . . .

Six days passed. Then the year. It was again winter, one which tragically summed up a concatenation of events from which France emerged diminished and again struggling for survival.

There had not been any coronation for the King of Rome and his mother. The Pope, under the pressure of his cardinals, had changed his mind and retracted the new Concordat. Rome should remain the See of Christendom, and the Church of Christ would not allow a temporal power to browbeat its anointed representatives.

Nothing had been accomplished, and the worst was yet to come.

On the floor of the Emperor's study, a little boy dressed in a green suit with gold buttons was playing with a papier-mâché horse. Father and son had been together for only two and a half months after a separation that had lasted over half a year.

Too much had happened in the interval. Once again, Metternich had scored against Napoleon. He had succeeded in isolating him from his allies, a feat that earned the ambitious Minister the title of prince and elevated him to the post of Chancellor of State. Prussia and Austria had made common cause with Russia and England, and they had declared war on France.

The Empire was now reduced to a tatter with the loss of Holland, Germany, and Northern Italy. Stripped of the territories that served as a buffer against enemy attacks, France was at present being invaded by a host of former vassals and allies.

During a stormy interview in Dresden, Metternich had slyly protested Austria's pacific intentions provided Napoleon would content himself with a France reduced to her pre-Revolutionary frontiers.

Napoleon thought the proposal an abomination, an act of treachery and the certain warrant for his deposition. So he had gone on fighting alone in spite of an alarming rate of defections. He had been beaten at Leipzig and had returned home to rally his forces still once again. . . .

The child went on amusing himself, humming a song while his father studied a map of France, which was spread over his working table.

With utmost concentration, Napoleon applied his mind to the business of war. St. Dizier, already in enemy hands, must be recaptured; the Russians and the Prussians would have to be repulsed beyond the

Rhine; Schwarzenberg's armies ought to be insolated from Blücher's as their joined force would surely ruin Napoleon's plan of defense.

Far from distracting the Emperor, the little boy's presence was to him a source of inspiration and strength. Besides, he could never see enough of his son, never touch him or kiss him to satiety. Since his return from Leipzig, they had been inseparable.

Presently, the infant King of Rome left his toy and gently tugged at his father's coat-tail. All the bustle since Napoleon's return had alerted his quick mind that something was afoot, and when something was afoot, Papa invariably went away.

Napoleon turned.

"Papa, will you be going again?" the boy asked looking directly into his father's eyes.

Blotting out the bleak present, Napoleon lifted him in his arms and tried to draw the boy's attention back to the papier-mâché horse, but to no avail.

"Will you, Papa?" the boy persisted.

That was like the turn of a screw, and Napoleon's throat tightened. "Only for a little while," he said hoarsely.

The boy locked his little hands behind his father's neck and began to heave until his sobs became audible.

The Emperior's face tensed. He tried to devise a game to create a diversion.

"Kings don't cry . . ." he admonished gently before asking, "Sire, do you know the name of that bird at the foot of your little bed?"

The King of Rome hiccoughed and directed at his father saucer-like blue eyes glittering with tears. He sniffled before answering. "A baby eagle."

"Yes! It is called an eaglet. That is what you are now. But someday you will grow up . . . and go up and up . . ." Napoleon's voice swelled as he lifted the boy over his head and proceeded to whirl him around in simulation of a flight.

"Now!" he boomed, and this was not all in fun, "Think of yourself as a full grown eagle, flying higher and higher. . . ."

No longer crying, the Prince squealed with excitement.

Beaming Napoleon asked, "Are you afraid?"

The child giggled. "No, Papa. You are holding me."

Napoleon pressed his face against his son's little chest, then he clasped him to his own. The most tangible and most precious of all his possessions! Only two years and ten months old! He would turn three while his father would be fighting the most critical of wars. . . .

The Emperor wished for the impossible. He wished that the hand of the clock on this evening of January twenty-four of the disastrous year of 1814 would just stop—if only for one hour—to allow him to enjoy the closeness of his son a little longer. . . .

A soft but firm and calm voice startled Napoleon. "It is long past the Prince's bedtime, Sire."

Punctual, conscientious, and dedicated, the child's governess before whom no doors giving access to the Emperor were ever to remain shut, had been let in by the grenadier on guard duty.

Napoleon swung about to see her straightening out of a curtsey.

Had Madame de Montesquiou not prepared herself, her tears could have flowed freely. This was the last evening the Emperor was spending with his son; in a few hours, at dawn or maybe sooner, he would be putting himself at the head of his armies to fight a war which this time would take place on the soil of France. He would have to defend his country inch by inch against an invading host of two hundred thousand. The staggering numerical superiority of the advancing foes was no secret; nor was the puny force he had at his disposal to repulse the enemy—fifty thousand men at the most, and for the greatest part, conscripts under twenty. They looked so terribly boyish and so inexperienced that they had been nicknamed *Les Marie Louises*. . . .

The Emperor smiled, a tired smile, but a warm, welcoming one. Invariably, the presence of Madame de Montesquiou put a balm on Napoleon's anxiety as a parent and a head of state whose concerns for his son's well-being and safety were constant. He depended on the governess without reserve to care for his son in his absence, and had grown to accept his wife's shiftless ways with fatalistic resignation.

Napoleon handed over his son and said in a steady voice, "Madame, I entrust to you the future of France. Keep the Prince well and safe until my return. Make a good Frenchman of him. And second to God, may he love this country above all else!"

The governess gazed upon her charge with absolute devotion. "My pledge and my love for the Prince are one, Sire."

Napoleon's eyes misted a little. That oath of allegiance she had had to take appeared to have assumed the sacredness of an indissoluble vow.

"Love him, then," he said with emotion. "This will always be my greatest source of comfort."

When Napoleon joined his wife after having carefully burned files of secret documents in the solitude of his study, he found her still crying. Her sobs were teary monuments to dismay and it began to wear on him. Marie Louise had been crying since morning. At supper her tears seasoned her pottage. Napoleon had invited his step-daughter, Queen Hortense, to share their last meal together to spare the Empress the trauma of eating alone with him. The Queen tried to be cheerful, but this had done nothing to alter Marie Louise's downcast mood. Her weeping and wailing assaulted Napoleon's confidence. He preferred to plug his ears to the persistent echo of *the thing* she had said and attributed this to an ordinary slip one might have, being so freshly away from one's native country. With time, he thought, she will come to feel more French and relegate to the background her ties to her family.

He tried horseplay to conjure away the oppressive disappointment that overtook him, pinching her cheeks and slapping her behind. She always loved that, but this time she cried all the more. He embraced her pityingly. Poor Louise! So ill-equipped to play the role of a tragic heroine as circumstances were placing her in the predicament of being the daughter and wife of two declared enemies.

He was not unfeeling about the tremendous stress his wife was being subjected to, and at best contrived to lighten the burden she would be called to shoulder in matters of government. During his absence, she was to exercise the duty of regent assisted by his brother, Joseph, the Arch-Chancellor Cambacérès, the Minister of Police Savary, and Charles Maurice de Talleyrand. But Talleyrand bore watching. A scion of France's oldest nobility, he was in fact a bishop placed under ban by the Pope for his republican tendencies. Gifted in the art of diplomacy, he'd proved to be all too pliant in his convictions when the lures of high-paying ventures presented themselves. Yet Napoleon thought it wiser to employ his diplomatic talent during these critical times instead of having him thoroughly embittered by a dismissal. Drawn into a close-knit nucleus of government, the ex-bishop could be watched more effectively. All these dispositions, Napoleon hoped, would only be in effect for a few months, after which all should be returning to normal.

Her face pressed against his shoulder, Marie Louise managed to gasp, "When will you be back, Nana?"

He had given himself three months to be victorious or . . . dead. But he preferred to reply, "Only God knows."

"I don't like secrets," she whimpered.

"Trust me. I have not forgotten to do my job. You'll see."

"Will you give my father a thrashing?"

He stroked her hair. It was the color of champagne and their child's was of that same exact shade. He thought passionately of his son and mumbled, "You came to me, I think, in a spirit of peace . . . But your father has forsaken us. Do you love me still?"

For an answer, her mouth tore into his in eloquent intimation of what he knew must be immediately satisfied. . . .

One hour later, Napoleon went to his own room to dress. His valet, Constant, helped him put on his boots and buckled his sword belt.

Menéval, called out of bed, was bidden to attend a once thorny matter, but one that was now of no great relevance. Murat's treachery had seen to that. Egged on by his ambitious wife, Caroline, the King of Naples had allied himself to Austria in the hope of retaining his kingdom and perhaps gaining Rome as well. So it would be better to let the Pope repossess Rome now, and pull the rug from under the traitor's feet. . . .

"Have Monsieur de Beaumont inform the Holy Father that he may set out for Rome whenever he pleases," Napoleon told Menéval.

It was three in the morning when Napoleon donned his gray field coat, tucked his cocked hat under his arm and marched himself out of his room. The valet preceded him carrying his small baggage. The Emperor followed halfway, then veered toward his son's quarters.

"Go on, Constant. I won't be long," he instructed.

But he could not help tarry in the nursery. By the soft light of a night candle, the angelic beauty of his little son's face in the repose of sleep brought Napoleon very near to a complete breakdown. The heart the Emperor boasted never to feel beat in the danger of battle, now hammered at the wall of his chest with the force of a battering ram. He stood by the cradle, the silver-gilt one that was being used in preference to the other two, and gazed at the little boy he so loved that his chest hurt. Then, carefully, he leaned over and touched his lips to the satin of the child's forehead.

Napoleon swore to himself that this was no good-bye, no farewell, but only that sort of parting for which the phrase, "until we see each other again" alone, was acceptable.

Dizzied with emotion, he whispered, *"Au revoir, enfant chéri . . ."*

On a nearby cot, the governess read the Emperor's lips and crossed herself.

6

At half-past eight on the evening of March 28, 1814, the Council met at the Tuileries palace. The persistent rumble of distant cannonades indicated that Marshal Mamont and Marshal Mortier were holding the invaders at bay. Paris was now the immediate target. The situation could not have been grimmer: Stranded beyond the river Marne, outnumbered, and in no position to depend on re-enforcement, Napoleon and his main army had been cut off from the capital by the forces of the coalition.

In the council chamber, Marie Louise had been given the chair at the head of the table.

Joseph, seated next to his sister-in-law, touched her arm and whispered, "Does Your Majesty feel well enough to lead the discussion?"

She shook her head.

Joseph turned to Clarke, the Minister of War. He would be the best qualified to get the debate started.

Clarke said without hesitation, "My recommendation is that the Empress and the King of Rome leave without any delay."

"If Her Majesty leaves," Savary objected, "the Empire is done for. The nation will lose all point of rally and will be engulfed in partisan intrigues."

Talleyrand coldly but sensibly added, "If Her Majesty goes, we will be plagued by another revolution. I strongly suggest that she stay."

Savary gave a start. Whence came this sudden interest in the preservation of the Empire?

Sitting across from him, the ex-bishop pretended not to notice. The fall of Napoleon, not the collapse of the Empire, suited his plan provided the Emperor's son could reign. The King of Rome was barely three. A long minority under the regency of his languid and vacillating mother would allow Talleyrand to regain an influential position and to grow richer. The Empire must continue, but under his aegis. . . .

"Paris is going to fall, revolution or no revolution," Clarke insisted. "And the Emperor, I am certain, will never agree to expose his family to the hazard of a capture."

Marie Louise remained silent. Lacépède, the President of the Senate suggested, "We should put this matter to a vote."

The Minister of War agreed: "All those in favor of the Empress and the King of Rome remaining raise your hands!"

All hands went up except for Clarke's and Joseph's.

At long last, Marie Louise said something in a timid aside addressed to her brother-in-law. "Why should you want me to leave, Joseph?"

Joseph, who had had to flee Spain and relinquish his kingdom in the general debacle of his brother's empire, intended to advise his sister-in-law to follow the same course of action. But he was spared offering his own counsel because her husband had done it for him. Tucked in his pocket was a letter he had received from his brother earlier in the month, a letter that precisely dealt with the issue they were debating.

In answer to Marie Louise's question, the former King of Spain held up the letter for all to see. Then rising from his chair, he said, "The Emperor, having foreseen the dreadful situation that we are now facing, has communicated to me the following instructions. . . ."

Savary swore under his breath. Why in the devil's name did Joseph let them rack their brains for a solution, when it had already been spelled out by the master at solutions?

Joseph read out loud:

> *Concerning the safety of the Empress and my son, and the proper continuity of governmental functions, the Regent, the King of Rome, and other members of the imperial family, the Great Dignitaries, the Treasury and the Archives—all must be removed from Paris. The seat of government will relocate in the region of the Loire. At no time, and under no circumstances must the King of Rome be allowed to fall into enemy hands. . . .*

Joseph broke off and lifted his eyes from the text to gaze at the assembly and paraphrased: "To such an eventuality, my brother proposes a rather ghastly alternative. He'd rather see the Prince drowned in the river Seine than be captured by the Coalition."

He paused for a few seconds and added, "The latter part of the Emperor's instructions, of course, must be taken as a figure of speech.

Nevertheless, this points to the Emperor's gravest concern: that of preventing his son from being taken hostage."

The Duke of Cador could not bring himself to bow to Napoleon's directives. "The Emperor's orders are not inflexible," he argued. "Under the present circumstances His Majesty does not expect us to follow them to the letter. After all, we are not facing a takeover, only a transition that cannot be rushed. A flight, gentlemen, is an abdication of power!"

Clarke said gloomily, "There is no remission in staying. Only disaster!"

Cambacérès injected with brisk practicality, "The Emperor always expects to be obeyed. For those who choose to disregard his wishes, I propose another vote."

That was a formality. Napoleon's imperious ways had worked wonders in bending to his will the minds of those who served him. They merely followed orders and dared not interpret them. When the ballots were counted his desires prevailed.

Marie Louise asked, her voice so strained she barely made herself heard. "When do we leave? Where are we going?"

"Tomorrow is not too soon," Cambacérès said, addressing her first concern. Then he glanced at the Minister of War who, guessing the Arch-Chancellor's assumption, nodded affirmatively. Cambacérès mentioned the castle of Rambouillet.

Quietly, Talleyrand had withdrawn from the debate. He had just divorced himself from the Empire. It was doomed. There would not be any regency to exploit. And short of advancing himself with the son of Napoleon, he would do so with the Bourbons.

On this pragmatic resolve, he no longer felt the anxiety that continued to grip the other councilors when they filed out of the room in gloomy silence.

In her apartments, Marie Louise shuddered and groaned, "Oh, God! How I dread tomorrow!"

The next day, to Madame de Montesquiou's dismay, young Napoleon woke up crying. She took him in her arms, at a loss to explain this strange outburst.

The little Prince held on to her as if a torrent was about to sweep him away, sobbing, "I saw Papa in my sleep . . . and he would not listen. . . ."

A sudden chill traversed her. With disturbing frequency the boy had been dreaming about his father, and the theme of those dreams, as the child revealed, was always the same—he had gone out to meet Papa and asked him to come back. So far the dreams ended there. But now. . . .

She kissed him. "You know it is not at all for real. . . ."

"He won't come home!" the little boy interrupted, and he seemed inconsolable.

"He will," she insisted. "He is trying to get home."

The Prince peered at her, loosening his little arms from around her neck. "Where is he now?"

"By the river Marne. . . ."

He was familiar with the Seine, having been driven along its pleasant shady quays in an open carriage, or as a special treat, driving himself a miniature calash drawn by two well-mannered sheep, a present of his Aunt Caroline.

Madame de Montesquiou proceeded to explain that at one point the Marne meets with the Seine, and that sufficed to convey to the Prince the idea of proximity. For the time being, it appeared to calm him.

But the day was beginning badly.

She had just received word to ready her charge to leave. She dressed him with care, selecting an outfit suitable for travel. After prayer and breakfast, she led him to his mother without telling him anything about the journey.

The sight of Marie Louise's floor length coat and poke bonnet immediately alerted the boy. He was used to seeing his mother leisurely breakfasting every morning clad in a dressing gown with no more than two of her ladies in attendance. But this time, they were all there and also wearing coats and looking glum. Glummer still was Mother who stood next to the window looking down at the courtyard.

He ran up to her and affectionately embraced her knees, his eyes following the direction of her brooding stare. Parked below were ten green berlins and the sumptuous coronation coach all loaded with baggage. The coaches had been there waiting since dawn. And since dawn, the distraught Empress had scarcely taken her eyes off them.

He glanced up at her with some anxiety. "Are you going somewhere, Mamma?"

"Yes, and you, too. We are going to Rambouillet."

"Right now?"

"In a while. . . ." Marie Louise chewed on her bulbous lower lip, "I think."

She still hoped that at the last minute a note from her husband would cancel the exodus.

But time was passing. Inexorably!

According to Clarke, she should have set off a while back when the sky had paled over the east, and before a deputation of the National Guard begging her to stay could compound her predicament. They had solemnly pledged to lay down their lives for the Prince and herself.

She had cried. . . .

At present she would have liked to scream.

Then she jumped at the voice beside her. "Your Majesty must not tarry any longer. . . ."

General Caffarelli spoke urgently, "The Cossacks have occupied Bondy yesterday. The longer Your Majesty waits, the greater the risk to run into them on the road!"

Marie Louise tried not to shriek. "Then is the Minister of War telling me to go?"

"With due respect," the General answered, "he does command it!"

Completely unnerved, she took her child's hand. "Let us go then!" she said with a heart-rending sigh.

To everyone's surprise, the boy suddenly wrenched his hand free from his mother's grasp and recoiled in the window embrasure.

"I don't want to go!" he declared.

"Oh, please. . . ." Marie Louise said weakly. She was so utterly disconcerted that she could only plead with him. She advanced holding out her hand, but the Prince clung to the drapes. "No! I want to stay here! This is my home. Until Papa comes back, I am the master!"

Madame de Montesquiou went to the boy and caught him by the wrists, whereupon he lowered himself to the floor refusing to walk. The governess managed to half-drag him out of the room, but when they reached the staircase, the child wrapped his arms and legs around the banister.

Pale and shaking, Marie Louise went down the steps with Menéval guiding her by the elbow. Napoleon's secretary looked even paler than the Empress. That infantile tantrum bore the sinister mark of an omen. Was young Napoleon having a premonition of never returning? God forbid!

Meanwhile, the Prince continued to resist fiercely. Sizing up the problem, one of the equerries took off his coat, wrapped it around the boy so as to straight-jacket him, and carried him kicking and screaming to the waiting berlins.

When cannon balls from enemy artillery planted on the heights of Montmartre began falling in the streets of Paris, Joseph decided that resistance would be futile. Shortly, he would be joining the Empress and her suite on their journey southward. Paris was nothing now but an empty shell.

"Marmont and Mortier," Joseph instructed, "are to withdraw. And Marmont may enter into parley with the Tzar."

Talleyrand rejoiced secretly. That meant capitulation! Seeking to elude suspicion, he made a feigned attempt to leave for Rambouillet, pre-arranging his arrest at the gate of the city. Then quite satisfied, he returned to his fine house and readied it to welcome Alexander.

Trying to outstrip the Russian's advance, Napoleon hastened toward Paris. The fate of his wife and son preyed on his mind. Soon, unable to surmount his anxiety any longer, he proceeded ahead of the troops in a modest and unmarked carriage having for sole companion a dispirited but still loyal Foreign Minister, the Marquis de Caulaincourt. Caulaincourt had no illusions left. Napoleon's star was plummeting with meteoric speed toward self-destruction.

But the Emperor had not given up. If only Paris could hold and allow him to enter it undefiled, then he could salvage something. . . .

Four leagues from Paris, the horses had to be changed, and while waiting, Napoleon impatiently paced the deserted road. In the direction of the capital, a faint glow colored the night sky. God! The enemy must be bivouacking at the city's gates! He realized he could even be straying into a highly dangerous sector. . . .

Suddenly, out of the gloom, a troop of horsemen emerged in a clatter of hooves. Immediately, he put his hand to the hilt of his sword. Oh, irony of all ironies that he should be so easily caught loitering in the middle of a by-road!

Then his hand went up commanding a halt as he recognized the leader of the company in the wan light coming from the posting house.

"Belliard!" he shouted.

General Belliard dismounted, surprised at finding the Emperor alone at ten o'clock at night, and in the middle of nowhere.

"Sire, Paris has capitulated!" he announced breathlessly.

Napoleon gasped, "The Empress? My son?"

"In safety at Rambouillet, Sire!"

"But what of the National Guard? Marmont? Mortier? Was Paris taken without resistance? And where are you taking your men?"

"Your Majesty's brother, the former King of Spain," the General said, avoiding Napoleon's eyes, "has deemed it wise not to resist. Consequently, Marshal Marmont and Marshal Mortier have received the order to . . . retire. As to our destination, Sire, it is Fontainebleau, the sole rallying point of the army."

"But this is a rout!"

Belliard coughed, visibly embarrassed. "A withdrawal, Sire."

Napoleon rapped out an oath and raged, "Joseph and Clarke are fools! I leave them alone and they hand everything over! I am going to retake Paris! Follow me with your men!"

"It's too late, Sire. By now the capitulation has been signed."

"Signed?" Napoleon cried out in disbelief. "Already?"

"Talleyrand has not wasted any time. . . . He stayed behind."

Napoleon's voice rose to a full-blown fury. "Do you really want to know what I see in this man?"

Given the Emperor's explosive anger, Belliard wasn't too sure he cared to. "Well, Sire . . ." he started lamely.

"A fancy stocking full of shit!"

"He is too despicable for words," the General interposed hastily.

To which Napoleon replied, "A turn-coat! A son-of-a-bitch!"

Then shaking with rage, he stomped back to the posting house with Belliard in tow.

"The bastard! The goddamn bastard!" Napoleon kept growling, slapping a map on a table. Caulaincourt raised his eyebrows and looked questioningly at the General. Over Napoleon's bent head, Belliard silently mouthed Talleyrand's name.

The Marquis nodded. By now Napoleon had stopped cursing, and began studying the map with absolute concentration. Caulaincourt looked on, mulling over a situation for which he could not see any solution.

"Fontainebleau," Napoleon finally said, "is an excellent place to recoup. Let's go!"

In the carriage, Napoleon gave Caulaincourt specific instructions: "You will go to Paris tonight. I give you full power. Try to interpose in the negotiations. For if the treaty is conducted according to the Coalition's whim, they're going to re-establish a monarchy, a desecration of our tricolor flag!"

It was a desperate proposition which caused the Marquis to stammer, "But Sire . . . whom shall I see?"

There was a short silence. Napoleon looked thoughtfully at his one-time Ambassador to Russia. His friendship with Alexander, which Napoleon had once railed at, might prove useful now.

He said, "Demand to see the Tzar!"

A bitter disappointment awaited Napoleon's emissary. As soon as Caulaincourt presented himself at the outpost of the city now occupied by the armies of the Coalition, and announced that he was being sent by the Emperor, he was given the curt reply: "We know only of two: the Emperor of Austria and the Emperor of Russia."

Shaken, Caulaincourt turned around. As he was galloping back to Fontainebleau with little hope to spare, he realized he was no longer riding alone.

A carriage accompanied by an escort of Cossacks sped toward him. It was too late to take cover.

Caulaincourt found himself surrounded. At that moment, a head leaned out of the carriage's window, and immediately the Marquis recognized Grand Duke Constantine whom he knew well. In happier days, they had pleasantly conversed and exchanged compliments in the salons of the Tzar's winter palace in St. Petersburg.

Something of those amicable moments must have survived, for there was no animosity in the way the Grand Duke looked at him. In the lights of the lanterns, Caulaincourt even caught a flicker of interest in the eyes of the Russian prince.

"Let the gentleman come hither," Constantine ordered.

Cautiously, Caulaincourt eased his mount alongside the carriage. "Your Highness is kind!" he said gratefully.

The Grand Duke smiled and made an evasive gesture. "Have you been in Paris?"

"Highness, I was not allowed to enter the city."

"Do you come in behalf of Napoleon?"

"I do."

Constantine sucked on his thick lips for a moment, then said sympathetically, "Then, as you have already discovered, you are wasting your time."

"I wish to see the Tzar," the Marquis confessed, encouraged by the Grand Duke's well-disposed attitude.

Constantine yielded after a brief hesitation. "I can smuggle you in," he proposed. "Get in my carriage. One of my people will take care of your horse."

Together they rode toward Paris in silence, a strange twosome caught up in an amity tossed now in the eddies of discord. Caulaincourt's affable dispositions toward the Tzar had kept him in Alexander's good grace as well as his brother's.

After a while, Constantine said dispassionately, "I shall be frank with you. The fate of your country is in the hands of the royalists. The restoration of the Bourbons is in favor."

Caulaincourt frowned. In favor by whom? The French people? That was utter nonsense! They might, in the weariness of having been dragged into so many wars, disown the Emperor, but they would never repudiate the Revolution! No doubt, that recreant Talleyrand must have been peddling the idea around with his pernicious know-how so as to make the desire of a few appear to be the ardent wish of a spurious majority!

"That is a mistake I have been sent to prevent," Caulaincourt responded firmly.

Another silence followed. Then Constantine took off his pelisse and astrakhan fur cap and heaped them onto Caulaincourt's lap. "Put these on," he told him quietly. "Before we enter Paris, I'm afraid I'll have to make a Russian out of you."

"Is that really you?" Alexander looked amused as he gestured graciously at Caulaincourt's Russian camouflage Then he laughed. "And where did you spend the night?"

"I slept in the Grand Duke's carriage, Sire."

Alexander smiled. "My brother is tender-hearted indeed. First, he would not bring you to me late in the night for fear of spoiling my rest. Second, he kept me up anyway pleading in your behalf. Had it not been for his pestering, I would not have consented to see you. Nothing personal, of course. . . ." A melancholy expression crossed over the

Tzar's delicate features, then he said brusquely, "Why have you come to me? Why me?"

"Your Majesty's willingness to grant this audience can solely be attributed to the Grand Duke's abiding kindness and indulgence toward me and his own power of persuasion."

The Tzar laughed sourly. He was not duped. Caulaincourt was trying to gloss over a foible that went far deeper than a mere feeling of sympathy for a former ambassador. There was in the Russian armor a chink in the favor of his master, an ancient admiration bordering affection. Now that things were going badly for Napoleon, that affection had reappeared. Some sort of stupid sentimental nonsense!

Alexander grew angry at himself and said huffily, "Why must your emperor always provoke me? My alliance with him has caused me much trouble! It has isolated me from my people, turned my family and my nobles against me. I can do nothing for Napoleon!"

"All the Emperor asks is that the throne of France be not taken away from him." Caulaincourt meant to temper that declaration by the possibility of a workable alternative, but Alexander did not give him time.

The Tzar's pink complexion turned red.

"That's preposterous!" he interrupted. "There will never be any peace so long as the Emperor remains in power and you know it!"

"A transfer of power, Sire. The King of Rome. The Emperor's son is only three years old. Surely he can present no threat to . . ."

"With the ever present shadow of his father behind the throne?" the Tzar cut in. "No! No! And no!"

At the risk of being skinned by Napoleon, Caulaincourt introduced the word "abdication," a sure way to play down the influence Alexander so perceptively dreaded. And the further mention that a monarchy would create more dissension among the French than it would bring about the stability sought after by the Coalition produced an encouraging change of attitude in the Tzar.

Alexander's face smoothed attentively and the color returned to a rosy hue.

Personally, he had no desire to force upon the French a regime contrary to their choice. On the other hand, the King of Rome being very young and malleable, and *related* by blood to the Emperor of Austria, was after all a rather sensible solution. His grandfather should influence him to adopt absolutism without openly repudiating a republic. And being a child of the Revolution through his father, the boy would certainly be acceptable to the French people.

Alexander spoke slowly, "Go back to the Emperor, and report to him what you have just proposed."

Caulaincourt thought, *I did it, Sire! I've put an end to your career! Oh, but you told me to save the Republic! How else could I have done this?*

Standing before Napoleon, he blurted out. "Sire, you are to surrender the crown to your son."

Napoleon leaped out of his chair. "Nonsense! Absolute nonsense! Who is talking of abdication?"

"I did, Sire."

"You?" the Emperor shouted.

"Sire, I had to! Or else the crown will be going to the Bourbons."

Napoleon fumed, pacing and gesticulating. "No abdication! Only if all is lost and that is not the case! I have fifty thousand men at my disposal. To abdicate now would be cowardly! Such infamous conduct will never strengthen my son's rule, nor will it add any luster to his reign. I'd rather have the crown taken away from the both of us by an act of courage on my part. I'm going to fight! Do you hear me? Fight! Fight!"

The marshals argued. There was fermenting among them, a mounting spirit of rebellion. What could fifty thousand men do against a host of invaders well-provisioned, well-equipped, and converging toward Paris from the four corners of France? They grumbled.

Napoleon told them with a drilling look, "If it is rest that you seek, take it! But you will force France to pay a dear price for your repose!"

Two hours later he handed Caulaincourt the abdication he had written in favor of his son. "Let's be done with this," he said sharply. "Go! Marshal McDonald and Marshal Ney will accompany you. Where is Marmont?"

"We don't know, Sire."

Pending Caulaincourt's return, word finally came that Marshal Marmont held a vital position at Essonnes with a contingent of twelve thousand men. He was presenting a buffer essential to the protection of Fontainebleau. Napoleon immediately issued an order to hold Essonnes at all cost. Marmont and his men spelled the difference between being hounded or captured and remaining the free leader of a sizable army. In the latter case, Napoleon would still be able to influence the negotiations by retaining some bargaining powers. Owing to Marmont, all was not completely lost. . . .

Marmont's Sixth Army Corps was on its way to Paris.

"We are marching against the enemy," the Marshal had said with a straight face, which almost immediately twisted into a grimace when the troops promptly responded with an enthusiastic acclamation: *Vive l'Empereur!*

The advance went swiftly. Too swiftly. Where was the enemy to bar their progress? Of course it was night and troop movements could not be easily detected. . . .

At dawn, Marmont's soldiers found themselves encircled by the Austrians. Realizing the dupery, the rear columns began to turn back with the desperate cry: "To Fontainebleau! Paris is a trap! We have been betrayed!"

As Marmont galloped alongside the rebellious soldiers, he was met with curses and imprecations. The soldiers had always admired his gallantry, but his conduct presently added to their anger a good dose of perplexity. They wanted an explanation or there was going to be mutiny!

Red in the face, Marmont obliged. "I have never shunned danger in the defense of the Empire! But Paris has already capitulated. A provisional government composed of Frenchmen has been installed. We must not fight against our own, and we are not going over to the enemy. We are only putting ourselves at the disposal of our compatriots. I would rather be shot now than suffer the infamy of having my actions misconstrued for an act of treachery!"

He waited. But no retributive volley cut him down. Torn between their devotion to Napoleon and Marmont's impassioned exposition of his motives, the soldiers wavered. Finally, Marmont prevailed, knowing full well that the evacuation of Essonnes was the death of the Empire.

Unaware of the new development, Caulaincourt hastened to see the Tzar. But when the Marquis handed over the fateful document, Alexander made no move to take it. "I am afraid we can no longer honor this," he said calmly.

"But, Sire, it is drafted according to Your Majesty's recommendations."

"The situation has considerably changed since our last interview. Marshal Marmont's troops are no longer to be counted among your emperor's adherents. Essonnes is now open, and Napoleon is in our power, if we choose to seize him."

Caulaincourt rammed a curse down in his throat. He rasped, "What is Your Majesty asking now?"

"We want an unconditional abdication."

"What will become of the Emperor? What will you do with him?"

"I shall endeavor to arrange an acceptable . . . sentence."

"What does that mean?"

"Possibly the sovereignty of the island of Elba and the retention of the imperial title," Alexander said, feeling magnanimous.

Caulaincourt cringed. Oh, how they were going to deride Napoleon! Turn the rest of his life into a farce! The sovereignty of Elba! A speck of an island off the coasts of Tuscany. He could feel the Emperor's humiliation and well imagine his rage at being so ridiculed.

He mumbled, "This is the end. . . ."

"At last!" Alexander agreed with a smile. "The end of strife and tyranny! What your emperor will suffer is an exceedingly mild punishment for the terrible wrongs he has done!"

Of all the evil conditions Alexander blamed Napoleon for having caused, tyranny was the most hypocritical accusation, especially coming from the Tzar. Caulaincourt was about to rise in his master's defense and say, "The monarchies of Europe are monuments to tyranny!"

But he didn't. What good would this have done?

Napoleon had somewhat prepared himself for the worst; but not for what Marmont did. His defection inflicted a deep, personal wound. Marmont, whom Napoleon always thought of as a brother, had delivered him to the enemy!

Bluntly, Berthier reiterated a strategic weakness: "Sire, without Marmont at Essonnes, Your Majesty could easily be captured!" He hesitated and added with genuine desolation, "It's no use, Sire. It's all over!"

Sullen and withdrawn, Napoleon wrote the final abdication, renouncing for himself and his heir the thrones of France and Italy.

In the early part of April, the Coalition sealed his fate. Alexander's influence was being felt, and Napoleon, it was agreed, would be exiled to the island of Elba.

He did not display any emotion. The hurt had imploded in a silent, heart-wrenching lament: *His little son's inheritance!*

Nothing!

Nothing left to pass on!

Nothing more than stardust!

7

"My father," Marie Louise said, "is a good man! He is fair and honest!"

Colonel Galbois preferred to keep silent. Sent by Napoleon, he had come from Fontainebleau and just caught up with the Empress, whose progress had taken her now to the town of Blois. Galbois had hastened to bear news that contradicted Marie Louise's complimentary statement about her father: The allied sovereigns, including Francis, had dethroned Napoleon and his son—Francis's own grandson.

In a letter, the Emperor apprised his wife of his fate and spoke of his father-in-law as their "most ferocious enemy." The Empire was dead, and her flight across France, pointless. To share her husband's exile was all she could expect.

"This can't be!" she insisted, holding up Napoleon's letter. "My father would not endorse an unconditional abdication! Is he in Paris?"

"No, Your Majesty."

Marie Louise's heart gave a hopeful jolt. All was not lost! Francis being absent, nothing must be final. And as soon as he was acquainted with the villainy perpetrated against his daughter's family, he would intervene. He would show himself as good a father as she would prove to be a devoted wife.

"Take me to the Emperor! My place is with him in these trying moments!"

"Majesty, I've not been given instruction to do so."

"Why not?"

"The Emperor realizes that his most ardent wish to be reunited with his family at Fontainebleau is impractical and ill-timed."

"How long, then, must I wait until my husband sends for us?"

"His Majesty will advise you in good time. Hopefully soon."

This cheered Marie Louise somewhat. In her heart of hearts, she could not conceive ever spending her life without the man whom she regarded as the most amiable of husbands.

"Colonel Galbois," she said earnestly, "do tell the Emperor that I shall be content only when I am with him!"

After the Colonel's departure, Marie Louise immediately wrote Francis four letters, which were entrusted to four emissaries so as to make certain that at least one of them would reach him.

Her present situation upset her and only being with her husband could restore her peace. Instinctively she mistrusted her entourage in general. Only two people had earned her confidence because of their unquestionable devotion to Napoleon: Baron de Menéval, and Madame de Montesquiou. As for the Duchess de Montebello, Marie Louise had placed her beyond any possibility of wrongdoing. The Duchess, in her belief, was simply irreproachable.

But her favorite, who secretly delighted in Napoleon's downfall, had vowed to aggravate his miseries mostly through his wife, and strained toward a goal for which she felt no qualm of conscience—the separation of the spouses.

She had long discerned in Napoleon's Austrian wife a weakness against which, she too, must guard herself. Whatever Marie Louise decided to do, she meant to do it with complete sincerity, until someone or some event would pressure her to swerve from her resolve. That unfortunate propensity came as no aid to those who depended on Marie Louise or sought to exploit her.

Taking no chances, Louise de Montebello decided she must play her part in stopping the Empress from joining her husband. Moreover, she might gain certain advantages in accomplishing this other than to gratify her own spite for not having been elevated to the rank of princess by Napoleon, and not having been chosen as his son's governess. She might even earn some recompense from Napoleon's enemies by working on distancing Marie Louise from her husband. It seemed the political thing to do.

Without wasting a minute, she sat herself down and wrote a letter, pretending to be sending news of herself to relatives in Paris. Only the letter contained a second message to be delivered to Prince Schwarzenberg. In that message, she urged him to prompt action. He must secure the custody of the Empress as it would be most unfortunate and embarrassing for the Allies if Marie Louise were allowed to espouse the cause of her husband simply by joining him in exile, especially since she was the daughter of one of the victorious members of the Coalition. The ambiguity and awkwardness of this situation, the Duchess further advanced, would be a sure obstacle to meaningful negotiations toward a lasting peace. . . .

In her bedroom, sitting in front of her mirror, Marie Louise despondently studied her reflection. It told her that the stress incurred by having to deal with the complications and the challenges of the unknown was obvious in the way she looked. Her lily-and-rose complexion had grown dull and sallow, little bags were pursing under her eyes. Her hair kept falling. She looked and felt like a wreck. Perhaps an hereditary weakness of the chest. . . .

She even began to cough, as listlessly, she rose and went to her drawing-room.

There she realized she had visitors.

Without having bothered to be announced, Joseph, Arch-Chancellor Cambacérès, and Jerome were waiting for her.

Joseph spoke at once. "Madame, you must come away with us." Guile thinned his voice but did not affect his manners, whose abruptness did not invite compliance.

"Yes! You must," Jerome seconded. And the two brothers exchanged a quick, concerted glance.

Joseph and Jerome had concocted a scheme because common sense and personal considerations told them that in the general collapse of the Empire, Francis's daughter could be used as a pawn to better their lots, provided she would not separate herself from them. She might, though, either by going to her husband or entrusting herself to her father, which in either case, would do them no service. On the other hand, if they were to secure for themselves the custody of the Empress and her son, they would save themselves from disadvantageous treatments as they would be in possession of something to bargain with.

But that "something" which Napoleon's brothers thought was docile and easily swayed, balked when Joseph added that Blois was no longer safe.

Marie Louise felt overcome with weariness. Again she must flee! She shrank at the idea and it injected in her unsuspected grit.

"Go if you want. I am staying here. I shan't run anymore!" she said, astonished at her own firmness.

Jerome declared superciliously, "We have orders to prevent Your Majesty and the King of Rome from falling into enemy's hands. We are thereby empowered to use force to accomplish this!"

Immediately she decided that Jerome was her most immediate enemy.

"I rather count on your devotion to let me await the Emperor's orders to proceed from here," she said trying to placate him.

Exchanging another quick glance, the two brothers stepped forward with perfect coordination. Cambacérès made at the same time a flanking movement.

Marie Louise panicked. They were really going to lay their hands on her! Frightened, she ran to the nearest bellpull and tugged at it, all the while screaming for help.

Surprised, the threesome drew back as the Empress's people erupted into the room, alerted by her cries. Baron de Bausset collided into the two dethroned kings, and General Caffarelli received Marie Louise in his arms.

Hysterically, she stammered out her brothers-in-law's misdeed. And immediately, they broke into vehement protestations.

Soothingly, Caffarelli said to her, "No one will go against Your Majesty's wishes. . . ."

Then de Bausset inquired ceremoniously, "What does Your Majesty want to do?"

Marie Louise repeated what she had told Jerome, that she wanted to stay in Blois and let her husband tell her when to go to him. Then, for the first time since her marriage, she felt completely estranged from her French entourage. Those dignitaries who were sworn to serve her, and who proclaimed their loyalty were foreigners and strangers for whom she might only be an embarrassment. The sole tie that saved her from a total feeling of alienation was Napoleon. But he was away and silent on the subject of having her come to him. Oh, if only he could say the word! How diligently she would comply!

Meanwhile the Baron assured her, "We will receive orders from Your Majesty only!"

Fuming, Jerome left the room with Joseph and Cambacérès on his heels.

Marie Louise now toyed with the notion that only her father, next to her husband, could put a stop to her tribulations.

Feeling homesick, she began to cry.

On April 8, Baron de Bausset's deferent words to Marie Louise proved to be nothing but words when the Tzar's aide-de-camp, Count

Shuvaloff, turned up in Blois. The Duchess de Montebello's message had been duly received.

"I have," the Russian said rather arrogantly, "come to conduct Your Majesty and her son to Orléans!"

Ruffled by his tone, Marie Louise snapped back, "And on whose orders are you so bold to advance this?"

Shuvaloff clacked his heels in a way which conveyed brutality rather than respect. "The order of the Allied Powers, Madam!"

Fright gave her a sinking sensation at the pit of her stomach. So Jerome was right after all. She was at the mercy of her husband's enemies, and in a way, she should be considering herself her father's prisoner, too! And where was Francis? Had he received her letters? And would he treat her like a rebel? But why? After having forced her to marry in the first place. . . . How could he fault her?

The authenticity of Shuvaloff's orders were beyond question and his mission signaled a general dispersion, for he had only come to secure the person of the Empress and her son. The others were free to part from her if they so chose. But the Duchess de Montebello was ordered to stay with her mistress. Her excellent work, Shuvaloff reflected. . . .

Of the throng that had accompanied Marie Louise thus far, only a handful remained with her. With dismay she watched the disbandment of her suite, and her feeling of estrangement deepened.

Letizia's most urgent care was to be with Napoleon, while Joseph and Jerome were arranging to go to Switzerland. The ministers and councilors applied to return to Paris.

Napoleon's mother lifted her grandson in her arms, made the sign of the cross on his forehead and kissed him for as long as she could. The little King had grown exceedingly fond of his grandmother. He hugged her as if he were never to see her again.

Throughout their whole ordeal, Letizia's love for the boy had deeply affected her perception. These events, which were to decide the course of his destiny, caused her unbearable anxiety for his future. She also knew that much of Marie Louise's conduct would determine the ultimate fate of her husband and son, especially through the influence the Empress could exert on her father.

Releasing the child, she cast on his mother a long, assessing look. Her daughter-in-law presented a pitiable sight. Marie Louise was deathly pale and shivered in spite of a heavy fur coat. She coughed weakly in her handkerchief.

Letizia embraced her. "Take heart, my daughter." Then she whispered in her ear, "Remember that Napoleon depends on you as he has never depended on anyone else before!"

Marie Louise's mouth quavered. She felt drained, and confused. With eyes downcast, she murmured, "I pray you will continue to keep me in your esteem and affection. . . ."

Letizia's features hardened imperceptibly. "This, my daughter," she said as gently as she could, "will depend on you, also."

In Orléans, Marie Louise kept waiting for a reply from her father to her plea to cancel the Coalition's pronouncements on her husband and to re-establish the Regency. But Francis was still in Troyes while Metternich had preceded him to Paris. In the absence of Francis, the messengers thought it quite logical and proper to pass Marie Louise's letters on to his Chancellor.

On behalf of Francis, Metternich penned a deceitfully reassuring message. The Empress and her son were promised an independent existence, and she would be free to either join her husband in Elba, or reside in the duchies of Parma, Piacenza, and Gusatalla, which the Coalition was willing to cede in a gesture of conciliation. Pending the final negotiations, she was to prepare herself to meet her father in Rambouillet.

When Prince Paul Esterhazy and Prince Wensel-Lichenstein came for her, she said the fateful words, "Take me to my father."

At Fontainebleau, about to set sail for Elba, a leave-taking worked havoc with Napoleon's emotions: the Old Guard.

Before climbing in the waiting carriage, he kissed the tricolor flag, looked at the silent, emotion-torn sea of faces and commanded with a carrying voice, "Continue to serve France!"

The men who'd served him for twenty years roared back, *"Vive l'Empereur!"*

No one acclaimed Marie Louise when she arrived in Rambouillet. Her Russian escort kept her under close watch, and all seemed to conspire to make her feel like the most abject of criminals. Was this, she reflected sadly, a foretaste of the kind of treatment her father reserved for her?

To her bitter disappointment, Francis had not yet arrived to keep their rendezvous. Unnerved and alarmed, she spent three long agonizing days. When he finally came, flanked by Metternich, she was waiting at the foot of the stairs, holding her son, Madame de Montesquiou standing a few paces behind.

"Oh, Papa! Papa!" she sobbed, thrusting the boy into his arms and slowly sinking to the floor embracing the Emperor's knees.

Practically nose-to-nose, grandfather and grandson peered at each other. Francis was instantly charmed by the child. The little King stared at the Emperor's incredibly elongated face and nose and let himself be kissed passively.

Francis couldn't take his eyes off the Prince as his governess led him away.

Metternich discreetly emitted a short cough.

"Oh . . ." Francis looked down and helped his daughter to her feet.

She threw herself on his breast. Metternich, calm and deferent, motioned Francis to one of the salons. Obligingly, he opened the door for them and then left father and daughter alone.

Francis asked dutifully. "How are you?"

"Not well. Did you read my letters?"

"I've been made aware of their contents, yes."

Still heaving, she said, "Can't you restore the crown to your grandson? You have seen him. . . ."

"Ah, yes!" Francis murmured dreamily.

"Poor little sweet boy! You can't wish him to have Elba for sole inheritance! You can't treat us like criminals! I've only done your will and he is the innocent fruit of my obedience. Oh, Papa, you owe us something!"

Francis stiffened. "I can do nothing for your husband. He is my enemy."

"I am not asking you to do anything for him, Papa! You must do something for *us!* You must protect my son's rights. Your blood runs in his veins!"

In the eyes of God, from whom derived his sovereignty, Francis would be justified in betraying the blood ties upon which his daughter and, no doubt, his son-in-law so depended. Pity! They should have understood that his office owed no liege to any mortal, not even kindred.

He said with grandiloquence, "I am above all the father of my people. Then and only then, your ever loving father . . . and your son's grandfather. So, when your interests and those of my people come into conflict, theirs must prevail. If you still have feelings for your homeland, you must also know that we cannot coexist with *any* of the Bonapartes *sitting on a throne!*"

Marie Louise looked at her father in an agonized way as if he had stabbed her. "So you will punish an innocent child for the sins of his father! Permit his exile to a miserable little island! Force him to live like a renegade for the rest of his life! Oh, Papa! I thought you did love us!"

"I do love you," Francis protested distractedly. That was because his ears had just caught something his daughter said, something of utmost importance for the future. She admitted to her husband *sinning!* If she so judged Napoleon, then she must have remained at heart an archduchess, her father's daughter. . . .

Francis spoke with genuine tenderness. "My dear child, must we speak of exile when you and your son are so near home?"

Marie Louise stared blankly at her father. At present she knew of no home. She was only aware of the availability of a place, Elba, where she and her son were to go eventually.

Francis smiled at her. "You need rest. And you will find Schönbrunn to be the perfect place to sort things out."

At this suggestion, her lids fluttered. "Thank you, Papa. I only intend to stay until I am rested enough to travel with my son to Elba."

"You really needn't rush," Francis said slyly.

She insisted. "Since my son's situation is without appeal, our places are by Napoleon's side!"

Francis worried. That was not what the oligarchy wanted! So far, he had made every effort to skirt certain considerations to spare her feelings for Napoleon, but now he could no longer afford to be so delicate.

"Louise, if you associate yourself with your husband, you are declaring yourself my enemy and that of the sovereigns with whom I have entered into a solemn and holy alliance."

She stared at him wide-eyed. ". . . now, must you turn away from so worthy a cause?" Uncertainly she shook her head. He pressed the point she was not to forget. "Remember that your marriage was intended to redeem our House." He gently took her by the shoulders as if to steady in her the realization of this wonderful truth. "Now this is done! And I do not wish to impose any additional sacrifices upon you. . . . As for your son—as you have so well understood—what future will he have with his father? He would gain much by staying with me."

A dull expression settled over Marie Louise's face. "Then you forbid us to go to Napoleon?"

"You are still free to decide. But it is your future, your happiness, your tranquillity, you are defining now. I offer comfort, consolation, and repose as a father knows how to give."

She heaved, "Oh . . . I am so terribly tired!"

"I know. And that is not good."

"Home is all I want, Papa!"

Metternich, a self-styled deus ex-machina, triumphed. The next day he approached Francis and said smoothly, "It behooves Her Majesty, seeing that she is accepting the hospitality Your Majesty is extending to her, to receive our Allies. A short audience would suffice."

Francis frowned. His daughter had been humiliated enough.

"Isn't this a trifle frivolous?"

"Alas, Sire, diplomacy is nothing but an exercise in frivolity!"

"Yet, so far reaching?"

"And often times, far more potent than armed conflict," added Metternich.

Francis thought briefly and smiled. Now he understood. Marie Louise's official interview with Alexander and Frederick William would go on record as the preliminaries to a willful disassociation with Napoleon's cause.

"Then by all means, this must be arranged," he agreed.

Apprised of her father's decision, Marie Louise protested loudly. The proposition was distasteful to her. Both sovereigns were the cause of all her afflictions.

"I don't wish to see them," she said. "They made me suffer enough!"

"Is that all that's bothering you?" Francis asked innocently.

"That is more than I can bear," she replied, obviously vexed by his lack of compassion.

"It's just a formality," he answered, relieved that she did not appreciate the true significance of submitting to the interview.

She pouted.

"It would please me that you see their Majesties without my having to order you to do so," he added in a tone of voice that gave her no alternative.

Marie Louise yielded. But when she asked if he would be present at the audience he shook his head "no." In truth, he was ashamed for her and made excuses. He told her he must return to Paris and tie up loose ends, then organize her return trip to Austria. At the mention of Austria, Francis was pleased to see her eyes brighten, and her indignation at receiving the sovereigns in whom she only saw her personal tormentors rather than Napoleon's enemies subsided.

Alexander showed Marie Louise much kindness and consideration. He called her son "King of Rome" as if nothing had happened; he even asked to see the child, and caressed the boy with genuine emotion. The King of Prussia's visit was more brief, much to Marie Louise's relief. She had no use for his condescending and patronizing attitude.

The next day, Marie Louise began to journey homeward, but not before writing Napoleon a letter exposing a happy and sad state of affairs—her father's kindness in insisting that she rest, but spoiling things a little because this must take place in Austria, after which she could go to Parma and from there to Elba.

She assured him that the delay would nearly kill her.

On a fair day in May, Marie Louise and her entourage of sixty-four left the soil of France. Then, four leagues from Vienna, Empress Maria Ludovica, elated by the ruin of Napoleon, came out sweet and mawkish to meet her step-daughter. They embraced and cried, Maria Ludovica gushing with relief as though Marie Louise—praise be to God!—had returned to the roost, safe from ill-treatment after four years of abject servitude to that ignoble upstart! Oh, how she hated him still! How she would go on detesting his son just as much! While hugging his mother, Francis's wife had consigned the boy to his father's lot, to annihilation.

Young Napoleon sat beside his governess in another carriage. Full of excitement at the beginning of the journey, he had grown progressively more quiet. Of late, he'd gone through frequent spells of melancholy. And each time this had happened, the governess became more concerned. She was racking her brain to find a consistent and calming answer to a question he kept asking her with redoubled frequency, why didn't he ever see his dear Papa anymore?

She always answered, "You will. It's only that he is very busy and the roads are bad in the winter." For a while, she blamed everything on the weather, but the winter had already passed. Now she simply kept telling him to be patient, that Papa would come. Or that he would go to see him.

Presently, the fuss caused by the two empresses meeting halfway before the end of the journey must have given the boy the impression that his own reunion with his father was imminent.

"Will we see Papa now?" he asked hopefully tugging at her sleeve.

She put her arms around him and tried to sound cheerful.

"Not today, but soon!"

Indeed there was no real indication that she could be deceiving him. No one had forced his mother to undertake this journey. She had only been persuaded. If Marie Louise should decide to set out for Elba sooner, it was commonly held that this option was hers to take.

Presently he snuggled up to her and appeared, for the moment, satisfied with the answer she had given him.

Soon, the caravan to which was added Maria Ludovica's equipage, resumed its progress. The dethroned French empress's twenty-four coaches, still bearing the imperial arms of France, wended their way along meadows abloom with wild flowers alternating with light forests suffused with the green twilight of an Austrian spring.

At nightfall, Schönbrunn came into view. Marie Louise pressed her face against the glass-plated window of her carriage to stare dewy-eyed at her beloved castle with its familiar, long, stately facade. The windows were ablaze with lights as though they had been lit to keep a joyful vigil, waiting for her to come home.

A tear fell.

8

That same evening at Schönbrunn castle, Madame de Montesquiou allowed her charge to stay up a little longer while the daughter of his nurse, young Fanny Soufflot, helped her unpack some of their baggage. Now and then, Fanny would glance sadly at Napoleon's son.

Seated on the carpet, the boy was engrossed with a mechanical bird, which properly wound up, sang and fluttered its brightly painted little wings.

Fanny adored the little Prince since the day she had followed her mother into his service. In turn, he grew attached to her girlish, lively ways—she was only fifteen. She spoiled him outrageously when the governess was not looking and he rewarded her by demanding that she hold his hand whenever they went for a walk. On those occasions, the servant girl felt immensely honored to stroll hand-in-hand with the heir to the French Empire.

Alas! she lamented silently, he was now the heir to great uncertainty! The two women did not speak. Once in a while, their eyes would meet in a mute exchange of shared anxiety. The strange language being spoken around them already accentuated an ominous change.

The Countess was beginning to realize its full and sinister significance. An exile in Elba straight away would have been proper and best. Whereas here, they were, in fact, in enemy camp. The hospitality offered them was deceptive, and she hoped it would not be too long before the boy could be reunited with his father.

Presently the Prince put down his toy and looked up thoughtfully at the white and gold ceiling. He startled his governess by asking, "Will we be staying here very long?"

A little pale, she answered evasively, "Don't you like this room?"

The boy glanced around. "I prefer the ones I had in Paris!"

That upset her. After leaving the Tuileries with so much reluctance, he had made no mention of preferring one place over another during their frantic flight across France. And some of the residences where they found lodging did not compare with the flamboyant luxury of the suite they presently occupied. It was even a little too gilded and gaudy for the Countess's taste.

Still, what is a child to know about such nuances? He most certainly judged by instinct, and that disquieted her. She realized with mounting dread that someday he would have to be told that he would not be going back to Paris at all. The disheartening prospect daunted her courage.

Trying to interest him, she said, "This is a beautiful room! Look again. And tomorrow you will see many other lovely things!"

But she purposefully did not tell him about the world-famous menagerie and wonderful botanical garden, hoping the boy's curiosity would be aroused.

"What other things?" he promptly asked.

Madame de Montesquiou smiled, relieved to have distracted her charge. "It is a surprise," she said. Then enticing him further, she added, "You will see tomorrow how wonderful it is!"

Overtaken by a sudden inspiration, the Prince said, "Coming here is also a surprise isn't it?"

Fanny made a sudden movement, but the governess remained calm. Her approbation was circumspect and quickly she moved on with a reminder the child appreciated. "It has been a long and tiring day, and you need rest."

Whereupon, with Fanny's help, she proceeded to prepare him for bed. The girl finished buttoning up the gown into which the Prince was changed, and this done, she kissed his hands as it was her custom. Then on an impulse, she pressed her lips to the enwreathed initial "N" embroidered on the collar, and ran out of the room.

The little boy watched her go, puzzled.

"Napoleon, our prayers!" Madame de Montesquiou said briskly, anxious to regain his attention.

As she had taught him to pray, it was her habit to pray with him also, because she did not believe in simply watching her charge deliver a pious gibberish no one could understand much less the child himself. To pray, she had explained, is a meaningful and simple practice. All one needed to do was to open one's heart to God. And God, she stressed over and over, is very loving and lovable. And once again, she said, "As we pray, know that God loves you."

Yet even as she reminded him of this, it was she who caused his baby heart to leap with an upsurge of affection for her. She was so completely a part of his life that she had become as dear to him as a real parent. He'd been calling her *Maman Quiou*.

He gave her a hug, which she returned while trying not to think unkindly of his mother.

Unlike Napoleon, Marie Louise did not require the frequent, if not constant, company of her son. She loved him with none of the concentration and vigilance the Countess lavished upon her charge; in return, the Prince demonstrated toward his *Maman Quiou* the instinctive appreciation of a bond only true parenting can provide: familiarity and tenderness, always guided by discipline.

Following a well-established ritual, she folded her hands over his, and they began to pray for the safeguard of all. At the mention of his father, the boy was fervent but calm.

When they had finished, he sprung out of his devotion with the liveliness of his tender age.

The last concluding "Amen" said, he asked, "Have I been a good king today?"

The Countess hesitated. That was a delicate subject that demanded that she put her reply in proper perspective. The child's standing had become problematic. He had no longer any right to the title of king because, since his father's unconditional abdication, he was now the son of a private person. But in the governess's eyes, the boy remained unquestionably a French prince. The idea that this singularity could be overlooked distressed her. A crown he might lose, but a citizenship, never!

"You have been a very likable prince!" she answered him, avoiding the word "king" to wean him from this notion. Then she went on to say that to reward him for his good behavior, she would sing to him and rock him to sleep, not in the cradle as Madame Marchand, his cradle rocker would do, but on her knees.

To fall asleep snuggled in the security of *Maman Quiou's* arms delighted the boy. He promptly clambered onto her lap and planted a grateful kiss on her cheek.

Rather large for his age, he made an armful. And gathering him to her, Madame de Montesquiou felt a sharp twinge of pity. It should have been Marie Louise's place to hold her son tonight, of all nights. But after a rather copious supper with her step-mother, Empress Maria Ludovica, Marie Louise had retired early, complaining of stomach cramps and nausea.

She kissed him back with great tenderness as if he had just been orphaned, asking softly, "What shall I sing?"

"Sing that song about rain and shepherdess."

"Ah yes! *Il pleut bergère!*"

That seemed to be his favorite *berceuse.* So she began to sing the old lullaby so familiar to little French children, and on a gentle tale of a soft rain falling on a kinder world, he drifted into sleep, dreaming of the marvels she had promised to him in the morning, and of a strange castle whose name he could not pronounce.

Schönbrunn castle, the Austrian counterpart of Versailles—the stately palace of France's Sun King—though not as grand, commanded a well-deserved fame of cozy magnificence. A beloved summer residence of the Habsburg emperors, it contained one thousand four hundred rooms, which were spacious and lavishly decorated in the Baroque-style that had been so dear to Empress Maria Theresa. In that ornate yet homey setting she had raised her numerous children, among them Marie Antoinette, who paid with her life for the distinction of marrying Louis XVI of France.

The gardens were laid out with studied elegance, formal and precise and dainty like the steps of a minuet. The lawns were shorn neatly to produce a smooth field of emerald, upon which flower beds formed intricate and colorful designs. There were broad walks lined with impenetrable clipped hedges of hornbeam and yoke-elm trees, which rose like walls to impressive height. Many birds nested in the tangle of their branches and usually at sunset filled the air with the din of their chirps.

Behind the palace and beyond the misty horizon marking the confines of the park, a graceful yet impressive porticoed monument called the *Gloriette* stretched elegantly on a grassy knoll, where one could enjoy a panoramic view of Vienna.

Just as Madame de Montesquiou had supposed, young Napoleon paid little attention to the landscaping, save to remark that trees in this country looked rather unfriendly. But she was correct in the assumption that the menagerie and the botanical garden would enchant him.

On his first day at Schönbrunn, young Napoleon would not hear of tearing himself away from the fascinating spectacle of animals from faraway places and the extraordinary display of strange tropical plants he had never seen. He only consented to leave the garden when told that at the stables a present from his grandfather awaited him. It turned out to be a little donkey adorned with silver bells and bright red pompons. Francis, everyone was quick to notice, already thought much of his little grandson.

But an old Queen who lived close to Schönbrunn, in the small castle of Hentzendorf, did not entertain such benevolent feelings. At least, in principle. She was Maria Carolina, Marie Louise's maternal grandmother. Now sixty-two, she had gone through her share of grief and trouble with France and with Napoleon. Her sister, Marie Antoinette, had died on the French guillotine. Then, with the advent of Bonaparte, she had lost her throne of Naples to the French Emperor's brother-in-law, Murat. As a reward for his recent treachery, Murat was allowed to retain his kingdom, to the extreme vexation of the old Queen.

Now, her rancor for Napoleon left no room for exception in her embittered heart, not even for a small child whose innocence she conceded without relaxing her grudge. Maria Carolina had not yet seen the son of that "devil" Bonaparte, but she had heard enough about him to harden in her resolve to dislike him.

It was in that hostile frame of mind that on a Sunday afternoon, shortly after Marie Louise's arrival at Schönbrunn, the unhappy Queen received the visit of her granddaughter and great-grandson. Although she never did approve of Marie Louise's marriage, Maria Carolina considered the obligations contracted by this union very much in force. There was no question in her mind that Marie Louise's place was at her husband's side, whatever the circumstances might be.

With this conviction, she embraced the young woman with an effusion that combined the element of a welcome with that of an adieu. Then she lowered her eyes and caught sight of the boy standing quietly beside his mother.

Paying no mind to her creaking bones, the Queen stooped for a better look at the little Prince.

"What a heavenly-looking child!" she exclaimed. "But why are we looking so sad?" she asked his mother.

Marie Louise tittered. "He just had a small run-in with my little brother."

"What has *he* done to your son?" Maria Carolina's tone intimated that already she cast the blame on the boy's young uncle, twelve-year-old Archduke Francis Charles.

Marie Louise was about to explain when her son spoke up.

"May I say something?" he asked politely, lifting his angelic face to the Queen.

Utterly charmed, she stroked his cheek. "Of course!"

"He called me 'that French boy,' which I am. But he looked so nasty saying that, I do not wish to see him again."

Maria Carolina hugged him consolingly.

"What he said was unkind and stupid!" she agreed, and for reasons that went beyond her own sudden benevolent disposition toward her attractive great-grandson.

Of mediocre intelligence, Francis Charles had been taught to hate Napoleon. Maria Carolina even saw him once roasting Napoleon in effigy using one of Marie Louise's dolls. And his mean attitude toward the fallen emperor's little son showed—in the Queen's judgment—a definite lack of discernment. Then she thought, I should accuse myself of the same fault! For which I *wholeheartedly repent!*

All in all, life was not unduly upsetting for young Napoleon. Cared for by a devoted governess, and fussed over by nurses and maids, there had not been any radical changes that he could perceive. He spoke French, was still surrounded by the familiar and friendly individuals who composed his immediate entourage, except that pages were no longer part of his suite.

On France itself, he had numerous books narrating her fast and fortune, and at every opportunity, his father's name was mentioned in nothing but glowing terms. From this arrangement emerged a well-delineated sense of segregation, which began to cause some frictions. Marie Louise and her French attendants were referred to as "they," meaning the foreigners, which placed a greater emphasis on the pronoun "us," meaning Austrians.

Empress Maria Ludovica mouthed that "us" with pride and vexation, for there should never have been such distinction had her stepdaughter refused to let herself be so shamefully Gallicized!

As for the child . . .

Consumed as she was by her hatred for Napoleon, Maria Ludovica could not and would not forgive him for being his son. She went as far as seeing in the Prince's surprising beauty the signature of some diabolical craft that must have presided over its formation. The boy, she maintained, was evil, like his father, and Francis was mad to dote on him the way he did!

Francis even felt sorry for having victimized a child whose only fault had been to be born. In view of the losses his grandson had already suffered, it was a small compensation to let it be known that the little boy ranked high in his affection. The Emperor's sentiment, however, did not overstep the limits set by politics, and Metternich was already authoritatively disposing of Napoleon's son's future.

It was not enough to have exiled the eagle; the eaglet, in turn, must be a cageling! In complete agreement with his Chancellor, the Emperor was convinced that he was doing his grandson a favor by keeping him confined. But while he would term the "hospitality" he offered the boy to be a generous arrangement, he knew the little Prince's civil and pecuniary situation to be a sorry one. The child might be his grandson and live in comfort and luxury at his court, but the fact was that he was left without a country and without a sou.

The fortune his father had acquired over a period of twelve years had been unlawfully confiscated by the French provisional government, for Napoleon had made no claim on assets that were not legitimately his. Francis was informed that at the time of Napoleon's abdication, the deposed French Emperor had returned all the crown jewels and expenses money to the National Treasury, quite confident that his personal savings amassed from the salary he drew from the civil list would be going to his wife and son. Instead, he had been robbed.

Swallowing her pride, Marie Louise had even written to Francis and begged him to intervene. But he was still in France and she had not heard from him.

At long last, news of Francis's homeward journey heartened her. In her impatience, she went out to meet him. In Siegartskirchen, she sank to her knees once more before Francis.

The Emperor looked down at his daughter and remembered. On that very same location, nine years ago, attended with the pomp that celebrated Napoleon's victory over him, the capitulation of Vienna had been laid at her husband's feet.

Now, to behold his enemy's wife in that humbling posture, pricked him somewhat pleasantly. But Francis was not a cruel man, and with kindness he made Marie Louise rise and clasped to his breast a confused young woman whose personality was much like his own. They shared the same naive streak, the same irresponsibility in the hurt they inflicted on others, persuaded as they were that in the last resort, God gave them very little initiative in the conduct of their own lives.

As father and daughter rode home in the same carriage, both reflected on the working of Providence. Francis's interpretation was simple: Napoleon's downfall bore all the marks of divine retribution. But God's designs were not so clear nor so fair to Marie Louise. To be tossed in the eddy of her husband's misfortune seemed a harsh and unjust punishment.

After a few inconsequential exchanges of words, she mentioned again her stolen fortune. Francis pulled on his lower lip, showing that he was thinking deeply. The provisional government of France had indeed acted shamefully. On the other hand, it was expedient that anything connected with Napoleon's personal affairs be left alone. So far as the Emperor of Austria was concerned, his daughter and grandson had nothing any more to do with France and the Bonapartes.

"I only know you as my daughter. In this context, and this context alone, rest assured that what is mine is also yours. As for the rest, I have knowledge of nothing," he finally said.

Marie Louise clenched her teeth. How little her own sufferings counted! All she had already lost meant nothing to her father, drew no consideration from him!

He gave her a sidelong glance and felt compelled to offer a lame expression of regret. "I am sorry," he mumbled.

But she heard him and did not desist from showing her father that as a human being, she could feel as well as obey. His being sorry took nothing away from the reality of her hurt. Her chin went up, her face took a set and hard expression.

That worried him a little. A feeling of rejection could bring on defiance and ruin everything.

"I shall see that you are well provided for," he assured her.

She seemed to relax a little.

But then he hastened to caution without sounding judgmental. "For your own good, I am advising you to be more discreet concerning your deportment. . . ." Her stubborn attachment to all things French had filtered down to him through Maria Ludovica's correspondence.

She gave him a blank, uncomprehending look.

Choosing his words as one treads a scabrous terrain because the subject was delicate, Francis explained that he did not mind so much his daughter's predilections for French dishes and French ways, and would have overlooked her overt Francophile attitude as well, but if it were to cause serious embarrassments, he would intervene. He hastened to add that so far, the displeasure his daughter seemed to have incited was only a minor imposition. Nevertheless, he envisioned the possibility of incurring the censure of his allies. To obviate this, he advised her to be unobtrusive and attract the least possible attention. He impressed upon her that her situation was difficult, and her allegiance subject to extreme scrutiny. Finally, he asked her to trust him, and assured her that he would lead her out of the impasse with dignity.

The whole time her father rambled on, Marie Louise listened, eyes downcast, with a pained and resentful expression on her face while repeatedly biting on her lower lip.

Noticing her unhappiness, Francis lapsed into an admission. "Perhaps I have laid too heavy of a burden on your shoulders?"

Marie Louise rejoined crisply, "Will you also lay the blame on me for not having prevented this last war?"

Francis shook his head and squeezed his daughter's hand with all that he could deliver in warmth and affection. He must not antagonize her. The existence of her son posed serious problems as it was. There was no need to compound this with a rebellious mother on his hands.

"I can only commend you for everything you have done. I want to help you find happiness within the bounds of the power for which I am answerable to my people and to my God."

When Francis, a direct descendant of seventeen generations of Habsburgs, spoke with that celestial emphasis on the nature of his commitment, he awed his daughter.

She stared at him for a moment with her almond-shaped heavy-lidded eyes. Then with a clear and steady voice she said the words he hoped to hear: "Papa, I have decided to put myself and my son under your gracious protection."

Francis's eyes glinted. "You have a fine son. *He will make a good German.*"

Marie Louis thought, But what of Elba?

Under the mantle of wifely devotion, the archduchess in her recoiled.

Elba!. . .

A rock in her way over which she had just stumbled.

9

The announcement caught Marie Louise by surprise.

"Louise! How could you think of leaving me now?"

The Duchess of Montebello composed her features into an expression of sorrowful regret. "Your Majesty will be shortly joining the Emperor in Elba . . . and my own family needs me."

She had thought about tending her resignation for some time. She saw no point in remaining any longer with Napoleon's wife. Her interests lay elsewhere—in Paris, where she could further her cause with the Bourbons and secure favors with the new regime in France. Corvisart had connived with her all along, having himself no personal interest in staying with Marie Louise. As she kept bending his ears with complaints of experiencing spasms in the chest—which he had stopped taking seriously—he authoritatively declared that only the watering place in Aix-en-Savoie would cure her. The plan was to lure Marie Louise to Aix, which was on French soil, in order to speed up the time of their own departure with the enticing promise that the Duchess and himself would meet Marie Louise there. And she had accepted the proposition with enthusiasm.

"But I still need you, and I am not well!" Marie Louise protested.

Montebello considered her mistress with feigned sympathy. Like Corvisart, she was not blind to the transformation she had seen in Marie Louise since her return to Austria. The comfort and quiet of the days so far spent had had restorative results. The ex-Empress's colors and appetite were returning; the despondency given way to indolence. Her ardor to join her husband appeared to have considerably lessened.

"But as agreed, I shall be seeing Your Majesty in Aix," she reminded Marie Louise. Then with an anguished look, "Alas! Madame, circumstances are forcing us to part!"

Marie Louise stared at her through teary eyes. Louise de Montebello felt a flicker of compassion. Her mistress's lot was not enviable—the daughter of an emperor having to live the life of an exile with her husband on a tiny island!

She put her arms around the ex-Empress and said consolingly, "We'll have a lovely time together in Aix!"

For Marie Louise, going to Aix-en-Savoie had taken the form of an obsession. No less obstinate, Queen Maria Carolina became the most ardent champion of her granddaughter's reunion to her husband, a pursuit Marie Louise was obviously putting off. Setting aside her personal dislike of Napoleon, the Queen endeavored to instill in Marie Louise the urgency of sailing with her son for Elba.

"You must pull yourself together," she told Marie Louise, "and go about your business of joining your husband!"

Marie Louise made no reply.

"Now," the Queen went on briskly, "if diplomacy fails, and if I were you, I would tie my sheets to the post of my bed, climb out the window, and be on my way. It has been done before!"

Wide-eyed, Marie Louise stared at her grandmother. Such a picaresque vision of her departure for Elba was contrary to anything she might be inclined to imagine or do.

"But Grandmamma, I don't feel well enough. I haven't been sleeping much to speak of," she whined, coughing for emphasis.

Maria Carolina glanced at the tea tray she had ordered. The rich pastries were nearly all gone, and not due to her own voracity.

She wanted to say, "But you eat like a horse!" Instead she said, "You look fine to me. Your cheeks have filled out as well as some other parts of your body! It's time to go, girl! And don't be timid about doing what is right! Take me, for example. Do you think my coming to Vienna was easy? Particularly for a woman my age? Now just listen to what I had to go through to get here."

Marie Louise listened politely. Maria Carolina's journey would have exhausted even someone young and robust. She had stolen away from Sicily, then under the domination of the English, whom she loathed. Fearing arrest by their vessels, which swarmed the port of Malta and patrolled the Adriatic Sea, she'd hastened without stopping to Constantinople, crossed the Bosphorus, then sailed across the Black Sea to finally land at Odessa, and from there, proceeded to Austria.

"And do you know why I undertook this long and dangerous voyage?" she asked ebulliently.

Wearily, Marie Louise asked, "Why, Grandmamma?"

The Queen slapped the flat of her hand on her bony knee. "Because I intend to demand the return of my kingdom at the upcoming congress. And I will put up a fight for what I want! And so must you!"

"I don't anticipate any difficulties in obtaining what I want," Marie Louise said, her voice flat, her eyes lost in the contemplation of her hands, which she kept clasping and unclasping all the while her grandmother grew hoarse recounting her peregrination.

For a few seconds Maria Carolina eyed her granddaughter with a pitying expression laced with a soupçon of exasperation.

Then she demanded brusquely, "Has the Emperor approached you on the subject of Elba?"

"No. Not yet."

"Well," the Queen puffed with a rush of impatience, "are you not eager that he should?"

Marie Louise sighed. "Yes, of course."

A broom, Maria Carolina thought, could not have been less motivated. Something was happening to that long-limbed, somewhat torpid girl. And the Queen disliked it.

"Believe me, if you really want to see your husband again and give him the consolation of hugging his son, you will have to fight like a lioness!" she said tartly. Then her eyes narrowed and fixed Marie Louise with indicting insistence. "Are you willing to fight?"

Her lips quavering, Marie Louise averted her face. These last sheltered months spent at Schönbrunn, instead of helping her regain some stamina, had instead reinforced her natural pattern of do-nothing behavior. She realized this and it troubled her. Abruptly, she burst into a loud wail. "Oh, I am so unhappy!"

Until then, her little son was playing at the other end of the vast salon with the new toys his great-grandmother had given him. But alerted by Marie Louise's outburst, he left his game and came from across the room. Anxiously, he laid his hand on his mother's arm.

"Why are you so unhappy, Mamma?"

Maria Carolina said decisively, "Because she is thinking of your Papa."

The boy asked with excitement, "Will we see him soon?"

Seized with a sudden inspiration, the Queen said, "That depends . . . you may not see him at all!"

Meant as a goad, the reply produced the desired effect. Marie Louise, feeling challenged, came out of her apathy, while her son, to

Maria Carolina's desolation, burst into tears. His mother snatched him into her arms and protested vehemently, "Yes! We are going to see Napoleon!"

That was precisely what the Queen wanted her to say.

"We are going to see my papa very soon!" young Napoleon happily told his governess when he was returned to her care.

She was surprised. "How can you be so sure?" she asked, not having herself heard anything on the subject.

"My mother told Great-grandmamma we would," he replied confidently.

Madame de Montesquiou took this declaration with more than a grain of salt. Napoléon's wife—in the governess's daily observation of her deportment—seemed anything but interested by the prospect of joining her husband. At first, the Countess tried to find excuses, which she had well exhausted by now. And she was so terrified by the possibility that Marie Louise would abandon her husband to live out alone his life of exile, that she'd drawn a curtain over the whole matter and turned to praying.

Not to disappoint her charge, she said, "But you must be very patient. It takes time to organize everything . . . especially for someone as important as your mother."

"Is she important because my father is important?"

"Yes . . ." She hesitated only briefly. "And *he will always be important.*" She wondered if he would ply her with more questions concerning their situation. He didn't. He seemed content.

That night, watching the Prince drift into sleep, Madame de Montesquiou was also satisfied that, so far, all she had explained to him would suffice for the time being.

By now, he had some notions of what had happened to his family. It all boiled down to essentials she had succinctly put to him in order to ease his curiosity. Accordingly, he was aware that there was a king in Paris because his father had lost a war. At which point he'd asked, "How could my dear papa lose a war? He is a clever emperor!"

She answered that it was because some of his marshals and trusted relations had betrayed him and let him down. Then gradually, too, the idea that his father was being detained and that he was no longer ruling over France, just as his own kingship was something not to be mentioned, were concepts the child seemed to have accepted.

Certainly, to the babe that he was, the loss of a kingdom did not affect him as much as the loss of the toys he had to leave behind in his gay and sunny nursery at the Tuileries palace. She recalled the little Prince only remarking that the new king of France must be a nasty person for having impounded his toys, as he was told he did. Then one day, Louis XVIII must have reconsidered. The toys arrived in crates along with the silver-gilt cradle, which was placed in her charge's bed room at Schönbrunn. He was much too grown to sleep in it now, but he would lean over the nacelle and playfully rock the crib. Once, she found him doing this, singing softly to himself, "*Je ne suis plus roi . . . Oh, lala, la . . .*" I am no longer a king. . . .

Madame de Montesquiou gazed devotedly at the sleeping little boy, no longer a king to the world, but in her heart, always enthroned, and crowned with the glory of a magnificent heritage.

The reality of Marie Louise's dethronement was, for her husband, a rather thorny matter. From not too distant Elba, Napoleon scowled upon learning of his wife's intention to take the water at Aix. Aix-en-Savoie belonged to France and was naturally at present under the rules of the re-established Bourbons. The choice, he thought, was in poor taste and would give rise to all sorts of embarrassments.

In a letter to Marie Louise, Napoleon strongly advised her to please pick Tuscany instead as a watering place. Diplomatically, Tuscany was not a controversial location, and it was ideally situated so that from there, at the conclusion of her cure, she and their son could easily proceed to Elba without inconvenience. . . .

But Marie Louise would not hear of Tuscany. It had to be Aix-en-Savoie because the Duchess de Montebello had promised to be there. And because Corvisart recommended it highly, and because . . . her mind was made up!

Francis, who tended to liken his daughter to a weathercock, did not believe his ears when she said, as she sought his permission to go, "I don't wish to pick any other watering place but Aix. I am your daughter, and there is nothing wrong with the Emperor of Austria's daughter spending her holiday on the soil of France."

Obviously, she had abjured all allegiance and all claims over her former territories. Things were going smoothly, Francis thought.

Then she said, "I shall take my son with me."

Francis took a good, long look at his daughter. Then certain of the correctness of his judgment, he addressed the Habsburg and not Napoleon's wife.

"That is not possible," he answered. "As my daughter you can go anywhere you please. But too many political implications are attached to your son for me to allow him to go with you to France. It would be a gross breach of . . ." He hesitated. About to say the word "security," he selected instead another, just as valid, ". . . diplomacy."

Unimpressed and uninterested, she replied, "Papa, he is only three!"

"That makes no difference," Francis answered patiently.

"And what does?"

"He is Napoleon's son!"

Proudly, Marie Louise asserted her motherhood. "And mine, too!"

Her poor understanding of the political problems caused by the birth of her son appalled Francis. The young Prince already inspired enough fear to spoil the Coalition's exultation over his father's ruin. His existence held explosive potential. And that potential threatened the survival of the oligarchy, which Francis protected of sorts by holding hostage a three-year-old boy. The fate of Napoleon's son was that he remain under the close guardianship of his mother's kindred.

He tried to put this to her as gently as he could.

"Go to Aix. Take care of yourself. Your son will be well looked after here. Remember that you will never be separated from him *unless you choose to be.*"

Still, Marie Louise seemed not to have understood. "But you just said that. . . ."

Francis heaved a sigh. "There are watering places in Austria as well. . . . If you had chosen Baden, the situation would have been different."

She thought for a few seconds, but held steadfastly to her decision to go to Aix.

Metternich's countenance clouded as soon as Francis told him that he had approved Marie Louise's travel arrangement. "Aix-en-Savoie?"

"I see nothing wrong with her going there by herself," Francis put in weakly.

"What if the Archduchess decides to run off to Elba?" the Chancellor objected.

Surmising that his daughter was a good mother, Francis reassured him. "She won't, Clement. We have her son."

Metternich was partially convinced. But never leaving anything to chance, he decided to quickly put in motion a *modus operandi* based on the dictate of the following principle: where it concerned Marie Louise, never allow a vacuum. She was in absolute need of constant guidance. To be more exact, the young archduchess ought to be put under surveillance. She was, after all, the wife of their enemy.

He threw Francis a lead, saying casually, "Her Majesty is weary and overwrought by the recent events, and might appreciate the company of an escort, a *chevalier d'honneur.* Someone on whom she could rely for advice and *the kind* of directions Your Majesty deems pertinent this individual should give while the Princess is traveling."

"A kind of spy?"

"Sire, a go-between would be more befitting the Princess," Metternich offered tactfully.

"Whatever!" Francis rejoined with good humor. The idea of spying on his own daughter did not offend him. As long as Marie Louise had not declared herself against her husband, she remained a potential adversary. He thought he would propose a name.

"I think Prince Esterhazy should fulfill this role well!"

Metternich smiled thinly, praying, The Lord save us from such a choice! Personally, he had nothing against the noble gentleman. All members of that ancient princely family from Hungary had always been staunch supporters of the Habsburgs. But Prince Esterhazy was venerable in years. The choice did not suit at all Metternich's conception of what that escort's role should be. His designs pointed to the desirability of a relationship that would not be entirely innocent. He already had someone in mind.

Once more he set on manipulating Francis.

"Your Majesty could not have chosen anyone more trustworthy. In view of his old age, however, Prince Esterhazy might not be so inclined to help the Princess see the brighter side of life. She is still very young and must not be left to pine overmuch. Sadness begets all kinds of thoughts. Some may run counter to Your Majesty's plans for her happiness."

Francis stroked his chin, nodding. His daughter's status as Empress of the French had served to promote Austria's interest. As soon as circumstances would permit, she must be claimed back and made to disown her past. This was the happy plan Francis had in mind for his daughter.

"So you think someone younger. . . ."

"No more than twenty years the Princess's senior, Sire. A mature adviser who can also amuse and distract while being influential and discreet."

Francis smiled knowingly. "And I suppose you have decided on such a person?"

Metternich affected an air of humble confusion at being found out. "Your Majesty is perceptive. I recommend that you approve. . . ."

Francis cut him off with a chuckle. "Of course! Since you recommend him. Who is he?"

"Adalbert Adam von Neipperg, Sire."

On the last days of June, the Duchess of Colorno was journeying to France in the oddest possible equipage. Her name was assumed, of course, taken after one of the pleasure houses in Parma. But by some embarrassing oversight, the imperial arms of France had not yet been removed from the doors of her carriages, and so proclaimed her true identity. In the same manner, her suite gave her away as her retainers' liveries were still those of Napoleon.

Significantly, her progress had mostly been an excursion in bygone days with the prefix 'ex' strewn along her way. Prince Eugene, ex-Viceroy of Italy, entertained her in Munich. In Baden, the ex-King of Holland, Louis, claimed that honor in turn. Then ex-King Joseph of Spain wined her and dined her at Prangins. Finally, at Payerne, it was Jerome, ex-King of Westphalia who had her for guest.

Marie Louise shed a few tears on her brothers-in-law's shoulders. In their company, her mind became saturated anew with her French past as she would respond to the closest pull. She thought often of her husband and felt the urge to correspond more assiduously with him. Nevertheless, couriers headed for Portoferraio tended to become less and less reliable. It was with great difficulty that a simple lock of her hair finally reached the exiled Emperor.

By the time Marie Louise neared her final destination, she had again recaptured a strong desire to join her husband. Given such longing, she felt quite morose and dispirited when about to enter the town of Aix. Then melancholy made way to ill-humor the moment General Count Neipperg rode up to meet her.

•

As he dismounted and stood, framed in the opening of the carriage's door, which an equerry had opened to allow the General to present his credentials and respects, his appearance displeased her. His sudden intrusion offended her. He had come unannounced, and his person was unaccounted for in the chosen members of her suite.

Despite a resplendent Hussar uniform, the black patch that covered his right eye gave him a swashbuckling air Marie Louise did not appreciate. What did this fancy highwayman want with her?

Before she could address that question, he had deferentially introduced himself and explained that he had been commissioned by the Emperor, her father, to escort her to Aix and put himself at her disposal as a permanent attendant.

Frowning and sulking, Marie Louise gave Neipperg a second look. She thought he must be in his middle forties, judging by the scanty blond hair graying at his temples. His features were quite ordinary. She earnestly hoped he would not be too much of a nuisance.

"I shall submit to my father's wish," she said curtly. "You may follow me, if such are your orders!" And leaning back inside the carriage, she did not accord Neipperg another glance once the door was closed.

Perspiring heavily under the noon sun, Neipperg vaulted his horse, his pride nicked, but his determination undaunted. He entertained great expectations. Neipperg's essential role was to prevent Mary Louise from attempting to join her husband by providing her with *all manner* of consolations. "*Seduce her! And that's an order!*" Metternich had said. Given this incredible license, Neipperg's ambition leapt from the not too exciting prospect of aging with a modest pension to the rewarding prospect of a stable opulence by becoming intimate with the Emperor of Austria's daughter!

While he trotted alongside her carriage, Marie Louise remembered now having met this unpleasant man once in Paris after her wedding, then again, during a visit in Prague with Napoleon just before his Russian campaign. At the time, she recalled, Neipperg had acted as her honorary chamberlain. He had only been another face in a crowd of numerous attendants and she had quite forgotten him. Until now.

Glimpsing the Emperor's daughter's sullen, rather longish profile in the recess of the carriage, Neipperg would not have judged Marie Louise suitable for seducing. He favored small, dark and provocatively attractive women. The former Empress was substantial and colorless.

Moreover, he detested the French and her connections with France were distasteful to him. Neipperg had lost one of his eyes in his first brush with Napoleon's Grand Army, and after recovering from the wound, he'd worked relentlessly to help bring about the downfall of Bonaparte. Although married, his numerous extramarital activities caused considerable scandals. He had just left his latest mistress in Milan.

The cold reception he had just received was not an insurmountable challenge to his hard-set intention to carry out Metternich's order to the letter. The General gave himself six months to worm his way into Napoleon's wife's confidence, heart, and bed, knowing himself to be suave, even tempered, well mannered, and daring in love. He could dazzle women as a fine musician and amateur poet. He would give Marie Louise time to appreciate him.

Late in the afternoon, he led her to a quiet and restful Olympian dwelling, a rented villa on a hilltop ringed by stately mountains whose summits rose above the clouds. The house overlooked the town of Aix-en-Savoie with its celebrated Lake Bourget, which reflected the changing hues of the sky. The air was sweet and pure to breathe, and Marie Louise was enchanted with the site and felt less ill-disposed toward her official curator when she learned upon her arrival that the selection of this delightful abode had been his responsibility.

By evening, she already called him not "General," but "My dear General."

They supped on the terrace, as she insisted that he share the meal with her—though such was not his intention. Not yet. His preliminary tactic was to play the benevolent genie, seldom seen, but whose good turns would constantly remind Marie Louise of his presence.

And more than willingly, she promptly left everything to him. He ran her household with finesse and competence. As she was gourmand, she delighted in finding that he'd hired the best cooks. As she was reputed to be an accomplished musician, she found the piano turned to perfection. And then there were flowers! A profusion of them in every room. When she complimented him for this attention, he smiled saying, "They should brighten Your Majesty's days. And I dare hope, as much as my serving Your Majesty brightens mine."

She thought his teeth were dazzling, and even more so his smile.

Whenever he could, Neipperg continued to stay out of Marie Louise's way. He played the invisible host to the company she enjoyed having. On such occasions, he did not mind being the "foreigner", the lone Austrian in a crowd of guests who were French nationals.

As the summer wore on, Adalbert Adam von Neipperg ceased to be the odd and inconspicuous man at the *soirées* he organized so brilliantly. While Marie Louise sang, he accompanied her at the piano, and soon she would ask him to give small recitals. As the rippling notes of a sonata flew in delicate and sensitive peals from under his agile and strong fingers, she looked out into the moonlight over Lake Bourget thinking, *What a wonderful life this is!*

In August she confided to Neipperg, "I am greatly concerned about my son. This concern takes priority over my going to Elba. I believe that it would be wiser to *give up* the idea of going there so I can devote myself entirely to the education of my little boy."

Neipperg only bowed in assent, saying to himself, "It might not even take six months!"

Then Marie Louise moved next to a subject that had been preoccupying her. "Since I shan't be going to Elba from here, I must confess dreading to return to Vienna. As you know, a congress is about to be held there, and I would be the target of derision. Oh, if only confirmation of my entitlement to the Duchy of Parma could be expedited so I might go there!"

"Madam," Neipperg responded, delighted that she should think enough of him to consult him on such grave matters, "I would defer to His Majesty's counsel on such questions."

So she wrote her father. By return post, Francis enlightened her. Staying away, he insisted, would seriously jeopardize her success in securing the Duchy of Parma and Piacenza. They were only Marie Louise's in a matter of form. In fact, the congress had yet to finalize such acquisition and there were other contenders. Her presence would be essential to the recognition of her claim.

By September, all the guests had departed and Marie Louise gave order to pack her trunks. On the day of her departure, a visitor came who requested a private audience with the Duchess of Colorno.

"And whom might that be?" she asked languidly.

"Captain Hurault de Sorbée," was the reply.

"I don't know him," she said with annoyance.

"The Captain is here to visit his wife, one of Your Majesty's ladies," she was informed.

"Then let him visit her," she replied with indifference.

"But he insists, he must see Your Majesty."

Marie Louise sighed. "Oh, well, show him in."

After having presented his compliments, Hurault de Sorbée said gravely, "I've come straight from Elba, Your Majesty."

She looked at him with a vacant expression.

Disconcerted, the Captain drew from his tunic a folded sheet of paper.

"I have been entrusted to deliver this message to Your Majesty," he said, not concealing his eagerness.

Without a word, or the least demonstration of interest, Marie Louise took the letter as if she had no idea whom it might be from.

Annoyed at such inexcusable behavior, the Captain said flatly, "The Emperor requests an immediate reply to this message. Your Majesty, according to his instruction, is to read this letter in my presence and act upon it forthwith."

Marie Louise drew herself up and looked coldly at the messenger her husband had sent her. Then, with no sign of emotion, she began to read Napoleon's letter.

It said:

Come to Elba at once. No one has any right over you and our son. If anyone prevents you from coming to me, the bearer of this letter will assist in your escape.

Her hands began to shake. The whole idea, she thought, was a hare-brained move. Then the possibility of an abduction caused her to take a few backward steps.

"Give me at least a few minutes in private," she faltered, and left the room to find Neipperg.

With great agitation, she showed him the letter and told him who had delivered it, thus betraying Hurault's part in Napoleon's plan.

In her drawing room, the Captain waited and waited, wondering what might cause such delay. After nearly a half hour, the door opened. Neipperg stood on the threshold flanked by two local gendarmes.

"Captain Hurault?" one of them inquired perfunctorily.

"I am," Hurault acquiesced, completely stunned at seeing them.

"You are under arrest!"

That evening he was transferred to a Paris jail. Upon his release, Hurault returned to Elba not quite knowing how to explain to Napoleon the failure of his mission.

Marie Louise set off for Vienna in easy stage by taking a detour through Switzerland. Niepperg now traveled in her carriage and she no longer sulked in her corner. Her gloomy outlook on life had lifted because Neipperg's nearness and devotion illuminated an existence she had thought forever dreary and dull. Like a beacon, he adroitly flashed a happy prospect, that of her establishment in Parma.

He mentioned its mild climate as compared to that of Austria, which was so very severe in its extremes. He also lauded the amiability and friendliness of the Parmesan people. Above all, he emphasized the independence, she as the sovereign of the duchy, would enjoy.

She listened, captivated.

In Switzerland, having Neipperg in constant attendance besotted Marie Louise though no improper thoughts came flitting through her mind. But she began to fantasize being held by him. It had been so long—eight months—since she had felt the arms of a man around her!

I am still young, she thought, shedding a private tear, I have not yet lived!

On a golden September day, the last of Marie Louise's vacation before returning to Vienna, Neipperg took her to visit the ruined castle of Habsburg, the cradle of her ancestry. They came upon a narrow ditch filled with rainwater. She could have easily jumped over it, but being that they were alone, Neipperg dared take at long last the liberty to lift her in his arms and carry her across. He held her long enough to precipitate a denouement master-minded by Metternich.

By the time he put her down, all the repressed sensuality Napoleon had awakened in Marie Louise and left untended, surfaced. Still dizzied, she did not pay any attention when Neipperg said, noticing the clouds which began to form blotting out the sun, "We must take cover, the rain will soon follow."

But there wasn't even time to find shelter. A sudden torrential downpour drenched them. Stranded by the violence of the storm, which showed no sign of abating, Neipperg suggested they spend the night at the nearby Inn of the Golden Sun.

Marie Louise stood in a puddle widening at her feet, while the General took diligent care of their accommodation for the night. Then he ordered logs to be sent to Marie Louise's room, and on his knees, expertly set them afire himself.

Still shivering, she watched him tend the blaze, swathed in a blanket that covered her nudity, because the hostelry maids had taken her clothes to dry them on the General's orders, as he feared she might catch pneumonia if she kept them on.

She admired his strong, athletic build. The press of his taut chest and the brace of his muscular arms were still a vivid sensation embedded in her flesh since the moment he had held her.

She stretched a well-formed, small foot—which Napoleon admired—toward the warming glow of the fire.

She brushed her toes against his arm, an inviting, consenting glimmer in her eyes.

Emboldened, he took her foot between his hands and proceeded to rub it gently. Then, moved by some chivalrous inspiration, he opened his wet tunic and placed it against his chest.

From that instant, he did not remember how it followed that Marie Louise was encircling his neck with her arms while murmuring incoherently something he interpreted as fear of being left alone in a strange place.

The blanket slipped from her shoulders baring lusciously white, bouncy, large breasts, and she made no attempt to cover them. Aroused and surprised, Neipperg thought, *That* soon?

Vaguely, he heard himself stammer, "I shall sleep in front of the door, if this can reassure Your Majesty."

For an answer she pulled herself closer as if something was already menacing her.

Neipperg initiated a daring caress. "Majesty . . ." he murmured, and reverently closed his lips on her hardened, bright pink nipple.

Marie Louise let out a little pleading cry, wishing that he would see in her the woman brimming over with passion, and not cold and abstract royalty. "Oh, Adam!" she gasped, clutching at his head.

Kissing her breast with unrestrained desire, Neipperg triumphed with a whisper, "Here, always!"

10

During her step-daughter's absence, Empress Maria Ludovica put forward the suggestion that Napoleon's heir should dedicate his life to the service of the Church. The desirability of having the Prince enter holy orders in adulthood amounted to the political and virtual personal castration of Bonaparte's son, which would insure the complete annihilation of Napoleon's direct descendant.

Francis found the proposition shocking and gruffly told the Empress to hold her peace on the subject. Notwithstanding the Emperor's generous intervention, Queen Maria Carolina's reflection on the child's future took on a gloomier cast whenever she thought of him or saw him. Few mortals had such a dazzling beginning in life, and very few had known so severe a reversal of fortune at so young an age. This disquieted Marie Louise's grandmother, who perceived in the disastrous conclusion of Napoleon's stellar career nothing very encouraging for his son.

Then her opinion of the Prince's mother sank to its lowest when Marie Louise left Vienna to go to Aix.

As she observed the boy playing with a new set of toys, which she kept plying him with, she whispered to the child's governess, "I tell you, Madame, the dear little one's mother is soft in the head! What in Heaven's name is she doing in Aix?"

Not wanting to divulge her own reprobation, Madame de Montesquiou said charitably, "Her Majesty is not well."

"Nonsense!" the Queen hissed. "You are kind, I know. And I also know that there is nothing really that wrong with her. She and the boy should be with Napoleon by now!"

"Her Majesty has not yet obtained the permission to go," Madame de Montesquiou observed, not without deepening misgivings.

Maria Carolina shrugged casting a pitying glance at young Napoleon and wondered how his mother could make so light of leaving him in such political chaos.

"My granddaughter wants everything to be handed to her on a platter," she fumed. "And when things aren't going her way, she just puts her head in the sand! Or runs off somewhere!"

Later at the conclusion of the visit, she tearfully kissed her precious great-grandson.

Shortly thereafter, the Queen was spared any further anxiety concerning the fate of her protégé, for she died of a stroke during the night.

Queen Maria Carolina's demise plunged the Court into a period of mourning. The respect paid to the dead, however, could in no way interfere with the preparations that had been set in motion for the congress to be held in Vienna. The magnificence attending that event was to eclipse the gravity of the matters whose disposition and promotion had necessitated the gathering. Europe was about to bind its wounds and undertake the arduous task of patching up the territorial havoc created by Napoleon's conquests.

Back from her journey, Marie Louise had retired to Schönbrunn with her son and followed her father's orders to the letter. And those were strict. Though Francis deemed his daughter's presence mandatory, she was not to take any part in the event. Neipperg, now officially her chamberlain, would be her representative and manage her interests.

Neipperg was having difficulties safeguarding those interests against the attack of none other but always provident Talleyrand, who, like a buoy, kept surfacing after the worst of disasters. Reverses could never sink him, and successes never cloyed him.

Forever pursuing fortune, Talleyrand was now cheek by jowl with the newly enthroned King of France, Louis the Eighteenth. Having secured the influential honor of being the French King's plenipotentiary, he was suggesting persuasively that the Italian Duchies of Parma, Piacenza, and Guastalla be bestowed on the Spanish Bourbons. Like the rest of the oligarchy, he shared the same determination to oust Napoleon and his son from the arena of politics. The boy could never be allowed to even enter into the possession of any independent states. He must be barred from inheriting whatever domains his mother might receive.

On this point, Metternich felt quite comfortable in giving the impression of doing ill-office to his master's daughter for the sake of Europe's tranquillity. He told Talleyrand the suggestion deserved much attention. That remark, passed on to Neipperg, came to Marie Louise's ears.

She went to her father and vehemently pleaded her cause. "I have already sacrificed much! Please don't let them take the duchies away from me! They are all I have left!"

Francis seemed not to have heard, bringing up instead a subject she judged utterly trivial. The emblems painted on the doors of her carriages and the liveries of her servants! They were the talk of the Congress, Francis said. People, he told her, were sneering at the ridiculous display. Would she please have the good taste not to disgrace herself and cease to cause him any more embarrassment!

Humbly, she said, "I shall have the emblems erased and do away with the liveries. . . ."

Then he left her abruptly without another word, giving her a quick kiss on the forehead, a mark of affection she felt was sterile. She began to believe her father was deserting her, and her only friend in the world, she reflected sadly, was a stranger—a man with whom she had slept on a wild impulse in a moment of weakness, a man of good counsel. . . .

Indeed, Neipperg had suggested that she appeal to the Tzar for help and this turned out to be excellent advice. Alexander, who entertained no particular fondness for the French or Spanish Bourbons but cherished the prospect of being known as the champion of ladies in distress, readily promised to intervene. With much good grace, he'd agreed to lend his aid to foil Talleyrand's brazen attempt to nullify the validity of a compact signed at Fontainebleau. She'd hoped her father would join force with the Tzar. . . .

Yet Francis had made no mention of any progress having been made on this issue. All he found important enough to say to her was that she should get rid of her servants' liveries!

Neipperg found Marie Louise in tears.

She was despairing of ever seeing her tribulations come to an end, of obtaining the duchies as a sure guarantee against the misery of facing serious pecuniary problems. As Neipperg had pointed out to her, she could not draw on the revenues of the duchies until Article V of the Treaty of Fontainebleau was duly recognized.

She was crying with short little gasps, and rubbed her eyes with her fists like a child.

Neipperg felt a certain tenderness for her. He no longer performed his assignment with detachment. In a pitying sort of way, he was beginning to care for her. Her helplessness, the need she had of him, flattered and touched him. He was ambitious, but cynicism was not a part of his nature. Moreover, his future was now clearly tied to hers. Her gain would be his gain. And Parma must not be lost to Talleyrand's perfidious machination, which proposed the cession of Lucca to Marie Louise to compensate for the duchies. Again, on Niepperg's advice, Marie Louise had energetically rejected the proposal.

Only he'd just come away from a meeting in which there had been a new development that would settle the dispute. It was a concession freshly formulated by the commission charged with the territorial arrangement of Italy. That concession was the condition without which Marie Louise could not count on retaining the duchies. Neipperg wondered if she would consent to it.

At his entrance, Marie Louise gradually calmed down. Even his absence—in these trying days for her—put a salve on her irritated nerves because she knew that he was away defending her interests while attending those sessions where kings and emperors were tearing and pecking at the carcass Napoleon had left them, as though the territories and the people they contained were mere carrion.

At once Niepperg said, gently dabbing her cheeks with his handkerchief, "I have comforting news! It has come to my knowledge that much depends on Your Majesty to put an end to the state of affairs which so offends you." He took her hand and respectfully raised it to his lips. "Parma is going to be yours!"

She gave a start. "How?" she gasped, her countenance brightening. Then, seized with a sudden apprehension she blurted out, "Will I be going there without you?"

"I shall accompany you. Your august father's wishes," he answered.

"How," she exclaimed with a fire which for a few seconds illuminated in Neipperg's mind intimate scenes of her passion, "can Parma be mine, with you at my side?"

He did not smile as probably any lover complacent of his success would have. She was, in fact, the one who had thrown herself at him, given herself to him with a fire he could not so far comprehend. Ever since that night of torrid lovemaking, she had withdrawn into a strict reserve while constantly seeking his company. So he'd had to content himself with a circumspect handling of his prize, half-won, and half-possessed. But now he wanted her completely, even though she was not exactly the fresh bride Napoleon had caressed at Courcelles. Her complexion tended to blotch and her chin had grown a little heavy, but her bosom was superb and her sensuality, a sample of which she had accorded him that one night, matched his own lusty appetite.

He could see by her eagerness to retain him that her attachment for him was not one of a flirtatious nature because she was too scrupulous. She must be having pangs of conscience, and he was willing to wait. Adultery, so readily committed, must evolve in good time, and at her own pace, toward a proper liaison.

But this, of course, could not develop in Vienna. Parma again would be the solution. Parma, in truth, was offering the panacea to the problems of her financial difficulties and the embarrassment of her infidelity. It would anchor her in a mode of existence that would also satisfy the oligarchy and give it what it desired—a Bonaparte family torn asunder, and a boy deprived of all chances of ever reigning even over the pettiest of dukedoms. Parma would accomplish all this and for the good of all. But only if Marie Louise would go along with the newly proferred concession, or condition, however she chose to see it.

Like Francis, Neipperg was unsure of Marie Louise's other persona, the one he had not yet tested. Knowing only the volcanic sensualist he had found her to be.

He proceeded gingerly, not wanting to appear to pressure her, saying, "The Congress is reluctant to recognize Your Majesty's sovereignty over Parma because it does not wish to see your son accompany you to Italy. If you were to leave without him, the duchies are yours. This is the very best the Tzar can do and that is about all the delegates are asking of Your Majesty . . . aside from the stipulation that the Prince is not to inherit the duchies, either."

Marie Louise murmured, visibly tormented, "So I am to sacrifice my son for Parma. . . ."

"No," Neipperg answered with contrived pathos. "Your Majesty will be sacrificing yourself for your son."

This seemed to disconcert her utterly. And Neipperg came to the conclusion that she was much too naïve and slow-witted to be truly guileful and pick out deceit in a well turned discourse. He was even more convinced of this when she said, looking frankly puzzled and sounding quite amenable, "I will?"

Neipperg saw his chance and explained. "With Your Majesty as Duchess of Parma, a wealthy state, your son is at least assured of considerable material independence. I should think that Your Majesty would want to secure this assurance now, since the Prince's future welfare depends on your prompt acceptance of the terms I have been asked to put before your consideration."

Marie Louise visibly relaxed while thinking over what Neipperg had said. The personal sacrifice demanded of her never looked so appealing, so consistent, this time, with her inclinations. She could already see how intolerable her life would be by staying with her son in Vienna. She and her son would be poor, depending on Francis's charity. Petty vexations would abound because her close association with her son was certain to stigmatize her as the vestige of a distasteful interlude on the scene of political affairs. And she would be an object of curiosity and pity, if not scorn.

By staying, Marie Louise would be immolating her youth, and giving up her chances to secure some happiness in compensation of having gone through so much aggravation. It would also jeopardize her son's financial security. And to bring such ills upon the two of them by remaining with her child? How wasteful and how unwise!

On the other hand, their separation would not be without appeal. Once in Parma, she could visit her son every summer without fail. With her revenues, she could work at setting up a trust fund for his needs.

Suddenly, another enticing consideration came to her—the dear child should be favored by an early separation. At his tender age, she reasoned, parting would not affect him as deeply, as his attention could be easily diverted. She remembered how, upon her return from Aix, he had let himself be kissed without any demonstration of having missed her, so dazzled he had been by Neipperg's gorgeous uniform. Yes! Leaving her little son behind was truly the heroic thing to do!

Neipperg caught the favorable turn of Marie Louise's mood and settled himself beside her on the sofa, one knee touching the floor as if making obeisance to her. He said softly, "I know Your Majesty's decision will be an excellent one!"

She took a long look at him, her expression reflecting the emotions she felt for him—gratitude and a sense of indebtedness that overrode all compunction. He was her knight; gallant, courteous, devoted, and of good counsel. He offered her salvation from wants, loneliness, turmoil, and humiliation. The remembrance of his caresses was driving her mad, mad enough to long to renew them away from all cares and spying eyes . . . In Parma!

Parma obliterated Elba and the existence of the man she once professed to love so deeply. In the course of her separation from her husband, she had ceased to think of him as a person of flesh and blood. Neipperg, though, was sensuously real!

Neipperg felt drawn to the center of a tempest. The violent, devouring passion with which Marie Louise kissed him required no further persuasion and gave him no more doubts as to what her decision would be.

"I," said Marie Louise solemnly, "am deeply grieved to leave my son behind."

"I understand," Francis responded.

"I consider it my duty to fix and establish in my lifetime the basis of my son's future," she explained.

"Assuredly," Francis agreed, "you are doing well to work toward that end. It is your duty to claim your due also. That is why, notwithstanding the restrictions you are asked to observe, I am pleased with the outcome of your affairs. Your decision to go without your son is wise."

She smiled, and he had almost forgotten that she could.

"You always know what is best for me and my son," she said cheerfully.

"I shall be a father to him," Francis promised with complete sincerity.

At this, she chirped, "Do you know what I desire most for my son?"

Francis said guardedly, "No, tell me, dear."

"I want him to become a German prince. He should make a name for himself. A new name that is. Because the one he has acquired by birth is unfortunately quite undesirable!"

Francis's mouth hung open. His daughter was incredibly amenable, volunteering to turn her son into an Austrian, going so far as to favor the repudiation of his father's name. "This is a noble goal," he finally agreed.

"Oh, Papa," she enthused, "he will be so much happier with you!"

"I hope so. I do care for him." Francis meant what he said, and for the first time in his life he found himself loving deeply, and completely.

That was saying much, as the sentiment made ample demand on a nature basically as niggardly with feelings as it was with money. Francis, transfixed by a pompous sense of duty, had grown mentally and emotionally rigid. To discover now that he was mollified added an element of guilt to the pleasurable affection he felt for Napoleon's son. This was going to torment the Emperor in years to come.

But not thinking that far ahead, Francis, for the moment, delighted simply in a little boy he would always hug and kiss with a particular tenderness that never failed to amaze those in attendance.

In more than one way, irony was invading the young Prince's existence with insidious little forays. On twelfth night, at a party his mother had given at Schönbrunn for the occasion, the boy the oligarchy never wanted to see sit on a throne found in his portion of the traditional cake the bean that made him king.

So it was on the afternoon of a carnival, in the midst of his Austrian relations, that Napoleon's little son was crowned with a coronet of gold paper.

He wore it proudly and with charming distinction.

11

"I wish," Captain Hurault concluded sadly, "I could say more."

Napoleon stopped pacing and jerked his chin upward. "So! The Empress and my son won't be coming after all! You know what this means, don't you?"

"Sire, I . . . I . . ." the Captain stuttered, feeling utterly helpless.

Napoleon turned his back on him and ordered in a low strangled voice, "Just leave me!"

Hurault left in a hurry, dreading to witness a complete breakdown.

Slowly, Napoleon sank into a chair. A modest world built in a spirit of resignation was crumbling around him. The notion that he could live on the island of Elba in quiet domestic felicity and humble renunciation was a delusion, his wife's loyalty a fantasy. And had he not deliberately refused to read between the lines, he would have recognized in her letters a dismaying, distant tone. In the last one she sent him on the occasion of the New Year, her good wishes for him in 1815 were that he should submit to his fate because the peace he would derive from such acceptance "*would give joy and comfort to those who were devoted to him.*" Without even hinting at a reunion, Marie Louise only stressed that he must not concern himself with the way his son was being treated. The boy was well looked after and accorded all manner of considerations.

He hadn't heard from her since.

For a moment Napoleon just stared into space. Then he took out his snuff box and fell in anguished contemplation before the miniature of his son inset on the lid. It was time, he thought, to make a thorough evaluation of their respective situation.

He had been patient, docile, and trusting. In a treaty. In a wife's protestation of affection. In the humanity of his jailers. But he was being deceived and made to look like a fool! Yet he would not begrudge Marie Louise's faltering ardor in sharing his captivity. He would gladly release her from carrying out their original plan. He would agree to a separation. The bonds that united them, he admitted now, had never been stronger than the self-serving means that went into a political match. And politics change.

But the boy was stranded in enemy camp! The thought was revolting! Unbearable!

He must rescue his son!

To do nothing but lament would shamefully and cowardly abet a monstrous coercion! And to loudly decry the Coalition's ruthless disregard for the sacred bonds of parenthood would never give him back his son nor free him from the clutches of his enemies!

Unless . . .

Suddenly, the desperation that had gripped him at the outset of his interview with Captain Hurault made way to an upsurge of optimism. But that was because he'd just decided on a plan—a plan he knew was bound to succeed thanks to a situation his foes found quite laughable. But this time the laugh would be on them!

Considering the dread he still inspired, his present position paradoxically allowed undue freedom of action. In derision, as it were, for his having once been master of half a continent, the Coalition had agreed to let him rule over a petty kingdom under rather lax supervision. Situated in the Tyrrhenian Sea off the coast of Tuscany, mountainous Elba covered only eighty square miles. And there, the Allied Powers were willing to let him play kinglet. They even allowed him to have a personal standard!

From where he sat, Napoleon could see his *new* flag! A diagonal red band sewn with three bees on a ground of gold fluttered now above the forts that were delivered to him along with all their munitions of war. He was the sovereign of twelve thousand enthusiastic and flattered Elbans, and was permitted to keep a few hundred soldiers of his ever faithful Old Guard.

But that was not all. He was even allowed to retain the officers, aides-de-camp, and familiars, who refused to abandon him. Letizia lived with him, and members of his family were permitted to visit him. On the whole, he thought his captivity had taken the aspect of a comedy under the direction of Neil Campbell, the English commissioner who was a man much too well-disposed to play the role of a warden. The commissioner had been amenable to Napoleon's suggestions of remodeling a modest island to his specifications. Napoleon was proud to have contributed his own money toward public constructions by minting uncoined gold he possessed. In return, the people lauded his generosity and industry. Portoferraio was transformed into a flourishing town where workers of all trades found it lucrative to establish themselves.

The people would certainly never foil his plan. . . .

Nearly leaping out of the chair, Napoleon put away the snuff box and went to his appointed lunch with Neil Campbell.

Lunch with the English commissioner had become a ritual without ceremony. Both men began to companionably chat on various topics, mostly the work being done, the weather, the food, and the local wine.

Napoleon raised his glass to the sunlight, turned, then tilted it, admiring the rich carmine color of its contents. It reminded him of the wine produced on his family vineyard of Sposenta back in Corsica. But that wine, he recalled with nostalgia, had a special goodness. Perhaps that was only an illusory aroma extracted from sweet boyhood memories conjuring up a rugged land of calming and arid purity. He decided to use an innocent gambit to relax the Englishman's vigilance.

"In the state of retirement in which I find myself, I should like to try my hand at wine-making. What do you think of this one?"

"I find it quite good," Campbell went so far to agree. But his mind was not on the subject. Nor was he debating whether or not Napoleon was capable of producing a palatable wine, for the commissioner had no doubt that he could.

What he kept questioning was Napoleon's sincerity in wanting to embrace such a prosaic vocation. He might rather attempt to shake the fetters, much too light, that strapped him to a life much too quiet to suit a hyperactive and aggressive temperament. Other than this premise, upon which Campbell based the possibility of an evasion, nothing in the prisoner's attitude suggested that he could be contemplating anything of the kind. Napoleon appeared to make the best of his situation. Campbell decided for the moment to enjoy his lunch.

Later, Napoleon went for a solitary stroll to the edge of a cliff and stood there looking out at the sea, remembering the fall of the year just passed when on a September day, a woman and a child had set foot on the shores of Elba.

At the time, the visit of Marie Walewska had stirred to a paroxysm his longing to see and hug his only legitimate son, all because of the little boy the Countess had brought with her. That boy was their child,

Alexander, a year older than the other son stranded in Vienna. His reunion with Marie had taken place on a solitary stretch of beach, in a tent pitched under a huge chestnut tree, and for two days and nights, no one but an orderly was allowed to approach.

He wasn't too surprised to find that at twenty-five, Marie Walewska still retained the shy, sweet seductiveness of her teens. She had never asked any favor of him and at the start of their emotion-filled reunion he'd seen that she had come with the sole purpose of offering consolation. When he embraced her, he wished that Marie Louise could have possessed one smallest fraction of Marie Walewska's forbearance and fiber. Moved to tears, he had whispered, "So you've come! You, Marie! Of all people!"

"I would never forgive myself for staying away, Sire. Even if my doing so might have pleased you!" she answered, hugging him back with all her strength.

"Marie, to hold you pleases me . . . and don't give me that title. Not you. Did you ever believe in it?"

"I believe in you," she said simply.

He'd smiled, appreciating the choice of the present tense. And unforgetful of something hinted at but never done, he mumbled with a belated feeling of indebtedness, "I should have liberated Poland."

"I would like to see you free," she replied.

Napoleon set the idea aside. Enough! I will content myself with leading the life of a family man with my wife and my son. And Marie had left him without rekindling the old adventurous flame.

Such was his frame of mind a year ago.

But no longer.

Napoleon scanned the misty horizon. The year just gone by left no traces of its passage on the swells of the waves, the course of the clouds, the shifting direction of the winds. But it had plowed through his life, leaving deep furrows from which sprouted only bitterness and sorrow.

There was no longer any doubt that he'd lost his family. *His son.* And his stay in Elba was fraught with uncertainty and danger. There were unmistakable signs that the Coalition had no intention of honoring the clauses of the Treaty of Fontainebleau, which had disposed of his fate. News from the continent was proving this as Talleyrand was reported to be clamoring for his removal to the more distant Azores.

Money was scarce. Not one fraction of the sum drawn from the revenue of his estates in France had been paid as promised by the Allies.

There also existed a danger his jailers tended to conveniently ignore—the ever-present risk of assassination by rabid royalists. He had also learned that the French were growing rapidly disenchanted with the monarchy. Under the regime of the reinstated Bourbons, tithes and privileges profiting the interests of the nobles and the clergy were being revived. There were contestations over the peasants' rights to hold on to the lands distributed to them after the Revolution.

He'd heard that the king of France offended his subjects mostly because he was not of their own choosing. They didn't appreciate his powdering his hair as it was the fashion under the Old Regime. His antiquated clothes, which seemed to have been borrowed from the wardrobe of his late brother, the ill-fated Louis the Sixteenth, displeased them because they reminded the people too much of an abhorred institution, and the population looked upon their present king as an agent in the pay of foreign princes foresworn to resurrect and maintain a system that had convulsed a nation to the point of regicide. It was also rumored that the army's loyalty to the crown was dubious.

Then there had been a great deal of gossip, which, like pollen traveling in the wind, had crossed the sea and reached his ears.

A certain General von Neipperg. . . .

Napoleon did a brisk about-face, and picking his way through the rocks and brambles, headed for the Palazzina die Mulini, where he had taken up residence.

He was surprised to find a visitor patiently waiting for his return. Formerly a member of the Imperial Council of State, Baron Fleury de Chaboulon jumped to his feet to greet him.

Heart thumping, Napoleon gave the Baron a powerful hug. "You!" he exclaimed. "Here? How did you manage? I am only allowed 'non political' visitors!" Then he noticed Chaboulon's rumpled and plain clothing. "Have you fallen into penury?"

The Baron smiled. "Not quite that low, Sire. A convenient disguise, I passed myself for a trader to escape the scrutiny of spies. I come straight from Paris!"

Napoleon fixed his eyes on the visitor. The happy glint in them was dimming. "It's already February," he remarked with a sigh. "Anyway, happy New Year, Chaboulon!"

"I wish I could say the same, Sire," the Baron replied pulling a long face.

Napoleon showed no immediate reaction. He filled a glass with wine. "A little cordial," he said, and presented it to Chaboulon.

"Am I drinking alone, Sire?"

"I've had enough at lunch," Napoleon answered, motioning him to sit down.

The Baron raised his glass. "*A votre santé!*"

Napoleon nodded absently in acknowledgment and watched Chaboulon drain his glass to the last drop as though he needed the comforting vapor of an alcoholic drink.

Then, no longer calm and composed, he said, hanging by the edge of his own seat, "Tell me everything!"

"Ah, Sire! Nothing is the same!" Chaboulon complained. "France is in dire need of assistance!"

"France," Napoleon observed flatly, "has a king and enjoys peace. And I am quite forgotten!"

"The throne of the Bourbons is wobbling, Sire."

"It will steady."

"It's on the verge of collapse. I am here because . . ."

"No collapse," Napoleon interrupted bitterly, "can be in my favor. If and when the King falls, there will probably be a republic!"

"I am here," Chaboulon insisted, "because there is no consensus on this opinion, Sire. A kind of . . . regency is very likely to be established then, just to provide for the contingencies created by your absence."

"Are you suggesting that I go back?"

"Ah, Sire! I speak for many!"

"Do you really?"

"On my honor, Sire!"

Napoleon's eyes narrowed as though focusing on a newfound ploy. Evasion, nebulous beyond the physical act of escaping with the sole purpose of reclaiming his son, was now taking definite shape. A more comprehensive plan was being laid out in front of him. And everything would fall into place, provided his return be approved by popular will, and not least, given the support of the French troops.

"The army," he asked breathlessly, "what does it think of me?"

"The army," Chaboulon said without hesitation, "knows of no commander but you!"

During the fortnight that followed Chaboulon's departure, Napoleon said to Campbell in the presence of his mother while the three of them were taking an evening stroll on the beach: "I know of no more pleasant place than Elba!"

Letizia smiled joyfully at her son. She was quite ready to accept this declaration at face value. She had watched Napoleon go about his daily routine. He seemed to have adapted well to an uneventful pace, and the numerous projects he had undertaken to improve the quality of life on the island kept him occupied enough to give him some sense of purpose. She was contented. Her mother's heart had found peace. Her son was safe from the danger of war and she'd ceased to experience the nagging fear of being told that he had been killed in battle, or suffered some great calamity. That great calamity—her son's downfall—had come to pass, and thank God! his life had been spared. Yet, being a wife and a mother, she bemoaned the tragedy of a husband torn away from his wife and child.

The commissioner contented himself to scratch the lobe of his ear. By a curious concurrence of thought, Letizia's sorrowful appreciation of Napoleon's ruined prospect of ever having his family with him, was a situation that kept bothering Campbell. His good sense and sensitivity told him that a man forcibly separated from his family and under such frustrating conditions is likely to become a restive prisoner. In the eventuality Napoleon did intend to escape, the commissioner felt that the English cruiser, *The Partridge,* could not adequately foil the attempt. He had just made plan to go to Leghorn to consult with the British envoy in Florence on the subject.

"I'll be away by month end," he only said after they had taken a few paces. "I do hope nothing untoward shall spoil Your Majesty's tranquillity while I'm gone."

Napoleon laughed. "I don't believe anything will!"

After Campbell left, the first thing Napoleon did was to give a banquet and a ball hosted by beautiful and effervescent Pauline, who had come to visit her brother. All the prominent persons of the island and visiting foreigners of distinction had been invited. Affable and relaxed, Napoleon circulated among the guests joking and telling anecdotes.

Then in the middle of the festivities, Letizia received word that she should wait for her son in the garden. Her intuition told her that his jocular mood was a sham.

Napoleon found his mother standing statuesquely, facing the sea. Tinsels of lights from the illuminated shores hemmed the waves' somber crests, and the surf gave out a soughing, cadenced noise that drowned the sound of his footfalls. Yet she must have felt him coming.

"Napolione?" she called softly to him without turning.

The melodious language in which she chose to say his name—a language that so accented his French when he'd spoken it in French schools that he'd been mercilessly teased by his classmates, stirred remembrance of bygone times. Suddenly, the fading aura of a humble childhood, of Corsica, enveloped him.

Moved, and letting himself be led back to the ancestral mood, he murmured in Italian as he came up to stand by her side. "What I have to tell you, Mother, no one but those whom I have chosen to share this with is to know. And I especially mean Pauline."

Letizia said quietly, "Paolina is a lovely bird. One sings to her. One does not speak." Then she turned to face her son and closed her fingers around his wrists. "Napolione, you are going away."

"Yes."

"Where?"

"I must fetch my son and finish my work," he said with a little break in his voice.

Letizia crossed herself, calling upon the little boy she had left in Blois, a distant blessing she never ceased to invoke in her daily prayers. Then, lifting a trembling hand to Napoleon's cheek, she said, "Follow your destiny, for a compulsion such as yours can only be God's will."

"God," he asked gently, careful not to allow skepticism to creep into his tone, "speaks to you about me?"

Letizia did not answer at once, then averting her face, she said, looking back at the sea, "God speaks to all of us. Including you!"

That same night, after the servants had put out the candles, General Bertrand and General Drouot were secretly summoned to the Emperor's room. They found Napoleon seated on his bed, arms folded across his chest, eyes fixed on an invisible, yet all-absorbing point in space. But as soon as the door shut behind the two men, he snapped out of his contemplation and asked briskly, "Has everyone gone?"

"Everyone, Sire," Bertrand answered. "The governor of the island and the mayor have expressed their deepest regrets."

Napoleon repressed a smile. In a way, the situation, though grave, contained a dash of comedy. A prisoner turned guest courteously tells a few chosen people of his decision to escape to hear them express with the same civility "deepest regrets!"

"Gentlemen," he said, with a sharp commanding tone the generals had heard before, resurrecting an epoch they thought had forever ended, "the day is set for tomorrow. We seize the vessels tonight and embark in the morning. No ship is to leave the harbor before we are at sea!"

At sea. . . .

It had been incredibly easy. With a wharf full of well-wishers, Napoleon had embarked with some four hundred men of his Guard on the brig *Inconstant.* A schooner, *The Caroline,* and five smaller vessels accommodated the rest of the troops, which amounted to seven hundred grenadiers.

They had been thirty-six hours at sea now and Napoleon hadn't said a word about his plan to anyone. Some conjectured that he might have in mind to "colonize" some out-of-the-way place and establish himself there as a free landowner.

Finally Bertrand dared ask what everyone was anxious to know. "Sire, where are we going?"

"If you will assemble the men, Bertrand. What I am going to announce is also to be communicated to the rest of the flotilla."

As he looked at his grenadiers, Napoleon felt a severe pang of anxiety. Back home, their brothers-in-arms, who once had composed the Grand Army of the Empire, were wearing the King's color. Yet Chaboulon had assured him that beyond that filmy horizon something waited, unfinished.

Into the wind he shouted, "Soldiers! We are sailing for France! We are going to retake Paris and save the Republic!"

A deafening roar of approval greeted his words, and sea birds hovering over the ships dispersed in fright to regroup at some distance, uttering plaintive little cries.

On the first day of March the ships set anchor in the Gulf of Juan. Before landfall and in the privacy of his stateroom, Napoleon had taken out his little snuff box and smiled at the picture of his son. March was the month of the Prince's birthday. On the twentieth, to be exact, his son would turn four. He thought of the occasion he would be missing and the presents he could not give him. But *his return* would be the very best present he could ever offer his son. Kissing the miniature, he whispered, "Happy birthday Napoleon!"

By dusk, bivouacs were established in a nearby olive grove and Drouot brought a lantern and set up a table upon which Napoleon spread a map which he studied at length. After a while he said with a metallic tone heralding the resumption of an epic, "We are going to take the road of Dauphiné. Provence would be easier, but we might encounter difficulties there with the King's partisans. I want to avoid a fratricidal war at all costs!"

The road Napoleon chose was in effect nearly impassable. A rugged terrain covered with ice and snow added to the hazard of trails bordering precipices. Yet he trudged along with a hundred men as a vanguard, a battalion of the Old Guard at the center, and another bringing up the rear.

Up to Grenoble the march was uneventful, save for the heartwarming reception the peasantry gave him. At Saint-Bonnet, the population even lamented the paucity of his troops. Mountain folk were his most ardent supporters. For twenty years their memory of him had not ceased to be a pleasant one. He had protected the lands given to them. Without him now, they were living in the dread of losing all to the King and his nobles. The sight of him lifted their spirits, and they hailed him as their savior. May he deliver them from King Louis!

King Louis. . . .

Six leagues from Grenoble, the King's troops were blocking the highway. An ominous order rang out, "Draw back, or we will open fire!"

Napoleon dismounted. At a glance, in spite of the distance, he recognized the Fifth Army Corps. Once those troops would have gladly died for him, but now he could perish at their hands if they executed the dramatic command:

"Present arms!"

A fearful murmur broke out around Napoleon. "Sire, stop! What are you doing!"

"I am going to talk to them."

"You will be killed! Order the charge instead!"

"I will not. They are our brethren!"

"They have sworn allegiance to the King!"

He knew that. Poor devils! Had they any choice? Had he not told them to serve France? But now came his chance. Their oath to the crown was no longer binding, because he had come back to liberate them.

"Tell our men," he ordered, "to keep their rifles' point down."

Then, in a jingle of spurs he advanced on the road. After ten paces he stopped far enough not to provoke, but close enough to be heard and scrutinized.

Napoleon was aware of ravenous eyes fixed upon him. A nostalgic hunger, he could tell. He capitalized on it. The bayonets leveled menacingly at his chest did not point too steadily. Again, Chaboulon's assurance crossed his mind.

He shouted, "Soldiers of the Fifth! Do you hear me?"

Silence.

"Of course you do! And let any of you who wishes me dead, fire! My life is in your hands! Not under the protection of these people behind me. Kill me now, if you wish!"

Once during a tiff with Josephine, she had thrown objects at him, missing him, but hitting a mirror. He'd seen how it broke, chinks radiating from the stricken point of impact.

Something similar was happening to the veneer that had been covering the magic of old. With the surrendering of his life as the epicenter, the veneer cracked before his eyes in a sudden uproar of frenzied acclamations. Muskets now pointed upward topped with blue caps. White royalist cockades were tossed over shoulders as tricolor ones were conjured up from the bottom of knapsacks.

Then pandemonium broke and troops from both sides mingled in a delirium of fraternal embraces. And caught in the middle was the commander they did not imagine ever to see again.

"Welcome home, Sire!"

A fugitive mist dimmed Napoleon's vision. Sweet words! Sweet France! He wanted to kiss the ground on which he stood, but found himself being held aloft. A hero's welcome indeed!

The Emperor marched on. . . .

At the news of Napoleon's triumphal progress, the King would not chance being caught in Paris. When he realized that the roads to the capital lay wide open, Louis the Eighteenth decided to flee back to

England, where he had once sought refuge in the aftermath of the Revolution.

King Louis had fled on Palm Sunday in a heavy downpour and Napoleon promised himself to be at the Tuileries on his son's birthday.

He kept his word.

On the evening of Monday of Holy Week, March twentieth, the Tuileries was ablaze with illumination, ready for his return. As soon as Napoleon stepped down from his carriage, he was enthusiastically seized by his Guard and carried triumphantly on their shoulders to the foot of the grand staircase his son had descended so reluctantly.

The Court, the grand dignitaries who had managed to keep an honorable balance between duty and inclination, pressed around him and jostled for a chance to offer congratulations and compliments.

Berthier squeezed his hands shouting hysterically, "You, Sire! My God! It's really you!"

Light. Glitter. Homage. Joyous trepidation. Once again, against great odds, Napoleon had succeeded. The moment was just too incredible not to intoxicate. Had the past year really ever taken place? Had he only dreamed of treason, defeat, and exile?

Then the absence of Marmont and Talleyrand, sobered him.

But something else too, was *terribly* wrong!

It struck him with devastating force once the ovations and the general exhilaration had quieted down, the candles were snuffed out and the throng had departed. . . .

That was when dawn began to rosily color the facade of the Tuileries, shedding a pale light in its deserted interior where once the presence of his wife and little son made the palace his home.

Head bent, Napoleon trod the silent corridors and hurriedly walked along to a point. There, he stopped and pressed his forehead against a gilded door no longer guarded by a grenadier.

Heart pounding, he pushed it open.

The room smelt of dust and its furniture covered with cloths—which to him looked like cerements—was almost all gone.

He recoiled with superstitious fear and began to shake violently. Incapable of taking another step, he just stood on the threshold and wept as he had never wept before, staring at the vacant space where once stood a silver-gilt cradle.

why?

12

"It won't be much longer, Monseigneur. Please, try to remain still," Isabey said patiently.

He had come to Vienna with the express purpose of consigning on canvas the likeness of the Congress's eminent participants. Then a remorseful Marie Louise had asked him to do her son's portrait, which she intended to send to her husband as a token of her good will. Isabey had obliged.

Looking on, Madame de Montesquiou, quietly signed to the boy that he should mind the painter's request, and he did, holding to his end of the bargain. Her charge had submitted to the tedious sittings on the condition that he would be wearing a military outfit similar to the hussar uniform he had admired on his mother's chamberlain. His taste for all things of a martial nature had not lessened. On the contrary, it grew stronger with the passing of time—a penchant in which Madame de Montesquiou saw an ominous streak, probably inherited from his father. She could explain why the boy had taken so well to General Neipperg. The child's fascination with the General's uniform had, by transference, earned the wearer of this dazzling outfit, the Prince's friendly reception. As for her own sentiments toward Neipperg. . . .

They were muddled by upsetting jabs of suspicion, though Madame de Montesquiou could not have known yet how well things were going for the General. Neipperg was indeed a very contented man. He had finally succeeded in convincing Marie Louise to accommodate the demands of her sensual temperament with passionate threats of blowing out his brains if she resisted them much longer. They were now lovers with all the connotations of intimate permanency the General desired. Neipperg's constant presence at Marie Louise's side, and her evident all-consuming attachment for him had sufficed to alert the pious governess to the possibility of a sinful relationship.

As she admired the magnificent uniform the child was wearing, the thought again entered her mind. She tried to banish it by turning her attention to the work in progress.

She went to stand behind Isabey to take a look at the canvas. Instantly her mood lightened as she became completely captivated by what she saw.

Isabey had captured with expert brush strokes the Prince's loveliness. All was there: the lily-and-rose complexion; the golden curly hair; the fire in the sky-blue eyes; the straight tip-tilted nose with delicate and well-formed nostrils, and the beautifully delineated mouth with a cherry-red lower lip divided by a charming dimple.

The governess had no difficulty guessing how such a face would look in adulthood. . . .

For the moment, she could only enthuse. "Ah, it's him! How very skillful of you, Monsieur Isabey!"

Isabey smiled, as pleased by the compliment as he was proud with his work. Then he asked, "Of what order shall I decorate the Prince?"

She answered in a low voice that quavered with emotion. "The order of the *Légion d'Honneur.* It has been conferred upon him since birth!"

Isabey emitted a slight embarrassed cough, for he had been given certain instructions and the Prince's portrait had to receive clearance from Metternich. Egged on by Talleyrand, Metternich had readily agreed that the order of the *Légion d'Honneur* be taken away from the child.

"Madame," he whispered, "I am not at liberty to satisfy this suggestion."

She had lived in such dread of what was to become of her charge since the Congress had convened that it did not take her long to realize that her fears were not unfounded.

She said with a point of exasperation, "But it's only a picture!"

Isabey sighed in commiseration. "It may be so," he agreed sadly, "but in matter of politics, virtuality, too, has its importance."

She felt so overwrought that she thought it best to hold her peace on the subject and tried to calm herself, not wishing to upset the impressionable little boy whom she had kept isolated from the general commotion that had spread to the castle's staff.

Repeated by a coachman who had heard of it at the Chancellery in Vienna, the report of Napoleon's escape and his outlawry pronounced by the members of the Congress had reached Schönbrunn that afternoon. And rumors were that Talleyrand had declared Napoleon an escaped convict to be hunted down as an outcast and vicious criminal.

Marie Louise, gone riding with Neipperg, knew nothing of the news. Her ignorance did not preoccupy the governess nearly as much as the light interest the former Empress seemed to be taking in her son. She would see him briefly in the morning and caress him distractedly, returning him afterward to the care of his governess for the rest of the day.

Glancing up at her charge, Madame de Montesquiou wondered with a knot in her throat how a mother worthy of that name could display such indifference toward a child so exceedingly lovable. No doubt, the governess concluded with utmost reluctance, the Prince's mother must *have engaged* in an illicit relation that was driving her to distraction. Marie Louise appeared to have abjured all sentiment of motherhood. And as events were sure to grow even more chaotic, the governess's feeling of devotion for Napoleon's hapless little son deepened.

So did her distress.

Isabey put his brush down. "We are done for today," he told her. So she went to the Prince, who continued to mind her and sat very still. "Come," she said lovingly, holding out her hand. "You have been very good!"

To ease her mind and amuse the boy, she took him for a stroll in the park. Hand in hand, they walked to the vast pond of Neptune. The Prince enjoyed feeding the swans and also the carp, whose undulant shapes he liked to watch weaving along the bottom. They had taken along some bread crumbs, and two majestic swans took quick notice of the brilliantly-clad child as he dipped his small hand into a bag containing the treats and tossed them in their direction.

Quickly, they glided toward him on the mirror-like water. Outracing the graceful birds, the carp came up pouting gluttonously to the surface disturbing with silvery ripples the reflection of the adorable face that so haunted Napoleon.

Haunted were the eyes of his wife. When Marie Louise learned of her husband's disappearance from Elba, she lamented on Neipperg's shoulder, "That is not true! It's a joke and it's in very bad taste!"

But her lover's prolonged silence dispelled her incredulity.

"I am lost!" she cried.

Her dismay augured well. Neipperg spoke excitedly. "No! Nothing is lost! Not if Your Majesty place yourself, and without any reservation, under the protection of the Coalition!"

She did not appear to be listening. "He will come after me . . . pursue me . . . ruin everything!"

These were beautiful words. Neipperg quickly capitalized on her fear, her reluctance. "Nothing of the kind is going to happen to Your Majesty if you do as I say!"

"What am I to do?"

"Renounce all claims on France. Put a stop to the still prevalent idea abroad that you are being detained here against your will. Disavow what Napoleon has just done. This way, you will remove the pretext he may use to justify his aggression. Your peace and tranquillity depend on the severance of everything that might link you to him."

"But I already have . . . I think."

"Do all this *in writing* and your trouble will be over!"

"But will my father go along with this?"

"I believe so. Your Majesty must seek an audience with your father as soon as possible!"

The Emperor of Austria was not immediately available because Francis was engaged in a squabble with Alexander and Frederick William over who should shoulder the blame for having allowed the prisoner of Elba to enjoy a freedom downright incompatible with a state of captivity. Francis had come to the conclusion that Russia and Prussia were the chief culprits. Why, he argued, had they accepted the motion to establish a foreign garrison on Elba? Why did they agree to permit a few hundred French soldiers to live there with Napoleon? And England, too, had acted irresponsibly. Why did Lord Wellington thwart the plan suggested by Talleyrand to exile Napoleon further away, to some more remote island in the ocean?

So words bounced back and forth in a tempest of recrimination and tempers grew hot. Everyone could see that the intended harmony of a triumphant and grandiose gathering was being totally wrecked by confusion, bitterness, frustration, distrust, and uncertainty. The latter maddened nearly all the Congress's participants.

No one had been able to find out for certain where Napoleon had gone. Reports kept coming which contradicted one another. One said he had landed in France, the next that he was re-embarking, and still another that he had made the King of France a prisoner. The last rumor was that he was marching on Italy.

Italy! Francis, having shifted and swayed so far, would suffer no hesitation. On the question of Italy, his son-in-law better back down. He would oppose him ruthlessly. On the other hand, if Napoleon wished to reclaim France and demanded to have Marie Louise back, and if she herself expressed the desire to be reunited with her husband, notwithstanding a decree of outlawry against him, well, perhaps. . . .

"Perhaps," Marie Louise glumly said to Menéval, "I should have gone back to Napoleon!"

Left to herself with only Neipperg to furnish an anchoring element in the midst of mind-boggling problems, she was totally unsure of what to do. Until she could see Francis, whose last word would absolve her from all responsibilities, she felt extremely uneasy. Her attitude was scrutinized by her French suite, and their evaluation of her conduct worried her.

Menéval listened with consternation. What she had just said to him was the opposite of what she had told him earlier in the day. Earlier she had said, "I can't return to France. There is nothing for me there!" and "My son must not be told anything. His father's actions hold no future for him!"

No doubt now, Menéval thought, she felt ashamed and sought to curry his approval. As if it mattered at all at this point! He had many other concerns and every reason to be preoccupied by them.

Austrian hospitality toward the small French colony at Schönbrunn had turned sour if not downright hostile. All communication with France had stopped and the prospect of arrest faced anyone caught trying to pass a message or receiving one.

Presently Marie Louise asked, sounding his own feelings, "Have you no hope? No gladness?"

"We are all to hope for a peaceful settlement," he answered carefully.

She grew alarmed, "Settlement?"

"There are indications that the Emperor comes in a spirit of peace and that he has won the overwhelming support of the French nation."

"How do you know this?" she demanded. "Only my husband's outlawry is common knowledge."

Menéval had managed to secure his own source of information and tried to repair the slip as best he could. "I believe a little time should be given the Emperor to prove the rumors that his intentions are pacific. For the time being, I beg Your Majesty to sign nothing that might force you to take side."

Marie Louise wrung her hands. "Alas! I am not mistress of my action. No princess is! We all owe obedience to the head of our House!"

By nature gentle and even-tempered, Menéval felt a surge of anger and contempt. Marie Louise was using paternal authority as a shield and a crutch.

"Madame," he replied, struggling to remain calm, "I commend you for those sentiments. Yet you have been engaged in a contract that has freed you from that tutelage. Your Majesty is the co-initiator of a new dynasty. You are a wife and a sovereign, the mother of a child who needs your protection. . . ." He also burned to say, "And a married woman whose duty is to cleave to her husband for better and for worse, so long as he lives, and not be swayed from honoring a marriage vow by the dictates of a father!"

But she spared him the trouble of biting his tongue and cut in, saying testily, "It is my son and I who are in need of protection! As for my sovereignty, it is a mockery! All I have is my family to which by tradition I owe absolute submission! And I cannot, Monsieur, rebel against my father! This is contrary to the principles in which I have been raised."

At this point, Marie Louise began to cry and concluded, "Of my own I can do nothing. For you see, I am doomed to be put under a yoke! I have been born under a fatal star! Oh God! I shall never be happy!"

Unmoved, Menéval watched Napoleon's wife cover her face with her hands.

Then something he saw, or rather failed to see, numbed him with shock. Marie Louise had taken off her wedding ring! She had for all intents and purposes divorced herself from Napoleon and his cause!

The Baron could have pointed her out as a traitor worse than Marmont, because without her complete support as a consort and a wife, the ignominious and ruinous ban placed on Napoleon could never be revoked. Under such a ban, he would be the quarry of Europe. But had she stood by her husband, and with all of the restraining factors her Austrian parentage could have brought into play, few members of the oligarchy, including her father, would have pursued the idea of ostracism.

Without a word, Menéval left Marie Louise to her crying, looking upon her tears as a spilling of some sort of morbid humor from whose riddance one should feel purified. But Menéval entertained no such hope. The woman had declared herself Napoleon's enemy!

Marie Louise was still shaking with a chestful of sobs when finally Francis found time to grant her the audience she so earnestly sought of him. She rushed to her father, crying hysterically, "Oh, Papa! Why must this happen? Please save me from this terrible man!"

Francis's mood splintered. Fragments of it lay chipped and unmendable as her declaration ran counter to his new-found spirit of conciliation. He just had intelligence that Napoleon was limiting his ambition to France. Given Napoleon's assurance of espousing a pacific policy, he, Francis of Austria, was on the brink of allowing his poor daughter to go back to her husband if she so demanded. But what of this outcry? This aversion! Not in the least suspecting his daughter of being Neipperg's contented mistress, he asked nonplused, "Do you realize what you are saying?"

He had never seen her that way, resolute in her vehemence. Marie Louise even stamped her foot! "Yes! I decline to have any part in what Napoleon has just done!"

"You repudiate him?" Francis exclaimed, sinking in deeper astonishment.

"I do!" and almost accusingly, she dared him to criticize her: "Isn't it your wish that I do this?"

Francis considered his favorite daughter in silence. Indeed, she was a true Habsburg. In her mental make-up was ingrained the dynastic conscience. He kissed her. "You are doing the right thing." Then softly, "Tomorrow you will take your son to Vienna. The Hofburg is better guarded than Schönbrunn."

She exclaimed, wide-eyed, "Is my son in any danger here?"

"Of being abducted by his father's agents or supporters, yes!"

"Oh, no!" she moaned. The possibility that the boy could be reunited with Napoleon struck her as a gross impropriety. "This must never happen, Papa!"

More softly still, Francis added, "And another thing, a trifle to you perhaps, but a matter of importance that would lend credibility to your renunciation in the eyes of our Allies. It is time to dismiss your French attendants."

"All of them?" she asked, stunned.

"I can't say that you are to forgo the services of a good valet or those of a good cook, but the others must go. I am sorry to bother you with such details."

Marie Louise thought of Menéval, of her gentlemen and ladies. They stood for a past that would only lay her open to censure. But with them gone. . . .

Already, some invisible hands seemed to have lifted a heavy weight off her chest.

She nodded. "That is a sensible suggestion, Papa."

"I shall attend to it, then," Francis said with a honey-sweet smile.

On the eve of her charge's fourth birthday, Madame de Montesquiou was unpacking once again, this time at the Hofburg palace situated in the heart of Vienna. The foreboding which had beset her while doing the same thing at Schönbrunn less than a year ago now congealed to a certitude of impending doom.

Presently she caught herself laying out the Prince's clothes as one would handle some relics. A wave of desolation broke over her. A quick glance in the direction of the window eased this a little. Young Napoleon was there, a few paces away, reachable and embraceable and completely engrossed by a scene in the courtyard below—the changing of the palace guards.

He had begged her to let him watch it, and kneeling on a chair she had pulled near the embrasure he was now gazing with rapt attention at "the ceremony" as he called it. This unrelenting martial inclination of his set her thinking again: like father, like son. And look where all this has led!

She had never concerned herself overmuch with the complex ingredients that went into the making of a war. For whatever causes or reasons, war to her was evil. Another war, it was rumored, was about to flare up. Everything heralded its imminence. She had heard talk of Neipperg going to Italy to fight Murat, who had been reported to have sided now with Napoleon, no doubt to regain his favor.

Presently the child climbed down from the chair, and mimicking the close-order drill he had just observed, asked, "How soon can someone become a soldier?"

She looked at him pensively, remembering how he cried once at the sight of a bird eating a worm, and how his sensitivity extended to others' misfortunes at an age when most young children knew nothing of altruistic sentiment and tended to be naturally self-centered and reluctant at giving. He was not like that at all.

One day in the park of Saint Cloud, she recalled the incident vividly, a small boy in mourning clothes had arrested the Prince's attention. Then, upon learning that the boy was a war orphan, he had wasted no time to ask his papa to grant the child and his mother a pension. This had already been done, but it was increased, so touched had Napoleon been by his infant son's goodness.

How was she to reconcile this gentle, compassionate side of his nature with this martial propensity?

She answered noncommittally. "As soon as you grow to be as tall as those soldiers you have just seen."

That seemed to distress the Prince. "This will take a lot of eating!"

"And not the sweets you like so well, but the vegetables that you detest," she added.

"And how long will this be, if I eat the things you say I should?"

As it was, his growth had been rapid regardless. She had noticed this by the frequency with which his trousers had to be lengthened or replaced. "Soon enough," she assured him.

The very next day he would be growing a year older. Then she wondered with gripping anxiety, *How well will he fare as a young man?*

Next morning, Madame de Montesquiou forced herself to think positively. The day, despite the present difficulties, should be a day of *quiet* rejoicing. Quiet, because the date of March twentieth would most likely go unnoticed. In the commotion following their move to the Hofburg and the current state of alert, there had been no word from Marie Louise that any special celebration would be held for her son's birthday. Accordingly, Madame de Montesquiou made up her mind to mark the occasion with the resources at her disposal—an extra helping of sweets for the Prince, longer playtime and, above all, an outpouring of all the love her heart contained.

When the boy came to her for his morning kiss and hug, she held him longer. As though touched by some premonition, he clung to her convulsively and kissed her again.

That unnerved her, but she made herself smile and it came, she felt it, all crooked.

"Do you love me that much?" she asked.

"I love you more than much!" he answered gravely.

"For how long?" she asked, fighting back the tears that stung the back of her eyes.

"All my life!"

She smiled. "A long life. . ." And her voice trembled as she cupped her hands over his smooth rosy cheeks and declared with tender solemnity: "You are four years old today!"

That day began as it ordinarily did; with a prayer recited aloud and together. Then, as this would not ordinarily happen, a personage was ushered into the antechamber by a footman who lost no time informing Madame de Montesquiou that Count of Urban, Grand Chamberlain of the Emperor, was requesting to see her.

The governess received him holding her charge by the hand, her knees bent in a curtsy. The visitor looked grave, but the Countess only thought of acknowledging a considerate gesture.

"How kind of you to come in the Emperor's behalf on the morning of the Prince's birthday!"

The Grand Chamberlain grimaced a smile. "Madam," he said, avoiding eye contact, "what I have come to say is a private matter."

Save for the boy whom that visit directly concerned, there was no one else with them.

"We are quite alone," she replied squeezing the little hand nestled in her palm.

Urban looked at Napoleon's son. "Not quite," he said.

"Surely, the birthday greetings that you so kindly bring can't be delivered but in the presence of the Prince!"

"The object of my visit does not relate to the Prince's birthday. Please, have him removed."

Shakily, she tugged at the bellpull.

When Madame Marchand entered answering the call, Madame de Montesquiou blurted out without thinking, "*Vite! emmenez le petit roi!*"

Take the little king away . . .

The Grand Chamberlain's eyebrows went up. Was the child still addressed as "king" by the small nucleus of devoted attendants?

It was high time he deliver his message.

As soon as they were alone, he came straight to the point.

"Madam, it is my duty to inform you that the Emperor, as of today, is releasing you from the task of looking after his grandson. You are to leave immediately for France!"

For a moment he thought she was going to faint and extended a helpful hand. But she refused it, and far from swooning, entreated with dignity: "I shall wholeheartedly comply with the Emperor's wishes. But for the sake of the child to whom His Majesty has shown so much affection, I should like to leave him . . . later. When he will be the least aware of my departure. Tonight, after I put him to bed. This, Monsieur, is to be a happy day for the Prince!"

"I realize that," Urban said, with a conciliatory nod. "A nightly departure would not be objectionable in this case." He gave her the letter of dismissal.

Concealing her agitation, Madame de Montesquiou pretended to read slowly, but she was skipping every other line. She wasn't missing much. And what was there to miss? The finality of their intent had already lodged itself in her heart like the poisonous barb of an arrow. The few sentence fragments she caught were honeyed words coating the poison. Francis praised her out of her post, out of the boy's life!

She folded the letter, which she would have liked to crumple and stamp her foot upon, and said, "I leave the Prince in good health. I ask that this be verified by the Emperor's First Physician, the child's own physician, and the Empress's surgeon. I further request that a certificate attesting to their findings be issued to me, duly signed and sealed!"

"This shall be done," the Grand Chamberlain said, only too anxious to give the proceedings the legality that would silence any allegation of foul play. And wasting no time, he went to fetch the doctors while the boy was returned to the room by his cradle rocker.

Hemmed in by serious-looking men towering over him, the Prince made no move to seek refuge in his governess's arms. That filled her with tender pride. Thank God! He had been spared his mother's spinelessness! And to see him so blissfully ignorant, so brave, so beautiful, and so forsaken broke Madame de Montesquiou's heart. It was she who felt in need of comfort. Parting the intimidating ring formed by the doctors, she knelt in front of Napoleon's son and hugged him to her with infinite tenderness.

To feel the child in her arms soothed her, enabled her to speak to him calmly. She said after releasing him, "We are going to show these gentlemen how big and strong you are!"

Without preamble one of the doctors ordered, "Please, undress the Prince."

In silence, she did this, her movements slow and maladroit. Her fingers were shaking a little as she thought, This time, and once again tonight, for the last time. . . . Then she surrendered the naked child to probing hands and assessing eyes. That miniature of a man, the doctors agreed, was indeed in excellent form.

Within the hour, the examination was completed and the certificate signed and a copy given to Madame de Montesquiou.

The day passed.

Too rapidly! Time did not stretch. On the contrary, the hours seemed to have been compressed in a moment.

But nothing, so far as the child could tell, seemed to be amiss save that his dear *Maman Quiou* kept glancing at the clock she had brought from Paris. It was significantly adorned with two eagles guarding the sacred fire. Every time it chimed she would give a start and grow a shade paler.

Madame de Montesquiou's face was constantly turning to the window. Her wish was an impossible one: that the sky could stay bright indefinitely. Never had the light of day seemed so precious to her. When it began to dim, she truly thought she might lose her mind.

Dusk descended over Vienna on March twentieth, 1815, unmindful of her desolation. Lackeys in powdered wigs brought in lamps, and that increased her torment. The Prince's bedtime was fast approaching. Too fast!

In haste, she whispered her last recommendations in the serving women's ears. In tears, they nodded to the sweetest of commands—that of loving the little one over their own private interests, of fostering in the Prince love of the fatherland and remembrance of the father whose name no one dared pronounce.

They solemnly swore to do so, huddled in the safe recess of an alcove for fear of being overheard or observed. For walls had ears and keyholes had eyes. Their days, too, they felt, must be numbered. Then the great Emperor's son would be on his own and may God protect him!

Madame de Montesquiou fearfully peered into his future while observing him that night happily going to bed, older by a year, unaware that being four was precipitating the moment when he would have an inkling of the drama that could so seriously affect his life.

As she watched him pass from sleepiness to slumber, she decided to leave her charge's room only when she was absolutely certain he was sound asleep.

When he slept, she crossed herself and began to pray silently. May life be kinder to him than it had been. May his name never be used as a tool to perpetuate dissension. She could see so much goodness in him! Yet again, she recalled the violence that had surrounded him like a fatal aura. The example of Jesus came to her mind as she observed the child clutching the small crucifix she gave him to hold each night.

He had been pestering her to have it "permanently" as he would say, and she had been reluctant to give it up. It was an heirloom she did not want to part with. Now she would gladly surrender her dearest treasures. But a little cross and a farewell kiss were all she could leave him.

For the last time she gently touched her lips to his forehead. If he woke, she would simply coax him back to sleep. If he didn't wake, she *must go!* He did not stir, plunged in a deep sleep, which in little children suffused the face with blissful serenity.

Next morning, after Madame Marchand finished dressing him, young Napoleon saw a strange woman entering his room. Instinctively, he felt her hostility. He stared at her with wide, worried and uncomprehending eyes, for he expected to see his *Maman Quiou*.

He did not like the way she looked. Her lips were pinched and she stared back at him without warmth. Her dark, coal-black eyes, which he thought resembled the buttons on his shoes, shone meanly. She seemed to be taunting him.

But he stood his ground and demanded, "Who are you?"

She returned sharply, "I am Countess Mitrovsky. You are to obey me from . . ."

"I want *Maman Quiou!*"

Countess Mitrovsky drew herself up and disdainfully looked down at the little boy who dared challenge her. Empress Maria Ludovica, to whom she owed this appointment, had warned her against the child. Spoiled and nothing but trouble for the future, she had told the Countess, who shared the Empress's vitriolic dislike of Napoleon.

She said sternly, "She is gone!"

Young Napoleon stamped his foot, not realizing the finality of this statement. "I want her back!"

Countess Mitrovsky had a child of her own whom she would not have hesitated to slap had this tone been used with her. Her hand itched and her tongue grew barbed.

She snapped, enjoying being cruel, "You will never see her again. She has left you forever!"

With complete indifference Mitrovsky watched the little boy gasp, heave, and then burst into violent, spasmodic sobs.

Alarmed, Madame Marchand made bold to intervene. "Madam, I would have broken the news to the Prince more gently," she said, putting her arms around the boy.

"This child," Mitrovsky hissed, "is being excessively coddled. And I won't have it!"

He would not have any of her ill-humor either. He ignored her and buried his face in the maid servant's neck. "Oh, Chanchan, I thought she loved me!" he sobbed.

Taking advantage of the fact that the Countess had turned her back on them in annoyance, Chanchan whispered into his ear to set the record straight. "She will love you always! She has been made to go!"

Immediately his sobbing eased. He pressed his forehead to the maid's and looked into her eyes, so closely that his eyes crossed. He mouthed the small consolation she gave him, "She did not want to leave me?"

Chanchan breathed, "Never!"

Her back still turned, the tormentor waited. She waited until the wails and whispers had quieted down to a few jagged sighs. Then she swung round and proceeded to lay down new orders.

"It is the Emperor's command," she said severely to the maid, "that from this day onward, the name 'Franz' is to be used exclusively as opposed to 'Napoleon' when addressing His Majesty's grandson by his surname. Your name," Mitrovsky went on, directly speaking to the boy, "is not Napoleon, but Franz. Is this understood?"

The Prince wiggled himself free from his cradle rocker's protective embrace and declared, "I like being called Napoleon!"

Worried by his boldness, Madame Marchand stretched out her hands to him in a restraining gesture even as she grasped the futility of all resistance.

Mitrovsky confronted her recalcitrant charge with the ultimate weapon. "Do you," she said to him, "dare say 'no' to your grandpapa?"

Silence. Napoleon's son looked away, presenting a profile of such captivating purity in its curves that the new governess could not help but stare. She surprised herself talking gently to him.

"Now," she asked, "what is your name?"

Still, he did not move his head and appeared to gaze into some distant, secret dimension of his own.

Mitrovsky felt as though she was trespassing on a mysterious domain when she urged again, her tone subdued, almost respectful. "What is your name?"

"Franz," he finally answered with a faraway little voice.

Thus, four-year-old Franz was born on the same day four-year-old Napoleon was given the foretaste of certain problems. From that experience undergone with the trauma of a loss, the persona of Franz emerged, reflective, cautious, casting off like a molt the lightheartedness and spontaneity of a childhood that had scarcely begun.

In the days that followed, the Prince refused to eat and declined to play. Overnight, he seemed to have mentally aged. In a wounded but proud reserve, he grew attentive to the gradual crumbling of a comforting and familiar world.

The next to go was Menéval. Before leaving, the Baron made a last, desperate effort to dissuade Marie Louise from abandoning her husband. When this had failed, he pleaded the young Prince's cause, begged her not to consent to separate herself from her son.

But Marie Louise exhibited a mulish obstinacy and Menéval had no difficulty guessing why. Her head must be filled with the enticements Parma offered her. The duchies had been given to her with the explicit proviso that upon her death not one parcel of her domains would go to her son, but would revert instead to the heir of the Queen of Etruria.

"At least this way," she told Menéval, "I will have a revenue. I can set aside for my son's future use five hundred thousand francs a year! Whereas if I refuse that condition, I am left without anything at all."

That had made Menéval's blood boil. She had France, a sovereignty awaiting her there at the side of her husband if only she would take up Napoleon's cause and make it her own. So he had tried to goad her back to that resolution in a roundabout way.

"Think, Madam," he argued, with redoubled vehemence, "the Prince is already deprived of his paternal inheritance as it is. He has lost his titles. He has been taken away from his native country, and his own father is condemned to live outside the pale of the law. A million, two or three, all the riches of the world for that matter, will remedy nothing at this point!"

And what will? She had not asked this, but he could guess by her deeply troubled air, that unbidden, from some obscure reservoir of guilt, well hidden and never quite drained of its bothersome contents, that question like a dim point of light at the end of a tunnel, had beamed an answer at the very same instant it had set a spark in her conscience. That answer must have angered her. It lent a belligerent pique to her reply.

"Don't you think that *my sacrifice,*" she had said sounding out each syllable, "has been costly too?"

Then he had bluntly told her that she had been misguided and deceived by unreliable counsels.

"But that is all that I am allowed to do!" she stated flatly.

"Not at all!" he contradicted her. "Please, consider an alternative that has always been open to Your Majesty. It is . . ."

She must have detested him for what he was going to suggest and did not let him finish.

"Enough! Monsieur!" she cut him off haughtily, then went on to say something that reminded Menéval of a famous retort: "What I have signed, I have signed!"

He hung his head, and looking at him sideways, she had mumbled. "I pray you to remember me with indulgence."

It was at that instant that Menéval put Marie Louise out of his mind. She was, as far as he was concerned, *une cause perdue.*

A lost cause!

His preoccupation was now centered on her son and he felt helpless, as the boy's own cause was without appeal with the defection of his mother.

Now on this sad day, Menéval stood in a roomful of people, the Austrians outnumbering the French, and closely watched the little Prince to whom he had come to say his good-byes. His eyes made contact with the boy's, but the child acted as though he had never known him before.

That strange attitude deeply disturbed Menéval. In the past, the Prince would run up to him with spontaneity and soft exclamations of joy. But now, he stood by the side of his new governess, withdrawn and with a melancholy air which somehow made him look more attractive than ever. In a fit of sadness Menéval imagined seeing in the Prince a sacrificial victim chosen because of its flawless beauty.

Slowly, he made his way to his master's son, took his hand and asked with a voice dulled by emotion, "I shall be seeing your Papa very soon. Is there anything you wish to say to him?"

The boy made no reply and withdrawing his hand, moved toward the window embrasure.

This was not the little Napoleon he once thought he knew so well. Gone were the spontaneous and familiar playfulness, the endearing loquacity he used to display with charming infant grace.

Menéval was so worried about the transformation that he scarcely paid much attention to what he said in his leave taking as he made the rounds of the drawing room. He kept glancing furtively at the Prince's small figure standing alone at the same place where he had inexplicably turned down Menéval's friendly greeting. With a heavy heart, the Baron went back once more to the child to bid him his final farewell. He did not attempt to touch him. He only bowed ceremoniously.

"Monseigneur . . ." he murmured, and overcome with grief he made to walk away.

"Monsieur Méva . . ."

The Prince reached for his hand and drew him deeper in the window's recess.

Menéval's heart gave a jolt. Young Napoleon was opening up to him! Still, he was not the same child he once knew. This little boy seemed to have suddenly learned the value of secrecy and dissimulation.

Menéval bent down to look with deep affection and concern into a pair of sad and thoughtful eyes. "Yes, Monseigneur?"

After a brief hesitation the Prince whispered as if what he had to say was censurable. "Monsieur Méva, be sure to tell my dear Papa that I love him very much!"

13

Napoleon slammed a balled fist against the palm of his hand. "All I want is peace! And only peace! I want to be left alone and complete the establishment of a democracy in France! That is my goal. No more wars!"

Caulaincourt listened, pulling a long face, the sight of which inflamed Napoleon.

"Nothing will deter me from accomplishing this! My promises are not empty. I will keep them! Is this so difficult to believe? Is it?"

Caulaincourt hesitated voicing his own misgivings.

This time the Emperor was pitting himself against a moral vengeance which made no allowance for his credibility. Who would dare lend support to an outlaw who had become the quarry of Europe? No one! And once again, France—isolated and shunned, was readying herself for war because her outlawed emperor refused to allow any foreign powers to force him out of his throne. Even though Napoleon kept proclaiming his pacific intentions and shouted himself hoarse over it, the armies of Europe were banding together to be rid of him.

The Marquis began with the most immediate contention. "Sire, the Powers are animated with such a terror of you!"

"I had to rule aggressively!"

"They associate your very person with war . . . never ending."

"That is utterly stupid!"

Caulaincourt went on to recite a litany of misdeeds leveled at Napoleon by his critics: "It is generally held that Your Majesty has no conscience, that you care for no one, that the blood of many innocent people is on your hands, that you hate humanity and that in order to save it, you must be neutralized."

For a moment, Caulaincourt thought the Emperor was having a stroke. His eyes bulged. His speech seemed to be impaired as he appeared to gag.

Finally he exploded.

"Necessity! That is my conscience! And I know all about humanity! There is nothing inherently noble about it! When the mob was running amuck in the name of liberty, I saw a man soaking a piece of bread in the blood of a noble he had just hacked to pieces before shoving it in his mouth. . . . The *ideologues* are fools. Circumstances alone make a man what he is, and I have never been cruel without absolute necessity!"

Then, catching his breath, Napoleon emphatically stated: "I have been forced to make war as I am forced now into this one!"

A grim probability went through the former ambassador to Russia's mind: This one might be the emperor's *final defeat* as well.

The odds against him were so staggering!

The same consideration lanced Napoleon's brain, a brain whose care-worn lucidity had to work in a body slowed by approaching middle age and its infirmities. He had been suffering from intermittent gastric pains, but they did not prevent him from planning this final campaign.

He said, "I am going to attack before being attacked! I have no alternative but to win brilliantly and *immediately!*"

"Sire. . . ." It pained Caulaincourt to mention this, "I do not mean to speak disparagingly of the army. Still, Your Majesty must realize that your best generals are dead, a handicapping factor as Your Majesty can see."

Having said this, he bit his tongue to stop himself from saying more: Like Moloch, Napoleon's wars had consumed the flower of France's youth.

Napoleon glared at him. "What do you suggest? That I do nothing when I am told of the inhuman proceedings directed against me? Proceedings which are to be implemented by aggressive means!"

Caulaincourt remained silent.

"June 12," Napoleon said, speaking to himself.

"Sire?"

"I'm setting out for the front."

Waterloo! A dark star of catastrophic proportion had blotted out the light in the glowing firmament of Napoleon's victories. This time, the defeat of his army was total and its rout complete.

In a borrowed carriage, Napoleon rode back to Paris. He could have wept oceans of tears over the greatest of all ironies: The boundless courage and spirit of sacrifice that had animated his troops were elevating a defeat to an indisputable level of glory!

As for his own. . . . He promised himself, he would reshape his destiny. He would think of something!

His Parisian palace was still a haven. The outer world coalescing against him had not yet announced itself. Only the haunting recollection of those fateful few days—nine to be exact—which had seen the total collapse of an empire whose existence depended so exclusively upon his victories. In such fashion he had seduced France. And France, in the aftermath of Waterloo, might repudiate him.

Napoleon found his brother Lucien waiting for him. Lucien's arrant penchant for adventure had prompted him to re-appear in Napoleon's life.

Lucien had not changed. Hot-headed and impetuous, he planted himself in front of his brother and asked point blank, "What are you going to do now?"

Napoleon clasped his hands behind his back and looked straight ahead. "I shall give an account of what has happened and return to battle."

"With what, Sire?"

"I can call up a hundred and fifty thousand men. I can also use the National Guard. That should suffice to prevent the enemy from advancing any closer."

"You are not going to give up?"

"Certainly not!"

"There is a great deal of dissension in the Chambers on how to proceed. You will have to do a lot of convincing to get your way," Lucien cautioned.

Napoleon winced as though Lucien had bumped against a fresh wound. For the first time in his life, he had been thoroughly beaten.

He had to admit. "I am tired, Lucien."

"Of course!" said Lucien sympathetically. "You ought to be!"

Napoleon shrugged, then let his shoulders sag. He had not meant to indicate the wearisome burden of one's own mass, the aching muscles and back, or the pain sometimes dull and other times sharp in the pit of his stomach that interfered with the working of his mind. Those were all there, of course.

He had also meant emotional exhaustion brought on by the fruitless sacrifice of so many lives—by the tens of thousands, by the trauma of betrayed trust and hopes, and by something else. Something unfinished weighed him down: he had failed to rescue his little son, whom he so dearly loved, and in whom he saw the repository of his revised political ambition and ideals. And there was France for which he considered himself very responsible. Yes! Very responsible. Yet, it seemed as though the sincerity of his concerns was being put into question.

Napoleon turned his back on his brother and moved to the window, to the high rectangle of light whose glare made the gilded molding on the walls and ceiling look faded, and these were not the suites he used to have. Since his return from Elba, he had abandoned the Tuileries for the Elysée palace. It suited him. The surroundings did not evoke any poignant memories.

Lucien studied the figure of his once formidable brother clad in a plain dressing gown. A warrior wearing slippers! The man was balding and pot bellied. He presented a rather pathetic sight. Yet he spoke of going back to the front, of levying new troops! He talked confidently as a mighty commander-in-chief to whom all would still give obeisance.

My brother is deceiving himself, Lucien thought, having no illusions left. For he knew of a few machinations being set in motion. Some had suggested disowning the Emperor outright as the best way to secure peace and tranquillity for the nation since the Coalition directed its wrath against Napoleon alone. The Marquis de Lafayette had clamored for the abolition of the empire and ardently recommended the institution of a republic, while Talleyrand was plotting the restoration of the Bourbons. . . .

No longer could Napoleon have his way on a word and at a glance. Still, out of habit, Lucien made use of a superfluous conditional. "If the Chambers were to oppose you," he asked, "what will you do?"

"That," Napoleon answered crisply, without turning round, "is a problem I shall deal with when the time comes!"

Time, Napoleon quickly realized, was a fast diminishing commodity. If no decisive actions were taken at once, France would once again be conquered. Blücher and Wellington could reach Paris in a matter of days. A quick agreement to a fresh offensive was urgently needed.

He sat surrounded by grim-faced councilors he had summoned to an emergency session, confident they would support his plan.

"In eight days," he told them, "we will find ourselves facing the enemy's bayonets. And I say to you, there is no time to debate. There is barely time to act. I call upon your patriotism to invest me with the power of temporary dictatorship. I need full freedom of action in order to carry on the defense of France!"

At this declaration, everyone's noses pointed downward and chins sank faintheartedly into starched neckclothes. No one dared volunteer a word.

Napoleon grew impatient. "I do not sham necessity to stifle liberty! You will keep it! My asking for this extraordinary power is proof that I am not acting deceitfully. Trust me!"

"The Chambers," one of the councilors made bold to say, "no longer dare put any trust in Your Majesty's intention!"

Napoleon darted a sharp look at the speaker, a look that conveyed the irrefragable admission of a change he had encouraged. Once he had possessed so much power, no one dared contradict him, much less question his motives and demand that he justify them. Now that he had relinquished a great deal of it by redrafting a new constitution upon his return from Elba, no one had the nerve to put any confidence in him.

"The Chambers," he retorted with a metallic tone redolent of despotic days, "must trust me or I may very well dissolve them!"

Seated at the end of the table, Lucien bit on his knuckles, wishing the dissolution of the Chambers had already taken place. Napoleon had to contend now with a liberated democracy whose fierceness in safeguarding its rights had translated itself into alarming declarations the Emperor seemed to disregard. The Chamber of Deputies had proclaimed itself in permanent session. It also warned that any attempt to dissolve it would be considered an act of high treason, liable to impeachment. To make matters worse, the Minister of War also declined placing the remnant of the army at the Emperor's disposal.

You can't be delicate about this! Lucien thought. *Might* dissolve the Chambers? No! *Ought* to!

Beside himself, he took the floor. "Dissolve them!" he urged. "They will be the ones accountable for the crime of high treason by refusing to grant Your Majesty the only mean to save the nation!"

"Lucien . . ." Napoleon calmed.

Lucien had set aside all restraint. "Dissolve them! You have that right!"

"No," Napoleon said, having weighed the consequences.

"You must!"

"Lucien, you don't understand. We will cause a civil war!"

"That is something to chance!" he persisted.

All eyes were riveted on the Emperor. No one spoke.

Napoleon declared in an oppressive hush. "I wish to reiterate to the Chambers, through you gentlemen, that my intentions are inspired with the same spirit that has so inflamed France, the spirit of 1789."

One of the councilors said, "Sire, the Chambers have requested that Your Majesty appear before them!"

Napoleon clenched his teeth. His appearance, disgraced by defeat, would certainly not help much in obtaining a vote of confidence.

"The Chambers," he said airily, "have no need of me to value the necessity to repulse the enemy!"

Several councilors put forward another alternative. "The Chambers request that you send your ministers."

Napoleon bristled. "I forbid this!"

They persisted. "Sire, if you do not allow your ministers to go, the Chambers have sworn to depose you."

Lucien started clamoring again, "Dissolve the Chambers! They are rebels!"

Napoleon rose and squarely faced the tempter. Beads of perspiration shimmered on his forehead.

"Go with them then," he said breathlessly, "and tell the Chambers I am considering forming a commission to negotiate with the enemy. Report to me in the garden!"

On that warm summer day, the chestnut trees of the Elysée's grounds forced Napoleon's thoughts back to a tender time. He recalled another summer at Saint Cloud, a hastily eaten lunch in the garden, and a fair and lusty little boy drinking out of his wine goblet with an adorable grimace. He tried to imagine him now, at this hour, much grown, attractive, and wise.

Menéval had told him so. Menéval had also passed on to him the moving infantile message of love and Napoleon had wept while repeating the child's words. And as his eyes misted now remembering them, in his mind he was devouring the boy with kisses. Until they became real. . . .

So much depended on what the Chambers would decide. If they did not accede to his wish to take up arms to save France, then they might agree to a parley with its enemies. He would continue to protest his pacific intentions and he could have his little son back. Arrange a separation with Marie Louise, but *get his son back!*

Lucien's footfalls crunching the graveled walk, accelerated the beats of Napoleon's heart. He hastened to meet his brother half-way. At forty, Lucien panted a little too heavily. Or was it because what he had to report ran the breath out of him?

Napoleon's fingers dug into his arms. "Well? What will it be?"

Pale, Lucien stammered, "The Chamber of Deputies said that because of your outlawry, the Powers will not treat with you. And . . . and . . . that consequently, there is nothing more for you to do but abdicate."

"Abdicate?"

Napoleon shook. Once this renunciation wrenched from him by the treachery of Marmont, though infamous, had been tolerable. It was then no more than a tactical loss. But now, it represented the sneer of the nation turning away from a derelict. Disowned by his own people! Was this the verdict of France?

He looked his brother up and down as if the archetype of an ungrateful humanity had been presented to him. "I lost a battle!" he raged. "And they are sending me away like a mercenary! Have I been all that bad?"

He gripped Lucien by the shoulders, that part of the anatomy so symbolic of support and consolation, which was so utterly denied him. "Have I spent sixteen years of my life in blazing incompetence?"

And quicker than his brother might be attempting to assess, it all lay before his mind's eyes. He had done work of monumental proportion and remarkable diversity. He had brought about the swift suppression of a decade of hopeless disorder, the preservation of the civil conquests of the Revolution, the conservation of social equality, the establishment of a paternalistic regime accepted and hailed as the best remedy to dissension and bankruptcy, the stabilization of the finances and regeneration of the industries, the promulgation of a new, more efficient, code of laws of far reaching influence, the rise of France to a respected world power and the creation of the *Grand Empire!*

Well . . . maybe too grand. But he had adjusted his vision to more modest proportion and shouldn't have been humbled at Waterloo, losing all credits and respect.

And to all this, Lucien only found to say, "You will be remembered. Posterity. . . ."

Incensed, Napoleon danced with furor on his short legs, shouting, "I don't give a damn about posterity! Is this the verdict of France?"

A large crowd of Parisians composed of humble workers and Veterans had assembled outside the gates. They craned their necks, shoved, and pressed. They followed with intense curiosity and interest the bobbing of the famous cocked hat above the top of the ornamental shrubbery. At the turn of the walk, Napoleon, still shouting his indignation, came into their full view wearing his customary costume, the no less celebrated uniform of the Colonel of Chasseur.

A booming cheer broke out. "*Vive l'Empereur!*"

Napoleon gave a start. He realized how much for granted he had been taking that acclamation. And now, more than ever, it meant that in spite of all. . . .

Lucien pounced on what it meant. Frantically he clutched at his brother's elbow and yelled, "Listen to this! They have not abandoned you! And they represent France in her most guileless and truest expression of appreciation. Don't listen to the Chambers! Do away with them!"

"Lucien, calm yourself!" Napoleon ordered.

Inasmuch as Lucien recklessly flitted from one possibility to another, Napoleon reined his impulse, remembering that a little over a decade ago the Senate had solemnly declared: "Glory, gratitude, devotion, reason, the interest of the state; all unite to proclaim Napoleon, hereditary emperor. . . ."

But now, defeat, suspicion, fear, disloyalty and reasoning that ran counter to his own, all conspired through parliamentary processes to point out that his leadership was no longer acceptable on the grounds that he was an enemy and a disturber of the tranquillity of the world. Well, he was not! He would not use these good folks in a conflict which had taken the twist of a personal vendetta.

"Lucien!" he said firmly, jerking his elbow free, "put this into your head. No civil war! Under my command thousands have died for France. But no one is going to die on my personal account. I am not a demagogue, nor am I an adventurer! Put that into your head, too!"

A look of utter disappointment broke over Lucien's face. "You are going to abdicate then?"

Still followed by cheers, Napoleon turned around and without another word strode back to the palace.

The Chambers, Napoleon was informed, gave him one hour to abdicate. In one hour, the grand story of his life which had reverberated through a continent would end.

Later that same day, June 22, Lucien's quill screeched plaintively as Napoleon dictated his final abdication. The fact that the Chambers had not refused to recognize his son as Napoleon II as the consequence of his abdication gave him some hope of an official proclamation. But then, rumors were already going the rounds that his son's reign was a sham. Appalled, Napoleon kept asking himself, What would become of the Prince, whose own countrymen had disdained to reclaim, now that he could no longer go to the child's rescue?

On the third day of his abdication, Lucien asked, "Where will you go?"

Lost in thought, Napoleon did not appear to hear his brother. He was thinking of the plea from a deputation of the workers of the faubourgs. They had urged him to assume the dictatorship they were convinced would check the enemy's advance on Paris. They had begged in earnest to bear arms under his command and leadership!

But he remained steadfast in his resolve—no civil war! He would not instigate one, nor would he, by his availability, encourage hopes of a *coup d'état.* He must go away, remove himself from a hotbed of controversies. No one as yet had told him where he could go. No one so far seemed to care. He thought of faraway places. Of America. . . .

"Where," repeated Lucien, "will you go, and for that matter, can you go?"

"Malmaison," Napoleon finally said. "For the time being," he added, not concealing his emotion.

When he was still on the island of Elba, news of Josephine's death deeply affected him. She was said to have died of a chill caught in her beautiful rose garden at Malmaison, the country estate he had given her. Now the circumstances that brought him back to Malmaison stirred anew memories of earlier times when his love for Josephine was vibrant with passion and when fortune was smiling upon him.

But the choice wasn't a sentimental decision. He had decided on Malmaison knowing that this move only meant a step toward an uncertain destination. He had no illusion that sooner or later he would be apprehended. Nevertheless, he still clung to the tenuous hope of being allowed to take up arms like a simple commander, to help repulse the invasion. He had sent a letter outlining this proposal, but was ordered to leave France and quickly.

Caulaincourt took that order very seriously. An increasing number of deputies were in favor of handing Napoleon over to the Coalition.

"Sire," he urged, still according Napoleon the title which legally was no longer his upon the signature of his abdication, "you cannot tarry any more and stay in France. Your Majesty knows as well as I that you are now being hunted."

"Then where to, from Malmaison?" Lucien wanted to know.

Napoleon made a decision. With no safe conduct to take to sea, he must somehow secure passage through bribery or subterfuge. The first thing to do was to flee to the coast.

"We will go to Rochefort next," he said.

That evening, Malmaison was bustling with activity. Alas, Napoleon sadly mused, the pother was not one of the kind which attended Josephine's brilliant *fêtes* when Murat, shimmering in green satin and gold braids, stood out from among the guests and postured like a peacock in front of every mirror partly to admire his reflection and also to assure himself that not one lock of his scented hair was out of place.

The mirthful excitement and glitter of the consular days had long vanished. Instead, the lights were dimmed and one could hear the rumbling of enemy cannons toward the plain of Saint Denis.

Hortense was sewing her diamond necklace into the seam of his belt.

"You don't have to do this," he told her gently.

"I want to," she said stubbornly. "You are going to need some money! This world is cruel and cold, and full of brigands!"

He thought, I know that world, dear . . . . I held it in my hands. Once!

When Letizia joined them, she led him to a corner of the room and sat him down beside her, studying his clothes.

Napoleon had discarded his uniform for mufti.

"Where will you be going, Napolione?"

He didn't have any idea. In his wildest dreams, short of America, there had been other places where he would have wanted to find refuge—Mexico, Caracas, Buenos Aires. . . . Now any place would do.

"I don't know, Mother. I should be content to sail away, even if this were on an endless sea."

"I am going with you . . . anywhere you choose to go."

"No!"

"I'm going with you, Napolione," Letizia repeated quietly.

"I have taken you on a very long adventure. And it must end here and now! I have made arrangements with Lucien to have you go to Italy."

"Napolione . . ." Letizia stroked his cheek with the back of her hand. "In time of difficulties a mother should always be with her child!"

Napoleon's features contracted as he thought of his little boy and the mother he had given him. Tears she had not seen since his father's death, were welling up in his eyes. Quickly, he averted them.

She looked at him in silence. Then she said simply, "May God go with you."

At the port of Rochefort, the sea beckoned only to tantalize. A problem had arisen—if Napoleon were to board either French frigate, the *Saale* or the *Meduse,* orders had been given that the ship was not to leave without a passport duly approved and provided by Wellington, who in turn was said to have referred the application to London.

As his suite was quick to point out to him, Napoleon could have disregarded this ordinance and taken to sea without too much difficulty had he reached Rochefort a little earlier.

But he'd lost two whole days in Nior where the population and the soldiers stationed in the town gave him a warm reception.

And the French coast was now blockaded by the British.

There were talks of chartering a fishing smack, which the British would hopefully not think of searching.

Joseph suggested, "I think you should consider disguising yourself. Perhaps a mustache, or a beard?"

Napoleon grew indignant. "Never! I will not leave France all made up to deceive! I am not, I repeat, a criminal!"

Bertrand said, "By virtue of the decree of outlawry directed against Your Majesty, you are a wanted man. You could be murdered and your assassins would be rewarded instead of being prosecuted!"

Dejectedly, Napoleon took mental count of those of his suite who had volunteered to share his proscription: General Bertrand, sensitive and proud; Count Las Cases, an amiable man of the world who happened to be fluent in English; General Gourgaud, high-strung, devoted, but whose youth demanded constant recognition of the sacrifice he had consented to make; Count Montholon, simply loyal. . . .

Bertrand declared without ceremony, "Sire, we are stuck!"

Napoleon thought of the French frigate *Saale,* anchored in the roadstead of Aix. He could still take it and chance eluding the pursuit of the English cruisers. He said, "We will leave Rochefort for the island of Aix tonight, board the *Saale* on arrival and set sail as soon as the winds are favorable."

Gourgaud said, "Suppose we can't get away."

There was a pause. Napoleon looked his companions straight in the eyes. "If I am not free to go to an exile of my choice, I'll surrender myself to England."

Mouths fell open in response to the sinister implication of that choice.

Napoleon kept them in suspense, thinking. The Chambers of the Hundred Days, that very brief interlude marking his return to power after escaping from the Island of Elba, had died, and along with it, all the constitutional provisions which guaranteed the reign of his son as Napoleon the Second. From the current royalist regime, he could expect no quarter, and from France no further considerations. Now, with the only avenue of flight barred by an enemy of twenty years, he had no other choice but to bank on England's generosity. It could only enhance her luster. After all, England was a nation of grand and distinguished renown!

Gourgaud was first to recover his wits. "England is known as the most perfidious of nations."

To everyone's complete astonishment, Napoleon mumbled that he was quite aware of England's perfidy.

"Then why?" cried Gourgaud, "Why England?"

"I put my trust in her basic, elemental sense of rectitude. Her laws show this. . . . By the way, that business of passport. . . ."

Indeed, this had to be verified. If by now the safe conduct was in the possession of the commander of the British Fleet, it ought to be ascertained in case the latter might not be inclined to volunteer such good news. At least, if asked, his gentleman's honor would forbid him to dissimulate its existence.

And if the answer were to be positive, with the freedom to take the sea, Napoleon would definitely choose to sail to America.

"*En destination pour l'Amérique?*" Captain Maitland, commander of the *Bellerophon,* wetted his lips. He spoke excellent French and continued with an almost imperceptible accent, "I don't believe our country would allow General Bonaparte to go to America."

Las Cases and Savary exchanged a weary glance. They had boarded the *Bellerophon* with some hope. That hope dwindled considerably when Maitland, upon being apprised of the disposition made by the now-defunct Provisional Government regarding Napoleon's departure by sea, pleaded complete ignorance of the safe conduct. "I only know of Waterloo," he had said, adding much too graciously, "I shall notify my admiral of the application you have mentioned and I shall let you know the answer as soon as I receive it."

Las Cases thought, How convenient! But we can't wait for an answer!

Savary, who by occupation was conditioned to be suspicious, sniffed deceit. Maitland's ignorance may have been purposefully contrived by Admiral Hotham, his immediate superior, in view of letting a misunderstanding go conveniently unsolved.

To test the Englishman's stance, the former Minister of Police said, "We have established with you that the Emperor does not want to steal away or resort to any kind of trumpery. Now, if before you receive that answer, he should decide to go, what will you do?"

Maitland rubbed his chin and said rather pleasantly, "As we are at war, I shall prevent him from leaving, seize him, hold him, and refer the matter to my superior."

Las Cases interjected with a point of impatience, "All well and good, Captain, but *where will the Emperor be allowed to go?*"

"I don't know," Maitland answered with apparent honesty. Then struck as it seemed by an attractive idea, he offered, "If, however, General Bonaparte would not mind coming to England, all the present difficulties might be obviated."

The two Frenchmen exchanged another glance. Again, Savary thought the proposal had the flavor of a conspiracy.

"The Emperor is not a well man," he said, "the damp climate of England may not be good for him."

Maitland protested engagingly, "England's climate isn't all that bad! In fact, the county of Kent is blessed with a very mild one."

"Suppose," Savary said, wishing to gauge the extent of Maitland's authority, "the Emperor should adopt your idea, the supposition prohibiting him, of course, from seeking passage on a French frigate. Should he contemplate being taken on board your vessel with his suite?"

"Well," said Maitland, "I still must ask for instructions." He smiled. "But if they do not reach me when General Bonaparte expresses the desire to come on board, I shall receive him and his entourage nevertheless."

"I see," said Savary, now utterly convinced of England's perfidy. They were trapped with or without permission!

Las Cases kept a despondent silence.

"In any case, gentlemen," Maitland offered, all smiles again, "do feel free to communicate with me whenever you please."

"Savary!"

"Sire?"

"You will communicate to Captain Philibert the following order: we are to sail now!"

Swiftly and silently, Savary swept out of the cabin.

Napoleon joined Las Cases at the porthole. Night had fallen about a half-hour ago. The *Saale* would take advantage of the darkness to gain the high sea, even if that meant an engagement with the Britannic vessels. That was a risk Napoleon had finally decided to take. The more he thought of Maitland's suggestion the less he cared for it. The Captain's initiative in proposing an easy solution was nothing but a trick to catch him. Exile did not mean captivity, at least, not in Napoleon's understanding. Why should he be held prisoner? He had put an end to his political career and only wanted to go peaceably away, nullifying the crime of which he had been accused.

His epaulette brushed against the Count's sleeve. He had felt the urge to put on his uniform because of what he was about to do: put up a last fight! The realization that his freedom had been in very real danger of being taken away shattered him.

He said, ruminating still, "What is that place our Britannic friend said was mild?"

"Kent, Sire."

"No, thank you!"

"We didn't think you'd like it."

"I wonder if President Madison would mind terribly my settling down in America instead . . . America has what Kent has not."

"What is that, Sire?"

"Space," Napoleon said wistfully, "and plenty of it!"

Las Cases said, keeping his eyes on the obscure aperture. "You will be happier there, Sire."

"Somewhat," responded Napoleon, wondering how much happiness he would ever have the capacity to feel when a part of him had been torn away with his boy, now a prisoner of Austria.

Then, aware of a movement behind him, he turned around. Savary had just returned from his errand looking perturbed.

"Sire," he said nervously, "Captain Philibert refuses to sail on the grounds that his orders forbid him to do so if such a move is going to endanger the frigate."

"I can't believe this!" Napoleon exclaimed in disgust.

"Sire, we have been deceived. All the Provisional Government really aimed to do was to place Your Majesty under the necessity to give yourself up to the British."

He had a point. On the mainland, just before sunset, the Tricolor had been taken down and the white royalist flag fluttered in the sea breeze. It would be only a matter of days, nay, of hours, before the Bourbon King would take Napoleon into custody.

Napoleon held his peace only for a moment and then declared, "I've decided to turn to the British."

"Oh, God!" lamented Gourgaud.

Napoleon ignored him. He had resolved to be hopeful while everyone else, he could see, thought he had lost his mind. He proceeded to dictate to Las Cases a letter Gourgaud would be taking himself to the Prince Regent of England.

In less than ten courteous lines he called upon George IV to grant him the protection of British law and the hospitality of his land.

Napoleon's entourage shuddered at the idea. The Prince Regent was notorious for his dissolute habits and meanness of character. He was certainly the last person from whom one should expect a noble gesture. Moreover, England too, had signed the decree which outlawed Napoleon. To secure his person was in perfect accord with that compact. Clemency would be a folly and a breach of contract. How could Napoleon delude himself to such a point?

Napoleon staked his whole future on clemency. In closing his letter to the Prince Regent he had Las Cases write the thought so dear to his heart: Like Themistocles, who was welcomed by his erstwhile enemy, the king of Persia, he was going to sit down beside the hearths of the British people.

Las Cases wrote it all down with imperturbability.

Napoleon appeared calmed and confident. England would understand. She would receive him with kindness.

Once Napoleon had said: "I am the Revolution."

By an odd turn of fate, this letter was signed, "Island of Aix, July 14, 1815."

Bastille day!

Next morning, Napoleon was informed that King Louis XVIII's emissaries were in Rochefort with orders to arrest citizen Bonaparte.

Napoleon hesitated no longer. Captain Maitland was approached immediately, given a copy of the letter Napoleon had written to the Prince Regent. Gourgaud, in possession of the original, had sailed ahead to London on the corvette *Slany*. There was no time to wait for Gourgaud to come back with a reply. The *Bellerophon* with Napoleon as passenger was sailing for England, too.

Las Cases had said to Captain Maitland on that second interview, "I wish to emphasize that my master, of his own free will, is seeking the hospitality of your country as a private person."

Maitland nodded. He felt so comfortable with the supreme authority vested in his captaincy that he spoke as if the intentions of his government reflected his own benevolence.

"There is no question in my mind that your master will be well treated in England, sir."

And now, at sea, on open water, Napoleon reiterated his faith in England's clemency. He said to Maitland, "I put myself under the protection of your laws."

Maitland found it difficult not to stare. Napoleon was in uniform, his hat planted transversely on his proud roman head. He appeared even shorter than he was because of his corpulence, but he looked formidable even as he spoke the words of his own surrender.

The captain of the *Bellerophon* inclined his head and introduced his officers assembled on the deck before rows of soldiers drawn up in Napoleon's honor.

Afterward, Maitland courteously accompanied Napoleon back to his cabin. On their way, Napoleon remarked, "You have a different way of charging bayonets."

Maitland, struck with reverential admiration, shot a quick glance at the "Disturber of the Peace", "the brigand of Elba" as the Coalition called Napoleon. In the presence of this small man whose very name made the kings of Europe quake on their thrones, he would not even think of altering protocol. He accorded Napoleon his former title saying, "That's because we are English, Sire!"

"Ah!" Napoleon shot back with a half-smile. "How could I forget?"

Most of their conversation during the voyage related to the various merits of the French and British navies. Napoleon pointed out to Maitland, "Our ships are stronger." And the captain of the *Bellerophon* replied, "Perhaps, but our seamen are more experienced and can shoot better!"

After ten days at sea, the vessel docked at Tor Bay. The port, with its picturesque shores that lay at the Southwest tip of the British Isles, seethed with curiosity. The crowds that had massed on the quays hoping to glimpse Napoleon were disappointed. Lord Keith, Admiral of the Channel Fleet, had issued strict orders. No one was to disembark from the *Bellerophon* and no one was permitted on board except Gourgaud, who stepped on deck as soon as the ship had dropped anchor.

He looked glum and impulsively seized Napoleon's hands. "I am sorry, Sire. I never saw the Prince Regent. I had to surrender your letter to subalterns."

Napoleon tensed. "What else do you know?"

Gourgaud shook his head. "Nothing, Sire. Except that we are to wait."

"I wonder why," Napoleon said between his teeth.

Unable to sleep that night, he was already on deck at the first light of day. A thick fog shrouded the harbor. Napoleon scowled. Something was afoot. The sailors were unaccountably busy. Then out of the mist, Maitland materialized beside him.

At the same time, Napoleon noticed that armed boats had surrounded the *Bellerophon*, which began to move. And all the captain found to say was, "Good morning, Sire. You should go below. It's a trifle damp up here at this early hour."

They stood side-by-side, their arms almost touching. Napoleon took a deep breath, the humid air filling his nostrils with what he called "sea-smell": salty, pungent, evocative of open oceans' awesome liquid mass and depth.

"Not at all like Kent," he said evenly.

Maitland coughed, hemmed and in obvious confusion stammered, "I wish it were Kent, Sire. I presume . . . this suggestion has not offended your taste."

"Captain," Napoleon asked quietly, "where are we going?"

The figure in the fog coughed again. Then with a touch of apology said, "To Plymouth, Sire."

"Plymouth," Napoleon responded with a calm that made Maitland's uneasiness worse, "is further south. Further removed from London where this business should be taking me. Hasn't my letter been delivered to the Prince Regent?"

The Captain only answered, "I am sorry. But those are my instructions received from the Board of Admiralty. Lord Keith. . . ."

"You have received communication from Lord Keith?" Napoleon interrupted.

"Aye, Sire, in which he also asked me to convey to Your Majesty his gratitude for the good treatment you gave his nephew in the aftermath of Waterloo."

Napoleon clenched his teeth. Such civility on the part of Lord Keith was aimed, no doubt, at covering some sinister undertaking.

He asked sharply: "And what exactly, are we supposed to do in Plymouth?"

"Sire," Maitland answered, and he spoke the truth, "I do not know."

When Napoleon went up to the windswept deck clad in his rumpled gray field coat, his hat tucked under his arm for the gale would had blown it away had he worn it, his eyes blinked in astonishment. The harbor of Plymouth offered an incredible sight.

By the thousands, as far as he could tell, people packed in boats of all description had come to witness his arrival. Oars-to-oars and poops-to-sterns, everyone tried to catch a glimpse of him from a platform of oscillating yawls, skiffs, and barks that completely covered the water from view.

The second most extraordinary thing Napoleon slowly became aware of was the absolute silence that greeted his appearance. Not even a jeer could be heard, and as far as his eyes could see, all heads were bare. He knew that this was a gesture of homage.

If such was the reception of the English population, he thought, George IV's conduct would certainly reflect the same magnanimity.

Still, the Prince Regent let five days pass without sending word. Then on the sixth, Napoleon received two official visitors in his cabin. The resolution taken by the English government was solemnly read to him by Sir Henry Bunbury in the presence of Lord Keith.

Impassive, Napoleon listened to the Under Secretary of State's impeccable French.

"Il ne serait pas conforme aux obligations contractées par la nation Anglaise de permettre au Général Bonaparte. . . ."

As England's answer to his plea for clemency rang out word after word, the ferocity of the verdict numbed him. For the sake of safeguarding the peace of Europe and in keeping with a solemn international compact, his liberty was to be restrained to whatever extent necessary. Even to the extent, therefore, of confining him to the God-forsaken and minuscule island of St. Helena!

Only when Sir Henry had finished reading the document did Napoleon break out in violent reproach.

"You want my death! And you want to wash your hands of it! Come! Why not kill me now? Or is a lingering end what you have chosen for my death sentence?"

Once in his studious youth and visionary curiosity, he had noted the location and size of an island called St. Helena. He had even at one time contemplated using it as a base. Of all the irony! St. Helena spelled a drawn out agony for certain. The climate of the island was known to be deleterious to one's health, and its size horrified Napoleon. Compared to the vast uninhabited prairies of America, St. Helena measured a puny fifteen miles long and three to five miles wide. Inactivity alone was sure to kill him, for he was accustomed to ride twenty leagues a day!

"General Bonaparte," Lord Keith interposed, "You are dramatizing simple but indispensable precautionary measures."

"There is enough material here for a great drama!" Napoleon retorted vehemently. "I have paid England the highest compliment by voluntarily putting myself under her protection! By deceiving my trust, your government is irreparably disgracing a great nation whose future generations might not look so kindly upon the damage you have done to her glorious reputation!"

"I am sorry," Sir Henry said, "we have not come to estimate the judgment of posterity." He looked uneasily at Lord Keith.

The latter understood. He must put Napoleon through a ritual prisoners of war have to undergo.

"General Bonaparte, I have orders to demand the surrender of your sword now!"

"That," Napoleon snapped, closing his hand on the hilt, "you can have only when I am dead and cold!"

The sword hung at his side for all to see when he boarded the *Northumberland,* a newer, larger vessel better suited for a long voyage. On that fateful evening in August, Napoleon stood on the deck, glumly listening to the sough of the surf. The sound evoked a long, unbroken sigh of anguish he acknowledged as his own. For he had lost everything but his life.

As he began losing sight of Europe, his fingers convulsively closed on the hilt of his sword. When the continent he once ruled sank beneath the horizon in the afterglow of a spectacular sunset, having nothing left to fix his eyes upon, Napoleon raised them to the stars.

14

Francis could not have been more pleased with his daughter. The satisfaction Marie Louise openly expressed over Napoleon's defeat at Waterloo, and her relief upon learning of his captivity, were perfectly attuned to her scornful reaction regarding the nominal reign, however brief, of her son as Napoleon the Second. Napoleon was now a nuisance of the past, a nuisance that had been dealt with—and quite successfully.

Heartened by his daughter's unwavering resolve that her son should be raised as a German, Francis felt entirely comfortable in undertaking the complete obliteration of his grandson's ties with France. He did not expect to encounter any difficulties. The boy was very young and consequently malleable.

He reached for a memorandum in which Metternich had delineated a very detailed plan of action. To the memorandum was attached a list of tutors whose duties were directed to bring about the Germanization of a little child of four. The name at the head of the list was that of Count Maurice Dietrichstein, the chief tutor responsible for this transformation. "I think," Metternich had said, while discussing the matter earlier, "Your Majesty will find him suitable." Francis had no doubt that he would, putting his trust, as usual, in his Chancellor's counsels and decisions.

As he read the memorandum in preparation for the interview that would soon take place, he was exceedingly pleased to see that every provision had been met to comply with his wishes—that above all, his grandson's schooling would single him out as the most enlightened prince in the realm. That wish, Francis was not ashamed to admit, came in a sincere spirit of reparation. He had taken the boy away from his father and was about to force upon him a German education. But that education would be the best he could offer.

When Metternich entered accompanied by Count Dietrichstein, Francis wondered if the sight of the designated chief tutor would displease his grandson. The Count was extremely thin, with angular features whose contours seemed to have been sharpened with a pumice stone. His piercing eyes were deeply set under projecting brows bristling with thick, wiry hair, and a large hooked nose overhung lips that cut a mean looking line.

But Francis knew the Count to be of the highest nobility and that credential, coupled with his reputation for possessing great culture, quickly eased his mind out of speculating on the child's reaction to Count Dietrichstein's desiccated and forbidding appearance. Graver matters were at stake.

He greeted him affably while Metternich placed before him the Count's application detailing his own plan concerning his pupil's training.

Francis gave a cursory glance at the document. He had informed Metternich that he preferred to have the Count present his view *de vive voix* during the interview.

"Tell me, Count, how would you go about this assignment?" he promptly asked him.

Dietrichstein had well prepared himself for this question, but not without having pondered at length the reasons for having been singled out for such a task. Since his selection, forty-six-year-old Count Maurice Dietrichstein-Proskau-Leslie kept interrogating himself on the strange turn of fortune that had earned him this appointment. He was a retiring and introspective man who knew enough of his own character to recognize that his inclinations and emotional makeup were not suited to befriend any child. The Count was painfully aware of his saturnine disposition. Smiling was an exercise he seldom practiced, a trait which did little to assuage his morbid preoccupation at wanting to be liked. His true passion in life was to collect rare objects d'art and organize concerts. Schubert and Beethoven had often performed at his house, the finest in Vienna.

In truth, Count Dietrichstein did not think of himself as an educator. Yet his dedication to learning had never stopped. It was probably this distinction at scholarship that had been the decisive factor in his selection for this position in which he immediately recognized grave political implications. He admitted being rather apolitical. His artistic temperament drew his attention away from worldly affairs, but having a rigid sense of duty, he had fought for the fatherland against the French in Napoli in 1798 with patriotic courage. When he had retired with the rank of major, his personal fortune was sufficiently large to permit him to indulge his passion for the arts. Until this happened.

The full realization of his responsibilities gnawed at him like a toothache as he answered: "Being issued of two different races, so significantly apart, the Prince's qualities are also dual. With Your Majesty's permission, I propose to foster the Austrian traits he possesses and suppress those that are French. The process should be conducted in such a manner as to ease the Prince into a gradual assimilation with no harm done to his sensibilities." He paused, then concluded, "I am honored to be of service in this undertaking and I should like to pride myself on having contributed in the effort to turn Napoleon's son into a fine German subject who will serve Your Majesty loyally."

Francis nodded his assent. The grim-looking Count with his bitter mouth met all his expectations. But there was one item whose importance was not to be overlooked and it needed to be addressed as well.

"Concerning the Prince's opinion of his father. . . ." Francis said, and his voice trailed off as he looked at Metternich in a way that intimated that his Chancellor had liberty to speak on the subject.

Metternich spoke with calm gravity, "Under no circumstances must the Prince's natural filial piety be allowed to evolve toward inordinate feelings of devotion or compassion. He is to be instructed in a fashion that will extinguish any admiration he may tend to develop for his father. The peace of Europe depends on the fact that the Prince must never entertain any idea of emulating Napoleon or of avenging his memory. There must be no sequel to Napoleon. One has been quite enough."

Amen! exulted Francis, relishing the thought. Since Napoleon's defeat and the subsequent re-installment of Louis the Eighteenth in France, there was no longer a republic within the nucleus of European monarchies to threaten the continuation of absolutism. Now, Francis felt free to shed all the worries that had beset him and spoiled his sleep. He could turn his attention to enjoying his grandson.

The thought of the boy always had a mellowing effect on Francis. He said warmly, addressing Dietrichstein, "The Prince is a delight to be with. You will like him."

In a happy mood, Countess Elise Mitrovsky hummed to herself while methodically pulling every piece of clothing that bore a monogram "N" from the armoire that contained her charge's apparel. Fanny Soufflot, pale and with a deadpan look on her face, held a box into which the Countess tossed the garments while she gave the maidservant her instructions.

"Be sure to have the seamstresses remove the current initial on these items and replace it with an "F," she told her.

Fanny nodded and managed a half-audible "*Oui, Madame la Comtesse.*"

Mitrovsky then rummaged through the outfits of various French military classes that the little Prince was so fond of wearing, and removed every one of them, flinging them into the box.

"You will see that these are destroyed," she commanded.

"*Oui, Madame la Comtesse,*" Fanny croaked.

Mitrovsky turned around. "Are you crying, Fanny?"

"A sore throat, Madame," Fanny lied, trying her utmost not to burst into tears at the thought of what had already taken place.

A few days ago, the systematic stripping of all that could remind the Prince of his origin had been set in motion. She had been ordered to surrender the child's books and albums that dealt with France and Napoleon along with his medals and decorations, which consisted of the *Légion d'Honneur* and the Iron Cross of Italy. The lead soldiers wearing French uniforms had just been painted to resemble Austrians. And now, the monograms "N" for "Napoleon" on his clothes were about to be removed and replaced with "F" for "Franz" which wasn't a name at all!

Mitrovsky pitched the last outfit into the box, not bothering to ascertain if the maid was telling her the truth. She did not really care. She was just doing what she had been told and her mind was busy planning her upcoming wedding to Count Scarampi after a widowhood that had lasted long enough. She was excited by the prospect of following Marie Louise to Parma. Her assignment as governess had been taken over by a tutor.

And that just reminded her. . . .

"Fanny, ask your mother to bring the Prince to me at once."

Fanny made a slight curtsy and left, straining under the weight of the box.

Moments later, Madame Soufflot entered holding Franz by the hand.

When they were sure of not being overheard, the French serving women still called him Napoleon. They also kept telling him about Paris, the Tuileries, and Saint Cloud; about his father and how much he loved him, and about the splendor of the imperial days in France. When they played little childish games with him, they contrived to lose so he could win and be proclaimed "emperor" in a chorus of laughter and compliments. They were spoiling him utterly, but they could not help themselves. They had promised his *Maman Quious* to love him above all else, and the boy responded to their adulation with happy abandon. Only with them was he open and playful, and at times a little tyrannical.

But away from them. . . .

At the sight of his governess, Franz let go of Madame Soufflot's hand and assumed an aloof and self-sufficient stance.

Mitrovsky looked at him absently and said, "I shall no longer be your governess and we are going to meet the gentleman who will be taking my place."

She held out her hand. "Come!"

He followed her quietly, feeling no particular emotion about her leaving him; no relief, no satisfaction, nothing. She had made such a bland impression upon him that he had shut her out of his concern. He was, however, curious about the gentleman she had mentioned and also felt apprehensive.

Franz's first encounter with Count Dietrichstein augured the coming of more separations and the unpleasantness of incipient problems. He accorded the Count a distant and haughty look that left the tutor profoundly hurt.

Several weeks after taking up his duties, Dietrichstein had made no inroad in gaining his pupil's acceptance. At every opportunity, Franz would run back to his French maidservants. Dietrichstein put two and two together and brought his grievance to Francis.

"I beseech Your Majesty," he wrote in a memorandum, "to send the French women away. Their presence and attitude are a continual reminder to the Prince of the very elements in his life I have been entrusted to eradicate. The longer they stay, the more difficult it will be for the Prince to conform painlessly to Your Majesty's designs."

A few days later, Franz noticed that Fanny's eyes were quite red. When he asked her why, she told him the sandman had put too much sand in her eyes, whereupon she burst into tears.

"Fanny . . ."

His small voice, choked with alarm, brought Fanny down on her knees and clasping him in her arms, she sobbed, "Mother and I have been asked to leave. We are going back to France!"

In a matter of seconds, Franz, too, was in tears, gagging and convulsively clinging to her. Then, still crying with little gasps, he brought out all his favorite toys and heaped them in the girl's apron.

"Take them with you, Fanny!"

"No, no," she protested. "These are your toys!"

"Take them!" He sniffed. "I am too sad. I'll never play with them again!"

"Oh, but you will! You like them so much!"

In spite of two teardrops running down his cheeks, he said gravely, "Fanny, am I your emperor or not?"

Fanny would rather die than deny this, and she gazed upon him worshipfully. "Yes!" she cried with fervor. "Yes, you are! And always will be!"

"Then you must do as I say."

Still on her knees, Fanny let go of the apron she had gathered up. The toys spilled on the floor as she folded her little emperor in her arms once more. They started crying all over again.

"Oh, Fanny. . . ." Franz hiccuped on the maid's shoulder.

Fiercely, she pressed him to her bosom. "Oh, Sire!" she lamented. And kept repeating this as if it could conjure away all the terrible things that were being done to him.

Christmas, the second to be celebrated away from France, cumulated the changes in Franz's lifestyle. In September he had been given a second tutor, Captain Jean Baptist Foresti. Franz could not warm up to the Captain either. Foresti's attitude was correct but distant and lacked flexibility. So far, he tolerated his tutors and only looked forward to being with Chanchan or his mother, whom he saw not often enough for his own liking. He had heard talk about her going to Parma and he imagined he would be going with her there, too.

In itself, the holiday was filled as in the previous year with sweet pleasures. Franz nibbled on the candied apples and cookies that were used to trim a huge Christmas tree. In the evening, he was allowed to share with Bonpapa and the whole imperial family the traditional meal, which consisted of a plump roast goose, pancakes, stewed plums, and baked bread all twisted and knotted and filled with almonds. Franz's impeccable table manners delighted his grandfather. On this special occasion, the servants were given the signal treat of dancing afterward with members of the imperial family if they so desired, and so he took a graceful spin with the cook's daughter.

But on this Christmas, Franz, as he was growing accustomed to be called, could keenly sense an enormous difference. This time, the festive day did not prolong itself in his chamber among the women who used to attend him. Tonight, alone with the humble and sole female servant left to him, he experienced an upsetting feeling of isolation.

Presently Chanchan undressed him with crushing sadness, even though she tried to smile while preparing him for bed. She knew that soon she would be asked to go. The fact that she had been allowed to stay on longer after Fanny and her mother's departure had been a concession to Franz's young age, a concession won, she had heard, by the child's mother so that the Prince wouldn't be totally bereft of female companionship. But Franz was growing older.

With special tenderness she tucked him into bed, stroked his head and raised his little hands to her lips. Contrary to her habit, Madame Marchand wasn't going to sing a lullaby. She could not, for the simple reason that her throat was so constricted by emotion that her warm and distinguished voice, which seemed ill-matched to her rather coarse and common features, would have sounded like a pitiable croak.

Too much went through her mind to leave any room for rejoicing during this holiday season. Her own son had followed Napoleon into captivity as his valet, while she remained the only French national attending the deposed emperor's hostage son. An immensity separated both parents from their children and the fate of Napoleon's son tormented the cradle rocker more than her speculation on the eventual return of her own son to France. She perceived for the little Prince greater desolation to come. It was a threat that lurked unseen, yet she could feel it like the plume of a breath, sour and malevolent.

She kissed the Prince's hands with fervor, realizing that she had been remiss.

"Guess what?" she whispered.

"What is it, Chanchan?"

"We have forgotten to say our prayers!"

Tonight of all nights! God forgive her! But her mood on this celebration of the Birthday of Christ was downcast, besieged by distracting worries and heart-breaking sadness. Sadder still, was the *Our Father* they recited together.

"Notre Père qui êtes aux cieux . . ."

God forgive her again! She was not concentrating properly. Each sentence pointed to no heavenly matters but rather to earthly contrasting truths. To a Father who dwelled in the heavens she considered the boy's own, thousands of miles away and so impossibly out of reach, that to speak in terms of the feasible, communication with God seemed incomparably easier!

"Que votre nom soit sanctifié . . ." Hallowed be Thy name!

Ah, but Napoleon's was unutterable as if it were a foul word! So foul, his son could no longer be called by it!

"Que votre règne arrive." Thy kingdom come. Alas, the Empire has crumbled most tragically!

"Que votre volonté soit faite . . ." Thy will be done.

Yes! That, she had heeded!

Madame de Montesquiou had related a father's wish that his son be a good Frenchman; and the cradle rocker had fulfilled this wish to the best of her ability by keeping in the child's young and impressionable mind, memories of his past as vividly as she could. But Madame Marchand recognized that her efforts were being challenged by the child's tutors. Distant, icily polite and speaking to the boy in an unintelligible, guttural and harsh sounding language, they would take the little Prince away from her each morning to return him to her only at nightfall.

They had been doing this for about four months now.

"What do you think, Captain?" Dietrichstein asked, rubbing his chin.

Captain Foresti reckoned silently. This was February, 1816, and he had been the Count's deputy tutor since September of last year. Barely six months had passed in educating a little boy, soon to turn five. And long before those six months were up, the Captain was able to form a rather firm opinion of their pupil's potentials. He thought these to be remarkable. The child was astonishingly articulate and used expressions far beyond the normal reach of children his age. He could recite verses from French classical plays, and knew an impressive number of *La Fontaine's Fables* by heart.

The Captain's military background centered on mathematics, which would be a complementary adjunct to the Count's specialization in the humanities. Given the boy's intelligence, Foresti had no doubt that he would master this science effortlessly.

He declared tersely, "He will do all right."

"Better I know, when the French influence will be gone," said Dietrichstein.

Foresti gave him a knowing glance.

Franz's predilection for Chanchan's company set his tutors thinking of a young tree being unsuccessfully uprooted for transplant. A few tendrils still clung obstinately to the original soil, and it was not at all the soil which should be nourishing the sapling. For all her unobtrusive ways and docility, the French cradle rocker had to be removed.

"Has the woman been told yet?" the Count asked.

"Yesterday. She is to leave tonight. I did not want to give her too much advance notice. Her unhappiness might show and this might upset the Prince."

Dietrichstein shrugged. "I don't believe he has any feelings."

Sometime during the fateful evening, Chanchan, under the pretext of arranging Franz's hair, quickly cut off one of his locks intending it for Napoleon. Franz did not feel a thing.

But the simple operation was so symbolic of the irreparable finality of her severance with the child that Madame Marchand almost betrayed her grief. With the necessary effort, however, she proved herself in better control of her emotion than Fanny. All had gone smoothly until Franz sleepily closed his eyes on her gentle homely face embellished by love and devotion. Then she fled, not daring to kiss him. Had she done so, surely she would have broken down and wept.

The next morning, Franz woke to a cool, crisp sunny day. Snow had fallen during the night as the winter had some twenty more days to run its course until spring, the month of his birthday when he would be turning five.

For a moment he lay quietly; and as it was his habit, he called softly. "Chanchan. . . ."

A movement in the bed placed in the corner of his room where his cradle rocker usually slept caught his attention. His eyes widened in surprise upon seeing Captain Foresti slowly sit up rubbing the stubbles on his chin.

His little heart sank. A panicky sensation made him heave, but somehow he was able to say calmly, "She has gone, too."

Expecting a scene, Foresti braced himself and replied, "You are too old for a nanny anyway."

Dry-eyed, Franz flinched nevertheless. He felt very small and very lost. But that was no longer anyone's concern. Throwing off his cover he declared, "I should like to get dressed, sir."

Foresti gaped, astounded by the child's composure. When he recovered, the Captain went about the established routine of having his pupil recite his morning prayer with a slight variation. Whereas the serving women had prayed with the boy, continuing a habit the Prince's governess had fostered, the tutor stood with grave remoteness watching the child at his devotions.

As Franz recited the *Hail Mary*, a thought suddenly occurred to him, a thought he was quick to communicate to Foresti when he had finished the prayer. How was it, he asked him, that the Holy Mother of God could be addressed as a mere woman? That seemed so disrespectful for someone so special.

Foresti calmed his pupil's scruples. If the Pope, he assured Franz, can pray and say, "blessed art thou amongst women," there was absolutely no need for anyone to worry about doing the same thing. Such reverence, Foresti had noticed, extended to womanhood in general. On several occasions, Franz categorically refused to enter a room first if there were ladies present at his side. He gallantly backed away to let them go in first. That was a trait Foresti deemed remarkable for a child so young and yet unschooled in social manners. He imagined this sensitivity would in some way smooth the path toward his own effort in managing the Prince.

Dietrichstein was in a remarkably positive frame of mind himself when he entered Franz's room. No other influence than his own could come now between him and his pupil. His first order of business was to have the Prince start speaking only German. The child understood most of what was being said to him in that tongue, yet so far, he had managed to avoid conversing in it.

The Count was surprised to find Franz quite calm as if nothing had changed. He congratulated himself on his perspicacity. The boy, obviously, had no feelings, indeed.

Without preamble, the tutor asked, "*Wie heissen Sie?*"

That was an easy question intended to ease the Prince into speaking this tongue; but it was nevertheless an important one. The Emperor of Austria's grandson must condition himself to respond properly by saying the surname of his grandfather, after whom he was being called. Besides, no one really knew what to call him. "Napoleon" was absolutely out of the question. "Prince of Parma" was unacceptable, seeing that he had no rights whatsoever to the succession of that domain. In fact, Francis's ward had no appellation of his own other than a namesake, which was being assiduously drummed into the Prince's head to the point where he should automatically answer: "Franz" when asked.

But Napoleon's son took his time. Then he began reluctantly, choosing to speak French.

"*Je. . . .*"

Dietrichstein bent and hissed in the child's face. *"Ich! Ich!"*

Without backing away, his pupil drew in his little chin. The Count sounded like a frightened, sputtering cat.

Annoyed, Dietrichstein lifted an admonitory finger declaring that he would listen to no more French.

After another hesitation his pupil obliged saying with an excellent accent, *"Ich heisse Franz."*

"Good!" the Count encouraged in German, and proceeded, warning Franz in that tongue, "We are going to speak German all the time. Is this understood?"

Silence. Franz looked Dietrichstein straight in the eyes, lips compressed.

"Well?" harried the turor, "Is this understood?"

"*Non!*" said Franz at last.

"*Nein?*" Dietrichstein almost shouted.

"*Non,*" Franz replied innocently. "Why should I speak German? I am French!"

"You are . . ." the Count's voice came out strangled with vexation, ". . . mistaken! Just like your mother and His Majesty, the Emperor, you are German!"

Franz thought briefly and said with assurance, "But my father, the emperor. . . ."

The tutor interrupted sternly, "Not *that* emperor! I am referring to your grandfather, the Emperor of Austria!" And Dietrichstein risked a deceitful logic a child nearly five might find adequate. "All his relatives," he said, "are German. So you see, being his grandson, you are German, too."

Too young to debate on this, Franz took the simplest of options. "Well, I don't want to be German," he replied. "I am going to stay the way I was in Paris. And in Paris I was French!"

This established, the hostility began. Franz chose to rebel for a cause that was rather obscure to him. He was primarily moved by instinct, and his instinct told him that he was being tampered with somehow. So he defied his tutors and continued the usage of French.

Furious, Dietrichstein complained bitterly to Francis. The Emperor thought a while and declared with an obvious touch of regret that he would permit some light corporal punishments if this would help.

Teeth clenched, Franz submitted to the whip without renouncing, as his tutors put it, "his evil ways."

"That little devil!' Foresti said, half in anger and half in awe when he was done administering the lashes.

The little Prince's stoicism during the punishment haunted the Captain. And more disturbing still, there was about Franz an aura of elusive charm that could be distracting. Often times, when the child was studiously bent over an assignment, his tutors watched him stealthily from a distance with uncontrollable admiration. Everything about the boy exuded some peregine grace and singular distinction, which his physical beauty seemed to enhance. In those moments, they had the sentiment the Prince might never blend with the Habsburgs. He was of another race, of another world. And their only defense was to underplay their fascination by a show of greater severity.

At a loss to obtain satisfaction on the problem of having his pupil abandon the French language, Dietrichstein, as a last resort, went to the boy's mother.

"Your Majesty alone can convince the Prince that we do not wish to torment him."

In all sincerity, the Count deplored the whippings. The issue, he reflected, was not worth such heroism on the part of a child so young. Growing up a German was the only natural thing for Napoleon's little son to do under the circumstances. And only in this manner could he dissociate himself from his father's disgrace by becoming a less conspicuous member of the prestigious Habsburg family. Few political hostages could boast a more felicitous arrangement.

Marie Louise sent for her son and drew him on her lap. Whenever Franz saw his mother, an occasion that he considered a treat due to the brevity of the visits, his heart welled waves of happiness. She continued to belong to a world he understood, and her proximity evoked the restful familiarity of the home life he used to know. For all her estrangement from him, she was above all the mysterious, distant, and sweet mother, good and kind in her indolent and distracted sort of way.

She said pleasantly, mussing his curly hair, "You must do as you are told, or you will sadden your Bonpapa. You will also sadden me very much. You do love me, don't you?"

Seated on his mother's lap, Franz's little bottom still hurt from the whipping but he did not mind. The circle of her arms about him immediately re-established inner harmony and compliance. He gazed intensely into his mother's eyes and snuggled up to her. She was soft to cling to and reassuring to have near. Often, when his young mind grew tired of the constant efforts of coping with his anxieties, he longed to be able to run to her for a hug and a kiss. Oh, he loved her immensely! The mere sight of her filled him with precious joy and confidence. The very thought of paining her would make him cry.

He flung his arms around her neck and said in German as a pledge to abide by her wish, "*Ich liebe dich, Mutter!*"

She smiled, pecked him on the cheek and returned him to his tutor. She felt at peace. Her affairs were in order. Denouncing Napoleon had earned her praises from her family and the long awaited ratification of her possession of the duchies. Very shortly, she would be leaving for Parma. March seventh had been set for her departure. She would miss the celebration of her son's fifth birthday, but that couldn't be helped.

She did not want to think otherwise because in Parma she would be completely free to give herself to Neipperg. Conveniently, her ardent lover's wife had passed away. At long last, she could be happy! Her son's situation was settled, pending a few details she would attend to, but those could wait. In the meantime, he was well cared for and on the road to becoming a well-educated and contented German prince. His willingness to do her bidding added to her satisfaction. Obviously he did love her, and more intensely than she could have imagined. This set Marie Louise thinking. Perhaps it would be best not to tell him anything about her going away without him; best to leave him *after he would have gone to sleep.* To leave without saying good-bye would save him much grief.

Faithful to the promise he had made to his mother, Franz set aside his repugnance to learn and speak German. But to yield for the love

of Marie Louise demanded compensations he would exact at his tutors' expenses. He teased them with deliberate mistakes. Dietrichstein, apt to lose patience easily, one day declared the Prince a complete failure. More perceptive, Foresti said, "he is failing out of spite."

At this startling revelation, the Count exclaimed angrily, "What an insolent imp!"

"And he is just too clever for his age," Foresti admitted gloomily.

"Is he," asked Dietrichstein, "ever playful with you?"

The Captain shook his head. "No. He only acts like any frolicsome child with Emile."

Dietrichstein frowned. Since Foresti mentioned it, the presence of Emile, who was the Prince's only playmate and classmate, presented another obstacle toward the Germanization of Napoleon's son. Emile was allowed to share Franz's lessons in order to provide the proper emulation to the learning process. At six, the boy proved to be ideal. He was bright and offered the right degree of competitiveness. Unfortunately, and this was the fly in the ointment, he was the son of a Frenchman, Marie Louise's valet. He spoke only French and kept a perfect recollection of his companion's former status. As children are wont to do, he played at paying court to Franz by calling him "Imperial Highness" during their games and kissed his hands in homage.

More than once, the Count had remonstrated on the use of the title, but Franz came to Emile's defense with a quip that made his tutor cringe.

"Emile can't help himself, sir. You see, it is like *a catechism* with him. There is nothing one can do about it."

As this incident came back to the Count's mind, he said with a sigh of relief, "Emile will be leaving soon and we have the Prince's mother to thank for this."

Emile, to the satisfaction of the tutors, was indeed going away. He would be following his father to Parma, Marie Louise having been permitted to retain her French valet.

The preparations for her journey were conducted in earnest. And as planned, on the night of March seventh, while her son slept unaware that she was leaving him, Marie Louise made her good-byes to her family and, accompanied by Neipperg, went to her new life, carrying off in her baggage her son's silver-gilt cradle.

Franz was devastated by his mother's secret departure. He melted in a torrent of tears, moving his tutors to genuine pity without causing them to moderate their severity.

With Marie Louise gone, Dietrichstein undertook the complete reorganization of his pupil's schedule. Breakfast, which in the past might be postponed until nine so Marie Louise could have her son share hers, was set precisely at eight o'clock. Dinner was served at two, and supper at half past eight.

A third instructor soon joined the teaching staff, a quiet man of gentle mien and manners, a bit of a dreamer who had authored a tragedy. Mathias von Collin, it went without saying, specialized in literature, history, and philosophy. And seeing that he professed these sciences, his benign disposition and easygoing ways were accepted as a matter of course.

Collin's gentle and sensitive soul was immediately stirred with much compassion for the little boy. From the outset, something tender and delicate passed between the Prince and the eminent professor of the University of Vienna. Franz and Collin took to each other nearly at first sight.

Francis was far gone in his attachment to his grandson. He thought about him a great deal, and at times, with less lightheartedness than others.

That morning, alone in his study, his reflections like a hand rummaging through the contents of a drawer, turned up more than his own guilt for having separated the child from Marie Louise. Feelings toward Napoleon's son were mixed among the Habsburgs. Most considered the young Bonaparte as an intruder in their clan. They thought of him as having strayed into their midst by mischance and their attitude was one of haughty tolerance. Luckily, for the moment, Empress Maria Ludovica was ill and away in Verona. At least Francis was assured that the Prince would momentarily be spared the scourge of the Empress's malevolence. Francis had caught Maria Ludovica calling Franz "that Corsican bastard," and that had pained and angered him. He honestly admitted to himself that the Corsican blood his spouse so disdainfully regarded as vile, did impart brilliance, a smattering of which he would have liked to observe in his own two sons.

Francis had serious reasons to be envious of bright children and to feel concerned about the quality of his offspring. The ancientness of his race entailed certain penalties of which he was ashamed. The thought of Archduke Ferdinand, the heir to the Habsburg throne, set him on a repeated excursion into the history of his famous ancestors.

The beginning had been humble. The first to assume the Habsburg name was Otto, lord of the modest castle of Habsburg in tenth-century Switzerland. But Otto had raised the family to unparalleled prominence and power through a series of judicious marriages, a trend that had continued through the centuries. Yet to Francis's chagrin, no splendor is without chinks. And like a worm hidden in the core of a fine-looking fruit, subsequent excessive inbreeding had eaten away the vigor of Otto's descendants. Untold numbers of Habsburgs had died early in life of consumptive diseases. Others had suffered from mental instability. Mad Queen Joanna, a princess of Spain who married into his family, must have passed this on to the members of his race. Joanna was blamed for adding a dab of idiocy to the Habsburgs' strain, thus, causing Ferdinand's feeblemindedness. Ferdinand, called Ferdi in the imperial circle, was also an epileptic, the victim, Francis felt, of an accursed atavism. Even Archduchess Marie Anne's eccentric behavior hinted that she, too, might be wrong in the head. But the condition of Crown Prince Ferdinand was Francis's true cross, on which his fatherly pride had been crucified. At twenty-three, the pivot of Francis's dynastic hope, though gentle and docile, had not mentally developed with his years. Not without disgust, Francis remembered how, wedging his buttocks in a trash basket, Ferdinand had amused Franz by rolling in it on the floor. Thank God, his other son, Francis Charles, while far from brilliant, was at least normal.

Whereas Franz. . . .

Francis smiled to himself.

At barely five, the little Prince was so clever! Everything about the boy enchanted Francis; his amiability, extreme politeness, and incomparable ease in deportment; his arresting beauty; the facility and sophistication with which he could express complicated thoughts; his precocious wit. . . .

Francis's smile changed to a chuckle as he recalled a recent incident Count Dietrichstein had reported to him in a rush of indignation he could not completely share. It appeared that France continued to hold a special place in Franz's esteem. And those who spoke ill of her were putting themselves at risk to incur his infantile displeasure. On several occasions, even in Franz's presence, sharp tongues wagged freely on the assumption that his tender age went along with a modest comprehension. In the course of a conversation, as retold by the tutor, France was mentioned and the boy exclaimed, "Oh, what a beautiful country it is!" Whereupon a lady of the court countered sourly, "Perhaps! But that was a very long time ago!"

At this point of the story, Dietrichstein had to explain to Francis that the lady in question had bags under the eyes and a triple chin. The Prince, the tutor continued peevishly, retorted without hesitation, "The same can be said of you, too!"

Dietrichstein had demanded that his pupil be punished and suggested that the Prince's customary visits to his grandfather be canceled until Francis himself would decide to reinstate them. "This," Dietrichstein said, "is a punishment, the Prince would feel most keenly, given his deep affection for Your Majesty."

Francis agreed only to soothe the irate tutor. As it turned out, he felt just as much penalized having to forgo seeing his grandson. For weeks he had pined. Then, unable to endure his own unhappiness he had called the whole thing off. In a little while he would be seeing him. At long last!

With the prospect of a tender reunion, Francis left his reflection and turned his attention to police reports neatly placed on the top of his desk. Soon he grew absorbed in the meticulous study of pages and pages of documents, which his master spy Baron Kobielski had compiled for his review.

There was much work to be done, and Francis rang to summon the Baron who following an established ritual, came to stand behind him, prepared to clarify a point or offer a warning.

Francis was quite satisfied at the way he was managing his empire. His paternalism masked an iron rule, which relied heavily on the secret police. Owing to this all important organization, he felt the pulse of his people and monitored the private lives of his own relations. No one, not even his wife and brothers, were exempt from the vigilant scrutiny of Kobielski's spies.

Presently the Baron thought it opportune to call his sovereign's attention to an academic trend that could have undesirable repercussions.

"The universities are devoting much time to the study of philosophy and literature, Sire."

"How much?"

"Too much, Sire . . . To the near exclusion of science!"

"I certainly don't want my subjects to be taught to think."

"True, Sire. But how are we to dispose of bright minds?"

"Re-channeling," Francis said. "Concentrate all teachings on the disciplines of mathematics and the sciences. When one reckons or grapples with a theorem, one does not philosophize."

"Will Your Majesty approach the subject of theology with the same caution?"

"Most certainly! Let religion be the exclusive province of the Church. Individual mysticism is unwholesome. It should be wiped out and regarded as an infraction liable to prosecution. We are the guardian and the keeper of the populace's innocence. I am the father of my people. It follows that they should be treated like little children!"

Francis and his master spy conferred gravely for over an hour. Kobielski had just departed, when, suddenly, the door of Francis's study opened even as the call rang out.

"Bonpapa!"

Breaking away from Collin, Franz threw himself into his grandfather's outstretched arms.

Collin withdrew quietly leaving a rectangular box on the console near the door.

Francis clasped his grandson to him and said in a tone that gave no indication of reproach, "I heard you have been naughty!"

Franz said against the Emperor's chestful of medals, "Were you very angry with me?"

Francis stroked his head. "I should . . ." He smiled in Franz's soft hair and inhaled with relish the sweet and fresh scent of childhood. "What you said was pretty nasty," he chided weakly.

Franz drew away a little to peer at his grandfather and Francis wondered how such long and curled up lashes could belong to a boy. His grandson's reply startled him.

"I had to. She has insulted my country, Bonpapa!"

"I see you have a sense of obligation," Francis responded a little disconcerted. He paused, reflecting with some anxiety on the consequences this could possibly hold for the future. Then meeting some vague, unproved threat, he murmured, "I, too, have mine."

"How do you mean, Bonpapa?"

Francis cringed a little. He had addressed this last remark to himself. Franz seldom passed up anything. An explanation would be difficult in this case.

Instead, he said, "I mean," and he jerked his head at the pile of documents on his desk, "I have not yet finished my work and I must go back to it. Did you bring anything to play with?"

"A whole regiment!"

Francis laughed and watched fondly as Franz ran to the box Collin had left. Its contents were promptly emptied, and little figurines whose variegated uniforms lent so much color to a real-life Austrian battalion, spilled pell-mell onto the floor along with cannons, ammunition wagons, and standard bearers.

Francis's New Year's gift. . . .

Soon the Emperor of Austria and Napoleon's son became totally absorbed in their respective occupations. Francis signed with care the official documents drafted by the chancellery while Franz disposed with perfect assurance his battalions in battle array. A war raged at Francis's feet on a plain of thick wool pile. It was a war born of a little boy's imagination with the images and the noise that must accompany such operations.

But the noise only filled Franz's head. He played so quietly that after a while, without even looking up, Francis called out, "Franz?"

Franz promptly answered, "Yes, Bonpapa?"

"Oh, nothing," Francis said. "I just wanted to know if you were still here."

"Still here, Bonpapa!"

Francis smiled. And each returned to what he was doing. A moment later Francis became aware that his grandson was observing him.

"What is it, Franz?"

"Bonpapa, I should like to ask you something."

Francis put down his quill, stretched his cramped fingers and beckoned his grandson to come to him.

Franz folded his arms on his grandfather's knees and looked confidently into his eyes. His own, of a bright blue, sparkled like jewels. Golden baby hair frizzled on the edge of his forehead. Francis gazed upon Napoleon's son in complete thrall and said absentmindedly, "Speak . . . I am all ears."

"When I lived in Paris, wasn't I a king?"

That returned Francis to an alert state of mind. "Yes, you were once a king."

"And I had pages?"

"You did, yes."

"But I lost them. So that does not make me a king anymore. Is this possible?"

"It's quite possible."

"Just because I lost some pages?"

"Kings do have pages," Francis answered gravely.

"Was I not called King of Rome?"

Francis swallowed hard. "Yes. That is how you were called."

"And what does it mean to be King of Rome, Bonpapa?"

Inwardly Francis winced. It meant a quake that had irreparably cracked his empire. It was the marker of its dismantlement. Though the perpetrator of this evil deed was in captivity, the harm had been done and could never be repaired. Europe was scarred and the Holy Roman Empire extinct. The title Napoleon had given his son epitomized a historical upheaval never to be forgotten. If the child's tenacious retention of the past could not be done away with . . . yet, this past must be re-interpreted.

"Just as I am King of Jerusalem without any power over that city, so you were King of Rome. It's only a fancy name, Franz. Nothing more."

"Ah," Franz said, obviously satisfied, and returned to his game.

But Francis wondered what else will he be asking next time? And how long will it take for his tutors to dull his childhood's memories.

It was nearing autumn when Franz met his *new* grandmother—that was how he thought of her. The *old* one, the one who was so mean to him, had died in Verona, where she had gone to get better. That was how this was explained to him and it did not make any sense.

He did not think his new grandmother looked pretty at all. But when he had been presented to her, she exclaimed, *"Er is ein schöner Mann!"* and hugged him and kissed him, and he liked her at once. Not because she found him attractive but because she considered him a man, and showed genuine marks of affection.

A princess of the ancient house of Wittelsback, Francis's fourth wife, young Charlotte of Bavaria, suffered none of the acerbity that plagued the character of her predecessor. Where it concerned Franz, whom she found irresistible and fondly called *Franzchen,* Charlotte had no reason to dislike his father to whom her own father, Maximilian, Elector then King of Bavaria, was allied up to the time of the French

Emperor's Russian campaign. Thereafter, Maximilian continued to conserve pleasant memories of Napoleon, for he owed him his royal title, territorial gains at the time of his association with him, and the leadership of the Confederation of the Rhine—while it lasted. Under much duress, Maximilian was finally forced to abandon the French alliance. The rupture with Napoleon was all the more painful, as one of his own daughters was in fact married to Napoleon's stepson, Prince Eugene.

Given such good rapport, the King of Bavaria's children were not taught to abhor, but on the contrary, to respect an ancient amity. Charlotte, known as Carolina Augusta since her marriage to Francis, was raised in that observance, and so was her half-sister, Sophie, whom the new Empress left in Bavaria with the joyful anticipation of seeing her at her side as a daughter-in-law when she would be of marriageable age. At present a little girl of eleven, Sophie was being groomed to become the future wife of Francis's son, Archduke Francis Charles, to whom she had been betrothed.

With a loving grandmother and a doting grandfather, Franz was beginning to experience the calming effect of living somewhat *en famille.* Only somewhat, because the sense of truly belonging still remained uncertain. He felt this more than he could explain it, and he had this sensation because his solitude continued to be very real. Those by whom he felt loved were few, and the times during which he could warm himself to such generosity were of an occasional nature. He was also conscious of a great hush over his past. As the hush seemed to have taken the flavor of a conspiracy, his curiosity increased. His head was filled with notions cobwebbed by a faltering understanding of what had happened. Why not ask? he thought, instead of wondering when he would be told, if he was going to be told anything at all.

The lessons had gone well that day and Foresti seemed to be in a fairly good mood. So Franz decided to make his move.

"Is there an emperor in France now, sir?"

Foresti's mood wasn't so sunny anymore when he responded laconically, "No. A king."

"What is his name?"

"Louis the Eighteenth."

"It seems to me that there was an emperor before."

Foresti wondered how much his pupil remembered. He also went over his instructions. He should not lie. If the child insisted, he should tell what could be told. What couldn't, he must meet with evasion or silence.

He said, "So there was."

"Was it my father?"

"Yes."

Franz allowed a silence and advanced tentatively, "My father must have been a great man to be an emperor. Don't you think so?"

"I have no opinion," Foresti retorted losing patience.

"And why isn't he there anymore?" Franz pressed.

"Your father had an inordinate passion for war. Because of this, he lost his crown!"

Obliquely, Foresti watched his pupil's reaction. Franz appeared to be thinking this over at some length. Then he asked, "Where is my father now?"

Foresti grew rigid. That was the question he feared the most. This time he said with absolute honesty, "I cannot answer you, Prince."

Franz insisted on a dare, "And why not?"

Cornered, the Captain resorted to absolute authority. "Because I say so. And as your master, you are to mind everything I say!" He gave his pupil a sidelong glance and was amazed at Franz's apparent imperturbability.

Franz decided in his simple wisdom to let the matter rest for now. He switched to another topic.

"I used to have many picture books I brought from Paris, all about my father and France, and I can't seem to find them anymore. Do you know where they are?"

"I never saw them."

"But I had them, sir. And I am sure I did not give them away."

This time Foresti took the liberty to lie. "You must have misplaced them or lost them."

Franz heaved a deep sigh. "That's a pity! If only I had them I would remember better!"

The Captain made a careful note of that remark.

15

As stiff as a ramrod, Count Maurice Dietrichstein stood by the open window overlooking Schönbrunn's formal gardens. Spring had come and gone, and it was again summer. Though his eyes stared abstractly into the distance, his attention did not wander.

The year 1817, the second of his tutorship, continued to challenge his resources. Now a new problem he never contemplated having to address had just arisen. Dietrichstein thought himself quite capable of coping with matters involving discipline; he had not yet been confronted with the situation of having to alleviate his pupil's despair, the despair of a six-year-old boy who, for hours now, had locked himself up in his bedchamber to cry seemingly without interruption.

The Count shook his head and remarked with a touch of commiseration, "I am afraid we won't be able to do anything with the Prince today."

From the back of the room, Foresti, who was perusing their pupil's notebooks, mumbled that he'd never seen such a violent outburst of grief. He regarded this as disruptive and wasteful and said with no show of compassion, "I had no idea this would affect him like this! Every time I have been listening at the door of his bedroom, I heard him crying!" Then he added with annoyance, "It's a pity Her Majesty cannot come. The Prince has really worked himself up to a frenzy at the prospect of seeing his mother."

The Count nodded, thinking, And with equal transport he is showing his disappointment! After one full year of caring for the youngster, Dietrichstein was beginning to gain some insight into the working of a child's mind. Having repeatedly promised to visit her little son every summer, Marie Louise had just reduced Franz's expectation to nought in a letter of cancellation invoking ill-health incurred by absorbing affairs of state. Given the peculiar intensity of infantile credulity, the child considered her promise as binding as a holy vow, and in the candor of his heart, he made no allowance for any contingencies as an acceptable reason to break such a promise.

The Count also noticed that Marie Louise's absence exalted the deep sentiment of affection Franz already felt for her. When he spoke of his mother he credited her with all manner of perfection. He well-nigh venerated her. And for having been let down by his idol, the boy was presently crying his heart out. . . .

Dietrichstein decided to pass to action. "We can't leave him like that," he said firmly. "Somehow I must appease him or he is going to make himself sick!"

With the Captain on his heels, Dietrichstein marched himself to the door of his pupil's bedroom. He put his ear to the gilded leaf, and not liking what he heard, commanded, softening his voice, "Franz, please open up!"

Foresti, breathing curiously into his neck, was waved away. Then more softly still, the Count coaxed. "Open the door, Franz. I just wish to be with you."

The tutor wondered if this initiative meant anything at all to his pupil, as there continued to be no warmth in their relationship. Not without reluctance he imagined having to threaten to break down the door if the boy persisted in being unresponsive.

To his relief he heard the telling "click" of a key being turned in the lock and expected to see the door open. As this did not happen, he hesitated a few seconds and then went in to catch Franz clambering back on his bed. The Prince pulled up his knees and touched his forehead to them, giving Dietrichstein enough time to glimpse a face disfigured by tears.

"Oh, God!" he breathed, walking over to his pupil.

In answer, Franz heaved, "You don't have to bother with me. I can be by myself!"

But you want me to, thought the Count. Or you wouldn't have let me in. He sat himself on the bed and lay a hand on Franz's shoulder saying, "You have been left alone too long. Won't you let me stay?"

Franz trembled. A part of him, which in self-defense relied less and less on his male entourage for the solace of human tenderness, surrendered. He ached to be hugged and consoled. He threw himself in Dietrichstein's arms.

Moved, the Count murmured words he did not think himself capable of uttering, "Always remember that I am a friend in whom you can confide. . . ."

Franz did. With his tutor's arms about him, he told him how much he wanted to see his mother, and wished he were dead!

"Now, now," calmed Dietrichstein. "You must realize that your mother is the sovereign of an important duchy. She has obligations and she can't leave just like that!"

Not to worry the Prince, Marie Louise's indisposition was not mentioned, and the tutor wondered if Franz would have borne his disappointment better had he been told that Marie Louise was sick.

Franz looked up at him. He had been told that the reason why his mother had gone to Parma was to do good work. So with this in mind, he asked, "Is Mother busy taking care of the poor?"

"That, too," answered the Count, after a brief hesitation.

Somehow, he had reservations concerning the real reasons which prevented Marie Louise from coming, and he was not wrong for being suspicious. She had given birth to Nieperg's child in May, a girl named Albertine. In deference to Francis's ignorance of Marie Louise's relationship with the General, the birth was kept secret. In a way, Marie Louise could say she was ailing, as she was recovering from childbirth. But everybody at her little court in Parma knew that this was not the only reason why she would not undertake the journey to Vienna. That baby girl, conceived and born in a climate of her own choosing, captivated her. To leave her infant daughter to the care of a wet nurse obviously distressed Marie Louise more than forgoing a reunion with her lonely little son.

For all the Count knew, Marie Louise was not coming. The only thing he wanted at present was to calm his pupil and re-establish their normal routine.

He gave Franz one of his rare smiles. "You must come out of this crying. If I were to tell your Mamma how unhappy you are, that would make her unhappy, too. You don't want to do that, Franz. Do you?"

"Ah, no!" Franz protested, resolutely rubbing his eyes dry.

Hoping to be right, Dietrichstein said, "You shall be seeing your mother next year."

The following year, the seventh in is life, Franz's joy knew no bound upon learning that his mother would be spending her summer holiday with him. Dietrichstein explained that they were to travel to the small village of Theresienfeld to meet her. From there they would go to Baden, and then to another of Francis's summer residences, Persenbeug castle.

In his excitement, Franz paid no attention to the Count's preoccupied air during the preparations for the journey. Dietrichstein had begun to worry the minute he heard the name of the village. He knew the village itself was insignificant, but he also knew that it happened to be the place where some of the Bonapartes had chosen to exile themselves.

Jerome, Caroline, and her children, and a colony of retired officers of Napoleon's disbanded Grand Army lived in its vicinity. The thought that his pupil, though for a very short time, would be taken to such a rendezvous point sent chills up the Count's spine. He earnestly hoped that as planned, they wouldn't have to stop any longer than to transfer the Prince to his mother's carriage and get on with the rest of the trip.

During the first leg of the journey, Franz fidgeted, all given up to the happiness of seeing his mother. Dietrichstein chewed on his knuckles. As he'd feared, Her Majesty's coach failed to materialize at the appointed hour. So they had to wait.

Soon the idle equipage with its liveried outriders began to attract a small crowd of curious. Dietrichstein dreaded the possibility of the crowd swelling to a mob as soon as the identity of his pupil was found out. Already, the nudging, pointing of fingers, and muffled exclamations of surprise augured an interest the imperial crest painted on the carriage's doors only partially explained. It was the boy seated beside him who had become the center of attention. Thank God! Dietrichstein thought, *The child has no conception of the significance he has assumed since his arrival in Austria. And hopefully, he would not come into contact with his Corsican relations.* The only thing to do to end the staring was to find the shelter of a walled place where they could wait in privacy.

Looking around, he caught sight of a farmhouse nearby and decided that it would serve this purpose well.

"Come," he said taking Franz's hand. "Walk fast and don't speak to anyone."

Franz obeyed, but could not help asking if there was something wrong. The Count did not bother to reply.

The Prince walked at a quick pace, but quicker was the equerry who preceded them and rapped on the door of the farmhouse. Without giving it a thought, he told the proprietor to let in the child, who was expecting his mother, the Duchess of Parma.

Immediately, the man exclaimed at the sight of Franz standing on the threshold, "So this is Napoleon's little boy!"

"Hush!" Dietrichstein silenced. "I ask you not to give us away!"

The farmer smiled broadly, looking over the tutor's shoulders. "There is no harm, sir. You are among friends here!" He stepped aside. "Please, enter. I am Bernard Petri. At your service!"

To Dietrichstein's dismay, the crowd, which had gathered behind him while he waited at the farmhouse's door, followed them inside also, owing to Petri's good grace. In a matter of minutes, Franz was surrounded. Suddenly, in the language he had very nearly completely forgotten, came a loud cheer. *"Vive le fils de l'Empereur!"* Long live the Emperor's son! The Count cringed. Adding to the general commotion and increasing his panic, Napoleon's sister, Caroline, and her brother, Jerome, chose to arrive at this precise moment.

A hush fell over the assembly as the crowd parted before them. Horrified, Dietrichstein could see the moment when, after years of jealously guarded care, some utterly stupid mischance would effectuate an unthinkable encounter—Franz meeting eye-to-eye his paternal relations! Frantic, the tutor stretched out his hands in a forbidding and at the same time pleading gesture.

"There is no need to speak!" he cried. "The Prince understands only German!"

But the dreadful Bonapartes kept advancing. Caroline had lost much of her ambitious virulence, having also lost her husband, Murat, shot three years ago as he recklessly attempted to recover his Neapolitan kingdom. The former queen, now living under an assumed name, was exceedingly curious to glimpse her long lost godchild and had a good look at him when suddenly, a man wearing a black patch over one eye lifted the boy off the ground and carried him outside.

Franz found himself sitting beside his mother with the accompanying mention that there was some sort of disturbance inside the farmhouse.

"How do you mean?" wondered Marie Louise.

Neipperg backed out saying before closing the door of the berlin, "I'll explain later."

Intrigued, she watched her lover climb into another carriage, joined by a bedraggled-looking Dietrichstein. Finally, she turned her attention to her child. Her first words to him after two years of separation were, "Franz, what happened?"

Speechless, Franz stared at his mother. He'd been befuddled by the fuss from which he had just been extricated and also stunned by the joy of being with her at long last.

She decided not to press him any further. Playfully twisting his long, blond curls around her fingers she said with a slack, understanding smile, "You are nervous. . . ."

She was amazed by his size. She had left a baby not yet five to find now a prodigiously grown boy of seven. A very quiet boy. Marie Louise wondered if he had gone mute.

Privacy and a return to the familiarity of his own sheltered little world at long last untied Franz's tongue. Giving free rein to an overwhelming rush of affection, he flung his arms around his mother's neck and covered her face with kisses. Then in a fluent and beautifully spoken German, he proceeded to tell her about all the things he could not have shared with her during the two years they were apart.

In the weeks that followed her reunion with her son, Marie Louise picked up the thread of a nagging worry. She was concerned about the confirmation of Franz's status. Though he was never to possess a foreign estate, he could own some lands in his grandfather's realm, and Francis had promised to look into the final and honorable settlement of his grandson's position. Marie Louise was still waiting.

Finally, on a bright and sunny morning while she and Franz were in Baden, the letters patent arrived. Francis was true to his word. As Marie Louise carefully read the official documents whose stipulations were saving her son from the shame of being related to an international outlaw, she saw the realization of her plan for Franz's future.

He was granted a new, suitable identity. From now on, he was to be known as the Duke of Reichstadt, a germanized name taken after one of the domains located in Bohemia, which Francis had gifted to his grandson. Franz was to be addressed in direct discourse as "Your Highness" and on more formal occasions as "Serene Highness." He was entitled to a ducal blazon and ranked second at court and throughout the empire after the other archdukes. All of this, decreed and duly authenticated by: "*We, Francis, by the grace of God, Emperor of Austria, King of Jerusalem, of Hungary, of Bohemia. . . .*" There was no mention of the boy's father anywhere. In the preamble, Franz had solely been born of "Our beloved daughter." Francis refrained from saying any more. . . .

With quiet elation, Marie Louise glanced at her son. She had just shown him how to form words with freshly picked forget-me-nots. Bent over the table, Franz was thus occupied, puffing now and then on strands of hair, which kept tickling his nose and lips. Marie Louise made a note that something should be done soon with those somewhat girlish curls. Franz had definitely outgrown this sort of hair style. Her fine-looking little duke!

She promptly sent for Count Dietrichstein, wanting to share her joy by apprising him of the recognition conferred upon his pupil by her father.

Dietrichstein beamed reading the letters patent she'd handed over to him. When he finished, she called softly, "Franz!"

The Prince was so engrossed in his project that he did not pay any attention to his tutor's entrance. But his mother's voice, the signal that she needed him for whatever reason, he would mind.

Immediately, he stopped what he was doing and crossed over to her, wearing an attentive expression that pleased her.

"Now, listen to this," she said jubilantly. "As of today, you have a new and wonderful name."

"I won't be called Franz any more?"

She laughed. "Of course you will, silly dear! But you are now a Bavarian duke. The Duke of Reichstadt! Isn't this splendid?"

Dietrichstein watched is pupil with smug gravity. Judging by Franz's serious air, it appeared that he was having some difficulties sharing his mother's enthusiasm. He did not reply at once, either. So the tutor urged, making use of his pupil's newly acquired privilege, "Well, what does *Your Highness* say to this?"

Franz cast a placid glance at the Count. The title was not at all unfamiliar really. It wasn't that. But the resumption of its usage had exhumed something. Something laid aside, but by no means voided. On the contrary. Its validity was to him irreversible.

He said, "So I am a Bavarian duke and at the same time a French prince."

Marie Louise paled and gulped down her disappointment. "Franz, how can you say that?"

Dietrichstein promptly scolded, "How is this at all possible! Can Your Highness speak French?"

Silence. Finally, Franz spoke, his voice flat, acknowledging what had been done to him. "No, sir. I can't speak French anymore."

"There you are!" concluded the tutor. "You can see that speaking only German and thinking in German makes you German and not French. You are a duke, for which you should thank your grandfather!"

"I am most grateful," Franz said, directing at his mother an anxious look.

Some color had returned to her cheeks. She asked hesitantly, "Franz, you do think in German, don't you?"

He took his time answering. So much so that when he finally said that he'd never given any attention to the language he used to form his thinking process, she sensed a resistance that troubled her. As it was in her character to flee from trouble without putting up much of a fight, she recoiled inwardly at the challenge of confronting her child's reticence. Let those in charge of changing him handle this!

Affecting a brisk and insouciant tone of voice, she abruptly turned to Dietrichstein and said, "I rely on you, Count, to show my son the spelling of his new name. I should like to see him sign it on the next letter he will be sending to Parma!"

The mention of Parma made Franz shudder slightly. His only consolation for now was to look forward to this holiday not yet ended. Baden had been their first stop. Persenbeug was next.

Built on a rocky promontory overlooking the Danube, the romantic castle of Persenbeug was Francis's favorite haunt. The surroundings always impressed him as exuding a unique kind of peace, and at Persenbeug he felt less an emperor and more a carefree, well-to-do country gentleman. Yet up to the town bearing the same name, this valley, according to a legend, was once the tumultuous abode of the ill-fated Nibelungs, hoarders of an accursed gold whose possession led them to perdition. The tragedy, of course, had dissipated itself in times forever gone. If the memory still lingered, it was solely to evoke the gentler side of romance immortalized in long-extinct and harmless pathos. The ambient legendary air did not affect Francis in the least. He was not a dreamer, nor was he a poet. His tastes did not tend toward the fanciful. They were earthy and simple. And Francis that summer, like any other summer, enjoyed passing time walking and hunting with the added pleasure this year of overseeing his grandson's initiation to manhood.

First, this was marked by a haircut, which delighted Franz. Collin suggested a *titus*, which was promptly adopted and suited the Prince perfectly. Short locks curling above the ears abolished the nuisance of having Franz's hair rolled each night in well over forty *papillotes.* He disliked the tedious ritual of letting his hair be wound around little pieces of paper at the end of each day. It might produce a well-arranged cascade of curls next morning, but it was an operation he grew to regard as futile and unbecoming a boy.

Next, Francis took him to a hunt, not as a spectator but as a participant. Franz's eyes lit up with excitement when he was given his first rifle and Francis Charles, with whom he had made his peace, showed him how to use it. It was not long before his aim became deadly, and never before had Franz so enjoyed himself. With his mother near, always available, most appropriately when he had killed a partridge or a hare to marvel at his excellent marksmanship, life was sweet and beautiful. He felt as if he had a true home life again, and his attitude underwent a remarkable transformation. He became spontaneous, docile. Dietrichstein thought he was hallucinating.

This was too good to last!

Franz said the same thing to himself when the Court moved back to Schönbrunn. His hourglass of happiness was running out. It was now September and Mother would be leaving soon. He tried to maintain a cheerful exterior so as to not upset her. When Marie Louise left, he accompanied her as far as Persenbeug. From there, she was to take a boat to a point further up the Danube, then land to proceed to Parma by coach.

Franz took leave of his mother without undue transport and waved at her with liveliness from the quay. As soon as the distance began to blur the lines of her face, he quietly left the jetty where her family had assembled to see her off and sadly went inside the castle. Climbing many stairs, he burst into the room that gave the most commanding view of the river and rushed to the window, sobbing. Impatiently, he wiped his eyes with his fists. He wanted to see the small speck that transported the being that was infinitely dear to him. A whole sweet world was sailing away, and his most ardent wish was to be a seagull, like those hovering over the boat, which was quickly disappearing from view.

Adulterated with considerations at variance with the pursuit of her own happiness, Marie Louise's love for her son was no match for his unrelenting devotion, which she put to a grueling test. Nothing could be more erratic than the times set for her visits, which were the focal point of Franz's anticipation at the beginning of each year. In the year that was to mark his eighth birthday, a letter pleading ill-health canceled her trip to Vienna, which at first had been confirmed only to be postponed.

Marie Louise had reasons enough to stay away from her son and her family. She was again pregnant and too far gone with the child to put up an appearance. The baby, named William, was born in August. Francis was a little perplexed by these convenient yearly bouts of illnesses. Metternich, in better position to suspect the causes, did not volunteer any explanation.

Franz underwent the painful process of bemoaning his mother's absence, but this time instead of locking himself up to cry, he sent Marie Louise a letter letting his pen convey what tears could never impress upon her. He wrote:

> *You must know, dearest Mamma, that the sight of you last summer, the remembrance of each minute spent in your beloved company, continues to abide with me. Perhaps at times, I may have annoyed you with my childish anxieties. But I have resolved to grow in wisdom. Oh, if only I were older than I am! I could be to you a more interesting companion. Until such time comes, until in your kindness I shall have the joy of being with you again, I am overcoming for your sake the sadness of not having you with me while restraining none of my anxieties concerning your health. Do get well; and pray, remember me a little. I beg you to think kindly of a son who loves you without measure. . . ."*

When Marie Louise read those lines, she stared at them breathlessly. Franz's passionate protestations of affection swept her in a whirlwind. He was disquietingly eloquent for his years, inexorably loyal, constant, and giving. She had reached her prime and her fill, and she knew not what to do with the ocean of love he was offering her. And he was only eight!

It soon became evident to Count Dietrichstein that Franz's emotional stability was undergoing serious strains. From one year to the next he would be wondering at the beginning of each spring if his mother would be coming. She did come in the year of her son's ninth birthday and brought him a playmate, Gustave, Neipperg's son from his late wife. The boy was not much older than Franz and the two children became inseparable. They went fishing and acted out the adventure of *Robinson Crusoe* under the expert directions of Collin. Happily, Franz had found a perfect "Friday" as he wanted to be "Robinson."

Again, he was cheerful and outgoing, but then his mood would shift and Dietrichstein worried as this condition gave rise to a problem of an academic nature. For as soon as his mother was with him, Franz would begin to fret because she would have to leave him. Then after she had gone, he would worry himself to distraction to the detriment of his studies because he was not sure of having her back next year.

By mid-summer, the tutor looked forward to an event that would take his pupil's mind off worldly preoccupations in favor of heavenly ones. As Franz was of age to make his First Communion, a half-hour was added to his religious instructions. He listened to pious discourses on the evil of sins, their degrees of virulence, and the means to remedy their devastation. He was told of the blessed virtue of charity, of the abomination of man's cruelty to man, of God's justice, His mercy, and all-abounding love in the gift of the Eucharist. He was taught the prayer to merit that gift.

His heavenly blue eyes fixed upon the priest's lips, Franz conscientiously repeated after him: "Oh my God, I am heartily sorry for having offended Thee. And I detest all my sins. . . ."

16

When General Gourgaud set his eyes on the wind-swept island of St. Helena, he had but one comment: "That rock is only fit for the damned!"

No one contradicted him. Everything about the island evoked death and disintegration. The aura of malignity that seemed to envelop St. Helena projected the sinister impression of a relentless pursuit at punishing. All because hundreds and hundreds of years ago, in that part of the Atlantic Ocean two thousand miles distant from Europe, the seas had parted under the explosive forces of an erupting volcano, which spewed forth the materials to form land. The molten rocks, long petrified in time, presented now a jagged, gloomy mass of black, steep cliffs rising from the waves like glistening ramparts which seemed to have been erected by the labor of demons. The sun rarely shone, but the heat was fierce briefly tempered by frequent cloudbursts which chilled one to the bones. England had lost scores of sailors because of these erratic changes in temperature. The locals, consisting of Negro slaves and Chinese coolies serving the white, did not fare any better. Their masters managed to survive because they only stayed a year at a time. The servants were not so lucky. So death, to those who could not leave at all, came at an early age.

In his dilapidated house, Napoleon also suffered from the onslaught of a climate he foresaw would get the better of him. Now in the sixth year of his captivity, his entourage had considerably dwindled.

Gourgaud's intense devotion for Napoleon and his disruptive jealousy caused such intolerable dissension that he was sent back to France. Las Cases—who carefully recorded Napoleon's recollections and observations—having had the temerity to try smuggling a message to Europe describing the hardships inflicted on the Emperor, was caught and deported during the first year of his voluntary exile. Bertrand and Montholon were still there, putting up a valiant front despite frequent bouts of dysentery. They were indeed selfless men, but they had grown irritable.

Promiscuity, discomfort, privation, and the regret for a better life they could have chosen, soured their mood and set their nerves on edge. An innocent remark was taken as an insult, or a look, inasmuch as it was given asquint, started many altercations. Bertrand often stomped out of the room with so much outraged vigor that his foot went through the rotten flooring. The irony of it all, Napoleon often thought, was that he who, as Emperor, stirred so many conflicts, now thoroughly enjoyed the role of peacemaker by settling innumerable squabbles.

Above all, it gave him something to do, for idleness sapped his spirits and gnawed at his bones, which he thought were going soft. Once he said to Bertrand, "Do you realize I am the richest man in the world?" Naturally Bertrand looked at him as if he had just taken leave of his senses and told him frankly he did not see at all how this could be.

"Time," Napoleon answered, "I have so much time!" And placing his hand against his stomach, he grimaced. "If this old mechanic holds, I shall have plenty more. Oh, how I hate having so much time!"

It wasn't so bad at the beginning when his pent-up energy found an outlet in the dictation of voluminous memoirs. But six years are more than one needed to reminisce. Soon the minutes, the hours, the days, began to drag endlessly. Time seemed to spawn time like the earning of a judicious investment. But that was accursed wealth, a nightmarish bounty that cloyed Napoleon to the point of nausea.

In April of 1821, he realized that there would not be so much time to while away after all. The excruciating cramps that sent him writhing in agony on the floor of his room warned him that it was no longer a matter of waiting for time to pass, but rather, for death to come. The sight of him filled his companions with profound sadness. He had almost recaptured the leanness of his youth, but it was an unhealthy loss of flesh accompanied by a wax-like complexion and the graying of the skin under his eyes.

The Irish surgeon O'Meara declared that the prisoner was suffering from a liver disease that could only worsen in view of the damp climate of St. Helena. A report supporting this statement was dispatched to London without eliciting any reaction. Meanwhile, Napoleon continued to endure ill-health along with much hardship and many vexations inflicted upon him by a skinny, freckled, red-haired Englishman on whose watchfulness depended the peace of Europe.

Hudson-Lowe took his mission to heart. He turned the whole island into a prison that swarmed with spies who spied upon one another. He believed that all prisoners, as such, must be made to feel utterly miserable, this one in particular. Consequently, the Emperor had been moved from a fairly decent dwelling to Longwood, where a stable built on a wind-swept plateau was hastily transformed into a house. "House," everyone agreed, was a euphemism for pigsty. Not only did the place look like one, but it smelt like one as well because the flooring had been laid over cattle dung, which no one had bothered to remove.

Lowe gloated over the fact that Napoleon was left for weeks without fresh water and milk, that his meat was spoiled, and his wine went sour. With fanatical thoroughness, Lowe also undertook to torment Napoleon in spirit. For six long years, anything that in any way could relate to the captive's son was systematically proscribed. The child, for all Napoleon knew, might as well be dead.

This situation constituted Lowe's greatest source of satisfaction because it sent his prisoner into severe fits of depression. At such moments Racine's verses from the play *Andromache* haunted Napoleon. They seemed to have been written especially for those dark hours as the plight of a heroic Trojan family became the model of his own glorious yet tragic destiny. He knew those verses by heart, and in anguished moments of longing for news of his son, he would recite them to himself:

I am come to the place where my son
lies captive: for a moment only,
allow my tears to flow with his!
This is all that is left to me
of Hector and of Troy. Permit me, Lord,
to visit him once every day. . . .

Those were the lines of a wife to the victor who had slain her husband. Those were Andromache's admirable words. But Napoleon had long recognized Marie Louise's inability to fit the part, so drinking the cup to the bitter dregs, he made those lines his own.

It was in a state of utter dejection that Count Montholon found the Emperor when he answered an urgent summons. It was already noon, which said much for the pitiable condition into which the prisoner had sunk. Napoleon was sitting up in a four-poster iron camp bed hung with faded green silk curtains. His legs, swollen for lack of exercise, were propped on a pillow.

A near invalid now, there he sat. And for the celebrated commander that he once was, looking a bit ridiculous with a red-checked Madras kerchief covering his balding head. That proud Roman head, Montholon noticed, was sinking forward and the imperious eyes, which had commanded the world, were now dull and staring absently at a brown nankeen all spotted with saltpeter stains hanging on the wall facing the bed. It was the same camp bed Napoleon had used on the eve of his glorious victory at the battle of Austerlitz. From this last monument left to him, Montholon had observed how, each night before closing his eyes, Napoleon would melancholically survey one by one all the souvenirs he had been able to bring with him and fought to keep.

The room was the shabby repository of a grand epic that had shaken the world, and regardless of the judgments to be passed on Napoleon, Napoleon *had happened* and would never be forgotten. Montholon took a visual inventory of Napoleon's treasures.

Set on the mantelpiece were the two silver candlesticks the Emperor had brought from Saint Cloud. Between them, stood his most cherished possession: a marble bust of his son. It depicted him as he should have looked at the age of five from a mold of clay alleged to have been executed in Livorno, where the little Prince was said to have stayed with his mother. The lie, perpetrated to suit a fraud, had overwhelmed Napoleon with unquestioning joy. Of course, this had enraged Hudson-Lowe, who demanded that the statue of the boy be thrown into the sea. Montholon, who had witnessed the delivery of the hoax, would long remember the violent altercation that had ensued between the prisoner and his jailer. Lowe finally capitulated, but not before declaring that the statue was a piece of junk. The boy, he also told Napoleon, for news that was certain to pain the Emperor would not be kept from him, was not free to travel and therefore could not have gone to Livorno. Moreover, he was barred from the succession of Parma and at present no longer retained his name, but was called Reich-something.

Napoleon refused to learn how to pronounce the name. This abomination done to his son drove him to near despair and Montholon remembered how he and Bertrand spent watchful nights listening at his door for fear their emperor might attempt the unthinkable. In their presence, Napoleon gloomily vented his fears. His heir, arraigned before the tribunal of politics because he was the vessel of a new covenant, so very young, abandoned by his mother and helplessly isolated, was being made to renounce his name and surely his country of birth as well. They must be schooling him in all the ideas the Revolution had sought to eradicate. In an outburst of sorrow, Napoleon had wondered how much damage would be done. . . .

Four more pictures of the infant Prince, painted in miniature by Isabey, hung on the wall along with a portrait of Marie Louise done by the same artist. Next to it, held by a nail, a gold watch was suspended to a chain made of her plaited hair. A little above, from a tarnished gold frame, Napoleon's first empress, Josephine, stared down in languid abstraction. Reality and its flux were relentlessly measured and recorded by another souvenir, a trophy acquired in Potsdam—Frederick the Great's silver clock. Often Montholon asked himself if instead of consoling the Emperor, these beloved mementos were not in fact aggravating his spleen. . . .

Then the Count caught a sudden movement on the sideboard where Napoleon's worn cocked hat was set. Seemingly by itself, the hat was moving quite ludicrously and soon ran itself off the shelf and fell to the ground. Rats! That one, doffing the famous chapeau as both hit the floor, scurried across the threadbare carpet to disappear under a battered daybed upon which Napoleon lounged more and more frequently.

Reverently, Montholon retrieved the hat and placed it back on the shelf next to a row of books whose bindings were corroded by mold. They were rotting like all that he walked on or sat on.

Napoleon had not moved and kept staring at the nankeen. Count Montholon concluded that the Emperor must be stupefied with pain.

"Should I send for the doctor, Sire?"

Had the doctor been O'Meara, Napoleon might have said yes. O'Meara might be an Englishman, but he was nevertheless sincerely devoted to his patient. In fact, he had demonstrated enough fondness for the prisoner to displease Lowe, who had sent him back to the civilized world. Napoleon did not like O'Meara's replacement even though his mother, Letizia, had recommended him, mostly because he was

Corsican. In spite of his mother's good intention, he found doctor Antommarchi pretentious and totally unsympathetic to his sufferings. Antommarchi had the gall to insinuate that Napoleon's pains were simulated for political reasons.

Napoleon shook his head. He pointed to a chair drawn up against a rickety table. "Sit down, Montholon. I have work for you to do."

Montholon obliged, surmising he had been called to write down more memoirs or record more revealing truths such as the avowal by Napoleon that his greatest enemy had been none but himself.

"You are going to draw up my will," Napoleon announced.

The Count made a movement of protest, but he was not too surprised. Napoleon looked so wretched . . . and he had been passing blood.

"Don't look so glum," Napoleon said. "Now write."

Napoleon declared first that he would die in the Roman Apostolic religion in which he had been raised. Next, having become French by choice, his wishes were that his remains be interred on the bank of the Seine.

For his wife, there were kind words with no allusions, however light, to her betrayal. He asked that she never consent to have their son used as a tool in the hands of the powers that were oppressing the people, and that above all, she must remind him never to contemplate bringing harm to France or bear arms against her.

To his son, the principal legatee, his bequest consisted of mementos. When the boy reached the age of sixteen, he was to receive from his father's executors all of Napoleon's arms among which figured the Consular sword and the one he had worn at Austerlitz, his saddles, spurs, snuff-boxes, books, body linen, and a bracelet made of his hair.

Napoleon further commanded that a collection of pictures, medals and books be assembled and presented to the Prince. These would provide him with sound ideas concerning his origin and destiny.

Then, last but not least, when the boy came of age, he should resume the name of "Napoleon."

"Do you have it all, Montholon?"

"Yes, Sire."

"Now go fetch Bertrand and Marchand."

When all three men stood before him, he said quietly, "I am naming you my executors."

Marchand made an involuntary movement of surprise. Napoleon noted this and he knew why. To the humble valet, this was indeed an honor, and it was well-deserved. Marchand had served him with absolute and unconditional devotion.

Napoleon watched with satisfaction the servant affix his name to the will, a plain monogram next to the arms of two counts of the oldest nobility.

Later, after Montholon and Bertrand had gone, Marchand, who had stayed on to help his master change into fresh and dry clothes said, on the verge of tears, "Your Majesty's confidence overwhelms me. In other circumstances that would have gladdened my heart. But in this situation, if I may make bold to say, Sire, I wish I did not have to be so distinguished."

"You have a noble heart, Marchand."

The valet shook his head. "No, Sire. It just aches."

"I want you to be comfortable," Napoleon rejoined thoughtfully. "When I am gone, I desire that you marry and start a family. I think the daughter of an officer of my Old Guard would be a fine match for you. . . ."

Marchand began to cry. Napoleon gave him an affectionate chuck under the chin. "Now Marchand," he scolded gently. "Is this any way to envisage matrimony?"

"I don't want to get married, Sire!"

"And one must be practical," Napoleon continued. "You will be needing some funds to set up house, buy yourself a little cottage, maybe."

"I don't want anything. I only want to serve you, Sire, to make you comfortable!"

"You are quite a remarkable person," Napoleon said softly. Then he commanded, "Marchand, fetch my belt. The one I brought from Malmaison."

The valet did as he was told.

"Rip open the seam," Napoleon instructed.

As this was done, a dazzling flash of precious light half-blinded the valet.

"Marchand," said Napoleon, "this is your wedding present from me to you."

Marchand stared incredulously at Hortense's magnificent diamond necklace. His tears redoubled. "It's . . . it's splendid, Sire!" he stammered. "But it is too sad a present. It just pains me too much. . . ."

"It pleases me to see you accept it. Can't you believe that?"

Bleary-eyed, Marchand looked at the Emperor and saw a countenance suffused with peace. He is content and so must I be, he told himself.

Indeed, a remarkable serenity had come over Napoleon. His will had been witnessed, signed, and sealed. Now he could wait for death to set him free. . . .

Then the nagging fear of not having done enough, and said enough, transfixed him. How could he rest certain that his son would become an ardent champion and proponent of democratic ideals? This had been a presumption that did not take into account the inevitability of certain ugly proceedings. Proceedings he had to counteract. The boy was too conveniently young and isolated. His still malleable mind was sure to be seeded with the poison of decadent notions such as the principle of legitimacy. This was nonsense! Yet who would impress on the Prince that true legitimacy does not evolve from a family name, but primarily and ultimately resides in the assent of the nation? Had he not himself been *elected* emperor? And would his son, by himself, ever see and recognize the marvel of this? Would he think kindly of his father? What if they were teaching him to abhor him? What if they were going to put into his son's head the notion that he would have to do a lot of atoning for his father's "crimes" so as to earn for himself a "respectable" standing?

Unfortunately, saddles and swords, snuff-boxes, and medals would never adequately convey his father's philosophy. To accomplish this, Napoleon decided to draw up a political testament as well. . . .

Once again he summoned Montholon; this time at three in the morning. The lateness of the hour alarmed the Count, and he hastened to the Emperor's room thinking, This must be the end! He practically ran in.

He found Napoleon sitting in front of the fire.

"I am sorry to have upset you like this, Montholon. I don't feel any worse, really. I have just been thinking. . . ."

"I am glad," panted the Count, sitting down to catch his breath.

In deep thought, Napoleon's hand crept to his throat and his fingers began to toy with a small pouch that hung around his neck. Once it had contained the poison which would have robbed Alexander of the satisfaction of capturing him alive, but it held no such lethal power now. On the contrary, its deadly contents had been replaced with a hope-giving, life-sustaining relic of sorts.

Montholon watched the Emperor carefully loosen the string; and more carefully still, pull out a tiny packet of neatly folded paper, which he unwrapped with trembling hands.

Napoleon stared down with tear-filled eyes at a golden lock of hair still lustrous with vitality. He savored a few seconds of humble triumph recalling how he came to have it.

No system is foolproof and no misery is ever complete. Five years ago the silky lock had made its way to the island in a letter Madame Marchand had addressed to her son. Speaking of that fine strand of hair, she had written, "It's mine, in exchange for a portrait of you. Have it painted soon." But Napoleon's faithful valet knew better. The sheen, the supple, and exquisite texture of that lock could only belong to a young child. When he brought it to his master, Napoleon had wept openly.

Now, as he contemplated his son's lock of hair, he thought of all the possibilities that had been put before him to plan an escape and reflected on his decision to forgo trying them out. Many proposals of evasion hatched by admiring and sympathetic travelers had been secretly submitted to him. In those days, he was still healthy and the risks such enterprises entailed did not discourage him in the least.

Yet to those who would have applauded at reviving the Hundred Days, he did appear somewhat aloof. He had seen some of his secret supporters shake their heads in disappointment because he seemed to eschew the chance to be free. They did not realize that he had carefully weighed the advantages of remaining chained to the rock of St. Helena. Simple observation had demonstrated that there is, in over-exposure, an attenuation and eventually a loss of charisma. His, as a captive, kept all of its potency. He knew himself to be right in creating a mystique from which his son would profit tremendously, a mystique born of the depth of a dereliction that would equal the apogee of his fame.

An evasion, possibly a re-appearance on the international scene, would only disturb the pathos his present fate evoked, a pathos that could only enhance his son's chances instead of discrediting his name. For the boy's sake, he wouldn't act. Enwreathed with the nimbus of his father's martyrdom, his son would have a better chance to be called upon to carry on a work of regeneration so that the seed sown in strife would bear in peace the fruit of a new order.

"This," he said in utter desolation, pressing the lock to his lips, "is all that I ever will see or touch of my little boy!"

Montholon scrambled to his feet. "Sire, you mustn't. . . ." He went over to the bed and placed his hand on Napoleon's arm, pleading, "I pray you to consider that the Prince needs you!"

"It is wise that I die," Napoleon said, convinced of the absolute necessity of a personal immolation. He folded the lock in its protective wrapper and returned it to the pouch. Then his gaze wandered back to the focal point of the dingy room, to his son's bust.

"Look at him, Montholon," he murmured, tears running down his cheeks, "Isn't he absolutely beautiful? *Mon pauvre petit diable*. . . ."

"The fairest child I ever saw, Sire," Montholon agreed, moved himself to tears by the term of endearment the Emperor used, calling his little son "my poor little devil."

"Indeed . . ." said Napoleon. He paused, and a light smile passed over his mouth, hinting at the enormous pride any doting father would have for a lovely child. Then he continued with a contented sigh, "I bet by now those Austrian lasses must have succumbed to his spell!"

Smiling along with the Emperor, Montholon observed, "His Imperial Highness is only ten years old, Sire."

Suddenly Napoleon's countenance darkened. "Do you suppose he remembers me?"

No one knew. The child Menéval had left must have changed. And God alone could tell how much and in what way. Montholon only hoped that somehow the boy would never disappoint his father.

He said, hoping to be right, "He most certainly remembers you, Sire. And may the Good Lord look after him."

Saturated with grandiose tragedies of ancient literature, Napoleon had come to look upon his career as the unfolding of a grand and somber drama in which brilliance and gloom were inextricably joined.

He said gravely, "When you pray, Montholon, pray that my son be set free soon. Remember, the Greeks killed Astyanax."

"Heavens!" cried Montholon, "with due respect, Sire, you are pushing the analogy a little too far!"

Napoleon spread his hand in a gesture that commanded attention, immediately followed by a chilling declaration, "My son . . ." he seemed to be looking into a concrete future, "is destined to be the man of the people. For this reason he will be used as an instrument of intimidation. And if he remains in the clutches of Austria, he will be destroyed! I must guide him, warn him. That is why I wish to draw a political will for him."

Napoleon waited for Montholon to take out paper and ink.

Then he began:

> I do have supporters. Not all of France has rejected me. Therefore my son must not seek to avenge my death. I die so that he may reign in peace. He must not make war for the sake of war in imitation of what I had to do under compulsion. The throne of France should not be so precious to my son as to cause him to ascend its steps with the help of foreign influence and power. He is to remember that no party is so powerful as to entice him to rely on factions for support.
>
> The true gauge of popularity is in the masses. He should never despise the will of the people. He should listen to them through a free press and may he be the selfless exponent of new ideas, of doctrines that are sound, and of principles which are the genuine expression of human dignity. May he be the rallying point of concord throughout Europe. . . .

Twelve pages of lofty counsels. Montholon carefully numbered them while Napoleon, looking somber, stared again into the smoldering fire. His mouth was drawn in a line that expressed anything but satisfaction, and Montholon wondered why. Had he not said everything that needed to be said?

Napoleon had just realized how naive he was. How could he, for one second, entertain the hope that words such as the ones he had finished dictating would ever be of any inspiration to his son? The boy would never be allowed to read them!

Shaking from head to foot, Napoleon made to rise.

Leaping from his chair, Montholon said thoroughly frightened, "I am going to call the doctor."

"I am going to bed," Napoleon rasped. "And I don't need that charlatan to hold my hand!"

"I'll fetch your medicine, then," Montholon suggested, rushing over to help him.

"No good, Montholon." Napoleon clutched at the Count's arm. "You," he said feverishly, "the three of you . . . Bertrand and Marchand . . . I trust you to do it!"

"Do what, Sire?"

"Get to my son . . . directly. If not, he will never know anything of what I've just said."

"Aye, Sire. We will try the impossible!"

Immediately Montholon repented the choice of that last word. Yet, however indelicate it might have sounded, he believed it to express an unfortunate truth. For unless there were a war or some manner of upheaval in the course of which diplomacy could be bypassed, the chances of ever approaching Napoleon's son were practically nil.

Two weeks later, on the fifth of May, death came to Napoleon at sunset. It came attended by a tropical storm of uncommon violence. By contrast, he spoke his last words in a soft slur. He spoke a woman's name, the first to reign over his heart and his empire. He called his army. And he gave his last look to the bust of his little son.

That was at ten past six in the evening.

Tears streaming down his cheeks, Marchand stopped the hands of the mahogany clock.

At long last Hudson-Lowe was given the satisfaction of setting his eyes on a dead General Bonaparte. Disregarding the deceased's wish, the body, following an autopsy, was not shipped back to France, but buried on the spot under six stone slabs and three glazed tiles taken from a cooking stove. Lowe's malevolence pursued his captive beyond the grave when the mention was made that the inscription "Napoleon" alone would suffice for epitaph.

The governor was furious. He countered mordantly that it was going to be "Napoleon Bonaparte" or nothing.

Bertrand bristled saying, "We take you to your word. It shall be nothing. For even then, it will still eloquently say *it all* and *to all!*"

Accordingly, there was no inscription on the grave dug in a secluded valley of the island. For nineteen years it was to remain nameless, with nothing to mark its place but wild geraniums, a nearby spring, and two weeping willows.

17

The news of Napoleon's death reached Europe in the first days of July. Smugly, Metternich said to Francis, "With the death of Bonaparte, Your Majesty can count on the extinction of false hopes and the futility of more conspiracies!"

Francis responded with a staid "We hope so."

Unlike his Chancellor, he did not find it easy to look upon the death of his son-in-law with carefree detachment. A small boy whom he tenderly loved had not yet been told of the loss of his father while for over two weeks the entire staff at Schönbrunn knew of the event though they were ordered to keep quiet about it.

Francis needed time because he found himself in a terrible predicament. Marie Louise had stayed away this year, once again indisposed, so he could not count on her to break the news to Franz. And for all his affection for his grandson, he was incapable of mustering enough courage to discharge himself of this task. He still refused to have anything to do with Napoleon, and did not want to be forced into sharing Franz's grief over the death of the man whom he had consigned to a cruel exile. The very idea made him cringe. That left the Prince's tutors.

That summer, Dietrichstein had been given leave to visit his family. As the boy's deputy tutor, Foresti was the logical alternate; one which the Emperor deemed correct. But he recognized that sending Foresti was a poor choice as news of this sort should be revealed in an atmosphere of love and caring which only close relations can provide.

Francis vacillated, torn between the desire to preserve his own tranquillity and a nagging reluctance to entrust the painful duty of telling the Prince of his father's death to a total stranger whose feelings could not be expected to provide the tender climate of consolation Franz would find instead in the comforting presence of his grandfather.

He finally decided that his own tranquillity would prevail and chose the cowardly way out.

"I don't care," he emphatically told Foresti, "how long it will take you to prepare yourself for this, but the important thing is that the news be broken to the Prince gently. I insist upon this!"

Foresti nodded. He would do his best. He intended to carry out the assignment as smoothly as circumstances permitted.

"I shall tell the Prince at sundown," he announced.

Francis's eyebrows lifted. "Sundown? Why sundown?"

"It is a peaceful and soothing time, Sire."

"Indeed!" Francis hadn't contemplated this alternative, and the fact that Foresti would pick a certain moment showed consideration.

Then Foresti thought of something else he was sure would ease the Emperor's mind. "It might interest Your Majesty to know that according to my observations, the Prince is at this point rather indifferent to the past."

"He has not asked any more questions?"

"Not since last year. And we have managed to keep the subject of General Bonaparte's place of detention from the Prince in spite of his repeated attempts to find out."

"Ah, yes," Francis sighed. "Did he not also think that his father was living in misery?"

"If Your Majesty will recall, this was caused by the Prince overhearing a conversation which, to our dismay, took place between two individuals discussing Napoleon on St. Helena. To the Prince it sounded like our German word for misery, *Elend,* hence the confusion. Somehow this was clarified without giving away the location where the Prince's father was detained nor the conditions in which he lived."

Francis was relieved. "Then everything is under control."

"I do not expect the Prince to be unduly upset by the news," Foresti said confidently.

The Emperor scowled. The well-meaning Captain had offended Francis's sense of decorum. Had he ever instructed that the boy should become so detached from his father as to be totally devoid of filial feelings?

"No child should be indifferent to a parent's passing!" Francis said icily. "I hope your zeal has not caused the Prince to trespass the bounds of decency!"

Foresti protested. "I pray Your Majesty to rest assured that the Christian principles the Prince has been taught to observe would never allow him to default in that respect."

"Well, then," Francis said somewhat appeased, "proceed without undue delay."

But the Emperor's passing concern had just dropped a tiny seed of anxiety into the Captain's mind. Suppose the boy just took the announcement of his father's death dry-eyed, looking merely surprised and pensive at the most?

The Emperor would be furious! And there would be no one else to take the blame but Foresti.

From the window of his apartments on that evening of July 16, 1821, Franz watched a tranquil dusk slowly settle over Schönbrunn park.

So far as he was concerned, the day had been uneventful in the sense that the academic burden placed upon him continued in full force with no relief in sight. It was all Dietrichstein's doing. Franz had overheard the Count saying to Foresti: "I am perfecting for the Prince a course of study that will span ten more years, and of so vast and fearsome a scope that he will have me to thank and remember!"

The way his studies were already progressing made Franz flinch. Since he had forgotten French, he was forced to learn it all over again. Dietrichstein was terribly vexed when Franz could not say a word of greeting in French to Tzar Alexander when the Russian emperor passed through Vienna and came to see him.

After that incident, the Count declared that since no person of good breeding should be ignorant of the French language spoken throughout the courts of Europe, he would make arrangement to give the necessary lessons. Accordingly, two professors native of France, but living in Vienna, were put in charge of "refreshing" Franz's memory. It was also decided that other lessons would be conducted in French as well. So while still struggling to master his native tongue, Franz was learning Latin, Greek, Italian, history, religion, ancient literature, and some elements of strategy and tactics.

Somehow, it was a welcome switch when the distinguished and pompous Professor Baumgartner conducted his classes of natural science, chemistry and physics exclusively in German, as well as the arts which were not forgotten subjects since they were most dear to Dietrichstein. Although he showed remarkable talent in drawing, Franz disappointed the Count most severely in music. He only enjoyed military tunes—anything else left him totally unresponsive. He had no ears for notes, and when he would make an attempt to sing, which was rare, he'd seen his tutor, plug his ears. . . .

Presently, the garden walks were turning pink and the box trees were graying rosily. In the fading blue of the sky, a star—the same Franz saw summer after summer—twinkled.

He heaved a sigh at the prospect of an evening that promised boredom. He did not relish listening to his grandfather make music. Grandfather would most likely tackle pieces by Mozart, and Franz only managed to endure the Emperor's labored virtuosity by having perfected the technique of yawning with his mouth closed. All in all he did not feel terribly unhappy.

Yet in the back of his mind, like a tiny splinter too deeply embedded to be excised, fuzzy memories of his father lingered. He could not remember from his childhood what Napoleon looked like. There was a picture of his father hanging over his bed, but the painted face did not awake any sensation that he really recognized the features. Still, he had the abiding feeling of a deeply caring presence. His tutors seldom, if ever, spoke of Napoleon, and Franz had long ago decided not to ask any more questions. They were always met with evasive answers anyway.

Only the secrecy, the fact that his father and mother were separated, and that he no longer lived in France were circumstances that he could never completely put out of his mind despite all the distractions which attended his daily activities. Naturally, he missed his mother, and with no hope of seeing her that summer: He'd been told she was so overworked that her condition required rest, which a journey to Vienna would severely hamper. . . .

The garden walks were turning gray, and the trees took on what Franz called the color of the night—and so had the room when Foresti entered and found him still daydreaming, leaning on the window casement.

Resolutely, the Captain came forward and proceeded to light the candelabra, while making a mental note to upbraid the servants for their tardiness in providing this service.

At the tutor's entrance, Franz turned halfway to say brief words of greeting. Foresti continued to find him distant and this attitude was not particularly conducive to make his task any easier.

He tried to sound natural. "Did Your Highness find your geography lesson interesting today?" he asked in a manner calculated to ease his pupil into the unpleasant subject at hand.

This time Franz turned full circle to regard him with a mixture of surprise and suspicion. It was not in the Captain's habit to show much interest in what he thought of his lessons.

"I always like geography," he replied truthfully. "It does open many horizons."

Unbearably nervous now, Foresti raced toward his objective. "Your Highness realizes that there are many islands that we have not yet studied."

Franz watched him attentively. Something told him that there was an ulterior motive to this line of conversation. "So there are," he said, and crossed his arms over his chest, waiting.

Wearing long trousers and a jacket, and having grown prodigiously since a bout of the measles, Franz looked older than ten. His posture and the poised inflection in his boyish voice denoted more maturity than the tutor desired.

Foresti wetted his lips and found himself sputtering, "I should like to mention an island in the Atlantic Ocean called St. Helena. It is the place your father and a few chosen friends have been calling their home. . . ."

Franz recoiled toward the window.

The Captain hurriedly went on speaking. "It is a warm place. There is no winter there. But in spite of a mild climate, an illness . . ."

At this instant, the Captain's voice seemed to have faded away. His back turned on his tutor, Franz faced the imperturbable serenity of a star-spangled firmament. Like consoling fingers, a gentle, rose-scented breeze from the garden ruffled his fair hair.

In his clear boy voice, Franz said to the arbors and the fountains, "My dear Papa is dead. . . ."

Intuitively he knew this to be true. Because at long last they spoke of Napoleon and told him *where he was!* His heart sank. What difference did it make now to keep it a secret, unless . . .

Unless!

Franz's heart skipped a beat. What if the illness only meant that his father's condition warranted that he should be taken to him because it was the decent thing to do? Maybe Papa was ill but still alive! How far was St. Helena?

Franz swung round torn between alarm and happy anticipation, but Foresti saw nothing of Franz's hopeful expression. The Captain's eyes were fixed on the parquet and he rushed on with an aching urge to be done with it all, relieved that his pupil had taken the terrible announcement out of his mouth.

"Yes! Your father passed away in a Christian fashion," he said in one breath.

With the news off his chest, the Captain looked up to glimpse his pupil tottering to lean against the window sash.

Stunned with an excruciating sense of loss, Franz stared into the night. The heavens emptied of stars. They all compacted under his lids and liquefied into shimmering tears, which poured down onto the front of his shirt, his hands, soaking them.

"I am sorry," Foresti nearly implored. "Truly sorry. . . !"

Franz could only gasp, drowning in tears. "When?"

"In early May," Foresti said in a low voice.

Franz shuddered violently, feeling irreparably cheated. All this time, while he studied, played, ate, and slept, Papa had quietly closed his eyes on the world and left him for good. *Forever!*

"We shall pray for him," Foresti said with genuine compassion.

The Captain's words brought no comfort. The belief in an afterlife Franz so readily accepted as a matter of faith, lay like a mutilated bird in the hollow of his grief, its wings clipped, never to take flight, never to lift him to heavenly consolations. Paradoxically, the terrible void he experienced smothered him.

Foresti realized that his pupil needed tending. "If I can be of any help . . ." he offered, meaning what he said. And he crossed over intending to put his arms around the grief-stricken boy.

Franz shrank back. Some wounds cannot be tended. His was too profoundly personal to suffer a stranger's intervention. Pressing his hands against his mouth to stifle the sobs, he ran to his bedroom and quietly closed the door behind him.

No one dared enter.

Then when it became very late, Collin, carrying a candelabrum, tiptoed in, dabbing a few tears of his own, weeping over Franz's sorrow. He found the boy sprawled across the bed, motionless. Thank God, Franz had cried himself to sleep! His lashes and cheeks were wet and a tear drop, diamond-like, scintillated in the small hollow at the corner of his mouth.

Next morning, Franz woke to a state of high sensitivity. As soon as his tutors spoke to him, he began to cry all over again and went on weeping nearly without interruption for the rest of the day.

Meanwhile, Francis debated whether or not the Court should go into mourning. Metternich settled the problem by pointing out that it would be improper to give any mark of consideration to an adjudged outlaw. However, to accommodate a minimum of decency, it was decided that the young Duke of Reichstadt and the members of his household could wear black on the condition that they refrain from appearing in public.

Still reeling from the shock of his father's death, Franz walked about, head down, and spoke only when spoken to. Often during his lessons, his attention would leave him completely and he would stare into space with a faraway look. At such times, his tutors had the unpleasant sensation that their toil and dedication had suffered a setback. In grief, Franz seemed to drift into a mood they feared might be dangerous.

Franz also ached from grieving all alone. His heart would not have felt so unbearably heavy had he been able to cry in his mother's arms and mingle his tears with hers. A week had passed, and still no word had come from Parma. He wondered if his mother was sad, too. Or did she know yet?

Finally, in the last week of July, Franz heard from Marie Louise. At this point, though, the letter he was about to open did not do much to lessen his hurt. The stress of a prolonged solitary state of bereavement had put him beyond the reach of the comfort he longed to find in a special message from her.

Besides, his tutors would not let him read her letter in privacy. They insisted that it be read aloud, in their presence. Franz faulted them for having no compassion, no respect for his feelings and no mercy. . . .

So he read Marie Louise's letter without showing emotion, and not much of what she wrote could elicit any. But Dietrichstein gave signs of transport when Franz came to a passage in which his mother wrote that although it would be commendable for her son to remember the kindness his papa had shown him during his infancy, the resolve never to follow the example of Napoleon would be even more praiseworthy.

"Ah!" Dietrichstein enthusiastically exclaimed at this, "your mother is positively genial and her affection for you is admirable!" He turned beaming to Collin and Foresti. "Isn't Her Majesty absolutely adorable and wise?"

In unison they responded, "Most adorable and wise!"

Franz said nothing. He just felt numb.

Dietrichstein was never so perky. "May this letter," he said positively glowing, "be a model upon which to base your conduct! You should read it over and over again and thank Providence for giving you so perfect a mother!"

Franz remained silent with a distant stare again, and the Count's good humor soured. Was his pupil questioning that statement?

Seeing Dietrichstein's lips compressed in displeasure, Collin decided to speak for the Prince. "His Highness is well aware of Her Majesty's goodness, aren't you Franz?"

"I love my mother," Franz murmured feeling the sentiment was too precious to share.

Dietrichstein's mood brightened anew. "I should hope so!" Then he took the letter from Franz and began folding it quasi-religiously for safekeeping. "You will write presently to Her Majesty," he added.

Franz nodded, but the "presently" was drawn out to a fortnight. Finally, Franz confided to Collin, "I don't know what to say to my mother."

Collin asked, after allowing a silence for careful deliberation, "Is it so difficult to express that which your heart feels?"

"Yes," Franz confessed, surprising himself. He found his mother's expression of grief so composed and so rational! She would never understand his sorrow unless he could present it in the same fashion. He could never tell her about the tender fragments he remembered, however dimly, of his childhood impressions—his papa's wonderful smile, the way his eyes filled with love when he looked into them, the strong arms that held him, the kisses and the games; the fellowship and the constant attention his papa gave him at every available occasion. Other than those things, what could he tell his mother?

"Could you please help me write this letter maybe?" he almost pleaded.

Collin agreed. He understood. He even enrolled the services of Foresti with Franz's assent. Foresti was very good at composing fine, proper letters, and the whole thing would be kept secret between the three of them.

Going over the finished letter, Dietrichstein declared:

"These are not your ideas. And what an atrocious handwriting!"

"That's my third draft," Franz answered.

"Still atrocious!"

"My last draft, too," Franz said flatly.

"You will send *this* to Her Majesty?" Dietrichstein asked incredulously.

"This or nothing!" And the tone of Franz's voice left no room for argument.

"*Herr Gott!*" Dietrichstein never swore, and never let Franz have his way. Now he swore because Franz's imperious streak came as a vexing revelation.

And the letter was sent just the way it was.

Nevertheless, Dietrichstein did not consider himself beaten. Instead, he took upon himself to institute a course of remedial penmanship. So over and over, Franz was made to write a sentence which the Count thought suited his pupil admirably: *"I know my duties but neglect to fulfill them."*

When Marie Louise read her son's letter, she found it pleasingly adequate. The Count had added a note pointing out the poor handwriting and apprised her of the corrective actions he had taken, quoting the edifying phrase that went along with the exercise. At this, Marie Louise cringed a little.

Speaking of duties. . . .

She could not face in good conscience her years of adulterous relations with Neipperg and the birth of the children born out of wedlock. But at long last, four months after Napoleon's death, she and Neipperg were married. Francis did not dissimulate his surprise while giving his consent, and stressed that Franz be spared the news of his mother's early re-marriage "for the time being" as he had put it.

Marie Louise was growing weary and resentful at the thought of having to tailor her private life to the susceptibility of her son. Franz had no valid reasons to exact from her any more demands. He was titled now and surrounded with honor. Learned men looked after him and numerous servants waited on him. He lived in the luxury and glamour of the court and was his grandfather's darling. Rather, her heart went out to Albertine and William. They were the ones who needed her most for their station in life would be modest and tainted by illegitimacy.

In the summer of 1823, Franz's appreciation at seeing his mother surpassed all the gratitude he may have had for the elaborate dispositions taken for his welfare. When he finally loosened the ring of his arms from around her neck, he gazed lovingly at the woman who, unbeknownst to him, now bore Neipperg's name.

He had not seen her in two, long, and lonely sorrow-filled years. She was approaching thirty-two; many lines had appeared at the corner of her eyes; her complexion was no longer so clear and her jaw lines blended into the shortening stem of her neck. But he saw none of those things. Her presence was all he cared about.

Marie Louise found him much grown for being only twelve. And so very fervent!

To evade the tender scrutiny of a pair of worshipful eyes, she drew his head to her bosom and ran her fingers comb-like through his short, thick curls which felt silken to the touch.

"You should not miss me so much!" she said reproachfully.

Franz threw his head back and looked at her with an expression of pained incredulity. Instantly Marie Louise realized she must have scandalized him by suggesting such restraint, knowing the way he felt about her.

He said gently, "I do miss you. And I understand the heavy responsibilities you have running your duchy; and how difficult it must be for you to stay by yourself in Parma. Would it help you to know how much I am aware of your unhappiness?"

He noticed a sudden pallor spreading over her cheeks.

Marie Louise imagined herself being put through the inquisition of a heavenly tribunal, and God had the face of her son! His eyes were Franz's eyes, dazzling blue and pure. Their innocence transfixed her, wounding her serenity. Was God using her child's devotion to exhume her faults?

She said weakly, "Franz, you may not see me again for perhaps another two years."

Immediately the lights went out of his eyes. He looked away, and his voice came muffled: "I see."

This upset her. Would he go on tormenting her on the subject of their separation? It could not be helped! Yet every time, his pain seemed to indict her.

A touch of annoyance crept into her tone. "Did you not promise me to accept this situation gracefully?"

Franz remembered making such a promise in a letter he wrote when she hadn't come last year. He nodded. Then on a sudden inspiration he proposed, "Can't I go to Parma with you? Just for a little while?"

Heaven forbid!

"No, Franz," she said flatly. "Your grandfather desires that you remain in Vienna. Princes of your importance receive a better education by staying at court."

Franz frowned, thinking. He was not aware of being even as important as his uncles and cousins who seemed to be able to go wherever they pleased. Moreover, he detected a certain inconsistency in his mother's declaration. For if he were to spend his holiday in Parma, there could be no question under such condition of his education suffering any setback, seeing that he was enjoying an academic intermission anyway.

"I mean," he said, wishing to clarify this point, "I could go there only for the summer, if for some reason you cannot come here." Why hadn't anyone thought of that? he wondered.

Marie Louise was sorry Franz had. Disconcerted, she blurted out, "That is impossible!"

"Why, Mother?" he asked puzzled. It was a such a perfect and simple solution.

"Because. . . ." Her mind reeled, an empty spool that spun sheer panic. It pricked her cheeks like those Parmesan mosquito bites, and she likened her discomfort to their noisome sting. The analogy quite unexpectedly gave her a reason.

"Because Parma," she declared with more vehemence than she would have cared to project, "is not at all pleasant in the summer. It's dreadfully hot and you might catch a fever there because of the mosquitoes!"

Franz pondered that answer. The way it had been delivered did not really convince him. A few years ago maybe. But now, it did not sound quite right. He began to experience the odd sensation of fitting into some particular and yet unclear dimension.

With resignation, he said, "Well, whatever the reason, it is plain that we cannot be together."

"Don't take it like that, Franz!"

"How else?" he asked with a touch of frustration.

"Really, dear, you are not making it easier for either of us!"

Had she not sounded so argumentative, sharp at times, had she not given him the impression that she found their situation quite acceptable and in no need of alteration, he would have felt somewhat better. . . .

He had to ask. "Mother, do you love me?"

Franz saw a flicker of confusion pass over his mother's face, a face she promptly hid against his shoulder as she pulled him to her in a display of effusion he had never yet seen. Her voice combined indignation with considerable warmth. "Franz, you are impossible!" she complained, and caressed him as she would have William.

When Marie Louise left at the beginning of September, Franz never felt so miserable. Nothing that reminded him of his mother was of any consolation. On the contrary, the sight of a flower she had given him only aggravated his sadness.

Then another loss, added to his pain that winter—Collin suddenly died of a stroke. Franz mourned the passing of a dear friend. And it seemed as though fate had decreed the systematic elimination of all those he cherished and trusted.

18

"How can I possibly marry that imbecile?" thought the nineteen-year-old Bavarian princess on her way to wed the son of the Emperor of Austria, twenty-two-year-old Archduke Francis Charles.

Lining the streets to watch the bridal cortege on that bright and cold day of November, 1824, the people of Vienna cheered. They could only assume that she was happy. She waved and smiled graciously at her well-wishers from behind the glass-plated window of her gilded carriage.

Under the smile, Sophie of Bavaria hid a gamut of unpleasant emotions: distaste for her husband-to-be, frustration at being utterly helpless to change her lot, and resentment for having to submit to the inescapable bondage attached to her gender. She would gladly have traded her marriage for a secluded life in a nunnery had that alternative been available to her.

No such option had been proffered. Princesses got married on command and for convenience. Accordingly, Sophie was ordered to put aside all resistance and wed her intended for the good of her House.

"Now, look at Charlotte," her father, Maximilian, had said when Sophie did not conceal her reluctance upon learning of the match, "she went through with it. Didn't she?"

Poor Charlotte! Her marriage to Francis of Austria only demonstrated that Bavaria was marrying its princesses to ruling monarchs whenever possible, whether they liked it or not. Now it was Sophie's turn. Caring nothing for a marriage without love let alone respect for the groom, Sophie did try to trap her ambitious father in his own logic. And so it went: Since her half-sister had become Empress of Austria, why should she, Sophie, have to marry a dull archduke who would not even succeed his father because his brother, Ferdinand, was first in the line of succession anyway?

"Would you prefer to marry Ferdinand then?" Maximilian teased mercilessly.

Sophie had shrunk in horror. The Habsburgs' occasional visits at the Bavarian Court had acquainted her with Francis's sons. The pitiable sight of the crown prince uttering disjointed phrases and displaying an embarrassing mixed-up behavior made his brother, Francis Charles, look more acceptable, although she found him less than passably intelligent, disgustingly coarse, and insufferably arrogant. But at least he was *compos mentis*. "No," she had said, vanquished, "I'll marry Charles."

Whereupon, to impress upon her the weigh of a quasi-international entente, Maximilian told her that her marriage to the archduke had been long ago foreordained by the Congress of Vienna. Still, that left Sophie unmotivated. All she knew was that she was forced to bend before her father's will, and by extension God's.

But she was not done fighting—fighting her own reluctance. She would renounce happiness with militant resignation. Profoundly pious, Sophie embraced the Roman Catholic religion with passionate zeal, yet a docile acceptance of the crosses—light or heavy—that went along with her steadfast adherence to the tenets of her faith ran counter to her grain.

So she had decided to take the unpleasantness of her marriage as a challenge and strove to overcome her dissatisfaction with equal ardor and determination. She would be gracious in her misfortune and turn it into an appreciable success. Her resources, she knew, would help her in that endeavor. Short of fulfilling her romantic inclinations, the aridity of her marriage would be offset by dedicating herself to raising her children while giving free expression to other traits in her character, without shirking her duties as consort. With a nature that was dutiful, tender, gay, and warm, and with a love of poetry, music, and the theater, Sophie faced her married life with the reasonable assurance that it would not be totally unbearable.

Moreover she had already found a soul mate.

While growing up in Bavaria, Sophie knew of Napoleon's son's cloistered life at Francis's court, and of the peculiar situation in which politics had placed him. When she finally met the son of her father's one-time benefactor during the bustle of the wedding preparations, the youngster's character and personality delighted her. She thought him the model of a perfect prince—grace, good looks, exquisite manners, intelligence, wit, sensitivity, and originality. He stood out from amongst his Austrian relatives to such a striking degree that Sophie found him much too different to really ever fit, just like herself, in a milieu that she discovered lacked taste, humor, and imagination. A friendship already flourished between them, and she knew the friendship would last forever.

Presently, the thought of the thirteen-year-old boy who would soon become her nephew by marriage, comforted her. Heartened, Sophie's smile was no longer forced. But her arm began to cramp from the non-stop waving at the cheering crowd. She folded her hands on her lap, and leaning back, let her eyes rest upon the homely face of Empress Carolina Augusta seated opposite her.

The Empress had been studying her with simple, good-hearted envy. She imagined their physical dissimilarities must have been caused by the fact that they were related only through one parent. It was more than evident to Carolina Augusta that she was the one short-changed. Everything about her was plain and nondescript, even the color of her hair. It was not really brown, yet not fair. Whereas Sophie had grown into a comely young woman, sensibly tall and gracefully proportioned. She was favored with liquid doe eyes, a fine and straight nose, and a small mouth with delicately outlined lips. Her hair was lustrous and of a rich brown color that had a glimmer of copper in it, and her neck was slender and graceful like that of a swan.

But the Empress noticed that on this, her wedding day, Sophie did not display the effervescent radiance generally observed in young women about to be married. And as a caring half-sister to her future daughter-in-law, she asked, "Are you happy?"

Having made up her mind, Sophie answered, "I will be happy."

At the ball that concluded the wedding festivities, the Marquis of Caraman could do no better than nervously chew on his appetizing canapé. His anxiety reflected the very mood of his country, France.

France had a new king now. Louis the Eighteenth had died that year without leaving a direct issue, and his brother, the Count of Artois, ascended the throne under the name of Charles X. Charles, with utmost diligence, pledged to support Metternich's relentless efforts to stifle all liberal movements.

In view of France's cooperative attitude, Charles's ambassador, the Marquis himself, had been cordially invited to the wedding of the Austrian Emperor's son and given all manner of assurances that the monarchic regime of France had nothing to fear from the Bonapartists.

Yet the Marquis could not shrug off a feeling of extreme uneasiness. For one thing, since Napoleon's death, and despite the assumed name of "Reichstadt," his son had become an object of international concern. In Paris, pictures of him were being clandestinely sold in vast quantities and reprinted faster than they could be confiscated by the royal gendarmes.

Moreover, since the uncovering of a plot that purposed to abolish the monarchy in France and proclaim the empire with young Reichstadt as emperor, the French king slept fitfully.

Something else bothered the French ambassador. Since the beginning of the reception, he had not ceased to observe Reichstadt, who was, as expected, the cynosure of all eyes. The Marquis himself could not help but admire at length the youth's good-looks, his elegance in movement, and the poise with which he deported himself, but it was his mature appearance that rattled Caraman. He half-choked swallowing his hors d'oeuvre at the realization that Napoleon's son was fast approaching the moment when his mind would inevitably wake to the call of dangerous thoughts.

Caraman's apprehension took another twist as he watched the Emperor of Austria approach his grandson and drape his arm around the Duke's shoulders in an unmistakable display of affection.

"A touching sight, don't you think?"

Caraman gave a start and turned, nearly bumping into Metternich, who had come up from behind him undetected.

Metternich was also surveying the scene with private misgivings. A few things about Reichstadt were seriously worrying him. Count Deitrichstein's written observations on his pupil—observations which constituted an increasingly voluminous dossier over which Metternich kept poring with intensifying attention—attested to a willfulness that boded no good.

To make matter worse, the professors reported that the young Duke cared little for frivolous pastimes. His mind, they said, turned most naturally to serious subjects, which he would research and explore thoroughly. His curiosity was all-encompassing and he acted much older than his age.

Armed with that information, Metternich braced himself to face greater difficulties than he could have envisaged, and he cursed Franz's heredity on the father's side. His task would have been considerably easier had Napoleon's son taken after his vapid mother and been contented with a life of ease and dissipation.

And then there was another matter that continued to trouble Metternich, a matter which Caraman presently voiced for him. "His Majesty seems to hold the Duke in great favor."

"So you have noticed," Metternich admitted dryly.

"Under the present circumstances I find it most . . ." Caraman hesitated to say "alarming" and chose instead, "interesting that His Majesty would bestow so great a sympathy on . . . should I say it?"

Metternich's eyes narrowed. "By all means do."

"Well, on an object of such contention."

"A bone in your throat and in ours as well."

Caraman was startled by the Chancellor's blunt observation.

"Your Excellency says it so well!" he blurted out with an approving nod.

Metternich put in aggressively. "And you are saying that His Majesty's good grace toward His Highness is not in keeping with our policy. Are you not?"

"I mean no offense . . ."

Metternich's expression grew stern, almost menacing. "You are vexingly forgetful that the stability of your government rests solely on the Emperor's fondness for the Duke, a fondness that is naturally expressed by his desire that the Prince remains with him. I suggest that your government cultivate this desire!"

Caraman made an appeasing movement of the hand, protesting, "I would never contest that. But what kind of precautions have you taken to guarantee that His Majesty's wish to keep the Prince will be . . . respected?"

"The Duke is very well . . . looked after," Metternich replied, understanding the allusion.

"How well, Excellency?"

Metternich wondered, How well, indeed? Reichstadt's tutors and servants had sworn to keep an eye on the Prince's activities. Even his relations engaged in performing that service. The imperial police possessed a very good description of him, so he could never escape physically. . . . But what of his mind? Would the trammel-net of his education hold up against the push and pull of external influences?

But he only replied, "The Duke is under constant surveillance, I assure you."

Waltzing with Franz eased the mounting panic that took hold of Sophie when she had danced earlier with her husband. She had to tilt up her head to look him in the eyes.

"I assure you I'd rather dance with you than with any of those gentlemen!" she said smiling.

Franz sighed, "In spite of my lack of years?"

"With your lack of years, Franz, well compensated by your height!"

Franz sighed more deeply. "Perhaps! But I wish I were older!"

"Why?"

"Youth is said to be shallow."

"Well, let me fathom you just as you are!"

Franz's gilded brows came together. "Do I interest you that much?"

Her sprightly expression changed to gentle contemplation. There was not a trace of self-importance in this boy; no vanity despite the complimentary attention being paid to him in society. She could not recall having met any individual more modest and mindful of others, or more fascinating to be with!

"You interest me immensely," she responded seriously.

"Then I am not such an insignificant fellow?"

"You could never be insignificant. And least of all, to me!"

Franz turned his head to the side trying to conceal a rush of overwhelming emotion. There was something terribly heady in discovering that he could be of importance to someone already very special to him. Somehow it displaced the dregs of lonely years.

Until now he had had no one with whom he could talk to heart-to-heart, trust, laugh with, or feel accepted by. And the only person he could count on now as a friend was Sophie! He thought her beautiful and found she was clever. She had a great sense of humor and was kind and sincere. He felt she was God-sent. And he feared losing all self-control and making a spectacle of himself by weeping for joy.

He steered her to the precarious privacy of a corner of the ballroom, and there, under hangings and surrounded by potted plants, let his arms fall away without daring to look at her and started to turn away, not from her, but from his own inability to cope with her caring declaration.

Gently, she caught him by the sleeve and in a manner which showed that she understood, took his face between her hands and turned it towards hers, "Franz, don't ever be uneasy with me," she told him gravely.

"I am not used to . . . to being . . . meaningful," he stammered, the wound of his separation from Marie Louise lancing him anew and casting doubt on his self-worth. For if his mother did not think well enough of him to visit him at least every year, who would?

"I know what you mean," she said softly, correctly assuming that his abandonment, of which she was aware, must have profoundly affected him. For a few seconds, she studied him, thinking how much alike they were in their own respective sphere—self-reliant and isolated. And since they were now kindred, for the first time since they had met, she took him to her and embraced him.

While a marvelous harmony existed between Reichstadt and Sophie, Dietrichstein's persistence at being unbending and critical only succeeded in alienating himself from his pupil. More inhibited than ever, Franz presented his tutors an impenetrable exterior that became a reef upon which the Count repeatedly wrecked all his efforts at taming a boy he deemed insolent, lazy, and devious.

Dietrichstein's ideas of what constituted the Duke's deficiencies were alarming. Listening to his complaints, Marie Louise, in faraway Parma, formed a rather distressing picture of her son's character. Franz, it appeared, was unfeeling, rebellious, and insufferably fastidious about the clothes he wore. He also seemed to have some warped notion of personal freedom which, according to the tutor, was the source of all the boy's "vices" and "contumacious behavior."

In the month that followed the death of Collin, Joseph Obenaus, appointed to replace the professor, corroborated emphatically the criticisms Dietrichstein had directed against the Prince. He treated Franz with undiscriminating harshness and severity.

Franz retaliated the only way he knew how: Poor performance. Obenaus vented his exasperation in a carrying voice, which made the servants press their ears to the door.

"You can't make me believe that you are a dunce!"

"You may believe what you want," Franz shot back.

"It's sheer wickedness that is prompting you to do so poorly on this assignment! None of the rules you seemed to have perfectly mastered have been observed! Do you want the world to laugh at you?"

"The world couldn't care less about my breaking a few grammatical rules."

His face turning red, then purple, Obenaus bellowed.

"Go on then! Stagnate in mediocrity! Bring shame upon your name! Disgrace yourself, if that amuses you!"

"I don't intend to amuse myself at my own expense, sir."

Obenaus made a contemptuous snorting sound.

"And you should know that," added Franz.

The master drew himself up. "I know nothing about you," he countered accusingly. "Nor do I perceive what Your Highness's intentions are, given the repugnance you seem to have in communicating your ideas!"

Franz took a long look at his professor. Then he said seriously, "My ideal is to be another Prince Eugene."

Obenaus's mouth fell open. The Duke had said something quite remarkable and very encouraging. If Reichstadt so sought to identify himself with Prince Eugene, then his tutors' labors were well-directed. The Duke could not have picked a better role model than the illustrious Prince of Savoy, who had fallen away from allegiance to France in the course of a dispute with King Louis the Fourteenth. Eugene was the perfect and often cited exemplar of valor! He was an expatriate who eloquently demonstrated that a French-born nobleman—Eugene was born in Paris in 1663—had in fact renounced the country of his birth to serve Austria with steadfast zeal and devotion. The Duke's desire to emulate such a brilliant military figure was the epitome of good sense. Something could be done with him after all!

Obenaus's tone softened. "I can't deny that Your Highness will be called to play an important role in Austria. Your education is designed to prepare you for this. It is not too late to reassess your attitude toward learning."

Franz thought, Is the world really watching what I am doing?

He ventured out of his shell, "What do people think of me?"

Obenaus did not answer at once. Only after a few seconds of staring at his pupil's face he said, "Outwardly . . . Your Highness raises favorable comments."

Then he immediately lifted a finger in warning, and gruffly scolded. "On the other hand, you must be wary of flatteries, which are the scourge of princes. It is the inner person that Your Highness must cultivate." After a pause he challenged, "Now, how do you feel about yourself. . . . Give me an honest evaluation!"

Obenaus had lapsed into his familiar provocative style and that put Franz on the defensive. Had the tutor's mood not shifted, his pupil would have admitted that he needed guidance versus criticisms, understanding instead of being accused of insubordination.

"Well, are we thinking?" Obenaus asked impatiently.

Obenaus's face reminded Franz of some busy nuts-gathering rodent. Well, he might not like what he was about to collect!

"Answer me!" Obenaus insisted with irritation.

Franz flung the answer to his tutor, head high, with a clear and assured ring in his voice, just as another sweet voice had inspired him. "In truth, sir, I feel quite outstanding!"

"Franz, did you really tell him that?" Sophie asked, laughter in her voice.

There was laughter, too, in Franz's life since his aunt had become a part of it. "Certainly," he chuckled. "And to my sin, the man absolutely hates me now!"

Sophie clapped her hands, feeling the same lightheartedness she experienced in her girlhood after having played a good prank. Then with the same spontaneity, she hugged her nephew saying with lively warmth, "Oh, I do love you!"

Franz hugged her back not yet believing what he had heard. For as far as he could remember, no one had said to him "I love you."

And it had to be Sophie. . . .

Sophie did something for Franz that Marie Louise had not done—she mothered him and took an interest in everything he cared to share with her. Together they went to plays and to the operas, rode on horseback or went for a drive in her carriage. She read poetry to him and he talked of becoming a fine soldier. He discovered that she was infinitely wise, tolerant, and patient. He had found a companion of esteemed quality.

Then for the first time, she brought warmth to the celebration of his fourteenth birthday. Franz's upbringing by an all masculine staff had successfully dulled much of the susceptibility that so wounded him in the beginning when he had to face, as a matter of course, the repeated absences of his mother on his birthday. He was still deeply hurt by Marie Louise's failure to visit him the year Sophie's marriage took place.

Somehow, his aunt's caring observance of his birthday painfully revived the feeling of abandonment. Sophie was quick to detect this, whereas nobody else noticed anything because no one cared for Franz the way she did. His snips of melancholy mood made her sad beyond words. And words did not come easily to her when she had to broach a sensitive subject.

She tried her best to tell Franz as naturally as she could that she would soon be going to Mantua and meet Marie Louise there. Did he have anything he wished to say to her?

Franz tried to sound composed but only succeeded in saying woodenly, "Tell her I miss her. Tell her to come this summer . . . if at all possible."

With a lump in her throat, Sophie promised to deliver Franz's message.

As if this had become a too familiar refrain, Marie Louise once again declined to come to Vienna for the summer, having terminated another pregnancy with a miscarriage, which of course was not mentioned as the cause for her decision to stay away.

But Sophie returned from Italy with matters for thoughts she carefully kept to herself. Her meeting with her sister-in-law had sadly enlightened her. No admissions, or even passing reflections of any kind on the part of Marie Louise were needed to open her eyes; it was rather her silence, her inconceivably insouciant, self-centered behavior which betrayed her.

Franz, upon learning that he was not to see his mother that summer, took the news badly. Opening up and divulging feelings he had never voiced to anyone, he told Sophie of his pain half-choking on the words, "I have not seen her in two years . . . and *it always hurt* . . . You don't know *how much!*"

Sophie could well imagine. His sensibility, as she had discovered, made him all the more susceptible to his mother's unforgivable neglect. She was appalled by Marie Louise's infrequent visits to her son, having discreetly acquainted herself with their occurrences. In all the years she had lived in Parma, Marie Louise had seen Franz only three times!

Sophie put her arms around him. "I know it's been a while . . ." Then anger flooded her. And the tone of her voice conveyed an implacable demand for redress. Her lips brushing against the fine golden fuzz which had begun to appear on the sides of his cheeks, she said, "Next year, dearest, she *will* come!"

19

When Marie Louise saw her son in June of 1826, she could not believe her eyes. The extraordinary transformation caused her to doubt the reality of their meeting.

Slender, a head taller than Dietrichstein, who stood beside him, a radiant youth wearing an elegant double-breasted dress coat and trousers with underfoot straps briskly strode toward her. Though clean shaven, golden sideburns reached to the edge of a high collar held rigidly against his cheeks by an artfully knotted white cravat. This completely upset the image of the boy of twelve Marie Louise remembered from her last visit.

"Franz?" she wondered out loud.

He held her in a tight clasp and assured her between kisses, "Yes, Mother. It is I!"

His voice had broken; verging on a baritone with a warm and rich resonance that was so precociously virile for a fifteen-year-old that she was disconcerted.

"Franz, you are smothering me . . ." she protested weakly, feeling awkward as though this effusion came from a strange boy.

He apologized and let go of her while she continued to stare at him, her mouth half-open. His features had shed their childish beauty, becoming instead more defined in their perfection. She found him incredibly handsome.

"I have grown since you last saw me," he said with a gentle hint of reproach. "I hope to have become wiser, too, for your comfort."

She gave him an uncertain smile, not knowing what he exactly meant and only hoped that the comfort of which he spoke would conform to her desire to see him well-established and contented with his situation.

During their holiday she was pleased to observe that Franz appeared to have passively settled into his role of a perfect archduke as he kept harping away on his ambition to serve Austria like Prince Eugene. To her immense satisfaction, the tutors told her that her son referred to the French as the "enemy" in his essays on historical events and assured her that years of relentless indoctrination had numbed his childhood love for his father.

They further called her attention to the positive result of such indoctrination by pointing out that his attitude toward Napoleon was one of objective awareness. Franz gave every indication that he felt quite comfortable with the notion that his father was an extraordinarily gifted tactician whose excessive lust for power caused much sufferings and brought about his own ruin. He did not exhibit any signs of feeling any affinity with Napoleon's tremendous impact on history.

In a private conversation with her father, Marie Louise's peace of mind was complete when he told her that in view of her son's cooperative attitude, his own apprehension of seeing him grow into an inquisitive manhood had considerably eased. "Franz considers Austria his motherland," Francis told her smugly. "And no other powers can dispute this!"

Until that incident in August.

While still on holiday in Persenbeug, Franz was riding in an open carriage with his great-uncle Archduke Louis when someone from the crowd lining the roadside managed to toss a small parcel which happened to land on Louis's lap. As Franz was looking the other way, Louis promptly hid it under his coat and secretly brought his find to the Emperor.

When the parcel was opened, it revealed a tricolor cockade and a message in which Reichstadt was accorded the title of "Sire". It invited him to return to France with the assurance that thirty million subjects were waiting to welcome him home and closed on a lyrical phrase: "*I have come to present Your Majesty with the morning star!*" There was no signature.

Deeply shaken, Francis groaned, "This is awful! Absolutely awful!"

Everyone present pulled a long face. The town of Persenbeug was thoroughly searched and all the frontier guards alerted, but the conspirator whom Archduke Louis described as young and elegantly dressed, seemed to have vanished.

The minister of the imperial police said, "We do know who the man is, Sire. His name is Joseph Romain Doudeuil and he paints houses."

"But you have not caught him!" Francis lamented.

"The French authorities will, Your Majesty."

Later Francis learned that Doudeuil had been indeed apprehended by the French royal gendarmes upon his return to France and sentenced to spend two years locked up in the fortress of Ham for conspiring to overthrow the French monarchy.

Francis was only mildly pleased at the news. A chink had appeared of which he should be wary: his beloved grandson, for all his good intentions and innocence, would go on inciting what Metternich had hoped would not happen: a revival of "false hope."

And that was a jarring awakening.

Kept in complete ignorance of the interest he inspired, Franz felt now at home right where he was, in Austria. He had no inkling of occupying an ambiguous position in the politics of his time, nor was he aspiring after any lost rights to be reclaimed. He only concentrated on getting through the complex transition of changing from a boy to an adult.

Growing too rapidly—he had gained twelve centimeters in one year—he seemed to be plagued by colds and chills, for which Dietrichstein held him personally responsible. "If you weren't standing as you so often do, with your shoulders all hunched up," he grumbled, "you would be healthier because your breathing would improve."

Franz retorted that there was nothing wrong in the way he breathed, and that his posture would definitely thrill the Count if he could be given a uniform to wear! There, he had touched upon a subject the tutor considered in much need of redress.

At fifteen, Reichstadt had not yet been appointed colonel of a regiment, whereas, according to custom, that promotion was commonly conferred on archdukes barely thirteen years of age. In all fairness, the Duke deserved such recognition as his knowledge in military science was already quite remarkable.

Reichstadt's serenity in the face of this great injustice done to his talents, infuriated Dietrichstein. But Franz was not envious of others. He had promised himself to merit all distinctions even if this demanded twice the time to be recognized. Rather than boast a rank he had not earned, he much preferred to appear retrograde. So while the Count fumed, he waited patiently.

Waiting had become a way of life for Franz. And waiting again for

Marie Louise in the summer of the following year renewed an exercise in forbearance that went without recompense. She found some pretext to stay in Parma, and Franz managed to control his disappointment. But his sadness, because of his maturity, assumed a more wounding quality.

He spent the summer of 1827 in Baden without Marie Louise with fatalistic resignation and consoled himself with the prospect of enjoying Sophie's company while avoiding that of her husband, if at all possible. Except this once.

Archduke Francis Charles held on to his seat as he had never done before only because Franz was the one driving a team of four horses at an infernal speed.

After another hair-raising turn he cautioned, "Franz, I don't think you should go this fast!"

His eyes on the road, Franz smiled, but did not slow down.

"What are you trying to do? Kill us?" Francis Charles's voice had risen to a falsetto.

Franz laughed and said glancing up at the dusky sky, "That's so prosaic! Can't you see? We are riding through heavenly prairies on the chariot of Apollo. We are herding that bright star called the sun to bed! This shall be accomplished just in time for supper!"

Sophie's husband glimpsed his nephew's profile etched against the backdrop of a glorious sunset whose slanting rays put a halo about his head. Franz's allusion to the young sun-god Apollo's mythical chore could not have found a more entrancing illustration. But in the grip of a mounting terror, all Francis Charles saw was a mad youth about to have them both killed. "Damn your lyricism, Franz!" he shouted. "If you don't slow down, there won't be any supper!"

Franz cast a quick glance at his uncle. What an unimaginative fellow! He could never expect to have any fun with him. But he was Sophie's husband. Franz never thought of Francis Charles as Sophie's spouse in its literal sense. He considered him more like something that was part of her possessions, like a piano, or a pet. As far as Franz was concerned, Sophie just kept his uncle around, and for her sake, his welfare was paramount. He could not be responsible for damaging his aunt's property by breaking Francis Charles's skull or his neck, whichever came first.

"Very well," he relented. "We are going home *au trot*, and nothing is going to happen to us."

But something went quite wrong when later, Franz sat down to supper. Luminous spots flashed before his eyes like exploding stars and the whole room seemed to be turning upside down. Frantically he gripped the tablecloth. A glass nearby tottered, spilling its contents before Sophie could prevent this from happening. Instinctively, she had reached out and tried to steady Franz instead. When he felt her hand take a firm hold of his arm, his equilibrium returned somewhat.

"What has he been up to this time?" Francis asked to no one in particular, yet to everyone in general.

Francis Charles put in testily, "Driving the carriage in which we rode like the devil was after us! I didn't think we'd come back alive!"

"You shouldn't have let him," Sophie reproached gently.

"Easier said than done!" Francis Charles retorted with irritation.

All eyes were on Franz. He was taking shallow breaths, head bent forward, swaying a little. Empress Carolina Augusta left her chair and came up to him to feel his brow.

"Poor little dear," she concluded. "You should go lie down."

Struggling to regain an air of normalcy, Franz straightened. Humiliation burned his cheeks. The Empress had failed to adjust her speech and mannerism to the progress of her favorite archduke's growth, and she talked to him as if he were a crybaby.

Protesting with all the manly eloquence his sixteen years could muster, he said, "Absolutely not! I am just a little tired. This will pass!" Then, smiling wanly, he proceeded to unfold his napkin.

Concerned, Sophie watched him closely. This sort of malaise in one so young must signal something was amiss, something that should be taken care of. To her relief, Francis intervened.

"Franz," the Emperor ordered in a tone that admitted no discussion, "go immediately to your room! I shall send the doctor anon."

Biting down on his lip, Franz slowly rose to his feet and strode away from the table with a slight lurch, energetically refusing the helping arm of a footman.

Doctor Straudenheim found him stretched fully dressed on his bed and in a bad mood. At the sight of the physician, he rolled over on his stomach and buried his face in the pillow. He was furious at himself. Questions were going to be raised as to the general fitness of the future commander of a regiment! It was such a stupid moment of weakness. Only girls get dizzy! Young, growing boys only hurt because of an accident. He wished he had broken a leg. . . .

Dietrichstein, who had escorted the doctor to his pupil's bedchamber, stonily looked down at the stripling. As the Count was prone to find the past more delightful than the present, he said with a touch of nostalgia, "Your Highness is acting like a child." Then sternly: "Take off your coat and your shirt!"

Sulkily, Franz complied. Straudenheim repeatedly felt his throat, took a long look at his patient's slender frame, and declared, "Your Highness must eat more to offset a rapid growth. There will be no fencing for a while. Dancing and riding can continue, but in moderation. For now, I urge Your Highness to rest."

With a heart-rending sigh, Dietrichstein rang for the valet. Moaning and groaning about all the unnecessary fuss, Franz had to change into comfortable breeches and a linen shirt. After he had been made to climb back into bed, Straudenheim put a glass to his lips. Soon afterward, he fell into a drugged sleep.

Sometime later, Franz woke to the manifestation of a balmy summer evening. The sky, velvet back, was studded with stars; and through the windows which were thrown wide-open, came the faint pulsating shrills of crickets singing their mating songs. A few candles had been lit in the sconces beside his bed, and their soft spent glow made him wonder how late it was.

Presently their flames flickered from a draft caused by the door opening and closing noiselessly behind Sophie. On the tips of her toes she trod lightly, head bent as she was absorbed gathering the ample folds of her gown so as to not make a sound. Her lovely face, Franz noticed, was tensed.

He raised himself on his elbows to sit against the pillows. Sophie caught the movement and looked up. Quickly she crossed over to him and took his outstretched hands.

"Franz, you gave me such a fright! How are you feeling now?"

He looked at her pensively and gave her a wisp of a smile. "Let me think," he said, only to give himself time to savor a private joy.

An appalling realization had just come to him. In a span of some twelve years, bouts of the various indispositions peculiar to childhood had only brought to his room servants and tutors with their efficient but impersonal ministering. The care and tenderness of a mother's presence on such occasions had been denied him. But now Sophie was changing all this! That discovery suffused his face with an air of such contentment that it dispelled Sophie's initial anxiety.

"When will you know?" she teased, letting go of his hands and pulling up a chair close to the bed.

"I am cured," he declared with a grin.

But that assurance put a little frown on her brow. Surely Franz jested. Straudenheim's mention to Francis, and in her presence, of a predisposition to "scrofula of the trachea" gave Sophie little cause to accept that affirmation.

"Franz, be serious!" she chided. "You know how much I care about you!"

"I know," he said softly. "You are here. . . ."

Sophie suddenly realized she was seeing Franz in an unfamiliar and intimate setting: abed, half covered with a sheet, and wearing an open neck shirt revealing a smooth adolescent chest.

"I have invaded your privacy," she said apologetically. "But I had to see you. What is wrong?"

"Nothing that can't be cured if I refrain from fencing and only ride and dance in moderation for a little while," he said without any trace of concern. "I am growing up too rapidly . . . or so I am told." He chuckled. "Dancing I can go without. I have better things to do!"

"Such as?" Sophie asked brightly, somewhat relieved.

"Studying. I never seem to have enough time to study. Hopefully, seeing that the court is full of old kings and princes, and with a mortality rate especially high in winter time, I might be able to skip a few balls when the court goes into mourning. Then my studies progress in leaps and bounds. For instance, when the Duchess of Nassau passed away, I managed to finish at long last the complete translation of *Julius Caesar's Commentaries!* I commend the Duchess for leaving this world for a better one, while mine could stand some improvement."

It began with a smile that rippled to Sophie's eyes. Religion, she reflected, had not cast upon Franz the somber pall of rituals regarding death. His logic was to the point: Heaven being so wonderful, then why all the doom and gloom about death? The Duchess of Nassau had gone to her reward and done him a favor for which he was thankful.

He could be so disconcertingly droll. . . .

A peal of laughter shook her.

Pleasantly surprised, Franz watched her. As laughter is contagious, he joined in, soon out-laughing her.

At this point, Sophie remembered the doctor's prescription: rest and quiet.

"Franz, you must be tired," she said rising from her chair.

"Oh, don't go yet!" he pleaded. "Don't you want to know how I can steal the pleasure of your company?"

A mischievous glint danced in his eyes and the vivacity of his tone convinced her she could tarry a little more. She resumed her seat. "Very well, show me."

Franz allowed a few seconds to pass. He seemed to be thinking hard. Finally he said, "Ever try to hold a moment? Or observe, if you prefer, a 'now' never caught and only measured in the extent of its loss? Well, behold a sophisticated munching on duration such as that of a clock, this being the most elusive form of gluttony! And you have. . . .?" he paused dramatically. ". . . a few seconds gone by!"

Sophie smiled. "And I am still here!"

"Precisely."

"You are much too young to be such a philosopher! To lead such a retired life. You should be consorting with young people!"

"I am consorting with you."

"That's very sweet of you, Franz. But I mean people of your age."

"Age has nothing to do with my interest in people," he rejoined. Then he leaned over and putting out his hand, touched the tip of his fingers to her mouth to gently trace its contour.

"Only you, can laugh with me like this . . ." he murmured.

Then settling back against the pillows, he said with gravity, "I must thank you."

"For what, Franz?" she asked, moved by the delicate way in which he expressed his appreciation. The feel of his fingers still lingered on her lips.

"For everything! I never had anyone . . ." his voice broke off.

Coming to grip with her own loneliness, she said on a die-away breath, "Now we have each other, don't we?"

"Yes. And I must thank Karl, also."

She studied him with fond curiosity. "Tell me why."

"He brought you to me."

She marveled at his artless gratitude for her coming into his life, his purity of perception, and youthful innocence. Never had he been so precious to her. Yes! had it not been for Karl, for her life-long commitment to him. . . .

The thought that her own misfortune could have brought them together appeased her.

She pressed a tender good night kiss to his forehead. "I wouldn't have planned it any other way," she answered.

Reichstadt's fit of dizziness was soon dismissed as an incident of no consequence. When he developed a dry and dainty cough, Doctor Straudenheim prescribed cold baths. Dietrichstein promised to have one brought up to the Prince's bedchamber every day.

"No tub," said the physician. "His Highness is to bathe in the Danube."

"The Danube? But he cannot swim!"

"It's time that he learns. There are very special properties in the water of the river."

A stickler for cleanliness, Dietrichstein objected, "But the water of the Danube is murky . . . it even smells!"

"All the better!"

Later, remarking on Franz's success, Straudenheim asked how it was like swimming in the river for the first time.

"I thought I was going to drown," Franz rejoined honestly.

"Nonsense!" snapped the doctor. "We would never allow Your Highness to attempt anything hazardous! We were well prepared to rescue you. But you did so well. Nevertheless, considering the severity of your apprehension, you should have told us how you felt about the whole thing."

"Never! I'd rather drown than do such a thing!" Franz retorted with indignation.

"But why?"

"Because," he said coolly, "I had an audience. That's why!"

Strangely, the therapy, which soon became a ritual, produced salutary results. Franz, feeling in excellent form, pursued his studies with unabated zeal. The subject of strategy began to absorb him considerably. At the same time, he felt an intense desire to master the language he had been forced to abandon: French. It was in French that his father's tactical genius had found a brilliant vehicle of expression, and it was in French that he wanted to read every available publication concerning Napoleon's mastery of strategy.

In the summer of his seventeenth year, Franz passed again through the usual anxiety of waiting for Marie Louise. The Duchess of Parma, yielding to the open criticism of her family for staying away so often, met Franz halfway at Molk. In her own self-centered and practical sort of way, she cared about him. And now, as she faced a towering seventeen-year-old, she felt she had a perfectly legitimate bone to pick with her father. Franz still held no commission in the Austrian Army. She took this as an affront. Was her son treated differently because he was only a half-Habsburg?

Feeling personally insulted, she promptly took up the matter with her father. Francis apologized and mentioned the Prince's rangy and delicate build. Franz might become easily fatigued.

Marie Louise remained unconvinced. From glaring precedents, promotions bestowed on archdukes, especially young ones, were purely honorary. "Papa," she complained, "you are ridiculing him! Me!"

Francis gave in and immediately granted Franz the captaincy of a regiment of Tyrolean cavalry.

Franz reached the extremity of joy.

To mark the memorable event, Marie Louise gave her son the curved saber his father, Napoleon, had raised under the hot sun of Egypt.

Shaking and hoarse with emotion, Franz asked, "Will my uniform be ready for the upcoming maneuvers at Munchendorf?"

The Emperor beamed a fond smile. "You will be outfitted in time, Franz."

"Oh, you will be proud of me, Sire!," Franz enthused, his eyes flashing fire. "I am determined to live up to the honor you have so graciously bestowed upon me!"

Franz, being the least favored, exhibited an appreciation far beyond the importance of the gift.

A little ashamed and moved, the Emperor said, "I am already very proud of you, Franz!"

Franz continued grandly as if reciting an oath, "The glory I will endeavor to earn for Austria will not only be offered as a tribute to Your Majesty's kindness, it will also, to your satisfaction, reconcile the world with my father. I will make amends!"

"You will?" panted Francis.

"Yes!"

Francis experienced an elating sense of triumph.

Dear, sweet, wonderful Franz! His impassioned pledge to make up for his father's sins proclaimed a total rebirth. And the delivery itself! In impeccable German! No metamorphosis could have been more complete. . . . He will fit without difficulty in an order Napoleon had defied and defiled. And not in mind alone. Tall, fair-skinned, and radiantly blond, Franz had scared away the ghost of the short and swarthy Corsican upstart.

Francis placed his hands on his grandson's shoulders. "Your goal is a noble one, Franz. You have my blessing and my prayers!"

Within less than a week, spruce Captain Franz von Reichstadt eagerly discarded mufti for a beloved uniform, which he got into the habit of wearing all the time except in the evening. On ceremonial occasions, Napoleon's sword hung smartly at his side. That sword, a talisman auguring future military exploits in the service of Austria, was precious to him only in that context. He never let it out of his sight.

Soon, another memento, this one touching him personally, was added to his collection—the silver-gilt cradle Marie Louise had taken to Parma was returned to him. Franz wanted it back, driven by a sense of purposefulness. Until he could earn some recognition through his own accomplishments, he regarded the cradle as the only significant monument to his existence. His earnestness to reclaim his baby bed had been dutifully brought to Metternich's attention.

Metternich lifted his eyebrows in surprise. What could the Duke possibly see in a cradle which, to add to the oddity of the request, was to be placed in the young man's bedchamber at the Hofburg? Such intimacy with an object so closely related to one's infancy struck him as somewhat unwholesome. Nevertheless, Metternich found no valid reason to veto the transfer.

The Chancellor's curiosity had come to Franz's ears. He satisfied it with the quip: "Please assure Prince Metternich that there is no chance for me to return to my cradle."

Metternich made a careful note of that remark. Reichstadt's witticisms, as everything else about him, deserved scrutiny.

The feeling that Metternich might be a threat to his self-realization had begun to worm itself into Franz's consciousness. The reason for such an assumption was totally unclear to him. Nothing warranted that sort of misgiving seeing that his only ambition was to carve for himself an illustrious career in the service of Austria. The uniform which he wore quasi-religiously vouched for the sincerity of his intention, an intention momentarily jarred out of focus by a curious incident which occurred at the conclusion of Franz's holiday in Baden.

While he was taking a stroll accompanied by his tutors, a carriage overtook them. At that precise moment, a torrent of invectives made him look up. A young woman was leaning out of the coach and glaring at Franz, her comely features momentarily distorted with anger. The noise of the wheels trundling on the cobblestones drowned most of her words, but the few he managed to hear, uttered in French, were "uniform" and "shame". After the carriage had passed, Franz wondered if the woman could have mistaken him for someone else. A lover's quarrel, perhaps, with an officer of his own regiment? That may have prompted this angry outburst, and hence the misdirected insults because of the uniform he wore. But why had she chosen to address herself in French to an Austrian officer? They were on German-speaking soil.

In any case, for all he knew, his own conduct was beyond any reproach . . . or was the reproach addressed to him because she knew who he was?

And *who* was he? An odd sensation of being faulted for something he had neglected to recognize suddenly coursed through him. Dietrichstein, who made light of the incident, noticed that Reichstadt looked preoccupied for the rest of the day.

20

Count Dietrichstein's first impression of August Marseille Barthélemy was not a favorable one. He prized reserve and poise. When he came into the drawing room, he expected his visitor to calmly rise from his seat and behave decorously. Instead, he found Barthélemy briskly pacing the floor, and upon seeing the Count, he greeted him with inconceivable familiarity with the exclamation: "Ah! At long last!"

Dietrichstein refrained from showing any sign of displeasure and looked him over, not deigning to respond as yet. Of medium height and delicate frame, Barthélemy was modestly but neatly dressed. He held in the crook of his arm a small packet whose shape indicated that it might contain some printed materials.

This was a logical assumption because Dietrichstein knew the man to be a writer. Indeed, his reputation as a libeler even overshadowed the notoriety he earnestly sought as a poet. Barthélemy, whose previous work included several political satires, had recently published his latest creation, an epic poem entitled *Napoleon in Egypt.*

The Count summed up the opinion he had formed of Barthélemy as an author in one simple proposition: the man was a rebel, a literary *franc-tireur.* He could only anticipate problems in consenting to receive such an individual in his private drawing room at Schönbrunn.

He said staidly with a slight bow without extending his hand, "In the Emperor's behalf, I am pleased to bid you welcome to Austria, Monsieur." His French was excellent, which added some amenity to the greeting.

Barthélemy had had to overcome many difficulties to obtain a passport to travel to Vienna, and thus far, he had only met with hostility. By contrast, he found the reception to be relatively friendly. He let his appreciation be known with too much directness.

"Thank you, Count! It is very comforting, indeed, to hear you say so."

Dietrichstein caught the slight mordancy of the undertone. He feigned commiseration. "I suppose you must have encountered some . . . obstacles. What a pity. . . ."

"Let me only say that your police are thorough," Barthélemy replied with a tight smile.

"Nevertheless," said Dietrichstein, forcing himself to smile in turn, "we are glad to have you, Monsieur."

That was another perfunctory amiability. A direct referral from the Grand Master of the Court offered no other alternative.

Without wasting any more time, Barthélemy said, "I have come to Vienna to present you with copies of my latest work."

Wearily Dietrichstein eyed him and ventured a guess he felt was correct. "*Napoleon in Egypt?*" he said in a flat, noncommittal tone.

Flattered, the Frenchman beamed, ignoring his interlocutor's obvious lack of enthusiasm, "You've heard of it! How wonderful!"

"I am aware of your work," Dietrichstein mumbled, bending his head. He seemed absorbed in the contemplation of his shoe buckles.

The visitor cranked up his courage. "I should like to give a copy to the Duke of Reichstadt myself," he said.

Startled by the directness of the request, Dietrichstein replied with calm nevertheless. "I am afraid that is not possible, Monsieur."

"May I ask why?"

There was an arrogant edge to the question and it annoyed Dietrichstein. "A person as intelligent as you are, Monsieur, should be able to supply your own answer. And I have no doubt that you can."

Barthélemy ignored the gibe, "I am sorry. I do not understand."

Dietrichstein decided to shame him. "And I am not sorry to contradict you. I am certain you do understand."

Flushing, Barthélemy protested, "I represent no faction, I assure you. I only wish to see the Prince as a private individual. I shall gladly speak to His Highness in front of fifty witnesses if you so desire. Certainly, you cannot tell me that he won't receive me under these conditions."

"His Highness will not see you," Dietrichstein declared categorically.

Indignation flashed in the Frenchman's eyes.

In an attempt to forestall further unpleasantness, the Count elaborated. "We have to consider the Duke's safety. You must keep in mind that while people such as yourself are friendly to His Highness, others are eager to see his . . . permanent removal. The Emperor . . ." he made a gesture intimating that the decision did not rest with him, "refuses to take any chances. His orders are very strict regarding such matters. No one is to disregard the precautions the Emperor has personally established to protect the Duke's life even with the most convincing proof of benevolent intention."

Barthélemy grew bold, vexed by this arbitrary rule which, in his opinion, lacked discernment. "I believe His Highness is kept isolated for fear that any contact with his compatriots might awaken his hopes. But what guarantee have you anyway that the Duke will never receive any communication either openly or clandestinely?"

"That is no concern of yours," Dietrichstein replied, his voice shaking a little.

"My concern," the poet retorted defiantly, "is to report to my countrymen that our suspicion regarding the Prince's situation is correct. He is a prisoner! The dispositions taken to insure his safety cannot conceal this fact!"

Dietrichstein bristled. "The Prince is not a prisoner. Only his situation is . . . particular. That's all!"

"Which says a great deal!"

The scoff was not well taken. Dietrichstein drew himself up, his expression surly, his voice cutting. "The Duke is a very contented individual who entertains no other ambition but that of distinguishing himself in the exclusive service of this country. This, I urge you to report to your countrymen, because the truth will spare them much disillusion and troubles. Good day, Monsieur!" And nodding curtly, he turned to go.

"The poem!" Barthélemy aggressively called at him. "Won't you take it?"

Dietrichstein hesitated and decided to oblige to be rid of the visitor. "Of course," he said coldly; and went away with Barthélemy's long epic on Napoleon's Egyptian expedition.

The assurance that Napoleon's son had been successfully Germanized, as reported by Dietrichstein, preyed on Barthélemy's mind. This disturbing possibility spoiled his sleep and impelled him to see if not approach the product of this detestable transformation. He would not leave Vienna without setting his eyes on the elusive and disappointing prince. The most likely place where he might catch a glimpse of Reichstadt was the Burgtheater, assiduously frequented by the members of the imperial family.

The theatrical season was at its height during the winter, and Barthélemy congratulated himself for having chosen to visit Vienna during the month of January 1829.

So, night after night, he scrutinized the imperial box. But this compelling curiosity soon drained his financial resources and so far the Duke of Reichstadt had not turned up.

Then it occurred to the poet that were the Prince to appear in a crowd, he would not even know him. The pictures that circulated in France usually represented the son of Napoleon as a child, or if they offered any likeness of him as he was now, a couple of months shy of eighteen, they were most likely more fanciful than true. He was said to be fair-haired and well made. . . .

That night, seated in the parterre, Barthélemy had just about given up when finally Franz came in causing a small commotion. As usual, Reichstadt—this was indisputable—had his own audience. Like everyone else, Barthélemy's eyes were riveted on the dimly lit recess in the first tier of boxes close to the stage.

Three figures emerged from the shadowy backdrop of velvet hangings and moved to the seats. Barthélemy recognized Dietrichstein and that left no doubt as to the identity of the youth who was with him. The third man, he was sure, was a mere attendant. His manners, as he waited for the Count's companion to take his seat, were deferent and watchful.

Barthélemy studied the archduke with avidity, intent on memorizing what he saw. The Prince sat down, smartly tossing the skirts of his coat from under him. Two bejeweled stars sparkled on his breast, which was crossed with the red and green sash of the Order of St. Stephen. His features from that distance were only remarkable in so far as they gave an exceedingly pleasing impression.

The most salient characteristics were the young man's height, his light complexion, and golden wavy hair. The poet had not expected to find in Napoleon's son the duplicate image of the Emperor, but such crying dissimilarity!

I am too far, he thought. Surely at close range, something in the face would recall a glorious parentage!

But then to what avail?

Barthélemy paid little attention to the program. A more relevant drama held his interest and put a strain on his emotion, for he remembered the Count's words: "The Duke is a very contented individual."

Yet in spite of that proclamation, the poet could not bring himself to accept the fact that the youth who sat in the imperial box draped with Austria's emblem, a bicephalous eagle, could be forgetful of his native ties and indifferent to his heritage while in France, his father's legend, like a phoenix rising from his own ashes, had ignited the nation's imagination rekindling the hope of seeing the return of his son to power!

Barthélemy's gaze remained trained on the youth's profile. With intense longing, he hoped to see it graven on French coins.

Suddenly, his imagination started to spin wildly. A vast lyrical composition, charged with fiery exhortations and extravagant accusations, began germinating in his mind.

After the performance, Barthélemy's determination to gain an audience with the Duke of Reichstadt firmed. He must try to speak to Dietrichstein's pupil. Only then could he assess the extent of the damage done to the character of Napoleon's son.

Dietrichstein received him mindful of avoiding any demonstration of ill-will. But he asked without preamble, "Have you come to seek again an interview with the Duke?"

"I have," the poet answered with the same directness.

Dietrichstein shrugged and said, "I find your persistence disturbing, Monsieur. Someone or some faction must have sent you."

"No one has sent me, Count. I swear!"

"Still, I cannot grant you that audience for the reasons I have already explained."

Barthélemy clenched his fists. Like the Count, he too, could be stubborn. "I believe your refusal is not in keeping with the protocol that governs accessibility to princes. What I am encountering here presents all the aspects of a sequestration, and I will not desist from this conviction."

"That is regrettable," Dietrichstein responded flatly.

Then he walked over to a richly inlaid desk and unlocking the center drawer, withdrew the poet's gift. "You have talent, Monsieur," he said picking up the two copies, both of which he handed to Barthélemy, "But I cannot allow the Prince to see this. It would put into his head ideas that might be . . . distracting."

"Distracting!" Barthélemy blared.

"Not so loud, Monsieur."

"But," he protested thoroughly incensed, "there is absolutely nothing reprehensible in what I have written!"

"The evocations nevertheless might cause His Highness to become unhappy with his present mode of existence."

"Ah-ha! So you do admit having no assurance that the Prince's quietude is genuine!"

Striving for self-control, Dietrichstein rasped in a low, hoarse voice, "I pray you to reconsider what you have just said, Monsieur."

Barthélemy clutched at the unwanted gift. His parting word sounded like a battle cry.

"Never!"

Never before did Barthélemy feel such a pressing need to combat the insidious and odious complacency that seemed to have taken hold of Napoleon's son. After returning to Paris, which was to become the epicenter of a political tremor, Barthélemy set to work. It took the calming influence of his friend and sometime collaborator, the poet, Merry, to help him sort his ideas. The person of Reichstadt had assumed in his mind the part of a tragic character, which he intended to reveal to the French public. Barthélemy would picture the son of Napoleon as the victim of a sinister revenge, besotted by lies and imperiled by poison. He would, above all, endeavor to stir the Prince and wake him from a dangerous apathy.

What did Merry think of all this?

Merry quipped, "I think you should prepare yourself to spend some time in jail!"

Jail was the least of Barthélemy's worries. The title of that new, startling composition in verse became the focal point of his preoccupation. Such a title should catch the imagination of the readers. The two men racked their brains, then agreed to exploit the analogy to the fullest. Napoleon's dereliction, the mental and physical suffering he had endured during his last captivity, already evoked in the mind of the French people the notion of martyrdom. Now, in turn, his son was marked to be crucified by Austria!

The two decided that the poem should be entitled "The Son of Man."

In February, Franz wrote his mother upon learning that Neipperg's health was failing: "I envy you. At least you can look after the General and visit him. Whereas all I can do is worry. . . ."

In mid-February Neipperg died, leaving a will that caused Marie Louise considerable embarrassment. The document disclosed who the parents of Albertine and William were. It also enlightened Francis about the age of the children.

The Emperor was appalled. His daughter had placed herself in a situation that was an abomination to God and to man. He forgave her, but not without impressing upon her the enormity of her offense. Then, to aggravate her plight at being found out, Francis declared that it would be impossible to conceal her morganatic marriage from Franz any longer.

Marie Louise was panic-stricken. What of the children? Should Franz be told about them, too?

Francis only promised not to mention their ages for the sake of conserving the exalted sentiments Franz felt for his mother, but this concession took nothing away from the fearsome task confronting Francis. *He would be the one* to inform Reichstadt of his mother's remarriage, and in the least damaging way possible.

Francis swore to himself that his grandson should never learn of his mother's adulterous relations with Neipperg. The children's ages held the key to that secret, so all those who knew of it were ordered to keep mum on that detail.

When the dreaded moment came, he broached the delicate subject of the marriage and the existence of Albertine and William with every intention of being subtle. Yet he began awkwardly.

"Franz, is everything well with you? Do you need any money?"

Franz glanced obliquely at his grandfather. This was so unlike the Emperor, a veritable miser, to encourage expenditure. Instantly, he knew something was amiss.

"I have just received my allowance, Sire," he reminded him with his habitual honesty.

"So you did," Francis muttered with agitation. Then he gave up trying a slick approach and said with haste, "What I have to tell you, concerns your mother. . . ."

Neipperg's recent death had put into Franz's mind the notion that anything connected with Parma would spell some new catastrophe.

"Is my mother seriously ill, too?" he interrupted thoroughly alarmed.

"No, no," Francis waved energetically, "she is quite well. Only . . . the question here, Franz, dear, is that you are not an only child. You have a sister and brother . . . well I mean. . . ."

"I have what?"

The Emperor stammered, "I meant . . . a half sister and a half brother. Oh, but don't be shocked!" He hurried on, feeling a rush of irritation at being forced to lie. "It's all very proper. You see, after your father died, your mother remarried. A normal occurrence, you must understand. And . . . General Neipperg was your mother's choice."

"General Neipperg? Neipperg took my father's place?"

Somehow Francis said with profundity, "No one can ever take your father's place, Franz."

There followed a silence.

"Your mother was very lonely . . ." Francis, said in his daughter's defense.

Franz shuddered. Neipperg, his stepfather! That struck him as totally incongruous.

"When did my mother remarry?" he asked tonelessly.

Francis squirmed, and his mouth opened and closed without emitting a sound. Finally he said evasively, "After . . . after your father's death, of course. . . ."

Inwardly, Francis groaned. I don't deserve this! I have raised her boy, loved him, and now I should be the one to conceal her shameful conduct . . . marrying Neipperg at a time when she should still be in weeds! And leave it to Franz to ask for more precision!

In Franz's tone, as he pursued this grueling interrogation, a new edge entered his voice: that of suspicion. "I pray you to tell me," he demanded, "exactly when did this marriage take place."

Francis gave up. He said almost inaudibly, eyes downcast, "When you were ten years old."

Sensing no reaction, he looked up. Franz was staring past him, jaws taut, nostrils pinched, and eyes glistening with tears. Then he turned away, head bent and shoulders trembling.

"Oh, God! This is terrible!" Francis heard him moan.

"Franz!" Francis warned. It was a call to order, a reminder that filial respect forbade that sort of inference.

But Franz paid no attention to his grandfather's reproof. With his back still turned on him, he asked with bitterness, "Why wasn't I told about it then? Was it because the marriage took place the same year my father died?"

"You were still a child then."

Franz swung round, his tone biting, "Oh, so I am supposed to understand better now that I am almost eighteen, is that it?"

"Be kind to your mother," Francis could only beg. At all cost he tried to avert a calamity no parent would wish to see befall another parent: that of being an object of contempt to your own child. And Franz's contempt for his mother would be the most dreaded form of detestation. Francis winced at this possibility.

Franz looked at him with pain-filled eyes.

Quickly Francis put his arms out and drew his grandson against his breast, thinking of the man he had outlawed and allowed to die longing for a word from his little boy—a word that never came. It was said that Napoleon idolized his son, a son Francis now clasped ever so fondly. The irony jarred him a little. But he did not repent. He never could.

"Be kind," he repeated in earnest.

In their ill-mated embrace, Franz broke down and cried. He wept for his father whom, over the years, his entourage had exiled away into silence and utter oblivion. And while his mother had not waited to remarry after at least a year before banishing him from her memory, had he, himself, not been guilty of allowing that memory to fray and fade in his own mind? Then Franz wept for his mother, a shattered idol. He wanted to make it whole again. If he failed, something in him could never be mended, never be the same.

"I love my mother . . . I only care to love her," he sobbed.

And what of Father? Would his love for him be limited to pious reverence? No! He decided he owed it to himself to learn more about him. The whole of Napoleon's once existing personality should be exhumed, revitalized with a comprehensive understanding of the dynamics which had made him the sort of man he was. And in this undertaking there could be no place for tears! Away with them! He had cried his fill for two!

Breaking the ring of Francis's arms, he said, "I am sorry, Sire. I have overreacted."

Francis said soothingly, "And I commend you for being so understanding."

Marie Louise did not share her father's confidence. She could not bring herself to face her son that summer. Her health, she informed him, required a cure in the salubrious mountain air of Switzerland.

For the first time, Franz showed resentment. His mother was avoiding him because she put little faith in his capacity for forgiving. To her note of cancellation, he replied offhandedly: "I do hope, dearest Mamma, that the Swiss air will be as effective in providing you with the relief you seek as the company of those who love you might have."

As a counterpoint to his hurt and disappointment, and inflamed with reparative zeal, Franz undertook another pursuit. Until now he had been satisfied with an abstract, ill-defined image of Napoleon, a caricature of ruthless ambition at its worst. He had accepted that image unquestioningly.

Not anymore. There existed in his past a complex person who had loved him, a man whose brilliance couldn't have been totally dedicated to evil. In all fairness, he must get reacquainted with that person.

How? Questions would avail him nothing. Long ago he had given up asking them. To arrive at the truth, he would have to rely on his own ingenuity.

The search began in Schönbrunn's vast and well stocked library, which oddly contained quantities of publications relating to Napoleon. No one had deemed it necessary to remove them because Franz had never demonstrated any interest at finding out more than what he was being told about his father, which amounted to very little. If he was given anything to read on Napoleon, the material had been carefully expurgated.

Stealthily, Franz immersed himself in forbidden reading. The first book to fall into his hands was the most apt to enlighten him: Las Cases's memoirs published shortly after Napoleon's death. It was entitled: *The Memorial of St. Helena: Journal of the Private Life and Conversation of the Emperor Napoleon at St. Helena.* The subtitle alone already set his heart pounding.

Eagerly he leafed through the book. Then he found in the appendix the will of his father, printed in full. Reading it, he came upon the message addressed to him beyond death:

"I command my son never to forget that he is born a French prince. . . ."

Reading on, the mention of the objects he should have received upon reaching his sixteenth birthday affected him deeply. Where were those things bequeathed to him? He had just turned eighteen!

Save for the sword his mother had finally given him, why wasn't even one of those other items delivered to him? Was it because they were considered the dangerous repository of a mystique that could draw him into a warmer evocation of his father's memory? But the harm was already done! To know of their existence sufficed.

Within a week, an avalance of facts gleaned through furtive reading relating to his parents' marriage, the pomp that had attended his own birth, and the events that had taken place in his early childhood opened up new and unsuspected prospects. Now his future troubled him as it no longer seemed so clear.

Franz longed to recapture the intelligibility of a portrait: that of his father painted by Gérard and set in an oval frame which had hung since the days of his boyhood in his bedroom at the Hofburg palace. Francis had deemed it decent and proper to allow his grandson to possess a picture of Napoleon. Franz had not paid overmuch attention to the brooding face looking down at him. Napoleon dead nearly a decade, merely elicited from him a limbic interest. But this was no longer so. . . .

Sophie's attention began to focus on her nephew's frequent abstraction and faraway look. Seeing that he had not yet cared to confide in her, all she could do was to conjecture. He might be experiencing the unsettling process of falling in love, perhaps. Indeed, a particular Polish canoness at court was quite brazen in the interest she took in him. And so did other ladies for that matter.

At dinner over which Francis presided with the gravity of a patriarch, Sophie watched Franz with some anxiety. He picked at his food and so far had only answered in monosyllables when something was said to him. Then Francis, too, noticed his grandson pondering over a plate nearly untouched.

"Franz, you have hardly eaten anything," he remarked.

In reply, Franz took a hurried bite. Despite Doctor Straudenheim's recommendations, he still ate very little.

By her absence, Marie Louise had relinquished all parental attention to such details. Determined to offset her sister-in-law's most glaring and deplorable shortcoming, Sophie, taking on the role of a surrogate mother, did the worrying for her. She nodded her approval when glancing up at her, Franz took another bite.

Now she thought of her own unfulfilled yearning for motherhood. She so wanted to have a child of her own! After five years of marriage and despite her strong aversion to Karl's sexual prerogatives, her childbearing years did not show any sign of fertility. Of course, not to be derelict in her duties, she ardently hoped for a boy and looked forward to grooming him to ascend the Habsburg throne as he would be third in the line of succession. . . .

Presently she caught Franz's eyes fixed upon her, their expression grave and brooding. Intuitively, she felt sure now that those expressive eyes had not seen the dawn of any sentimental upheaval. A lovesick boy doesn't look troubled in this sort of way. There was something else. And if he wanted to confide in her, she would leave the initiative to him.

After the meal, he said to her with an urgent tone, "If you are not busy, I should like to talk to you."

Sophie surveyed the drawing room where the imperial family had scattered in small groups. Francis Charles was playing pool with his father.

"You can talk to me in the garden," she said, trying to conceal the apprehension in her voice.

Franz followed her, taking with him the image of the Emperor leaning over the pool table and squinting at the billiard balls for a perfect shot. How would he call his own shot in the private game into which he felt drawn more and more deeply every day?

As they walked side by side, he said following that same train of thought, "Chess is a very interesting game. One can play it alone by pretending to be two different people at the same time. . . ."

Sophie looked up at him lifting her eyebrows.

He smiled apologetically. "I am sorry. I must sound a bit incoherent."

"Not at all," she encouraged. "Tell me more."

"I must confess it is a trying experience for me."

Obviously what he'd said was only a figure of speech. She asked cautiously, "How long have you been at this game?"

He kicked a pebble and blurted out, "Long enough to start wondering!"

"You have been thinking . . . "

It was a leading statement and she knew it.

Franz answered with all the impetuosity he reserved for her alone. "Oh God, yes! I have been thinking about a sense of direction!"

"Direction . . ." she repeated thoughtfully.

"Does this surprise you?" he asked, looking away into the distance.

"No, Franz," she replied firmly, studying his profile. From the domed forehead to the determined chin, its curves were arranged with dynamic determination. "No," she repeated resolutely, "you should be wanting something of life . . . and something meaningful."

"I should. I am old enough!"

"Eighteen years and four months old," she said softly, feeling more than ever conscious of her own age and barrenness.

Yet at twenty-four, Sophie's youthful look was on a par with Franz's. More exactly, he had caught up with her, maturing faster in appearance. She was very much aware of this. The mirrors told her so whenever their reflections appeared in them. Franz had grown so tall that the top of her head did not quite come to the level of his shoulders. At times she chided herself for continuing to see in him the thirteen-year-old boy she had met five years ago. But that impression provided a familiar and comfortable dimension within which her affection continued to thrive with artless security. Intellectually, she had always regarded him old beyond his years and, as she suspected, inclined to speculate on the outcome of his destiny.

"Franz, what do you want of life?" she felt compelled to ask.

He rounded on her and seized her by the shoulders.

"Who do you say I am?"

Without hesitation, she replied, "Who you are is not in the least changed, just because your name is different. At least, I have never thought of you any other way."

He stared at her, and she stared back. He looked haunted.

Letting go of her, he resumed walking and said, "I am trapped!"

A hint of alarm thinned her voice. "Franz, what is happening to you?"

Somberly, he replied, "Nothing and everything!"

Sophie kept silent because the gravity of what he'd just said was immediately obvious to her. His terse assessment encapsulated the magnitude of some soul-searching she should not intrude upon unless he invited her. To show him that she was there, ready to listen and comfort, if not counsel, she took his hand. He squeezed it hard then relaxing his grip he murmured, "What will become of me?"

Sophie trusted herself to say the right thing. "Only what you want to become."

For a second, Franz was tempted to tell her about his secret reading, but he reconsidered. He must give himself time to evaluate his own goal. Her own insight, he could tell, had already glimpsed the nature of his unrest.

And again, he thought her infinitely wise.

Having champed at the bit for so long, Franz did not find it at all inconvenient to have to rise four times a week at four o'clock in the morning to take up some of the duties attached to his promotion. On the parade ground at five, he was totally oblivious of the world so passionately did he give himself up to executing the drills until half-past seven. Then, back at Schönbrunn, he felt too excited still to breakfast and went instead horseback riding.

While galloping, he meditated on his vocation. An obscure urge beckoned but the undertaking itself had no definite substance; only one realization was absolutely clear to him. He was destined to become a soldier and an excellent one, he decided.

Dietrichstein seemed to have found new causes for aggravation when Franz found him waiting for him in the castle's courtyard upon his return. The Count's expression was anything but cheerful or welcoming. He snapped as soon as Franz had dismounted. "I hear you have run off to the woods after a strenuous session of exercise without so much as a cup of chocolate in your stomach!"

"So?" Franz retorted airily.

"There won't be any more riding immediately after maneuvers," the Count declared with a scowl. He allowed a brief pause during which he assessed the damage done. The Prince was disheveled, bathed in sweat, and looked spent. Then he concluded, "You are abusing your strength!"

"I have plenty more to spare," Franz replied confidently.

The Count insisted with mounting irritation. "Your Highness doesn't know the first thing about husbanding your energy. Look at yourself! Thin as a reed! Yet you are acting as though you were made of steel!"

"I don't believe I will ever get fat!" Franz said with equal irritation.

Dietrichstein decided to choose sentiment over reason. "Have you no regard for your mother's concern about your well-being?"

"My mother," Franz answered between clenched teeth, bending his riding crop to a perfect circle, "doesn't seem to know that I exist!"

She should have come to him instead of sending him, as a sop, a dozen Parisian cravats and four walking sticks! For the first time, Franz wondered, Do I really mean anything to my mother? And did Father ever mean anything to her?

Dietrichstein went on defending Marie Louise in his courtly and impersonal way. He said emphatically, "How unfeeling of Your Highness to contemplate such thoughts! Her Majesty has nothing but your welfare and happiness in mind." Then in a last ditch attempt to entice Franz to compliance he thought of something else very dear to his pupil's heart. "Her Majesty. . . ."

Franz clenched his teeth. Her Majesty! He wondered why Marie Louise clung to that title. She did not cleave overlong to the man!

". . . may not at all approve," continued the tutor, "of an early emancipation if Your Highness goes on overtaxing yourself that way."

At this, Franz forgot his hurt. He said passionately, "I wish we were at war now! I wouldn't need anyone's consent! I'd be drafted. And what a glorious occasion that would be! Oh, how I could fight!"

"And pray, against whom?" Dietrichstein asked sourly, thanking God for Francis's peaceful reign.

But well aware of political ferment, Franz declared with impetuosity: "Russia and Prussia! And I'm ready to earn my epaulettes against them!"

Dietrichstein threw his hands up. "How can you take any pleasure in killing?" he lamented.

"I don't! But it's a job. A soldier's job," Franz responded with gravity. After a pause, he added melancholically, "Somehow, I have the presentiment that I won't be given a chance to do that job. . . . I may just die without receiving my baptism of fire."

"Nonsense!" Dietrichstein snorted.

Franz continued wistfully. "In which case I should like to have my coffin carried in the midst of the first available battle. What a splendid requiem this would be!"

"You are talking utter nonsense! That ride in the woods must have given you a fever!" Dietrichstein scolded.

Then, mindful of the fact that his pupil was drenched and stood in a draft, he ordered him to go change into dry clothes.

With some apprehension, he watched him ascend the perron, nimbly taking two steps at a time, spurs jingling. The idea that Reichstadt might soon gain his emancipation—the goad he had used earlier—did not strike him as a sensible one. At least for the time being. Given the Prince's ebullient temperament, he would spend himself beyond all reasonable limits.

And the Emperor, Dietrichstein recalled without much enthusiasm, was talking about sending his grandson to a garrison in Prague next autumn!

21

Merry's prediction came true when, in the summer of 1829, the publication of *The Son of Man* so upset Charles X that its author, Barthélemy, was sued for seditious intent. On the day of the trial, Paris was in a turmoil. Before a packed courtroom, Barthélemy insisted on delivering his own defense in Alexandrine verses. His appointed lawyer, Merilou, backed his client's eloquence by saying to a glum, looking magistrate, "What crime is there in exposing the plight of a young man whose sole inheritance is a name through which he is not permitted to seek glory and fame? I say, none! His father, Napoleon, came into our midst and we have not shut him out, nor did we think of dissociating him from the past of France! Yet we should keep silent about his son! A son whose misfortune, unparalleled in the records of our time, it is forbidden to lament!"

An ominous murmur of commiseration rose from the crowd. But the judge, being a dutiful servant of the Crown, sentenced Barthélemy to three months in jail and made him famous!

In Vienna, Metternich flew into a rage. Austrian hospitality had been repaid with an insult and a call to rebellion! And suppose Reichstadt should come by *The Son of Man*? The thought that he might, horrified Metternich. Copies of the poem were already circulating in Vienna and the imperial police were hard at work trying to prevent them from reaching Reichstadt.

Sitting in on the Chancellor's tantrum, his secretary and long-time advisor, Friedrick von Gentz, said quietly, "Let the Duke read it."

Metternich stared at his trusted alter ego as though the man had taken leave of his senses. Gentz scratched his head, and since it was covered with a wig, the gesture invariably irritated Metternich. Nevertheless, he bore with that annoying habit as he would patiently suffer Gentz's constant and noisy sucking on various candies to which he was addicted. Theirs was a long and fruitful association, tested and secured by a natural compatibility. Metternich could not do without the worn sexagenarian who chose to dress in baggy trousers and old-fashioned suits and delighted in showing off a collection of reddish wigs that had become a part of his anatomy.

Yet what Gentz wore, his decrepit appearance, and the scandalous way in which he lived was unquestionably redeemed by superior intellectual talents and a geniality that endeared him to everyone. His conservatism espoused Metternich's own fierce opposition to innovation. But the suggestion he'd just made did not at all fit the dispositions the Chancellor knew Gentz to have. Could he have misunderstood his advisor?

"Would you mind repeating what you've just said?" he asked him.

"The Duke," Gentz obliged, "should be allowed to read *The Son of Man.*"

"I was afraid you'd said that!"

Gentz smiled. "Don't be."

"But that would be disastrous!"

Gentz's watery eyes, considerably enlarged through the lenses of his pince-nez, intimated by their expression that this was not the opinion he held. His hand went up signaling the imminence of an explanation. But he took his time.

From a jeweled little bonbonnière which he always carried in his capacious pockets, he picked a candy and tenderly examined it before putting it into his mouth.

"We must," he finally said, "capitalize on the defamatory elements contained in the poem."

He paused to switch the candy to the hollow of his left cheek. Metternich wondered how, with such passion for sweets, Gentz had managed to keep most of his teeth.

"Well?" he urged. "What is your scheme?"

While sucking on the bonbon, one that was exotically flavored with ginger, Gentz explained: "For one thing, the insinuation of foul play and the allegation that the Duke is being purely and simply poisoned is absolutely preposterous. His Highness's affection for the Emperor will not allow him to accept this cheap sort of sensationalism with indulgence.

"Furthermore, the Prince will not appreciate being portrayed as a sickly youth without much fiber. If such is the opinion the French have of him, he can only look upon them with scorn and anger.

"And lastly, seeing that he is bound to hear about the poem, the very discovery that it was kept from him will surely arouse his displeasure and ruin our credibility. By allowing the Duke to read the poem . . . under guidance, we would be vindicating ourselves."

"Saved by candor," commented Metternich.

"Spared . . ." Gentz felt a crying need for precision, ". . . by the Duke's fondness for His Majesty; by a rootage that cannot exist without pride. The pride of belonging. This is only natural."

Metternich meditated on the proposal. Gentz's arguments were cogent. They relied heavily on the permeating influence of education and placed much faith in habits. But that faith, Metternich could not bring himself to accord Reichstadt. The Prince was the product of a dangerous seed and must bear within him the germ of peril no matter how reassuring the appearances might be.

With feigned lightness he asked, "You have not yet met the Duke, have you?"

Gentz laughed softly and confided with a hint of regret, "No. I have not."

The Chancellor's lips tightened. Obviously Gentz did not share his aversion for Reichstadt, whereas his strong dislike of Napoleon's son kept increasing with each passing year. The fingers of one hand would amply suffice to keep count of the times Metternich and Reichstadt had met, so seldom this had happened. And though he remembered well having saluted the Prince's birth with a toast: "To the King of Rome!" he continued to rue the day Reichstadt had been born and kept avoiding him whenever possible.

Caustically, he cautioned. "When you meet the Duke, beware Gentz! He is false—a play actor like his father!"

The delicate task of discussing the merit of *The Son of Man* fell to Obenaus. As Gentz had so well deduced, Franz's first reaction was one of indignation. He ran to the mirror and studied his reflection, asking his tutor, "Do I look sickly?"

The Prince's irritation augured well. Obenaus advised him to pay no attention to a single word of the poem, the whole object of their examination of the work having precisely to do with exposing the author's bad taste and poor judgment.

At this, Franz ranted, "Imagine! Me, in danger! Marked for destruction and by my own family! What an utterly ridiculous idea! What crass ignorance! Don't *they* think us civilized? Decent?"

Obenaus thought happily, Case closed! He tucked the pamphlet in his coat pocket, noting with satisfaction how Reichstadt had said *they* in contemptuous opposition to a proud *us.* The rather superficial study of Barthélemy's poem had produced such positive results!

"No need to dwell on this any longer," he said.

"On the contrary," Franz replied, startling him, "I intend to undertake a comprehensive criticism of this despicable libel. I owe it to His Majesty. I should like to have that pamphlet, sir."

"Really," Obenaus demurred, "I do not see the necessity. . . ."

"Oh, but I do! For my own peace of mind!"

"Peace of mind?" Obenaus spluttered, feeling a mild panic invade him.

"Certainly! No one can insult my family, question my worth and expect a simple outcry. Now if you please, the pamphlet, sir!"

That was an unimaginable command. Yet a refusal might create complications. Obenaus surrendered the pamphlet, saying shakily, "In this case. . . ."

"I do have a case!" And Franz clutched the pamphlet with such anger that for an instant the Baron feared it would be torn in half.

In any case, reflected the professor, this was a good sign.

Left alone, Franz read *The Son of Man* in its entirety. And after having read it from cover to cover, not once, but twice, his anger ebbed. Aside from gross exaggerations, there emerged a message—a message Franz found impossible to ignore.

True! He had inherited a great name. Yet he should not be content to shine through its reflection. He should wake to the significance of his assigned place in history and merit recognition through personal commitment! Only by being a son of France could he fulfill his destiny and truly vindicate himself by living up to the expectations placed in him as *The Son of Man*, the son of Napoleon!

With mounting agitation, he perceived in himself a dangerous dichotomy: How could he aspire to such a re-orientation and continue to be an archduke?

Confused, he sought guidance and inspiration by poring over *The Memorial of St. Helena,* which he had smuggled into his room and hidden on the top of the baldaquin over his bed. Again, he studied his father's will.

For a long while he meditated on this entry: "My son must adopt the motto: 'All for the French people!' "

Then a sudden peace flooded him. He'd found a path in the twilight of a forest through which he had been straying all along. He also recognized a warning he ought to heed: he must be very careful from now on. . . .

The next day, returning the pamphlet to Obenaus, he declared, "You were right. I have decided not to waste any more time on Monsieur Barthélemy's poem. It really doesn't deserve any further consideration."

On the surface, that summer, Dietrichstein could find nothing to carp about and consequently felt useless while Franz found himself holding a sort of vigil, briefly interrupted by Gustave Neipperg's short visit on his way to Vienna.

Franz welcomed Gustave with mixed feelings. By association, his boyhood playmate reminded him of Marie Louise's painful shortcomings. Dietrichstein's reception was lukewarm. He felt no ambiguity in his attitude toward Gustave. Neipperg's son had already earned the reputation of being a profligate young man. His favorite haunts were dance halls and fashionable taverns, where he drank to excess and caressed girls with equal abandon. He was boisterous, and in the Count's judgment, lacked breeding. The tutor thought him a bad companion for his pupil and dreaded the thought of a close association. Fortunately, such possibility was unlikely as there seemed to be no true affinity between the two young men, and circumstances caused them to live separate lives.

At the sight of Gustave, Franz began scheming. When they were left alone, he thought, Maybe, *you* can tell me something. . . .

He gave him a vigorous handshake, playfully boxed his ear and said, "Welcome, stepbrother!"

Gustave blushed. He keenly felt the incongruity of their parentage.

"My father is dead," he mumbled. "We don't really have to put up with . . ." He wanted to say "this nonsense," but in tactful deference to their respective parents' conduct, chose a simple, ". . . this."

"That's very sensible of you," Franz said, going along.

Gustave blushed a shade deeper and Franz decided not to wait a minute longer to obtain a few facts which had not been made clear to him, facts he knew he could only learn by guile. So he said casually, "But we just can't forget Albertine and William."

Gustave tensed. All the exhortations to prudence regarding any mention Reichstadt might make of his half sister and half brother rushed to his mind: Watch your tongue! Play dumb! Evade! Never, never give the children's ages away!

But incredible as this might seem, and to his immense relief, Franz added with an accepting smile, "I know *all* about them, Gustave. *Everything* . . . and I don't mind. I wish I could meet them. Until such time comes, I want to amuse them with a little gift. Tell me, seeing that you are closer to them than I ever could be, what would be a suitable present for a girl and a boy their age?"

Falling headlong into the trap, Gustave answered obligingly, "Nothing out of the ordinary, really. Any twelve-year-old girl would still enjoy a doll. As for a boy, well, just think of yourself. What was your favorite toy when you were ten?"

Franz seemed to ponder the suggestion. Actually, he was reckoning and in doing so became ghastly pale, shocked by the results of his calculations: Both children were born *during* his father's lifetime!

Watching Franz's expression alter, Gustave sensed disaster. The enormity of his blunder hit him like a slap in the face when Franz said, his voice dulled with pain, "When I was ten years old, I longed to see my father, Gustave. But he died. And until today, I did not know that before he even closed his eyes on this world, his wife had already given him up for dead—and had children!"

Then abruptly, he turned away. "God! Oh, God! How could she do this!"

"I am so sorry, Franz!" Gustave cried, his consternation laced with vexation for having been duped. "But you told me you knew everything!"

Franz swung around, eyes blazing with cold anger. "Damn, no! All lips are sewn on the subject! And yours, too, if I hadn't tricked you!"

"And of course, you hate me now for telling you what you wanted to know in the first place!" Gustave accused hotly.

Clamping down his hands on Gustave's shoulders, Franz shook him and there was furor in his denial. "I don't want to hate anyone!" he said violently. "And I shan't hate you, least of all people!"

Then releasing his stepbrother, he panted, "Now, just forget this conversation ever took place between us!"

"All right," Gustave groaned, massaging away the pain that burned his upper arms.

But Franz roared, "No! Swear!"

"I swear!"

Once again Franz grabbed him. "Make that oath good, Gustave! Or I shall cut out your tongue if I have to!"

Gustave winced. "You do hate me! And you are hurting me!"

Franz let go of him and took a few tottering steps back, looking deathly pale. "You will never hurt as much as I do!"

Thereafter Franz spoke incessantly of Prague. Francis's "official" mention of sending him there, was to Franz a buoy to which he clung. It enabled him to turn his thoughts away from the shattering discovery of his mother's infidelity. Being posted in Prague also related to his emancipation, which had become the subject of a raging controversy.

Dietrichstein still balked at the thought. He told his pupil that one who continues to misspell belongs in a classroom and not in a casern. Franz only admitted to being careless.

"Careless?" scoffed the tutor. "Is this how Your Highness explains spelling the name of your mother backward?"

Franz shrugged. "How else?"

How else? The effrontery of this lad! On the other hand, the Count reflected, no other explanation would do. Reichstadt was definitely not a dunce. He had won the admiration of older, experienced men whose opinion of him was laudatory. Besides, other than writing *Luoise,* the tutor conceded that his pupil's qualities deserved far more notice than an occasional inversion of letters.

In truth, Reichstadt was Dietrichstein's ideal of an accomplished prince: learned, lofty in character, refined, and chaste. It pleased the Count to see that Franz's susceptibility to feminine allurements had not evolved beyond the stage of social gallantry. His overriding interests were horses, casern life, drills and prowesses of a purely military nature. Such as he was, unsullied and protected from the corrupting influence of the outerworld, the Prince kept the tutor in a constant dread of seeing such perfection ruined by a slackening of his own vigilance.

Without admitting this to himself, the Count had become extremely protective of his pupil. And so the objection he'd proffered was totally inadequate. It was but a straw he had seized upon for want of a better way of stilling his own anxiety.

But Franz did not take the Count's evaluation on his fitness to become a soldier lightly. His temper flared. "Damnit! What has the spelling of my mother's name to do with my ability to perform in the army?"

"Your misspelling of her name," Dietrichstein corrected dourly.

"My father wrote badly too, so it is said, yet what a great warrior he was!"

"That is no excuse for Your Highness to be sloppy. Sloppiness is not inherited."

"You can't possibly oppose me on such flimsy grounds!"

Dietrichstein took a martyred air. He did not care to clarify his intention. "My task is thankless," he said tragically.

This only infuriated Franz. "If you thwart me because of this," he warned him, "I shall never forgive you! I shall banish you from my esteem!"

"I am only acting in your best interest," the tutor whined feeling wretched for being so completely misunderstood.

For an answer, Franz stormed out of the room and slammed the door behind him.

Franz hastened to the Emperor's study, fearful of the damage his tutor's retrograde appraisal of his capabilities might have done to his chance of going to Prague. The thought of the excellent recommendations he knew Francis had received from various quarters must count for something! Why, General Prince Alfred von Windischgratz had warmly welcomed the possibility of having him in his brigade! Count Feodor Karaczay had offered to become the intendant of his household. And the Emperor himself, thought him responsible enough to have said to him: "Whatever you do off duty is your private affair. I'll see to it that in Prague you have your own house."

Francis's long face which normally wore a rather dull expression, immediately lit up when Franz was ushered into his work room. Nothing had changed much in the study since his grandson had played on the carpet with painted Austrian toy soldiers. Only there was no little boy to rush into his arms.

Instead, a splendid looking young man clad in the dapper Austrian uniform of captain of the Tyrolean cavalry strode in and saluted smartly. Francis felt an overwhelming sense of pride and accomplishment.

Franz immediately noticed that the Emperor's desk was covered with heaps of documents.

"You are busy, Sire. I could have waited," he offered considerately, though he entertained no such intention.

"Not at all," Francis beamed. "For you, I can always find time."

"You are most kind, Sire."

"And you are very formal," the Emperor said, smiling fondly. He motioned Franz to a seat. "What is the nature of this pleasant visit?"

"Business, I am afraid," Franz said, twisting his sword knot.

Francis rose from his chair, walked around the desk, and briefly touched the back of his hand to the firm clean-shaven chin jutting over the high, stiff military collar.

"What sort of business?" he asked softly.

"I need Your Majesty's solemn assurance that the plan of sending me to Prague has not been canceled."

"Canceled? Hardly! What gave you this idea?"

"Count Dietrichstein seems to suggest this possibility."

Francis studied his grandson's upturned face. It was a little pale, a result, he was sure, of those repeated colds that had plagued him on and off for a period of two years now.

He said cautiously, "Only if your health requires it."

Franz jumped to his feet. Dietrichstein must have magnified a little cough or a sneeze out of proportion, and he made a mental note never to complain of the slightest indisposition, even to conceal it if at all possible.

"I am in perfect health, I assure you!" he protested vehemently.

"I believe you," Francis soothed. "By next autumn, given the same situation, you will indeed be free to go."

"There won't be any restrictions?"

"None that I can see," Francis said prudently, not discounting Metternich's say in the matter.

The catch word in Franz's life, he was sorry to admit, was: *Waiting.* A sorry state only supportable because Francis reiterated that his emancipation was a sure thing. Encouraged by this prospect, he prepared himself for the examination that was to mark the official end of his schooling. Then on the first of March, three weeks before his nineteenth birthday, he caught a cold. It could not have happened at a worse time, for on that day, at Schönbrunn, an impressive panel of eminent professors and high-ranking officers had assembled to test him in the presence of the Emperor and the Empress.

A stuffy nose, a voice that had become deeper, more resonant, and not unpleasantly nasal, were impossible to conceal. So it was plain to Francis that his beloved grandson was once again suffering from a too familiar ailment.

Anxious to divert attention from his condition, Franz surpassed himself. When questioned on military law, he began a brilliant explanation of the penal code, but at that moment, a dispatch was hastily brought to the Emperor.

Reading the message, Francis paled then rose to announce a sudden flooding of the Danube, which had caused considerable damages and casualties in the suburbs of Vienna.

All present got to their feet while Francis gave order to make ready to leave immediately for the capital. In the tumult, Franz rushed to the door. On the way, his grandfather caught him by the sleeve.

"And where are you going?"

"To pack," Franz said. "I am going to Vienna with you, of course!"

Francis tightened his grip. "You will do nothing of the kind."

"Oh, but Sire!"

"Not with this cold!"

"Franzchen, you mustn't," the Empress chimed in.

Franz sniffled involuntarily. "I want to help!"

"No!" Francis said. "You cannot take part in the rescue operations. You'll catch pneumonia for sure."

"Blow your nose, my darling," the Empress enjoined sweetly.

Franz groaned in his handkerchief, "I am not helpless! And I am not a child anymore!"

Francis shook him affectionately. "I know that. And there will be plenty of other occasions to prove that you care, that you are useful!" He winked. "Remember, I need you in my army . . . soon and in fine form!"

Reluctantly, Franz submitted. Moreover, there were many ways to dispense relief, to lend help.

"If you would consider this as an advance, Sire," he offered, "I request that my next allowance be given to the homeless."

"Oh, Franz!" The Emperor gave him a quick, hard hug. "I am so proud of you!"

And Francis, habitually so niggardly, was so moved by his grandson's offer that he promised himself to double that allowance so as to not deprive Franz of his due.

There were even moments when Francis imagined it painless to give his grandson the world. . . .

22

C*ome, daughter . . . Come home with the child. He is mine to keep. Your work is done . . . done . . . done . . .*

It was the mew, strangled and cat-like, which woke Marie Louise. After a few seconds, she realized the sound was of her own making and found that her bed-gown was drenched with sweat. She sat up wondering where she was. This was not the bedroom in which she slept in her ducal palace in Parma. As her eyes focused, it all came back to her, and she wondered if reality wasn't worse than the nightmare from which she had emerged.

On this morning of June 18, 1830, she had awakened in the bedroom of Baron Mandl's villa, requisitioned for her use during her stay in Gratz. Gratz! That's where she was. And on her father's direct orders to join the Court in the Styrian capital. She would have much preferred to spend another season in Switzerland instead, given these trying circumstances.

Anxiety skewered her. Her son was giving her nightmares, needlessly reminding her of his imminent arrival after a two-day journey from Vienna. What was he going to say to her? The Neipperg "issue" hung over her like a pall. The marriage, the children . . . How well had the shameful irregularities been kept from him? She dressed hurriedly and skipped breakfast.

When Marie Louise entered her drawing room, Reichstadt was already there. Immediately he sprung from his seat and practically collected his mother in his arms as her knees grew weak at his sight.

"Mother?" The caring inflection in his voice revived her somewhat and she steadied herself. Her nose, in her near collapse, was crushed against the posy he wore on the lapel of his frock coat and that made her realize how tall he was. She had to look up to see his face.

She was dazzled by the Nordic radiance of his hair. Her Habsburg contribution!

Gently, he held her away, holding on to her shoulders. Bright blue eyes smiling, he said, "This may sound conceited, but must I have that effect on you too, Mother?"

Marie Louise heard herself laugh. The sound pleased her because with it came a tremendous sense of relief. He wasn't going to reproach her. His banter and relaxed manners pointed to—if not absolution, forgiveness at least.

In her gratitude, she indulged an impulse that might have been the manifestation of an emotion ill-conceived, but not totally lamed. She took her son's face between her hands and kissed him repeatedly, saying, "Don't be so sure, Franz. I hadn't had breakfast yet. I must have felt dizzy!" A perfect explanation, she thought, "But yes! you are the most handsome young man I have ever laid my eyes on!"

"Mother, please . . ."

"Modest at that?"

Franz smiled ruefully. "I can't even take any credit for the way I look."

What he'd said, the hint at some eddying dissatisfaction, had of course eluded her.

"Have you been waiting long?" she asked.

"Only five minutes at the most," Franz replied, opening a little box he had picked up from a chairside table. From it, came a nosegay which he pressed into his mother's hands.

"For you . . . a little different from mine," he said softly, looking at her with a pensive, melancholy air.

All these years, he thought her virtuous, a bit forgetful of how he'd longed for her nearness, but undefiled. And she had deceived him. He still loved her. The simple, childish love he'd felt for her still warmed and nourished his soul. He would keep banking this fire no matter how much he hurt now.

"Franz, that's sweet!" he heard her say, as she held the nosegay to her nostrils.

"Let me fasten it for you . . ." he offered, returning to the blunt reality of her limitation.

A little cross-eyed, she watched his long, nimble fingers work on the delicate task. The storm she had dreaded did not shatter her peace, and her appetite had returned with a vengeance. She rang for a footman.

"Have you had breakfast, Franz?"

"At six o'clock this morning at the inn before setting out for the last leg of the journey."

"That was a long time ago! Would you like to share mine?"

"I'll have a cup of tea, please," he said, as he settled down beside her and thanked her for the parcel of Parisian cravats she had sent him.

"You are such a smart dresser," she said, studying the stylishness of his frock coat and pin-striped trousers. "I knew you would like them!"

"I would have liked your coming to visit me better," he said gently.

Her voice took on a whine. "I wasn't feeling well last year, Franz," she replied with a touch of asperity. "That's why I chose to go to Switzerland."

"I am sorry, Mamma. That was thoughtless of me. I imagine the fresh mountain air must have done you much good."

The entrance of a footman answering her summons put an end to the silence which had followed. Marie Louise welcomed the interruption and took more time than necessary to give her instructions.

After the flunky had left, she worried about what to say next to a son she so seldom saw. By pure chance, Reichstadt created another welcome diversion when a mild coughing fit shook him.

"Have you taken another cold?" Marie Louise's tone was inquisitive, but bright, almost cheery.

Catching his breath, Franz rasped, "It's only a tickle."

"When I had my last cold," his mother went on chattily, "I was given a white powder. Oh, that was horrid! It made me sicker than I was! I hope you won't ever have to take that nauseating medicine. I just can't imagine people having to get ill in order to get better. That's absurd! Don't you agree?"

Franz nodded obligingly, and from behind his cupped hand quipped, "It might be hazardous to be well."

"That's just my point. . . ."

But Franz was not listening. He thought, *The real point is that we have nothing to say to each other. Long ago you shut me out of your life. What have I done?*

". . . Now mind what I am saying. . . ."

The guttural, harsh sounding German issuing from his mother's mouth reclaimed his attention for no other reason than she spoke with jarring volubility.

"It is wise to look after one's own health, like I am doing. So instead of defying your doctor's advice like Count Dietrichstein writes you are doing, you should heed them at all times. This would please me!"

"I don't consider a cold an illness, Mother," he objected patiently. "And I don't care to be pampered and coddled like an invalid."

"Colds can develop into something serious," Marie Louise insisted, enjoying the security this turn of conversation gave her.

But the vapid remarks were grating on Franz's nerves.

"Colds are like diarrhea. They come and go like an over-indulgence in prunes."

"Franz, really!" his mother exclaimed shocked.

Presently the footman returned carrying a tray laden with cakes on doilied dishes and silver pots steaming at the spout. He placed it before Marie Louise and withdrew immediately at her signal. To help herself to the pastries and beverage gave her another means to secure a countenance. Before Franz could offer to perform that service, she poured herself a cup of hot chocolate and then tea for him.

"I am sorry to be so . . . graphic," he apologized, accepting the cup she handed him.

She bit heartily into a creamy *Kuchembacker* and indicated with a nod that he should indeed mind his language.

Between two mouthfuls, she said, "Really, Franz, you have developed such a style! I remember your writing me about Ferdinand's mouth. . . ." She filled hers again and was unable to continue for the moment.

"What about Ferdinand's mouth?" Franz asked absently, just to say something.

Marie Louise swallowed. "You wrote that Ferdinand's mouth reminded you of a funnel."

"Well it's true. It's not very kind, I admit. Poor Ferdi!"

"He might be your emperor some day. And you are fortunate to have all your wits and to be well made, not to speak of an enviable future in the bosom of my family as the ruler of appreciable domains in the Bavarian Palatinate when you turn twenty-one."

"I am blessed indeed," Franz said evenly, examining the tea leaves at the bottom of his cup. "How can I be so lucky?"

"There are a good many things you don't realize," Marie Louise continued with importance. "And it isn't your fault. You were much too young, a mere boy, when I took care of establishing your future."

"And we never had much of a chance to talk," he promptly rejoined.

"Even so," she allowed defensively, "you were not quite mature enough when I saw you last to concern yourself with what I have to say now."

Instantly, Franz's eyes focused attentively on his mother's face. At long last they were going to have a heart to heart conversation!

"What is it, Mother?" he said hopefully.

"Well, aside from making sure that you would be financially comfortable, I also saw to it that you wouldn't be given a ridiculous name like Duke of Kron-Porzitschen, or Chrustenitz, or Trnowan, or Buschtierad, which would have made me blush to see this printed in the Court Almanac. I fought and fought and finally got my wish by convincing your grandfather to name you after a domain that has a German name instead of one only Bohemians can pronounce. That is how you came to be called Reichstadt, which in Slavonic, mind you, is still frightfully unpleasant to the ear, 'Zakupy.' Imagine! Duke of Zakupy! Now this sounds absolutely ludicrous, whereas 'Reichstadt' is certainly acceptable. Don't you think so?"

Marie Louise's long tirade had nearly put her son out of breath. She had never said so many words to him in one turn. And what she had said showed him the chasm that was separating them.

From her side he had crossed to the other, and nothing she could ever do would bridge that gap. He was awed by his own progress and its tremendous implications. It took him a few seconds before he could react to his mother's smug evaluation on the choice of his name.

Coolly he replied, " 'Reichstadt' is not only pronounceable, it is meaningful with 'Reich,' and 'Stadt,' meaning 'City of the Empire!' What a glorious combination!"

"Well, at least it is a decent name," she said, a world removed from the reach of his sarcasm.

He could not help offering with a tight smile, "And Napoleon Bonarparte isn't?"

Marie Louise began worrying the corner of her napkin, Napoleon's name had been banished from all casual conversations and blotted out of their child's official records. So far as she knew, Franz seemed to have had no trouble accepting his new identity. He signed 'Reichstadt' with an elegant flourish enclosing the name with a possessive loop. . . .

Breathlessly she asked, "Do you think of him often?"

Franz gave a brittle laugh. "How often do you think of Valhalla, Mother?"

"Never, I am afraid," she muttered, taken aback. That was another aspect of their relationship she did not enjoy. Franz had a definite knack for disconcerting her.

Eyes flashing, he said, "Well, warriors do! And like Father, there is something of a warrior in my blood. I'll fight like a lion if I were given a chance to!"

"We are at peace," she said with a stiff upper lip. "And we should thank my father for this!"

"We should also thank Russia, Prussia, and England. They, too, have helped subdue France," Franz added to appear fair.

His mother only said blandly, "So it seems, Franz."

He went on with an animation that hid a bait. "But just suppose another war broke out between France and Austria. Do you realize I might be called upon to draw my sword against your *former* subjects?"

She looked at him with a blank expression.

Baring one wrist, he pointed a finger at a pale blue vein. "See what is flowing in here? Austrian and Corsican blood! So the French could not accuse me of fratricidal intent, could they?"

"I suppose not," she answered, wondering where this nonsensical talk of his was leading. "You should not concern yourself with thoughts of war," she continued, injecting in her tone a severity that she felt should put his aspirations in proper perspective. "Instead, you ought to recognize the blessing of bearing arms only during exercise!"

Franz readjusted his cuff. He had steered her exactly where he wanted. "I am not even that blessed!" he said ruefully.

"What do you mean?"

He pounced on the overture. "Mother, I have completed all my studies, successfully passed all the examinations, and I am quite ready to commence a military career in this . . . blessed peace time. Only so far nothing is happening but talks! But if you were to put in a few good words in my behalf, this can all change!"

"That's Count Dietrichstein's doing. Your tutor keeps insisting on the nomination of the best available candidates to form your military household, and those aren't easy to come by."

Franz rolled his eyes upward in annoyance. "He wants to give me a suite of officers descended from the gods!"

"You should be flattered! He always wants the best for you!"

"What's wrong with commoners of merit? As for rank, a noteworthy corporal would do very well. Father himself was brilliant at this early stage of his career!"

Napoleon, again. . . .

Marie Louise took a good, long look at her son . . . at *their* son. In spite of his blondness, the Habsburg's famous full lips and the slant of his jaws, there remained about him, a haunting and formidable emanation. A part of Napoleon was very much alive in his son!

But if that was all he wanted, *to play* soldier. . . .

"I'll see what I can do, Franz."

Metternich had convinced Francis that it would be unwise to surround Reichstadt with bright individuals whether they be of ancient nobility or of a lesser aristocratic vintage. Ultimately, the men chosen to compose the Duke's suite had to be Metternich's creatures and their roles essentially that of watchdogs instead of mentors.

At the conclusion of a private debate, with Count Dietrichstein holding on to his "unrealistic" demands, as Francis cautiously put it, nothing had been settled.

Frustrated and kept in ignorance of the real impediments, Franz moped. Feeling sorry for his grandson, the Emperor took him to various functions and parades, hoping to distract him.

With Francis standing beside him on the balcony, Franz moodily watched a magnificent and costly display of fireworks paid for by the city of Gratz in honor of the imperial visit.

Below, the crowds roared themselves hoarse waving at them. Francis was acutely aware that the presence of the young man at his side had much, if not everything, to do with the delirious ovation they were receiving. Reichstadt's immense popularity, he knew, originated from the mystique surrounding the circumstances that had brought him to Austria. His appeal was further enhanced by his striking appearance and winning manners, which endeared him to the populace. At this moment, Francis preferred to dwell on the two innocuous elements against which he, himself, was not immune. He would allow the Prince to favor the crowds with an acknowledgment.

"You may wave back, Franz. They are quite taken with you."

"I have done nothing to deserve such public homage," Franz said ceremoniously. "It is Your Majesty they are acclaiming."

The Emperor caught the curves of an impassive profile.

"You are sulking!" he exclaimed.

"Yes, I am."

Francis returned his attention to the cheering multitude.

"Is that why you are so darn formal?"

"Possibly, Sire."

"My dear boy, my not doing exactly what you want and when you want it, does not mean I love you any less!"

"I realize that," Franz allowed, a little mollified.

"Then do me a favor," Francis coaxed good-humoredly, "wave to these good people!"

Reichstadt raised his arm and waved. The salute was received with a thunder of acclamations. From various segments of the crowd came frenzied shouts of "Long live Napoleon!"

Francis gasped, and tottered. Livid, he choked out a rasping and dying, *"Es ist unmöglich!"* Impossible!

Franz came to his grandfather's assistance and lent him a steadying arm, putting the other around the aging Emperor's shoulder. His heart skipped and jumped and his head felt light.

"My God!" Francis panted. "Did you hear this Franz? Did you?"

"Yes," Franz answered with a lump in his throat.

"But why? Why?"

Francis's peevish question could only be addressed to himself, yet his upturned face distorted by what he had just heard demanded needless corroboration.

Franz looked down at the Emperor of Austria huddling in the vitality of his youth and seeking reassurance in his despoliation. The same man who had stripped him of every right he had and left him defenseless save for one weapon.

Quietly, and with implacable candor he said, "This is only natural, Sire. After all, my name is Napoleon."

That same evening before supper, Reichstadt sat down at his desk and wrote briskly:

My Dearest Sophie,

I wish Schönbrunn and its precious contents (meaning you, of course) could have been transported here like in the story of Aladdin so that without risk of hardship for yourself and for the baby you are expecting, you could have been with us in Gratz. Needless to say, I miss your company. I dare hope you are comfortable and resting in preparation for the great event in the pleasant surroundings of my favorite summer palace, so close to Vienna, yet so enchantingly bucolic that one can enjoy the quiet majesty of nature only a few miles from our bustling capital. So, do remember your friend if you happen to be walking up to the Gloriette, though such a long walk in the park might not be a good idea at this stage of your condition. I can't imagine the necessity for Mons. Malfatti to follow me here in Gratz, for though he is my physician, I have no need of him. Whereas if you recall, his specialization in obstetrics would be better suited to your present demands had he stayed at Schönbrunn to join forces with your own doctors. Forgive my concerns in matters such as these. But we have been friends so long. A lifetime for me, in any case. And a lifelong friend should be accorded some indulgence if he appears to fret needlessly or if he does become much too attentive in questions which pertain exclusively to the province of women. So just imagine that in this particular situation your devoted friend is the Princess of Venice (I shall explain later).

On the other hand, that individual known as Franz von Reichstadt isn't having much luck. Contrary to his fondest hopes, the "Congress" of Gratz has failed to settle the question of his emancipation. He is still being groomed to that end (doomsday!) pending the protracted selection of his military staff.

I shall be consoled somewhat when sitting happily beside you. Until then (Baden is next on our itinerary before I return), suffice to say that the old adage is still in full force: It is not the cowl that makes the friar. . . .

I kiss your hands and the tip of your nose.

At that precise moment, the Emperor was also sitting at his writing desk, pondering the problem of getting across to his people that under no circumstances should his grandson be called by his first given name. Such filiation had to be buried in the ashes of a defunct French Empire. One Napoleon was more than Europe could handle, Metternich had said. The Emperor of Austria wholeheartedly agreed. . . .

Later that evening, at a formal reception attended by members of the diplomatic corps, the "second" Napoleon did draw intense scrutiny. Franz was aware of being closely observed by his tutor's companion, whom Dietrichstein eased forward and introduced as Major Anton Prokesch Ritter von Osten.

Franz looked directly into large, dark expressive eyes with a slight flicker of recognition showing in his own at the mention of the name.

Chestnut-colored side-whiskers framed a face showing relative youth. The Major, Franz estimated, must be in his thirties. A well-groomed mustache shaded his upper lip, and his general appearance exuded sensitivity and refinement.

Anton von Osten smartly clacked his heels. Franz returned the salute with a slight bow, offering a few words of greeting that were courteous, but conventional.

To Dietrichstein's chagrin, Franz politely excused himself after the tutor announced that the Major would be sitting next to him at supper.

With glowering eyes, the tutor followed his pupil's exit from the drawing room.

"Now, what is the matter with him!" he fumed. "Why can't he show some interest in you? If he had any sense at all, he would appreciate the opportunity of becoming worldly-wise in the most accomplished sort of way by making your acquaintance."

It took Prokesch a few seconds to realize he had been enthralled at the sight of Dietrichstein's pupil.

He was aware of the Duke's particular circumstances, of the explosive implications linked to his very existence, which reaffirmed the Major's profound admiration for the audacity of Napoleon's tactical concepts. And now to behold the son of that great military strategist, apparently gifted and commanding such fascination!

Prokesch said at last, "You flatter me, Count."

"No, Anton. I've known and respected your family long enough and I admire you too much to waste my words in empty compliments. You are the kind of person I wish to see among the Duke's familiars now that your diplomatic peregrinations have at long last brought you back to Austria. And look what happened! He ignored you! Please, accept my apologies!"

"No apologies are needed, dear Count Maurice. Though I must confess, I had looked forward to conversing with your dashing pupil."

"Bah! I believe his extraordinary good looks is all he has after all!" Dietrichstein retorted, thoroughly roiled and well aware of his own deception.

Obviously the Count was overreacting. Prokesch reserved his judgment. He said quietly, "That would be regrettable."

"How can you be so calm?" Dietrichstein complained.

Prokesch smiled. "Call it an occupational ability."

Dietrichstein shook his head. "The Duke did offend you!"

"Oh, I wouldn't say that!" Prokesch soothed. "And I don't believe I deserve any special treatment on the part of His Highness after all."

Deeply disappointed nevertheless, and quite resigned to be ignored, Prokesch sipped his pottage while Dietrichstein kept glaring at his pupil from across the table as Franz began to exchange commonplace remarks with his other table companion, Colonel Firet.

By the end of the first course, had the tutor's gaze been as lethal as Medusa's, Reichstadt would have turned to stone. Once again, Count Dietrichstein's persecution complex flared up.

He is snubbing the Major because *I* was the one who introduce him, he thought bitterly. Anger gave the tutor an even more tantalizing vision of that life he had contemplated leading had he not been called to dedicate himself to the signal task of educating Napoleon's son. He could have organized many fine concerts and best used his talents as Director of the Imperial Theater. And now, as his blood pressure was mounting, he felt more honored having been the patron of the late Beethoven and Schubert than being tutor to this ungrateful wretch who couldn't even carry a tune and only liked military music!

The "wretch" whom Colonel Firet seemed to admire in a measure greater than Dietrichstein's ill-humor could endure, presently helped himself to a minute portion of the fish course and at long last engaged Prokesch in a conversation.

"And what brings you to Gratz, Major von Osten? Or is Gratz your place of residence?"

Surprised and gladdened, Prokesch answered pleasantly, "My family is from Gratz, Monseigneur. I am only here on a furlough of sorts. I am, one could say, an itinerant negotiator on international issues who is enjoying a reprieve."

Reichstadt's eyes seemed to outshine the crystal glasses set before them. He smiled. "Very diplomatically put. I suppose your wife and your children must be delighted to have you home for a while."

"My parents, Your Highness. I am not married."

"Forgive me, Major. I had no intention to pry."

"Not at all," Prokesch protested good-naturedly.

Only toward the end of the meal did Prokesch realize that the Duke of Reichstadt had subtly managed to interrogate him and learn that he was thirty-five years old, came from a wealthy bourgeois family with the "von Osten" short for Ritter von Osten—Knight of the Orient—standing for an honorary elevation to recompense services performed on fact-finding missions in the Middle East, that he had just returned after six years of extensive travel in the Balkans and Egypt, and last but not least, had also fought in the campaigns of 1813 through 1815 against the armies of Napoleon.

From his observation post, across the blossoms of an enormous centerpiece and between corpulent retired General Natzel sitting at his right and squeezing him against equally obese Major Jordis at his left, Dietrichstein began to calm down. Reichstadt, at long last, was conversing with his favorite diplomat!

Franz did even better. At the conclusion of the banquet, he warmly clasped Prokesch's hands.

Cursing the length of the table, the tutor hastened to the other side to find the cause of this miraculous change in his pupil's behavior. Dietrichstein's precipitation only partially succeeded in gratifying his curiosity. All he could ascertain was that Reichstadt had said something that delighted the Major, and at the same time left him deeply impressed.

"Thank you, Monseigneur," he kept repeating. "Thank you!"

Franz turned to his tutor, who had finally joined them. "I should like to see Major von Osten as often as circumstances will permit during our stay in Gratz. Do you suppose this could be arranged, sir?"

Dietrichstein's sour mouth formed a recognizable smile. "Certainly! If the Major is so inclined himself?"

"I have accepted the Prince's invitation, Count," Prokesch told him with a look of appreciation.

The tutor's smile broadened. "Tomorrow morning a nine o'clock then?"

As Prokesch nodded his assent, Franz put out his hand. "Well, it's settled. I shall be expecting you tomorrow. Good night, Major."

With visible pleasure Prokesch firmly pressed the extended hand. "Good night, Your Highness."

"Going to bed already?" Dietrichstein inquired, a little disappointed.

Franz only smiled before turning on his heels.

Brimming with indulgence now, the Count watched his pupil briskly stride out of the room.

He explained, a hint of affection creeping into his tone, "The Prince and I have been up since quarter to five this morning. Only I took a nap and he didn't. It's been a long day for him. . . ."

Then laying his hand on the Major's arm, he asked, "What happened, Anton? What brought on this amazing and sudden conquest of yours? Was it something you said?"

"Something I wrote, Count. Something your pupil read and assimilated extraordinarily well, and I assume, under your expert guidance. You ought to be very proud of him! He is, from the little I have seen, a very fine and exceedingly intelligent young man!"

Flattered, Dietrichstein pulled up his chin. "Of course I am proud!" And squeezing the Major's arm he added confidentially, "Coming from you, that sort of compliment certainly puts my mind at ease. I don't feel so . . . compromised by the Duke's progresses."

Prokesch's brows arched, "Compromised?"

"Come, Anton! In the Duke's particular position, brilliance is not exactly well-looked upon, nor is it to be encouraged."

"Oh, but that's utterly unfair!" Prokesch exclaimed with indignation.

"It's politics," Dietrichstein said pensively, "and I have no taste for that sort of thing! You have a noble soul, Anton . . . and so does the Prince, despite the white hair he had given me. You deserve each other, not to speak of the stabilizing influence you will bring to this relationship. . . ." The Count's voice trailed off. ". . . I can't claim any credit for guiding the Prince's appreciation of your work, of which I am familiar. He does a great deal of reading on his own. I can only assume he was impressed by your study of the Battles of Ligny, Quatre-Bras, and Waterloo. And there you must forgive me, Anton, my forte is not war."

"Those are precisely the ones! The amazing thing is that this study was published twelve years ago!"

"And reprinted since. The Prince is an avid reader of military publications and never forgets the name of an author!"

"Yet he seemed so . . . indifferent at first."

Dietrichstein affectionately slipped his arm under the Major's. "I suspect the disconcerting reception he gave you was nothing more than an indulgence in social tactics."

Without Reichstadt, the evening no longer held any interest for the Major although the Emperor and the Empress invited him to join their set. Carolina Augusta had taken quite a fancy to the well-traveled sloe-eyed diplomat whom the Emperor welcomed that very morning on a letter of introduction from Metternich himself. The Chancellor depended on Prokesch's evaluation of the political mood of various regions to direct or redirect Austrian policies.

The Empress looked forward to being entertained by anecdotes certain to abound with journeys to exotic places. Prokesch obliged, amusing everyone, including Francis.

Archduke John was the only person to sit quietly in the midst of a responsive audience. John and Francis were not exactly on amicable standing. Suddenly John decided to ask a serious question. "How close are the Greeks coming to being established into a monarchy?"

"By ridding themselves of the Turks, the Greeks have created a vacuum that is difficult to fill soon, since Prince Leopold of Saxe-Coburg has withdrawn his candidacy," Prokesch explained.

John made bold to comment, "The Greeks should be left to govern themselves."

Immediately Francis looked crossly at his brother. John should have held his tongue. Had he forgotten that his sojourn in Gratz was not meant as a holiday, but represented the serving of a sentence of banishment decreed by Francis himself? For John had committed a grave political sin. He was too close to the people.

Francis called him sharply to order. "John," he warned, "that is enough on the subject!"

Prokesch tried to clear the air by proposing, "I feel the throne of Greece will find a worthy incumbent in the person of the Duke of Reichstadt."

Immediately he realized having spoken under some totally irresistible impulse. To his relief and surprise, the suggestion did not meet with one of those frigid silences accompanying a *faux pas*.

The Empress was the first to express her delight, and Dietrichstein mumbled something undeniably pleasant, the near ecstatic look on his face was telling. John, having decided that silence is golden, contributed an energetic nod. John, naturally fond of Reichstadt, was so constituted he would commiserate with anyone ill-done by. As for Francis. . . .

The Emperor said dreamily that the idea deserved some consideration.

At precisely nine in the morning the next day, Prokesch paid his call. Reichstadt greeted the Major with effusion. Dietrichstein took a seat opposite the two young men looking on smugly. He had never felt in such excellent mood.

Once again, Franz voiced his appreciation of Prokesch's analysis of the battles he had read in the *Osterreichische Militarische Zeitschrift.*

"I can't thank you enough for defending my father's tactical competence when the general trend goes as far as denying him any at all," he said warmly.

"I only paid tribute where tribute is due, Monseigneur."

"And I wish to pay tribute to your courage for speaking up. I was so impressed with your article, I have translated it into French and Italian."

"You have?" Dietrichstein injected pleasantly. Franz took such copious notes while reading that the tutor was beginning to lose track of all his pupil's studious output.

Franz continued with excitement. "Sometime I should like to discuss with you the battle of Austerlitz!"

"War is all His Highness is thinking of," the Count put in with sustained good humor.

"The art of war," Franz corrected.

"All the same," Dietrichstein said affably, "it's a murderous hobbyhorse." His euphoria was such that anything his pupil might have said, if said in Prokesch's presence, would have his stamp of approval.

Besides, the Major's view on Reichstadt's future was in harmony with the Count's own idea of the place the Prince should occupy in life. By now, Dietrichstein had shed the fretful application he had used to transform a little French boy into an archduke and had reached the stage where his appreciation of his creation (for he did give himself considerable credit for his pupil's success and accomplishment) could not warm to the possibility of seeing so much potential go to waste.

Where Reichstadt would fit on the sensitive chessboard of politics did not faze his apolitical turn of mind. Somehow, something could be worked out. He just could not bear seeing Reichstadt's talents go unrecognized. The Duke deserved to be given a throne! He thought the moment opportune to bring up the subject of Greece.

"Anton, won't you tell the Prince of the suggestion you made last night to Their Majesties?"

Then he turned to Franz and explained, "That was after Your Highness had left."

Prokesch looked thoughtfully at Reichstadt. Facing him was a young man, paradoxically famous yet only known by very few people. And so misinformed was the general public about him that stories went the rounds describing the Prince as a poorly educated lad without much character. How utterly unfair! No youth had more impressed and inspired him! Even to the point of considering Reichstadt perfectly fit to wear a crown after having met him only a few hours before!

"Last night, Monseigneur, I proposed your candidacy to the throne of Greece," he said slowly.

Reichstadt stared at him with an expression of absolute incredulity. "You didn't!"

"I did, Monseigneur."

Smugly, Dietrichstein observed, "It is not uncommon for archdukes to accede to foreign thrones, you know."

"Oh my God!" Franz murmured running his fingers through his hair.

He was well-acquainted with the problems that beset Greece. Its current president's disdain for common people and strong Russian affiliations were creating considerable resentments. The Greeks no longer consider him suitable to help them attain complete nationhood. . . .

"What did the Emperor say to your proposal?" he asked at the height of excitement.

"His Majesty did not oppose it," Dietrichstein put in.

"Oh my God!"

Things were happening so fast! Sooner than Franz had anticipated. He had not yet emerged from that retired, sheltered existence he had often compared to that of a woman living in the seclusion of a zenana. Without warning, without giving him time for preparation, life was rushing upon him, assaying his talents!

With a surge of tender pride, he thought, Father became emperor at thirty-five. In a less grand manner, but earlier yet, I, his son, could be king at the age of nineteen! But what of France?

"General Prince von Holenhole!" a footman announced, breaking into Reichstadt's emotional moment.

An air of desolation broke over his face. The impromptu visit was ill-timed and ruining their meeting.

Immediately Dietrichstein came to his pupil's rescue. "I'll turn him away," he assured him.

Left alone with the Major, Franz asked, keeping his voice low as though he was acting in stealth, "Tell me the truth. Do you really think me fit to undertake anything of importance?"

Reichstadt's genuine ardor to excel, his total lack of conceit and candid offer to be evaluated profoundly touched Prokesch. Without hesitation he said, "I see a rare sincerity in you, Monseigneur, and an eagerness for self-improvement. Both of which are the marks of a worthy person."

On a dare, Franz took the unprecedented decision to come out of his customary reserve. "Alas! I have no one to prepare me to meet the crucial demands of a useful destiny. I am surrounded with mediocrity. I see no salvation but in you!"

"I am flattered, Monseigneur. And I value the compliment though I feel undeserving," Prokesch said noncommittally.

Wisely, Reichstadt chose not to press him.

When Dietrichstein returned, Franz interrogated the Major on his work and travel with intense curiosity. The diplomat was opening for him a window on the world.

Later, as Prokesch took his leave, Franz whispered while walking him to the door of the drawing room, "Will you come see me again?"

"I shall make every effort to do so," the Major answered conspiratorially.

When Franz met Prokesch again, he said soberly, "I have given much thought concerning the position you so generously wish to see me assume. And were I to be seriously considered for the throne of Greece, I have decided to decline that honor. My youth and inexperience would hamper my freedom to act. I wouldn't be allowed to take any initiatives. I would only be a figurehead. And who wants to be a figurehead?"

Prokesch glanced quickly at ever-present Count Dietrichstein. Reichstadt's independent closing remark could not have escaped him. But the tutor had decided that Franz did well not to engage himself, only because this would keep the way clear to merit the far more prestigious crown of France. He expressed his approval in the Prince's decision. Then convinced that his pupil was in good enough hands to dispense with a chaperon, he asked to be excused to dispatch some pressing household matters.

Franz felt free to elaborate. "And why should anyone want to bother with me anyway? I cannot expect to do much on my own because being the son of Napoleon would always prevent me from occupying an independent position. On the other hand, suppose that independence were granted. How could I possibly reconcile the two races in me? How could I satisfy this duality, being only one person?"

Reichstadt's amazing frankness, with all that it could suggest of problems and even danger, unsettled the Major.

Noticing his uneasiness, Franz continued with emotion, "If I were to count the hours we have spent together, they would scarcely amount to the necessary time one would need to debate the value of a newly made acquaintance. But I have completed my evaluation. I have such faith in the excellence of our association. Such faith in you! I can speak of unspeakable things!"

"I can assure Your Highness of my discretion," Prokesch offered nobly.

"Then, hear me out! Item: if France were to demonstrate that she believes in the Imperial principles and call me to power, I would answer that call! Item: if Europe were to prevent me from doing so, I shall draw my sword against Europe! But will France ever look more thoughtfully into the reservoir from which sprang my father's motivations? I, for one, can't imagine that his motives were ever base or totally centered on self-aggrandizement. Perhaps the worst of my father's sins was to have been a mercenary in the pay of glory. Glory for France, to be sure. And I can't really blame Austria for misunderstanding him . . ." his voice broke off and melancholically, he concluded, "Austria . . . the only home I know. Austria I have aspired to serve after the example of Prince Eugene. . . ."

Prokesch said soothingly, "Your Highness's attachment for Austria is only natural, for Austria is your country of adoption."

Franz laced his fingers and twisted them, wrestling with conflicting emotions.

"I love the Emperor! I feel bound never to break his heart, and mine is torn asunder! Yet Austria would have nothing to fear from me. If I am called to reign in France, I shall do all in my power to foster a fruitful and durable peace between our two countries." He paused to consider Prokesch. His eyes bore into the Major's.

"Ah, you inspire me so! And who will prepare me for the throne? You! Consider how providentially our paths have crossed! It's fate! That same predetermination that has ordained that individuals of consequence should be accorded the companionship and guidance of a wise and devoted friend. Telemachus had Mentor, Aeneas had Achates, and Schiller's *Don Carlos* had the Marquis of Posa! And how well, indeed, does a passage from that play conform to my own predicaments:

> *Let me cry, shed on your heart tears of fire, oh, my one and only friend! For in this whole world I have no one but you! I am an orphan on the step of a throne. I do not know how it is like to have a father . . . and I am the son of a king!*

Franz continued without stopping. "Major von Osten, I am asking you to be my Posa! Have faith in my star as I only vow to accomplish great and wholesome deeds!"

It took Prokesch a moment before he could answer. Reichstadt's passionate outburst had intensely moved him. But he was a cautious man. What the Prince was asking of him amounted purely and simply to a political betrothal.

Allowing himself some time for reflection, he said in good conscience, "The Marquis of Posa knew Don Carlos well. I have met Your Highness only recently. I am listening to a young man whose determination I have no means to ascertain and whose mettle I cannot test. Monseigneur, I cannot engage myself."

Instantly the radiance faded from Franz's face. He flinched only slightly to straighten to his full height, tight-lipped. The Major was surprised to see him bear with dignity and stoicism the blow of what must have been a monumental disappointment. Only his voice trembled a little when he said, "You are right. I have done nothing and proven nothing!"

"I meant no offense," Prokesch protested, sincerely pained.

"You did not offend me, Major. You have just sobered me."

"Monseigneur, I am sorry!"

"Why?"

Prokesch could not resist the valiant and yet hurt look directed at him.

"Because I do not wish to curb Your Highness's enthusiasm . . . if I am to become your Posa."

Franz checked himself. The wear and tear of mood changes had put a damper on his reaction. His tone was level.

"Will you?"

"Yes, Monseigneur! I cannot refuse you. I shall be your Posa on two conditions. . . ."

Prokesch could not complete his sentence. With youthful exuberance, Franz clasped him in his arms. He hugged him in turn, protectively, as one would a younger brother.

Once the effusion was over, he said, "I shall be your Posa for life! And for a full and rewarding one!"

Franz's eyes shone with renewed brilliance. "For a very long life indeed! Oh, Major! I feel as though I am born again!"

He was nineteen yet could indeed speak of rebirth because his life had assumed new dimensions; its purposes were redefined owing to the encouragement of an estimable man in whom he had found a true friend. A friend whom he hoped would become his companion and associate . . . soon.

But not soon enough. Prokesch received a new assignment and his impending departure for Switzerland was only tolerable in that he promised to write.

Before they parted, Franz said, "Slander is such a deep rooted evil once it has been sown. In the course of your mission, I beg you to dispel the falsehoods that have been attached to my person. . . ." He thought of Barthélemy's poem. "And one thing I can't bear is the stigma of degeneracy!"

Then with anxiety, he asked, "Where will we meet again?"

"I shall always find you, Monseigneur," Prokesch said warmly.

Franz looked at him, studying the gentle symmetry of the Major's face, the bright liquid dark brown eyes fixed amicably upon him. He experienced the infinite peace of being accepted for what he truly was. It took a stranger to do this. A stranger? No longer!

"Let us drop all ceremony between us," he eagerly suggested. "If you would please call me Franz in private, I should like to address you by your first name, too."

"Of course."

"Then, Anton, I wish you could find me in Baden instead of Schönbrunn next time we meet."

"Why Baden?"

Franz laughed. It was a happy, insouciant laugh Prokesch did not imagine could come from a youth so remarkably serious.

"Because," he answered, "I am going to Baden next. This simply means I shall be seeing you again shortly within the three weeks of my stay there before returning to Vienna."

Prokesch rubbed his chin, a fond smile pulling his elegant mustache. "I wish it were so. But I can't promise anything."

Then taking from his pocket a carefully folded piece of paper, he placed it in Reichstadt's hand. "I brought this for you. A souvenir of my Grecian voyage. It is very small and I did not want to lose it, hence the wrapping."

An exclamation of genuine appreciation escaped Franz when he examined a fine gold coin bearing the effigy of Alexander the Great. "For me?"

"Most especially for you, Franz. As a token of friendship and a reminder of the great future that awaits you!"

Franz looked up starry-eyed. "I'll wear it around my neck," he said solemnly. "Like a talisman. I'll never part with it as long as I live!"

23

Princess Melanie von Metternich was reviewing a list of guests she planned to invite to a dinner party at their magnificent castle at Konigswart near Marienbad when a footman breathlessly announced that something might be terribly wrong with her husband.

Immediately the Princess rushed to the study where Metternich had gone after lunch to pore over state documents.

Clement Nepomuch Wenceslas Lothar, Prince Metternich, who never failed to intimidate those who came in contact with him, was inelegantly hunched over his desk.

"My dear!" Melanie gasped, "What is it?"

Metternich lifted a fist, peremptorily waving the servants away.

Kneeling beside him, she asked, "Clement, are you ill?"

"Worse," he whispered to her. "Destroyed! All my life's work is ruined!"

"What happened, my precious? What could possibly upset you so?"

He responded with a groan. "France . . . King Charles X has been forced to flee to England. The fool! Now . . . they've put Louis Philippe Duc d'Orleans in his place! And I know the man is only a decoy to facilitate the implementation of Republican policies!"

He slammed the flat of his hand on the desk. "I won't stand for a Republic! Not ever! I have dedicated my life to uphold Conservatism! Legitimacy! The hegemony of Austria!" Another slam on the desk. "And the latter cannot survive if the mob is enthroned!"

Melanie tried to calm her husband. "The new king will mind you, for you are a powerful man! You'll have a proper monarchy and everything will return to normal."

"You speak as though I ran everything," he said with false modesty. "I am only a servant of His Majesty."

She disagreed with enthusiasm. "We would all be lost without you! If it weren't for you, Napoleon would have continued tyrannizing the world, or his son would be on the loose working havoc after the example of that upstart Bonaparte."

The mere mention of Reichstadt set Clement's irritation going again like the press of a bellows rekindling smoldering embers. His nostrils flared. "His son is my trump card. One which I can flash, and God help me, never have to play!"

"Soft, Clement. Soft," Melanie soothed putting a finger on her husband's lips. "Shall I cancel the dinner party?"

Metternich nodded. "I wish I were already in Vienna."

Disheveled and in the highest pitch of excitement, Franz erupted into his mother's drawing room after brushing past a footman who made a futile attempt to announce him. Marie Louise took fright imagining that her son had just met with some terrible mishap.

She made to ring for help. He stayed her hand. "No, please! Don't call anyone. I must speak to you alone. I have come to no harm!" Then urgently, "Mother, we must go back to Wien at once!"

Caught at one of her favorite pastimes, gobbling pastries, she lifted at him her slanted cat-like eyes and asked with a mouthful. "Why must we leave Baden?"

"Have you not seen the newspaper today?"

"Part of it," she answered, garbling her words.

"Have you not noticed anything . . . special?"

"Special?" She swallowed and licked her lips, thinking. After a few seconds, she admitted, "No, Franz. I can't say that I have."

"There's been a revolution in Paris and only in Wien can I find out more about what happened."

She said with genuine surprise, "I don't see how this should concern you."

Franz flushed. "Of course, you wouldn't!" he started impatiently. But immediately he checked himself, realizing with consternation that for the first time he was angry with his beloved mother.

He forced himself to speak more calmly. "That's unfortunate, Mamma. Because whether you see it or not, what is happening to France and in France ought to interest me."

"Ought?" Marie Louise said, taken aback.

"Mother, I wasn't born on the moon. Paris is my birthplace and I am the son of an emperor."

He saw her stiffened. "That's ancient history, Franz! The Duke of Reichstadt has no business bothering himself with the fate of a foreign country!"

In spite of the guard he'd set to spare her sensibilities, Franz's emotion brimmed over like water over a dam. His mother's repudiation of the past went outrageously too far, reaching to the unthinkable extremity of forcing him to renounce his origin! And if it were not enough that she should disown her husband, she dared negate his paternity! Damn her Habsburg arrogance! Curse their precious race!

"Did you say foreign?" he taunted her, raising his voice. "Then, am I to understand that I, too, have been conceived by the power of the Holy Spirit?"

Marie Louise glared at her son, her chin up, her lower lip quavering. "Blaspheme! Blaspheme all you care! But don't ever, ever, make light of the heritage I have given you! You would be all the sorrier without it! For there are those who, in spite of the status it has given you, call you a bastard regardless! Do you hear me, Franz? A bastard!"

"I glory in such bastardy!" Franz shouted. "I only wish I were wholly a bastard! With none of your blood!" Then at the peak of fury he exploded, "It stinks of decadence! Of stale and rancid antiquity! I would gladly rid myself of it! I care nothing for fossils!"

Her rage matched his. "Ungrateful wretch!" she spat out. "You care nothing for decency! At least you should have enough brains to appreciate the glory of the parentage I have given you!"

"I hate it!" Franz countered savagely. "Do you know what you have given me?" he stormed at his mother. "Poison! You have given me poison! You are filling me up with it."

Horrified, she threw at him the noblest of replies, "I have given you life!"

But that was an ill-chosen vindication. In the heat of the moment, Franz flung at Marie Louise words that showed he had pondered over the nature of his parents' marriage.

"You did not really want me! I was forced upon you! So what is there for you to give?"

"Franz!" she called sharply, reeling from the brutal blow of his accusation.

Unrelenting, he reminded her, "My name is Napoleon!"

"Oh, no!" she wailed.

"Ah, yes!" Franz said implacably.

Her anger gave way to deep self-pity and she whimpered, "God! What have I done to deserve this?"

"Nothing! That's exactly what you've done, Mother!"

Stupefied, she stared at him and burst into violent sobs that seemed to melt her whole countenance, capping a climax that left Franz stunned for a few seconds as he watched her shake and heave.

The loud sound of her crying overwhelmed him with regret. He would have gladly gathered all the words just said and return them unspoken to his heart. And it felt good to repent for having overrun her miserable defenses. . . .

Tentatively, he put his arms around her. "Mamma, I am so very sorry! I don't know what came over me . . . I was a beast!"

She shrank from his touch. "You have disowned me!"

"No, Mamma! Never!" he protested passionately.

"I have poisoned you! I have given you foul blood. You said so yourself! And you are loathing me for this!"

"I love you!"

"No! No!" she said with vehemence. "You can't!"

"Oh, but I do!" he cried frantically, "I do love you!"

With unexpected insight, and sobbing all the louder, she wailed. "I am not the mother you need . . ."

"You are the mother I love! Always!"

"You are only pretending," she countered harshly, her voice steely and steadying. "And I suppose I should thank you for that!"

"Mother, please, don't talk that way!" he implored.

"How else should I talk? There is nothing left between us!"

"There is love between us! Don't deny it!" Almost forcibly he took her in his arms. But she fought him, furiously trying to push him away. He was stronger and held on until she stopped resisting.

He said, "I worshipped you!"

She heaved, offering her own contribution "I want your happiness! I've done my very best to take care of you."

In his heart, Franz conceded that his mother's protestations were genuine. Within her limitations she had been called upon to cope with severe tribulations brought upon her by his own existence. His love for her now held absolutory compassion. Kissing her graying hair he said, "I know, Mother. I know. Please forgive me! I must have been out of my mind."

"You must have," she said, her tone softening, and looked up at him. Then, entranced by his remorseful beauty, she stretched herself on the tip of her toes, and quickly touched her lips to his forehead.

With the light brush of a finger, Franz wiped away from her cheeks the wetness of the tears, which he felt having so cruelly caused. "Mother . . . You must never doubt that I love you," he said. Then gently, "Will you do as I asked?"

Still spell-bound by the contemplation of his face, the request that had ignited their hurtful exchanges now came back to her as a distant echo. Appeased, she nodded. "We will leave tomorrow for Wien, if that is what you want."

In her private garden at Schönbrunn, Sophie was reading over the note Franz had sent her by special courier. In it, he announced his impending arrival, only saying that he was cutting short his holiday in Baden on a "whim." That puzzled her somewhat, but there were no other explanations.

So she waited in happy anticipation when suddenly she sensed a movement within her womb. She acknowledged the slight pain with delight and bravely welcomed all the attending miseries of pregnancy.

The baby was due in a couple of weeks at the most, and she looked forward to the joys and activities of motherhood. They would cancel that skewering sense of wasted youth and wasted years, which sometime so overcame her that she had turned more devoutly to religion.

Now with the pending arrival of the child and fortified by a deepening piety, she was able to regard her husband Francis Charles's distasteful personality with relative detachment. The thought of him made her briefly wonder where her husband was that afternoon. She assumed he might have gone to the Riding Hall. Karl had an irrational love for horses, even smelt like a horse, and like them, snorted with irritating frequency. He regularly spoke to his favorite teams of roans much too seriously for his own good. But whatever Karl decided to do to occupy himself, including frequent stops to local taverns where ale was served by accommodating and giggling wenches, mattered little to Sophie as long as he made no demand upon her time.

On that point she had no grounds for complaints. Finding nothing in common to share with her other than her bed, Karl made himself scarce when not required to appear with her at court functions, visits of state, or family meals. This estrangement had become so obvious in court circles that Sophie knew their marriage was generally looked upon as an expedient arrangement for dynastic coupling. . . . Which it was, she reflected sadly.

"Sophie!"

In seconds Franz was at her side and pressed a posy of violets into her hand.

Taking it, she opened her arms, and happily he stepped into them. Oh, how he'd missed the closeness and comfort of a long-established and irreproachable familiarity! He planted a kiss on her forehead, and more gently touched his lips to the tip of her nose before drawing away.

"You do keep your promises!" she laughed softly, remembering the closing of his message. She held the posy to her nostrils. "These are so lovely! Thank you!"

"Your favorite," he smiled, straightening to his full height.

Sophie never ceased to be amazed by Franz's passage from being a boy to adulthood. It was true that it had gradually taken place under her eyes, but still, there were moments such as this one, when the splendid transformation caught her by surprise as she found him towering over her.

"Don't loom over me like that," she said fondly. "Sit beside me, and tell me why you came back so soon. I did not expect you until late August!"

As he settled down next to her on the garden bench, Sophie saw him direct an interested yet concerned glance at her oversized girth.

"Now," she said briskly, "what is this . . . 'whim' you mentioned in your note? I was reading it again, just now."

"Well, it's not really a whim," he admitted. Then, with absolute sincerity he added, "Also, I didn't want to be away with the baby coming."

Her eyes misted as they rested on his face, flushed with the heat of the day. "That is above and beyond the call of duty," she said in a small voice, "and you are not even responsible for me!" Tenderly, she brushed back unruly blond curls clinging to his damp forehead. "How could I fear anything when you care for me to such a degree!" Then suddenly tears spilled over her cheeks.

He caught her hand and kissed it, "Sophie, what is it?"

She managed a smile. "It's all right . . . I am fine. I . . . just feel so blessed to have you, that's all! And tears do come easily these days.

Women carrying babies not only get tubby, they also become crybabies themselves!"

He thought she looked lovely. As was the fashion of the time, her sleeves of pale yellow tafetta swelled into the fantastic shape of a leg of mutton giving her a fragile and precious appearance. Her transparent complexion, enhanced by honey-colored hair pulled in tight bandeaux against her temples, accentuated that impression. But the impression was deceptive.

No, Franz decided, you are not a crybaby. You are a lily made of steel. You are the most valiant woman I know, and everybody can see that. . . . The way you put up with Karl's dullness and meanness!

He knew Karl too well. When he was a little boy struggling to learn German, Karl would take advantage of his naiveté and taught him improprieties so he would repeat them, not knowing what they meant. He had been punished for being too trusting . . . and Karl had not changed much.

"Let me dry those tears," he offered, taking out his handkerchief.

As she let him dab her cheeks, she said, "Every day I thank God for allowing our paths to cross!"

The suggestion of that fortuitous meeting set him musing on the question of belonging to the masculine gender. Being born a boy weighed enormously on the scale of his destiny.

"Think!" he said seriously, but also wanting to humor her, "You might very well be speaking to the Princess of Venice instead of me, your familiar duke!"

"Precious heaven," she exclaimed, remembering, "Who is she? You did mention her in your letter from Gratz."

"Why, me! Sophie, had I been a girl!"

"And what is bringing on this intriguing speculation?"

"I have read that had my mother borne my father a girl, he would have titled her Princess of Venice and that would have been the end of it!" Franz told her with a sudden flash of agitation.

She wasn't following him. "Calm yourself, Franz. The end of what?"

He had just thought of a disappointing scenario and went on barely taking a breath: "My father accepted to die in the most abject of conditions so that his sacrifice would start the dawning of a new era in which I would be the keeper of a new covenant. But don't you see? He could not have expected a *daughter* to carry on his work. It wouldn't have made any difference if she died in infancy or lived on . . . to even forget who she was. But I can't afford to forget. I have a mission. I have to leave my mark on the world! I am *his son* and I have to be *myself!* Do you think it's wrong?" he panted.

"No," she said, breathless herself and dizzied by this unexpected outburst. "I've always suspected you would eventually feel that way. Even before our conversation about your playing that game of chess. You are different from the others."

"Yes! And my life is going to be infinitely more complicated as I pass myself for someone I don't want to be anymore, wearing two faces and in the process confusing and even alienating those who still believe that I have a mind of my own and that I care to live up to their expectations! And with the revolution in Paris last month. . . ."

He stopped abruptly. "But why am I burdening you with such talk?"

"Is that why you left Baden so suddenly?" she asked gently.

"That, and to be with you. . . ."

"I know, Franz. Your affection is very dear to me. And that you should share with me your innermost feelings touches me deeply. They will be held in the strictest of confidence, of course," she promised, realizing how important that assurance was to him.

Franz debated whether or not he should let her in on something else. Then he confessed. "I had a terrible clash with Mother. How I feel and what I want are matters beyond her comprehension. Poor Mother! She should be paying you a visit some time today. I have persuaded her to come back with me. I'll have more information here about what happened in Paris."

Sophie's low opinion of Marie Louise had not altered over the years, because she had done nothing to improve her rating. It all revolved around her absence. Franz was now nineteen and she had visited him only six times!

"And how is your mother?" Her inquiry reflected mere charitable interest.

Franz thought a moment. Then he preferred to say, "She will tell you herself."

Then, not to be outdone in civility, he asked, "How is Uncle Karl?"

Sophie said evenly, "Karl is dying to know if I am going to give him a boy."

Prokesch had not been able to keep his tentative rendezvous with Franz in Baden, so he lost no time upon his return and rode out to Schönbrunn on August 16. He found carriages with splendid equipage filling the castle's courtyard.

After having sent his name, a few discreet inquiries explained why courtiers and prelates thronged the galleries while lackeys, minor palace officials, and servants bustled up and down the staircases: The Emperor's daughter-in-law Archduchess Sophie's lying-in had set the palace in effervescence and attracted a multitude of well-wishers.

While waiting, Prokesch reflected on the state of the Austrian monarchy. The outlook was bleak. Were Francis to die, Austria would have an idiot for emperor. On the other hand, should Ferdinand prove totally unfit, there remained the alternative of his abdicating in favor of his brother Francis Charles. No doubt, from the feverish activities surrounding Prokesch, the birth of the Archduchess's child, in many minds, hinted at that more reassuring option because if the baby turned out to be a boy, a wholesome continuation of the line would be secured.

"His Highness will see you presently," a voice announced beside him breaking into his reflections.

Prokesch nodded and followed the footman, who surprised him somewhat by leading the way, not to Schönbrunn's many sumptuous apartments, but to the stables instead. Midway, the footman explained, "His Highness was about to go riding."

"I see," Prokesch said, thinking of some amiable words to release Reichstadt from honoring an impromptu visit that might have perhaps come at an inopportune time. It was a perfect day for an outing on horseback and wide open spaces were not wanting.

Schönbrunn's grounds were of themselves vast. They comprised formal gardens, the world famous Ménagerie, the Botanical Garden, Palm House, and Tiroler Garten, ending with the *Gloriette* fanning its colonnades to a broad vista to the south. But beyond, stretched enticing expanses of gentle, undulating green meadows that reached far to the west toward the Wienerwald Range of low, wooded hills that hemmed Vienna and its suburbs.

The sky was cloudless and the sun shone at its most brilliant gold. Surely, Prokesch thought, Reichstadt would find it difficult to forgo galloping across this enchanting countryside for an hour or two.

"Major! Welcome back!"

Emerging from the deep shadow of one of the stalls, Franz briskly walked toward him, a smile of absolute delight on his face. He tucked his riding crop under his arm to press Prokesch's hand between his gloved palms. "You! At long last! A few more minutes and we would have missed each other. And I would have been inconsolable!"

"I am sorry, Monseigneur. I should have forewarned you of my visit. I am afraid I must have spoiled your plan. But please, think nothing of proceeding without me."

"Nonsense!" Franz was struck with an inspiration. "Why not join me? We will ride together to the woods!"

"I would like nothing better, if Your Highness will have me."

Franz beamed. "Come choose your mount! And I shall have it saddled for you."

"I am not particular," Prokesch laughed as Franz steered him toward the stalls. "Besides, with such an array of fine specimens, I would be at a loss to pick any horse. You pick it for me, Monseigneur."

"Then I'll let you have this splendid horse from Andalusia," Franz decided, and turning to the groom gave orders to ready the animal.

While his instructions were being diligently followed, Franz took the Major to a white Arabian. The horse let out a spirited snort as they approached. A stable boy led it out of the box stall. Franz grabbed the reins and fondly ran his hand over the Arabian's neck.

"Meet, Mustapha," he said proudly, then chuckled. "He has cost me a small fortune and I am left without a sou until my next allowance."

"I am sure Mustapha is worth your momentary ruin," Prokesch said admiringly.

"Absolutely," Franz replied, dismissing the stable boy with a smile. Then the smile vanished as he spoke, "When Mustapha takes me in a gallop, I think of nothing . . . I take wings, I soar above a trouble-free world. I am drunk with speed, and I don't care who I am. . . ."

"Franz. . . ." Prokesch said softly with a commiserative inflection.

Immediately Franz sought his hand and gave it a quick, hard squeeze before releasing it. "Anton," he murmured, "I've counted the days since we parted. So much has happened! I feel shut out . . . or in."

"I understand. I thought of you."

"That is kind."

"No. Only fair."

Just then a clatter of hooves put an end to their asides. Franz resumed an inconsequential cheerful exterior as the Major's horse was brought over to where they stood waiting. Prokesch sized up the Andalusian with the eyes of a connoisseur, himself being a fine horseman. Many horses had been killed under him in battles, and thrice this had taken place while he was engaged in combat against the armies of the very man whose son had won his heart. . . .

Another rider presently caught Franz's eyes, and he realized that he had forgotten Foresti was to accompany him. Fortyish, small-boned, and with squinty eyes, which he kept fixed upon the Major, Foresti approached them, leading his mount by the reins.

Franz claimed his friend's attention, "Major, meet Captain Foresti. Captain, this is Ritter Prokesch von Osten, Prince Metternich's most capable plenipotentiary."

Prokesch returned the Captain's stiff salute with a frank and direct smile.

"The Captain is my science teacher," Franz explained. "He taught me all the mathematics I know."

"I once taught that exact and marvelous discipline myself," Prokesch rejoined pleasantly. "I should not think it presumptuous on my part to salute you as a colleague."

Mollified, Foresti fell into the conversation. "And where, may I ask, did you exercise that professorship, Major?"

"I taught the cadets at the Military Academy of Olmütz."

"A prestigious institution indeed," Foresti said, obviously impressed.

Franz saw his chance to be rid of the Captain's company and took it. "As you can see," he said breezily, "the Major is going to accompany me, Captain. You needn't come along as you might have plans of your own."

Foresti indicated his relief with a grin. He hardly kept up with Reichstadt and could no longer pit his stamina against that of a nineteen-year-old.

"In that case," he said, "I shall remain here."

"We will be gone for a couple of hours," Franz informed him.

Automatically, Foresti pulled out his watch to glance at the time before leading his mount back to the stables.

With practiced ease, Franz vaulted onto his horse. Prokesch followed suit. Franz threw his head back and gave a happy yelp. "Just you and I!" he exulted. "And this, owing to your impeccable credentials!"

"I take it you are not very fond of the Captain?" Prokesch ventured.

Franz grimaced. "He is a bore! Has bored me for fifteen years! But he is not the worst of the lot. You should meet Baron Obenaus. Treated me like a rascal when I was a boy. Taught me history. . . . Oh, how he knew to bend the truth!"

"That is to be expected."

"Touché!" Franz rejoined appreciatively. "So I decided to get at the truth on my own. Every book relating to the time during which my father was rearranging Europe, I've read! At least whenever I could get my hands on one. Last year there was also this epic poem written by a Frenchman, Barthélemy. Have you heard of it?"

Prokesch thought briefly. "Wasn't it entitled *The Son of Man?*" he asked tentatively.

"Yes!"

"I am surprised you were allowed to read the poem," Prokesch commented.

"My tutors thought it best that I did, in the light of their own interpretations, of course. What hurts me most is to be thought of as a sickly and irresponsible whiffet!"

Mustapha punctuated those last words with a neigh and balked under the restraint of any easy trot. The riders were leaving Schönbrunn's grounds proper to enter open meadow lands.

Franz leaned over Mustapha's powerful neck, closed his eyes and said, "Mustapha is the extension of my desires, of my pent up energy. As I, he chomps at the bit and I won't hold him back!" Then straightening, he gave the horse its head and shouted, "To the woods!"

The Arabian took off as if shot from a cannon, and Prokesch realized what a magnificent horseman Reichstadt was. Not to be left behind, he spurred his Andalusian to a gallop and followed his companion full speed toward the distant hills.

Moments later, they were cantering in the middle of a winding path shaded by a thick canopy of leaves. Twigs snapped under the horses' hooves, and other than the calls of thrushes they found themselves surrounded by a pristine silence.

Franz reined in Mustapha. "Let's walk," he proposed. "It's just too beautiful here not to linger."

"Let's!" agreed Prokesch, pulling his horse to a stop.

They dismounted and secured the horses' bridles to a low lying branch. The winded animals began to chew on tender ferns with snorts of satisfaction.

Loosening his neck scarf, Franz inhaled deeply and lifted his face to a shaft of sunlight. "There is such peace and serenity here!" he sighed. "And I needed this! Particularly today."

"I know your heart is troubled," Prokesch replied.

Franz pressed his hand against his mouth, from which issued a short broken cough, after which he said, "It isn't only politics. Today I fear for the Archduchess Sophie's life. My aunt is about to have her first child. Did you know that?"

"Yes. I have inquired as to the reason for the commotion at the castle."

"And she is in agony," Franz added somberly.

"Childbirth is not a disease," Prokesch observed.

"But she is twenty-five," Franz countered with agitation. "Isn't it a little late for a first lying-in?"

"That is the prime of life," Prokesch told him. "Even for a woman." He smiled. "Of course, since you are only nineteen, you might tend to look upon those in their mid-twenties as having passed that milestone."

Somewhat reassured, Franz said as they sauntered along, "I want to ask you something of utmost importance. Promise to answer truthfully. Even if the truth isn't what would please me."

"Ask, Monseigneur."

The terse and formal assent to his request indicated unconditional frankness. Franz could not help feel a pinch of anxiety. "Can I rule? What does the new regime in France hold for me?"

"Statesmanship is a skill that does come with maturity. This, you will achieve in far less time than any above-average individual. Yes, you can rule. And brilliantly, I am certain! But you need a little more preparation. Consider what has just happened in France a necessary transition to help you acquire such maturity."

"Yet, in *The Son of Man* I am portrayed as a degenerate Habsburg. Is it what people think of me in the outer world?"

Prokesch shook his head. "When I was in Switzerland, your name was mentioned with respect and sympathy. And believe me, you are not thought of as Reichstadt. Foreigners have never forgotten your true identity!"

"I don't think my entourage has forgotten this either. Everywhere I go, I must be accompanied. Today, my escort would have been the Captain. If it hadn't been for your close connections with Prince Metternich, he wouldn't have so easily desisted from coming along. And even so, you must have noticed that he looked at his watch when I told him how long we were going to be away."

"What do you think of His Excellency?" Prokesch put in carefully after allowing a short pause.

Without hesitation Franz spoke his mind, realizing as he did so that he trusted his friend completely; that his sentiments would not be repeated.

"I consider him my sworn enemy. I am not blind, Anton. I recognize that my life so far has been governed by his dictates, which, by the way, bring my fondest hope of having you with me on a permanent basis to naught! My request of including you in my military household, as presented by Count Dietrichstein, has been rejected!" He clenched his teeth and added with contained rage, "By God! someday my will, and not the Prince's, shall prevail!"

Prokesch laid a hand on his arm, "Calm down, Franz. It isn't worth such a tantrum. You must strive to exercise the virtue of restraint and patience. That will serve you well, believe me!"

"Speaking of patience," Franz said easing into a calmer mood, "The Emperor is finally talking of establishing my military household in Prague, and I am looking forward to going there."

"Don't go, Franz," Prokesch said decisively. "Stay in Vienna. You will be forgotten in Prague. Vienna's diplomatic milieu is the setting you need to further your good reputation. In Vienna you can avail yourself of an opportunity Prague will never give you: consorting with influential and distinguished personalities such as diplomats, ambassadors, head of foreign states, financiers, statesmen, and scholars. They will do you far greater justice than the visitors of Bohemian spas."

"I hadn't thought of that," Franz said reflectively. "But suppose I am forced to go?"

"Didn't you say Prague was the Emperor's idea?" Prokesch asked cautiously.

"Yes. He is the one who suggested it."

Thoughtfully, Prokesch ran a finger over his mustache. "Bear with me for saying this, but if you haven't heard anything on the subject from Prince Metternich, I doubt very much if your reluctance to go is even called for."

Franz frowned. "Do you mean there is no substance to this project?"

"No, Franz. Not unless Prince Metternich also agrees to it."

Franz's irritation flared anew. "I should have known it! How can I be so naive? I love my grandfather dearly, and he loves me. But not enough to go over Metternich's head." Then in a resigned tone of voice, he conceded. "No matter! In this instance, it's all for the best, then."

Prokesch nodded, and for a moment they walked in silence.

After a while, with a slight hesitation, Franz asked, "I am putting you in a difficult position, aren't I?"

"I don't see how," Prokesch answered calmly.

Franz gave him a sidelong glance. "You know what I want."

"I would have been disappointed to find Napoleon's son wholly Austrian," the Major admitted.

Just to be sure, he said, "I believe in the sovereignty of the people. Don't you find this heretical?"

Prokesch drew a deep breath. "We live in a dynamic and changing world. You are the product of that change. I can't close my eyes to it, and France has set the pace since the Revolution of 1789. It would be foolish to force her to revert to her old form of government." He stopped, then decided to reveal in turn his innermost belief. "I consider the restoration of the Bourbons an anachronism. It hasn't worked with Charles X, and it won't work with Louis Philippe!"

Franz grew excited. "And with me?"

"You are the best possible alternative as the head of a republican state."

This declaration sent Franz into a paroxysm of exhilaration. He gave a shout of joy and threw his riding crop in the air, caught it deftly while laughing, a devil-may-care laugh full of youthful zest and abandon.

Prokesch watched him with fond pleasure touched with a twinge of sadness. Reichstadt looked so vulnerable yet so driven . . . so much in need of assistance.

Then, following a pattern Prokesch would soon come to recognize, Reichstadt's rare moment of lightheartedness evaporated. The formidable odds that confronted him, ever present on his mind, put a damper on his elan. Abruptly, he grew somber. In a halting voice, he said with growing agitation: "Take this situation for instance. Suppose France is encouraging other neighboring countries to revolt against the existing order. A war ensues between France and Austria. I shall be torn between two contradictory obligations! That of defending Austria and that of respecting my father's dying wishes; and I consider those, sacred rules that are to direct my life! Don't you see? Two races in me are at variance, and the loyalty I owe to both sides places me in a state of indefensible indecision! And if I can't decide, I am totally worthless!"

Firmly, Prokesch took hold of his arm, squeezing it. "Franz stop!" he entreated. "Don't give in to such pernicious speculations. When the time comes, you will make your choice. Your anxiety shows that you already have. And never forget this: you are invaluable to those in search of a new definition!"

Franz gave him a penetrating look. "Do you really care to pursue this with me?"

"Am I not your Posa?"

Nearly choking with gratitude, Franz could only nod.

Closeted in his office at the Ballhaus in Vienna, Metternich was reviewing the latest reports on the political developments in Paris when he was informed of the arrival of Louis Philippe's Ambassador Extraordinary, General Belliard. Already displeased by France's choice of Louis Philippe, Metternich was even less inclined to receive her plenipotentiary in the person of Belliard.

Out of spite he said, "Have the General wait for five minutes."

"The General is on time, Your Excellency," the functionary respectfully pointed out.

"Then make him wait ten minutes!" the Chancellor snapped.

"Very well, Excellency," the functionary replied, withdrawing with precipitation.

Alone again, Metternich opened the center drawer of his desk and took out Belliard's dossier, which he placed before him. Then he stood up, walked around the desk and crossed over to the window.

The chancellery building adjoined the Hofburg and from where he stood, he could see a wing of the palace and part of the facade of the Duke of Reichstadt's apartments.

A palace's drudge was sponging the window panes. Metternich congratulated himself. Not only was he in absolute control of the young man's destiny, he could also conduct the business of manipulating it within sight of the Duke's quarters. How ironically appropriate! Reichstadt lived in those suites eight months out of twelve, spending the remainder of the year at Schönbrunn from June to September, a long established arrangement which followed a cycle as predictable as the seasons which directed it.

Metternich enjoyed a moment of titillating triumph, deriving much satisfaction in knowing precisely where the Duke spent his time of gilded confinement: The Hofburg, Schönbrunn and occasionally in trouble-free and well-policed locations as he followed the Court on its summer holiday progress to Gratz, Baden, or Persenbeug. Reichstadt's next "approved" trip on the calendar this year was Budapest, where he would accompany the Emperor to attend Crown Prince Ferdinand's coronation as King of Hungary. That was about the only important travel in the Duke's existence, which Metternich would countenance for tradition's sake. Once the ceremony was over, Reichstadt would return to his usual place of residence, the city palace or the summer palace in either of which the Chancellor intended to keep him as long as circumstances would accord him the power to do so.

The drudge finished his chore, closed the window of Reichstadt's apartments and drew the drapes, a significant disposition, which meant that the Duke's suites were being tidied and kept in readiness for his return in early fall.

Reichstadt, by Metternich's reckoning, must presently be at Schönbrunn, which was best considering the fact that the Ambassador Extraordinary would have come too close for comfort had the Prince been occupying his quarters now. The Chancellor winced at the possibility that Belliard might have caught a glimpse of Napoleon's son by chance leaning out the window during the course of this interview.

The General's ten minutes of waiting were up, and a nervous cough reminded the Chancellor of that fact, when the same functionary as before timidly poked his head from behind the door, which he held ajar.

Metternich gave permission to admit the unwelcome visitor with an impatient fillip.

As Belliard entered, Metternich had resumed his seat behind his desk. Formal introduction would have been futile. Belliard, like countless Frenchmen who had held a commission in the army or served as civil servants in position of influence, was a familiar carry-over from the defunct French Imperial Republic, which Metternich considered an abomination never to be resurrected. He likened men such as the Ambassador Extraordinary to the dregs found at the bottom of a cask after all the soured wine had been poured out.

It made not much of a difference how Metternich proposed to refill the vessel of French power. He was woefully aware that no monarchy in France would ever be free from the contamination its officials would carry with them by virtue of a former connection to Napoleon. Belliard, for one, had never veered in his loyalty in the service of his imperial master. His name and face, like the names and the faces of so many others, were etched in Metternich's memory. He had seen Belliard often enough among the cohort of marshals and officers surrounding Napoleon. Belliard had commanded his armies and wholeheartedly espoused his cause to the end. And he had not given up. . . .

General Belliard saluted briskly in a military fashion, clacking his heels and producing a pistol-shot noise not quite congruent with his civilian attire and mission. The latter should have called for a more bland and currying form of greeting. He was dressed in ceremonial frac, knee breeches, and hoses, and held in the crook of his arm a plumed tricorn hat prominently displaying the white royalist cockade.

"Excellency," he said with a steady, resonant voice, "I have come to inform His Majesty, the Emperor of Austria, of His Majesty King Louis Philippe's official accession to the throne of France!"

Metternich motioned the General to a seat and said, coating the sarcasm with an icy smile, "Frankly, with your background, I am surprised to see you as the King's envoy. I suppose congratulations are in order!"

"And recognition of our government, Excellency," the General retorted unruffled and striking a prepossessed pose. Although sixty-one years of age, Belliard was still spry and lean and could do so with dignity and elegance.

In these circumstances, dignity was paramount. France was in a sorry state of affairs; in constant strife; weakened and ill-spoken of, and brow-beaten into the position of a minor nation. Since the fall of Napoleon, her kings were treated with contempt, toyed with, and never seriously minded. Her representative could do no less than exhibit presence and aplomb.

This irked Metternich. He could have taken the man and his cocksure attitude, his credentials, and fancy dress, and stuffed the whole exasperating lot into a bag to be thrown into the Danube.

Anger pinched his nostrils and put barbs in his tone.

"The Emperor absolutely abhors what has taken place in Paris! Austria will recognize the new regime at the express condition that France will continue to follow a policy of restraint. Any attempt at expansion, any propaganda adverse to the preservation of the status quo as laid down by the Quadruple Alliance will not be tolerated. Am I making myself clear?"

The former General of the Empire pulled up his chin. "Those are conditions I cannot personally guarantee."

Metternich glared at his interlocutor as if the Ambassador had uttered a profanity. "Personally?" He stabbed a finger at the cover of the dossier. "I have enough damning evidence in here on the nature of your *personal* undertakings to have your king arrest you for treason!"

Belliard remained impassive. "And what do you know of them, Excellency?"

"You have affixed your signature to a document that outlines explicit plans to bring the Duke of Reichstadt back to Paris!"

"My congratulations to your secret police," Belliard said evenly, refusing to allow Metternich the satisfaction of noticing his surprise.

"So you admit conspiring against the King!"

"That is beside the point," Belliard retorted, unruffled. "Prince Napoleon François Charles is a recognized political figure whose candidacy to the throne of France is no more subversive than that of the Marquis of Lafayette, whom my compatriots might have elected president of a new French Republic!"

Metternich blanched, but kept his temper under control. "General Belliard," he said at his smoothest, "the person whom you refer to as Prince Napoleon François Charles no longer exists. A child once was called thus, a child whom His Majesty the Emperor has taken under his protection and nurtured with fatherly devotion. Now, you know perfectly well that we are the product of our culture. Would you want to lend support to a German prince? For what you propose is tantamount to inviting Austria to annex France."

That rattled Belliard, but on a dare, he replied with complete self-possession, "I would like to be granted an audience with His Highness."

"That is impossible!" Metternich returned shortly. "You have forfeited your official status of ambassador since the beginning of our interview. The Duke of Reichstadt will only see foreign diplomats. He will not receive petty conspirators!"

"Then Your Excellency should denounce me," Belliard taunted.

"Don't be ridiculous! The Bonapartists' cause would get a new lease on life were we to make any ado concerning individuals such as yourself, General. But it will become extinct for lack of recognition.

Conspire all you want, and be assured that we will never acknowledge a movement that springs from sentimental caprices!"

Sentimental caprices! For a moment Belliard felt tempted to respond to the Chancellor's condescending and offhanded dismissal of a cause which, he believed, now focused on the awakening of national self-determination as opposed to dynastic oppression. Then he thought better of it. There was no point in prolonging the discussion. As Metternich rose, intimating that the interview was over, Belliard stiffly saluted and left.

Moments later, the functionary announced the unexpected arrival of Prokesch.

"I am sorry to have missed our rendezvous at Konigswart," Prokesch said immediately after the door had closed behind him.

Metternich lifted his hand, indicating that he understood. "And I apologize for not keeping it, Anton. But the latest events in Paris, as you may have learned, necessitated my immediate return to Vienna."

Prokesch nodded. "I heard of the Revolution while I was in Zurich."

"A despicable occurrence!" Metternich commented with acidity. Then his pale blue eyes which could turn icy cold, cast a benevolent and trusting gleam on his favorite diplomat. "What is your appraisal of the reaction at Charles X's overthrow in Switzerland?"

"Enthusiastic."

Metternich clenched his fists. "I knew it! And I don't like any of it. The July Monarchy owes too much to the Republicans and the Liberals! They have accepted Louis Philippe as a revolutionary monarch!. . . . Ah, but with the Duke . . ." he stopped in mid-sentence, watching the Major.

The cue, if it was so intended, alarmed Prokesch a little.

"The Duke?" he rejoined as innocently as he could.

"Your friend, Anton," Metternich prompted, his voice soft, his expression unaccountably benign.

"My friend. . . ." Prokesch repeated, as though trying to place a close acquaintance, an effort that appeared futile, for his voice rose questioningly. "My friend?"

Levelly, Metternich said, "Did you not befriend the Duke of Reichstadt while in Gratz?"

"I have called on the Prince several times." Prokesch only went so far as to confirm.

"Not without assiduity, so I am told. And I expected it," Metternich said, flashing an encouraging smile. "What can you tell me of His Highness's outlook on . . . life?"

"The Duke wishes to emulate Prince Eugene, Your Excellency," Prokesch answered, feeling comfortable enough.

It wasn't a lie. Only the focus had shifted and that shift had been made known to him in the strictest of confidence. He intended to keep it that way.

Metternich's face registered disappointment. "Is that all?"

For good measure, Prokesch threw in, "He has also expressed deep sentiments of affection for His Majesty the Emperor."

"A sentiment that is more than amply reciprocated," Metternich admitted sourly. "And unless the Emperor's affection is well placed, irreparable harm could result from it."

Prokesch contented himself to say, "The Duke is a young man of excellent address. And His Majesty's fondness could only be rewarded by the Prince's eagerness to dedicate his energy and talents to serve Austria."

Rising and smoothing his silk waistcoast, Metternich moved to the nearby console and picked up a heavy crystal decanter. "Would you care for some wine, Anton?" he offered, his tone ominously soft.

"No, thank you, Excellency," Prokesch replied, watching Metternich's jaw grow taut as he slowly began pouring himself a glass.

Then abruptly he set the decanter down, spilling some of its contents on his braided cuffs and slammed a balled fist on the marble top of the console. "It's all a pretense!" he spat. "The Duke is much too intelligent to find contentment in his present situation! Who is he trying to dupe?"

Prokesch threw himself headlong into a duplicity of his own by pretending to have been duped. "I, for one," he said. "But with time and *savoir faire* I might be given some evidence of his dissimulation."

Metternich regained his calm. He took a sip of the mellow wine. "I am granting you that time," he said. "If you can win the Duke's confidence and penetrate his mind, I should be in a better position to deal with him."

"Your Excellency speaks as though the Duke were an enemy of the State," Prokesch could not help remark.

Metternich snapped, "He is a Bonaparte! Isn't this sufficient ground for indictment?"

"But his education . . ." the Major slyly offered, not minding the falsehood of this observation, since he knew Reichstadt's true feelings. "Surely his German upbringing. . . ."

Metternich had used this argument with Belliard in a bluff, but he wouldn't put much credibility in it himself. He interrupted, "I'll never know how much he has assimilated. But through you, Anton, I will."

Since the moment Metternich had made mention of Reichstadt, Prokesch knew he was treading on dangerous ground. Now he felt slowly sinking into quicksand. He tried to steer the Chancellor away from relying on his own contribution in what he perceived to be an outright betrayal of the Prince's confidence in him.

He said, "And what of your own appraisal, Excellency? Through your conversation with His Highness and your personal contact with him, might this not give you an idea of the Duke's state of mind?"

"I can't abide the sight of him," Metternich confessed with a nasty curl of the lip. "Just as I could not abide that of his father! I speak to the Duke on very rare occasions. Besides, I am certain that he looks upon me as Napoleon's hangman. With me, he can only put up a front. But with you that would be different."

He directed at Prokesch a look of such intense curiosity that it nearly discountenanced him. "Do you," he asked slowly, "find the Duke engaging?"

Prokesch sought refuge in an evasive answer. "Seen through the eyes of any ladies, I would venture to say that His Majesty's grandson is regarded as a prince charming par excellence. For my part, I can only observe that his winning manners have earned him favorable notice."

Metternich grimaced. "Ah yes! He knows he can manipulate people with his looks and charm! But we can't let this happen to us, can we?"

Prokesch never doubted Reichstadt's sincerity and the nobility of his conduct, but he caught the insinuation. The *us* was obviously intended as *you*. Metternich expected him to stay clear of Reichstadt's winsome personality and spy on him.

Not caring to sound repetitious, he said, "The Duke is His Majesty's subject. His life-long goal can only be one of dedication to the service of this country."

"And as a patriot," Metternich said, pointing at Prokesch a finger that might have appeared accusatory had it not been for the cajoling tone in his voice, "you are to ascertain the veracity of this statement."

He resumed his seat, folded this hands, and considered Prokesch with unblinking concentration for a moment. "You are perfect! I should have used you sooner," he said at long last. He smiled. "May your friendship flourish . . . I count on you."

That was an order which Prokesch understood too well. It chilled him. After he left, for the first time in his life, he pondered over the true meaning of being a patriot. Did this mean the betrayal of a trust? The turning away from certain convictions his own reason did not consider blameworthy? To what extent does a man engage himself, if not for the realization of a noble dream? A dream to see a world in which all people counted, such as Franz saw it. . . .

Franz's immediate dream, that of commanding an Austrian regiment, no longer represented an end in itself. He knew a higher destiny awaited him. A niche in the history of his time had been assigned to him, and his allegiance belonged to the country from which he had been torn away since infancy. France still held the ferment of a new order. The Age of Revolution had only begun, and he recognized in himself a child of that age. He theorized that the Holy Alliance's anachronistic tenets would precipitate its doom. Europe was balking at enduring the shackles of oppression. He could see in the unrest in Greece, France, Belgium, and more recently in Poland, that the twilight of Divine Despots was at hand; that his time would come.

Still, in more than one way so much conspired to douse his hope with unrelieved frustrations! Francis had begun to openly support his return to France if the French were to strongly express the desire that he come back to them. On the other hand, Metternich's ever watchful presence would never allow his grandfather to act on his own. Aware of this, Franz's restlessness grew.

Then there was the vexing business of his physique. Height had not been compensated by the filling out of his body. He continued to look girlishly slender. Malfatti kept cautioning him with glib politeness and Franz argued that he could not be expected to live like an old man just because he was underweight. "It's not only that," the physician pointed out, "Your Highness has a cough. . . ."

Malfatti had even dissuaded Francis from allowing him to enter the army for awhile!

Mortified, Franz reluctantly submitted to the doctor's prescription and had to drink a disgusting mixture of milk and salep. Nauseated and dispirited, he began to wonder if after all, his desires and aspirations were sound. Perhaps they were mere vagaries only inspired by demons intent on tormenting him.

24

Stalking is usually done best on foot, and location was important to the young woman who busied herself dressing warmly to go out in the November sleet. She knew she would not have too much of a distance to cover, because upon her arrival in Vienna, she had selected to stay at the Swan Hotel, conveniently situated on the Kärtnerstrasse, a broad thoroughfare that gave easy access to the city residence of the Habsburg emperors.

Rented lodgings are not particularly significant beyond the need travelers have of them for shelter and creature comforts. But that evening the impersonal hotel room, expressly chosen because it suited her plan, assumed in her eyes the peculiar importance assigned to places that are linked to events of great import. This room was the starting point of a venture whose success would eclipse in brilliance the light of a thousand suns!

"Why a thousand suns?" one might have asked her. And she would have answered, with a proud toss of her dark head, "Because, like my famous uncle, I always think in grand terms!"

The woman held her head still as she pulled the hood of a voluminous tartan over her black hair. Her movements were slowed by the contemplation of her image in the mirror of the dressing table.

At this crucial moment of her life, Countess Camerata savored with fanatical pride the resemblance she bore to her uncle Napoleon. It was remarkable. By some quirk of heredity, Napoleon's sister, Elisa, had produced a daughter who did not look even remotely like her husband, Felix Bacciochi. The girl, who was consistently called *Napoleone*, had turned out to look like the feminine counterpart of the late Emperor.

This astonishing likeness titillated the Countess, for who could be better qualified to rescue the son of Napoleon than a relation who not only closely resembled the father of the luckless prince, but also venerated the Emperor's memory to the point of idolatry? One thing bothered her, however. That cousin, for whom she was willing to risk the censure and punishment of a political tribunal, hardly exhibited any of the Bonapartes' physical characteristics in which she took so much pride. She found him looking too German: tall, blond, light-complected, and if this were a redeeming grace, impossibly handsome!

To have glimpsed him again on the Prater, clad in that despicable Austrian uniform, made her question day after day the worth of his character. Save perhaps for his immediate entourage, no one really knew much about him as he was unapprochable, even through proper channels. He was always surrounded by attendants, never strayed from what appeared a regimented schedule, which this time, would serve her plan.

The Countess had come to extricate her cousin from the clutches of his wretched guardians and help him reclaim his birthright—provided he hadn't grown cold in the heart and weak in the head. That question kept popping up in her mind, sidetracking her concentration on the preparations at hand.

They had been underway for sometime, for her ambition to restore her cousin to his former imperial status had kept her busy over the span of many years. So engrossed had she become with this project, that her already troubled marriage to Count Camerata had ended in separation.

Like her grandmother, Napoleone had something of an Amazon in her. She passionately deplored the limitations that went with the condition of being a woman. So, where tradition and custom failed to apportion the desired latitudes, she simply followed her inclinations and never yielded to the inhibitions which afflicted the members of her sex.

Accordingly, Napoleone often wore clothes with a masculine cut, finding them more comfortable for riding and fencing. She could shoot a pistol with deadly precision and master the most difficult of horses. Those were skills she felt fortunate to have developed as she already pictured herself disguised as a man and riding beside her cousin toward the frontiers of France. Dangers of all descriptions would be awaiting them, but she was confident she would meet every peril with more than adequate competence. She could, if bad came to worse, fight, sword in hand, at her cousin's side as a capable escort should.

So far, all had gone well.

Obtaining a passport to Vienna was not difficult. There were no questions asked. Having earned the reputation of being an eccentric person, she knew that individuals of that sort were actually considered harmless. Full of fiery zeal and confidence, she had left her home in Rome in a frenzy to meet again, this time face-to-face, the long-lost relative she had verbally attacked in Baden.

Two years had passed since that unhappy day for her, and the mystery that surrounded the young man living under the irrelevant name of an obscure Bavarian duchy remained undispelled. In the back of the Countess's mind lurked that same needling question, that same unknown quantity that was part of an equation upon which depended the success or failure of her sacred mission—how was he going to receive her proposal?

She had heard many distressing rumors about him. It was said that he cared nothing for his paternal relations, that he had detached himself completely from the country of his birth, that he was content to be an archduke. Would he refute all those things? And what if he did not?

Shuddering at the thought, Napoleone turned away from the mirror and began to fasten—in precise order—blue, white, and red ribbons to her wrists. This ornament was an innovation of her own. In Rome she wore ribbons the same way, and even girthed her waist with them.

On this particular evening, the ritual proclaimed more than her political conviction, it lifted her soul to superstitious reliance on good luck. Napoleone's fingers worked through the silky flosses so arranged as to represent the revolutionary and imperial colors of France, grasping for a felicitous outcome. In her head, she challenged with Latin passion, "Cousin, here is your chance! Within a few hours, please God, I shall have the whole truth about you!"

Her plan to meet Reichstadt was really simple. To accost the Prince in public was, of course, out of the question. But since she had begun watching him come and go from afar, she had acquainted herself with certain of his habits, and in that manner discovered a way of approaching him privately, if only briefly.

Just as she finished securing the ribbons with the comfortable assurance that her scheme would work, the bells of St. Stephen Cathedral sounded the Angelus. Countess Camerata gave a start and paled under her cowl. It was the signal she had set for herself. A signal that now started her heart pounding despite weeks of relatively calm anticipation.

It was time she left.

The orange sun had long set behind the hills of the Wienerwald. Pulling the folds of her cloak around her, Napoleone walked decisively out of the room, down the stairs and out into the street.

A fine, freezing drizzle continued to fall chilling her, but Napoleone did not walk hurriedly as this might appear suspicious. Nevertheless, she looked over her shoulders now and then, but no dogging shadows trailed after her own.

Soon the Hofburg loomed ahead, massive and permanent behind heavy wrought iron gates. At this point, Napoleone advanced no further, praying that of all times, this time would be the one Reichstadt would choose to go out. From what she had observed, chances were that he might. She had seen him go on foot, unaccompanied and rather regularly, to a nearby house in the early hours of the evening. So she waited out of sight, huddled under a porch.

After what she estimated to have been a half hour, the stone-like sentries posted in the guard boxes suddenly came to life. Glimmers of silvery steel flashed faintly as they saluted a tall figure wrapped in a flowing overcoat. An escort of lackeys bearing lamps went no further than the gates which ponderously swung open under their concerted effort, to shut with a cryptal clang as soon as the figure had passed.

Despite the darkness, the distance, and the fact that thus far Napoleone had not had an opportunity to look closely at her cousin, the erect and graceful carriage she had admired on the Prater promenades convinced her that her prayers had been answered.

Indeed, it was Reichstadt! He walked fast, nimbly strode over puddles. She feared she would lose him in the chase. But she decided to let him outdistance her for now, not wanting to attract the guards' attention. Only after she was certain of escaping their notice did she dare follow, quickening her pace. When he reached the Ball Platz, she finally ran to overtake him as he entered the dimly lit vestibule of a private residence.

Under the overhanging lantern they stared at each other.

The expression of melancholy hauteur with which he regarded her enraptured the Countess. Unable to speak, she could only seize his hand and press it fervently to her lips.

It was more than a kiss. It meant a solemn recantation of all doubts, a total acceptance from which questions and reproaches had been banished. Humbly and tempestuously, Napoleone admitted a surrender to absolute devotion. In her mind and heart, she was saying to her cousin: My Lord and Master!

A harsh, indignant call abruptly ended her trance. From the landing, an ill-looking middle-aged man was shouting menacingly at her. "Madam! I demand the meaning of this!"

It was Obenaus, who had been expecting his pupil. From the top of the stairs, he stood arms akimbo and glared down at the Countess, who still clutched at Franz's hand. She held her ground and said defiantly, "I am paying homage to my gracious sovereign!"

Puzzled, Franz began to climb the steps backward, thus providing a screen to give himself a fleeting instant during which he could investigate that strange encounter.

Whispering as he gazed searchingly into the face whose classical features reminded him of an incident, of a portrait, too, he asked, "Have I seen you before? Who are you?"

"I saw you in Baden! I am your cousin, Countess Napoleone Camerata," she whispered back.

"Ah, yes. . . ." Franz mumbled startled, looking deeper into her eyes. They glinted at him with a sorry and somewhat adoring expression as her mouth quavered. For a moment he thought she was going to throw her arms around him.

Then Obenaus impatiently growled above them. Franz tore his hand free from the Countess's grasp and turning round ascended the rest of the stairs under his tutor's inquisitive and disapproving scrutiny.

Stepping into Obenaus's apartment, he made to glance behind him, but dispensing with ceremony, the Baron slammed the door shut.

"She is gone," he said casually. "And if this will satisfy your curiosity, Your Highness has just seen Elisa Bacciochi's daughter. She is known to be rather . . . unconventional in her ways. Some even say that she is crazy. Which might explain this. . . . incident."

Franz gave his professor a remote look and said nothing.

Obenaus went on pleasantly, "Well, Monseigneur, so much for the lady. Did you bring some notes this evening?"

"Right here," Franz said, giving a tap on the pocket of his overcoat.

"And relating to what question this time?" The Baron asked with an affability Franz felt was forced. It looked to him as though the professor was doing everything possible to gloss over what had just happened.

Distractedly, he said, "The Spanish colonial system."

"Ah!" said Obenaus exhibiting, so Franz thought, an improbable delight for the topic at hand, "let us see. . . ."

For the rest of the evening Countess Camerata was not mentioned again. But her sudden appearance in Franz's life brought to his attention a deficiency he sincerely deplored. He had lost track and count of his paternal relatives. He knew nothing of them except what had been said to him: that they were never to be trusted, that they were rash and devious and selfish, and had contributed to his father's ruin.

Certainly, Napoleone's hot-headed approach did little to lift the generally unfavorable impression he had of the Bonapartes. Besides, what could this totally unknown relation want with him? In Baden she had been far from friendly.

Napoleone walked back to her lodging with a modified opinion of her cousin. In Baden, she had spoken abusively to him and driven away hurt and embittered. All was different now. Unknowingly he had worked his charm on her and she wasn't going to pass any judgment on him. She would hold out doing so.

Instead, she would be attending to more urgent matters. He needed help, and needed to be made aware of her design. Napoleone reflected that the impossibility to approach her cousin for any length of time said much for the climate of suspicion that surrounded his person. She was certain that the man who had shouted at her must have been watching for the Prince's arrival from the window of his dwelling to make sure that he would come straight up. More than likely, another attempt to speak to him again would fail.

There remained one alternative that might prove successful. She could write to Reichstadt. But to whom would she entrust the safe delivery of her message? No doubt, with the promise of a handsome reward, the servant of the man the Prince visited regularly could do this readily if she pretended to be enamored of the Duke. That would explain the letter and the secrecy that must accompany further communications. And not for a second would the messenger question her motive. The attraction Reichstadt exerted on women was notorious.

In the Prater, Napoleone had noticed how the ladies looked dreamily at him and how, when he looked at them, they would blush while their eyes filled with stars.

Her plan proved to be judicious. Not knowing who the Countess was, Obenaus's servant gladly obliged. He was generously paid for a small service, and said he would go as far as arranging a tryst if that was requested.

Franz had quite forgotten Countess Camerata. She belonged to a clique for which he felt no affinity. Moreover, he had not seen her nor heard from her in the two weeks that followed their encounter. As such, he dismissed her from his thoughts with the disheartening impression that the "sovereignty" she alluded to solely reflected a clannish notion of rulership.

He did not blame her, though. After all—and the apprehension of that truth crushed him—the son of Marie Louise and Napoleon had no French blood flowing through his veins. Strictly speaking, Franz was a cross between Italian and Austrian. This was a mixture the French might not be liable to forget and hold as evidence to contest his nationality.

But like his father, Napoleon, Franz believed the willful choice to belong to a nation is infinitely more meaningful and binding than a citizenship acquired by way of biological fortuity. True citizenship resides in the mind and the heart, not in the blood. His father seemed to have been accepted that way. . . .

An insistent knock at the door of his bedchamber interrupted his reflections.

Quite naturally he answered, "*Herein!*" Strangely, it struck him as odd and false to hear himself utter the permission to enter in German. He had never experienced such sense of incongruity before. He had spoken German for so long. For as long as he remembered the whippings. . . .

Built like a wrestler and looking ill at ease in Reichstadt's braided ducal livery, the valet entered and bowed respectfully. Franz looked vacantly at his cipher embroidered on the servant's uniform.

"What is it, Titz?"

"Baron von Obenaus's servant wishes to see Your Highness."

A little perplexed, Franz cocked his head. "Isn't he delivering a note?"

"It does not appear so."

Franz frowned. The only thing Obenaus might have wanted to communicate to him would be to change the time or postpone their evening meetings, which were held for the sole purpose of expanding Franz's understanding of world history. A simple message to that effect delivered to his own servant would have sufficed, unless the Baron had some confidential matter to share with him. Franz was hard put to envision anything confidential being passed on to him through Obenaus. Yet, if this were the case, why send a domestic of all people?

Thoroughly intrigued, he told Titz to send the messenger in.

"Here? In Your Highness's bedchamber?" asked the valet after a brief hesitation.

"Of course," Franz replied casually. "It is more private."

The valet returned ushering in Obenaus's servant.

As soon as he found himself quite alone with Reichstadt, the messenger pulled out a letter from his sleeve and handed it over without saying a word.

Franz took the folded piece of paper and examined the seal. It wasn't the Baron's. The wax bore no identifying impression and was crudely affixed.

"Who gave you this?"

"A lady," the servant replied, in a low conspiratorial tone of voice.

"Do you know who she is?"

"No, Highness. But I am to wait for a reply."

Not so fast! Franz thought. He reasoned that were he so much as to show the slightest interest in anything underhanded he could be accused of conspiring.

He said, "Do you know many ladies write to me?"

"Scores of them, I am certain," was the candid reply.

"And they do not do this secretly. Nor do they presume to demand my immediate attention. So I am going to disappoint you. I also suggest that you serve your master exclusively. You may go now."

"But," the messenger began with humble insistence, "I was expressly instructed. . . ."

". . . By me, to leave presently," Franz interrupted, finishing the sentence for him. Then he called: "Titz!"

At once he started to count in his head. If Titz had been listening at the door, he might in a reflex open it too soon. For from where the valet was supposed to be, stationed in the antechamber, it would have taken him at least fifteen seconds to leave the entrance of the other room and cross over to Franz's bedroom door. Franz could be precise about this timing because he had tested it before himself.

Titz did not enter until Franz had counted to eighteen. Either the valet walked slowly or he had in fact outsmarted his master. For some time now Franz had come to grips with the realization that his own servants were spies.

Titz opened the door and stood in a servile and deferent stoop, waiting for his master's orders. But Franz had no illusion that he took only those that pertained to trivial domestic matters, while discharging himself of a more sinister assignment whose ramifications led straight back to Metternich.

Concealing the message, he said with a wave toward the messenger, "Show this man out, Titz. And I don't want to be disturbed anymore this evening!"

Left alone, he turned the letter in his hands, hesitating. Should he open it? He also wondered if Obenaus was not using his servant as an agent provocateur.

He decided to break the seal. Before even reading the first line, he glanced at the bottom of the last page. The letter was signed Napoleon C. Camerata. Franz noticed the omission of the feminine ending vowel "e" after the word "Napoleon". She was indeed odd.

He began to read. The letter opened with an invective. Why had he not answered the two previous letters she had sent him? A chill crept through him. So far as he knew, this letter was the first he had received.

This outrageous silence, she wrote, reflected the shameful mentality of the Austrian archduke he must have become and not the noble identity he should have kept as a French prince. Was he seeking to establish himself in the favors of his German keepers at the expense of her ruin by forwarding those letters she had sent him to the police? Wouldn't he choose to act as a gentleman instead, and find a way of communicating with her? And could he, in good conscience, be indifferent to the fact that by turning away from the country of his birth and by repudiating his paternal heritage he might as well consider himself dead to the French and dead to the Bonapartes?

Then came the exhortation: in loving memory of a father who had so adored him, in the name of his sacrifice and the torments he had suffered, he should remember that he is Napoleon's son and as a sacred duty, dedicate himself to live up to this status. But if he preferred to act like a coward and denounce her to the authorities, then she would find her misfortune more bearable than the discovery of his total lack of integrity.

Lastly, if he had any honor at all, she should be accorded the courtesy of receiving at least one reply.

Franz was stunned. The mordant tone of the letter, the ferocious accusations and the revilement shattered him. What Napoleone wrote smarted all the more because prudence dictated that he should not attempt to defend himself. Yet, in the face of the damaging opinion the Countess had formed of him, he would also be committing political suicide by remaining silent.

Then it occurred to him that at no time did his cousin make any mention of strong partisan support, supposing he had remained a French prince at heart. How many people in France cared enough about him as a political figure to concern themselves with his future and the place he should assume in the world of international affairs? For all her zeal and fire, Countess Camerata might be acting only as a private person. And Franz did not have any intention of becoming embroiled in a mere cloak-and-dagger adventure whose impact on the scene of European politics would mean little, if anything at all.

Another possibility dawned upon him. He might be walking right into a trap set by Metternich, who undoubtedly must have intercepted the two missing letters. Perhaps he had allowed this third one to reach Reichstadt to bait him and ferret out his true feelings. For there was enough in what Napoleone had written to set the blood of an upright Bonaparte boiling and crying for a fair hearing.

Yet if Franz were so naive as to speak his mind and open his heart to his cousin by a written refutation of the shameful stance she accused him of holding, that confession would never reach her. Instead, it would find its way to the Chancellor who would show it to Francis with a triumphal comment: "Just as I suspected! Your Majesty's grandson is an enemy of the State! I have proof of this now! See for yourself, Sire. He wrote this!" Then farewell to the little freedom Franz still had. Security around him would be doubled. Farewell, also, were he to keep silent, to the good impression he was trying so desperately to project for those who might put their faith and trust in Napoleon's heir. Either way, Franz felt condemned.

Feeling trapped and unable to decide on the proper course of action, he turned to Prokesch for counsel.

They met in the Wolksgarten. Within walking distance of the Hofburg, the park seemed to afford greater privacy than a closed room. Out in the open, it would be difficult for anyone to overhear them, though the exchange must not betray any sort of excitement for fear that the conversation might indicate something of import to the watchful eyes of Francis's ubiquitous secret police.

As they ambled along the path, Franz told the Major of his strange encounter with the Countess, of the letter and its contents.

He purposefully spoke in a quiet, conversational tone.

"I have said nothing of this to you until now," he concluded, "because I had no idea I would be hearing from the Countess again."

"Do you still have the letter?" Prokesch asked.

"Yes," Franz answered somberly. "I have it on my person. And if I were to destroy it, I still would remember every word."

"Please smile," Prokesch said, glancing watchfully around.

Smiling, Franz lamented, "How can I enlighten her without compromising myself?"

"The problem," Prokesch commented, while keeping an unclouded expression, "is that your cousin's proceedings seem highly unreliable."

"I agree! Yet I share and respect the expectations she entertains concerning my place in history. Meanwhile, what am I going to do with the Countess? I can't ignore her."

Prokesch thought for a moment and sighed. "No, Franz. You cannot ignore her."

"The more I think about the whole thing, the more I am convinced that she is not acting as a decoy," Franz said.

Prokesch regarded him with commiseration. The Prince's isolation, the boundless confidence he had placed in the Major did not make it easier for him to say, "You must send her a reply; but in a manner that will clear you of all blame as Duke of Reichstadt. You must, in short, ask her to leave you alone without further explanations. Besides, her interest in you, as I see it, can lead you nowhere."

A groan escaped Franz. "Then I ought, using her words, reply as an archduke!"

"But just for the time being," Prokesch hastened to add. "If you do not compromise now, you will, I am afraid, put your whole future in jeopardy."

At long last a letter came bearing Reichstadt's ducal seal. Napoleone, forgetful of her ire, kissed the rectangle of cream-colored vellum before starting to read the message. But when her eyes fell on the opening paragraph, the rapture immediately deserted her as it said:

Madam,

It is neither as an archduke nor as a French prince that I wish to treat the letter I have just received. But courtesy compels me. . . ."

Napoleone's hands began to shake so uncontrollably that she had to set the letter down on the table before her in order to real on. What she read appalled her. While claiming to be neutral, Reichstadt's partiality was blatant. For obviously, a Bonaparte would never have dared deny having received any of her previous communications. The son of the Archduchess Marie Louise would, though. And that despicable son further declared finding no sense whatsoever in the note that did reach him and which only honor obliged him to acknowledge. But he declined having anything further to do with her. And would she please cease writing to him!

Now Countess Camerata could have spat on her cousin's signature—a shameful one at that, as it was signed: *The Duke of Reichstadt!* Her Latin temper overtook her. Duke of Reichstadt! The devil take him! Certainly, his poor father, had he lived, would have disowned him and damned him, too! And France! France needed no longer place any hope in him. The French people would do well to forget Napoleon's son! He never had a son! That son was only a myth nurtured by the devotion of those who respected and admired his father. But in reality, the great Emperor's son wasn't worth anything. To consign him to a place of eternal detestation was all he deserved!

Already, Franz felt hopelessly damned. As soon as his reply had gone out to the Countess, a torturing remorse took hold of him. He had just ruined himself in the eyes of those who, like Countess Camerata, continued to keep some faith in the Duke of Reichstadt. He had abandoned the people, who like her, were willing to suffer hardship and imprisonment by lending him aid and support. For he was certain to have some partisans.

But now that he had betrayed their hope and trust, he would be left alone indeed! And if not totally forgotten, then accursed and held in utter contempt, alive or dead.

He said to Prokesch, "I am finished! The Countess, I know, will spread this advice around: 'Don't bother with Napoleon's son. He is a German!' And that will make me a double bastard! I can't bear this! I just can't! I'd rather go mad and be put away!"

Prokesch hesitated but one second and said, "We can still repair this."

Franz stared at him wildly. "How?"

"For the sake of your sanity, I'll go to her. I'll explain everything!"

Franz lunged happily at his friend and grabbed him by the shoulders. "I'll go!" he proposed impetuously.

"No, Franz. Let me do it. My whereabouts are not so stringently scrutinized . . . not to my knowledge anyway."

"But I don't want to compromise you! Not any more than you are already!"

Prokesch smiled comfortingly, "I will be careful."

Becalmed, Franz let go of him. "I have taken a few precautions myself," he said.

He went on to explain that he had shown the Countess's letter to Obenaus and Dietrichstein, as well as his own reply to it. The professors had approved what he had done.

"You've acted wisely," Prokesch told him. "By bringing the whole matter into the open, Metternich would have no evidence upon which to build a case against you."

As for Napoleone, he thought, seeing that her undertaking had not met with the Prince's consent, the only risk she ran would be to receive a notice of expulsion, but expulsion without prosecution. By an open refusal to have any part in her scheme, Reichstadt was protecting her.

Countess Camerata did not see things that way. She received Prokesch badly and wondered how he had obtained her address. Evidently, she suspected he must be with the police, for only the police kept a record of all foreigners' places of residence in Vienna. In a sense, she was not entirely wrong as the Major's occupation and importance gave him easy access to such records, being himself a sort of politically-oriented policeman.

Without meaning to, Prokesch projected an official-looking air, which prompted Napoleone to peep past him as he stood in her doorway. In the dark hall might lurk some unpleasantness, such as a detachment of Austrian policemen waiting for a word to come forward and arrest her.

But her visitor was quite alone, and he introduced himself, adding that he had come in her cousin's behalf.

At this declaration, the Countess let out an exclamation of anger while eagerly asking him to enter. After the door closed, she accused, eyes blazing. "So you, too, must be responsible for what has been done to the son of Napoleon! And why have you bothered to come here?"

Prokesch thought she was reckless, indeed. He said calmly, "I have come to caution you against erroneous judgments as well as to warn you that you are putting the Prince in a very compromising situation."

"I don't see how I can compromise a devoted member of your citizenry!" she snapped.

"Madam," Prokesch said patiently, "in spite of what you may think. . . ."

"I don't think," she interrupted, dramatically crossing her hands over her chest. "I know! His heart is perverse and things being as they are, you would call that patriotism! But at home, where he was born, we call this treason!"

"Have you thought of dissimulation, Madam? I am surprised this possibility has not occurred to you. I myself, am here clandestinely."

Napoleone reconsidered. "Are you really?"

"Yes."

A complete change came over her. "Merciful God!" she cried, a half-smile smoothing away the expression of contempt and anger from her face.

"And the letter the Prince has sent you does not express his sentiment," Prokesch added.

Transfigured with joy, Napoleone declaimed, "Oh, I should have known! My cousin is too fine looking to be false! And may the star that presided over his birth forever shine upon his brow! He shall walk in glory and greatness! I dedicate my life to this end! You will assure him of this, won't you?"

"The Prince is aware of your dedication, Madam," Prokesch answered cautiously.

With pride, she announced, "I have come to take him back to France!"

The Major thought the moment opportune to gauge the extent of her resources. "And how do you propose to do this?"

"I shall find a way," she replied, as though this consideration was of secondary importance.

Prokesch's brows shot up. "You have devised no plans?"

"Oh, but I will!"

He put her through the ultimate test. "I suppose you are acting as the delegate of a party powerful enough to guarantee that the Prince will be welcome in France."

Drawing a deep breath, Napoleone declared with grandiloquence that her cousin's presence alone would suffice to rally the French nation around him. *The Hundred Days* gave her faith in personal magnetism. Like Napoleon, all his son needed was first to wrench himself free from the clutches of his Austrian family, and all the rest would fall into place. The transition from the monarchy in France to the Empire would be smooth, blessed, and acclaimed. . . .

Realizing that there was no plan, and no backing, Prokesch had to curb her enthusiasm. He told her that Reichstadt was not a criminal, and only criminals abscond. As a true French prince, and only as such, did the son of Napoleon wish to leave Austria. In the open and with the consent of the Powers.

"He is constantly looking forward to that day," the Major assured her. "To rush matters as you are proposing to do, would only ruin its advent. I am certain you would not want to spoil anything by an untimely move, however generous are the impulses which direct you to help the Prince."

"Of course not!" she replied hotly. "But what need has he to wait? Those who long for justice have already consecrated the son of Napoleon! And I have so much faith in my cousin just as things stand now!"

"Madam, faith in matters of politics is not enough."

Napoleone thought a moment, then moodily: "I presume my presence here is no longer of any use."

How easily she could drop everything after embarking on a venture she hadn't even bothered to think through!

He said diplomatically, "Your presence has given much comfort to the Prince."

She looked pleased. "May I," she asked with an accent of total devotion, "see him sometime soon?"

Prokesch shook his head. "That would not be advisable. I strongly suggest that you leave Vienna as soon as possible. To tarry any longer could be . . . unpleasant."

The Countess frowned. With a touch of anxiety she said, "Do you suppose. . . ."

Prokesch nodded. "You know," he said gravely, thankful for remembering to mention this to her, "the two letters you sent the Prince have never reached him. He was not being untruthful when he wrote you that he had never received them."

"For the love of God! Where are they?"

"We don't know, Madam. That is why we are here, meeting on borrowed time."

"Then I'll leave," she said, utterly alarmed and compliant. "I give you my solemn promise!"

25

With unadulterated pride Dietrichstein gazed at his pupil's reflection in the mirror of the cheval glass. Franz had recently been promoted to the rank of Lieutenant Colonel of the 20th Infantry Regiment of the Duke of Nassau, and in two more months, he would be twenty.

The uniform he wore on this particular evening of January 25, 1831, reflected the importance of his rank and the glittering allure of military calling. It consisted of a white tunic with coattails. The collar, a choker high-up under the chin, was dark green. Facings of the same color with cuff patches ornamented with silver braids ended long tapering sleeves. The breeches, skin-tight, were sky blue and decorated from the waist down to mid-thigh with silver lace embroideries. The rest of his legs were encased in high boots whose spurs had been removed as this was a non-military function. In similar consideration, a brocaded cummerbund replaced the sword belt. The red and green sash of the Order of St. Stephen crossed his chest to which was pinned, on the left, the star of the same order and the medal of St. George.

The Count's gaze continued to linger on the shimmering apparition, then pleased to see that everything was satisfactory, he motioned the valet to bring the gloves. Franz stepped away from the mirror and jerkily proceeded to slip them on.

"Don't be too outgoing tonight," Dietrichstein admonished. "But don't be too withdrawn either. And please, do not shake hands with everybody as you tend to. It is a despicable habit of the British that does not become an archduke."

He paused, watching Franz fumble with the buttons on his gloves.

"You are nervous," he observed.

"Only because you are driving me crazy," Franz retorted, letting the valet help him.

Since morning, Dietrichstein had been insufferably fastidious. Several times, he had inspected every article of Reichstadt's clothing, fussing then as he was fussing now, and he did not mind the rebuke. In fact, he was much more nervous than his pupil. Lord Cowley, the British Ambassador in Vienna, was hosting a ball in Reichstadt's honor to mark his debut in Viennese society.

The irony of being the guest of such a personage was not lost on Franz. England, after all, had been his father's jailer, but he refrained from dwelling on the dubious quality of the favor done to him. The choice of Lord Cowley was obviously intended to demonstrate his total assimilation into the Habsburg rank. And as a Habsburg, there could be no offense taken at being a guest at the British Ambassador's ball.

"Your Highness must shine!" the tutor said.

Franz almost snapped at him. "I'll be at my scintillating best!"

In the carriage, Dietrichstein uttered a cautious reminder, "Marshal Marmont will be at the ball."

Sinking deeper into the cushions, Franz made a faint acknowledging sound. He had quite prepared himself for the meeting. Prokesch had warned him about Marmont's presence at the reception, and the Major's contempt for the Marshal had prompted him to say, "Marmont is not worthy of meeting you face to face, Franz. Not after what he did to your father!"

But that only firmed Franz's wish to be presented to the infamous Marshal who had betrayed Napoleon. Marmont, Franz reasoned, was a precious well of information. The details he could provide would far surpass in originality the great many reports published on the late Emperor; and Franz could never pass up the opportunity to question a man who had actually *seen* his father.

Furthermore, it was important that Marmont's opinion of him be based on premises other than mere hearsay. When speaking of Reichstadt, the Marshal should be able to affirm, so Franz hoped: "*I have met the Emperor's son, and he is very much part of France's national heritage.*"

Lord Cowley's balls were always the talk of the season, and on this particular evening, the British Ambassador to Vienna offered his guests added thrill and excitement: the presence of a young man whose sheltered life foreign plenipotentiaries likened to a sequestration. The powerful mystique, which, for some, ominously surrounded the name of his late father cloaked the youth with enough importance to titillate everyone's curiosity.

Marmont was one of those for whom the occasion could not be missed. He had come early, eager to witness the guest of honor's arrival and made every effort to still the pangs of a guilty conscience, which could not be assuaged no matter how much he tried to persuade himself of the validity of his actions.

The betrayal of Napoleon was not all. During the July revolution in Paris—and as a result of having passed into the service of Charles X—he, Marmont, a marshal of the Revolution and of the Empire, *had ordered* the Royalist troops to open fire on his own countrymen! They who were offering up their lives in the name of liberty! Abhorred and called fratricide by the French, he had been forced to leave France and seek refuge in Austria. And tonight, he was about to meet the son of a master he had twice betrayed!

He began to perspire heavily. Waiting for Reichstadt's appearance was slowly destroying his composure. Nervously, he ran a finger inside the rim of his stiff collar and brushed the back of his hand over his forehead glistening with sweat.

"A little uneasy, perhaps?"

Marmont turned, startled. Metternich stopped a footman carrying a tray of champagne glasses and took one for the Marshal and one for himself.

"I think the occasion calls for a private toast," he said engagingly, raising his glass.

Marmont hesitated.

"To your success and to a continuing peace for Europe!" Metternich toasted grandly.

Silently, Marmont held up his glass and drank. The champagne gave him no pleasure and its fizz recalled the ephemeral effervescence of his own career.

Life had not been easy for Marmont. While the dapper Austrian Chancellor of State had climbed to the pinnacle of success, power and prestige, and earned Austria's highest honor: the Order of Golden Fleece, the former Marshal of the once mighty French Empire had tumbled from the lofty post of governor of the Illyrian Provinces to the lowly position of an exile. Austria had ingratiated herself to the hapless Marshal by offering him asylum, and Marmont felt indebted and more than eager to return a favor. It was a small service, really, which Metternich had asked him to perform as "a necessary precaution."

"Excellent champagne!" Metternich observed.

"Indeed," Marmont said distractedly, and craned his neck, directing his eyes toward the far end of the vast salon, ablaze with the light of hundreds of candles burning in crystal chandeliers.

As he watched, more guests were arriving and descending the stately staircase through an entrance draped with crimson damask fringed with gold tassels. A majordomo announced each arrival in a grand and sonorous tone. But despite his carrying voice, most names were drowned in the noise of the conversations and the strain of a waltz.

"Isn't the Prince late?" Marmont inquired, trying to sound casual.

Metternich's lips curled into a fleeting smile that was anything but pleasant. "I suspect His Highness wishes to create a sensation by arriving last. Now remember. I welcome the idea of Napoleon's son gaining insight into his father's character through your eyes. They have beheld a truth which you must help him see. The son of Bonaparte must not entertain illusions—or I should say delusions—of grandeur like his late father! He must be made to realize the enormity of his father's folly."

Marmont relaxed a little At least from the Austrian's perspective he was not the traitor, the turncoat, and the renegade the French people made him out to be. Austria understood his motives and by doing so, absolved him of all wrong.

Yet, will the Prince extend to him this sort of indulgence? Will he look with tolerance upon a man who had grown weary of wars, of violence, even if such violence had been fueled by the philosophy of the Revolution? A man who, in a moment of utter lassitude and discouragement, helped depose Napoleon, and by doing so robbed his son of a crown?

"Does Your Excellency think the Prince would care to notice me this evening?" he asked, not concealing his misgivings.

"You *will* be noticed."

As Metternich spoke, something quite out of the ordinary was happening. Marmont sucked in his breath. He had never seen Reichstadt, but he was sure that the exciting moment had finally arrived. The orchestra stopped playing, the couples on the dance floor came to a standstill. All conversations quieted down. And this time, the name being announced came loud and clear: "His Serene Highness the Duke of Reichstadt!"

Marmont stared thunderstruck and panic-stricken. He turned to Metternich for succor, but the Chancellor had vanished into the crowd.

At the top of the stairs, Franz steeled himself, his cheeks burning, aware of the sensation he was causing. He tried to stay poised and calm by concentrating on Prokesch's precious advice given to him in preparation of this momentous occasion: "Your surest guide to a satisfactory conduct, Franz, is to keep in mind that you are the son of Napoleon!"

Descending the steps with martial grace, Franz greeted the intense attention directed at him with a faint smile.

The conversations resumed and the orchestra started playing again. Beaming at his side, Dietrichstein moved in an aura of enchantment. In an exultant mood, he took Franz round the salon and began the introductions.

"Your Highness . . . the Count of Artois's special envoy, Baron von Kentzinger . . . and His Majesty King Louis Philippe's Ambassador, Marshal Maison."

Franz thought they formed an odd pair, for both men represented rival claims. Charles X, Count of Artois, presently in exile in England, had sent an envoy who was rubbing elbows with an official attached to the service of the man who had taken his throne. Neither diplomat seemed ill at ease, however. They amicably drank their champagne from long-stemmed glasses.

But the sight of Reichstadt deeply troubled Marshal Maison. Nostalgia gave the French ambassador a jolt. Maison, who had replaced General Belliard, was another unrepentant Bonapartist. He bowed, stammering a compliment, which to his delight was returned in fluent French without a trace of accent. Franz expressed his pleasure, intentionally glossing over Maison's present position while stressing his former ties, and that set the ambassador speculating. By alluding to the past, wasn't the Duke pointing to an enticing future from which Maison might not be excluded?

As Marmont intently watched the exchange from a distance, he also wondered if he would be playing a favorable part in Reichstadt's future. Not even the curse of his countrymen could extinguish his hope of vindicating himself. Did he not save Europe from further carnage by abandoning Napoleon? A lasting association with his son would also exonerate his conduct in 1814 once and for all, while at the same time discrediting the Prince in the eyes of his supporters. Marmont owed Metternich too much not to enter into such a scheme. . . .

Having recovered from the initial shock of beholding the splendid youth he had only known as a baby swathed in lace, Marmont managed to draw close enough to be spotted by Dietrichstein. The Marshal's heart began to palpitate when the Count beckoned for him to approach while whispering something into Reichstadt's ear.

Immediately the Duke looked up in his direction and walked toward him with an outstretched hand meeting him halfway, saying with a smile, "I am delighted to meet you, Marshal Marmont!"

Marmont shrank. That voice! Those eyes—direct and penetrating! The tilt of the head!

He sputtered nervously, "Your Highness is most kind. . . ."

Reichstadt's handshake possessed a forceful grip to which Marmont responded in kind, but out of desperation. During a very tense moment, the Duke of Ragusa stared avidly at the Duke of Reichstadt. There was no trace of Napoleon's lackluster ivory tan in his son's complexion; by contrast, the youth's skin seemed to glow and the faint blush of coral on his cheeks made his eyes appear more dazzlingly blue. And in those eyes, which quietly transfixed him, Marmont confronted the ghost of another visage. Emotion cramped the Marshal's chest as memories of an epic filled his head.

Experiencing a smarting sense of lost innocence, he faltered, ". . . most kind indeed!"

Franz put him at ease. "I delight to see in you my father's oldest associate."

"Thank you, Monseigneur," Marmont muttered, felling the sting of a blush.

"You were with him from . . . the very beginning," Franz said evenly. "There are many questions I should like to ask you."

"I am at Your Highness's disposal," Marmont replied with a deep bow.

Turning, Franz addressed his tutor with pupillary deference. "Then, we ought to set a date."

Expressly warned of Metternich's approval, Dietrichstein nodded in assent. He went as far as to invite Marmont to call on the Prince three times a week. This settled, the Marshal shakily saluted and moved on.

At that same moment Prokesch emerged from the press. At the sight of the Major, Dietrichstein smiled approvingly and left his pupil to mingle with the other guests.

Franz briefly squeezed his friend's hand. "Anton, where were you?" he asked hoarsely, realizing how tense he had been.

"Stranded in that corner because of the general push in your direction. I saw you come in."

"Am I behaving properly?"

"You have charmed everyone and obviously deeply troubled Marmont. From what could be observed, some already pretend you must have reproached him . . . Did you?"

"Nonsense!"

"I thought not. That is not like you to do such a thing."

Under his breath Franz said, "Marshal Marmont is an orange from which I shall extract all the juice, then discard. No, I am not going to reproach him. I am going to squeeze him dry!"

"You are going to see him again?"

"I am going to listen to him. Find out what he has to say. Everything is already arranged . . . just like that! It's very easy for Marmont to meet me because . . . the man is a traitor!"

Prokesch began to steer him through the crowd.

"You ought to put Marmont out of your mind for now, and enjoy yourself a little. After all, we are at a ball. . . ."

"Where are you taking me?"

"Over there, where Maurice Esterhazy is standing."

At the mention of Maurice, Franz relaxed somewhat. The young aristocrat possessed such a zest for life! With him, Franz discovered his own capacity for merriment. The two had met at a Court ball, and ever since, Franz kept cordial relations with the young man, who had embarked on a diplomatic career.

They found Maurice in animated conversation with a young woman whom Esterhazy hastened to introduce as Countess Naudine Karolyi. Franz's first glimpse of her captured the essential details which made her look so ravishing: the becoming color of her mauve silk ball gown; the parure of opals and diamonds, which enhanced the own luminescence of her clear porcelain complexion; and her raven-black hair in which clusters of fresh camellias seemed to have spontaneously blossomed.

He bent over her extended gloved hand, but only half way, as etiquette did not permit that he kiss it. Then straightening, he said, "I felt a little anxious coming here tonight. Meeting you, Madam, convinces me I would have felt sorry had I not been able to come after all."

The Countess gave a soft, throaty laugh and turned to Esterhazy. "I give you permission to repeat what I have said to you earlier concerning my being here, too."

That was an enormous concession to feminine vanity on her part. Issued from the princely house of Kaunitz, she led a brilliant and independent train of life and her palatial house in Vienna was the rallying point of the capital's gilded youth. Being beautiful and feted, she possessed an assurance and ease that, at times, could pass for conquettish condescension. But on this occasion, she had confided to Maurice, whom she knew well enough, that if the Duke of Reichstadt did not pay her the compliment of noticing her at the ball, she would never be the same woman again—a confession hardly expected from a woman as courted as Naudine was.

Esterhazy hesitated. "Should I, really?"

Franz kept gazing at her with attentive admiration, almost touching in its candor. She noticed in him a refreshing absence of affectation, which amazed and disarmed her in a pleasant and novel way. All her feminine wiles and arts to seduce and ensnare seemed to have made way to girlish timidity.

"Ah, do!" she urged, and even blushed.

Esterhazy obliged. When all was told, Franz smiled and said, "I have caused you needless alarm and I should feel forgiven if you would consent to grant me the next waltz . . . unless it is already claimed?"

She told him without hesitation he had the first choice.

Watching them dance together, Maurice Esterhazy remarked, "What a splendid pair!"

Prokesch made no comment, gauging much of what he observed against the discipline that directed his personal life. He had not married yet because the demands of his work, in his judgment, would have precluded a normal family life. But certainly, Reichstadt needed the company of women. His childhood and adolescence had been unnaturally bereft of feminine companionship. Yet if some serious sentimental experience were to appear in his life, few women would fit adequately in his very uncommon destiny. The Major even wondered if such a woman existed, one who could understand Franz's aspirations, relate to his needs, adjust to his frustrations, and stand by him in time of trials.

But Franz would not brook any of those considerations. His first impression of Naudine stirred in him feelings that transcended reflection. . . .

Later that night, in the familiar surroundings of his bedroom, he kept gazing at a new and exciting object—a flower. It was the camelia Naudine had taken from her hair and given him with a parting promise, which, like the flower, was perfumed with enchanting possibilities: "There shall be another, and it will bring us together again," she had said.

On the appointed day, Marshal Marmont arrived punctually, refreshed and fortified by a sense of mission.

Since Reichstadt was not yet in the room, Marmont curiously looked about him. On the top of a massive desk, obviously cleared to provide adequate space, a large map of Europe lay unrolled. To hold it flat, a curved saber sheathed in its scabbard and two exquisitely inlaid pistols were placed on the edges. A second desk bore the additional load of the objects that had been removed from the first one. It was heaped with books, piled in precarious pyramids, topographical sketches, rulers, compasses, and more maps. He'd seen such disorder before: Napoleon's war room.

The Marshal's shoulders drooped. He felt the grip of an acute need to be understood and, above all, absolved. For on this very spot, miles away from France, all because of an action he still maintained was justifiable, he was about to greet a young man he could have addressed as "Sire" or "Your Majesty."

"*Monsieur le Maréchal, je vous prie de m'excuser . . .*"

The mellifluous, deep-toned voice and the use of the French language in the purest of accent startled Marmont. He turned, his face ashen.

Advancing toward him, Franz amiably repeated, "Please excuse my tardiness. Punctuality is the politeness of kings . . . I beg you to forgive my not being a king and thus, my being late."

Marmont grew agitated and took the gambit as a veiled indictment. "It is I who must beg forgiveness. My watch must be fast."

Then, unable to bear the stress of a mounting tension, he added at the risk of seeming to rush things, "Where would Your Highness wish me to start?"

Franz walked up to the desk, motioning Marmont to follow. He pointed to the map.

"I have set the stage for us. This is Europe such as it was in 1789. Notice the frontier lines. Here is France. Still unassuming, but fermenting and falling prey to a remarkable . . . pestilence. Some call this phenomenon an incendiary enlightenment, other a *heresy.* How would you describe this occurrence?"

Intensely moved, Marmont answered, "I would describe it as a splendid upheaval, Monseigneur!"

"And you witnessed it!"

"I witnessed the best of it!"

"Then speak!"

"I would like to clarify my position in 1814, however."

Reichstadt's eyes fixed him coldly, but his voice was soft and his tone patient. "Clarify, if you wish."

"Monseigneur, it was against my better judgment to let your father retake Paris. His life was in peril. And the situation had so deteriorated that it would have been futile to prolong the hostility. Something had to be done. And somebody had to do it!"

Franz's lips compressed. That was no excuse. Soldiers should not dabble in political decisions. That sort of initiative never deserves praise. Marmont will always be guilty of betraying a soldier's most sacred trust—a strict observance of orders. Marmont, like Judas, would have done well to hang himself, too, he thought.

"You were weary, tired of it all," he preferred to say.

"We were all tired, Monseigneur! So many lives lost. . . ."

"*Monsieur le Maréchal,*" Franz interrupted. "What you did, I am certain, was decided *en connaissance de cause.* This being established, I pray you to proceed."

As the Marshal spoke, the incredible Napoleonic saga began to unfold in words Franz never hoped to hear. Marmont, too, was caught up in the thread of his own narrative and grew animated and fervent.

"Monseigneur, those were heroic times!" he concluded enthusiastically, noticing that Reichstadt was himself enthralled, with a blush on his cheeks and fire in his eyes. Then, remembering his mission, he curbed his own emotional outburst and added, "But what a terrible price!"

Franz came out of his euphoria. "Terrible?"

"Ambition . . ." Marmont commenced dutifully.

"Oh, please, spare me! I've heard all about it."

"I trust Your Highness understands what I mean," Marmont insisted, slightly discountenanced.

Franz objected testily, "Why this obsession about my father's ambition? What of his genius?"

"Alas! Your father's genius fueled his insatiable drive for power. This led him to commit monumental miscalculations. With all due respect to his memory, Monseigneur, I humbly urge you to avoid the scourge of a similar passion."

Franz flashed a bewitching smile. "You must not trouble yourself with that sort of thing. I am not. And please! Rest assured of my deepest appreciation!"

With those last words, Marmont's qualms of conscience were dispelled. By the time he left, he considered himself in favor. If by some lucky turn the young prince were to reign after all, he, Marmont, would enjoy the prestige of being recognized as the son of Napoleon's friend and his hidden protector!

Insinuating itself in Franz's political agenda, a name would enter his mind with increasing frequency. A name that evoked a sensuous presence he could still embrace with the strain of a waltz playing in his head.

Naudine. . . .

The camellia she gave him after the ball was still in a small crystal bowl he religiously kept filling up with fresh water every other day. The flower had long wilted, brown, limp, shapeless, and emitting a dead odor. But woe to the servant who might imagine doing him a service by throwing it away! Franz refused to part with the desiccated evidence of the Countess's favor. He recalled what she had said and waited and waited. . . .

Since the ball at the British Embassy, he had not seen her again, but he did send her tokens of his admiration. It was nothing extravagant by the ordinary standards of gentlemanly courtesy, but to him it had always been something of significance. This could be traced back to his adolescence, when he gave his mother posies and extended that same attentive compliment to Sophie and still was, even more frequently since the birth of her child. Whenever he passed through the streets of Vienna during the warm season, he would not fail to stop to buy her nosegays of lavender and herb peddled by humble housewives with their lilting chants.

That winter Franz sent Naudine long stemmed-roses wrapped in lace paper. Grown out of season, they disclosed, so he intended, the sentiment that he regarded her as a precious and extraordinary creation.

But having not heard from her, he began to wonder if she cared as much for him as he did for her. He grew impatient and felt as though he was running a fever.

Then one evening, in the beginning of the month of February, at a time of wild general carousing because Lent would soon impose on everyone a godly restraint, a small box was brought to him. It contained a fresh camellia and—surprisingly—a note from Maurice Esterhazy inviting Franz to meet him that evening at ten o'clock in the Redoutensaal. The message ended with precise instructions: he should wear a domino and mask, and attach the flower to the lapel of his costume.

Franz's heart leapt for joy. The flower indicated that Maurice was acting as Naudine's intermediary.

Never had the Carnival season so excited him and he felt genuinely frivolous. When, at the appointed hour, he entered the ballroom, a vast dancing hall located in the Hofburg palace, Esterhazy immediately came up to him and whispered, "Who knows you are here?"

"The secret police, I imagine," Franz whispered back. "What difference does this make?"

Maurice shook his head disapprovingly. "My plans were that you would be finishing the night somewhere else. But that is still possible. I have anticipated that difficulty anyway. Here!" He thrust something fuzzy into Franz's hand.

Looking quickly down, Franz saw that it was a black wig. What did Maurice have in mind? And where was he taking him afterward?

"Put this on now," Maurice instructed, without giving him a chance to ask. "Just pretend you lost something on the floor. Bend low. This crowd is so dense, it will serve as a screen."

Franz obliged without attracting anyone's notice and, in a matter of seconds, he straightened, looking completely changed.

"Well?" he inquired, curious as to how he looked.

Esterhazy's eyes registered immense satisfaction. "Splendid and unrecognizable!" he answered jubilantly.

The transformation was truly remarkable. Reichstadt's black velvet mask conveniently covered his fair eyebrows, and only his blue eyes shone with arresting contrast under a thick mass of black curls that nearly hid his forehead. Maurice thought the Prince resembled those dashing romantic heroes of the Italian Opera. Even Naudine could be fooled! He had not told her about the wig.

With as much grace as her natural demeanor would permit, Countess Karolyi elbowed her way through the mirthful throng, advancing straight toward Maurice. She wore an emerald green domino, a loup of gold cloth trimmed with pearls concealed the upper part of her face.

At the sight of her friend's companion, she stopped for only a few seconds, then resumed her slithering approach. Her mouth did not smile, but Franz saw a glint of surprise and pleasure flash in the twin almond-shaped obsidians that were her eyes.

As soon as Naudine reached them, she slightly flexed a knee before Franz and breathed, "Highness. . . ."

"Shhh. . . ." Maurice cautioned.

Naudine ran the tip of her finger over the fragrant petals of the camellia attached to Reichstadt's breast.

"My favorite flower," she murmured, smiling.

Franz put out his hand upon which she rested hers and said ardently, "Madam, had I been born in the age of chivalry, no lady's sleeves, as this flower, would have been worn with greater pride and joy!"

There followed a silence during which Franz and Naudine stared at each other starry-eyed.

Maurice suggested, "I hear music . . . shouldn't you be dancing?" That was all the prompting needed. Reichstadt and the Countess came into each other arms.

After the second dance, the two young men took turns dancing with Naudine. Then at midnight, she announced it was time they left for her residence where she herself was giving a masked ball.

"Will Your Highness accompany us?" she asked hopefully.

Franz inclined his head in the affirmative. The invitation answered the question he had asked himself earlier.

Quite thorough about masterminding his companion's escapade, Esterhazy suggested that Franz hide the flower under his cloak. That would further confuse the agents, for they had been aware of a blond masker wearing a boutonnière entering the hall. They would not see anyone answering that description leaving the building.

Maurice's stratagem proved completely successful.

Naudine did not introduce Reichstadt to her friends. A masquerade waived such formality. As Maurice pointed out, it was better for the Countess's special guest to remain incognito. No place would be free from spying eyes were the identity of such a guest known.

As a result, everyone was left to wonder who was the handsome dark masker the Countess had brought with her. While Franz was the object of much speculation, Esterhazy was satisfied to discreetly fade into the mirthful background leaving him to dance exclusively with the Countess.

As they spun round and round, Naudine kept her face upturned, staring through the peepholes of her loup into the blue depth of her partner's eyes.

After a while, she said a little breathlessly, "I cannot decide which side of Your Highness I prefer . . . the dark one or the fair one!"

"Which would you choose if you had to?"

Naudine laughed. "Do I have a choice?"

Below the black velvet mask she watched Reichstadt's lips accord her a pensive smile. He said, "Either way, there is always a dark corner in a man's soul. Mine is no exception."

Naudine felt a twinge of anxiety. Somehow, in the thrall of Reichstadt's embrace she was allowing herself to dance out of the easy and mundane world in which her sense of security was rooted, and follow him to some untested dimension that his extraordinary beauty and charm offered, but where in return, she would be caught in unforeseen complications.

"I am afraid of shadows," she confessed.

Franz bent his head. His lips almost touching her forehead, he said with sudden desolation, "You are afraid of me. . . ."

She felt the warm plume of his breath on her mouth. "Yes," she gasped. "Yes, I am!"

Pulling her closer, he asked urgently, "Oh, why?"

Naudine surrendered and slid her arms across his back, letting her body press to his. "Because there is something fearsome and sweet in discovering you!"

Instantly she felt him tremble and sensed the light touch of his lips on her hair. She heard him murmur her name with such amorous inflections that she shivered in turn as they twirled into a deserted salon adjacent to the main reception hall which was now empty of guests. Only sleepy musicians remained playing the last measure of their waltz. When the music stopped, neither made a move to draw away.

In silence they stood in front of a ceiling-high window garlanded with paper roses. A wintry moon wanly shone between silver edged-clouds. But the sky had shed its nocturnal depth and its milky pallor hinted at the apparition of a crisp and frosty morning.

Slowly Naudine removed her mask, then Franz's. Next, she took off his wig letting it drop to the floor and ran her fingers through his damp, blond curls.

"Dawn. But don't go yet. You might catch a chill. . . ." she whispered, offering her lips.

As she felt the pressure of his mouth against them, she responded with adroit movements, surprised and charmed by his inexperience. But he was an avid learner and their kiss lasted as no other she had received.

Afterward, Franz crushed her to him while whispering her name over and over to the great silence of the house and to the fading moon beams. Chanting Naudine's name, he discovered the wonder of all wonders: there was definitely more to life under the heavens of the world than being the son of the Great Napoleon.

26

The July Revolution in France spawned intolerable difficulties for Metternich. In early February of 1831, Italy took up arms in the name of liberty and called upon the immortal blood of Bonaparte to avenge the iniquities suffered at the hands of their oppressors. To Metternich's horror, the fire of dissent was rapidly spreading to Bologna, Ferrara and Ravenna. Parma was in danger of falling into the hands of the insurgents.

Franz stormed into the Emperor's study demanding to be sent to Parma.

He'd heard rumors that his mother was being held captive by her rebellious subjects. The fact that she could be endangered by an undertaking he secretly held virtuous, did not alter his determination. Regardless of his convictions, filial devotion required that he be among her rescuers.

Persuaded that he would be damned if he acted in his mother's behalf, and equally damned if he didn't, he left his grandfather little latitude to engage in a sensible conversation.

Francis heard him raving about something he vaguely understood—in a disjointed discourse—as referring to honor and infamy, and it took him a while before he could calm his grandson.

"Now, listen, Franz!" he finally managed to interject. "I assure you that your mother is in no danger. Contrary to what you've heard, she is not being held against her will. She has gone to Casal-Maggiore and is quite safe there. *I should know,* don't you think?"

"But Sire, I just want to see to her personal safety!"

"I commend you for offering to defend your mother, but really, Franz, this is not necessary."

"I am also a soldier. If you took my commission seriously. . . . If you could realize that parade-ground soldiering is not my goal in life, you would let me go!"

Francis regarded his beloved grandson with a queer defeated air. "I believe in your valor and goodness, Franz," he said almost plaintively.

"Then this belief, Sire, should be my passport to Parma!"

"Franz, I mean . . ." hedged Francis.

For the first time Franz dared confront his grandfather with a truth he'd pondered for some time. "If I were any other archduke, you would not hesitate to send me there!"

An expression of melancholy chagrin settled over Francis's face. Grave and daring thoughts passed through his mind. Franz was so vibrant with vitality. What was he going to do with him? How long and how stringently must he hold him back and keep him in political quarantine?

Suddenly, all these talks of impending disaster and doom should Franz be allowed to sit on a throne, no longer impressed him as being realistic. And why should Louis Philippe conserve his crown when he dared put forward that disgraceful theory of non-intervention regarding the Italian upheaval? Whereas Franz would be so much better suited to rule in his place! Habsburg blood flowed through his veins, and the deep affection that united them offered the pleasant prospect of a peaceful and fruitful coexistence between Austria and France. Meantime, all the dear and brave youth asked was to lend his service to help rescue his mother from the perils of a revolution. What better indication should he need to convince himself that their views, like their hearts, were in perfect harmony?

Francis, Emperor of Austria, decided to assume the awesome authority he had relinquished to his Chancellor.

"I may just do that," he said.

At first, Franz was too stunned to speak. Only after having half-smothered his grandfather in a frenzied hug was he able to urge him with childlike exhuberance, even reverting to a once and long-abandoned familiarity. "Oh, do it, Bonpapa! Do it, please!"

Completely charmed and mollified, Francis chuckled, patting his shoulders. Then suddenly, he tensed and grew still.

Franz sensed another presence. He backed away and swung round.

Metternich stood in the doorway.

"I am sorry," the Chancellor said with suavity. "I was not aware Your Majesty had a visitor." He bowed toward Reichstadt, all smiles. "Your Highness!"

"Highness . . ." Franz returned distractedly, his eyes on his grandfather.

Francis felt cornered. Franz's gaze begged for support with such wrenching intensity! He braced himself. He would have to inform Metternich. And the sooner the better.

"Clement, do stay. The Duke was just about to leave, weren't you, Franz?"

Franz's heart leapt. There was in Francis's dismissal a tone that betokened a decision in his favor. He inclined his head in assent and without a word left the room.

"I do apologize for the interruption," Metternich said, concealing his anxiety. In truth, he did not feel regretful at all. He might have come at a very opportune time. The tender scene he had just witnessed could indicate a concession, one which Reichstadt might have exacted from his grandfather. The Emperor's incurable and dangerous affection for the son of Napoleon kept Metternich in constant alert.

"No. Not at all," Francis answered a little shakily, berating himself for being so nervous. Then summoning all his courage, he announced: "I have decided to allow my grandson to go to Parma. It is important to him. He wants to see to his mother's safety, personally."

Metternich felt a strangulating fear creeping up his throat but managed to remain impassive. He reminded the Emperor that the Archduchess Mother was quite safe where she had sought refuge, and Austrian troops had already been dispatched to Parma to re-establish order without the official consent of the Parisian Cabinet—a move he had taken the liberty to risk, even if this would mean a diplomatic break between France and Austria.

This eventuality did not seem to interest Francis. And for once, he showed unusual tenacity.

He said proudly, "The Duke is after all an officer eager to test his talent. And I don't want to disappoint him!"

"If His Highness is allowed to set foot in Italy, Your Majesty may have much cause for regret," Metternich answered with ominous gravity.

But Francis held his ground. "The Duke would never join the revolutionary movement. My grandson is not unprincipled!"

"Sire, His Highness's mere presence in Italy will put an end to Your Majesty's dominion beyond the Alps."

"That is a gross exaggeration!"

"I even predict a general revolution this time. His Highness might very well receive, as a result, the Iron Crown of Italy. France will overthrow the King and proclaim the re-establishment of the Empire, joining again the two kingdoms together. And again, there will be strife, and wars and utter anarchy!"

"No . . ." Francis said weakly and shuddered, aghast at the horrifying picture of Europe Metternich had summoned to his mind.

Francis so detested change of any kind! Change which he equated to sin. If his Chancellor was right, and he trusted him to be, his golden boy would be the ruin of his policy and his snare. Once, in one of those disquieting moments when he'd tried to plumb the extent of his affection for Franz and stopped half-way, unable or perhaps afraid to ascertain its depth, he remembered having said to Metternich in an aside which he only intended to be light and amusing: "You must protect me from the Duke."

He realized now that his order had been followed, and breaking into a cold sweat, he finally admitted, "You have made your point, Clement. I thank you."

Franz had gone straight to his apartments, taking a passageway which few people knew about and no one, so far as he could tell, ever thought of using anymore. The Hofburg Palace was ancient, and with the march of time had sprawled to accommodate legitimate needs and imperial caprices. Endless corridors shimmering with mirrors and gilt were not the only way one could access a suite. If one should stray or methodically explore, one would soon discover a warren of narrow, winding staircases, treacherous trap-doors and mazes of dank and obscure subterranean passages interconnecting the apartments.

Franz liked to use them because he could come and go without being noticed by the numerous servants staffing the palace, and this gave him a pleasant illusion of privacy and freedom. He often took these passages to go to Sophie's apartments.

Entering his bedchamber, he found his valet, Lambert, laying out his clothes in preparation for the ritual supper at the Emperor's table. Francis's male relations would be committing a grave infraction by coming to the familial meal dressed in military uniforms, and attendance at those meals was mandatory. Every member of the Habsburg clan, even those who were married or maintained an establishment of their own, had to comply with the routine of assembling for a common repast. Men's clothing had to conform to those worn in an ordinary household at such occasion. Only guests who might happen to belong to a military unit were exempt from appearing in mufti. And the guests were rare.

Franz had long ceased to find any enticing quality in such gatherings. With the exception of Sophie, the company was uninteresting, the conversations were anything but stimulating, and though his appetite was light, the little he ate gave him frequent indigestions.

But this evening, he did look forward to the meal with a mixture of happy anticipation and severe anxiety. He wondered if Francis would be true to his words. Metternich more than likely had been apprised of his grandfather's intention, and the Emperor never issued direct orders. They would have to be reviewed by Metternich. Did Francis stand up to him this time?

"Does Your Highness wish to be dressed presently?" Lambert asked.

"I'll dress myself," Franz answered, as usual declining the valet's offer. He considered this form of ministration unmanly and frivolous. "You may leave me now."

Left alone, he undressed and dressed himself all over again, speculating on the answer Francis would give him. And the longer he dwelled on the matter, the more apprehensive he became. Then he found himself staring at his image in the full length mirror and the reflection did not quite please him, even though the tall and slender youth with aureate hair staring back at him looked dreamily attractive in a midnight blue cutaway tail coat. He compressed his lips with a slight scowl, wishing they weren't so full. He had hoped to look more like Napoleon.

As Franz entered the drawing room where the imperial family usually gathered before the evening meal, Francis was finishing the last chords of a simple composition at the piano, surrounded by a respectful if not captivated audience, which was composed of the Emperor's brothers, Archdukes Joseph and Rainer, and Empress Carolina Augusta. Her homely face brightened as soon as she caught sight of Franz.

He went straight to his grandparents and noticed the absence of Crown Prince Ferdinand, who, he imagined, must have had another epileptic fit. All his other uncles and aunts presently in residence at the palace were there, except Francis Charles and his wife. Franz felt a sharp twinge of disappointment. Was Sophie indisposed? Or only late coming?

Pivoting on the piano bench, Francis stood up just in time to receive his grandson's greetings. Franz gave him a searching look, but the Emperor's expression gave nothing away. Franz's heart sank and he barely paid attention to the Empress's effusive display of affection as she kissed him with ever increasing relish.

"How elegant you are, Franzchen!" she beamed, looking him up and down.

"A fashion plate," Archduke Joseph observed with the assurance of a connoisseur, although he tended to dress too garishly for Franz's taste.

Archduke Rainer injected staidly, "It is a wholesome pastime to follow the latest mode. One can never go wrong." Saying this, he significantly glanced at his brother who immediately caught the allusion. Joseph emitted an acknowledging grunt thinking of their other brother, Archduke John, whose continued exile from court pointed to the danger of deviating from innocent pastime.

At this point, Franz was past guessing what Francis's answer would be. He already felt betrayed. The hurt made him feel puckish and he found in deviltries an outlet for a strong undercurrent of exasperation.

"Not quite so," he returned. "One can certainly err by conforming blindly. I submit that a dash of individuality is the most valuable accessory in a gentleman's wardrobe."

Having no inkling of his grandson's descent into a whorl of utter frustration, Francis exclaimed jovially, "Well said, Franz!" Yet the light turn of the conversation did not deceive him. He knew that later, when he would have to tell Franz that going to Parma was out of the question, he would have to contend with his grandson's disappointment. For the time being he felt comfortable going along with Franz's apparent levity.

He moved to the sofa, and the Empress took her place beside him while he motioned his grandson to an armchair. "Join us, will you, Franz?"

Joseph and Rainer, having received no such invitation, dispersed to another corner of the drawing room. Francis still put off the announcement and was intent on making conversation.

"We did not see you at Mass, this morning," he remarked with a wink intimating that no reproach was intended.

Recalling the proposition put forward in his childhood that he should consider entering holy orders as a career, Franz said with a straight face, "That goes to prove how bad a priest I would have been, Sire. Daily Mass, with your gracious indulgence, is not my forte."

"Poor Franzchen!" the Empress sighed, eyeing him with unreserved admiration. "Inasmuch as I pray daily for the salvation of your soul, I certainly can't picture you in a soutane."

"Ho! Ho!" Francis guffawed. "You do remember, Franz! What a silly idea that was!" And with a dash of lewdness in his eyes, he said, "God, forbid! With your looks, you would be damning more souls than you would be saving!"

"Sire!" Franz blushed. These sorts of allusions made him squirm. The irreparable wound inflicted upon him by his mother's adultery had deeply influenced his perception of sensual gratification. As an antidote for the profound distaste his mother's betrayal had inspired in him, and in the ardor and idealism of his youth enhanced by his sensitive and high-minded nature, Franz had raised physical love to a level of romantic perfection—all enduring and ennobling. Physical love taken in jest, or placed in the context of mindless coupling like satisfying basic human lust, was repugnant to him. Realistically, if lust had to be satisfied at its germinal level, he simply loathed talking or boasting about it.

"Now, now," Francis insisted. "You are full grown. This is a matter for consideration. And to make it all good and proper, we shall find you a buxom wife!"

Inwardly, Franz cringed. Francis spoke of a wife as if it concerned the acquisition of a brood mare!

"I don't wish to marry anyone at present or in a near future," he said, weary of the direction the conversation was taking him—nowhere, as far as he was concerned.

But Francis had embarked on a subject he thought eminently apropos, and wished to give it further consideration. He lived in fear of sins and eternal punishment, and worried about the salvation of Franz's soul. And only a proper wife could lead his beloved grandson down the path of connubial delights with complete peace of mind. Francis saw himself as a shining example of such sagacious lust.

Placing his hand on the Empress's knee, he fondled it, musing out loud, "A tour de force, Franz . . . A tour de force, indeed! Do you think you can stand . . . err . . . being single and remain virtuous?"

The Empress became absorbed in the contemplation of her fingernails, feeling self-conscious because her husband's hand was now running up and down her thigh. Francis was incredibly candid about fondling his consort in public. It seemed as though he utterly enjoyed the legality of his carnal instincts at the risk of appearing downright lecherous and indecent.

Fortunately, Franz was spared the ordeal of having to respond to the Emperor's tactless prying into his private life. Sophie had just arrived on Karl's arm and both were walking toward them.

"Excuse me, Sire," Franz said, rising to his feet to offer Sophie his seat which was the most comfortable of the ones available. He acknowledged Karl with a polite, perfunctory nod.

Karl returned the civility with an ever present touch of condescension. He was intensely jealous of Reichstadt's privileged position in the Emperor's affection, and in spite of all the shining qualities he recognized in his nephew, he felt definitely superior by virtue of his own noble antecedents. The blood that ran through his veins was unadulterated, and one of the oldest in a mighty line of divinely appointed rulers. It was an ichor of which he was so proud that he had managed to tolerate Reichstadt with relative calm. The Duke could not earn the signal distinction of being regarded as a rival in any aspect, save for being Francis's favorite. This was the attitude Karl fostered with an obstinacy which was going to dim his perception.

Full of self-importance, he perched himself with studied nonchalance on the arm of a fauteuil. The posturing was totally lost on Franz, who had only eyes for his beloved aunt. Sophie looked ravishing in a rust-colored dress whose wide but modest neckline accentuated the graceful slope of her white shoulders. Motherhood seemed to have put a special radiance to her complexion.

Franz placed himself behind his aunt's chair, his forearm resting somewhat protectively on the curved backrest. Sophie tilted her head to smile up at him before answering a familiar question put to her by Carolina Augusta: Yes, her baby was doing well, and mother and child had a good day.

Whereupon Karl began blustering. "A bad one for me!" he put in. "A dratted groom was responsible for my falling when I got out of my carriage this afternoon! I got muddied and my arm still hurts!"

"It was raining," Sophie said quietly, "and you must have slipped."

"I say the son-of-a-slut did it on purpose by not pulling down the folding steps when he should have! I'll have him whipped and returned to that farm where he belongs with the rest of his kind. Peasants are shifty and incorrigible!"

"I have the utmost respect for peasants," his wife said, not changing her tone. "Without them we wouldn't have any food on our tables. As for the boy, I have already given instructions to dismiss him. He is to receive three spanks on the bottom for not knowing how to ingratiate himself to you, and he will be placed in the service of Princess Grassalkowich."

"That is not what I wanted!" Karl whined with irritation. But the blustering subsided, leaving only a residue of ill-humor, which Sophie ignored with admirable serenity by not bothering to answer.

Francis hoped to give his son a chance to shine by saying, "Good work, Karl, for fathering a lusty son!"

Karl seized the opportunity only to blunder, "I should think so! I've tried often enough, long enough, and hard enough!"

From where he stood, Franz could not see Sophie's expression, but she went absolutely rigid in her chair, and a telling vivid blush began to spread over Carolina Augusta's cheeks. The Empress lowered her eyes and a nervous ghostly smile twitched her pale mouth.

Immediately Francis laughed heartily and was joined by Karl.

Utterly disgusted, Franz thought it best not to add to his aunt's embarrassment by staying a minute longer. Excusing himself, he walked away and almost bumped into the head steward, who came to announce that supper had been served.

Everybody began to pair off. Franz noticed that Sophie barely allowed the tips of her fingers to touch Karl's sleeve as they took their place in the procession which filed into the glittering dining hall. Having no one to escort, Franz brought up the rear.

Stunned by the incident, he made his way to his assigned seat, one which Francis wanted his grandson to occupy. It was next to him as a special honor. What Francis had to say needed to be flavored with a little coddling.

The meal began, Francis had waited long enough and wanted to dispatch the unpleasant task of saying "no" to Franz's ardent request. Leaning sideways, he murmured, "Franz, I am sorry. There is no real need for you to go to Parma."

"Fine," Franz responded absentmindedly, still reeling from the shock of hearing Karl speak so crudely and publicly of an intimate act without any consideration for his wife's modesty and sensibility. Franz was not a prude, nor was he totally innocent in mind and body. There existed inherent raw needs that would even flare at an inadvertent touch, and he recognized their pleasure. But the coarse delectation people seemed to find in talking openly and lightly about sexual traffics filled him with revulsion. Sadly, lewd, and vulgar conversations were much appreciated in imperial circles. He had heard quantities of smutty jokes told in his grandfather's presence because Francis himself enjoyed them with little discretion, and on too many occasions. Karl seemed to have followed his father's poor example to an even worse degree. He had behaved like an absolute brute!

"Franz, you must not have paid any attention to what I've just told you," Francis said.

This time, Franz gave a start, "I'm sorry."

"There is no need for you to go to Parma," Francis repeated.

Franz had already prepared himself well enough to remain calm. "Why did you change your mind?" he asked, defeat and resignation dulling his tone.

"I have reconsidered," Francis preferred to say.

"'As you wish, Sire."

For the rest of the meal, he ate little and spoke even less. He glimpsed Sophie from across the table, and their eyes met. Hers smiled at him. Outwardly she seemed perfectly composed, as if the horrid episode with Karl had never taken place. Franz's admiration for her sangfroid deepened.

After they left the table, Francis drew his grandson in a window embrasure and said consolingly, "Franz, don't be discouraged. I have something to tell you in the strictest of confidence."

Franz's face was expressionless. He had been frustrated and disappointed often enough, and mistrust froze its mobility.

"If you as much as appear in Strasbourg," Francis continued, "The Bourbon-Orléans family is done for."

"I am not going anywhere, Sire," Franz bitterly reminded him.

The Emperor's mouth twitched. There was pain in his eyes. He sighed and said with genuine regret, "Ah, Franz! If only you were a little older! You must learn to wait."

Franz made no reply. He did not dare speak. One word could release a gale of wounding remarks and their mutual affection might not withstand the damaging blow. Something between them would break, never to be mended if, for instance, Franz were to say that he did not give a damn about living long enough to grow older seeing that the life he was made to live was so hopelessly stagnant; that Metternich's counsels should be called into question if only to stimulate the latter to offer some variation to the sempiternal argument that nothing ever good could come from Napoleon's son; that Francis should be able to make up his own mind once in a while. . . .

Francis touched his arm, thinking of an anodyne. "I am giving a ball tonight, just for the family. It is my wish that you attend it."

Franz was about to make some excuses, when his grandfather heaved a pitiful sigh saying, "Please. I would feel so much better. And it would do you good. You should amuse yourself for a change!"

And do you think that *a ball* would help *me* feel any better? That Francis should offer such a lame consolation and be relieved by it angered Franz. But that was all he should expect. He said drily, "I shall try my very best, Sire."

The Emperor's private balls, *Kammerballe,* were not exactly Franz's idea of tasteful and stimulating entertainment. As he entered the ballroom, he would have been hard put to find any redeeming grace in the graceless and dull assembly that composed the imperial family. The only feminine presence that showed breeding and commanded admiration was Sophie's. The other archduchesses spoke and laughed too loudly, uttered platitudes, and picked their teeth. Surveying the people dressed in their fineries, Franz decided that all those present—including himself—were special only because through no merit of their own, they had been born to a pre-acquired level of social superiority that had nothing to do with personal excellence.

To him, this status had to be earned and, in fact, was within the reach of any naturally well-endowed individual. There was no pre-ordained mandate bestowed from the Heavens to become a leader, or to belong to an elite. If there were any predestination at all, it simply originated in one's own ability, like his father had so brilliantly demonstrated. Or in one's own infirmity, like poor Uncle Ferdinand so pitifully revealed. "Blue Blood" never guaranteed superior qualities. Those qualities could be found in every stratum of society, in the nameless, faceless masses which the aristocracy regarded as chattel. . . .

"Cousin Franz," a high-pitched voice said at his side.

Franz turned to look down at a simpering girl of fifteen with a long face, almost carrot-red hair, and round dark-blue eyes. She was the daughter of Archduke Louis and had earned the nickname of "The

Infanta" because she bore an uncanny resemblance to a portrait of the seventeenth century Spanish princess, the Infanta Margarita Maria, painted by Velazquez.

As her glance met the absent stare of her dream prince, she piped, "You look so serious. Isn't any of this," she gestured with an ostensible flutter of her dance program which was held open to a blank page, the movement encompassing the glittering salon and all the uninspiring company it contained, ". . . amusing you?"

Franz forced a smile and conceded. "Yes, somewhat."

Encouraged, she asked if only to make conversation, "What were you thinking about?"

"The popular elite."

The young archduchess screwed up her face. "What is that?"

"An untapped commodity," he responded, well aware that she couldn't possibly know what he was alluding to.

Utterly disconcerted, she observed a short silence; then plaintively, she announced, "I had a birthday, you know. But you missed my party."

"I am sorry, Henrietta," he said with sincerity.

He was really contrite not about missing the party, but because he had sported with her simplicity and perplexed her with considerations far beyond her reach. Her own world would always be far more limited than his, with boundaries set by the small range of her understanding; and like too many of her kind, regardless of gender, her mind was enjoying a gilded and well-guarded quietude that put her in a lethargic state of grace. She could find perfect contentment in her privileged status, all padded with comfortable traditions to which one could warm oneself and feel protected from the harsh and challenging reality experienced by ordinary people.

So Henrietta had a birthday that, by pure luck, had been celebrated in princely fashion. With many more to come, she could look forward to a lifelong procurement of luxury. Her needs were simple, yet ravenous in terms of excesses, and her cares were enormously trivial. Franz felt he should make an effort to bring himself down to the level of her miserable opulence.

"I'll dance with you, if this can make up in some way for my not being present at your birthday," he said pleasantly.

Henrietta was ecstatic. "This dance, and the next," she said, holding out her arms as the musicians struck the first measure of a waltz by Josef Lanner.

Tittering, she came more than readily into the circle of Franz's arms and let herself be swept into the seventh heaven of delight when they began to spin around the salon.

Henrietta said breathlessly, "No one dances the waltz as well as you do!"

"You are doing very well yourself," Franz said absently, spotting Sophie conversing with the Empress.

Karl was nowhere in sight. And he found himself wishing, *If only Sophie had a husband who could command respect and treat her with regard. . . .* The abomination of what he had said!

Henrietta giggled. "I love to waltz! My head spins and I love it!"

"*Schwindelig?*" he inquired with deceitful solicitude. "If so, we can stop right now if you like."

"No, please! I am not that dizzy!" she protested in earnest.

To her disappointment, the next dance was a quadrille, which meant that partners would have to interchange in the course of intricate movements. Franz's last contact with Henrietta ended with the tips of their fingers touching, before the ladies sank into a shallow curtsey in front of their gentlemen partner at the end of the piece.

But Henrietta demanded her due to the last farthing. Straightening, she said with a bright blush coloring her cheeks, "Since you were not present at my birthday celebration, you do owe me a happy birthday kiss!"

"All right, Henrietta," he said with even greater abstraction and made to hold her by the shoulders in a playful sort of way to peck at her cheek.

She stopped him. "Not here, Cousin Franz," she squeaked, taking him by the hand and dragging him after her. "Out there!"

Acceding to her girlish caprice, Franz followed her to the door that led onto the Hofburg private gardens. It was shut because of the chill, but Henrietta tugged at the handle, opened the pane a crack and squeezed through with her catch in tow. Pulling Franz a few more paces away from the illumination of the ballroom, she swung round, and with unbridled effrontery and womanly wile, stood on the tips of her toes and pressed herself against him. Her mouth came up to his to claim her due in a clumsy and delirious wet kiss. Then she backed away giggling, pirouetted on her silk slippers, and was gone.

Henrietta's impish retreat left Franz to return to a meditative mood. Slowly, he moved to the far end of the terrace to gaze at the dark symmetry of clipped yews and ghostly statuaries which lined the geometrical network of paths that seemed to lead into endless gloom. The strain of another waltz barely intruded on his perception of other sounds, the sounds of Vienna.

The familiar noises of the bustling city were thinning because once again this side of the earth turned to face the unfathomable night of the universe. Its vastness and mystery crushed him and he felt utterly abandoned and alone.

Desperately, he clung to the anchoring succor of some echoes of human activities that still lingered: the distant rumbling of carriages, the cadenced clatters of horse hooves on the cobble stones, dogs barking. . . . He thought of France and wondered how Paris would sound settling down to sleep? Perhaps the very same way.

"*François?*" The quiet, caring voice did not startle him, and the use of French to call his name with uncanny timing entered unobtrusively into his melancholy reverie. This only provided a kinder bridge to reality.

Crossing it by half-turning, Franz held out his hand, grasping a gentle consolation—he was no longer truly alone!

Thin and soft fingers laced into his.

"Sophie, you will take a chill!" he chided gently.

"You, too," she said, drawing up to his side.

"You came to rescue me?"

"God, forbid! I would never presume. Only I saw you and Henrietta go outside. She came back in and you did not."

"Henrietta dragged me out here to steal a kiss," Franz chuckled, without the least trace of amusement.

Sophie eyed him and said cautiously, "You are preoccupied . . . upset. You hardly ate anything at supper. Something the Emperor said to you perhaps? Oh, but you don't have to tell me anything! The last thing I want to do, is to pry."

It would have been totally inappropriate and tactless to mention Karl's odious bragging, so he answered, the ember of his frustration flaring up anew and injecting a huffiness in what he had to tell her, "I have been denied permission to go to Parma!" He laughed, but so bitterly, the sound came as a sharp series of mirthless staccatos. "I'm not even allowed to go to my mother and assure myself of her safety!"

Sophie hoped to soothe him by saying evenly, "I understand matters are well under control. Your dear mother is in no danger. . . ." Then with anxiety, "But it pains me to see you so hurt!"

"I'll get over it," he said, his voice softening. "You have never given me anything but encouragement and support. How could I continue feeling sorry for myself?"

Trying to repress a slight shiver, she commiserated, "You are going through a difficult time, I know."

Instead of elaborating on her observation, he only remarked, "You are cold!" and put his arm around her bare shoulders. "We'd better return inside."

Halfway before entering the ballroom he asked, puzzled, "Why did you say my name in French?"

She seemed sincerely nonplused. "An inspiration perhaps?" she offered.

They had always deeply cared for each other and nothing seemed more simple and natural for him to acknowledge how blessed he felt. He drew her against him and kissed her forehead saying, "You will always be an inspiration to me!"

For a brief instant Sophie wrestled with the fear of losing self-control. Karl had deeply wounded and humiliated her. The crude means he had used doing this could never be forgotten; and Franz, she knew, must have been appalled by what he had witnessed. The consummate gallantry he exhibited by refraining from even making the slightest of allusions to the incident—though praiseworthy, left her stranded and alone in her pain. But she quickly stamped down an intense longing to let herself be consoled by sobbing against his chest.

Instead, they parted with a simple "good night," both intending to leave the ball early.

Sophie retired to her bedchamber which she occupied alone, a temporary arrangement she had succeeded in securing after the long-awaited birth of her first child. That birth had been particularly difficult, and the physicians attending her strongly recommended that she not get pregnant too soon afterward lest complications might develop. Recovery would be slow and Karl was amenable to the idea of sleeping in separate quarters. Sophie suspected he was not wanting for sexual amusements in the libertine milieu Vienna had to offer, and she would not deny being relieved that he did not shun them. She more than welcomed having her bed to herself. And while it lasted, she would make the best of it.

She was enjoying her solitude, reading a book of poetry by candlelight when Karl startled her by boldly walking in, wearing a dressing gown. He fumbled at the sash with a look she had never liked; a look, she had hoped she would not see for a while. It was too soon. And what of the truce he had agreed to?

She strove for calm, but her hands were shaking as she dropped the book on her lap to gather the bedclothes about her.

"Karl, it's late. And you should be in bed," she managed to say quietly, pretending to prepare herself for rest.

"This bed will do just as well," he returned with a smirk, finishing to untie the sash and shrugging off the garment.

Naked, he advanced toward the bed.

Shuddering, Sophie jerked her head to the side, pulling up her knees. "Karl, no. Please! Not now. . . . Not yet!" She had never felt so used and abused. Her own welfare meant nothing to him!

"You are my wife!" There was something gloating and vengeful in the way he said this, and his hard hands clamped down on her shoulders.

Wincing, she crossed her arms across her chest. "I gave you a son. And I'll give you many more children, but they must be spaced," she pleaded.

"Ah, don't be so coy!" he growled. "What makes you think I am only interested in having children? What of the rest?" Violently he tugged at her wrists forcing her arms apart and dipped his head to her breasts, his mouth opening and closing on them through her night shift with gluttonous sloppiness. In her over-wrought state, she imagined only a pig could be expected to do this the way he did: gorging on slops.

Writhing, she taunted, "Then get yourself a whore!"

Karl gave a cackling laugh and forced his wife back against the pillow, pinning her hands down on either side of her head.

"Ah, but whores don't resist! And I have not found one as satisfying as you!" His breath on her face was sour and his hooded eyes with their habitual dormant bovine expression similar to that of his sister, Marie Louise, were now aglow with sickening lust.

He had a few scores to settle with her.

"You may run your life the way you please and treat me with that distant primness of yours, but remember, in the bedroom I am the master! The one to whom you have pledged the sacred oath of wifely submission and obedience! Have you forgotten this? And doesn't your bigoted conscience have any qualms consigning me to the ministration of sluts? Where are your saintly concerns? What of me? What of the salvation of my soul, eh? I have seen you pray at Mass with the devotion of a nun, and surely you wouldn't want to have me damned? . . . ."

He clambered onto the bed and straddled her. "And now that your belly is empty, I'll fuck you and none other, and as often as I please!"

"No!" she cried buckling against the hard press of his thighs that held her as in a vise. "Karl, no! . . . Not like this!" Tears blinded her, and through the stinging veil of unspeakable hurt, she glimpsed his triumph.

Then an inspiration made her say, "I can't let you. I have my menses!"

"You are lying!" he snarled. But his buttocks lifted in instinctive disgust.

"It's true, Karl," she gasped, knowing that she was breaking every rule by which she lived and hallowed. Yet could God and the Church sanction the abusive use Karl made of her body? He was not lying earlier when he dared speak of their marital congress in front of Francis.

Under the pretext of producing an heir, Karl had ruthlessly forced himself upon her. For so many years he had poked fun at her bareness after loveless sessions during which he alone took his pleasure. While he worked himself up to a climax, she would bite her tongue and pray with a fierceness bordering on revolt that his ferocious entries would this time impregnate her and put a momentary stop to his abuses, restore peace to her nights and dignity to her womanhood.

The arrival of the child had changed nothing. Her physicians' recommendations were being disregarded. Unless she feigned an indisposition, pretended irregular periods, he obviously intended to continue finding a sadistic satisfaction in mastering her the only way he knew.

But Karl wasn't that easy to fool. He grew suspicious.

"Why didn't you tell me when I came in?"

"You caught me by surprise," she stammered helplessly.

He sneered. "And you are holding one in store for me, my deceitful wife!"

Then before she had time to realize what he was going to do, he yanked her night dress up to her waist, exposing her complete nudity.

"Ah-ha!"

Sophie tried to push him off, but he lowered himself over her, squirming, bearing down with his full weight. Vanquished, she lay inert thinking of the child, the fruit of countless other rapes.

How she loved that child!

Yet the face of its father, contorted in the frenzy of conquering her, was that of an enemy. Karl's frantic toil was a defilement to which she offered a passivity borne of the only recourse left to her. The least she would resist, the more likely—she prayed and hoped, he would tire of these punitive assaults.

Karl began to utter a series of grunts, and after a last spasm rolled off her seemingly in a stupor. Satisfied and exhausted, he lay motionless.

In shock and nauseated, Sophie waited, shaking. Her most ardent wish was to be spared his proximity; but the room that she had thought a refuge offered no such possibility. She could not abide remaining in it. A sense of utter helplessness engulfed her. Ironically, she lived in a luxurious series of rooms, yet was denied sanctuary in any of them. She just wished she could run to a cellar, a labyrinth, a passageway. . . .

Karl began to snore. Seizing the opportunity, Sophie got out of bed. In a somnambular trance she made her way to an available escape which she now remembered existed; to the dank haven of ancient masonry tunneling under the suites. Her bare feet padding over cold flagstones, she began running until her breath came in short dizzying gasps. Then she collapsed sobbing at the bottom of a narrow stairwell.

The walls echoed her lament and she found relief crying loudly with explosive breaks in the voice that half-choked her. This was a perfect place, one of absolute and priceless privacy not even a chapel could give her.

Suddenly, the door on the landing plaintively creaked on its rusty hinges, but she did not hear it open. It was the dim, rosy glow of the light of a candle which put a hiatus to her desolate wailing.

Startled, Sophie looked up and gave a whimper of recognition as a familiar voice exclaimed in muffled alarm, "Dear God!"

Instantly, the candle was jammed into the sconce which clung precariously to the wall, and a few nimble bounds brought Franz crouching on the last step. His hands lightly ran over her undone tresses as if to smooth away his bewilderment at finding her there.

"Sophie, what happened? What are you doing in this place?"

She was conscious of sounding somewhat incoherent. "I have nowhere else to go," she said, lifting toward him a face glistening with tears.

In the semi-darkness, she saw the movement of his eyes sizing up the possible reasons for her disarray. But he only asked, "Are you hurt?"

"Yes," she blurted, admitting a mental anguish, which to her was even more damaging than physical harm. Then realizing what he meant, she shook her head. "No, no!"

Franz gave her a searching look then said decisively, "I'm taking you away from here, you will catch your death."

"Please don't take me back to my apartments!"

"No, I am not." He took her face between his hands. "I will not leave you."

Perhaps it was the caring, protective tone in his young voice, his abiding goodness and decency, which completely broke her down. Giving into despair was her only way to acknowledge her vulnerability, her need for consolation. "I wish I were dead. . . . If I didn't have you!" she said, turning her head to stifle a sob against the hollow of his palm.

"Shhh . . ." he soothed, lifting her in his arms. Then cautiously, he ascended the steps. Sophie realized that the room into which Franz was carrying her was his bedroom. On a large desk stood a candelabrum which shed a soft yellow light on sheaves of paper half-covering an open book. The bed was turned down, but not slept in. A velvet housecoat was draped over the gilded backrest of a rococo fauteuil nearby.

For the next few minutes, Franz proceeded with speedy efficiency. He deposited her on a sofa and went to close the door of the passage, retrieving the candle and rearranging the hangings that concealed the entrance. This done, he moved to the washstand behind a screen at the far end of the room to fetch a towel, which he wetted with water from the ewer. Then snatching the housecoat, he crossed back over to her and gave her the towel to hold while wrapping the garment around her.

Still stunned, she followed each of his movements, docilely holding the towel and doing nothing with it.

"There . . ." he murmured, taking it from her hand. And delicately parting the hair from her face, he began dabbing her tear-glazed cheeks with complete concentration, watching, she could tell, for telltale signs of violence.

But there were none. The trauma Karl had inflicted upon her was only evident in her complete loss of self-control—the realization of which was now slowly dawning upon her. There she was, haggard, disheveled, and scantily clad, and having no idea that the intimate and sordid episode with Karl that evening would take her to Reichstadt's bedroom!

"Your hands," he said, dropping on one knee and wiping the dirt off them.

She noticed he was still wearing day clothes, though they were casual, the sort of attire men would wear for comfort at home—knee breeches, waistcoat over a white linen open-neck shirt, and long flowing sleeves completed with ruffles cascading over the hands.

By some grateful alchemy of perception, Sophie found herself gazing upon a consecrated being no longer clad in ordinary clothes, but arrayed in an effulgence radiating kindness and grace.

"Now, your feet," he said, proceeding to clean the soles.

"Oh, please," she protested, having composed herself at long last. "I have caused you enough trouble!"

Shaking his fair head, he looked at her with a puzzled and worried expression. She felt ashamed and sensed the heat of the blush rising to her face. "I had no intention of ending up here!" She made to rise. "I must go!"

But Franz laid a hand on her arm, staying her firmly: "You are not going back in the passage. . . ."

Sophie saw the hesitation in his eyes, which now struck her as being peculiarly brilliant.

"You ran out of your room. And . . . whatever the reason, I know you do not wish to return . . . just yet," he concluded tactfully.

"I can't stay here!" she objected.

He said matter-of-factly, "Yes, you can. For awhile. Rest on my bed. I promise to be very quiet. I am only taking notes. And if you wish to sleep, I'll wake you at dawn."

"Franz . . . I can't sleep here!"

"I understand," he said with a contrite little smile. "I am offending your sense of propriety. I confess it isn't exactly a conventional offer, but it is an honest one."

She shook her head, for such was not her real concern. "It isn't that at all! But you speak as though you were going to stay up all night! Do you have any idea what time it is?"

"I find lucubrating very rewarding," he replied.

Her fingers reached into the fob of his waistcoat and deftly fished out a watch, which she consulted. "It's nearly three in the morning!"

He took the watch from her and put it away. Then he held her hands as if to communicate to her by touch the persuasiveness in his voice. "Don't fret about how much sleep I need!"

A moment ago his hands had made contact with her face, that was through the insulating strands of her hair. But now she could feel the skin. With a slight frown, she said, "Your hands are hot! Are you running a fever?"

He withdrew them from her insistent grasp and stood up. "Of course not!" He stared down at her and asked patiently: "Shall I help you to the bed?"

This situation, she thought, was incredibly awkward! All because of her utter failure to cope with her private life, her marital problems. She should not have let this happen. For a few fleeting seconds, unbidden, the idea of Franz being married crossed her mind. And for the first time she realized that she was seeing him not as an adolescent but as a man.

"I'll rest here if you don't mind," she decided, snuggling under the housecoat.

"With a bit of improvement, I am sure," Franz rejoined fetching a pillow from his bed, which he fluffed before slipping it under her shoulders. "Are you warm enough?" he inquired next, rearranging the housecoat about her.

"Franz, please stop fussing!" she begged, placing both her hands on his arms to keep him still. "I have totally disrupted your evening plans and I don't intend to make a nuisance of myself!"

"You are never a nuisance," he said with tender gravity.

Her own tenderness for him overwhelmed her. The contrast between his gentle, attentive manners, and Karl's coarse and rough comportment glared at her with all of its imponderable heart-warming and heart-breaking irony. And she knew she had found a refuge that could never be taken away from her. He was her solace, and though his physical presence might be denied her in the course of other tribulations, the thought of him would give her fortitude and abiding comfort.

But right now, he was so close, so within her reach. She wished she could hold him to her. There had been so many other times when she would have thought nothing of drawing him in her arms, as he drew her in his, earlier on the terrace. But somehow, this did not feel right to her at present. . . .

She lifted her hands from his arms. "I am sorry for having made such a spectacle of myself."

He did not respond, studying her intently. She felt his gaze slowly moving over her face, her hair which was undone in a lustrous auburn spray on the pillow. And she knew with absolute certitude that *not only he had an idea of what happened, but also grasped the savagery of the act.* Tears began welling up in her eyes, and she fought them back with all her might.

He must have sensed her painful attempt to conceal her shame for having made him privy to a very intimate tragedy.

"Rest," he finally said, placing the palm of his hand on her forehead as though he wanted to exorcise the evil that was causing her so much agony.

Sophie closed her eyes. She heard his light footsteps recede to the desk where he had been working before her untimely interruption. But something of him remained with her—the housecoat that trapped her body heat. He must have warmed it, too. She felt as though she was falling asleep with the protection of Franz's arms about her.

When Sophie woke to the pallid light of dawn, the room was absolutely quiet. Her eyes, still blurred by sleep, repeatedly blinked for a clearer look around. The bed was empty, the sheets still crisp, taut, undisturbed. Then she saw Franz asleep at his desk, his blond head resting on his forearms crossed beneath it. He must have been exhausted and quite unable to keep watch as he had intended.

Quietly she got up and approached the desk for a silent good-bye. Franz slept soundly, looking as though he was hugging the volume that had been the object of his study. Glancing at the heading on the open page, she read: *The Memorial of St. Helena.*

Now the full impact of the staggering complexity of his concerns, their danger, and the impossible odds he was pitting himself against, hit her. How insignificant her own problems were in comparison! And how patient and courteous he had been with her, as always!

For a moment, she fell in rapt contemplation of his profile in handsome repose, relishing the intimacy of seeing him asleep. Then she had to tear herself away as a rush of emotion such as she had never experienced before nearly suffocated here. . . .

When she returned to her bedroom, she found Karl still there, awkwardly sprawled across her bed and still sleeping like a sated beast. He had stopped snoring, emitting instead an irregular whiz. She averted her gaze, unable to bear the sight of her husband's naked body a second longer and hugged her shoulders, feeling as though the very atmosphere of the room had been contaminated.

Then she glimpsed the familiar prie-dieu and the sumptuously carved crucifix hanging over it—a gift from the Abbot Rausher who had brought it back from Spain to grace her private little oratory. Each time Karl took her, she had felt no disrespect fixing her eyes on the crucified corpus, likening her torment to that of Christ's Passion. Her marriage was also a cross from which she could expect no relief. She must accept it. She must beg God for this grace in all earnestness.

Sophie flexed her knees on the padded kneeler. And for the first time in her life, realized she could not pray.

Franz's day was not going well. The issue of Parma returned to haunt him as well as Francis's observation that if he were not so young, things could have been different. How different? In the meantime, while he was being forced to watch life flow by from the bank of untenable prohibitions, too much was happening.

In desperation, he had sent a note to Prokesch that morning begging him for help. Perhaps the Major could incline Metternich to reconsider on the question of Parma, thus allowing the Emperor to follow his initial impulse. The Major returned a message that said that he would try his best.

Later that afternoon, Prokesch stood before Franz, head bowed, the bearer of disappointing news.

"Franz, I really tried!" he said with genuine regret.

Franz stopped in the middle of a furious pacing, striking a balled fist to his forehead. "I was a fool to hope that anything could be changed!"

"I am so terribly sorry!"

Franz continued in a rage, "I find obedience loathsome! It's wrong for me to just stand on the sideline! Do nothing!"

"You are not to blame, Franz. And you could be blowing this all out of proportion simply because you are impatient to gain the freedom to prove yourself!"

"And why shouldn't I, Anton? Life is too short for pussyfooting. I just won't have it! If I can't be free soon, I can't answer for my actions!"

"You are not making much sense," Prokesch said respectfully.

"Sense?" Franz laughed hysterically. "How could I make any sense? I am a walking nonsense! My very title . . . *Duke of Reichstadt* is an absurdity! And I don't care if I just reach a miserable consummation by revolting even if it's all in vain! For I cannot be helpful! My efforts are wasted! My protests impotent! All I can do is beat my fists against bars. Oh, Christ! Why was I born? Why? Damnit! Why?"

"Franz, stop it!"

Franz began to cough. The paroxysm was prolonged into a hollow inner tearing sound that worried Prokesch.

"Have you been ill?"

Catching his breath, Franz poured himself a glass of water. "Absolute not! But I am sick of the futility of wanting what is right!"

Prokesch watched as he took a few gulps. His concern deepened. A few days ago, having come into Reichstadt's study unannounced, he had caught him sleeping at mid-day in an armchair. He remembered how pale and tired the Prince looked then. Might something be wrong in spite of the emphatic denial?

Setting the glass down, Franz went on. "I don't want the flavor of hope. I have been starving on that for too long. I want the taste of liberty! And if this longing becomes such that it could force me to go against Austria, I still might render her a great service! And Anton, I am going to take my due!"

"How do you mean?"

"Get away!"

Prokesch stammered. "You . . . you can't be serious."

"Oh yes, I am!"

"Oh, my God . . ."

"You don't approve?" Franz asked defiantly.

"Let us think this through."

"But you don't approve. Isn't that right?"

The Major shook his head. "I don't know what to say."

Franz's hands clamped down on his friend's arms. "Anton, take a good look at me!"

Prokesch not only looked at Reichstadt's face, he scrutinized it. Its planes were chiseled to exquisite proportions and contours; and under this generous gift of nature, there was so much more to admire! The youth had character and mettle. His intense sense of mission and the unflagging drive to fulfill it amazed the Major. It would have been so easy for Napoleon's son to stop caring and indulge, *with absolute freedom,* all the hedonistic pleasures at his disposal.

Franz said, "Anton, knowing me as well as you do, you must have considered the possibility that I might want to break away from my gilded cage sooner or later."

"Better later than now," the Major muttered. He needed time. Time to re-examine the nature of his feelings toward Reichstadt. To what depth must his commitment to their friendship go? As a servant of the Crown, Prokesch could not condone Reichstadt's idea of escaping. That would be treason. It would also be just as treasonable to have knowledge of the Prince's intention to run away and do nothing to foil his attempt to do so.

But that would mean an abject betrayal of the absolute confidence Reichstadt has placed in him. This, the Major felt, was an unthinkable alternative. There was something else, too. Prokesch foresaw enough difficulties to objectively explain his genuine lack of enthusiasm.

"Why wait?" Franz erupted. "What in damnation are we waiting for?

Trying to speak calmly, Prokesch put forward objections which he felt were free from personal bias.

"Let us assume you elude the German and the Swiss police. That is, if you manage first to get out of Austria at all. Then you have to keep in mind that at present, the strength of your supporters is puny. Moreover, the French people at large do not know you and do not expect you. With no friends and no money, assuming again that you also do not die at the hands of assassins, to whom will you turn and where will you go? Think, Franz! By right you do not have to stoop to employ means that only adventurers would think of using. You don't have to conduct yourself like a wandering waif! You are legitimately a figure of consequence, and in time the position you represent will prevail. Time, Franz—and I am sorry to sound repetitive—is your surest and best ally!"

After a thoughtful silence, Franz asked sullenly, "And when will this ally deliver me, Anton?"

"I am sure, in less than ten years."

"Christ!"

"Franz, you are only nineteen."

"Fine! And I'll be *only* twenty next month!" Franz groaned, looking utterly disgusted. Then gloomily he said, "If France should want me back, Prince Metternich would never consent to my release. I have reached this certitude. You are asking me to wait. You are asking me to believe that some day he will change his mind. That, Anton, he will never do!"

"He may not want to, but he might be forced to! Events abrade the fibers of policies, or Prince Metternich could very well not be in office at that time."

In exasperation, Franz caught himself doubting his friend. Was Prokesch speaking his own thoughts here? Or was he merely repeating something Metternich suggested he say in the eventuality that he might become restless? Prokesch, after all, was German and his involvement with him could only go so far. Beyond that, the Major had the perfect right to abandon him.

Yet he did not believe in a betrayal of trust. Instead, Prokesch might withdraw all supports by being constantly negative, or over cautious maybe? That would be the pattern Franz should be looking for . . . and seemed to have found.

Abruptly he said, "I have made excessive demands upon you, Anton. But I won't anymore. It is not fair."

Prokesch's soft dark eyes looked steadily into his. By their expression it was evident that sadness and not relief made him say, "We should have met under happier circumstances, Franz."

Franz flinched, sank into a chair; elbows on his knees and head between his hands, he mumbled, "Had my mother been Empress Josephine I would not have met you. I wouldn't even be here. . . ."

He paused. A shiver rippled across his shoulders before he could sum a tragedy whose magnitude he now fully comprehended "My father's marriage to my mother was a terrible mistake. It was his undoing and . . . mine. It has ruined us both!"

"No, Franz, no!" Prokesch protested warmly. "You are not ruined! You are only feeling a little low!"

"I feel forsaken," Franz said dully. And why not admit it? He had suffered about all that he could endure. Calumnies, mistrust, discrimination, isolation. Now Prokesch's measured advice, this talk of abdicating all initiatives in favor of time! That sort of speech sounded ominously too similar to the one Francis gave him! Franz felt having grievously erred in imagining that the Major could wholly espouse his cause.

But Prokesch was saying, "You are wrong! I have not deserted you!"

Not quite convinced, Franz nodded. He forced out of his throat a faint, "Thank you." Then he rose smiling wanly, wishing for the first time since they had met that Prokesch would leave. He extended his hand intimating that the interview was over.

"If you will excuse me, Anton. I must pay my respects to a little baby."

Since Francis had become for the second time the grandfather to a boy through the male side of his offspring, a notable change had rocked the routine of the imperial household.

The fuss over the birth of Sophie's son extended now to every facet of the infant's existence. The rigid ceremonial attending the upbringing of an archduke was set in full motion. At all hours of the day, courtiers would flock to the baby's room to pay the child a visit as it was the custom. A small legion of flunkies and chamberlains would usher the visitors in and out while maids and nurses came and went in a steady bustle. The confusion was unimaginable.

As a result, the baby's *aja,* Baroness Sturmfeder, was exceedingly appreciative of small considerations. In that respect, the Duke of Reichstadt held an unchallenged place in the governess's esteem. Of all the visitors, he was the only one to make it a rule never to disrupt the demanding business of caring for the infant.

So when Franz appeared in the doorway of Franzi's quarters, the Baroness gave him a warm welcoming smile and sank in a half-curtsey. "Your Highness could not have come at a more opportune time," she beamed. "Franzi is fully awake and in a playful mood. This way, please. . . ."

Franz followed her into the nursery where the late afternoon sunrays slanting through the windows lent a halo to a charming scene. Bent over the cradle, Sophie was cooing softly to her baby.

He had not seen her since the previous night. And he now recalled the difficulty he had experienced trying to concentrate on his father's words as he would glance in her direction now and then while she slept curled up on the sofa. Fatigue must have overcome him and when he had awakened, Sophie was gone. Had it not been for the crumpled housecoat or the scent of her hair on the imprint her head had left on the pillow, he would not have discounted the possibility that what had taken place in his bedchamber was all a dream.

"Hello, Franz!" Sophie said softly looking up and motioning him to join her.

Seven-month-old Franzi—officially known as Franz Joseph—and fated to end his reign in the middle of the First World War, emitted a light gurgling sound, which his governess explained as indicative of unusual contentment. She had no sooner said this than the baby grinned toothlessly and put out his arms to Reichstadt.

"You are in favor, Franz," Sophie remarked happily.

She looked radiant and exuded so much joy! The thought of what she must have gone through for this blessed moment confused Franz. This violent side of sexuality. . . . Would men do *this* to women?. . . .

"Franz?. . . ."

"Yes, Sophie."

"Pick him up," she suggested.

With amazing dexterity he scooped up the baby, careful to support its neck before tucking Franzi in the crook of his arm.

Franz gazed down at the child and thought of his own birth and its formidable and perhaps fatal significance. "Oh, Franzi," he murmured, lost in a private anguish, "where will I be when you grow to be my age?"

Sophie heard him well enough to spring to attention.

These kinds of remarks were signals she must mind. How many others had there been when she was not around to notice? She felt having sorely neglected him. Oh, but this will change! Now that the initial commotion that went with parenthood was settling down to a more organized pace, she could devote not only much of her time to Franzi but also to Franz.

She held out her arms. "My turn, Franz?"

Carefully he passed the child to her.

From under the light burden that linked them for an instant, their hands touched in the fumble of the transfer. And for a few inexplicably tensed seconds, they looked deep into each other's eyes.

Then Franz leaned over and kissed the baby already nestled against his mother's bosom. His curly head briefly brushed against Sophie's cheek. She felt the silken texture of his hair, its fresh, clean smell and not the artificial scent produced by oily macassar widely used by young men. A bizarre, upsetting, but not unpleasant sense of disorientation, of loss, and paradoxically of gain came over her.

She forced her attention back to the baby. She would never know afterward whether what she did was conscious or just happenstance. She kissed her little son on the spot Franz's lips had just touched.

As they left the nursery together, they did not speak for a few seconds. Her confinement, then a recent tour of the Tyrol with her husband must have disrupted the habitual comfort they felt in each other's company.

"Franz," she said at last. "Have you a little time to take tea with me presently?"

He looked at her, a hard and almost bitter twist curling the corners of his mouth in a smile that came all wrong. "I have *all the time* in the world."

A tea tray awaited them and Sophie dreaded pouring the fragrant brew because to her dismay and in spite of her efforts, she found that her hands were shaking.

She said awkwardly, "I must thank you . . . for last night. . . ."

Gently, Franz interrupted her. "Don't say another word. . . . I won't. Ever!"

"Thank you," she whispered nevertheless. "Tea?"

"None, for me," he declined, sitting down on the sofa and leaning his head on the backrest. He closed his eyes. His abandon exuded intense weariness.

"Play something for me," he asked her.

Sophie hesitated. Franz continued to exhibit a predilection for the brassy sound and cadenced beat of military music. He had never asked her to play for him.

Half-opening his eyes he said, "Play something you like."

Though Sophie played a soothing piece, Franz could not relax. The interview with Prokesch had deeply upset him. His emotions were in a shambles. Even his sentimental life offered no true solace. At this point, it revolved around Naudine. He often wrote to the Countess and she wrote back in a vein he would have wanted less superficial. Their chaste embrace on that night of Carnival had begun a relationship to which he could not adjust completely. He did not question the possibility of consummating that relationship, but the way Naudine seemed to regard its eventual completion—a fling—disconcerted him. He even wondered if he was not falling in love with perhaps a need rather than with a person.

The notion jarred him. His lids fluttered, then lifted.

Noticing this, Sophie immediately stopped playing. "Poor Franz, I am boring you!"

She did not believe him even though he shook his head and rose to briskly walk over to the piano, placing himself behind her. She felt the congratulatory press of his hands on her upper arms as he bent over to study the music sheet.

"Cimarosa," he said. "That is beautiful!"

She turned up her face to meet his eyes and let her head rest in the hollow of his shoulder. "Oh Franz! You may be a renegade, but you are a true gentleman!"

Gently, his hands tightened on her arms. "I don't lie very well, do I?"

"Badly. Which confirms my suspicion. I really must have bored you."

Impulsively, he touched his lips to her temple and held them there, murmuring, "Never!"

"Franz . . ." she said faintly.

Something she had fantasized in her maidenhood, something never realized, came over her. Fearfully, she stamped it down and relegated the feeling in the compartment of her mind where all that could not be undone was kept like letters of a long-dead love—locked up and tied with faded ribbons.

She rose abruptly.

Franz moved away, resuming his place on the sofa.

In his eyes, she read a flash of panic. She thought, *Something is coming between us!* A strange sinking, yet elating sensation stayed her breath for a moment. This she could not control, but the idea that something could have changed was repulsed with utmost determination.

Yielding to a calculated decision, one that she knew was sound, she came to sit beside him and took a firm hold of his hands. Her voice steady and her gaze direct, she set the tone so they could talk of this and of that as they always did.

"You have to blame me for something, Franz. What are friends for?" she said, trying to sound her habitual, cheerful, and natural self.

He averted his eyes and looked down at their intertwined hands. Then slowly, he stretched her fingers to their full length, rubbing his thumbs over them to give himself a countenance, and because he wanted to feel those gentle hands, which had led him away from complete isolation.

Then he felt it.

He felt the ring.

"Sophie . . ." he began, but his voice drifted into silence. He had never paid any attention to her wedding ring before; not even last night when he had full concentration while cleaning her hands. Now looking down at it, he was shocked by the sudden realization that not until now had he thought of her as a married woman. Somehow that status had bypassed his consciousness. Since the day of her marriage, he regarded her as a relation, but oddly, not as Francis Charles's wife. She had appeared in his lonely existence owing to the working of some extraneous agreement that still put her beyond the pale of any specific appropriation, save that of his tenderness for her. Not even her pregnancy, then the birth of Franz Joseph had altered that unattached image he had of his aunt. Until now. . . .

"Yes, Franz. What is it?" she prompted softly.

He sprung the question at her with the incautious curiosity of youth. "Do you love Uncle Karl?"

She stared at him mutely, giving herself a moment to recover, after which her voice came hushed and thin. "Why are you asking me this?"

"Being married . . ." he blundered, and immediately cursed himself for committing a monumental indiscretion. "Please, forgive me!" he said hurriedly.

Sophie tensed and lowered her eyes. "That is all I am, Franz. Just married!

"Oh, Sophie!"

All these years, while she thought of nothing else but of giving him comfort and solace, he'd only taken. Only now, to share her pain was all he could give her. Spontaneously, he put his arms around her and drew consolingly her head on his shoulder. "I am sorry . . . so sorry. God! I'm such a bungling dullard!. . . ."

She pressed her face against the crisp serge of his uniform and felt all her miseries melting away.

Then some prohibition made her pull back.

Franz looked deep into her eyes. "You have never been happy?" he asked with desolation, not yet fully believing that she could have quietly borne such misfortune for so long.

She pulled up her chin. "I am not complaining, Franz."

"You never do."

"I have no reason to. I feel blessed to have our precious friendship."

"Seven wonderful years."

"Yes. It has been that long. . . ."

There followed a silence.

Suddenly, Franz felt miserable. He caught himself, *willing* the thought: *It is Naudine I should pursue!*

Huskily he said, "I want our friendship never to end."

"I want this, too," Sophie echoed in a whisper.

"Even after I take a wife . . . if I ever do."

“I hope so Franz. It is ours to keep.”

“Always?”

“Yes, always!”

Despite a natural repugnance in meddling in others’ private affair, Prokesch had begun to follow the progress of Franz’s infatuation with Countess Karolyi with the concern of a physician feeling a sick man’s pulse. The Major would not have minded a superficial attachment. He would have welcomed a passing liaison. Reichstadt needed some respite from an all consuming concentration on his future, and he certainly deserved to find enjoyment in the company of young women.

But Franz’s assiduity where it concerned the Countess gave no indication of being a mere pastime. Naudine, in Prokesch’s opinion, could neither stabilize, let alone inspire the Duke. She was, in his opinion, a fizgig upon whom Reichstadt wasted excessive attention, to a point, the Major strongly felt, which rather hinted at compulsion. In any case, she was not worthy of him and might possibly weaken his character as he was young and impressionable. But so far, Prokesch had not dared say anything.

Unwittingly, Franz provided that opportunity. After having given much thought to his friend and confidant, he came to the conclusion that the Major’s honesty and loyalty were beyond question. He also took the resolve to be more tolerant of Prokesch’s viewpoint concerning his welfare. But he continued to believe in the possibility of an escape. The incredible ease with which he had eluded Metternich’s spies the night he had gone to Naudine’s house enforced this opinion. Moreover, no one had missed him at the palace when he had returned to his apartments at daybreak.

Franz had said nothing of this to Prokesch as yet, but the more he thought of that successful escapade, the more tempted he was to mention the incident. That would show the Major he disposed of some freedom of movement after all. If such a latitude was given him to employ it in frivolous sports, he could just as easily use the leeway for serious undertakings.

He told him point blank, “Do you know that I was out all night on one occasion and no one took notice of that?”

“When?” Prokesch wanted to know.

Franz colored a little. “Sometime ago,” he answered evasively. “It’s not important. But what is, though, is the fact that I could have been away for so long without being missed. I could have gone rather far, had I wanted to, don't you see?"

But that did not seem to impress the Major.

"And may I ask where you went?"

Franz declared in one breath, "I went to Countess Karolyi's masked ball and I did not leave until morning. Now, in my situation, I consider this a feat!"

"I am not so sure," Prokesch returned, looking thoroughly alarmed. A disapproving frown furrowed his brow. After a pause, he sighed, "You are deluding yourself, Franz. And I am sorry to add, you are deluding yourself doubly."

"I don't understand."

"That was an encouraging lapse, I admit. But you could not have gone very far. Believe me, I know. And that is not all. . . . The Countess, Franz. Where could your interest in her lead you?"

Franz answered stiffly, "Naudine suits me perfectly!"

"I don't think she does," Prokesch said with patience. He waved away Franz's movement of protest to continue in a forthright appeal. "And you know this perfectly well because you are too perceptive not to. The Countess is incapable of fitting into your world the way you would want her to. She can flit through it, but that is not what would content you. I can sense it, Franz. In the present circumstances there is too much at stake where your future is concerned to become that involved with her. What you need is a clear head and an unencumbered heart."

"I need to be in love," Franz said stubbornly.

"But not with the Countess."

"I have fallen in love with her already," Franz insisted with a boyish petulance in which passion was curiously lacking.

Taking notice of this, Prokesch remained unconvinced. This was not like Reichstadt at all to indulge in such capricious behavior.

"Franz, I don't know what you are trying to prove, but you are not yourself. And you must fall out of love."

"I am only human!" Franz protested.

"And you are different, too."

"So I must be denied everything?"

"Certainly not. But all that you do can never be inconsequential. You belong too much to history not to direct your actions in that context. You must submit yourself to the constraints and demands which are consistent with the lot of all those who are destined to leave their marks on the development of human affairs."

At this, Franz broke into a nervous laughter. "Submit! By God and by all the devils in Hell! I have done nothing but submit!'

Then in a disarming, childlike gesture, there he was, a dashing young officer in the uniform of a lieutenant colonel, wearily rubbing his fists over his eyes. This reminded the Major how very young indeed Franz was to shoulder such staggering expectations all on his own. He had been put through a rough and lonely school whose aim was to negate everything he strove to recapture. What youth wouldn't grow dishearten and balk?

Then Franz said in an exhausted, flat voice, as if all emotions had been drained out of him, "I am tired . . . Bone tired and brain tired. . . ." He sank into a chair and let his arms dangle, flexing his long fingers whose tips, Prokesch had noticed, tended to yellow. ". . . could we please postpone our discussion on the work of Jomini until tomorrow?"

That precipitated something Protesch had meant to tell Reichstadt. The moment was not particularly opportune, but he had no choice. "We can postpone it," he replied ill at ease, "until I come back."

"Come back?"

"I am leaving Vienna tomorrow."

Franz's moodiness and fatigue seemed to have left him. "Where are you going?"

"To Bologna. I just got word of this assignment."

Franz's expression grew somber and a disquieting thought crossed his mind. "Do you suppose this departure has something to do with me? With us?"

"I don't think so," Prokesch said, trying to be objective. "The presence of Austrian troops in Italy is causing considerable tension there. My mission is to pacify the Papal legate, and the need for this is pressing."

Franz's apprehension did not lift. "I foresee a separation of some length," he said fretfully. "But no matter! I want to tell you again how grateful I am for all the comforts and encouragement you have given me. I shall never forget what you have done. Never!"

Prokesch's calm and confident turn of mind suffered a setback. "Franz, you speak so . . . so irrevocably! Why? . . . We have been separated before, remember?"

Franz nodded. Of course he remembered. Prokesch had gone away on several occasions. But this time, he strongly felt inclined to predict a drawn-out conference any junior members of the diplomatic staff could have conducted satisfactorily. The importance of Prokesch's new assignment must have been exaggerated. Choosing the Major was a pretext to disrupt and eventually terminate their relation.

Often Franz had wondered how their friendship had been allowed to prosper so far without interference. Now he stopped wondering and started worrying.

"Anton, I fear this might be part of a plan to part us for good!"

Prokesch gave him a blank stare and then paled. It all came back to him now! There had been small, isolated incidents he ought to have recognized as leading to a definite separation: Metternich's gracious but firm refusal the past autumn to let him journey to France, then Metternich slipping thereafter from cordiality to studied courtesy whenever they met. In truth, Metternich must have reached the limit of patience with his favorite diplomat. The fact that Obenaus had shown Prokesch a memorandum addressed to the Chancellor in which he stated that the Duke possessed a vaulting imagination, and that he was much too spirited to ever find fulfillment in the routine of regimental life did Prokesch no service. Metternich must have grown wary of an association that wasn't producing any positive results. With appalling acuity, Prokesch realized he must have lost Metternich's trust. His ability was put into question, and his loyalty looked upon with suspicion.

With dignity and pride he said, "That is the consequence of an involvement in which concepts such as loyalty and integrity have been subjected to various interpretations. It appears that my superiors have a different idea of what those concepts should be. But I will not alter my convictions."

Franz looked at him with an awed and solemn expression. "Anton," he said in a clear, firm voice, "if you have any regrets at all, I beg you to yield to them. I will more than understand."

"I regret nothing, Franz."

With a hand which shook a little, Franz pulled out his watch saying, "My first. I've worn it faithfully for six years. You always speak of time. You have taught me to understand and appreciate its value." He handed him the watch. "My appreciation lies in here, with the tickling of this wonderful mechanic, a heart of sorts, which, like mine,will record with each second, the consolation, joy, and privilege of finding in you a true friend. The only friend I ever had. Please, I want you to have this!"

Profoundly moved, Prokesch received the gift with reverence, and even his speech reverted to formality. "Thank you, Monseigneur. I should like to offer you something in return. If there is any way I can further Your Highness's interest in the course of my mission, I welcome your suggestions."

Immediately a spark flashed in Franz's eyes. "Yes! There is something. You have a keen understanding of people. I should like to have an analysis of the causes which have led the Italian people to revolt. It is of utmost importance to me!"

They parted on a wary but constructive note.

With Prokesch away in Italy, Franz led an active double life. He became two distinctive personalities: a winsome archduke whom the social elite of Vienna lionized, and a prince deeply conscious of his secret calling. Though he was seen at many balls, at the theater, and at the opera, or supping late with Naudine, dawn would always catch him seated at his desk poring over books on strategy or political science. Marmont, who had not yet finished his lectures on Napleon, soon noticed that the late Emperor's son had developed an interesting pallor.

Dietrichstein's attention was exclusively engaged by his pupil's interest in Countess Karolyi. But where the confidant had cautioned, the tutor nagged. The Count judged Naudine severely. He thought her shallow and selfish. Thoroughly annoyed with her, Dietrichstein said to Franz with eyes downcast: "You can amuse yourself with the Countess, but you can't be serious about her," and kept ruing the day Maurice Esterhazy had introduced Naudine to Reichstadt.

In truth, Franz was willfully deluding himself into believing that he loved Naudine. By mid-April he stopped paying court to her.

That period also marked the conclusion of Marmont's lectures. The Marshal was complimented, thanked, and sent away. Franz had no more use for him. Nor had he much use for the whirl of social activities into which he was drawn. He kept seriously worrying about the real reason for Prokesch's departure.

When Gustave came to pay him a call, Franz was not quite able to conceal his overwrought state. Then quite unintentionally, he revealed something very personal about himself. Gustave's mouth fell open and he looked at him as if he were a freak.

"Mercy!" he exclaimed softly. "It's high time to complete your education. Why, you should have gotten on with it long ago!"

"My mind wasn't . . . on it."

"Ha! Ha!" Gustave guffawed, slapping his knee with the flat of his hand, "how very picturesque!"

"Gustave! Don't be vulgar!"

"I am sorry. But if you will allow me . . . I have excellent connections!"

Franz offered a closed face.

Gustave coaxed with a wink. "Oh, come! I assure you, it is a happy experience!"

"I have no doubt. . . ."

"So, will you, Franz?"

"I'll let you know."

27

It was not yet five in the morning when Lambert sleepily shuffled into Reichstadt's bedchamber. The valet had answered the bell call as fast as he could and finished buttoning up his livery, bleary-eyed and suppressing a yawn. Franz was already out of bed and impatiently rummaging through the armoire. "Where is my uniform?" he asked him.

"Everything Your Highness needs is in the dressing room. Will Your Highness have breakfast shortly?" Lambert also inquired.

Franz declined with an eloquent grimace. No breakfast. He was too excited to eat or drink anything. He had slept fitfully, wishing for the day to dawn quickly because it marked the beginning of a lifestyle after which he had been hankering a long time. In a few hours, he would officially be assigned the military staff Metternich had picked for him and obtain, at long last, full emancipation from the tutelage of his professors.

Franz considered this morning of June 14, a particularly auspicious date to embark upon a military career as it coincided with the anniversary of the battle of Marango and that of Fiedland, which his father had fought and won years before he was born.

As expected, General Hartmann presented himself at Reichstadt's apartments at precisely seven o'clock. Although this was their official meeting, the General had previously called on the Duke accompanied by his associates, Captain von Moll and Joseph Standeiski shortly after their appointment. Yet he was nervous. Being thirteen years older than Reichstadt gave him no comfort. Though an excellent soldier, he had received a simple education and felt at a crippling disadvantage having to associate himself with a much younger man reputed for his erudition and intelligence.

Napoleon's son—he could never think of the Duke in any other way—cut a splendid figure in his Austrian uniform of a Lieutenant Colonel. His erect posture added to his great height, and the resplendent white of his tunic seemed to enhance the sheen of his fair hair.

Hartmann wondered if he would have felt less intimidated or more trusting had Reichstadt been short, dark-haired, and of a stocky build like his father. But could appearance change in any way the inner self of a man?

For in spite of the youth's Nordic appearance and the military outfit he wore, Hartmann kept in mind Metternich's warning: a Bonaparte in an Austrian uniform would always remain a wolf in a sheepskin . . . and a fox. A fox the General's express duties were to outsmart. So bowing obsequiously, he could not help inject into his greeting a trace of the Chancellor's caveat. "No one but Your Highness could grace this uniform with so much distinction!"

Franz gave him an aseptic smile. "So you have noticed!"

That ambiguous retort convinced Hartmann that difficulties were already beginning. For Reichstadt might very well have understood the insinuation, and that put the General all the more on his guard.

Franz's excitement at the prospect of taking up quarters at the casern and his eagerness to acquaint himself with various details of regimental life offered a perch on which the General momentarily rested his worries and anxieties. The Prince bombarded him with questions. He wanted to know the years of service of each officer assigned to his companies and their respective backgrounds.

At one point he declared, "Mark my words, General. Laxity among the military in time of peace is a worse offense than desertion in time of war! And discipline should never be sacrificed to personal vainglory." Then remembering Marmont, he added, "A war can be lost by one single violation of that code."

Hartmann smiled thinly and nodded when at this moment, Count Dietrichstein and Baron Obenaus joined them. This occasion also marked the tutors' farewell call to their pupil. They would have many occasions to see him, but they would no longer have any jurisdiction over the conduct of his life. Hartmann, following Metternich's plan, would.

That morning, Count Dietrichstein felt a touch of melancholy. Fifteen years of friction had produced its peculiar chaffing. By force of habit, the sores had lost their initial stings to evolve into a condition the Count had learned to live with well enough to the extent of even enjoying it. Dietrichstein, in truth, ached having to let his pupil go, and not without a last confrontation.

After Hartmann and Obenaus took their leave, the Count tarried. Franz assumed the former tutor was staying to discuss some details relating to his new establishment. One particular item was on his mind.

"Are my rooms at the Alsler-Kaserne ready for immediate occupancy?" he asked excitedly.

Dietrichstein gave him a moody look, unreceptive to the fact that the Prince was all agog because of a simple move to the casern. The Count would have understood Reichstadt's thrill had that move meant leaving for some distant location, a move Metternich would never allow. But this was not the case. The barracks were only a few streets away from the Hofburg.

"They are all furnished and awaiting Your Highness," he confirmed without enthusiasm. Then he jerked his chin in the direction of the Prince's writing desk.

"That desk drawer . . ."

"What of it?" Franz retorted, immediately on the defensive.

"It's locked."

"Is that a crime?"

"Open it!" the Count commanded.

Franz clenched his fists. That drawer contained personal papers. They were letters from Esterhazy; letters which related to Naudine. He had kept them because of a sentimental attachment, not to the Countess, but to the feelings she had awakened in him—the magic *d'un premier amour.* That first love, however misdirected, had left an indelible imprint on his soul.

"Open it!" repeated Dietrichstein. "There is nothing you need to keep locked away."

"You have no right to invade my privacy!" Franz shot back at him, his eyes blazing with anger. "Have you," he taunted, "been passing time trying the locks on every desk and cabinet?"

"I can," Dietrichstein threatened, ignoring the sarcasm, "order the servants to force it open!"

At this instant, a footman crossed the room. Franz cringed. The humiliation of having domestics witness their dispute!

"Don't bother," he said sharply.

He opened the drawer and turned away in disgust.

Dietrichstein soon gloated over his find: a pack of letters bound with a string.

"A secret correspondence. . . ." Franz heard the Count grunt. Then a few seconds later, Dietrichstein exclaimed peevishly, "And through an intermediary I know and who has the impertinence of calling me the *Old Woman!*"

Franz swung round. "That suits you perfectly!" he commented testily. "Old women who have ceased to find any positive interests in their lives have the propensity to meddle in other people's private affairs!"

"I want these," Dietrichstein said, looking suddenly weary and uncontending.

Irritation and pugnaciousness seemed to have left them at the same time.

"You can have them. And you can burn them. . . ." Franz said dejectedly. He felt defeated. The incident reminded him that he would never be allowed to have any real possessions of his own, however insignificant. Whatever he had was merely *bestowed* upon him, and seemed to have the impermanent characteristics of a loan. And even that which he could manage to secure would be taken away.

But the next day Franz's spirits once again, as it happened so many times, lifted to new heights. At six o'clock in the morning he took command of his battalion.

The men, mostly young recruits, were completely awed upon learning who their commander was. To be sure, despite his tender age, the Duke of Reichstadt could not but be favored with a formidable heredity. Imagine! Napoleon's son! When they saw him, they decided they would like him.

Franz exuded a poise and a commanding air that was devoid of arrogance. He directed upon his soldiers a penetrating look that showed control tempered with care. Though they remained frozen in military impassivity, Franz intuitively felt that they were responding favorably to his coming.

As Hartmann delivered a welcoming speech followed by an introductory poem of his own composition, two hundred pairs of eyes remained trained on Reichstadt.

Gradually, Franz began entertaining unsettling thoughts: God! If father could see me now! Here! Dressed in *this* uniform! Christ! If this isn't treason! Slowly his fingers tightened on the hilt of his sword. It was the curved saber Napoleon had worn in Egypt. It had traveled far and fallen in sad and poignant custody. And well forgotten was the pledge to the Emperor to make amends for his father's sins. . . .

Meanwhile, Hartmann extolled with grandiloquence the Emperor's goodness, wisdom and pride in His Serene Highness's appointment as battalion commander. The General spoke next about dedication to the homeland.

Franz's heartbeats quickened as he recalled similar directions written in a book he took to consulting daily in a tongue he had been forced to abandon since early childhood and which he had to learn all over again! And with profound sadness, he realized that in spite of having regained complete fluency in French, he spoke it at times in a manner peculiar to German phraseology.

Then another dismaying realization came to him: though born a French prince, he would be serving under the banners of Austria's black bicephalous eagle! He whom the French called l'Aiglon, "*the Eaglet*", in recognition of an inalienable loyalty to the golden eagle volant of Imperial France!

If this wasn't treason! Then what would be?

Horrified by a situation over which he had no control, Franz sought refuge in achievement.

It was not long before Lieutenant Colonel Franz von Reichstadt's indefatigable zeal in the fulfillment of his duties became an exemplar of military dedication to excellence. Drills, parades, military functions, and resolutions of service matters absorbed his time and attention. Nothing was too insignificant for him to tackle. Much like his father, he wanted to be in control of every detail. He slept only four hours most nights and turned up at the palace on no other days but Sunday. To show off his newfound independence, Franz had also taken up pipe smoking.

The first time Count Dietrichstein surprised him puffing away in a window embrasure, he meditated dourly on the turpitude of the habit. When Franz once complained that his voice tended to become hoarse after several hours spent shouting commands, the former tutor countered without sympathy, "Smoking is ruining your trachea!"

Then he went on listing a few other ills for which he blamed Hartmann. If Reichstadt looked so frightfully tired, that was because he wore himself out in the performance of duties not consistent with his rank. Only a sergeant major drills troops, not a lieutenant colonel.

Something else also irked Dietrichstein. Reichstadt should not be a mere battalion commander. It would have been more fitting for a prince of his station to hold the honorary command of a regiment. Franz scrupulously clung to his ideas concerning merit. "Don't even voice any complaints of that kind," he advised peremptorily. "In view of the fact that my rank precedes my experience, I have to be a sergeant major and a lieutenant colonel at the same time. This is only reasonable and fair."

"That is a folly!" the Count grumbled. "Anybody with any sense, can see that this regimen is exhausting Your Highness!"

"I am in perfect health!"

"That is something I should like to hear from your physician!" retorted the Count.

Malfatti had gone hoarse too. That was because he kept preaching moderation which Franz went on ignoring. Nothing could have been further from his consideration than illness and mortality in general, and his own in particular. He was young and there was no harm in living with feverish ardor. So Dietrichstein fretted and hoped that Providence in some way would curb his former pupil's reckless neglect of his health. In a dire manner that wish was granted.

On a rainy afternoon in August, Dietrichstein took himself to the casern where he was certain to find Reichstadt. Had the weather been fair, he wouldn't have gone knowing perfectly well that the Prince would never miss an opportunity to spend the day out on maneuver. But it had rained so heavily all through the previous night that the fields were too sodden now to withstand the trampling of a large body of troops.

Dietrichstein arrived at Franz's quarters declining to be announced. He knew his way well for he had organized and supervised the refurbishing of each room himself. Franz had insisted on simplicity with the result that his home away from home looked austere and quasi-monastic. Dietrichstein had wondered if Reichstadt's severity in taste in the furnishing of his military surroundings intended to confirm a sort of sacred dedication to martial life and discipline.

In any case, the former tutor came upon a dismal scene when he opened the door after a knock that went unanswered. The room which was used as a parlor-study was bathed in a dim, cheerless gray light that came from a single window opening onto a drab looking little courtyard. As the clouds hung low and the rain came down again in sheets, the darkness was such that all one could possibly do in such a place would be to sleep.

And Dietrichstein had indeed come upon a sleeping prince. Wrapped in his regulation greatcoat, Franz was hunched over his desk, his head resting on his folded arms. Approaching quietly, the Count could see nothing of his face, only a crown of faintly glimmering hair with wisps curling boyishly on the nape of the neck. The sight took Dietrichstein back many years—years he would have called grueling, but upon which he now looked with a deep, mellowing feeling of nostalgia mixed with apprehension.

Somehow, Reichstadt's posture with the white billowing folds of the greatcoat reminded the Count of a mortally wounded bird with half-spread wings. This disquieting analogy elicited a jab of irritation. Only a fortnight ago, the Prince had refused to take Malfatti's advice to keep to his bed when a bout of catarrhal fever had weakened his constitution. Now, this run-down condition must have caught up with him.

I have come to remedy this, thought the Count. Your Highness will be forced to rest at long last after what I have come to say! For Dietrichstein was the bearer of bad news, news of a calamity which affected the lives of a great many people.

But mindful of the Prince's well-being, he decided to wait, and quietly took a seat.

After a few minutes, Franz woke with a start and noticing the Count's presence, he jumped to his feet and energetically rubbed his face with his hands.

"I am sorry to have surprised you like this," Dietrichstein said with his customary primness.

"A little catnap," Franz rasped.

The Count frowned. "What happened to your voice?"

Franz shrugged. "It will come back." But he wasn't so sure. When he woke up that morning, he could only speak in a whisper.

"Sleeping in the middle of the day is not . . . normal," the Count observed.

"My father, it is said, took little naps at every opportunity. It is a very restorative habit."

Dietrichstein regarded him skeptically. The room might be dark, but he could see that the Prince's complexion was sallow and that his eyes were bloodshot. And his voice was practically gone! The nap which might have been so beneficial to Napoleon gave no indication of having done his son a bit of good!

It was time he deliver his message. Without any further ado he said, "His Majesty commands that Your Highness go immediately to Schönbrunn. The cholera has reached Vienna."

Franz glared at him. "The Emperor cannot ask me to do that!" he exclaimed, indignation restoring some semblance of resonance to his vocal cords.

He'd heard of the epidemic which was ravaging London and Paris; and he never discounted the possibility that the disease could spread to Austria. Yet at no time did he imagine that such an eventuality would interfere with his occupation.

"You must leave," said the Count.

"I cannot abandon my battalion!" Franz protested, straining his voice. "If there is any danger, my first duty is to share that danger with my men!"

"I can only relay the Emperor's orders," Dietrichstein responded in a neutral tone of voice.

Franz slammed the flat of his hand on the desk. "I am staying right here! Besides, Schönbrunn isn't very far from Vienna. Do you realize that birds can just as easily carry the disease there anyway?"

"I wouldn't speculate on what the birds can do."

Curbing his exasperation, Franz declared, "I appreciate the Emperor's concern, but I will not leave Vienna, the barracks or my battalion. I will have to be taken away by force!"

Back to the Emperor, Dietrichstein groused, "The Prince is openly defying Your Majesty's orders."

Francis smiled. "I knew he would," he said, looking thoroughly satisfied.

Franz's rebelliousness and unwavering disregard for his own safety filled him with tender pride. He was also extremely pleased with his grandson's military accomplishments. In a special dossier kept in the War Office, Reichstadt's performance as a battalion commander already rated as excellent.

Despite the Emperor's mild reaction, Dietrichstein did not doubt he would recall his grandson to Schönbrunn. Only the Count cringed at the thought of Reichstadt putting up a fight and causing an embarrassing scuffle. He told Francis of his grandson's mention of forcible removal.

"Tomorrow," Francis said unruffled, "I shall personally see that he leaves immediately after the parade on the Schmelz."

The next day turned out sunny and hot. From a platform erected on the edge of the field, Francis watched Reichstadt move past the stand at the head of his companies, immaculately uniformed and sitting tall and ramrod straight on his spirited white charger. Every time, the glorious sight of his grandson taking a parade would plunge the Emperor of Austria into deep thoughts. At such moments his under lip would quaver and his pale blue eyes would set in a vague, wistful stare.

Malfatti found him thus, as he clambered onto the imperial dais panting an apology. "I am sorry to be late, Sire. It's that crippling gout again. I assure Your Majesty, I did try to get here as fast as I could."

Malfatti had hurried for nothing. Francis made a restraining movement of the hand without taking his eyes off the charger and its dashing rider.

"No need to rush," he said. "I'd rather see you later when the Duke will be joining me here. This must not look like a conspiracy."

The doctor mopped his face with a handkerchief and obediently retreated, feeling a little annoyed as he was sweating, in much pain and unnecessarily inconvenienced. Why did the Emperor have to go through so much trouble? He could have simply put Reichstadt in a carriage and sent him off to Schönbrunn.

Of course he knew this to be Francis's ultimate intention. Only the Emperor's affection for his grandson evidently compelled him to choose a roundabout way that would absolve him from having much to do with the decision, conveniently putting all the blame on the physician to whose orders he would appear to defer. Malfatti dreaded to think of his patient's reaction.

Francis had some qualms, too, but when Franz came to salute him after the parade, he was convinced of acting wisely in forcing the young man to take a furlough, cholera or no cholera.

Franz's face looked ashen and sweat poured from his forehead to which stuck tendrils of wet hair. Francis felt sorry for him, well aware that the uniforms of the Austrian army were not designed to provide suitable protection or adequate ventilation. They were gorgeously ill-adapted to Austria's bone-chilling, damp winters and stifling hot summers with the result that one would either freeze or stew wearing them.

He made a special point to compliment him warmly. "You were magnificent, Franz!"

"Thank you, Sire."

"Here," Francis said, handing him his handkerchief.

With a deferential bow, Franz backed away smiling. "Thank you, Sire, but I have my own."

"Heavens, Franz!" laughed Francis, "You are acting as though I were offering you a bribe!"

Any display of partiality, however well-meaning and inconsequential, when this related to his own personal merits in the discharge of his military duties, was something Franz would not countenance.

As graciously as he could he replied, "It is an unprecedented favor, Sire, for a member of your army to wipe the sweat off his brow with an imperial handkerchief. And I would not presume to rely on such kindness to leave my mark thus, in Austria's military annals."

The Emperor's entourage laughed appreciatively while Francis gazed at his grandson with intense satisfaction. Bypassing his many fears, words shot out straight from his heart.

"Ah, Franz," he said, and emotion boomed in his voice, "you don't know how much you mean to me!"

As if answering a cue, Malfatti came to stand beside him.

Startled at the sight of the doctor, Franz shrank, visibly embarrassed. The presence of his personal physician on the parade ground marked him again as an object of special attention which might even call his fitness into question. This was a situation he found utterly humiliating.

Confirming his apprehension, Malfatti began to recite a well-rehearsed discourse: It was his duty to inform the Emperor that in view of the Prince's overworked state, his continuing growth and his susceptibility to bronchial difficulties, a period of absolute rest at Schönbrunn during the present epidemic was in order. He further declaimed that his professional conscience and reputation. . . .

"You heard the doctor," Francis said. "Go to Schönbrunn immediately. My carriage is at your disposal."

And your equipage, my honor guards! Franz thought angrily. He could have wept for shame. His eyes blazed accusingly as they met Malfatti's. That confounded man was responsible for placing him under arrest!

Brushing past the doctor after sharply clacking his heels in sign of obedience, Franz said to him under his breath, "I will remember this, sir!"

With a grimace Malfatti mournfully looked at Francis as if to say, All is well! But Your Majesty just put me in the doghouse!

The Emperor only smiled as he watched Franz climb into the carriage. "Pay no attention to that show of ill-temper. You won't have a rancorous patient. That, the Prince is not. But willful and obstinate, he certainly is. This does not change in the least your previous difficulties with him, eh?"

Surrounded with quarantine posts manned by soldiers, Schönbrunn was no longer the quiet summer palace Franz knew and had grown to love. Servants bustled up and down the stairs readying every untenanted room for immediate occupancy. The imperial family, the court, the ambassadors and personages of influence in Vienna, all sought shelter from the cholera behind the palace's walls.

The castle reminded him of a monastery where during times of pestilence people would repair in the hope that the sacredness of the grounds would somehow protect them from contamination. But Franz still held to his theory of aerial infection and felt all the more mortified because Francis had chosen to tarry in Vienna for the same honorable reasons he had appealed to but without success.

So overcome was he with shame, that not even Sophie could appease him. Then adding to his miseries, Marie Louise would not be visiting him that year. Franz understood perfectly well that it would be quite impossible for his mother to travel at the present time, and he would have adamantly opposed her braving the danger of infection by undertaking such a journey. Only she had given no indication in her correspondence that she *had* intended to come to Vienna at all.

Just as Marie Louise completely divorced herself from her son's existence, so did Franz feel a deepening sense of being relegated to an ever shrinking corner of his mother's life. From her insipid letters, he only knew that she had returned to Parma and continued to ail from various afflictions which, she maintained, kept her from visiting him. He had no idea that his mother had come to an unhappy turning point in her life.

Her minister, Baron Marschall von Bieberstein, treated her harshly and severely, encouraged by the contempt in which Metternich held her. Moreover, Marschall was a man of principles. He could not forgive Marie Louise for turning away from Napoleon when his empire had collapsed, and least of all, for having had an adulterous relation with Niepperg shortly after.

Then he had been appalled by the discovery that Neipperg's widow's sex life had become unimaginably dissolute. The guard he had posted at her bedroom door was caught abed with her! The guard whose duty was to protect Marie Louise's virtue, however damaged, by barring the access of her chamber to the men of her household!

Fortunately, Franz was never to know the extent of his mother's depravity. But what he had discovered of her failings was enough of a burden. And for all his love and forgiving disposition, she had sown in his heart a wariness he had never thought he could feel toward women. There was one exception, however—Sophie.

Sophie alone was the repository of his childhood's reverence for womanhood, Sophie for whom his long-standing devotion was assuming troubling nuances. . . .

No longer did he dare think of holding her in his arms like he used to in those once spontaneous hugs. The last one, upon his unhappy return from the casern had confirmed the awakening of a special thrill he identified as no longer innocent.

He had fallen in love with her!

That enrapturing realization did not stun him as much as it alarmed him. So he speculated that maybe his feelings might have been diverted, even snuffed, had he remained at the casern, been kept busy with his duties, or been sent to some other places. . . . Yet he wasn't so sure. In essence, he had always loved her. Only the manifestation of that love had been scaled to keep pace with his maturation.

For several days, Franz's absent-mindedness had not gone unnoticed by his entourage. To his relief, the reason for such behavior was attributed to his disenchantment at having been taken away from his battalion. He was careful not to disabuse anyone, least of all Sophie. In the fear of betraying himself, he sometimes tried to avoid her. He felt trapped in a bewildering situation and thought of some possible places where he could escape from it. But where? And how far?

Close to Schönbrunn and within the limit of the quarantine posts, Malfatti had taken up quarters in his house at Hietzing after suffering from a more acute attack of gout which kept him house bound. He was surprised upon being informed that the Duke of Reichstadt wished to see him.

Malfatti imagined being needed at the palace, and he reminded his servant that an alternate physician had been assigned to the Prince in his absence.

"The Duke is waiting in the parlor," he was told.

"He is here?"

"Yes, doctor."

"I shall receive him, then."

Malfatti wondered if Reichstadt had come to reproach him at length and vent his resentment in private. As Franz entered, he made to get up from his armchair, apologizing, "Forgive me for seeing you in my bedchamber, Highness."

"Please! Remain seated, sir," Franz said amicably. "I have come to see how you were getting on. . . . I enjoyed the walk immensely." Actually, he chided himself for using the doctor's ailing condition as a pretext to get away from the castle. The emotions that wreaked havoc on his soul left him no alternative. And as Francis had predicted, his anger toward Malfatti had blown over and was well forgotten.

Malfatti had no such absolute assurance. "I sincerely deplore your removal from Vienna. I. . . ."

Franz made a dismissive gesture. "Don't give it another thought." He walked up to a chair. "May I?"

Malfatti gave a hurried assenting nod. "Do, please!"

Franz sat down and smiled at him. "I am the one who should be sorry. I have treated you unfairly. Do accept my apologies." Having said this, he drifted into deep thoughts.

"I realize this must be a difficult time for an active young man like Your Highness to be spending the summer cloistered at the castle," Malfatti said to set the conversation going.

"Horrid!" Franz responded with sullen intensity. "But I have been doing a lot of reading. Poetry. Byron. . . . The gloom, the mystery in his verses move me. . . ." His voice broke off. Bryon's verses were indeed consonant with the dark and passionate mood that hung over him like a pall.

"A despairing genius, Monseigneur," Malfatti cautioned. "Byron separates man from all hope . . . from a goal. He leaves us to the whims of a blind destiny."

Franz pondered the doctor's words. His own aspirations and his struggle to fulfill them seemed to have set the tone of this exchange. He had come to be distracted from a sentimental dilemma and found himself focusing once again on a no less all-consuming preoccupation. "Destiny. . . ." he mused out loud. "Does one have any say in the chain of events that will ferry us through this life?"

"To a great extent, Monseigneur, we are creating these events. History is a blatant example of this."

"So fatalism is nothing but an abdication of one's will."

"Precisely."

"The solution is in the will, then."

"Absolutely. And I should like to point out that the poet Lamartine, unlike Byron, sees in our existence an uplifting effort to rise above despair in believing that though limited in his nature, but boundless in his aspiration, man is a fallen angel who remembers Heaven."

"That is a magnificent thought! I regret to say I have not read any of Lamartine's poems," Franz confessed.

"I will be glad to lend Your Highness the volumes I have in my possession," Malfatti offered. "I shall have them packed and sent to the castle."

When Franz finally took his leave, he reflected that the afternoon had not been a total loss after all. His conversation with Malfatti had enforced the old adage: where there is a will, there is a way. He clung to the thought like a man set adrift on a turbulent sea would cling to a buoy.

In a swift, smoothing motion Sophie's fingers brushed over the lapel of Franz's frock coat so it would lay flat. Next, they gently fluffed little Franzi's hair, then deftly worked on the scarf tied around the neck of Princess Maria Carolina of Salerno, daughter of Marie Louise's sister, Archduchess Marianne. This done, she stood back and was pleased to see that the little girl held her rose gracefully.

Then she said to the court painter, Johan Ender, "Please proceed. We have so little time before the sun sets."

Franz was turning his forced inactivity to some good use by doing Sophie a special favor. He had agreed to pose for a group portrait which would represent on one canvas the likenesses of Francis's three grandchildren.

To paint young children was never easy, nor was it any less difficult for Franz to sit with them. Balancing young Franz Joseph on one knee, he tried to look steadily at the artist, because Sophie had expressed the wish that the picture, she intended for the Emperor on the occasion of his birthday, showed Franz with his eyes fixed upon the beholder. That way, when Francis would be looking at the painting, the Prince would be staring right back at him, thus enhancing the personal aspect of the gift.

While Franz's eyes were turned in the direction of the painter, Sophie kept hers trained on him. The stiff, upright points of the shirt collar framing his cheeks and the black silk cravat swathing his throat lent a special fascination to the distant and melancholy expression on his face. And she kept staring, oblivious of her surroundings.

When Ender spoke, he startled her. The children, he told her, were getting tired.

"And my foot has gone to sleep," Franz remarked.

Ender put down his brush signaling that his models were free to relax. Franz bent his head and touched his cheek to Maria Carolina's brow.

"And how is your arm?" he asked her.

She had been holding her arm upright with an elbow propped on his knee so she would be painted with the Emperor's canary perched on her finger. The pose would have taxed anyone, especially a child. She leaned her head on her cousin's chest and letting the cramped arm fall limply to her side said with a small, self-pitying voice, "It has gone to sleep with your foot, Franz!"

A snicker rose at the back of the room where stood the Archduchess's attendants.

Sophie glared at them.

Franz ignored the whole thing and stroked the little girl's head saying consolingly, "It will be well soon. You can go back to your game now."

The children were led away and Sophie came to the front of the easel to examine the picture which was nearly finished. Ender had painted Franz with the famous distinctive Habsburg under lip. The exaggeration was rather flagrant, and done for reasons she had no difficulty guessing. Court artists invariably emphasized "the lip" when they did portraits of the Duke of Reichstadt, as if to stress his Habsburg parentage.

Sophie glanced at a better expression of the truth—at Franz. His handsomely shaped lips with their full but firm and decisive contours, were nothing like the swollen underlip Ender had chosen to depict.

Franz had gotten up from his chair to stretch his legs and did not seem at all interested in the results of Ender's work. When Sophie's eyes met his, he said quickly averting his face, "I need to take a walk."

She heard herself timidly express a simple wish which in the past she would have put forward with spontaneity.

"May I come with you?"

After a slight hesitation, he held his hand out to her.

That particular summer of Franz's life, Schönbrunn's park—so familiar to him since childhood—was rediscovered through the eyes of love. The balmy breeze that mussed his hair, no longer mute, sang old romances, and the yew-lined avenue along which he and Sophie ambled, now led to unsuspected wonders.

In the gathering dusk, the air wafted a sweet, faint scent of vanilla. Swallows circled in flashing curves under the opalescent dome of a vacant sky over their heads. Toward the western vault of the firmament, a few stars had begun to appear as the red-hot summer sun slowly sank in a bed of persimmon clouds.

Franz forced himself to study their incandescent shapes which he likened to mysterious islands aflame, and drifting on imaginary seas. And he thought, I am not *imagining* my love. And, oh! . . . to speak of it now! simply! honestly! But that is impossible!

Instead, he would speak of wise and sobering things, of a sunset and its immanent beauty and truthfulness, of the one solace no one could ever take away from him. But he could not help saying all those things with the same passionate accents he would have put in a declaration of love.

He said, lifting his face to the heavens, "There can never be any deception in this sort of magnificence! Nor can there be any in the pursuit of knowledge. . . . That is where lies true bliss and nourishment until death comes! To blind. To silence. To still. . . . Blessed are the curious of mind!"

Startled by that somber proclamation, Sophie took a hesitant step. It sounded too much like a formal renunciation of youth, of life.

Gently, wary of his reaction, she said, "You speak like an old, world-weary anchorite. And you mustn't!"

Soberly, still staring at the sky, he answered, "I speak of consolation, Sophie."

"And what of joy?"

He hesitated. "And joy, too! My joys are austere."

She said with elan, "You are much too young to dwell on such alternatives. Your life is yet to begin!"

"Life is passing me by!" he said wildly, overwrought by her devoted nearness.

"Oh, Franz! How can you say that? You are merely twenty!"

Desperately he tried to contain his emotion, "I can say much more," he answered. "I can say that I am condemned to live a lie so that all that is left for me to do is to chase after chimeras. . . ."

They were presently standing in front of the *Gloriette*. Franz had always admired the elegance of its design. The structure, as its name indicated, had been erected to resemble a triumphal arch but in strict praise of aesthetic grace. Hence, the use of the diminutive French word for *gloire* to designate its limitation.

But *Gloriette*, as opposed to glory, had taken a very personal connotation where it concerned him. He was not superstitious, only hypersensitive to symbols. And that one, of late, haunted him. For was not the *Gloriette* symbolic of his own stunted self-realization? Of hindrances that even affected his sentimental life? That evening, the sight of the *Gloriette* embittered him. He stooped and took a handful of the sand that covered the walk.

"Look!" he said with suppressed violence, and let the sand slowly sift between his fingers. "This, Sophie, is my life! A hemorrhage!. . . ."

"Franz!" She felt compelled to sit on a nearby bench, shaken by the vivid imagery.

But he continued, propelled on an unstoppable course by an uncontrollable sense of failure. "All the things that are dear to me are slipping from my grasp! Just like this!" Then in a trance of weariness, and unable to check himself any longer, he blurted out, "Including the only woman I love. You!"

Sophie sat very still, barely breathing, speechless, stunned by a rapturous confirmation. It completely shattered the false tranquility that coated an inner conflict she had refused to recognize.

Franz misconstrued her frozen stance and her silence. Desolation choked his voice. "I have offended you! Forgive me."

The giddying tenderness she had begun to feel for him, and which had been tormenting her in an insidious, troubling yet delicious way compelled her to reach for him. When he sank to his knees locking his arms around her and burrowed his face into the hollow of her throat, she clasped him to her and broke into a fervent protest.

"No, my love! You haven't offended me! Never!"

And it felt liberating to be able to caressingly move her hands across his trembling shoulders, to run gentle fingers through his hair, let her lips brush over his forehead and cheek between her murmured words, *and not feel wicked or deserving of punishment!*

No! His substantiality was too precious to her to taint her emotion. Holding him now yielded such ineffable joy! She could not bear to let him go. She could only be attentive to the touch of him. Something long required of life was taking her by storm. Irresponsibility began to invade her. . . .

Franz tilted back his head, his eyes glittering. "You do love me! You are not turning me away. . . ."

She felt his breath on her lips. Her tender conscience at long last rose to her defense. A lifetime of pious and ardent practices placed before her a terrible and wounding alternative. Her love could only blossom in sacrifice. . . . She clutched at his head knowing that the slightest latitude in movement would cause their lips to blend and seal in a kiss, a situation from which she could never extricate herself.

Almost weeping, she acknowledged the difference he had made in her existence. "My life has begun with you. And my very first love is you! Not to end . . . ever . . . But I am not free, as you so well know. And though my love for you is immeasurable, it would be barren. Oh my Franz! You can't, and you mustn't accept that! Dearest, *it is you* who should be turning me away!"

He stared at her with an expression of ineluctable despair. "I can't stop loving you! Must I be ashamed of it?"

"No! Never!" she protested fiercely. Her fingers were tendrils of longing. Gently, lovingly, they began to trace his features and brushed over his lips. She had felt them many times on the back of her hands, but never this way, soft and quavering with passion. She heard herself without being conscious of actually speaking.

"My dearest love, what could I be to you?"

He closed his eyes briefly and breathed, "My heaven and my hell!" Then encouraged by her unavowed sufferance, he slowly lifted the shield of her fingers from his mouth and let his lips unerringly find their way, the warmth of them clinging to hers with unquenchable yearning.

Lost to an armful of love, to a passionate kiss she had never been given nor quite knew how to receive, Sophie surrendered to a moment of such bliss that time stood still.

When he pulled back, and slowly rose to his feet, she could still feel on her mouth the fiery imprint of the kiss. Entranced, she lovingly gazed at him as a heart-breaking realization came to her. Silhouetted against the evening sky, Franz presented a forlorn, vulnerable figure she was cruelly exiling into the corner of her observant application of rules.

Sophie wrung her hands in rebellious desperation.

"I can't be a torment to you! You of all people!" she lamented.

"And what of you?" he said, his voice hushed and shaky. "How could I be a lesser temptation?"

"Temptation is an evil word," she objected breathlessly. "It can't come between us!"

"Then what will?" he asked tensely. "What can possibly prevent me from kissing you again?"

"Never guilt!" she said fighting down a private agony. "Our love is above it! And like the constellations above us, it will leave its scintillating and indelible mark long after another love will flower in your young heart . . . as it should!"

"Stop giving me away to some nameless and faceless paragon!" he said disconsolately in a half-whisper.

She felt the tears of an unappeasable sorrow streaming down her cheeks, but it had grown so dark now that she was sure he could not see them. Springing to her feet, she impulsively threw herself into his arms.

"How could I give you so much pain?"

He clasped her to him, simply cherishing the moment, and not fearing of presuming too much, murmured against her ear, "I will survive. . . "

28

Franz and Sophie kept a conduct in which virtue was not a pretense. She wondered if love so stifled in restraint could ever endure. And the more she pondered their impossible situation, the more personally assured of the contrary she felt. She would love Franz forever! Where it concerned him, his plight filled her with overwhelming sadness. Least of all, should he be blighted in love! In selfless spurts of compassion she even prayed that he would stop loving her—for his sake!

Franz asked nothing, posed no penetrating questions and took each day as it came. The positive reality of Sophie's love for him mitigated the anxiety of facing an increasingly uncertain future.

Such as they were, events seemed to indicate that he would not assume any positions to the level of his aspiration. To his profound dismay, he learned that the Chamber of Deputies in Paris was actively working on a decree aiming to banish the Bonapartes from France. During a heated debate on this question, mention of execution by firing squad had even been put forward in the eventuality that members of that family would be caught on national soil. Evidently, the present monarchy was leaving nothing to chance! Rejected by the Legitimists, Louis Philippe had gone as far as inducing the proscription of the royal house of the Bourbons as well.

Still smarting from the sting of being disowned outright, Franz gave Prokesch a delirious welcome when the latter returned from Italy toward the end of September. After the initial effusions, the Major stepped back to examine him fondly. He felt quite satisfied with what he saw.

"You look extremely well, Franz!"

A wistful smile fleeted over Franz's mouth. And so he should have looked well! For the state of love into which Sophie had placed him was also a state of grace.

"I am well looked after," he said somewhat mysteriously. Then after a short pause, he resumed a grave expression. "I presume you have accomplished what you have set out to do?"

Prokesch understood. "All is calm," he replied.

Franz said in a monotone, "I know. Belgium has a king. Poland is once again subdued. Italy is quite safe, my mother has returned to Parma. France is self-sufficient and on best terms with Austria. I have to admit, the Congress of Vienna has done marvels. We haven't had a war for quite sometime, and that is a feat."

Knowing Franz's feeling regarding individual liberty, the Major wondered if he had heard well.

"A feat, did you say?"

"Only from the standpoint of cursory observation, Anton. For let me tell you that those who hanker after equality and justice must undoubtedly liken this quiescence to a state of induced constipation. . . " Franz paused briefly to apologize. "I pray you to excuse the coarse simile, but I find no other comparison that would be more appropriate. So let they who contend that the present situation is the panacea for Europe's problems take heed!"

"I am delighted to see you have not lost faith!"

Franz's lips compressed, his expression grew sullen. "Do you know there is a decree of banishment against the Bonapartes being debated in France?"

"Yes, I've heard of it."

"What is even worse is the suggestion that my foreign education might have left an indelible Germanic stamp on my character and outlook. If I were to tarry any longer in Austria, if I were to wait as you suggested, the credibility gap concerning my person would widen to an unbridgeable proportion."

Prokesch remained silent. He could understand such peril, but did not have any concrete solution to offer to counteract it.

Then decisively Franz said, "Anton, it is my sacred duty to force my destiny since all sensible avenues of fulfilling it are shut to me. What I have decided might seem aberrant, but it is sometimes wise to be mad. I have said it once, and now I am going to take action. I must get away . . . run away!"

In complete shock, Prokesch stared at him. Imagining Reichstadt going through such a perilous enterprise partly explained the pounding of his heart. But the underlying reason for the Major's overwhelming feeling of panic lay in the fact that he had persuaded himself to share such a venture should it become inevitable. Its imminence now terrified him. Often, he had pondered the nature of his deep attachment for the

Prince. In one short year it had become so strong that he was consenting to plunge headlong in an undertaking that held nothing for him.

On the contrary. To follow Reichstadt would turn him into a renegade, a traitor, and the penalty for those guilty of such offense meant proscription or death. Moreover, as an Austrian, his association with the son of Napoleon guaranteed a bleak future should his life be spared and their escape prove successful. Then, he would have to dissociate himself from Reichstadt shortly afterward in order to break him free from all tinges of Germanism.

This implied the loss of all possible compensations. Prokesch would become an exile, of no use to his friend and to a world of politics which he could so brilliantly serve. To a point, Franz's compelling charm, his nobility of character, and winning personality sufficiently explained the deep sympathy Prokesch felt for him. But there was only one glaring explanation for the immense sacrifice the Major was willing to make. Prokesch had yielded to limitless compassion.

Reichstadt's tragic fate evinced a pathos that was as sensational as his father's career was spectacular. There seemed to exist about this prince an aura of fatality often attached to being excessively endowed. It appeared as though his melancholy lot in this life was the result of some obscure and malevolent spell cast in protestation of an extraordinary convergence of qualities too generously lavished upon one single individual. He was a freak whose only deviation was to possess in form and content too many enviable traits Nature would normally sparingly bestow on one person.

And not least, Reichstadt was utterly alone with no one to turn to but Prokesch. His unconditional trust and complete surrender to their friendship touched the Major to the very core of his own noble soul. How could he fail to respond in kind? He could never abandon him!

Resolutely, after what seemed an interminable silence, he said, "If you go, Franz, I will go with you!"

Franz was thunderstruck. "I never implied that you should go with me, Anton!"

"I am going of my own accord, Franz."

The magnitude of the sacrifice he could never consider asking horrified him. "No!" he cried frantically, "You mustn't!"

"But I am!"

"That's madness!"

"You've just said that there was wisdom in madness,"

"In your case, Anton, it is utter madness! Your good name and your career will be ruined! I beg you to have also some consideration for your life! If you were to be caught, you could be shot!"

"We won't be caught."

"*We* . . ." Franz's eyes sudden filled with tears. He gripped his friend's shoulders, almost hurting him. "God help me! I can't let you do this! What you have given me, friendship, and unwavering support, are more than I ever hoped to receive. I ask no more. I beg of you! I implore you in the name of all I hold sacred and dear, let me go alone!"

Deeply moved, Prokesch stressed the irrevocability of his decision. "No, Franz, my mind is made up and nothing can change it. I am going with you."

In a paroxysm of emotion, Franz gave him such a fierce hug that he nearly smothered him. Almost immediately he backed away, seized by a sudden fit of coughing, a hand cupped over his mouth.

Prokesch watched him go through a series of short, dry-throated spasms. He recalled having witnessed other such episodes, mild, innocuous in their brevity, but now there appeared to be some kind of a pattern to this, and a latency no ordinary cold would sustain over months, even a year—as he remembered how Franz had been hacking as far back as last summer during their outing in the Vienna Woods. He grew anxious.

"You can't seem to shake that cough," he remarked with a slight frown.

Franz managed to gasp. "It's nothing! A scratch . . . It comes and goes . . . now and then."

The admission of that "now and then" raised in the Major's mind a concern he had not entertained until now. All other risks considered, there remained one that could never fit in the plan of a successful evasion—ill health. Franz's health, so far as Prokesch could tell, appeared satisfactory, due in all evidence to the restraints imposed upon him. But during the tumult of a hazardous flight, stress, and physical exertion would take a heavy toll on the Prince's endurance. So Prokesch felt obliged to impose some restriction.

Once Franz's cough had eased up, he said, "By next winter we shall have completed all the necessary preparations." He avoided saying anything about allowing Franz to rally his strength in the meantime. He only pointed out, "I say winter in consideration of the fact that you would be spending that season in Vienna. This will be perfect because in Vienna your movements are not so easy to track as they are at Schönbrunn. So wintertime, in my belief is best to carry out the execution of our plan."

"How I wish it were this winter!" Franz sighed, but he did not insist. He needed a few months to repair the tiredness he had begun to feel every time he exerted himself. Only a few weeks ago Francis had invited him to a hunt and the outing had left him utterly exhausted. He had kept quiet about it, but Malfatti had caught him stretched listlessly on a sofa, and more than once.

"In any case," he went on, "France is my long-range goal. The proscription against me might not take hold. Yet as you have said, I should not come to her by surprise. What I need is a temporary refuge where I can prepare myself for the opportune time, and it is quite impossible for me to achieve this here."

"I can think of such a place," Prokesch said.

"Where?"

"Rome. The Papal States by their neutrality would be perfectly suitable. I shall explore every possibility for us to steal away there after passing through Styria or the Tyrol."

"Anton . . ." Franz's voice came nearly inaudible, muffled by a powerful feeling of gratitude. He desperately searched for the right phrase to express this overwhelming sentiment. "I am indebted to you forever," or "I shall never forget what you have done as long as I live" were unutterable, so vexingly trite they would have sounded.

He decided to follow his instinct. Stylishness had no place in this declaration, and surely the sensation that his heart would burst could be translated in some fashion.

"Anton," he said forcing the sound out of his aching throat, "I want you to know that on this day, at this very hour, I have discovered many very precious and incomparable wonders in one word. Do you know what the word is?" By now, he let the tears come.

Prokesch took his hands which he found disquietingly warm.

"No, Franz," he said softly.

Smiling through his tears Franz whispered, "*You!*"

By November the threat of cholera had considerably eased and Schönbrunn slowly emptied of its guests. As in the past, the court moved to Vienna. Franz left for the capital in the first snow of an early winter, feeling reasonably assured that his future was definitely taking shape.

There had been a last minute change in his plan of evasion, however. Beset by a needling sense of urgency, he had said to Prokesch a few days after their momentous meeting, "If there is a possibility to escape this winter, I will not let the opportunity pass."

The Major thought it best not to contradict him.

Having reached a modicum of satisfaction in the course his life was taking, Franz soon began to agonize over the thought of leaving Sophie. Yet the pain that was tearing him asunder reiterated an implacable reality: a love without consummation and the utter hopelessness of its issue defied any sensible attempt at pursuing. It was just as well that he went away.

But not without telling her.

When they met now, her subdued amiability and his courtesy dissembled the passionate feeling they shared. When he would kiss Sophie's hand, he did so more fervently and longer; and when she talked, his gaze would change to a wrought-up stare as he would fantasize catching those very words on her lips with kisses.

When Sophie laid her eyes upon him across a crowded room, she would feel a renewed sense of plenitude in being loved and being in love; and when her sleeve would brush his, she longed to nestle in his arms. . . .

They had not kissed again since that incandescent summer evening in the gardens of Schönbrunn.

One week before Christmas, Franz finally found the courage to tell her of his plan. Again, he asked her to play the piano and he realized how much in love he already was when she had run her fingers across the keyboard playing that melody by Cimarosa.

After she finished, he made her sit beside him on the sofa, took her hands, and wordlessly began kissing each of her fingers separately. Then to Sophie's complete astonishment, he kissed her wedding ring and quietly said, "I shall be leaving you soon. For good!"

"Leaving?" she repeated faintly.

"Escape!" he said, watching her closely.

The color drained from her cheeks. She had adjusted to the impossibility of loving him lawfully and totally, but never contemplated losing him this way—and to the peril of his life!

As she seemed stunned and incapable of speech, Franz continued in a low, anguished voice, "I must. For your sake and mine."

"Franz," she said at last, slowly lifting her hands to take his face between them. And for a second, he thought she was about to kiss him as he hoped she would at the moment of their final adieu.

But Sophie grappled with far more sensual constraints—keeping herself from drawing his head to her breast, from letting him caress her as she had never been caressed, and allowing him to love her as she had never been loved. All these prohibitions were also the crux of his tortured and chivalrous restraint. She felt she ought to help him. And it more than behooved her to release him.

"Franz," she repeated, her voice dulled by the shock of acceptance, "whatever you do must meet with the approval of your conscience and the dictate of your reason. I treasure your happiness far above my own. And . . . going away, I realize, too, serves necessities that transcend our feelings for each other. So I wish you every success. Oh, but my very precious love . . . be careful!"

Then visions of him in some mortal danger raised a delirium of alarm. She drew him to her, heaving her fear, "I can't bear the thought of anything happening to you!"

She felt him press against her all his grief and hopelessness, then heeding a warning they both understood, he wrenched himself away and retreated to the window, touching his burning forehead to the cold pane.

His heart pounding, he stared absently at the twirling snowflakes, the foretaste of a tantalizing consummation of their desires monopolizing all his sensory faculties. Oh, how they would be tormenting each other by holding these desires in abeyance! Yes! It would be best that he leave. Never to return. . . .

In a flash she crossed over to him, sank to the floor embracing his knees and looked up at him with absolute devotion.

"Please," he begged her, "don't kneel before me like that!" Bending down he lifted her by the elbows and slipped his fingers between hers. They stood face-to-face, their hands locked in a desperate grip but their bodies did not touch.

Sophie made a supreme effort to regain her self-possession, to restore a semblance of quiet acceptance without which they could not function.

"When, Franz?" she managed to asked. She was going to ask, "How?" but refrained from doing so. Discretion, she reasoned, was not only prudent, but also mandatory.

"At the first opportunity. My position here is untenable," he said quickly. *And in more than one way,* he thought. *But don't be indelicate. Put it sensibly, rationally.* So he went on, "Because after all, I am not German. I have a homeland to go back to. I have work to do."

"God be with you," she murmured. And lifting both his hands, she, in turn, began to kiss them slowly in a selfless outpouring of generosity.

She felt like weeping, yet appreciated causes for rejoicing. For she was losing him to something that would be realizable. So these fine, young hands would be reshaping a much disturbed world, and for the better! She began with the back of them, then turning them over, kissed the warm hollow of the palms. The life lines, she noticed, were well-grooved and long. Offering up her sorrow, she passionately kissed them, determined to believe that soothsaying one's lifespan by their length was as sound as her faith.

In spite of Franz's ardent and secret hopes, the winter of 1831 promised to be uneventful. Once again he settled down to a pattern copied from that of the preceding seasons. It did not matter how often, or on what particular day Baron Obenaus or Count Dietrichstein would pay him a call, the fact remained, he could expect no surprises from them.

Nor could he find any break in the repetitiousness of his daily activities. He gave fruitless audiences to carefully screened visitors as he continued to be an object of attraction and curiosity; went riding to the Prater; sat down to supper at Francis's frugal table; spent afterward an hour or two at the opera or the theater. Then for his personal gratification and further edification, Prokesch would come to see him in the evening, and together they discussed the works of eminent authors.

Since the day of their compact, Franz would greet his confidant with an expectant expression. And so far, the Major had answered tersely: "Nothing yet."

One gloomy winter evening after having been given the same discouraging negative reply, Franz thought having nearly reached the limit of forbearance. A slow, relentless process of erosion set in. He began to feel as though he was drowning in a morass of insupportable restrictions. He saw his life at a dead end. Every single aspect of it was wrong. And he flirted with despair.

The signs were evident. Dietrichstein and Prokesch were quick to notice them. Franz's mood appeared to be smoldering like an untended fire. More and more, he preferred to shut himself out of the mainstream of daily activities and events, recoiling as it were, from a world tormented and tormenting. Prokesch soon detected in Franz's withdrawal a brutalizing, abdicative attitude. With increasing frequency, the Major would hear him say, "What good will this do?" or "I don't much care one way or the other!"

This sort of talk alarmed Prokesch and roused him to immediate action. Brushing aside his own reticence, he took the distasteful and difficult decision of resorting to a palliative he considered beneath Franz's dignity. That was the sort of vulgar consolation Gustave Neipperg kept suggesting after having made the remark to him that Reichstadt was "looking terribly down in the dumps."

Now Prokesch gave in.

Dissimulating his embarrassment, and not in the least aware of the part Gustave had played in Franz's initiation to the facts of life shortly after his break-up with Naudine, he told him: "You might be right. The Duke needs . . . satisfaction. He is of age. Find him a discreet, attractive woman who could catch his fancy without dragging him into a prolonged and torrid love affair."

Gustave thought briefly. One night at the opera, Reichstadt had lavishly praised a pretty cantatrice. And though he had expressed greater admiration for her talent than for her person, Gustave was certain the young woman would have no difficulty arousing the Duke's desire were she to become familiar with him.

He was quick to propose. "I know of such a woman. Her name is Thérèse Pêche. I could introduce her to His Highness."

Thérèse should be perfect if Reichstadt would have her. A tenderhearted girl with more tender forms, Thérèse sought above all to gain mastery in operatic singing rather than try to ensnare or dominate the men she was quite expert at pleasing. Gustave endeavored to explain this as tastefully as he could.

Prokesch replied in a business-like way, "These conditions are satisfactory. Proceed as soon as possible!"

It was further agreed that the young woman would be properly instructed as to the expectations placed in her, and Gustave would see to it that the meeting should not appear prearranged.

That night at the opera, after another of Thérèse's much applauded performances, Gustave turned to his companion and suggested: "Franz, you might want to congratulate Fraulein Pêche tonight. I could take you to her dressing room if you care to follow me as I am going there myself."

After a short silence, Franz said, "Why not? She deserves to be complimented."

Smugly Gustave proceeded with the introduction, "Your Highness, may I present Fraulein Pêche!"

Thérèse sank into a deep curtsy counting her heartbeats, and Franz noticed more than her grace as her reverent posture revealed the creamy swell of her breasts pushing against a generously low décolletage. She wore her hair drawn up into a high top knot secured with jeweled combs. Love curls coiled alongisde her cheeks, which were flushed with a peachy color slightly lighter in hue than that of her gown all adorned with a profusion of frills and ribbons. Named after the French word for peach, Thérèse looked as fresh and succulent as the fruit is reputed to be.

He bid her to rise and complimented her on her singing.

Gustave injected eagerly, "Fraulein Pêche sings like a nightingale!"

"Better! Much better," Franz said with gravity, "*Vox caelestis!*"

The cantatrice's cupid-bow mouth parted in a demure smile. She protested, "Your Highness is exceedingly kind!" Then, glancing hopefully at Gustave, she made her first strategic move. "Oh, but would Your Highness's indulgence allow me to sing for your private enjoyment in a less impersonal setting!"

Immediately Gustave chimed in, "A musical soirée with Fraulein Pêche is absolutely delightful. Won't Your Highness join us next week?"

The invitation took Franz aback. Its shocking informality, the rapidity with which the request was being put to him, suddenly struck him as odd. Odder still, now that his suspicion had been aroused, was the young woman's obvious lack of surprise to see him pay her a call. He realized that the instant he had appeared on the threshold of her dressing room, he was already expected.

Then accentuating this impression, Thérèse said as if she were in an advanced stage of familiarity with him, "Ah, do come, Prince! Grant me this happiness!"

"Your Highness will be charmed!" Gustave echoed. Only later, did he recognize that his eagerness in seconding every overture Thérèse made had contributed to give the game away.

Already Franz looked distant. He said smiling, nevertheless, "Alas! I do have a previous engagement and I deplore this mischance, Fraulein. But I shall always be flattered to be counted among your most ardent admirers!"

Thérèse curtsied, replying faintly that she was sorry he could not come. But sorrier than she was Franz, who, after a few perfunctory words of praise on her technique, left certain of having been tricked.

As they walked out of the opera house, Gustave had to double his steps in order to catch up with Reichstadt's. Once outside, the Prince climbed a little too briskly into their waiting carriage.

Gustave thought, He is crossed! So much for trying to amuse him! Franz had not even hinted that he could see Thérèse some other times, and Gustave puzzled over his reticence. Thérèse was a dish! Why wouldn't Franz go after her? This was not at all like him. Why, only in the spring of this year, Gustave had had ample proof that Reichstadt was extremely susceptible to feminine charms. The "initiation" he had discreetly arranged after Franz finally agreed to his suggestion seemed to have gone well. . . .

What was happening to him?

During the ride to the palace, Gustave's perplexity gave way to extreme annoyance. Franz still had not said a word, wouldn't explain what had gone wrong with his carnal inclinations.

Finally Gustave opened his mouth. His tone was querulous.

"Franz, did you really have a previous engagement?"

All he got was a sigh. Then he heard him mutter, "What do you care?"

"Did you or didn't you?" he persisted.

"No, Gustave, I did not."

"Then what the devil is the matter with you? Why did you refuse?"

"The lady is too forward!" Franz returned after a silence.

"She is," Gustave retorted with petulance, "a very pretty and much feted young woman. She derives a certain assurance in her success. Is this so terribly wrong?"

Franz leaned his head against the back of the seat. "Maybe not."

"So?" harried Gustave.

"This does not please me," Franz answered flatly. Then he added. "You set her up to this. . . ."

"Well," Gustave bawled, "I think it's high time you put an end to this continence of yours!" He gave his companion a nudge. "Damn it, Franz! It's obvious you've been living like a monk for a while now!"

"Gustave!"

Gustave hawked apologetically, but once caught trespassing the bound of good taste and decorum, he blundered on with no turning back. "You haven't touched a woman for sometime. And . . ."

"Gustave!"

". . . After a short . . . novitiate, which you seemed to enjoy! At least I thought so!"

"Gustave!" Franz protested again, irritation creeping into his voice.

"Or was it unpleasant maybe?"

Franz shot back at him, "I don't care to remember any of it!" He wholeheartedly meant this. With humbling clarity he saw his own hypocrisy in his earlier disdain for this sort of indulgence. He realized the rawness in the intense pleasure he'd taken and the demeaning and pitiful aridity of it all. With a superlative effort, he tried to block out the thought of how redeeming and meaningful making love would have been like . . . With Sophie.

"*Mein Gott!*" Gustave swore softly. And that was all he could find to say. Franz's incomprehensible recantation of past pleasures garbled his thinking process. He recovered, however, his lustful nature and coarse appreciation of sexual gratification summoning enough resources to insist on what he considered the essence of romantic fulfillment.

"But you can have any woman you want at a glance! Why stop now?. . . . Whereas the rest of us, we . . ."

"Gustave," Franz interrupted, "you are an absolute fool!"

Recoiling in his corner, Gustave said stiffly: "I am sorry to have displeased Your Highness!"

Franz gave him a sidelong glance. The deliberate choice of the formal address Gustave would only use with him in the presence of a third party indicated the condition of a deep hurt. Poor Gustave! Always full of good intentions, fundamentally harmless, and now bamboozled by nuances that were evidently beyond his comprehension. Franz felt genuinely sorry.

"Gustave, I called you a fool because I am fond of you. If I weren't that fond of you, I wouldn't care if you became a voluptuous idiot!"

"How very gracious of you," Gustave said, the sour trace of a sulk in his tone.

"Oh, come off it, Gustave! I just happen to feel . . . differently, that's all!"

"I just don't understand it," Gustave insisted, unwilling to drop the subject. Then having caught Franz's slight hesitation, the thought came to him. "Are you *seriously* involved with someone?"

Franz tensed. He thanked the semi-darkness enveloping them as he felt confusion, like hands, work on his face, reshaping it with an expression he would never want anyone to see.

Pulling his head in the shadow untouched by the faint light of the lamps mounted on the sides of the carriage, he said categorically, "I don't care to discuss my love life!"

Gustave answered with nothing more than a grunt; a welcomed indication that the inquisition was over.

29

On the morning of January 2, 1832, Franz opened his eyes, but not to the waking call of his orderly. It was the invasive chill creeping under his blankets which woke him. Immediately, the sight of his austere surroundings gave him a happy jolt. He was in his bedroom at the barracks! At long last!

The permission to return to his quarters at the casern with full resumption of service duties was Francis's New Year's gift to him, but Franz had had to resort to a ruse to obtain it. He kept concealing from Malfatti the fact that every evening, like clockwork, he had begun to run a temperature. Had the doctor detected this, Franz would have been condemned to continue a cure of restorative inactivity, which he couldn't bear contemplating. The deception had worked because fortunately by morning, like magic, the fever would leave him; and Malfatti after having conducted a routine examination *during the day*, had given his patient a clean bill of health.

Only Sophie seemed to have had an inkling he might have a fever. When in the evening he would bid her good night taking her hand to press it against his lips, she would remark, "Franz, *your* hand is burning hot! . . . and this is not the first time."

And he'd say, "It's only a natural thing with me," then wondered if indeed there wasn't some natural explanation for this. With her always so near and so far, so dear and growing hopelessly dearer, so embraceable yet untouchable, with the passion that flooded him with no possible outlet, shouldn't he be consuming himself?

They continued to keep that terrible self-restraint demanded by an exacting compact which repudiated all the sensual manifestations of love without renouncing love. It was a tantalizing and cruel romance, and in their guarded but tender moments he could sense her pain. For she must have related all too well to his once impassioned imagery of her role in their relationship when he had said that she was *his heaven and his hell.* As he did, she must have drawn in her own mind a graphic representation of their plight: there stood heaven, and there stood hell. The accessibility of the former logically excluded the possibility of visiting the latter. Yet they had both entered a heaven of sorts by passing through hell day after day. . . .

Franz rolled out of bed.

This morning, he'd been assigned to lead an honorary procession at the funeral of General Siegenthal. The frigid temperature in his room said much for what he would have to contend with outside when he looked out the window. Frost was everywhere, glazing the slates on the roofs, coating the bare limbs of trees with fanciful sculptures; and the sudden dip in temperature during the night had halted a thaw leaving festoons of huge icicles that hung like sword blades along the barracks' eaves.

The prospect of braving the cold did not dampen his eagerness to get up and get ready. At this point, nothing could deter him from plunging head-long into any kind of activities, no matter how adverse the conditions. He only sought to find something to distract him from the anguishing yet sweet throes of being impossibly in love.

In his "all season" dress uniform he set off at the head of his companies. The cold transfixed him. Yet he noticed how everyone rigidly sat on their horses, jaws firmly clenched, held by the undershin straps of their shakos. But Franz wore a cocked hat as this was indicative of his superior rank. His teeth began to chatter.

The thought that his soldiers' outfits offered the same inadequate protection spurred him on. To be that cold must be normal, yet he could feel an alarming numbness setting in his legs. Somewhere in the stirrups, some terminal parts of him, sheathed in ice-cold leather boots, were barely responding.

Normally, it would have taken little time to cover the distance between the Alsler-Kaserne and the Joseph-Platz where the ceremonial parade honoring the defunct general was to take place. But on this frigid morning, progressing in that direction became an agonizingly slow advance as the funerary cortege moved at a snail's pace.

Upon reaching the square situated on the north side of the Hofburg, Franz had the sensation that his tunic had turned into a crust of smothering ice.

When the moment came to raise his curved saber in salute and shout a command, he discovered to his consternation and utter embarrassment that he had no voice. A deep, savage anger shot through him.

He could only motion the officer riding abreast to take over while holding back tears of shame.

Then there was for all to see a minor commotion caused by a rider suddenly out of step, a horse pawing the ground in confusion and rearing with a whinny to swing round and dash away spurred into a furious gallop.

Franz did not have to go far. Home, around the corner, the all too familiar courtyard that lay beneath the windows of his apartments at the Hofburg, was reached just in time. His last coherent thoughts were self-deprecatory. He wasn't even an asthenic youth but a thin weakling! And put to rout by an enemy within, and by a constitution which was punishing him as if he was not being punished enough! He hated his body!

As he collapsed over the pommel, a groom hurriedly unbuckled his sword belt and eased him down into the waiting arms of his valet, Titz, who effortlessly carried him unconscious to his room. He was undressed, wrapped in hot compresses and put to bed. Bent over him, Malfatti reflectively chewed on his fingertips.

A moment later, the doctor said to Dietrichstein whom he found pacing the anteroom, "His Highness is warming up and resting now."

The Count looked at him reproachfully. "The Prince is ill," he grumbled.

Malfatti said frowning, "It seems to me that the Prince must have concealed from us a pre-existing indisposition. For had he been as well as he had led us to believe, he would have withstood the cold like the others."

"And now it looks like he has caught pneumonia," said the former tutor in an accusing tone of voice. Obviously, the Count held Malfatti responsible for what had happened.

Malfatti replied with asperity. "His Highness is suffering from a rheumatic chill, which is affecting his liver and stomach!"

"If that is the case," Dietrichstein offered, hoping to be helpful, "I know for a fact that the Prince's stomach is delicate, or else, Austrian cooking is upsetting his digestion, which is giving him constant trouble . . . and then there is this intermittent cough."

This made no impression on the doctor. A sinister case history of dizziness, repeated colds, laryngitis, poor appetite, and frequent indigestions could only point to a famous heredity.

"I intend to send His Highness to Bad Ischl as soon as possible. The waters there are said to work wonders on this sort of affliction. I tell you, Count, a faulty liver, like his father, and not the cold is the true villain!"

"Liver. . . ." mumbled the Count. He was not convinced. His common sense told him that Reichstadt had not quite recovered from his overspent condition. The Emperor should have questioned Malfatti's optimism, and the Prince should not have been allowed to go out in sub-zero temperature.

Francis, looking glum and walking with a slouch, came to Franz's bedside. He stood there without saying a word. As Franz was about to assure him that his indisposition had quite passed, the Emperor declared dully, "I have a gift for you."

Since Francis was empty-handed, Franz asked curiously what this gift might be. Francis smiled, "It is very large," he said. He motioned an invisible attendant. Then addressing his grandson, "Shut your eyes."

Franz complied. Almost immediately the Emperor said, "Open them now."

Franz did so to behold a magnificent thoroughbred with a satin smooth coat under which each powerful muscle seemed knotted in compressed energy. Francis whispered, laying a hand on the animal's haunch, "It will take you far. As far as you want to go. . . ."

Only Franz winced in horror and disgust. Something terrible was happening! At his grandfather's touch, the horse underwent a sudden and appalling change. Its shiny coat dulled, the racy elegance of its shape disintegrated into grotesque deformity. Meanwhile, Francis's cold, pale blue eyes were fixed upon Franz with a longing that was vaguely malevolent. . . .

With a start, Franz came to his senses and jerked his eyes open. He found himself lying in his bed, and Francis was nowhere to be seen. Seated in a chair drawn up close, Sophie was gazing at him with an expression of rapt concern. Her hands were tightly clasped against her breast as if she had been praying.

She had. And devoutly. A little over four years had passed since she had come to Franz's bedside, and never had this particular vigil been more distressing and unsettling to her. While he was having short bouts of delirium, she had spent long watchful hours racked with anxiety and tormented by an insufferable longing to caress him, wondering when he would come to, and hoping that there was nothing seriously wrong with him.

As his eyes showed sign of recognition, she placed her hand on his forehead. "Dearest, you have come back to us! Thank God!"

Emerging from a nightmare, Franz sought refuge in the only sanctuary he knew. He instinctively held his arms out to her. Yielding to an overwhelming rush of tenderness, Sophie came into his embrace and gently lay her cheek against his.

She heard him murmur feverishly and with a thready voice, "Precious love! It's you!" His first words in twenty-eight hours.

Angling his face so that his lips moved against her cheek, he asked, "Is the parade over?"

"My love, that was yesterday. . . ."

"Yesterday?" This revelation startled him, but only briefly. "I am sorry. . . ." But he wasn't. He held her closer. The incident had brought her into his arms where he felt she belonged.

The brush of his lips against her cheek dizzied her. "And you have been out of your senses all this time," she said faintly.

"Have I?" he breathed, slowly turning his head and trailing a kiss that sought her mouth.

"Franz . . ." she faltered, and drew away.

He released her and fumbled for her hands which he held in a tight grip, gazing upon her inclined face with an air of absolute desolation. She could feel his hurt and admired his valiant determination to respect her reticence.

"You have to promise me something," she panted. "You have to promise me to take better care of yourself . . . because I love you."

A flicker of annoyance drew his gilded brows together. He did not intend to discuss the shameful failings of his constitution. He had detected in Sophie's tender plea a dash of loving reproach. No doubt. Malfatti or Dietrichstein must have said more on the subject than was fair or necessary.

His eyes skimmed over the slender column of her neck and the dimple at the base of her throat, and he wondered how he would ever manage without so much as touching his lips to them.

Gravely, he said, "I have no promise to keep but that of conserving *your* love in God's grace."

Painfully, she caught the nuance. He could have said "our" love, but in all honesty, she knew, he strictly deferred to her own piety. She had long detected that his ethics were of an intellectual nature and not directed by religion.

She held his gaze, wanting to cry, to hold him again to her, kiss him endlessly, tell him how utterly unworthy she felt. And he seemed to have understood all those things. He even managed a weak smile saying, "Don't be distressed. The rest should take care of itself."

The "rest" meaning Sophie's concern for Franz's health did not live up to his optimism. He ran a consistent fever for a week and coughed by fits and starts. Sophie worried. Something else she would have to tell him threw her into a panic: her imminent departure for a state visit to Hungary with Francis Charles.

When Franz felt strong enough to leave his bed, she still did not find the courage to say anything. Meanwhile, he drew from her untiring attendance the energy to put forced physical idleness to some use by exercising his mental resources. He applied himself to the study of tactical treatises, learning also that he could be frugally happy in his love.

Since his illness, Sophie had gained unrestricted access to his room. At any given moment, he could lift his head from his work at the silken rustle which invariably accompanied her entrance. Her nearness wove about him a sachet-scented gossamer of feminine daintiness and devoted caring. Her presence alone, he felt, invigorated him.

One morning, Sophie found him busy writing at his desk. The sight comforted her and she had to pause to stay a breath-taking surge of love. Then she crossed the room and stood next to his chair to look at his work. None of what she saw made any sense to her. Yet, in spite of her complete ignorance on matters of such nature as equations and formulas, she was impressed.

She suggested, "You certainly know enough about strategy and tactics to write your own book on the subject."

He smiled up at her. How well she knew to put iron into him! "I intend to. I have already filled quantities of notebooks and my ideas can't be bad because Count Dietrichstein finds them absolutely incoherent and mad!"

"I am not surprised."

"Aren't you?"

Sophie said with tender pride, "Your ideas must be of great worth seeing that your *ex-wife* seems quite incapable of comprehending any of them."

Her cryptic reference to Franz's former tutor never ceased to amuse him. Since his adolescence, calling Dietrichstein his *wife* had been their secret code and private joke. The Count's close and well-nigh indissoluble bond with Reichstadt in his tutorial capacity, his well-meaning yet oppressive vigilance, his relentless carping and nagging had earned him the sobriquet.

Franz laughed. To hear the mirthful peal of his voice delighted Sophie. Such sound, she reflected, was not often heard from Reichstadt. Now it warmed her heart. Playfully, she pinched the swells of his cheeks and admired his strong, white teeth. They should be biting into life. . . .

Her worries were over. He was on the way to recovery and in good spirits. She laughed with him. When their gaiety subsided, she hesitated but a second then dared say with convincing lightness, "Upon my return, you may even have completed a rough draft."

Franz blinked. An air of absolute incomprehension settled over his face. In an almost inaudible voice he asked, "Where are you going?"

Briefly she told him. She had obligations and duties. She said visibly upset, "I can't put this off! I have to go!"

Franz's lips compressed in annoyance. He recalled how much he had enjoyed accompanying the Emperor to Hungary on the occasion of Ferdinand's coronation. But now he wished that country to nonexistence. This was puerile, he knew, but he did not care. Nor did he mind spoiling the neatness of his notes.

Morosely, he began drawing doodles in the margin. Soon they spelled Sophie's name. She saw the love scribble take form next to a terribly unromantic phrase: *The impact of an army, like the total of mechanical coefficient, is equal to the mass multiplied by the velocity.*

In his wrought-up state, she would have to be mindful of perilous indulgences. Gingerly, she dropped a consoling hand on his shoulder. At the touch, the pen fell from his fingers and his arms flew around her waist.

He moaned, nuzzling her stomach, "I wish you didn't have to go!"

Sophie drew a long shuddering breath and looked down a Franz's head. He made no further move. This again raised in her mind, by manner of contrast, unwanted recollections of Francis Charles's coarse handling of their marital relations. The contact of Karl's hands and other parts of his body had become even more repulsive to her.

Being in love with Franz had changed her formerly passive and long-suffering attitude toward Charles's assaults. A feeling of debasement overtook her whenever she had to comply with her wifely duties. And her submission to them had borne fruit. For the second time she was pregnant. Three months with child! And in no hurry to disclose her condition to anyone as yet because of Franz.

To her own astonishment, Sophie felt she had been unfaithful to him! In a small, painful concession to this peculiar loyalty, she welcomed their separation. When they would see each other again, her girth would say it all. Perhaps that would be kinder, more sparing. . . .

For the moment, she would subtract nothing from the loving but cautious strokes of her hands on his curly hair. All that she considered praiseworthy and good in this life was there beneath her breasts, preciously weighing against her belly with boyish abandon, and chivalrous restraint! There were so many small liberties Franz could have taken with her under the excuses of uncontrollable passion. Respectful of their compact, he had never tried.

Presently, he lifted toward her wide, anxious eyes. "When will I see you again?"

"In two months, maybe three."

"Three months!"

She placed a soothing finger on his mouth.

"Maybe, Franz. . . ." Then the pain of thinking that someday he would be the one leaving her for good woke again, tearing at her. She blurted out her poor consolation. "This is not so long, compared to the separation of which you have spoken."

Franz stared at her with such sorrow that she repented.

"I am sorry! I did not mean to accuse you of insensitivity!"

"No," he said hoarsely, suddenly remembering that he had been at his harshest with his mother during their stormy confrontation in Baden. "Don't apologize. I can be very cruel sometimes."

Her eyes misted, and her instinct told her she could not be wrong saying, "No, my dearest love. Not you! But life is!"

Franz's forced inactivity and bed rest produced some positive results. He slept better than he ever had to the absolute satisfaction of Malfatti and to the immense relief of Count Dietrichstein who remarked happily on the encouraging progress his former pupil was making toward a full recovery.

"Oh, I am quite cured," Franz assured him, hoping for a relaxation of the doctor's rules.

But Dietrichstein did not quite concur, knowing his former pupil's tendency to presume of his strength. He believed a touch of social gossip might divert Reichstadt's mind from dwelling overlong on his forced inactivity.

"A few gazettes are circulating the rumor of Your Highness's engagement to Archduke Charles's daughter," he said chattily.

Franz gibed at the news, "Without my knowledge? How amusing! That is pure fiction! Besides, I just can't imagine a Duchess of Reichstadt!"

"And why, in heaven's name can't you?"

Franz shrugged. "It sounds so awkward!"

"Nonsense!" Dietrichstein retorted. "Your Highness will eventually marry."

"It's absolutely out of the question now! And I am not interested in being engaged to anyone. I won't be going to any balls either," Franz declared categorically and concluded pointing at his mail. "Those are all invitations you see there. And they are all going to the basket!"

"Your Highness used to be sociable enough, if I recall," remarked the Count with an oblique look.

Franz caught the insinuation. Gustave's sedulous efforts in looking after his sexual "edification" must have caught the ex-tutor's attention. He preferred to ignore the encouragement if that was one, and said meaning every word, "To each season its mood. This year I prefer to keep to myself."

That worried Dietrichstein. He feared the onslaught of a fresh attack of depression. "I don't think such frame of mind is in keeping with Your Highness's age," he said.

Franz made no reply. Walking over to the window he stood there staring down at the courtyard.

Nothing had changed since the day of his early childhood when he had watched with curiosity the activities that went on at all hours. Carriages of all descriptions continued to come and go. The guards posted at the palace's entrances and at the gates saluted. And returning the civility, the windows of the vehicles were raised and lowered a prescribed number of times which were determined by the importance of their occupants. The changing of the sentries took place following a schedule that had been the same for seventeen years. Depending on the time of day, the shadows cast by the surrounding walls stetched or shrunk with the same mathematical precision. And moving in that immutable setting, Franz felt as though he was treading a millwheel. Only one thing would extricate him from the rut into which he was sinking deeper and deeper.

With an urgent inflection he finally said, "I need to go back to my battalion!"

"In good time," Dietrichstein responded cautiously.

Franz swung round not concealing his exasperation. "People must regard me with contempt for I must pass for a cripple or a sissy!"

"Not at all," protested the Count, but he had heard worse unpleasantness to report. The general opinion concerning Reichstadt continued to posit a fundamentally irrecusable situation: Habsburg and Bonaparte cannot mix. Consequently, the result of such a melange could only produce a hodgepodge of cross and counter elements.

Putting it not so bluntly, the former tutor volunteered, "People see Your Highness as a complex personality that cannot be pinned down to specifics."

Franz smirked at the declaration. "Oh, I see! Now I'm passing for a tower of Babel!"

Dietrichstein made a helpless gesture.

Unwittingly, Dietrichstein had rekindled Franz's doubts as to the political validity of his existence. Prokesch, never far to answer a distress call, tried to reassure his friend. In time, he told him, his position would become more and more defined. . . .

In the meantime, Franz thought, one has to contend with the present. And he began to entertain the distinct feeling of being marked for some propitiatory sacrifice. He even saw an indication of this in his daily attire. Was it not remarkable that the uniform he wore sported the sacrificial color white?

Then when he received an invitation to attend a ball given by the French ambassador, he became certain that being a victim was the only significant role he would be called to assume in his life. He went immediately to the Emperor and without explanation asked permission to be excused from going to the ball.

Francis did not appear surprised. His grandson's broken cough following the request revived his remorse for having allowed him to go out on parade in freezing weather.

"I understand," he said. "You are still convalescing."

Franz did not appreciate a permission granted on such grounds. To use his health as a pretext was an unacceptable falsification of a situation too intolerable to conceal. Vehemently he assured his grandfather that he had quite recovered.

"But that cough," Francis objected.

Franz resorted to his favorite explanation. "It's only a tickle, Sire."

"In that case," Francis pointed out, "I am certain you realize the propriety of honoring the French ambassador's invitation."

"On the contrary," Franz countered, "my presence at his ball would be shocking and utterly improper!"

"Shocking?"

"I cannot be a guest to a ball hosted by the representative of a government which is in the process of enacting a decree of banishment against my person."

The Emperor's eyes narrowed. All through the years he had nurtured a persona he had created to ensure the viability of keeping the son of Napoleon at his court, that of *Der Herzog von Reichstadt,* an archduke among the other archdukes. One who should have assimilated his Austrian parentage so totally as to have no qualm attending such an event. He had banked on it.

"I hadn't thought of that," he muttered.

"Well, I have, Sire."

"The Bourbons," Francis said conversationally, not quite knowing how to proceed, "are under fire, too . . . I suppose this business of banishment is bothering you after all, eh?"

"It is better to be disowned than forgotten!" Franz allowed, in meager concession to very little left to concede.

There followed a silence.

Then warily, Francis said, "Is this . . . proscription so important to you, Franz?"

On a wild impulse, Franz decided to assay the Emperor of Austria's understanding of his situation.

"The reason for my proscription is very important to me, Sire. The Bourbon princes are not wanted because they represent the legitimacy the current monarchy in France is lacking. The Bonapartes are also rejected because of their plebeian origins and inclinations."

"You don't belong to the plebes!" Francis retorted with pride.

"Then, I am probably destined to rule?"

"Perhaps," the Emperor conceded, lapsing again into that foible Metternich viewed as Francis's Achilles' heel. "And you must not only rule, but also master the populace with a steady and unflinching disregard for its caprices. Aren't those your inclinations?"

Franz drew a deep breath to fortify himself. He would carry out his resolve to do away with dissimulation. It had leached away the spontaneity he craved and shackled the care-free vital elan his youth demanded. Such dissimulation had not accomplished much of anything so far. Moreover, his frustration had reached a climax, and prudence was cast aside like a useless cloak.

Boldly he said, "I am inclined to respect the sovereignty of the people, Sire."

Francis gave out a gasp as if he had been punched. Reichstadt was defending the common people! He accorded the masses regards reserved only for an elite! Horror! Heresy!

He wailed, "Where in God's name did you acquire such corrupt political principles?"

Eyes flashing, cheeks aglow, Franz said wildly, "From the *Marseillaise!* From a last will and testament! From instinct!"

The Emperor lunged at him and dug his fingers into his arms. The youth must be raving! Fever was perverting his senses!

"You are still very sick and must be out of your mind!" Then he broke down moaning, "Oh, we were getting on so well!"

"Were we?"

Francis nearly wept, "Ah, yes! Yes! Yes!"

Franz remained unmoved. Intent on making a clean breast of things, he said, "You care for a different person."

"No!" Francis protested fiercely, tightening his grip on Franz's arms. "It must be you! There *can be only one* person!"

Wincing under the pain, Franz lashed out with punishing honesty, "You have me caged! Why is that then?"

"I am protecting you, Franz! Against assassination, for one thing! And I can say that I love you more than my own sons! And you find the heart to accuse me of treating you cruelly! Why must it be so unpleasant between us?"

"This is because I love you well enough not to deceive you, even if this means that I must become the object of your detestation!"

"I could never detest you," Francis said breathlessly. He put his arms around his grandson and held him in a tight, desperate embrace saying, "Don't ever think that I could! And forget this conversation ever took place. I command it!"

"I can't forget because you are forcing me to live a lie!"

Francis went into what appeared to be a spasm. Without relaxing his grip he said frantically, "There is no lie! Don't you see? There is only the question of making the right choice! And *I had* to make it for you! It is my sacred duty, Franz!"

Franz grew rigid, frozen in the realization that his own choice would be without appeal. Francis's implacable and fanatical adherence to principles in the conservation of which he saw the only reason for having been put upon this earth would never alter. Nor would the notion that his grandson should embrace them would ever suffer any compromise.

Slowly, he disengaged himself from the Emperor's clutch.

Francis managed to say evenly, "We have digressed from the business at hand."

Franz stared through his grandfather. "What business?"

"That ball at the French Embassy."

"Ah, yes. . . ."

"I leave you free to do as you choose."

It appeared that Franz's choices would continue to be limited to matters that could not leave much of an impact on questions that were of grave importance to him. Declining the French ambassador's invitation did not allay the provocation at being denied recognition and freedom. A freedom that continued to elude him. . . .

Prokesch went on preaching patience, and though Franz's was wearing down to a frazzle, his friend's company kept him hoping nevertheless. Then toward the end of January, the Major received orders from the chancellery to undertake a new assignment that would keep him away from Austria for an indefinite period of time. He said nothing of this to Reichstadt, dreading to upset him. Only three days before he was to take his leave, he finally stammered out the news.

Devastated, Franz collapsed into a chair and put his head between his fists, his body swaying as if in intense pain. Prokesch looked on panic stricken. The magnitude of Reichstadt's desperation corroborated some deep misgivings of his own.

After a long silence, Franz lifted a face completely drained of color. "You know what this means, don't you?" he rasped. "With you gone, I am losing all chance of getting away."

Prokesch could only nod, a deep wrinkle cutting a gash across his brow. The new mission might not be a mere coincidence. Perhaps in the course of a conversation with Gentz, whom he often saw, he might have made an involuntary and costly slip. Gentz was so shrewd, and they were on such friendly and intimate terms that the barrier of caution Prokesch was always careful to raise might have been lowered in the flicker of a passing remark. Gentz might have picked up a clue even though Prokesch always proceeded with utmost prudence whenever they mentioned Reichstadt. Could Gentz have communicated his suspicion to Metternich?

The Major felt utterly miserable. Self-reproach made him say with redoubled determination, "As soon as I arrive in Rome, I will prepare the way for us. I will also call on your grandmother, Franz, and tell her all about you. You can count on me!"

At the mention of Letizia, Franz seemed to revive a little.

"Will you do that, too?"

"Without fail!"

"Tell her, then, that the little boy she left in Blois remembers her, and that I love her. Tell her I am still my father's son despite all rumors to the contrary. That his dying wishes are sacred to me. That I will carry them out!"

"I will, Franz . . . And do take heart!"

Franz tried to smile. It came more as a grimace brought on by the lancing gash of a wound.

On the day which preceded their separation, Prokesch was profoundly disturbed by the resigned melancholy which settled over Reichstadt's demeanor. He often caught the Prince furtively staring at him with an expression of quiet despair, the way a person looks at another knowing that it would be for the last time.

When the dreaded moment came for the Major to take his leave, Franz solemnly placed his sword between his hands. It was not the curved saber Napoleon had used in Egypt. Franz would never part with that relic as long as he lived. Nevertheless, the weapon he was offering had its value. Issued by the imperial armory, he had worn it on the field and his name was engraved on the hilt.

"Take this to remember me by, Anton," he said, barely able to speak.

Prokesch took the sword with trembling hands. "Franz," he protested fervently, "I can't possibly forget you! Ever!"

"Good!" Franz half-choked, and his lips quavered. "I'll try to be patient."

Setting the sword aside with reverential care, Prokesch presented his own parting gift, a *gandoura.*

"I realize how much you are longing to see the world," he said softly, pityingly, too. "Here is a souvenir from faraway places, I brought this back from Egypt. The natives live in this sort of thing. I thought it might please you to have one."

Franz fingered the finely embroidered blouse. "It's beautiful, Anton. The feel of that cloth does make my mind wander. . . ." Then in a passionate outburst, "You don't have to espouse my cause to the extent you are doing! And your sacrifice is worth the world to me!"

"For you, Franz, that wouldn't be giving up too much!" Prokesch said in an all-engulfing surge of desolate devotion.

He had been wondering about Reichstadt's unconditional confidence in him. What manner of reasoning could sustain what might have turned out to be a dangerous and futile gift of trust? At that crucial instant, he felt the urge to probe.

"But surely you must have had many reasons to doubt my sincerity, Franz. Why didn't you? After all, I am Prince Metternich's errand boy."

Franz gave him a long, appreciative look.

"You are much more than his errand boy," he replied quietly.

"In any case," Prokesch pressed on, "shuttling as I do between the two of you might just arouse certain suspicion. Has it not occurred to you that I could be deceiving you under the pretense of friendship?"

"Nothing that despicable can stand between us, Anton!" Franz replied passionately. "There is no guile in you. My instinct told me so the moment I met you. And I can't be mistaken!"

"And the instant I saw you," Prokesch confessed huskily, "I was no longer master of my emotions. You were!"

For a moment they stared at each other. Then Franz tossed the *gandoura* over the back of a chair and they exchanged a brief and fierce hug.

"Will you," Franz asked, "defend the principles I represent whenever my name will be mentioned during the course of your journey?"

"Always!"

A clock chimed.

"I must be going," Prokesch said tonelessly.

Standing erect, Franz blinked away the tears welling up in his eyes. "Good-bye, my friend."

The friend froze. There was such an irrevocable quality in that farewell! Surely, they were going to see each other again soon enough. And there ought to be some parting words not charged with such terrible finality. Words a youth of only twenty should only use.

In a desperate effort to sound even more comforting, Prokesch said those words for him in French, "*A bientôt, Franz.*"

Franz only nodded. He couldn't even smile his appreciation. His throat hurt. In an agony of desolation he shut his eyes. When he opened them he was all alone.

Somewhere in the sumptuous succession of salons that led visitors out of the princely apartments, a door shut on the last audible footfalls. Then there was complete and deafening silence.

Franz rushed to the window and pressed his forehead to the pane, watching and waiting for a last glimpse of the only friend he had, the pounding of his heartbeats drumming in his ears.

In the courtyard below, Prokesch felt the crushing distress of a pair of eyes trained on the back of his head. He turned around before climbing into the waiting coach.

Reichstadt's slim figure with arms spread-eagle in the window-frame met his upward glance. The Prince was in uniform as usual, and catching the slanting rays of the afternoon sun, his tunic was respendently white. Like Dietrichstein, Prokesch imagined seeing a graceful bird, but one beating its wings against the bars of a cage.

He stared at the pathetic apparition until his vision became blurred with tears. Only then, did he remember to wave.

30

These gloomy days of early March had done nothing to improve Franz's mood. With Prokesch and Sophie away, the uninspiring company of his military staff aggravated a feeling of utter abandonment. Among the three men appointed to "guide" him, Captain Baron von Moll, his constant companion, was fairly likable but without substance. General Count Hartmann, acting as Chief of Staff, seldom seen, thought of nothing else but obstruct and thwart any attempt on the part of Reichstadt to deviate from the path of remaining a non-entity. Captain Joseph Standeisky, poorly educated, was too busy spying on the Duke to be conspicuous.

Incapable of concentration, Franz spent hours absently staring out of the window of his apartments at the Hofburg. The rooms he occupied provided no relief from the crushing realization that he was trapped in an inescapable situation from which, alone, he could never extricate himself.

The rich Gobelin tapestries that were gifts from Louis the Fifteenth of France, the costly meteorological instruments set in front of the window embrasures, the bookcases covering large sections of the walls and each piece of furniture, all posited the sterility of the existence he had led so far and the futility of turning away from it.

As his eyes rested on the magnificent silver-gilt cradle in which he had slept as an infant-king, on his father's sword, on a last will and testament he never parted with, he only thought of an ancient and cruel custom which condemned members of a household to perish walled-up in the funerary chamber of their departed master surrounded by earthly possessions forfeited by death. And Franz felt fated to end his insignificant life in the sepulchral shadow of his father's well-entombed legacy.

Indeed, to submit to his fate by deferring to Metternich's dictates placed him in *mortal peril!* For surely he would waste his youth away, languish and die. This would suit Metternich perfectly. Defeat by attrition might well be the Chancellor's intent. The removal of Prokesch must have been the final *coup de grâce*. . .

Franz clenched his fists, galvanized by the thought.

The battles his father had fought, as opposed to his own secret battle against all the powers ranged against him, seemed infinitely more preferable by comparison. Cunning, weapons and troops had been called into action to achieve the intended victories. But what did he have to fight with? Determination! Just plain determination! To go on struggling, hoping, watching for opportunities. And for now, getting out of these rooms!

Resolutely, he went to the bellpull and gave it an energetic tug.

"Cancel dinner. I'm going out!" he said, when Moll entered on his valet's heels.

"But Your Highness has gone riding twice already, today," the Baron objected after a slight hesitation. "It is not wise to overtax yourself for the sake of exercise."

Franz shrugged. He was convinced that if he coddled himself, his mind would fail him long before his body would—an opinion, he knew, was quite contrary to that of the ancient poet Juvenal, who maintained in his *Satires* that a sound mind needs a sound body. Rather, Franz clung to the proposition that in his case, the soundness of his mind hinged essentially on motion, on a vigorous regimen of physical activity. By remaining active he could stamp down self-pity and despondency; conserve his sanity. If he woke up tired and went to bed exhausted, kept vague recollections of having experienced in a half-agitated sleep a heaviness over his chest and queer spasmodic contractions in his legs, and noticed his drawn cheeks and the circles under his eyes, that was a price he was willing to pay. So his strength was diminishing! But paradoxically, it was in that slow process of debilitation that he felt in control, found a way to revitalize the pluck to go on.

"I won't be riding. Just order a carriage," he commanded. And to his valet, "I'll wear my uniform."

Baron von Moll insisted, "Doctor Malfatti must give his approval."

Franz repressed an urge to swear. A tantrum would accomplish nothing, as not much of anything else would. He could never give any orders. And those he gave would only be obeyed if they happened to agree with the directives set down by his keepers.

He only snapped, "Then fetch him, now!"

Confronted with his patient's decision to leave the shelter of a warm room for the inclement outdoors, Malfatti took Franz's pulse and finding nothing irregular in the beat raised no objections. He felt quite sure of having discovered the seat of all the Prince's ailments: a congenitally weak liver and a capricious and nervous stomach. So the doctor watched Reichstadt's progressive thinning and paling with temperate anxiety. Ischl, he'd decided, once the winter over, would set everything right.

In an open carriage, Franz and Baron von Moll drove off in an icy mist through which the setting sun rays shed no comfort. A cold wind blowing from the distant plains of Hungary chilled Moll to the bones. Seated beside him, Franz felt even worse. A dull and gnawing pain had started in his chest.

After riding for sometime, the calash suddenly seemed to be rolling unevenly. Franz felt Moll take hold of his arm and heard him hollering a warning. In a reflex, he leapt out and landed by the roadside on his hands and knees as a wobbling wheel rolled past him. The horses had skidded to a halt, neighing furiously. Moll, already at his side, inquired if he was hurt.

"No," Franz said, but he felt completely drained.

"We lost a wheel. I am afraid we will have to walk."

Franz's head dipped in a shaky assent. He reared on his knees to stand. To his dismay, he discovered he was quite incapable of getting up. At this, the driver who had run up to them, broke out in loud self-reproach, "Holy Mother of God! I am responsible for a broken leg!"

"There isn't any thing wrong with my leg," Franz told him. "Are you hurt? Is anyone?" he asked.

Moll shook his head. The coachman just stared and gaped. He expected imprecations. Normally that would be the sort of response a mishap of this nature would earn him. And to be shown any consideration at all. . . .

There followed a strange scene. Cap in hands, the fellow fell on his knees beside his august passenger in whom he recognized a Habsburg of very special standing. The young archduke was once a king in his own right. Simple folks in Vienna still called him King of Rome when they were certain of not being overheard by the secret police. The coachman had never addressed the winsome Prince whose kindness he wanted to repay in some way.

He made bold to say, "God has spared me from harm so I can carry *Your Majesty* to the palace."

The use of the title made Moll hawk in noisy protest, but to Franz, this miserable accident had redeemed the day.

He said to the coachman with an exhausted smile, "That's very good of you. But that won't be necessary. Just help me up and we shall be on our way."

They had to walk quite a distance. Franz hobbled between the two men with his arms slung across their shoulders. As they neared the palace, his most pressing ambition was to crawl into a warm bed. Once in bed he threw off the cover feeling too hot.

Next morning the fever did not abate and another morbid condition appeared. Franz found he had lost his voice once again and had gone almost completely deaf in his left ear. He was lucid, however. On a gesture mimicking what he wanted, Lambert brought him a sheet of paper and a pencil. Franz wrote: "I can barely hear and I can't talk. Why?"

The valet passed the note to Malfatti who after reading it said shouting a little, "Your Highness is suffering from the effects of an intermittent fever that should clear by the spring equinox."

Meanwhile Franz was again confined to his room.

On the morning of his twenty-first birthday, he dragged himself out of bed to sit in front of the porcelain stove. Wrapped in a blanket and coughing weakly now and then, he only wanted to be left alone. His hearing had improved and his voice had come back, but the fever had not left him. It clouded his head and made him somnolent. Soon, he began to doze when a murmur of voices in the antechamber disturbed him.

Then Moll came into the room to announce that his imperial relatives were here to wish him a happy birthday.

Franz greeted the news with a groan. The people he most longed to see were miles away, even Francis, who had gone to Trieste.

As for his mother. . . .

Since he had been ill, Franz kept receiving from her long letters of an admonitory nature advising compliance with his doctor's orders. She had made no mention of coming to Vienna that summer, let alone undertake a journey ahead of her normal schedule to see him or comfort him. Franz would have so much welcomed her presence! The rest of his Austrian relations meant nothing to him. But he could not be uncivil.

He signaled Moll he would see them.

They entered in a flurry with chamberlains and ladies-in-waiting in tow, all very pompous and conscious of doing something proper and decent. This had been the nature of their relationship with Franz, just perfunctory regards.

Ferdinand, now King of Hungary and duly married, had not emerged from imbecility. Franz felt sorry for him for the throne heir was good-hearted and had even shown occasional flashes of uncanny wisdom. That morning, however, was not one of those times. Ferdi hugged Franz and assured him that he should be feeling better if he were not so ill.

An embarrassed silence greeted that profound deduction. Franz tried to put every one at ease by hugging back the gentle King and thanking him warmly. Blushing, Ferdinand's wife delivered her compliments with a stutter. Archdukes Antony, Charles and Louis followed with glib haste.

Then came Franz Joseph. The little boy tore his hand free from his *aja's* hold, and rushed into Franz's outstretched arms, shouting happily, "Ava!"

Franz looked questioningly at the governess, "Ava?"

The Baroness explained smiling, "That is the name the Prince seems to have especially chosen for Your Highness."

"That's sweet," Franz said, having no idea why the child would call him "Ava."

He pulled Franzi onto his lap and fondly peered at Sophie's son, gently stroking his head. The boy was handsome, taking after his mother, Franz decided. He hugged him and kissed him longingly thinking of Sophie.

As the weeks passed, Dietrichstein reported to Parma that the Prince was having moments of deep depression. Malfatti assured Marie Louise in separate correspondence that her son's depression was nothing more than a reaction caused by a bilious attack that would clear once his patient would have ingested Bad Ischl's curative waters. Then in another letter, the former tutor raised a question which had been bothering him for sometime. Could there be something wrong with the Prince's chest? But by the next post, General Hartmann affirmed with military terseness that His Highness slept better at night.

And to all this, Marie Louis sighed, "Thank heaven!"

Franz gave thanks to a bittersweet surprise that came to him through a piece of mail—a letter forwarded by the chancellery. All letters received through proper channels were opened and read before they would reach him. This one, too, had passed through censorship but he appreciated having the letter because it came from Marchand. At long last he was in possession of a communication that came directly from one of his father's appointed executors!

He read it with intense emotion. Napoleon's faithful valet wrote that for many years he had solicited permission to execute the Emperor's bequest regarding the objects set aside for his son. "My requests having remained unanswered," Marchand candidly wrote, "I am addressing myself directly to Your Imperial Highness with the hope to learn the disposition you wish to make concerning the mementos the Emperor Napoleon had charged me to deliver into your hands."

As Franz read on, the elation he experienced made way to bitter rage. Metternich drove a hard and merciless bargain. The meager consolation Franz derived from receiving Marchand's letter had its price. At the bottom of the page, Metternich had scribbled a note to the effect that Reichstadt was not to expect anything more than the letter itself nor should he contemplate the possibility of replying to Marchand.

Franz's first impulse was to defy Metternich by appealing to Francis. For an instant he fancied the Emperor arguing the Chancellor out of so nefarious a rigor, or just meeting him halfway saying something like, "Keep the messenger away, but at least let my grandson come into the possession of a very small inheritance. I command it!"

Francis commanding Metternich? After a moment of reflection, Franz decided: No! It would be more realistic to envision the Emperor conveniently timid and petrified in antiquated notions of statesmanship. He would try to pacify his grandson by expounding political maxims with a flavor of his own, hedge, cajole, commiserate, but do absolutely nothing!

It was best to put the letter away and simply treasure it for what it was meant to accomplish. Only Marchand would never know of his late master's son's intolerable frustration and searing regret for not being able to write to him and say: "I have received your letter. I revere its intent!"

And Franz wanted to shout to the world: "I hear you! Do not misconstrue my silence! Do not turn away from me! Do not give me up for lost! Do not consign me to oblivion!"

Though burning with fever, he felt chilled by a terrifying and inescapable certitude. He was being sealed in complete isolation! This was the plan Metternich had devised for him, but that was not all. The failings of his constitution would serve that plan to perfection. He'd heard that General Kutschera even began suggesting that a military career might be too strenuous for him. With that insinuation, it would not be long before he would be treated like an invalid and *turned into a recluse* for the rest of his life!

This possibility so devastated him, that several times he caught himself staring at the silver-gilt cradle in the corner of his bedroom, thinking, *I am nothing but an encumbrance. . . . I should have died in infancy!*

On the first day of April, Dietrichstein said to Malfatti: "What the Prince needs is absolute bed rest instead of being up and about and going to the theater at night."

The doctor gestured impatiently. "Try to tell him that!"

Elaborating on his own observations, the Count continued unruffled. "The less the Prince moves, the less he coughs. I have noticed this repeatedly. But as soon as he is astir, rises from a chair, or goes down or up the stairs, he coughs and coughs. Last night, I heard him hacking away until two in the morning! I really fear he is getting worse."

Malfatti's ill-humor deepened. Dietrichstein did him no favor by pointing to the Prince's present condition. Reichstadt's birthday which, closely enough, coincided with the spring equinox had not brought about the improvement predicted by the physician.

He retorted shortly, "His Highness is not getting as well as he should because he won't stay still! But he just won't listen, and I can't tie him to his bed!"

"On the other hand," argued the Count, "have you not, just recently, urged him to lead a normal life? Isn't this encouraging him to commit the same excesses you forbid? Knowing as you do, how active he *normally* is?"

Cornered, Malfatti countered, "My observations are that His Highness, for some inexplicable reason, seems intent on punishing his body. He flouts my advice and does exactly as he pleases! In any case, I have welcomed the Emperor's suggestion to call two other colleagues in consultation."

Franz submitted to the examination with detachment. He staked his recuperative power on his youth, but the doctors did not have to debate overlong to arrive at a prognosis. It was grim, and of course, withheld from the patient. Malfatti's contention to have found a marked improvement in the condition of the Prince's liver, an improvement he affirmed having actually ascertained by touch, was given the go-by while mention of dire portent such as "abscess in the lungs" was murmured accompanied with grave nods.

Then Doctor Weihrer took a graver decision.

"The Prince," he said, "needs a warmer climate."

Not mincing his words Doctor Reiman injected, "His Highness must be sent to Naples before it is too late."

There followed a long pause. Deitrichstein paled. Moll heaved a deep sigh. Hartmann cleared his throat and announced with an official tone, "Gentlemen, I shall inform Prince Metternich of your suggestions at once."

Metternich had long learned the potency of time. In Reichstadt's case, a delayed decision was the only acceptable alternative. He could not afford to be hasty where it concerned Napoleon's son. Too much was at stake. He must be careful. A prompt assent to the doctors' recommendations might trigger a political disaster of monumental proportion should the Duke recover while convalescing in Italy. Then Metternich would be responsible for opening a Pandora's box from which would issue a calamity he could never repair. The idea of Reichstadt stretched out on a *chaise longue* under the warm, benevolent sun of Naples and growing stronger, conjured up visions of doom. Metternich saw the whole Italian peninsula in an uproar, clamoring for freedom and shaking off Austrian domination with armed insurrections while the multitude would be acclaiming Reichstadt as their liberator!

On the other hand, not to give scandal, he must present a compassionate front. He must also go to the bottom of things. How ill was Reichstadt? Hartmann had related the visiting doctors' findings. Metternich would not leave it just at that.

He sent for Malfatti wanting to sound out the Duke's personal physician. He began with circumspection. "Does the Prince cough much?"

"Only when he is active," Malfatti replied, willy-nilly concurring with Dietrichstein's observations.

"Fever?"

"Quite permanent at this stage, I regret to say, Excellency."

"Expectorations?"

"Some."

"And what do you make of those?"

A blank look greeted that query. "His Highness spits in a handkerchief . . . which I never handle."

Metternich's eyes narrowed. "You have not examined the Duke's spittles?"

"No, Excellency."

Metternich was astounded. Incredible! He was no doctor; yet as a layman, he was keenly aware of the existence of a baneful illness which reigned rampant and unchallenged by medical science in this fine century of progress. He had lost his first wife, Eleanore, and four of his children to its devastating sway. With such a prevalent illness one could hardly overlook investigating symptomatic evidences. Was Malfatti this blind? And if so, it would be wise to lay all responsibilities upon his shoulders.

"Then what *can* you tell me about the Duke's condition? About these coughing fits, for instance?"

Malfatti hurriedly replied spilling out his most profound convictions. "They are caused by changes of body temperature which the Prince's unrelenting activity keeps in a state of continual fluctuation."

Of course that told Metternich nothing. He gave Malfatti a long, calculating look. The physician's self-assured attitude and apparent determination to shut his eyes to disorders which pointed rather clearly to tuberculosis suited him perfectly. He would not press him to sound an alarm that might reverberate as far as Parma. Marie Louise might demand that her son be sent to Italy.

If she did, Metternich would have to comply because a mother pleading for her child's life would so stir public opinion that a refusal would cause enough of a scandal to ruin Metternich's position and credit. Never was he in such fear of Marie Louise's play on her maternal instincts to force his hand. For they might surface, and he would be a fool to discount that possibility.

"We shall endeavor to do everything possible for the Duke. Do tell His Highness's mother not to give way to anxiety."

"That is precisely the course I have followed, Excellency," Malfatti said smugly, savoring the satisfaction of being taken seriously for once.

Suppressing a contemptuous smile, Metternich chose to heave a sigh instead. The doctor was unbelievably inept. Yet the Chancellor suffered no pangs of conscience. He did not wish Reichstadt's death. Only that he be cured, if he could be cured at all, in Vienna, and as always, under close observation.

"I pray you to continue on that course," he said. "And let us hope for the best."

The best, Metternich knew, would have been to spare Reichstadt the rigor of the local climate. It was considered baneful for tuberculars, and Metternich had even sent his sick wife to Paris hoping to save her. But concerning Reichstadt this was absolutely out of the question, as it would be just as unthinkable to allow him go to Naples.

One thing kept Metternich from considering himself a cold, heartless executioner. In spite of the change of air, his wife Eleanore had not recovered while in France, and Reichstadt might not recover either by going to Italy. So Metternich felt his conscience was clear. . . .

"So, I shall be going to Italy?" Franz asked Moll.

The question startled the Baron though he had been expecting it.

All Vienna was talking about a journey that Metternich had been careful not to mention. But the solution to the Prince's health problems was so readily available that doctors seldom kept mum when they could think of a cure. So Reichstadt, who had been dragging himself about with anemic distinction, must have heard the rumor and taken it seriously.

"So it seems, Monseigneur," Moll replied on his guard.

"And when might this be?" prompted Franz.

"When Your Highness feels strong enough to travel, no doubt," the Baron hedged as no confirmation for the journey had yet been issued.

"I feel strong enough to go out every day," Franz suggested, envisaging all the advantages such a trip could offer. More than a curative expedition, Italy meant a run for freedom. Once there, with Prokesch's helpful presence, he could manage with good planning and an equal dose of luck to abscond from his keepers and never return to Austria. Falling sick was a blessing in disguise. . . .

Moll hesitated. Reichstadt's assurance of regaining his strength was debatable. He had seen the Prince break into a cold sweat at the least physical effort. So he said prudently, "That is for the doctors to decide."

Then he added cheerfully, "A period of rest at Schönbrunn will certainly do much to ready Your Highness for the journey."

Curiously, rest was constantly mentioned, but never stringently imposed. In that respect, there seemed to have been a complete breakdown in authority from the part of those in charge of Reichstadt's welfare. And not helping matters, Franz continued to live in such fear of being overcome with melancholy by taking to his bed that he did not care if his vital forces kept diminishing at a rate only Dietrichstein found alarming.

By mid-April, Franz woke up so tired one morning that he could not will himself to his feet. At noon, he felt asleep again.

Precisely at noon that same day, Sophie and Karl's traveling carriage pulled up in the courtyard of the Hofburg. Immediately she inquired about Reichstadt. Upon learning of his relapse, she addressed Malfatti with a taunt, "The Prince's current condition is your responsibility. Why has he not followed your directives? Or aren't you giving any?"

Malfatti broke into vehement protestations. He gave Sophie a long dissertation on the nature of Napoleon's last illness, drew analogies and concluded that in both cases, the liver was at fault. All other disorders, he declared, were related to that particular organ's malfunction. Moreover, he had had to contend with an extremely difficult patient.

As a concession, Malfatti mentioned the journey to Italy and confessed that so far, no permission had been given to proceed.

Sophie listened anguished and enraged. Who had ever heard that coughing was produced by a diseased liver?

She curtly dismissed Malfatti and turned toward the window to look sorrowfully at a glorious spring day.

Spring, so relentlessly vital with its proliferation of blossoms, sweet scented breezes vibrant with bird songs! Spring with all the promises it held as the season of becoming, of vigorous straining toward fulfillment whose force she even carried in her womb!

She looked down at her belly. She was visibly gone with child now, with a new life quickening within her. She closed her private ode to the loveliest time of the year with a silent lament: Why wasn't spring equally benevolent and generous to another young life barely on the threshold of adulthood? A young life in grave peril! And not much was being done to save it!

Metternich and Malfatti were evil! The first because of heartless calculation, the second because of total incompetence!

Then she had an appalling revelation: *I am injurious, too. I am about to confront Franz with . . . this!*

The prospect disheartened her. She could not dissociate the happy occasion of her reunion with Franz from the grotesque and painful element of surprise she would be forcing upon him; for her virtue had its incongruity and the comfort she was about to bring carried its own malignancy.

Seemingly out of harm's way, Franz slept on as Sophie quietly dismissed Moll and took his place by the bedside. She could not take her eyes off him. Blindly, she felt for the chair the Baron had just vacated, wondering if she should give up hope of ever seeing him well again. When she had left him he'd been ill, yet she thought, on his way to recovering. But now this! . . . A sinister pattern had returned.

Franz lay propped in a near sitting position on four tiers of pillows. His hair, longer than he ordinarily kept it, was mussed and stringy. He had thinned considerably. Shadows filled the hollows of his cheeks and temples and his once glowing complexion was sallow.

Sophie was aghast. Then it occurred to her that if one should waste away at all, it could also be from desperation and loneliness. With laudable perspicacity Dietrichstein had said to her before she came to see Franz, "Major von Osten's departure for Italy has deeply depressed His Highness who has been moping ever since and getting worse at the same time."

How right the Count was! Franz's appearance mirrored more than the havoc brought on by illness—it bore the stigma of betrayed needs and unrealized hopes. Sophie regarded her own absence as a desertion. She, too, must have driven him to this lamentable state, and by more than going away. . . .

Was this any way to love him?

Franz stirred.

Sophie froze, watching with trepidation his slow return to wakefulness. He stretched one arm toward the edge of the bed and turned his head toward her. Then his lids fluttered and his eyes opened to stare straight into hers.

Sophie forced herself to smile as naturally as if she had only left him for a few hours.

He continued to stare at her, a glimmer of joy slowly dawning in his eyes. Then, as they suddenly glittered with tears that began to spill over, he covered his face with his hands.

But to Sophie he was laying bare the breadth and depth of a devastation which completely overwhelmed her. She struggled to remain calm and dispensing with the futility of consoling words, clumsily sat herself on the edge of the bed and gently pried his hands apart. Then holding his dear face between her palms, she kissed him on the lips with a blissful sense of release. The salt she tasted on them sanctified the passion with which he responded as he threw his arms around her and clasped her to him with the fierceness of a drowning man.

His lips, soft and warm under hers were unrelenting in their demand until she gently pull away. But their gazes remained locked. And in a silence charged with wrenching perception, hers was bemoaning, Dearest, you were getting on well enough when I left. How could this have happened to you?

Franz's acknowledged the inescapable servitude of her lot as he had by now noticed that she was big with child. And though he felt an upsurge of acute, pitying distaste, it wasn't directed at Sophie. The state in which he found her in the passage that night sadly corroborated Karl's vicious and tasteless boasting of the way he handled her, and this had given him an insightful understanding of her own private torment.

He only deplored the cruelty of their fate and harbored no bitterness in seeing her present condition. The wonderful years they had shared together yielded the consolation of cherished memories which were, like in a marriage, exclusively theirs to recall. He found solace drifting back to the heart-warming past she had given him. . . .

When he was sixteen, she had visited him in his chamber and he had felt her lips with the tips of his fingers, touching off a sentiment he had not quite understood then. But it was then, he knew it now, that he had fallen in love with her. He knew this with unavoidable clarity. That was *when* it happened!

It was love, fully recognized in that special moment which had worked its gentle wonders and transformed his emotions. And now, love with all its peculiar strains of passion and compassion presently directed his hand to reach for her belly and cautiously feel its curve.

Franz's first words to the woman he could not lawfully love, were said in a low caring murmur, "How are you both?"

Sophie continued to gaze at him adoringly. A voice in her head cried, "*This child should have been ours!*" Then in a trance of excruciating regret, she looked down at the sinewy elegance of his fingers splayed over her stomach in a gesture she likened to a connubial caress.

"We are doing very well," she managed to gasp as he removed his hand.

He smiled wistfully. "I am very happy!"

Suddenly, she felt clear contempt for herself. "Franz," she pleaded, her voice trembling, "don't be so kind to me."

"I love you," he replied simply.

The adoring expression in Sophie's eyes intensified.

"Darling," she asked humbly, "have I given you any happiness? Have I really?"

His blue eyes held hers unblinking. In their limpidity she could see that he was struggling his way out of thinking that he had been cheated in every possible way—in his rights, ambition, his love.

And he just as plainly read in the sweet, loving and tormented expression on her face, a penitential intent to renew an intoxicating moment. "You always have," he murmured lifting his head from the pillow as she met him half way. "And you are now," he whispered against her lips.

He took them gently and long until the breath ran out of them both. Then he said, "Please, don't leave me."

"I won't," she responded with somber fervor.

Just then, a knock at the door intruded on their tender moment. Sophie returned to her chair and reluctantly, gave permission to enter.

Malfatti came in with Moll at a few steps behind.

Sophie scowled at the doctor. "I have not sent for anyone. I demand a reason for this interruption!"

"It's time for His Highness to take his potion," Malfatti replied.

"And what if the Prince were still sleeping, as you knew he was when I came in?" Her tone intimated that he should be minding her, and that she would be assuming an important part in the caring for his patient. "Would you have disturbed His Highness, nevertheless?"

"The medicine cannot wait once it is prepared, or it will lose its potency," Malfatti said with asperity.

Sophie glared at him. "Sleep," she retorted, "is a very potent remedy in itself. So I suggest you consider the possibility of throwing away your concoction when the time of its preparation does not coincide with your patient's awakening, and start a new batch at the proper moment."

The doctor made no reply. But by his air, one would have sworn that Malfatti was about to announce his resignation right then and there. Sophie wished that he would. Why one specializing in obstetrics had been assigned to Reichstadt defied all logic!

She turned her attention to Moll, who stood impassive, carrying a tray upon which were set a vial, a glass and a pitcher.

Graciously, she questioned him on the dosage to be given.

"The content of this vial mixed with water," Moll told her.

"I shall see that the Prince takes this," Sophie said in a tone that signaled a dismissal.

During the interlude, Franz had not cared to say anything. Sophie's nearness, her calm and efficient handling of the whole matter put a balm on his miseries. Life had accorded him little emotional satisfactions, and as in the case of those who have known severe wants, he was more keenly appreciative of modest gains.

He considered himself generously favored. The evanescent feel of her kisses could be renewed. Love, now, was so wonderfully tangible!

Once they were alone again she asked him gravely, "Have they been looking after you sensibly?"

"Only you, can."

She had hoped he could enlighten her as to the exact condition of his health.

"Franz, please tell me the truth! How do you feel?"

He said with serenity, "Never so well!"

He was not truthful nor very helpful. She scolded with a gentleness a mother would use with her child.

"I heard you have been naughty and unmindful of the doctor's orders."

"I won't be naughty with you."

That roused her into immediate action. "Then you have to take your medicine, and now."

With rapt concentration he watched her mix the potion.

He said with a childish anxiety, "I wonder if it's the one that is so terribly bitter."

Sophie directed at him a dewy stare. Happy memories crossed her mind, and they became more precious and sad at the sight of him stretched out in the white of rumpled sheets, looking weak and helpless.

She recalled seeing him in uniform, taking a parade, drilling his companies with dynamic efficiency. She remembered how intensely he spoke of becoming a fine soldier, how eagerly he welcomed hardship and how impatiently he longed to test his mettle in combat.

And here he was, dreading the bitter taste of a remedy!

Oh, how she loved him!

She said, matter-of-factly. "We shall see," and took a sip. Immediately she felt nauseated and her involuntary grimace was eloquent.

Franz broke into a soft laughter. "That's the one!"

"Do you have to take this often?" she managed to ask, nearly gagging.

"N . . . no," Franz said with an innocent air.

But the slight hesitation brought on Sophie's face a loving look of suspicion.

Immediately he confessed. "I spill most of it wherever I can. In a vase, the stove." Then with disarming honesty, "But that was before you came back to me. . . ." He held out his hand to take the glass. "I won't do it again, I promise!"

Sophie tried to appear stern, but love suffused her face with such a benevolent radiance that the effort was lost. Holding the glass under her chin, she said, "Wait." Then leaning over, she gently touched her lips to his, wishing that the kiss would lessen the bitterness of the medicine.

"That's for being honest," she smiled, drawing away, and gave him the potion.

"And this," he solemnly returned raising the glass as in a toast, "is for the love of you!" Then keeping his eyes on her, he slowly drained it, unflinching, to the last drop.

For the love of Sophie, Franz became a docile patient. She scarcely left him and made every effort to entice him to rest. But as April drew to a close, there was no marked improvement to record. Sophie hid her concerns under a cheerful exterior, and Franz kept believing in his own recuperative ability. Nothing could alter this conviction.

Not even the discovery one night, of a peculiar metallic tasting fluid filling his mouth after a coughing fit had shaken him to wakefulness. He spat it out in a handkerchief and by the night candle left burning by his bed, saw that it was blood. He thought, Must be my throat, raw from coughing so much. . . .

Metternich regularly wrote to the Emperor in a style that was concise, cool-headed, and designed to inform Francis of Reichstadt's state of health without alarming him. As a get-well present and hoping to cheer his beloved grandson, Francis promoted Franz honorary colonel of the regiment Gustave Wasa.

By now, Franz could barely hold a pen to thank his grandfather. At the same time, servants reported to Malfatti that the Prince spat blood.

On May 22, Malfatti decided to move his patient to Schönbrunn.

On the afternoon of Franz's departure, Sophie found him standing in front of the window overlooking the courtyard. The changing of the guards, then in progress, still exerted on him its old fascination. The sight of the men in uniform also exacerbated his impatience to recover soon.

Sophie briefly stopped and quietly stood in the doorway sadly admiring his elegant silhouette against the glare of a bright spring sky. But to see him in full skirted double breasted overcoat was distressingly unfamiliar now. He had grown so thin that he seemed to be floating in borrowed clothes.

Then she entered; and when he turned round, she rushed into his arms pressing her face against his chest.

Bending his head, he let his lips brush across her cheek, down her neck, and behind the shell of her ear. The tangible, and so longed for boon of holding her and kissing her was addictive. Now the mere idea of going to Schönbrunn only a few hours away from the capital, but without her, elicited a passionate wish.

"If only you could come with me!"

Sophie lifted her face and gazing at Franz's wasted handsomeness wished this ardently, too. Having just come back from a long and tiring trip, she had decided not to join the Court still in Trieste. Her pregnancy, with all of its accompanying discomfort, prevented her from subjecting herself to the fatigue of another journey. Nevertheless, this was not the principal reason for her reluctance. Franz was. He was ill and unhappily separated from his best friend, and quite alone in the midst of hired help. She would not abandon him. Where he remained she would also be.

But as in the past, the moving of a princely household still adhered to a time-table which did not coincide with Franz's unscheduled departure. He was leaving a month early, and she would not be joining him until mid-June.

This delay worried her as she recalled what had happened while she had been away.

"Still, you will get along until I come, won't you?" she asked anxiously.

"How could I?" he said softly with a lost-to-love look, tracing the contour of her upturned face with his finger.

Yes, you can, she thought, forcing her hopes as high as her opinion of Malfatti's professional ability was low. The doctor's flagrant, crass, and baneful incompetence impaled her with desperation. Short of removing the physician, which was not at her command, she promised herself to demand another consultation by two other reputable doctors as soon as Franz would have settled down at Schönbrunn. If at long last Malfatti could be forced to admit the terrible truth about his patient's condition, the choice of his remedies might, hopefully, prove more efficacious.

For what Franz had tried to conceal in his handkerchief was no longer a secret. All Vienna knew. . . .

Impetuously, she reached up to hold his face between her hands and breathed against his mouth a tender, fearful admonition before kissing it, "Please, don't talk like that!"

Franz murmured contritely when he could speak, "I didn't mean to worry you. But I can't bear being away from you. You are spoiling me so!"

Oh, God! she thought, disparaging her own virtue, *You are a saint!* Tears came to her eyes. She blinked them away and put all the fervor she no longer experienced in prayers in the most damning of all offerings. "Franz, I'll do anything for you!"

31

Franz arrived at Schönbrunn with a sun shining brightly in a sky corrosively blue. Even though the trip from Vienna to the summer palace had been short, he felt tired. His strides were no longer supple and brisk, and his breath eluded him at every step he took.

Overcome with pity Moll watched him trudge in the direction of his usual quarters and in his distraction, the Baron allowed him to go a little way before remembering that a slight change had taken place.

"I am sorry, Monseigneur," he apologized, "not that way. This way, please. Your Highness will be staying in the Archduchess Sophie's suite as yours is presently being repaired."

Franz came to a vacillating halt. "Those rooms," he remarked with more excitement than he would have cared to display, "were once occupied by my father!"

Encouraged by the positive reaction, Moll volunteered, "I've also taken the liberty to have your cradle sent along with your baggage."

Franz looked at him wide-eyed. "And why would you do that?"

"Since the Archduchess has given up those rooms for Your Highness's comfort, I thought bringing the cradle would be a . . . pleasant addition."

Franz appreciated the Baron's intention; and though he welcomed the idea of spending his sick days in the apartments Napoleon had once occupied long before his birth, the fact of having the testimonial of his own hapless coming into this world also included in the move, once again made him ponder the irony that seemed to dog him at every turn. To be surrounded by memories of faded glory—ill and isolated as he was—when he had no prospect of reaching out to any of his own, was another reality whose bitter dregs he had to swallow. But he made a point to thank Moll.

Coming half way down the corridor, they met General Hartmann who had preceded them at Schönbrunn to tend to some last details before the Prince's arrival. Moll let the General escort Reichstadt to his apartments.

"The rooms," the General said conversationally, "are sunnier than those Your Highness used to occupy."

Franz only nodded. What could he possibly share with Hartmann? Certainly not what was going through his mind.

He thought of a certain sun. A radiant sun, it was said, had presided over one of Napoleon's most brilliant battles, the battle of Austerlitz. Franz could recall every move which had led to the celebrated victory. In his mind's eye he could see through the lifting of an early morning wintry mist, Murat's glittering cavalry galloping in a thunder of hooves to cut down the Russian left. Meanwhile, Soult and Lannes were scaling the heights of the Pratzen to drive their center in retreat. Then Davout crushed their right in the icy marches between Telnitz and Sokolnitz. Franz's heart began to beat furiously. A glorious din rang in his ears and his nostrils filled with the acrid and stinging odor of gun powder.

Forward! To victory!

"Here we are," Hartmann announced, opening the double gilded doors in front of which they had stopped.

Glitter. Order. Silence. A sumptuous quietude leapt at Franz as they entered a gorgeous salon, the *Salon des Laques,* which, reflecting the fad of the time for *chinoiseries,* featured black lacquer inlaid with shimmering gilding, hence its name. Napoleon had used this room as a study as well as a war room, and Franz now imagined seeing his father pace the floor and hearing him issue orders and dictate dispatches in a sonorous and commanding voice.

He also heard himself cough.

Hartmann turned to express obsequious concerns. Franz waved him on impatiently and followed the General into the bedroom. It did not have the somber opulence of the *Salon des Laques.* The high ceilings were white and gold and light poured generously through the tall windows that looked across multicolored flower beds and on to the distant *Gloriette.*

A rich tapestry depicting the progress of Austrian cavalrymen across a mellow Italian countryside lined the wall against which, in a corner and facing the windows, was placed a massive rococo bed.

Franz ran a finger over the ornate footboard. "I suppose," he said giving in to a sudden, impish urge to annoy the General, "the Emperor Napoleon must have found this bed comfortable."

Hartmann eyed him warily. His left lid began to twitch. He said with military imperturbability, "Your Highness's father was known to prefer his own camp bed upon which he always slept no matter how adequate the accommodations at his disposal were."

"I want a camp bed also," Franz said. That was an aside. He had not yet finished with the General.

Slowly he walked around the room, hands clasped behind his back much like his father did, and continued as in a reverie, "So, my father slept here in 1805. Ah, Lord! What a magnificent year that was!"

"Magnificent?" objected Hartmann, his expression wooden.

Franz pretended not to notice. "Then in 1809," he went on, "my father stayed here again. That was the year of Wagram. I have visited Wagram when I was studying map-making. What a place! A vast plain, still brooding and still remembering the rumble of cannonade banging victory away!"

"Victory?" the General complained, half-choking.

"And what a windfall afterward!" Franz responded planting himself in front of the window, his back turned to Hartmann. "Lost: Salsburg! Berchtesgaden! The Innviertel! Half of the Hausrückviertel! West Galica, and a portion of East Galicia! All the lands beyond the Save! Thirty-two thousand square miles in all, and over three million people were taken away from His Majesty by the Little Corporal! With a bang and the scratch of a pen!"

Hartmann had turned beet red when another coughing fit interrupted Reichstadt's enthusiastic tirade and saved the General from having to decide what to do about it.

Franz clutched at his side and from his chest came a dreadful bellowing sound. Hartmann snatched a pitcher placed on the night stand and poured some water into a glass. Such a senseless outburst! he thought. And on whose side was he?

He said stiffly holding out the glass, "Drink. Your Highness must be tired from the journey. I shall send for the camp bed immediately."

As it turned out, Franz spent very little time in bed. No one saw to it. Malfatti continued to fumble lamentably for a cure. Instead of concentrating on a regimen of bed rest and substantial nourishment, he allowed his patient to go riding to the Kaninchenberg to drink cow milk and the milk from an ass which the doctor considered more regenerative than a solid and well-balanced diet.

The visit of two eminent physicians whom Sophie—faithful to the promise she had made to herself—had dispatched to Schönbrunn did not result in good news. Their findings were grimmer than ever.

"If the Prince holds out till autumn," Doctor Vivanot said, "he will have to winter in Italy."

"He might not even last until autumn," Doctor Turkheim injected.

Malfatti flew into a passion. He argued hotly, "The Prince's condition, I tell you, is not all that hopeless!"

Both doctors walked away shaking their heads.

Franz conceded nothing and accepted the sparing words that were spoken to him. Those who saw him were amazed that he could still be up and about.

One afternoon, as Franz clambered into his carriage, Moll watched him with a sense of impending disaster. But the Baron minded his tongue, knowing that if he as much as proposed to postpone the outing he would be provoking a heated counter proposal which in Reichstadt's state would most likely lead to a terrible coughing fit as this invariably happened when he grew excited, talked too much and too fast. So Moll only asked if they would be going to that fashionable inn *The Staehl Rouge*.

Franz shook his head. The inn no longer appealed to him. The last time he had gone there to peaceably drink an egg-flip, he had been the focus of pitying looks. He knew himself to be gaunt and felt unsightly enough without everybody staring in his direction.

"To the woods," he said hoarsely. "Haimlack!"

It was still early June and spring lingered in the Vienna Woods. They had enthralled and inspired Beethoven, and ambling under a lacy canopy of rustling foliage lanced with sunbeams, Franz also felt inspired and invigorated by the vernal exuberance of the lush undergrowth that surrounded him. Nature's rebirth was at its most vigorous stage. His own existence had barely commenced, its own spring still unspent. He should be looking ahead. . . .

But at less than fifteen paces from the coach, he had to stop and sit on a stump. Moll came to stand dutifully beside him.

"Moll," he asked after catching his breath, "what do you think of children?"

The Baron cleared his throat. "Err . . . they are nice," he ventured, completely taken by surprise.

Franz felt talkative and Baron von Moll was the only interloctuor he could find. By default, Moll was the nearest person to being a passable companion and he could show compassion.

Franz continued, "If I ever have any children, I'll raise them lovingly and correctly. I'll even establish a school they will attend. This will enable them to learn and grow up with companions of their age. I did not have that opportunity, and that is why I consider my education a failure."

"It is indeed sad to grow up alone," Moll conceded.

With complete abandon, Franz rejoined, "Terrible! I don't believe I ever recovered."

The Baron commiserated in silence. He could not remain indifferent to the Prince's isolation, nor was he callous to his physical sufferings. He had already seen a great deal of it. He even kept a diary in which he recorded the ups and downs of Reichstadt's temperature, the frequency of the paroxysms, and the composition of the spittles. And unless there could be some improvement, the details he would have to consign further to paper would not be for the squeamish to read.

Moll felt compelled to say, "You are still very young, Monseigneur. At your age, life is a constant recovering."

"Do you think so?"

This was not a question. Moll could tell by the offering tone of Reichstadt's voice that he had tended his trust in a humble and desperate cry for help. He needed comforting.

Moved, and foregoing all prudence, as nothing yet had been settled on the subject, Moll said, "Your Highness will be in fine fettle after a few months spent in Naples."

Franz sighed. "We have not received permission to go, Moll."

"It should not be very long before this permission is granted."

Moll had gone out on a limb, intent on being kind. Besides, he felt certain that this affirmation, though unfounded, would nurse an illusion that was no more than a dilatory move, which could serve Reichstadt better than the truth. Later, he would remember taking such liberty with great uneasiness.

But Baron von Moll meant well. Presently, and not without concern, he noticed a large bank of gray clouds creeping up overhead and quickly masking the sun. The woods instantly darkened and the air cooled down to a chill.

"I think we should be going," he urged.

Franz pulled out his watch. Only half-past two! A long and empty afternoon lay ahead, which he did not relish spending at Schönbrunn in the grating company of Hartmann and Standeiski.

"Let us go to Laxemburg," he proposed.

At ten miles from Vienna, on the road to Hungary, Schloss Laxemburg stood in the middle of a park laid out English-style which left nature free to landscape the grounds its own way. Hares and roe deers roamed in liberty, nightingales and orioles populated vast expanses of splendid timber and plump water fowls nested in the willowy reeds that hemmed the shores of a placid lake.

When Franz stepped into the castle's baroque hall, the guards on duty were absorbed in a game of backgammon. They snapped to their feet at his unexpected entrance.

Immediately Franz put them at ease, wanted to know their names, and soon began to chat amicably with them.

While he talked, melancholy observations crossed his mind. Those people had friends they could call on, a caring family and a home to go back to. They lived a normal and ordinary life. But my life, he thought, *is not even ordinary* to be normal!

He tarried. Any form of distraction was a boon. He had nothing to return to but a palatial jail and loneliness. He'd been caged, betrayed by history, by his health, and abandoned by his own mother!

Moll kept glancing out the window. The menacing clouds that seemed to have followed them were now reaching Cyclopean proportions. He began to worry all the more. A severe storm was in the offing. For the second time he urged that they go. Finally Franz consented to leave, but only after repeated entreaties.

Once they were in the carriage, the Baron's anxiety worsened. The air wafted with the unmistakable smell of rain and rolls of thunder with accompanying flashes of lightning were frightening the horses.

"Drive as fast as you can!" he told the coachman.

But the storm outstripped the horses' gallop. Suddenly the black, sagging clouds racing above them opened. Moll swore under his breath. There would be those who would not pass lightly over the improvidence of taking a sick man out in a carriage. Even with the top up, a torrential rain driven by gusts of wind was lashing out at them.

Franz stifled a moan as a skewing pain began to jab at his back. He shivered so violently that Moll had to lock both his arms around him to still the frightful spasms.

Had Malfatti not thought that stopping his ears would be unseemly for a grown man in his position and capacity, he would have plugged them with his fingers. He would have run out of the room as well.

From the *Salon des Laques* where he had just taken refuge, his patient's cough could still be heard. It was a sound the physician found unbearable. It had devolved on Moll to take charge of the distasteful details attending such paroxysms, and though this certainly required no particular skill, it made a terrible demand upon one's nerves. Malfatti's were much too shattered to even consider remaining in the sick room. He had retreated to the antechamber, and there, Mons Malfatti of Montereggio, far from doubting his abilities, decided that not even the most skilled of physicians could be right all the time.

This saving reflection coincided with a sudden dead hush which, contrary to the doctor's anticipation, unnerved him even more. He shot a glance in the direction of the bedroom and saw Moll coming out drying his hands on a towel.

Baron von Moll's face was ashen and hollowed out with fatigue, having slept fitfully while Reichstadt had passed the night enduring martyrdom. . . . Still was. Malfatti took cursory notice of the Baron's haggard appearance. It was the towel that captured his complete attention.

"How much?" he asked impatiently.

Moll gave him a churlish look. He was disenchanted. Playing nurse was something he never imagined he would have to do upon joining Reichstadt's military household. That was a depressing and distasteful duty. He began to have second thoughts on the validity of the prevalent belief that women have less pluck than men. Seeing that nursing was within the province of women, he understood now that this took a special kind of stoutheartedness to minister to the sick, especially after what he had just gone through.

"How much?" Malfatti repeated, irritation putting an unpleasant sting to his tone.

That irked Moll, whose opinion of the physician had sunk to its lowest. Somehow it gratified him to be blunt.

"Too much!" he answered. "At least a good cupful. My hands got a spattering of it, and there was also pus."

Malfatti could not suppress a grimace. Was he, Moll wondered, seeing at long last the nature of the Prince's true illness? Hartmann did. In fact, Hartmann at this precise moment came out of Reichstadt's room, rushed past the two men and left the salon without a word. The doctor seemed genuinely puzzled.

"Where is the General hurrying to?"

"To Vienna," Moll replied curtly. "As you should know, there is no hope."

Malfatti's dark eyes glowered with anger. Hartmann rushing off to Vienna to report, on his own assumption, that his patient was in imminent danger of dying was an unforgivable arrogation!

He burst into vehement denunciations. Hartmann wasn't a doctor! He wouldn't know how low Reichstadt was! How dare he meddle in Malfatti's affairs? Did Malfatti meddle in his?

Moll told him to lower his voice.

Malfatti shrugged off the warning. His patient's regrettable relapse did not warrant that sort of precaution. Besides, Reichstadt had had problems hearing and moreover must have been so weakened by the crisis as to be nearly unconscious by now.

Then he became aware of a movement in the direction of the bedroom door which Hartmann, in his precipitation, had left ajar. When Moll saw Malfatti's mouth fall open, he made a sharp about-face and swore softly under his breath.

Clad in the immaculate white of a flowing night shirt that reached down to his bare feet, and bracing himself against the door frame with his arms spread apart, Franz presented a startling vision of an appearing angel with outspread wings. But one who had been battered. And yet, he still looked commanding in his defiance.

Though by some incredible tour de force he had gotten out of bed, it was obvious that he conceded exhaustion by the way he clung to the door jamb, his knuckles all white in the effort this took.

Moll rushed up to him, "Monseigneur, you must go back to bed at once!"

"I want to go out," Franz rasped.

"Dear Lord!" Malfatti wailed. Then, unable to cope with the situation a minute longer, he ran out of the room.

Left alone to reason with Reichstadt, Moll could only plead, "After what happened? I beg Your Highness to reconsider. Please, go lie down."

"No! I want to perish standing up!"

"Your Highness can do that tomorrow," Moll said in a conciliatory tone, steering him back to bed. A touch of humor in response to a declaration he suspected was not totally lucid would only prove more successful than a logical argument.

To Moll's relief, Franz offered no resistance. But once under the cover, he said weakly, "Order my carriage, Moll."

This time, Moll asserted his authority. "Monseigneur, I cannot do that. It would be madness to take Your Highness out now."

"Then I shall order the carriage myself!"

"Don't! I would be forced to cancel Your Highness's order."

Franz did something he had not repeated since the age of three. He reiterated his rights. "I am the master! The servants will obey me anyway!"

Moll looked at him pityingly. His hair was a tousled mess and a slovenly fuzz covered his cheeks, upper lip, and chin. He could barely lift his hand in an attempt to reach the bellpull which he tried in vain to grasp.

Moll said as pleasantly as he could, "The servants won't obey you because you are ill."

"Oh, damn!" Franz groaned, attempting to sit up.

Gently, but firmly, Moll pushed him back. "Do you realize that the fuss you are at present raising should be witnessed by all those who accuse us of taking bad care of you? That should certainly throw some light on this unfair rumor."

Franz gave Moll a puzzled look. It had never occurred to him that people could be interested in the way he was being cared for while he was ill.

"Yes," Moll continued. "All manner of reproaches are being heaped upon us."

"What for instance?"

"We are reviled because we are letting Your Highness go out with a temperature."

"I always run a temperature."

The Baron hung his head. This was all too correct. Yet, had Malfatti been more firm and more competent, the Prince could have rid himself of that fever long before it had a chance to run him to the grave.

"Yes, Monseigneur," he admitted dolefully, smoothing the rumpled bed clothes, "you do." Then feeling a pang of guilt he said, "That is why I should have opposed your suggestion to go to Laxemburg yesterday. Your Highness wouldn't be so sick had we come straight home from Haimlack. Somehow, I had a premonition we would have a run of ill-luck. I should have said something, but then you would have become angry and done exactly as you pleased."

Utterly exhausted by now, Franz closed his eyes, the fan of their lashes casting a faint glimmering shadow against the feverish flush on his cheeks. His hand groped for Moll's. As soon as the Baron responded with a gentle squeeze, the ghost of a smile passed across his lips. "I am giving you a lot of trouble my poor Moll. I'll grant you a truce. . . . I won't be going out today after all."

Moll thought with sadness, As if you really could!

That evening, upon his return from Vienna, Hartmann immediately held a meeting to settle once and for all three points still in question: Since the Prince's decline was rapid, the Archduchess Mother should be notified so she could hasten to her son's bedside; the sick man should prepare himself to receive the Last Rites; and lastly, his worsening condition warranted a move to Italy, to which Metternich, at long last, had given his approval.

Count Dietrichstein went immediately to Vienna to see Sophie.

"Alas!" he deplored, after relating in that precise order the outcome of the General's interview with Metternich, "the Prince is so weak now he can't even travel to Ischl let alone to Naples!"

The next day, she was at Schönbrunn.

Sophie refrained from going to Franz at once. She needed time to prepare herself to face him and pretend that nothing had changed. Anxiously, she interrogated Moll who assured her that Reichstadt entertained hopes of recovering. "His Highness," he told her, "even talked of having children someday and spoke to me of the manner in which he intends to raise them. . . ."

Alone, Sophie let the tears come. She cried long and hard. Then gathering all her courage, dried her eyes, put quantities of cold compresses on her face to compose it anew, and watched herself smile convincingly in the mirror. She intended to look cheerful. If it gladdened Franz to turn to life when all were giving him up to die, she would defend his conviction with all her energy and the powers at her command.

But one power delegated from a higher authority challenged her determination when the Court chaplain asked to see her.

Monsignor Wagner immediately spoke of Holy Viaticum with detachment and urgency.

This horrified Sophie.

The priest hastened to explain, conscious of venturing on delicate grounds, for tongues were now wagging rather freely on the subject of Francis Charles's lovely wife's excessive fondness for her step-nephew.

"I would not have bothered Your Highness with this matter if it were not because of your . . . interest in the Prince. He would certainly take the suggestion well, coming from you."

Directing at the chaplain a sharp look for the innuendo had not escaped her, she replied, "The Prince will only recognize in such a proposition a death sentence."

An expression of mild surprise crossed Monsignor Wagner's face, for he knew her to be cognizant of the Church's stance in such circumstances. He said nonetheless to impress its necessity upon her, "To a Christian, death is not so terrible. On the other hand, readiness is paramount."

Sophie bristled. "He is an irreproachable, good young man, and quite ready," she retorted, immediately loathing herself for attesting to the terrible outcome the chaplain was placing before her.

"Highness," Monsignor Wagner chided respectfully, "The Prince's spiritual welfare must be tended by the sacraments of the Church . . . as a precaution, which in no way casts any doubt as to his goodness in God's eyes."

Sophie felt a rush of revolt. This pious, dogmatic sort of talk that she had accepted for so long, now offended her. And perhaps it did not behoove a devout person such as she believed herself to be to stray from absolute compliance with religious observances and to allow her rational mind to clamor: "Away with readiness!" For she held that it would be irresponsible and cruel to concern Franz with such rituals. He needed none of the so-called "precautions" the chaplain was advocating, to put himself in God's grace. He had *never been* lost to grace and must have merited an even greater abundance of it, if that was at all possible. She had been told by her confessor once that the more the Lord loves, the more He tries his beloved. If so, Franz must be well loved by God inasmuch as his whole short life had been nothing but a trial, his chaste passion for her being perhaps the severest of such testimonial to divine benevolence.

As for being good! He was the most sincere, generous, and noble of youths. She could find enough praises to compose a tender litany on the enviable qualities he possessed. . . .

With a welling of love, half cutting off her breath, she said authoritatively, "The Prince has well earned his Heaven! And as long as he is of good cheer and good hope, I forbid anyone to mention the Last Sacraments to him!"

Monsignor Wagner would not desist. He cited an oft forgotten benefit. "Holy Viaticum not only imparts spiritual succor, it is also known to have restored health in very sick people, and so does Extreme Unction."

Feeling like a heathen, but no longer caring, Sophie countered, "The Sacraments given at this time could only be indicative of an impending death!" Then glaring at the chaplain, whom she had so far regarded as a dispenser of kindness and compassion, she frankly accused. "The Prince is only twenty-one years old! He still believes he has a lot of living to do! How could you possibly entertain this heartless intention of disabusing him?"

"Faith should be guiding us in decisions of this kind," the chaplain responded unmoved.

Sophie tensed. Her face took on an anguished expression. It became plain to Monsignor Wagner that Reichstadt's death would be the Archduchess's despair. But she might grieve less bitterly comforted by the thought of having made allowances for a miraculous cure.

"I know Your Highness would never deny the Prince a supernatural chance to get well," he enticed.

Sophie wrung her hands.

The chaplain went on, assured of gaining a foothold, "I propose another approach which could ease all concerns. The Prince could take communion now; and later be given Extreme Unction."

Sophie dropped her face into her hands. Was the Archduchess crying? the chaplain wondered, but no tremor shook her shoulders. Then she lifted her head and looked at him dry-eyed and with an air of deep dissatisfaction. He could not imagine the reason why. What he had proposed eliminated the immediate administration of the Last Rites, the hinting at death she so vehemently rejected.

But only Sophie could have thought of a fresh complication. A complication that put them right back where they had started. Franz, though observant of his religious obligations, never received communion but on High Holidays. The last, Easter, was barely some two months ago. To ask him to communicate again after such a short interval might arouse his suspicion, as he was well aware of the customs that governed the dispositions taken in the event a member of the imperial family became deathly ill.

"It is not that simple," she said.

Misunderstanding her reservation, the chaplain harried with well-nigh impudence. "Your Highness's special attachment for the Prince should overcome any obstacle as Our Lord is forgiving!" Then realizing the enormity of his indiscretion, he hastened to add lamely, ". . . as we all need His forgiveness."

Sophie remained unperturbed. Her conscience reproached her nothing. And God knows what kind of cheap gossips Monsignor Wagner must have heard! To vulgar and coarse people whose exalted station at court did not necessarily guaranty nobility of character—and a lecherous and hypocritical lot they were—any interpretation of the tender passion she and Franz shared would inevitably be cast in a cheap and common light, no matter how sublime and heroic the truth might be.

Looking the chaplain straight in the eyes as if daring him to pass judgment, she stated emphatically, "Have no doubt. I love the Prince with all my heart and soul. I will think of a way."

Left alone, she went telling herself, *Cry all you care now. But before him you must present a valiant and blithe exterior. You must sustain in him the will to live.*

As this instant, the life within her stirred. The child conceived in lawful but loveless intercourse gave a sharp kick. The pain gagged her and as it subsided, she took stock of her own state of health. Twenty-seven already and only bearing a second child! Pray God she would carry the baby to term! Then an inspiration came to her.

Monsignor Wagner should soon obtain satisfaction.

On the afternoon of their reunion, Franz insisted that Sophie come with him for a walk in the garden. From the corner of her eye she watched him plod along. With the child she carried nearing delivery, her own pace had slowed, thus, it did not appear that she was hanging back to allow Franz to catch up. This suited her as she was mindful that he should not feel so enfeebled and inadequate as to be hampering their progress.

Franz walked erect and held his chin high. He never looked so tall. Heartbroken, she thought, *He must be still growing!*

Halfway to the Menagerie he so admired in his childhood, she caught a plurality of signals indicating that ambling was no longer a simple and effortless activity for him. To make him rest, she stopped, tactfully invoking her own tiredness and took him to an arbor laden with a spectacular array of cascading roses.

Once they were both seated on a bench beneath it, Franz started to reach up to pluck a blossom intending to present it to Sophie. But the movement triggered a coughing fit, he managed to bring under control pressing to his lips a handkerchief, which he quickly hid in his cuff. After catching his breath, he observed with a desolation that crushed her, "I'm not even able to pluck a flower for you!"

Ever present in her mind, the promise she had made to herself to bolster his spirits prompted her to force a lively smile saying, "Yes, you can! And without having to lift a finger."

"How?"

"Pick the rose you like with your eyes."

The amused expression on his face heartened her. "Go on," she urged, "pick one."

She watched the movement of his eyes as he made his selection then looking back at her he asked, "Now what is going to happen?"

"This," and she lightly kissed both his eyes shut. When he opened them she said, "I have the rose. You've plucked it, and I have just collected it!"

He stared into her face with such tender, wistful appreciation that again she felt in good part responsible for his ordeal.

"You amaze me," he murmured. "And I don't know what I would do without you. . . ." Then his glance dropped to her distended belly. "When exactly is the baby due?"

"Sometime in the middle of July."

He reckoned briefly: "That is only a little more than two weeks away."

Sophie nodded, dreading the prospect of having to leave his side.

"I shall be with you in thoughts all during your delivery," he said and added after a brief hesitation, "I shall be praying, too, although I am not very good at it."

Now! cried a voice in her head.

Cheerfully she proposed, "Franz, if you would consent to join me in taking Holy Communion, we could combine our prayers in holy petition for a prompt recovery for you and a safe delivery for me!"

Making no immediate reply, he looked at her with penetrating intensity; then with great calm and solemnity he said, "I don't believe I should take the Eucharist with you because I am almost certain my last communion was sacrilegious."

That declaration took Sophie's breath away. She gasped in absolute disbelief. There could be no evil in Franz and their love was, as the moralists would call it, "pure." Then, adding to her bewilderment, he declared bending forward and letting his head drooped, "Sophie, I have no religion."

"Oh, Franz," she protested, desolation toning down her vehemence, "How could you have come to this dreadful conclusion?"

He went on baring his soul to her in a voice dead with despair. "I find the taste of His body insipid. I find His love wounding, His justice tortuous, His mercy punishing, and His wisdom a maze of contradictions. And I have absolutely no desire that He should lie in me, nor I, in Him!" Then lifting his head he noted her distress and thought, *A priest should be hearing this in confession. I must have scandalized her!*

Sophie met his eyes directly and by their expression he knew at once that she had not been spared some soul-searching of her own. He felt encouraged to ask, "Am I making any sense?"

She took his hands and held them in a tight grip. "You do. I understand how you feel."

"I feel empty!"

"Even saints have felt that way! God's desertion! A wasting absence! Complete abandonment!"

He smiled sadly. "I don't deserve that signal distinction."

"Don't ever, ever, think yourself unworthy because of this!" she pleaded. "For you are the worthiest! Might you not want to reconsider?"

For answer, he leaned into her shoulder and kissed her cheek.

Franz thought about communion and put the subject out of his mind. It troubled him to engage in so serious a devotion given the state of spiritual desolation in which he found himself; and not content of avoiding heavenly sustenance, he had also lost all appetite for ordinary food.

Malfatti dealt with the problem by simply working around it. He left his patient free to pick at the dishes served to him. As Franz ate very little, variety, then portions steadily diminished. Soon he subsisted on a pittance, which too often consisted of three glasses of Mariendbad water or a bowl of broth for supper. If, in addition, he consumed two chicken wings and a few spoonfuls of cherries, it was considered a heavy meal.

Unwittingly, he once made the observation to Moll that he was being weakened to complete prostration. His changed appearance bothered him to the point of refusing to see Marmont when the Marshal came to Schönbrunn to wish him a speedy recovery. Moreover, all visits tired him and that of Marmont no longer held any attraction whatsoever. Nothing did.

Without realizing this, Franz began slipping quietly away from this world, passing long hours stretched on the *chaise longue* that Sophie had especially ordered for him. As his strength ebbed, he cared for no other presence but hers. She only left him to sleep, take her meals, and tend to minor yet unavoidable duties demanded of her station while enduring with undaunted valiance her own agony over the possibility of losing him.

She told herself that all was done that could be done within the limits permitted by Metternich. Then, by mere chance, she discovered Franz's appalling eating habits.

When Sophie came to be with him one evening, a sultry dusk was settling over the castle and an oppressive heat still packed his room. He was quite alone save for a lackey stationed in the antechamber, the rest of his staff having gone to supper.

Franz was availing himself of an accommodation Moll had devised for him. The Baron had arranged to have a small sofa placed on the threshold of the balcony. This way, he could rest with the advantage of being practically out of doors to catch a puff of air while retaining a certain degree of comfort and privacy.

Sitting on the sofa with a pillow behind is head, Franz stared at the mundane grandeur of the formal garden and reflected that he might never return to France.

It was at this instant that Sophie came to speak to him about a very special star.

He could not mistake her rustling tread for any other. Besides, there weren't any others. She was the only gentle element in his life.

The only woman. Without her, his deprivation from any meaningful feminine companionship would have gone unrelieved even though women's hearts would throb at the mere thought of him.

"Come sit near me," he said looking up at her, a quiet joy flooding him.

Sophie did so with that familiar clumsiness that set Franz in a pensive and rueful mood every time he watched her get around. She was quite shapeless now and awkward in her movements as the time for her delivery grew nearer. Yet, he never found her more lovable, more desirable, and restful to be with.

She lifted her eyes to a bright, outstanding point of light which had appeared above the darkening tree tops. "Look, Franz! There is your star!"

But he only looked at her. She was impeccably coifed. Her hair pulled up to form a cluster of curls carefully arranged in shiny tiers against her temples. Quietly, he savored the privilege of having seen her tresses undone on his pillow, much like a lover would have felt when recalling an intimate moment.

"How can you tell?" he asked distractedly.

Staring demandingly into the dusky firmament, she said, "Because it shines so! Because it stands quite apart from the others, as you do. These are your marks."

He kept gazing at her and murmured, "It is also a mark of defiance . . . or was. I am too tired now to defy anyone or anything." And with a break in the voice he said, "I only can love you!"

Then, in what Sophie perceived to be a capitulation to insurmountable miseries, he slipped his arm across her swollen stomach and pulled himself closer to her to lay his cheek on her bosom. Her breath caught, but only to acknowledge her own longing. She clasped his head lovingly and let her fingers stray in his hair which had lost its marvelous luster of silk.

She was past feeling guilt.

At this point, she would have denied him nothing. The contempt in which she held herself deepened. Scruples, conscience, were now senseless and empty considerations. Franz was dying and his tender abandon only intensified her regret.

Never had Sophie imagined finding virtue so loathsome. In any possible measure, the torment she had inflicted upon Franz must end.

He sensed her surrender in the way her heavy body settled more comfortably to cuddle him, and he let himself be told how much he was loved.

In an out-and-out rebellion against the norms she once held incontestable, she whispered to him, "And you are the life of my life. Think of that! You have such sway over my existence! Such absolute dominion you can claim over me! Your weakness is potent. . ."

Franz looked up at her with eyes whose brilliance passion alone could never conjure and touched her with a fleeting exhausted smile.

She bent her head to kiss him.

Right then and there he would have died without complaint. His arm tightened around her. His voice came muffled. "Hold me. . . ."

Gathering him to her as best she could, her heart sank. The emaciation which his clothes concealed was unimaginable!

Appalled, she said with as much calm as she could summon, "Franz, aren't you eating anything?"

She only knew that since his health had deteriorated, all his meals were brought to his room. She could never imagine that they would be anything but decent if not elaborate. Had she known!

Franz was of no immediate help. He delighted at her closeness. It wove about him a cocoon of numbing felicity. Finally, he said listlessly, "I am never hungry."

"You must try to force yourself," she entreated tenderly peering down at him.

An expression of calm and satiety suffused his face whose sharp edges had softened in the declining light. Franz at rest in her loving embrace and adorned with the illusion of health never looked so handsome and so reconcilable to life. Softly, she voiced her concern. "Have you had supper yet?"

"Yes."

"And what did you have?"

"A bowl of soup."

"And?"

"Just soup."

Surprise forced a little gasp, "Is this all you ate?"

"That is all I wanted."

"Oh, but my love!" She was becoming agitated.

Looking contentedly into her caring face bent over him he said, "I am making progress. Yesterday I could scarcely swallow two glasses of spa water, which composed my menu."

This horrified Sophie. "They are *feeding you water?*"

"Medicinal water," he corrected without much conviction. "I suppose that is what one would call it. . . ." Then blissfully, with a little crooked smile—it had been so long since he had given way to jocularity—he said, "But I can eat now. I can eat the whole of you!"

"Franz, you are being facetious!" But the rebuke was gentle with a hint of laughter attending it.

For a brief instant all their troubles seemed to have taken flight leaving them free to enjoy each other, to be amused by something quite silly he had said. She lightly touched her lips to his then began raining little kisses across his cheek, temple, and forehead until a clearer realization that something was terribly amiss, something which demanded her immediate attention curbed her own peculiar hunger to go on kissing him.

She said following a dismal train of thought, "I am going to speak to the cook."

And of course that made him chuckle, a quiet, cautious sound which she had learned to appreciate with a good dose of dread.

But when she made to go, he clung to her. "Please, not now. . . ." And as she relented, he began in a faraway voice, "I wonder if Mother will . . . *care at all* to come this summer."

When Franz mentioned Marie Louise, it was always in positive and guarded terms. He never gave the slightest impression of discussing her conduct, or of encouraging anyone to do so. Why was he doing this now?

Because Sophie thought bitterly, She is a selfish, spineless woman and an absolute disgrace to motherhood! Marie Louise had not visited Franz in two years! She knew how sick her son was but found all sorts of excuses to stay away! And Franz's inexhaustible indulgence for his mother's shortcomings had been so worn down that he could no longer endure the pain and sadness of meaning so little to her. His pathetic and generous effort to remain kind and unprovoked despite the cruel suspense in which Marie Louise kept everyone and more significantly her son as to when she would consent to take to the road to visit Franz, revolted Sophie.

"It will be so wonderful to have her this year," she managed to say charitably wanting to cheer him.

He tilted his head back to better look at her with eyes she thought were enormous as she realized how gaunt his face had become. He only said, "I have you!"

Her throat tightened into a knot and all she could do was to kiss his forehead.

He said, holding up a hand to stroke her cheek, "You are everything to me! Have I ever told you this?"

She was able to whisper. "You don't have to. Your love speaks to me."

The tips of his fingers traced the curve of her mouth as it had done once, and his voice, deep-toned, took a solemn inflection.

"Had there been a place for us in this life, would you have married me?"

"This very instant!" she breathed passionately.

Then, barely able to hold back her tears, she allowed him to lay an amorous claim on her acceptance to a poignant proposal when he dipped his head and pushed his mouth against the pliant swell of her breast for a prolonged kiss which she now considered his due.

Only after he had eased away and wordlessly nestled his head in the hollow of her shoulder did she say something. Something that would not destroy her precarious control over the tumult of her emotion. Something that also addressed a dear priority. She asked him, "Franz, how would you like to have *a real* supper with me, right here?"

Slowly he sat up and looked at her, his eyes wide and hopeful, a flash of vivacity she hadn't seen for sometime enlivening them.

"Could we really?"

She gave him a quick hug and rose. "I'll only leave you for a moment to order our supper."

But that was not all. Sophie intended to correct a situation she considered indefensible. This called for an immediate confrontation with Malfatti, whom she sought out for a direct upbraiding.

"Have you taken leave of your senses? I would like to see how you would fare on the ridiculous diet you have devised for the Prince!"

Like Franz's other attendants, the doctor had been at supper, which he had just finished and enjoyed when Sophie found him. Her reproach could not have been better timed and more to the point. His look of total incomprehension infuriated her all the more. She did not allow him to reply.

"You are not giving him an honest chance!" She further accused, "You are actually *starving him to death!*"

By now Malfatti's face was red with indignation. "Those are harsh words!" he bitterly complained.

"The Prince," she said glaring at him, "is no ordinary archduke. Because of him, the eyes of Europe are trained on this court. More so now, because he is not well. If . . ." her voice came in tortuous gasps ". . . some tragedy, if he dies, your ministering is bound to undergo some evaluation. Now I ask, wouldn't it be sensible and prudent to tend sedulously to a situation over which you do have a great deal of control? So for the love of God, feed him decently!"

"But His Highness does not want to eat!" Malfatti protested, throwing up his hands.

"Order him to!" she snapped at him. "You are the doctor! It wouldn't be any different if you were to prescribe a potion instead. And have you forgotten that food is also remedial?"

At this juncture Malfatti wanted to forget everything, pack his trunks, and go wait on a non-controversial patient properly afflicted with gout, an ailment all too familiar to him.

"Please try to understand . . ." he began, but doubted making himself clear. For how is one to explain concisely a complex and bizarre case in which the condition of an illness was intertwined with a peculiar psychosis? There existed—Malfatti's conviction on this subject was unshakable—a mental condition in the Prince that had precipitated his physical collapse. Reichstadt's persistence in the way he abused his body seemed to translate a subconscious wish to die, a wish only the promise of some other existential conditions not quite clear to the doctor could have canceled.

Malfatti put this to Sophie in terms she found only too explicit as they reflected a view that was, for once, in sinister accord with her own observation. "His Highness," he said carefully, "is a very disenchanted young man for whom life, so it appears, is a veritable tribulation. It seems to me as though there is in this amiable Prince, a principle that is driving him to self-destruction."

Sophie burst into tears.

Malfatti flinched. "I am terribly sorry," he muttered sincerely pained for he was not a heartless man. Nor was he, Sophie recognized, totally devoid of ability. Why couldn't Malfatti be as superior in medicine as he was astute in psychology?

She said, shaking with sobs, "If you are that sorry, you must heed my command. The Prince must be served normal, decent meals from now on!"

Malfatti promised to do so.

When Sophie came back to Franz, dry-eyed and smiling, a meal had just been laid out according to her instructions. Franz looked apprehensively at the food in quantity such as he had never seen since he had begun eating alone. This was because his conception of abundance no longer corresponded to ordinary standards.

Sophie had ordered a modest, but sensible repast of boiled beef, roasted sliced potatoes, sweet dumplings flavored with poppy seeds, fresh fruits and especially for Franz, an iced drink.

"Try to eat something," she coaxed, with an encouraging smile.

Franz ate to please her. It was a slow and laborious process she pretended not to notice, but she kept silent count of every bite he took.

By degree, he was rediscovering the social pleasure in the simple act of eating with someone, and Sophie's precious company enhanced his enjoyment all the more.

He began to perk up. He mentioned Italy, interpreting the permission to go there as a return to good sense. Sophie kept her opinion to herself. Franz, always so wary of Metternich's decisions where they concerned him, seemed to accept this one at its face value and gave every indication that he believed in recovering well enough to travel. And again, the resolve she intended never to abandon made her allude to France. She wanted to revive his spirits, and she succeeded.

With increasing animation, Franz told her that he favored a democratic type of government and began explaining how it would work.

Sophie listened caught up in his enthusiasm, and forgetful of the bleak present she even imagined him restored to the vitality and splendor of his tender youth. She was amazed at the rapid change which was taking place in his whole attitude, only because he had someone to share his thoughts with; and there was a future to discuss. . . .

Was it the lambent light of the candles that was putting a healthy blush on his cheeks, a vivacious glow in his eyes? Or was it a regenerative process, induced by a renewed sense of purpose that loneliness had corroded when he had been abandoned to the care of spies with no one to turn to?

Lured into the exhilarating prospect of a happy outcome, Sophie envisioned Franz dressed not in the Austrian white, but in the simple uniform his father had immortalized. Facing her now, was not the Duke of Reichstadt, but Napoleon, François-Charles-Joseph Bonaparte, ruler of the French by the grace of his own people! Her Franz, never so much loved and so irrevocably removed from her tenderness and from all claims to familiarity! Yet with pride, and profound joy she was willing to give him up to the life he was destined to live! Already, she had enthroned him.

Hopefully glimpsing a future Sophie so ached to believe possible, Franz said as if being twenty-one implied that he had already reached a venerable age, "When I was young, I misjudged my father's ambition. But I have come to a better understanding of who he was and what he wanted. I supposed I owe him this readiness to concede, when paradoxically he was so unyielding. Yet what Napoleon did or did not do was only part of a phase through which all schemes of any importance must be tested. I see my own passage not as a contradiction but as the completion of his wishes. I realize one cannot sow a seed without turning up the ground. My father plowed Europe because he was a man of great vision!"

He began to cough weakly in the napkin he had taken from his lap.

The interruption brought Sophie back to a stark and cruel reality. There wasn't any vigorous Napoleon the Second to give up to the claim of his native country; only a frail young man clad in a dressing gown coughing his life away.

To her immense relief, the crisis quickly passed. But she was already beside him, holding a glass of water to his lips and blaming herself.

As he drank, she said soothingly, "You have greater vision still . . . and much strength to muster in order to work toward your goal. Rest now. Don't talk anymore. If you care to lie down on your chaise, I could perhaps read to you?"

But he thought otherwise. "After I take a turn round the room?"

"Franz," she fretted, "should you really?"

"Please? With your help?"

Sophie lent him her shoulders, which he encircled with his arm bearing down on her a weight that was pitifully light. She held him by the waist and felt no need to adjust her waddling gait to his shambling walk. With infinite sadness she thought, *What a strange and lamentable spectacle we must be presenting! . . .*

Intent on walking the length of the room, Franz grew totally absorbed in placing one foot before the other. Each time he stepped on a twelve-pronged rosette of inlaid wood forming the parquetry, he felt gratified for doing so well. A child's game he would have thought in other circumstances, but now, it represented a daunting challenge to all his future accomplishments.

Three days later, after having given everyone the impression of rallying, Franz spent an appalling night. Monsignor Wagner once again came back to the charge. If the sacraments were deferred any longer, the Prince might die unconfessed.

Sophie unsuccessfully tried to stem her tears and breath eluded her as she gagged in the throes of uncontrollable sobbing.

The priest began to fear a nervous collapse.

When speech returned to her, she held her ground. "I have spoken to the Prince about communion. It is for him to decide." And she further told him how she had put the suggestion to Reichstadt.

In a spontaneous gesture of relief, Monsignor Wagner crossed himself. Sophie had just lifted in his mind troubling conjectures. The Archduchess could not have agreed to a joint communion with the purpose of calling down a divine blessing on an event which was the result of a sinful act. So her proposal undoubtedly meant that she had not committed adultery with Reichstadt. Francis Charles's wife's love for the Duke, if illicit at all, would only be so "in form". "In fact", it would be sinless. And in this respect, it could be considered her cross as well. A meritorious burden indeed!

Anxious to help, the chaplain said, "Young people are not generally inclined to be overly devout. Yet if Your Highness would allow it, I might point out to the Prince that he is not consistent in the devotion he bears Your Highness by persisting in a refusal which causes you so much anguish."

"He did not refuse," Sophie said defensively.

Actually, Franz had not made any mention of communion since the day she'd asked him to reconsider. He might be debating on the subject still, which in no way equated a refusal.

But the chaplain persisted, "Then he must say he agrees to Your Highness's proposition now."

Sophie balked at the idea. Through a subterfuge? Franz should come to God of his own volition and not for anyone else's sake. She would never ask him to communicate on such grounds, much less encourage an intervention conducted in the same misleading way.

"Don't press him," she pleaded. "Give him time!"

"But there isn't time!" the chaplain pointed out.

Stubborn, sanctimonious cleric! Sophie thought, relinquishing all effort at Christian charity. She felt drained and cornered. Years and years of tradition would eventually take matters out of her hands and override her orders; for no dying Habsburgs were ever exempt from the solemn ritual of a public communion. Then Franz would surely know how desperately ill he was.

Sophie reconsidered. It would be best to go along with the priest. Yet not without certain conditions, while she still had a say.

"If you succeed in convincing the Prince to take communion for my sake," she relented, "the ceremony must be simple and short."

But she knew that there would be a small crowd watching—clerics, archdukes and archduchesses residing at Schönbrunn as well as various dignitaries.

She added, "The Prince must not be aware of the others."

"I suggest we put up hangings," the chaplain offered.

"He will notice them," she objected.

"In Your Highness's private oratory that would not appear so out of the ordinary."

"No," she said firmly. "The Prince will take communion in his room. The door can be left ajar behind us so everybody can witness the ceremony from the antechamber."

"This can be arranged," Monsignor Wagner said, obviously satisfied.

"And another thing."

"Yes?" he asked with a slight touch of impatience.

Sophie said, letting her tears return. "I want absolute silence!"

Baron von Moll greeted the chaplain with an involuntary grimace. Clerics were not Reichstadt's favorite callers. Franz half-opened his eyes and seeing who was standing by his bed, shut them asking tiredly, "Have you come to comfort me, Father?"

Monsignor Wagner ignored the faint trace of sarcasm in the greeting. Reichstadt had never pretended with him and he would be equally honest.

"No, Monseigneur."

Franz managed a weak smile. "Thank you. . . ."

The priest said, "The Archduchess Sophie is causing us no small concern."

At the mention of Sophie, Franz jerked his eyes open and made an incautious attempt to sit up. There followed a fit of coughing which left him panting long after the chaplain had assured him that the Archduchess had not met with any physical harm.

"It is her spirits," he explained. "The Archduchess is heartbroken at the idea of taking communion alone. I learned of her hope to have Your Highness share her devotion, as she could no longer conceal her unhappiness at the likelihood that you might not do so. You must understand that in her condition, and so close to confinement, one cannot overlook the adverse effect of mental distress."

The priest did not have to go on elaborating what that effect might be. Franz gave in.

"I shall take communion," he said. Then reflecting on his spiritual inadequacy, added impatiently, "But I am such a miserable Catholic! You have noticed that, I am sure."

"Monseigneur, Our Lord will not fault you for trying to please Him, however faltering that effort might be. . . ."

"And you are not loath to hear my tales of woe?"

Monsignor Wagner took his hand and pressed it comfortingly.

Franz turned his face toward the wall. "Well then," he sighed, "tomorrow, you will have it all!"

The next day, after having heard Reichstadt's confession, Monsignor Wagner went to the chapel to fetch the Blessed Sacrament. Through endless corridors and up the main blue staircase, a silent and imposing procession accompanied him.

At Sophie's request, the priest wore his ordinary vestments while four acolytes held a sumptuous canopy of white satin shimmering with gold embroideries over the ciborium, which he reverently clutched to his breast.

In Franz's apartments, the throng of clerics, princes and princesses in residence at the castle, chamberlains, civil and military officials, and liveried servants quietly gathered in the antechamber. The chaplain went into the bedroom only attended by one of the acolytes carrying the paten.

Franz had gotten out of bed and waited seated in an armchair in front of which stood a prie-dieu.

A similar arrangement was provided for Sophie, for whom the moment was charged with emotion of a very special nature no one suspected, not even Franz. On this intensely sorrowful occasion, her love for him underwent a process of sublimation. Her heart breaking, she thought, This is our mystical marriage! Franz, and I. Secretly yet publicly. . . . And truly forever!

Monsignor Wagner held up the consecrated host. "*Ecce Agnus Dei,*" he softly intoned.

Franz sank to his knees and looked directly into the priest's eyes. "*Domine, non sum dignus,*" he responded, shuddering from weakness.

Immediately, Sophie slipped her arm around his waist and snuggled up against his shoulder to provide a prop. Leaning heavily against her, Franz took the host in a near faint, his cheek pressed to her temple.

At this moment, she said passionately in her head, *I, Sophie, take thee, Franz, my love* . . . Her mouth hungered for the touch of his lips and not for the Divine Victim which the priest placed next on the tip of her tongue.

And she who so looked forward to this communion, received the Body of Christ with no fervor at all. How well now she understood Franz's spiritual desolation! Yet, a giddying rush of love for him filled the void of her soul as she became totally forgetful of God.

Franz alone counted!

Oblivious of the priest and of his attendant, she pressed her face against the hollow of his jaw line and touched her lips to the warm skin under which she could feel the slow pulse of his ebbing life.

Only then did God mean something to her. Something her faith fiercely demanded as a just and undeniable compensation. In the Paradise Jesus had promised, the wonder most precious to her now rested in the assurance of the resurrection of the flesh, of a warm corporeality that would be eternal.

32

"Elise, my smelling salts. . . ." The vial was promptly proffered and held under Marie Louise's nostrils. The stinging vapor of ammonia revived her enough to cause her to regret not having swooned altogether so she could momentarily be spared the ordeal that awaited her. This was the culmination of other unpleasant situations she had had to endure since she had undertaken her journey to Vienna, Schönbrunn being her ultimate and much dreaded destination.

She was aware that her absence from her sick son's bedside was creating considerable scandal. Franz's communion had been witnessed by members of the court and the Imperial Family and many in her entourage began to loudly wonder if that meant anything to her at all.

Shamed by the accusation of being heartless, and cowering at having to face Franz in such dire circumstances, she had traveled in easy stages, first stopping in Venice, then in Trieste to meet her father, who did not receive her well. Francis upbraided her. "Why stop here? You should be on your way to see your son!" She told him she wanted him to accompany her. Francis declined and made excuses invoking matters of state. She did not believe him and was sure that, like her, he also cringed at the prospect of even coming near his grandson, whom everybody said was dying.

Now sitting in her landau which had just lumbered to a halt in Schönbrunn palace's courtyard, Marie Louise glanced up apprehensively at the interminable rows of windows fitted with the familiar green shutters. She shuddered violently and a moan escaped her.

Countess Scarampi made another pass with the vial. Marie Louise averted her face. "Enough!" Her voice was shrill and her hands nervously crumpled the muslin scarf draped around her neck.

Seated opposite her, her minister Baron Marschall and Count Dietrichstein who had gone to meet her at Guntersdorf, noted that she was much too agitated to faint. The Count feared a nervous collapse when she suddenly asked, her eyes wild and unfocused, "What day is this?"

"Sunday, June 24," he replied.

Elise Scarampi and the two men exchanged a perplexed glance. If they knew what day this was, so did Marie Louise, having herself attended Mass with them before setting off on the last leg of their journey. But in her overwrought condition, she could have uttered anything that came to her mind. And she seemed quite out of it. Looking haggard and seemingly in a trance, she was helped out of the carriage and taken to her apartments shuffling her way toward them as though she was being led to the gallows.

Once there, she broke down and wept.

Bones with moving parts hidden in long flowing sleeves bruised Marie Louise's ribs when Franz quite unable to lift himself up in bed welcomed her with outstretched arms. As she pulled away, he smiled sweetly at her, the white of his teeth offset by the ivory of his complexion.

She was aghast at his appearance, because now she saw nothing in him that she could any longer recognize as the radiant, handsome youth she once knew.

Intent on expiation, she said glibly, "I shall look after you now that I am here, any time of the day or night. Or I shall leave you alone if you so desire. Don't ever be afraid to speak your mind."

Feebly he only remarked, "I so wanted to see you, Mamma! . . . it's been a while."

"I am here," she heard herself declare a little too vehemently, "and if I ever tire you or bother you, just say so."

He drew her hand to his cheek. "You could never do any of those things."

But she did.

Something Franz thought indestructible had wilted within him. His beloved mother had neglected him for too long. They had nothing to say to each other and nothing to share. Even her presence, which he so looked forward to enjoying began to annoy him at times. Bitterly, he reproached himself for harboring such feelings, but when her visits grew short and spaced, he felt relieved.

Boredom had swiftly taken hold of Marie Louise. After having done a great deal of crying and praying, she believed she had received during her devotions a clear message from God, a message she accepted wholeheartedly and with unquestioning resignation: God wanted her son. Heavenly wonders and everlasting happiness would be awaiting him.

With a spark of queer compassion, peculiar to her amorphous nature, she thought, *This is about the only good thing that could ever happen to my poor Franz. . . .*

But until the liberating call came, what was she to do to pass the time of day?

Having given up her son in sickness as in health, Marie Louise went shopping in Vienna for souvenirs and gifts to take back to Parma. She could not return empty-handed to her duchy, where her life had taken a happier turn with the society of a new favorite, a certain Count of Sanvitale. . . .

She spoke often of him to all and sundry to the complete disgust of Baron Marschall, whose presence she positively loathed.

Moll and Hartmann also began to constantly speak of the situation which awaited them after Reichstadt's death. When Baron Marschall mentioned with detachment that the Prince's demise would not necessarily guarantee them a pension, Hartmann dared protest, "I can't believe Her Majesty would deny us a token of appreciation for all our troubles!"

"Perhaps," Marschall offered, "a complete inventory of His Highness's belongings, properly drawn and presented to his mother might enable you to secure something of value."

Hartmann cogitated and suggested, "The silver cradle could be sold. It is in fine condition and it would fetch a handsome price!"

"How much?" asked Moll.

"I know it cost over one hundred and fifty thousand francs. Taking into consideration its historical value, it would be worth much, much more. In my estimation, I would say . . ."

"The cradle is not for sale!" Baron Marschall interrupted testily.

Moll injected, being fundamentally a decent man, "I suppose not. That would be scandalous. For my part, I should be content with one of the Prince's thoroughbreds with saddlery. Maybe some kind of decoration and a few thousand florins."

Hartmann decided to speed up matters and announced, "I am going to draw up that inventory at once!"

Sophie alone kept careful stock of Franz's needs in a selfless and devoted vigil. Unlike Marie Louise, she fiercely opposed coming to terms with "God's will" and even found herself well on the brink of complete spiritual rebellion. Prayers no longer sustained her spirits. Only a frantic determination in willing Franz to live enabled her to confront each day.

When he would enjoy a reprieve, her heart would leap for joy, whereas everyone else would shrug, as if to say, "It's of no use. People with the cough often give the impression of rallying but die soon afterward." Such attitude infuriated her and hoping against all hope she fulfilled all the promises Franz's mother had made to him but did not keep.

On the eleventh day after her arrival, Marie Louise did not come to pay her son her customary visit at the close of the evening, sending word instead that she wished him "good night from afar."

Sophie practically lived in Franz's room and upon hearing Countess Scarampi deliver that message, she concealed her outrage. Her sister-in-law's inconceivable callousness made her wonder if Marie Louise had been born with half a brain which might explain why she was behaving with such cruel indifference.

Disheartened, she watched Franz's reaction, which amounted to a little trembling of the lips, a tired look of surprise in his huge blue eyes, which he rested on her as though saying once again "I have you" before closing them as Scarampi made a dignified exit.

Gently, Sophie took his hand and held it consolingly. In his exhausted state, she knew that emotions could subside to the level of a flame petering out, that he had lost all count of the days, and of the hours. Duration seemed to have slipped past his reckoning, and time, when it counted for something, must only be perceived as stagnant pool of pain which he would only express with a sudden twist of the mouth, a passing contraction of the eyebrows. But his sufferings endured with no complaints found an invisible channel that led to her own body, and his lapses into unconsciousness were her conscious efforts to repudiate despair.

And now, the imminence of giving birth firmed her determination to make good of all the time left to her down to the last hour. Childbed could separate her from Franz at any moment. So this evening, after Marie Louise had long sent her disgraceful good night. Sophie would not leave him, quite ready to sleep sitting in a chair by his bed if she had to.

Moll, who had been reading to him, began to nod sleepily over the open page. By signs Sophie indicated that he should retire. With obvious relief, the Baron silently obliged.

Sophie sank in sorrowful contemplation of Franz's face without being able to repulse a terrible vision. That unnaturally peaceful profile with the lid pulled down and the slightly parted lips might be the last image she would ever keep of him. And she thought, *If he dies, the person in me whom he loved shall die also. . . .*

After a moment, she felt his fingers move in the hollow of her palm. He opened his eyes and saw that they were alone.

"You are still with me. . . ."

She found the tone of his voice comfortingly clear. His true voice! No longer raspy and distorted, but warm and melodious, as she remembered in happier days.

"I won't leave until you are asleep," she told him, and she added, wanting to be right, "I hope you are not in pain."

"No."

"Honestly?"

He gave her a convincing smile. "Honestly." Then studying the dark circles under her eyes and the little creases at the corner of her mouth, he pleaded. "Don't stay. You have been with me since morning. You must get some rest."

She felt no fatigue. Perhaps that was because she was beyond the reach of such basic vulnerability with only love, impervious to stress, left to sustain her. Mutely, she stared at him, letting her gaze follow the outline of his head and shoulders scooping the pillow in a frail and light imprint. Then she caught a small detail left unaltered despite the ravages wrought on his face by a wasting illness. It was the little dimple which divided his lower lip, the same Isabey had faithfully painted in his portrait of him when he was a child.

An insufferable feeling of irreparable loss overcame her. She heaved herself out of the chair and leaning over, kissed him. Feebly pulling her to him, he kissed her back, trembling.

Alarmed, she drew away a little. "Franz, you *are* in pain!"

"No," he protested softly, looking at her with an expression of such complete serenity that she believed him. "No," he repeated, "I am in heaven!"

She thought with infinite sadness, "And a shabby heaven I have given you!" As for her, the heavenly place every good Christian looked upon as the ultimate repose after this life no longer held any bliss. Because all of a sudden, the heaven of her faith had lost its power of consolation. Franz's kiss and the warmth of his frail, emaciated frame suddenly proclaimed the inanity of disembodied love. She even questioned now the adequacy of the resurrection of the flesh. For such final incorruptibility entailed the exclusive adoration of the Divinity. In that glorified state, bosoms, it was said, were purged of the most celebrated, sung, and written about emotion ever to affect so completely the whole of humankind. Never carnal lovers, Sophie envisioned losing Franz twice. On this earth, to a mortal illness, and in the hereafter, to a jealous God.

"Heaven . . ." she repeated with an all-engulfing anguish.

"Yes," he assured her, not in the least concerned with Christian theology. "Your very special heaven. The one into which you have led me day-after-day . . . and now."

His contented surrender to the miserly dispensations she offered brought her no comfort. She sputtered, "I should have let it happen, and bear instead your beautiful child!"

For a moment, he kept silent. The thought of a possible parallel between his relation with Sophie and that of his mother with Neipperg crossed his mind. After all, wouldn't their situation become also tainted by the censure irrevocably attached to Sophie's infidelity? Oh, he desired her with all the imploding ardor of his youth! But not without nobility. He would have borne their lovemaking to such crest of romantic perfection that it might have stilled the fear that something highly esteemed would be destroyed.

But not now.

Broken in spirits, and utterly spent, he could honestly confront the damaging consequences of being Sophie's lover. By having withheld from him the ultimate favor, she had saved them both from subjecting their love to the same shame which besmeared his mother's early relation with Neipperg. . . .

A shame which had convulsed and devastated him.

He did something that recalled a time of unspoken sentimental trepidation, a summer when the precursory love they felt lay dormant and manifested itself by simple attentions and gestures; the summer he had given her a posy, come into her outstretched arms, and kissed the tip of her nose. . . . Only her nose.

Just as then, he now put a gentle kiss on the tip of Sophie's nose, feeling as though they were a married couple retracing the paths of smaller indulgences after having already explored the height and depth of their passion.

He said, "All children are beautiful. It doesn't have to be mine."

She wanted to protest *her* desolation despite the realization that they had achieved a truly blessed union. A union that would never compare with one sated in carnal gratification. Transcending that point, their love, unsullied, had reached its limited perfectibility because there was no place for it in this life.

She said with concentrated fervor, not quite reneging on her intent, and at a cost she would have gladly paid had he demanded it: "I do love you! In every possible and impossible way."

All he could say was her name. "Sophie. . . "

She saw his lids flutter, and mindful of the late hour and of the rest he so desperately needed, she consigned her bittersweet offering to silence. When she spoke again, her words tended to a practical matter. "Try to sleep, now. I won't go until you do."

For her sake, Franz felt obliged to comply but not without a sinking sensation. He knew the child she carried would be due any day. Even tomorrow. And he could not help recall those childhood separations from the women who cared for him and loved him. They had *all left him while he slept,* even his own mother.

Sophie would also be stealing away while he surrendered to slumber and he might not see her for sometime.

A premonitory fear of never seeing her again made him intertwine his fingers with hers as though this precaution might alert him of her departure.

But when she carefully disengaged her hand, Franz had mercifully fallen asleep, unaware of the movement and oblivious, for now, of all his pains and anxieties.

The next day, just as Franz dreaded, Sophie's labor commenced. Every hour he would send a footman to inquire on her progress. Every time, the same unnerving report would come back to him: Nothing yet.

Franz worried himself to distraction, thinking that men could claim a heroic death on the battlefield while women, in the throes of winning the grandest of battles, were given little if no credit at all.

He also realized how completely alone he was now. Even Dietrichstein had left him, called away to Würzburg to be with his daughter, Julie, who was also in childbed.

As for his mother, she had practically deserted his bedside. When Marie Louise came, usually no more than twice a day, but frequently only once, she would sigh a great deal, pat Franz's hand and ramble on in a weak monotone oblivious of his increasing deafness. Oftentimes, he had pretended to doze so he wouldn't have to tell her that he had not understood a word she had said.

Franz was left now with one solace: the extension of the woman he loved. He asked to see Franzi.

When the little boy was brought to his room, Franz sensed a slight reticence.

Young Franz Joseph approached him timidly. Ava's countenance was quite frightening. His blue eyes stared out of shadowy sockets, his temples were deeply hollowed and his cheek bones and jaw jutted with painful prominence. Franz tried to reassure the child with a smile, but it was the saddest smile Franzi had ever seen. Then when he was placed on the knees of the ghostly figure seated on the sofa, he wondered what sort of fun Ava had in store for him.

Together they leafed through fancifully bound albums like those Francis would use to press and catalogue his collection of herbs. They looked at colorful pictures of flowers and birds. But Franzi kept wiggling. Franz's skeletal frame made his lap uncomfortable to sit on. His chest against which the little boy leaned his head, seemed full of strange and inexplicable noises each time he took a breath, and peering at the gaunt face with that direct, penetrating artlessness of the very young, Franzi decided that Ava, in the twenty-second year of his life, was a withered old person.

A stripling himself, by more mature standard, Franz felt nevertheless, aged and decaying. At the limit of his strength, he began to let go of life. His eyes were full of twilight and his cautious and rare movements had the stamp of a fatal majesty inspiring in those who waited on him that peculiar awe the living feel toward the dying.

He experienced only a short reprieve when Sophie, on the day following her confinement, was safely delivered of a boy to be christened Maximilian Ferdinand Joseph. Maximilian would one day become the Emperor of Mexico.

Franz had abandoned all idea of ruling. Calm in knowing that Sophie and her baby were well, he became more aware of his suffering and loneliness. The pain was constant now, burning and gnawing at the wall of his chest and interminable coughing fits left him utterly exhausted and gagging on bloody spittles.

Once he said to Moll, "I am all hollowed out. Everything has gone out of me."

Moll made him drink some water sweetened with honey. "This will give you strength, Monseigneur."

"I am being punished," Franz reflected sadly. "Why? What have I done to suffer like this?"

And the Baron, who continued to keep a sharp eye on one of Franz's good horses, hung his head and said with great warmth and sincerity, "You are a gracious and kind prince. I would not serve any other more readily than I am Your Highness."

"If you think so well of me, Moll, how could I deserve to die like this?"

"Monseigneur," Moll protested, "you can't be dying! You are very young and . . ."

Franz interrupted him, "I am falling apart, Moll! So why pretend. . . ."

At long last, Franz confronted the certitude of his premature end with such burning regrets that no amount of human compassion and sympathy or religious consolations could relieve. The few people whom he deeply cared for had gone one by one, leaving him to die in abject abandonment and total isolation. Like his existence, the passages from life to death would be devoid of originality and notice.

He sought refuge in fantasy.

He was not lying in bed in this sumptuous room where his father had once slept, but on a litter made of boughs and muskets, which soldiers had just carried to a makeshift shelter under heavy shelling. The burning sensation in his chest and the blood he spat were the result of a serious wound suffered in the heat of battle. Suffering in that context was meaningful and grand and almost pleasurable. Death in such wise, in the prime of life, could be accepted with pride and joy. . . .

But the fantasy ended there.

The reality of what would be done to him afterward was too compelling to be ignored. There would be no martial parade for him, no tricolor flag to be draped over his coffin, and no Frenchmen coming to mourn over his grave. Instead, the laying away directed by century-old traditions must be that of an archduke. And he was thoroughly familiar with that sort of funerary pomp.

In logical sequence, the chapel at the Hofburg always received the bodies of Habsburg princes to display them at the close of their earthly peregrination. Clearly, Franz could see himself lying in an open coffin placed between three rows of silver candelabra, with draperies of crimson velvet gorgeously embroidered with gold threads draped around the bier. His coat of arms, leopards and chimeras on a field of ermine, would be displayed on the back step of the catafalque to the right side of which, on cushions fringed with tassels, would be placed his ducal coronet and the collar of St. Stephen, and to the left, completing the funerary layout, his sword and military hat. The honor guards would consist of German and Hungarian officers dressed in shimmering uniforms like the one he had so admired on Neipperg when he was a little boy.

And later. . . .

His coffin would be taken to the church of the Capuchin on the Neue-Markt where archdukes were laid to their eternal rest in a fusty crypt smelling of mildew. He had descended into those vaults with Francis, his first visit as a child, being on All Souls' Day. The Emperor had taken him by the hand as they followed the monks whose Order was principally dedicated to keep a perpetual watch over the remains of those born to the Imperial House of Habsburg.

While down there, Francis had pointed out to him elaborate sarcophagi reciting names august and revered. He also said proudly, "I, too, shall find my place in here!"

Franz remembered asking with infantile candor, "What about me, Bonpapa?" He had never forgotten how Francis had hugged him and stammered with a vehemence he did not understand then, "This is no place for you! You are so young!"

Twenty-one now since March, Franz reckoned, and still a very young age for a man to die. Then, as prescribed by etiquette, the Court would mourn his passing for six weeks. Long enough to close the inconsequential episode of a life which had been his misfortune to live. . . .

The former Rinuccini Palace held no particular significance for the people living in the vicinity of the Plaza Venetia. And even though Rome is celebrated for its many edifices that are hallowed because of their religious or historic importance, no one ever gathered in front of the weather-worn facade of the palazzo whose shutters were perpetually drawn as if the dwelling was untenanted.

Yet there lived inside a woman of international renown whom many of her contemporaries called the "Mother of Kings." She was content to be left alone as she had long ago shut herself up in the exclusive worship of the past, the present, as it was, being a source of unending sorrow.

Her family had been forced to disperse as far as America. After eleven years, the body of a son she had no desire to outlive, was still interred in a place of shame and desolation. Her grandson, following his father's tragic exile, remained to that day a prisoner at a foreign court, and his health, so the papers reported, was failing.

Many at her age would have succumbed to melancholy and quit this life, but Letizia endured in near blindness and bodily deterioration. Then a new development had put a spark in her day. Fresh anticipation of long-awaited tidings had been granted her in this year of her decline. So, thanking God, she patiently waited for a special visitor.

When Prokesch entered the silent palazzo, his steps hollowly resounded through the vast empty foyer. The date was July twenty-first, and the echo of his footfalls eloquently marked the fulfillment of a solemn promise. He had come this far, and the ground upon which he walked bore witness to the success of his mission.

He had planned everything with the circumspection attending a conspiracy; entered in discreet relation with Prince Gabrielli and met his wife, Charlotte, daughter of Napoleon's impetuous brother, Lucien. Through Charlotte, he had obtained this interview with Letizia.

Presently Charlotte took him up a flight of stairs and led him into the apartments of Napoleon's mother.

At first, Prokesch did not see her. The room was vast, sparsely furnished and plunged in sepulchral darkness. Heavy draperies, fully drawn, kept the daylight out and trapped an atmosphere that had grown stale. Set on the chimney mantel, votive candles placed on either side of a bust of Napoleon provided the only illumination. The Princess took him by the hand and guided his steps to a sofa upon which a form he had not noticed, stirred at his approach.

Charlotte whispered to him, "Madame is eighty-two and almost paralyzed." Then coming up to Letizia she said cheerfully, "*Grand mère,* here is Major von Osten, the King of Rome's most trusted friend!"

Letizia never called her grandson anything but by the title given to him at birth. She abhorred any other name. If someone in her entourage inadvertently spoke of him as the Duke of Reichstadt, her displeasure would long be remembered by the offender.

She motioned Prokesch to sit beside her and fixed upon him eyes that were dulled by the milky film of a cataract in its most impairing stage.

In a French still strongly accented with a Corsican inflection she said, "I have prayed God to grant me the consolation and joy to see my grandson at least once again. I am told you are here in his behalf, and I am very grateful."

He spoke his heart. "I am deeply honored and very touched to have been asked to come, Madame."

Her voice breaking, she replied, "You are very kind and courageous to have come here." Then she began to cry saying, "If I were to see my dear grandson now, that would be as if he were another person! You see, I remember him as a little child. That is how I saw him the last time I was with him. And I have never been permitted to write to him. But you are bringing him to me. I pray you, speak!"

Prokesch spoke and she drank his words. They eased some of her fears and misgivings. The Prince, he told her, was not ill-treated and he had received an enviable education. Then Prokesch repeated word for word the message Franz had given him.

Letizia now cried for joy. She tried to imagine her grandson as a young man after having not seen him in eighteen years. Then she grew agitated.

"The King of Rome is not well. How ill is he?"

Prokesch did not know for certain because he had not written to Franz knowing that their correspondence would be intercepted. They had been separated for a little over half a year and the Major preferred to hold to the assumption that the Prince would overcome any fresh crisis.

"He is young, Madame, and at his age, recovery is only a matter of time," was all he could say.

Letizia heaved a sigh and called weakly, "Charlotte, fetch the Emperor's game case and the miniature of myself, the one that has a lock of Napolione's hair inserted beneath the picture."

The Princess brought the objects to her and Letizia solemnly transferred them to Prokesch's hands.

"You will give these things to the King of Rome," she intoned softly. "You will also tell him that the silence and the separation to which we have been so cruelly subjected have increased a hundredfold the tender feelings I have always felt for him. You will tell him that I commend him for remembering so well; that such admirable fidelity is surpassingly valorous. The King of Rome is a gallant man. He will reign. All these things, you will tell him."

Deeply shaken, Prokesch promised, "Madame, I will!"

Then he rose to his feet, thinking the interview over and carefully tucked the miniature inside his tunic. On his person, the object was sure to reach Reichstadt. He imagined the Prince's elation receiving from his hands the most precious present Prokesch could ever dream of bringing back with him. As for the game case, he would have to think of something.

To Prokesch's surprise, Letizia got up with him, leaning heavily on a cane she had kept tucked away behind her on the sofa. He admired her majestic carriage. Draped in black silk and lace, Letizia, far from inspiring the sort of special compassion accorded to old and ailing persons, forced admiration and awe. She reminded him of a priestess in ancient times about to do something sacred and important. This impression was so compelling that he found himself kneeling before her.

He must have intuitively anticipated her intentions, for Charlotte, guiding her grandmother's hands, placed them on his inclined head.

The moment held such pathos that Prokesch made a conscious effort to remain calm. The best of imagination, he doubted, could not have contrived to produce a drama as poignant as the one he had so closely followed since his intimacy with a lonely Bonaparte. It was, alas, all too real! All laid out with calculated cruelty and unparalleled irony! And he, an outside observer of the family's incredible saga, by some strange quirk of fate had been so deeply drawn into it that he was about to receive the blessing of *Napoleon's mother!*

In a low voice, Letizia was intoning once again. "I cannot go to the King of Rome, and he cannot come to me. Thus, you will take my prayers and my love to him. You will take to him that which I call upon your head and entrust to your heart. . . ."

There followed a silence during which she must have been praying. Then her hands slipped down to Prokesch's shoulders and lightly pressed upon them intimating that some further acknowledgment was needed. He looked up at Letizia and saw now a broken old woman who asked him in a humble and pleading tone, "Will you do this for me?" Fresh tears gushed from her eyes and her sunken lips twisted wordlessly before she could add, "For him?"

Prokesch kissed her hands, and touching his forehead to them, he wept.

33

That same day Malfatti could have also wept, but in frustration as he scrutinized his patient's gaunt features gentled by the semblance of sleep. Thus far, his professional skills had not amounted to much. Crises, like so many traps set to test his science, had sprung in rapid succession and contradicted every single one of his predictions.

Flustered and steadfastly shirking all responsibilities, he mumbled addressing the second attending physician standing at his side, "All is failing. . . . The heat has upset all my calculations!"

Doctor Nickert thought it best not to comment. He had been called in to assist Malfatti in what appeared to be the final stage of the Prince's illness, which he had not had the opportunity to follow. But he knew that the heat had little if anything to do with the fact that their patient had lain unconscious for several hours.

At this moment Franz finally opened his eyes and moaned, startling the doctors.

"He is coming to!" Malfatti observed with satisfaction.

And to what avail? Nickert thought despairingly. The Prince seemed to have reached the limit of endurance, leaving his bed only to have it made, and having completely stopped taking solid food. Even the pap fed to him made swallowing unbearably painful, for his throat had gone raw from increasingly abundant hemoptysis.

Nickert was at his wits' end. The ingestion of live snails suggested by well-meaning charlatans no longer seemed an absurdity. All else approved by the faculty had failed; leeches applied to the Prince's temples, plasters and salves, potions and even human milk secured from available nursing mothers. Something yet untried, God knows, might do the invalid some good, and certainly at this juncture, nothing could do him much more harm.

Fortunately for Franz, live snails had not found a place in Malfatti's last desperate considerations for a cure. He resorted to more sophisticated means: hocus-pocus.

Bending over the bed and mindful of his patient's partial deafness, he shouted to be heard, "Your Highness should feel better after some magnetic passes."

Franz moved his lips with difficulty. "Just let me die. . . "

"Look at my hands, Monseigneur. And please, try to concentrate."

Franz averted his face. "No. . . "

"Monseigneur, I must insist!"

Franz shook his head. "Leave me alone . . . " he rasped and began picking at the bedclothes.

Malfatti panicked. Floccillation, it was said, presages imminent death. He hesitated and drew himself up.

"As Your Highness wishes," he relented. And for the first time he bemoaned his inability to provide any form of relief. He remembered that stimulating conversation he had had once with this radiant youth now a shell of a man whom he profoundly pitied. And for once, he did not like his profession. Death was an adversary he should never have taken on. With a stoop he left the room followed by his colleague. In the antechamber he dejectedly said to Moll, "The Prince has regained consciousness, maybe *you* can do something to help him . . . anything you can think of."

At Moll's approach, Franz relaxed. His hands grew still on the cover. Moll was not expected to cure him, and so he would not pester him.

Mindful of his instructions, Moll was racking his brain to offer some form of comfort to a very sick man for whom nothing could be proffered but only some illusory enticement that might still be welcome. And he had just thought of something.

He mentioned the special berlin, Koller the coach-maker had been commissioned to build in anticipation of Reichstadt's journey to Italy. "It should be finished any moment now and it is a veritable cradle, I am told. Your Highness will not feel a single jolt!" he cheerfully told him.

Having said this, Moll was saddened to have had to resort to deceit. What he had said was pure invention. Koller had not picked up his tools to work on that special coach. Like everyone else, he had been told to wait. Reichstadt's ordeal, everyone was convinced, would come to a quick close and the carriage would never be of any use to him.

With a wan smile Franz only requested. "Keep the doctors away. . . . Stay with me until my mother comes."

Marie Louise came after having offered her daily petition to God for a merciful release for her son. In craven deference to His will she felt absolved from all responsibilities. The sight of Franz's sufferings—those she could not at times avoid—had worn her nerves to a frazzle. It encumbered her ability to function adequately within the prescribed bounds of maternal devotion; and that devotion had never been tailored to fit Franz's situation or meet his needs and demands.

At his mother's entrance, he motioned Moll to leave. It was important that she be there alone with him. His time was running out. He was afraid of lapsing into unconsciousness again and of dying in the process without her nearby, without having her undivided attention and her hand to hold.

Reaching out to the ghost of a childhood love which had so inspired and hurt him, he lifted a bony hand to her. She squeezed it briefly, and delicately replaced it on the cover.

"How do you feel, now?" she asked. Her concern sounded frayed by habit.

He gave her a half-smile, very small and pleading.

"Better if you would stay a little longer today. You don't have to say anything."

She sat down, glad to see him shut his eyes. Their feverish glitter disquieted her in ways she did not wish to analyze. What more could she have done for him? Her gaze moved away from his emaciated frame barely pressing the mattress to look out the windows thrown wide-open on the formal gardens.

A leaden sky cast a pall of oppressive heat that even stifled the vesperal calls of song birds. Not a leaf stirred. There was an unnatural hush or rather one which Nature observed before it would go on a stormy, destructive rampage. For now, only the lulling sound of water gushing from the many fountains scattered over the palace grounds wafted through the gathering gloom.

Marie Louise turned her thoughts to the azure sky of Parma where her two other children whom she could love without compunction waited for her return. Three packing cases containing gifts she had bought for them and for her favorites were stored in her apartments ready to be sent when all would be over. She wondered if she had picked the right present for Sanvitale.

A sudden flash of anger lit a blush to her cheeks. She must mind her tongue and check herself. Too many mentions of her chamberlain Sanvitale in her conversation had drawn from her minister, Baron Marschall, abusive and humiliating censures. He had had the audacity to suggest that she had been conducting herself like a slut! Oh, he treated her harshly and disrespectfully! But she could never have earned anyone's respect.

She had married Napoleon and had outworn her use. She felt like an outcast even in Parma where Marschall, hand-picked by Metternich, continued to irritate her by spying on the most intimate details of her life. He had no right to! Neipperg's lovemaking satisfied her sensuality, which had been awakened by Napoleon's Latin ardor. But with her dear Neipperg dead, was she to consign her carnal appetite to the grave as well?

"Mamma. . . ."

Marie Louise gave a start. "Yes, Franz?"

Without opening his eyes he said, "Promise me to give Father's sword to Major von Osten upon his return."

Franz had recalled her to another unpleasant reality. Of a one track mind, he would only speak of preoccupations beyond the sphere of their influences and kept them alive with mementos to be passed around to a few chosen friends. This annoyed her.

Her breath caught as in a stumble and she steeled herself against the working of all the demons that had come between them. Her conscience gave her a jolt. She parried it with her own rationale: Franz had been part of a plan that had gone awry through no fault of her own. She had done all she could for him and God would be taking over.

In a pitiable attempt at candor she said, "You should be presenting that sword to the Major yourself, Franz."

He let a silence fall between them. Then fingering the medal bearing the effigy of Alexander the Great—he had faithfully worn it around his neck since the day Prokesch had given it to him—he said softly, "Mother, you do know what I mean."

The effort she made to spare him robbed her protest of tenderness. "You don't know what you are saying!"

He opened his eyes and looked straight ahead. He would not draw her in his private torment. Unrelenting disappointment, suffering, and isolation had borne him on an ocean of desolation he navigated alone. And he was past faulting anyone.

From where his head rested, he could make out the darkening outlines of the *Gloriette* on its hillock, its graceful porticoes etched against an evanescent plume of silver clouds. He looked upon the monument which once pleased him as a provocation which demanded surrender. And in body, he had been made to surrender. He would never fulfill his destiny. His solitary struggle would go unrecognized. . . .

And he had to acknowledge this.

Quietly he said, "I know I won't leave any mark on history. My birth and my death, that is my story. Not enough to fill one line. . . ."

Marie Louise made a lame attempt to protest, "Franz . . ." and then stopped at a loss for words.

But he continued gently as though he expected nothing else, "So will you do as I ask and give my sword to the Major?"

She nodded, tears welling up in her eyes. "I will," she gasped, wanting to flee to her apartments.

Franz turned his gaze on his mother and considered her with infinite compassion. The part she had been called upon to play in Napoleon's tumultuous career was ill-suited to her temperament and he had not done much to lighten her burden.

He said, "I am sorry to have caused you so much trouble and pain," and made a feeble attempt to lift his arms so she could hold him.

She fidgeted on her chair and his arms came down listlessly, empty of the consolation and tenderness he craved. Finally rising from her seat, she managed to deposit a quick kiss on his damp forehead, then began to gather her gown about her and appeared to pay excessive care not to knock over the dreadful cuspidor stored under the bed. But Franz knew this was mostly done to give herself a countenance.

It's all over. I must let go of her.

As a bait for a face-saving retreat, he murmured, "*Mutter . . . ich bin müde.*" This having barely passed his lips, he mused, *I, a Bonaparte born in Paris. I, a Frenchman, will die most likely uttering my last words in German!*

Another crushing irony!

Mary Louise pounced on the offer. "If you are tired, Franz, I shall let you rest."

"I love you, Mother," he breathed in a valediction.

For a moment she hovered over him then dropped a hand to stroke his cheek bristling with day-old stubbles. Grooming, at this juncture of his illness, had become ancillary to more demanding cares.

A little cry escaped her. "Oh, my poor, poor, dear boy!"

Franz shut his eyes and made no reply. In a few seconds he knew she had left him.

Immediately, he thought of Sophie.

His all-consuming longing for her nearness worked its relentless bane and aggravated his plight. Her absence had plunged him into Stygian depths of despondency. They had been apart for over a fortnight and had not communicated by notes because anyone would have been able to read them. Flunkies were trusted with terse reports passed to-and-fro such as: "The Archduchess and her baby are doing well," or, "His Highness has rallied somewhat."

Sophie was not told the absolute truth in that respect. Her entourage, well-aware of her deep feelings for Reichstadt, tended to gloss over the worse episodes of his battle with the illness. Franz himself had exacted from his staff the promise Sophie would be spared the ghastly details not to alarm her.

If she only saw him now!

He knew that his frightful appearance even stunned Metternich when he had come to Schönbrunn to glimpse his sovereign's grandson. The call had been dictated by etiquette and Franz had pretended sleep to shorten his jailer's stay.

As for the Emperor . . . Francis had stayed away altogether. State visits of paramount importance, Franz was told, had called him away from Vienna. For that long a time?

Not likely. His grandfather, too, had deserted him. . . .

Sinking into a merciful torpor, Franz was unaware that tears glazed his sunken cheeks.

When he woke to the distant rumbles of thunder, the sky had become as dark as pitch, a witch's cauldron brewing a storm of strange and ominous violence. That night, a bolt of lightning was to strike one of the carved stone eagles which adorned the palace's facade and send it crashing to the ground in pulverized fragments. And those who were inclined to read a message in like occurrences, would long afterward ponder its timing.

But no one looked for omens at the moment. Servants busily scurried about drawing the shutters close and lighting the candles.

Moll came in carrying Franz's supper. A glass of orgeat. The beverage which consisted of a mixture of barley extract and sweet almond was to act as a mild demulcent on the Prince's ravaged esophagus.

Franz was so weak he could no longer hold up his head. Without support it would dip and sway and taking nourishment had become a problem which Moll solved by holding him against his chest, using his own shoulder as a prop.

Presently he went through the motion with a caution that was not devoid of tenderness. Carefully he began feeding Franz the concoction.

Between two spoonfuls, Franz slurred, "Aren't people laughing at me for being so helpless?"

"If anyone does that in my presence," Moll said angrily, "I will knock off that person's teeth!"

Franz managed a smile. Human warmth, human kindness. . . . At times, he felt so utterly exhausted that all sensitivity seemed to have been drained out of him. At others, a terrifying sense of isolation would compel him to grasp at small good turns with overwhelming and disproportionate gratitude.

"I am terribly fond of you, Moll," he rasped.

"Your Highness," Moll went on soothingly, "should not pay any mind to what people think but rather look forward to convalescing in Italy." And up, went another spoonful.

This time Franz refused to take it. He averted his head and in an apparent trance, stared at the far corner of the room. Then with enfeebled exultation, he exclaimed, "They let you come!"

Puzzled, Moll looked in the same direction and saw no one; only the soft glimmer of the silver-gilt cradle with its ornate canopy upon which stood the winged Glory timelessly bestowing her triumphal wreath.

But from a delirious imagination, the figure of a man long dead had coalesced. A bright star sparkled on his breast, and his blue-gray eyes were fixed upon Franz with penetrating insistence. Joy inundated him. His childhood dreams had been fulfilled! His infantile plea of "Come back! Come home!" had been heeded.

Yet the apparition seemed restless as though it had only stopped for a brief passage much like a harbinger would on his way to secure more lasting accommodations. It beckoned with a jerk of the head which upset the little forelock which hung in the shape of a comma over a pale forehead.

Buckling with amazing energy and clamping down his fingers on Moll's arm, Franz panted frantically, "My carriage! Is it ready?"

Alarmed, Moll tried to hold him still.

"Not quite, Monseigneur."

"But you said . . ."

"I am sorry," Moll interrupted. "Surely tomorrow."

"Now!" Franz cried savagely. "I need it now! I must go and meet my father!"

"Your father is dead," Moll said, pinning him down on the bed.

Franz fought him in a demented frenzy. "I saw him! He has come for me!" Blood began to ooze from one corner of his mouth, then his writhing body suddenly went completely limp.

Horrified, Moll looked down as more blood kept coming. The macabre interlude had sent him into momentary shock, delaying his reaction. Then he realized something had to be done to stem the slow outpour that began to soak the front of Franz's night shirt.

Frantically, he called for assistance.

Malfatti was certain that the end was near. Franz lay inert, chin bloodied and drawing a hollow breath.

His hands shaking, Moll began to unbutton his shirt to change it. By now the bleeding seemed to have stopped.

Not unwisely Malfatti said, "Do not move the Prince! The hemorrhage may return."

Complying, Moll took a dampened cloth and began to clean the blood as best he could. When he finished, he sat down near the bed and waited. Franz appeared to be resting or perhaps, the Baron thought, going into a peaceful decline.

Not even a flogging rain which began to beat furiously against the closed shutters, or the night exploding with a close succession of thunder claps that rattled the panes seemed to disturb him.

And listening to all this, Moll wondered. There seemed to be an eerie similarity between the fury of this storm and the veritable tempest reported to have accompanied the death of Napoleon. Displays of Nature's violence such as this one, it was believed, were harbingers of death but only stirred up in honor of select individuals. In legends, demonds or demigods were said to depart in such a flourish. Demon? Reichstadt? Never! The Prince had never treated him with anything but consideration and respect and what had become of him was martyred and sainted.

Baron von Moll began to pray devoutly until the Prince's valet, Lambert, came to take over the watch.

Clocks also kept watch, ticking irreversibly the seconds, minutes and hours away in that relentless and mysterious process Franz had once pondered in jest to amuse Sophie.

He lay oblivious of time, unaware of the storm; of its gradual easing; of a sky awash with stars which soon began to pale. . . .

A new day was dawning and yet he still existed. His body also kept a wary watch over its life-line; the beat of a heart, the puff of a breath. . . .

His mind wandered and took him to other places, crossing all frontiers, man-made or natural.

He was free!

Running through open fields. Running toward the gay noises of a distant city, to its quays shaded with plane trees and to the gentle river along which he so often rode in a little calash drawn by two clever little sheep. He was running home to the pealing of Notre Dame's bells, to an airy palace he never wanted to leave.

But he had been running too fast. Breathing no longer came easy. His chest hurt. Then came the fall into a dark, interminable spiral and terror choked and convulsed him.

"*Mutter! Mutter! Ich gehe unter!*"

Mother! I am sinking!

Death by drowning in one's own blood and in one's own bed! The sensation of suffocating by immersion was vivid, and the struggle to get some air down his lungs was terrifying and very real.

Franz writhed, both his hands clutching at his throat.

Other hands touched him; raised him on the pillows. He gagged. "Poultices!"

The warm mush of herb applied to his chest enabled him to gasp out, "Call my mother!"

"Her Majesty is on her way," Lambert assured, wiping a heavy sweat off his brow.

Franz relaxed against the pillows. It was a familiar phrase but the deception, he was certain, had gone out of it. For to feel suddenly no pain at all attested to a warning. He thought calmly, I am dying. She will come. Everybody else is . . .

He recognized everyone: Sophie's husband, Francis Charles; Baron Marschall; Hartmann; Standelski; Malfatti; Nickert; Titz, as usual bursting out of his livery hastily put on, a button askew; and there was his other valet, Kolb, who seemed to consider this scene worth recording.

Kolb who could never draw a straight line and so admired Franz's drawings stood apart from the others with a sketching pad in the crook of his arm and a pencil in his hand.

Kolb was going to draw for posterity!

And Franz wondered if Kolb could capture on a sheet of paper death surrounded by strangers after a life spent among mercenaries. . . .

The one near-stranger Franz would have wanted close to him, close enough to touch and to hold, was just entering his room supported by Moll and Elise Scarampi. Mother's puffy eyes seemed haunted because of things undone and words unsaid.

No matter. Franz's own eyes smiled at her.

Marie Louise froze in her track and dared not advance any closer than to the foot of her son's bed. And there she sank heavily to her knees. She would not accord him a last healing kiss. She had relinquished her right to comfort. Religion would do that. Surely, her prayers must have gnawed her son free from the need of earthly consolations. The priest who followed her in the room would provide celestial succors that would be of far greater benefit.

The chaplain, surpliced, very young and of gentle mien, came up to the bed. A total stranger! Franz had never seen him before. Calmly he acknowledged a final desertion. For some reason, Monsignor Wagner who had heard his last confession must have been called away. Religious intimacy, that too, was denied him.

But no matter. This unfamiliar cleric proved to be a compassionate purveyor of God's final consideration for a hapless humanity. The light touch of his fingers smeared with sacramental oil moved gently from Franz's lids, to the nose, mouth, and ears. Next he felt it on his folded hands and then on his feet, which Lambert exposed by turning up the sheet.

A crucifix was delicately pressed against his lips, and with much feeling, the chaplain murmured, "My son, God is merciful. . . ." Then he laid his hand on Franz's forehead and asked softly, "Should I read the prayers aloud?"

Franz summoned enough energy to blink "Yes."

The chaplain began to recite the verses applicable to the sick and that was a thoughtful exception to the rules.

All present knelt.

An hour passed. Sunday July twenty-second began with precocious brilliance as days are wont to do in summer. The sky, cloudless, stretched rosily over the horizon colored by an early rising sun even too early for matins.

In a last wisp of consciousness, Franz thought of Sophie in recognition of a grace. Their meeting in this life must have been the working of Providence, a propitiatory boon to mitigate the implacable fatality attached to his destiny. Her tenderness and her love had lessened the rigor of his solitary existence.

If only she would come to him now! Her husband was there. She must have been told, too. Sophie! He clung to her name, the only thread that held him to this life for a little while, just long enough to give himself time to hear the rustle of her gown.

But he felt his lifeforce thinning like wine being diluted with water.

And he put up a last fight.

He turned his head from side to side. No! Not yet! She might come now . . . any minute . . . and he must keep his eyes wide open to acknowledge her, to greet her, to . . .

The Duke of Reichstadt's feeble shake of the head was interpreted by some of the people present as a pitiable and futile last attempt to denounce the inconceivable harm done to his young life.

It signaled Marie Louise's slow collapse to the floor.

Malfatti got to his feet and leaned over the bed. After a few seconds, he emitted a professional 'hem' which brought the lulling drone of the chaplain to an abrupt stop. The man of science looked at the man of God and claimed for himself a warranted gesture.

Much in a way of a blessing, Malfatti raised a hand over Franz's face and not without some difficulty gently closed his eyes.

"Franz!"

Sophie woke abruptly to the sound of her own voice. Lying-in is incapacitating business, and not being able to be near Franz for so many days—eighteen to be exact—anguished her even in her sleep. She had just seen him in a dream. A soft light shone on his fair hair, but his dear face was in complete shadow, concealed and mysterious. Yet she was certain he was smiling at her.

Still, a feeling of near terror began to overwhelm her despite the fact that last night, in reply to her inquiries she had been told, "His Highness is holding out."

Early that Sunday morning, Sophie's first born son, Franzi, drew his own childish conclusion. Once again he was taken to Franz's bedchamber where other people came treading lightly and spoke in a whisper. The shutters were still drawn and candles continued to burn hotly in every sconce. The room smelled of melted wax and holy oils. With a monitory finger held to her lips, his *aja* led him to the bed upon which Ava lay supine, his hands meekly folded over his chest. Sophie's little son gazed curiously at his face.

Gone were the elements that had upset his infantile sensibility. An exchange seemed to have taken place but the little boy knew not why. A restoration of sorts, a mysterious give and take process which had returned to Ava's appearance, its former arresting beauty.

Yet, in that handsome repose, a nearly forbidding majesty has settled over his features. The boy fidgeted. A primeval instinct surfaced, warning him away.

Franzi recoiled and clung to his governess's gown.

"Ava is not sleeping," he said.

In her lying-in chamber, Sophie asked the same customary question to her ladies. Was Reichstadt still asleep?

"No, Highness," answered the bravest among them. Then realizing the impasse into which she had engaged herself, the lady-in-waiting finished, floundering lamentably, "The Prince is resting quite . . . peacefully."

Sophie rolled in her bed and raised herself on one elbow to better look at the woman. What was the matter with her? What she had said was utter nonsense! Unless . . .

Her cry was agonized. "No! Oh God, no!"

"We are terribly sorry . . ." her ladies protested in a chorus.

Sophie screamed. "Not all alone!"

"It wasn't so! We assure you! The Archduchess Mother and your husband, the Prince's military staff . . . and his servants were all there!"

Sophie collapsed against the pillows. His servants . . . Even they were given this right . . . this last chance. *But not me!* A raging fury took hold of her and pulling at her hair she ranted.

"*Alone! Without me!* Why didn't anyone say anything to me? Why? Why? Why? . . ."

"You were sleeping so soundly. We did not dare wake you!"

She gasped. Franz died while she slept! Oh, the terrible, irreparable cruelty of it! And *they had let her!*

"When?" she demanded, tears streaming down her face which now wore an expression of demented grief.

Her ladies shrank in genuine alarm.

One volunteered. "At ten minutes past five this morning."

Sophie felt her own life ebbing and uttering a low moan she fainted.

When she came to, many feared her mind had gone. Some also thought she might even die. A high fever had set in, drying the milk in her breasts. For two whole days she lay utterly unaware, with eyes open wide, dry and soulless.

Then, when at long last some expression came back into them, so did the tears. She cried interminably racked with great sobs hugging a pillow. In a delirium of sorrow she imagined herself holding Franz in her arms whole and safe and forevermore hers to love and to keep.

She also wept for him.

To the bitter end he had been subjected to the dictate of a cruel and vindictive fortune. He had lived in an emotional wasteland, had suffered alone, and been foredoomed to die alone. If he ever found any solace in the course of his short existence, it had been in the form of fragments, like stolen morsels of happiness: the Emperor's affection adulterated by the dictates of dynastic and political considerations; Prokesch's precious friendship taken away from him. . . .

Even her own passionate gift of love to him was not unalloyed. It had a perniciously prohibitive element in it. Franz had emotionally subsisted on scraps and this had destroyed him. If only she had given herself to him! There would be now to counteract the terrible reality of his non-existence, remembrances of their caresses and surely a little child with his eyes or smile. Oh, rumor already went the rounds that the infant Maximilian was in fact that love-child, but the baby wasn't Franz's. And Franz wasn't in her arms. To touch him, she would have to go to his deathbed and kneel beside another world.

She threw back the cover and sitting up demanded to be dressed, unaware of having lost two days since her fainting spell. She considered dragging herself to the mortuary chamber unaided, if she had to.

But her orders could not be obeyed anyway, as another terrible revelation was made to her. Today was Tuesday the twenty-fourth, she was told. And the Prince's body was no longer at Schönbrunn. Placed in a litter, it had been taken to Vienna on Sunday, in the middle of the night.

Sophie knew for certain that she would never lay her eyes on him again.

In death, Franz's body became the exclusive property of another inescapable form of appropriation, an apparatus which was as inexorable as it was ancient. Surgeons, priests, and the trappings of an exact pomp would attend the disposal of his remains. An autopsy had been duly conducted, and to Malfatti's consternation it was found that his patient had died of consumption. The heart and the entrails were stored in separate silver urns. One would be preserved in the Loretto Chapel and the other in St. Stephen Cathedral.

For a whole day the people of Vienna were permitted to view the Prince dressed in his white uniform, booted, sashed and wearing the decorations Francis had bestowed upon him.

A great multitude of mourners filed past the open coffin and participated in the funerary celebrations which etiquette forbade members of the Imperial Family to attend. After the last Mass and prayers of intercession, a solemn-faced monk, guardian of the Kaisergruft, glimpsed the face of the deceased. The friar was discharging himself of a particular duty, that of verifying the identity of Reichstadt. This done, the coffin was closed forever and lowered into the hallowed crypt of the Capuchin Church, the final resting place of the Habsburg emperors and archdukes.

For sometimes it stood on a raised platform draped in a black velvet cloth. Then it received a casing of copper decorated with a trefoil cross. There were certain concessions to individuality, however. The inscription graven on Franz's coffin mentioned his former title and recognized his father by name. This time Francis had asserted his will.

"I command it," he had wept.

No one had ever seen the Emperor of Austria weep. He wept without restraint in front of Moll who had galloped all day Sunday to find his sovereign at Linz where the court was in progress. When the Baron arrived it was already dark but the whole town was aglitter in honor of the Emperor's visit. On the balmy air of a mellow summer evening wafted strains of music and peals of laughter.

As soon as the Emperor saw Moll, a stony look settled over his face. He knew. So without saying a word, the Baron handed over the letter Marie Louise had sent him to deliver.

"My very dear Papa," she wrote, "My poor son died Sunday at dawn. Heaven has answered my prayers and God has granted him a peaceful end. I can only bow to His holy will. . . ."

There were a few more lines, but Francis did not care to read on. His eyes were blinded by tears. His shoulders shook and his body slouched with that very same droopy carriage Franz had seen in that strange dream from which Sophie had lovingly rescued him.

Francis was utterly heartbroken. He experienced none of his daughter's fatalistic equanimity. He felt hollowed out. Franz's brief passage on this earth had profoundly affected his sentiments. And the world, he thought, had lost an extraordinary being whose brilliance it could not countenance. Franz had left him, bound for a loftier realm that would be kinder to him. . . .

When the Emperor returned to Vienna, he went to the Kaisergruft to mourn privately. A great fear had been laid to rest with Franz's death. But with that care removed, Francis was left smitten sick with frustration. He felt a torturing sense of waste in loving Franz in death with the abandon he had not dared accord him in life.

In the dank crypt Francis shuddered. The dust-gathering coffins save for one, projected the horrid reality of dissolution which assailed the tenacious hold he kept on the winsome image of a prince he thought so highly of and cherished. An image he so feared to see altered by a wasting illness.

He preferred to remember Franz as he was once, in the bloom of health and the glow of unblemished beauty, one so extraordinary that it must have been the enfleshed testimonial to his nobility of character, exceptional intelligence and remarkable aptitudes.

Heaving, Francis approached Franz's coffin and brushed a trembling finger over the inscription written in Latin he had composed himself for the son of his arch-enemy.

Aeternae. Memoriae . . .
In Perpetual Memory of Joseph Charles, Francis, Duke of Reichstadt, son of Napoleon, Emperor of the French and of Marie Louise, Archduchess of Austria. . . .
Hailed in his cradle as King of Rome. . . .

Endowed with every quality of mind and body.
Tall stature, a handsome face and singuler grace of speech. . . .

Francis suffocated under the weight of his grief. He felt victimized. The mandate he had received to rule despotically was God's ordinance and all he did was to carry it out faithfully. For this, he did not have to ask forgiveness.

Yet a private voice which he had stifled for so long under the gag of dynastic considerations rose in a crescendo of accusatory clarity: *Anything* for the monarchy!

Hugging the hard, cold coffin, Francis responded with long, spasmodic sobs gasping out the only excuse left to him.

"How ill you have been used, Franz! But that's all God's fault. . . . And may *you* forgive Him!"

Epilogue

"Between the melancholy fate of the Duke of Reichstadt, a prisoner of his own family, and the cruel fate of France, exiled in her own country by the arbitrament of war, history will note a moving analogy. . . "

—Marshal Pétain

A biting cold swaddled Paris on the night of December 14–15, 1940. The water of the Seine had frozen well over a foot below the surface, and a shimmering, intricate, lacework of frost covered the bare branches of the plane trees lining its banks.

It was a little past midnight when the snow—the first of winter—began to gently fall on a bronze coffin set on a gun carriage preceded by a motorcycle escort. The riders wore German uniforms, the Nazi emblem of a swastika on their arm bands.

The coffin was Adolf Hitler's "gift" to the French people, a "peace offering" to appease the population's deep hatred and feeling of revulsion since the Nazi occupation of its national soil.

One hundred and eight years after his death, Napoleon's son was finally coming home, still a pawn of politics. . . .

His father had already preceded him to Paris by one hundred years. In 1840, King Louis Philippe of France, in a desperate attempt to appease his malcontent subjects and infuse new life into a moribund monarchy, played his last trump. With great pomp and ostentation, Napoleon's remains were at long last exhumed from the solitary and shabby grave in St. Helena and brought back in triumph to Paris. He was entombed in a magnificent sarcophagus made of porphyry and placed under the majestic dome of the Invalides Chapel.

At that time, Prokesch and Sophie, who were to mourn Franz's passing for the rest of their long lives, pondered with renewed sorrow the implacability of his tragic fate. They did not believe that Franz, had he lived longer, would have been given the satisfaction of exulting over the long over-due honor and recognition accorded his father. That had only happened because Franz had died taking to the grave with him the threat of a Napoleonic revival.

The gun carriage passed the landmarks which had been so dear to Franz's childhood memories—along the Seine where he had driven his miniature calash; by the site where once stood the palace where he had been born and had refused to leave—the Tuileries, burned to the ground in 1871.

Finally, the procession came to a halt before the Invalides Chapel. On the shoulders of French soldiers, the bronze coffin was carried between a double line of Republican Guards in full dress, their uniforms bearing a vestigial resemblance to those worn by the soldiers of Napoleon's Grand Army. Covered with a huge tricolor flag to which Franz had so ardently pledged his allegiance, it was placed in a lateral chapel above his father's sarcophagus, which had been kept in an open crypt for the past hundred years.

To this day, reunited in death, Napoleon and his son are resting under the great gilded dome of the Invalides, built as a monument to the military glory of France.